"Sweeping . . . masterful. . . . Swerling tells of two men who straddle the white and red man's worlds, desperate to preserve the best of each culture, but fearful they will lose everything they love. . . . Readers . . . will be captivated by Swerling's intricate plot, colorful characters and convincing descriptions of colonial life."

—*Publishers Weekly*

"This spellbinding historical adventure highlights an often overlooked episode on the road to American independence."

—*Booklist*

"Vividly drawn characters. . . . A fine and warm-blooded book that offers more than a glimpse into a vital but nearly forgotten period in our history."

—*San Jose Mercury News*

Also by Beverly Swerling

City of Dreams: A Novel of Nieuw Amsterdam and Early Manhattan

Shadowbrook

A Novel of Love, War, and the Birth of America

BEVERLY SWERLING

SIMON & SCHUSTER PAPERBACKS

New York London Toronto Sydney

SIMON & SCHUSTER PAPERBACKS
Rockefeller Center
1230 Avenue of the Americas
New York, NY 10020

First Simon & Schuster Paperback edition 2005

SIMON & SCHUSTER PAPERBACKS and colophon are registered trademarks
of Simon & Schuster, Inc.

Manufactured in the United States of America

1   3   5   7   9   10   8   6   4   2

Library of Congress Cataloging-in-Publication Data

Swerling, Beverly.
Shadowbrook : a novel of love, war, and the birth of America / Beverly Swerling.
p.   cm.
1. United States—History—French and Indian War, 1755–1763—Fiction.
2. Indians of North America—Wars—1750–1815—Fiction.   3. Ohio—History—
To 1787—Fiction.   I. Title.

PS3619.W47S94 2004
813'.6—dc22
2003064127

ISBN 0-7432-2812-X
0-7432-2813-8 (Pbk)

For information about special discounts for bulk purchases,
please contact Simon & Schuster Special Sales at
1-800-456-6798 or business@simonandschuster.com

For Michael, R.I.P., and
for Bill, as always

These Things Are True . . .

About Europeans

Britain and France spent the first half of the eighteenth century fighting over empire. This story takes place during the decisive battle in that long conflict. In North America it was known as the French and Indian War, in Europe the Seven Years' War. It was a death struggle fought in a New World, the glory and extent of which the opponents did not imagine, and home to a rich and remarkable culture they did not understand.

About Native Americans

From the moment the Europeans discovered their paradise it was doomed, but the indigenous peoples—the Real People, as they called themselves—put up an immense struggle to hold back the tide. I have tried to be true to their history and customs, but this is a story and I am a storyteller. When I couldn't find details of a ceremony or a ritual, I made them up. My one rule was that I always extrapolated from what my research uncovered; teasing out the weave, never creating from whole cloth. Moreover, I never added or embroidered something that was by its nature pejorative. The bad stuff—or what seems so to us when judged by the standards of our culture and our time—is all there in the record.

About words

The linguists tell us that in the eighteenth century there were some hundred thousand languages and that now there are six thousand. Moreover, among all languages past and present, only two hundred or so have ever been written down. Native Americans had a complex and sophisticated system of pictographs, but essentially theirs was an oral tradition. Its strengths and its depth were wondrous, but much of it is lost. I worked with both Iroquoian and Algonkian dictionaries (all created in modern times to try and stanch the mortal wound) and have tried to give the flavor of the speech with some authenticity. I have, however, avoided the complicated accent marks that have been developed as pronunciation guides. They are beyond the scope of this tale and my ability. So too the grammar. I apologize for the inevitable mistakes.

ABOUT RELIGION

I know I have not been able to explain in proper depth or complexity the belief system of Native Americans. What the story contains is as true as my research allows; it is no doubt a vast distance from all truth. The rest, since it is part of my own Judeo-Christian heritage, is familiar territory. Here it is only necessary to say that Catholic theology is a long, ever-flowing river. What you see of the water depends on where you happen to be on the shore. The attitudes, customs, and practices, even some of the core beliefs described in this story, are accurate for the Church of that time and the religious orders as they were then. It is in many cases not the same now.

This Too Is True . . .

ABOUT US ALL

Love in all its many splendors has not changed in any fundamental way. Two hundred and fifty years ago it was as it is now—enough to move the world.

Contents

Important Characters
in the Story

The People of Shadowbrook, also known as the Hale Patent

AT THE BIG HOUSE

Quentin Hale: Also called Uko Nyakwai, the Red Bear, and very occasionally by his secret Potawatomi manhood name of Kwashko, Jumps Over Fire

John Hale: Quentin's elder brother

Ephraim Hale: Father of John and Quentin

Lorene Devrey Hale: Ephraim's wife, mother of John and Quentin

Nicole Marie Francine Winifred Anne Crane: A young woman of French and English ancestry, traveling through the American colonies on her way to Québec

Kitchen Hannah: The Big House cook

Corn Broom Hannah: A Big House maid

Six-Finger Sam: A general handyman

Clemency the Washerwoman: The laundress, and among the Patent slaves, the keeper of the oral history

Jeremiah: In charge of the stables

Little George: Jeremiah's assistant

Runsabout: A Big House maid and mother of the twins, Lilac and Sugar Willie

Taba: A young Ibo girl bought at the New York slave market in 1754

AT THE SUGARHOUSE

Moses Frankel: The chief miller, in charge of the grinding of wheat into flour and corn [Indian] meal as well as the production of rum and ale

Sarah Frankel: The wife of Moses

Ellie Frankel Bleecker: Their daughter, a widow

Tim Frankel: Son of Moses and Sarah; never married

Deliciousness May: The mother of Runsabout and a Hale slave assigned to the Frankels

Big Jacob: Husband of Deliciousness and father of Runsabout; a Hale slave assigned to the sugarhouse and gristmill. He is also the horse trainer of the Patent.

Lilac and Sugar Willie: Slave twins, children of Runsabout, but assigned to the sugarhouse. They are four years old when Quent returns to Shadowbrook in 1754.

AT THE SAWMILL

Ely Davidson: The sawyer

Matilda Kip Davidson: Ely's daughter-in-law

Hank Davidson: Ely's son

Josiah, Sampson, and Westerly: Brothers aged fourteen, twelve, and eleven; Hale slaves assigned to the sawmill

Solomon the Barrel Maker: A cooper, and a Hale slave born on the Patent

Sally Robin: The beekeeper and supplier of honey and various unguents and medicines used on the Patent; Solomon's woman since she was purchased at the New York Slave Market in 1720

AT DO GOOD—THE INDIAN TRADING POST OF THE PATENT, MANAGED AND STAFFED ENTIRELY BY MEMBERS OF THE SOCIETY OF FRIENDS, ALSO KNOWN AS QUAKERS

Esther Snowberry

Martin Snowberry: Esther's husband

Judith Snowberry: Their daughter; later Judith Snowberry Foster

Prudence: Their slave

Edward Taylor: Treasurer of the community

Hepsibah Jane Foster: Daughter of Judith

Daniel Willis: A Friend from Rhode Island who has come to bring an antislavery message given him by the Light Within

The People of the Town of Albany in New York Province

John Lydius: A trader and sometimes arms dealer

Genevieve Lydius: John's wife, a métisse who is half Piankashaw Indian and half French

Peter Groesbeck: Landlord of the Albany tavern at the Sign of the Nag's Head

Annie Crotchett: A prostitute who plies her trade at the Sign of the Nag's Head

Hamish Stewart: A one-eyed Scot, a Jacobite Stewart of Appin, and survivor of the infamous battle of Culloden Moor.

Assorted randy barmaids, crafty millers, entrepreneurial widows, drunken tars, layabouts and ne'er-do-wells; along with the many God-fearing huisvrouwen and burghers left from the days of Dutch rule.

The People of the Potawatomi Village of Singing Snow

Cormac Shea: A métis, son of a Potawatomi squaw and an Irish fur trader

Ixtu: The village Teller

Bishkek: The manhood father of the métis Cormac Shea, and of Quentin Hale

Kekomoson: The civil sachem of Singing Snow at the time of the story

Sohantes: The wife of Kekomoson

Shabnokis: A squaw priest of the powerful Midewiwin Society

Lashi: Bishkek's youngest daughter

Pondise: Her son

The People of Québec in New France

THE FRANCISCANS

Père Antoine Pierre de Rubin Montaigne, O.F.M.: Father Delegate of the Franciscans in New France

Mère Marie Rose, P.C.C.: Abbess of the Poor Clare Colettines of Québec

Soeur Marie Celeste, P.C.C.

Soeur Marie Françoise, P.C.C.

Soeur Marie Joseph, P.C.C.

Soeur Marie Angelique, P.C.C.

THE JESUITS

Monsieur Louis Roget, S.J.: Provincial Superior of the Jesuits of New France

Mansieur Philippe Faucon, S.J.: A Jesuit priest and an artist who documents the Canadian flora, called Magic Shadows by the Huron

Monsieur Xavier Walton, S.J.: An Englishman and a Jesuit, also a surgeon

THE CIVILIAN GOVERNMENT

François Bigot: Intendant of Canada, the steward and paymaster of the entire province

Pierre François Rigaud, marquis de Vaudreuil: Governor-General of Canada after June, 1755

AT PORT MOUTON IN L'ACADIE (NOVA SCOTIA)

Marni Benoit

Military Figures

Joseph Coulon de Villiers de Jumonville: A French officer; his death heralded the beginning of the Seven Years' War.

Tanaghrisson, the Half King: Born a Catawba, raised a Seneca; at the time of the story spokesman for the Iroquois Confederacy in the Ohio Country

George Washington: A colonel in the Virginia Militia. Twenty-two years old when the story opens in 1754

Pontiac: An Ottawa war sachem

Shingas: A war sachem of the Lenape, also known as the Delaware

Scarouady: Spokesperson for the Iroquois Confederation in the Ohio Country after the death of Tanaghrisson

Thoyanoguin, also known as King Hendrick: A war sachem of the Mohawk, also known as the Kahniankehaka. Members of the Iroquois Confederacy, they were called the Guardians of the Eastern Door.

Major General William Johnson, of the New York Militia (Yorkers): An Indian trader born in Ireland, in America since 1738 and married first to a German indentured servant, later to a Kahniankehaka squaw; adopted as a chief of that tribe

Major General Edward Braddock: Commander of His Majesty's forces in America at the beginning of the Seven Years' War

Général Jean Armand, baron de Dieskau: Commander of the French and Canadian forces at the beginning of the Seven Years' War

Général Louis Joseph, marquis de Montcalm-Gozon de Saint-Véran: Successor to Dieskau

General John Campbell, earl of Loudoun: Successor to Braddock

Major General Jeffrey Amherst: Successor to Loudoun

James Wolfe: A British colonel at the Battle of Louisbourg in 1758; a British Major General at the Battle of Québec in 1759

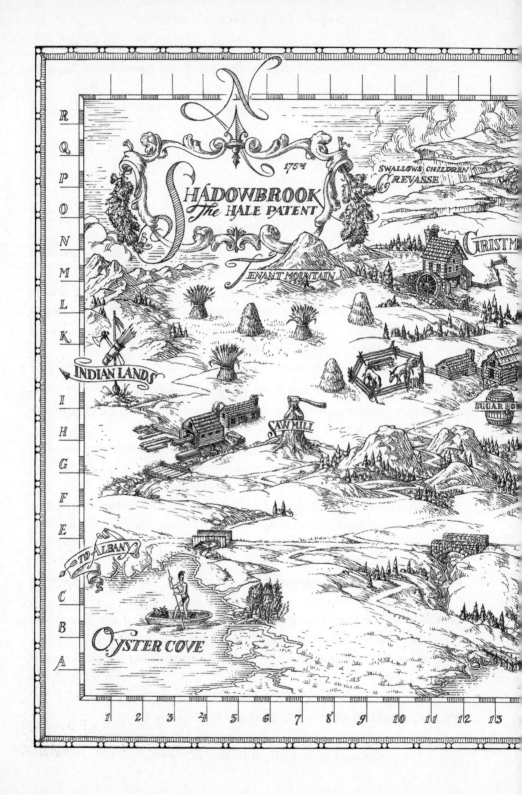

Book 1

Shadowbrook

1754

Chapter One

MISERERE MEI, DEUS . . . Have mercy on me, Lord, according to the greatness of Your mercy.

The five women had no mercy on themselves.

They beat their backs with knotted cords. Each wore a black veil, pulled forward so it shadowed her face, and a thin gray robe called a night habit.

The blows rose and fell, hitting first one shoulder then the other, and every third stroke, the most sensitive skin on the back of the neck. Occasionally a small gasp escaped one of the women, barely audible above the singsong Latin chant. *De profundis clamavi ad te, Dominum* . . . Out of the depths I cry to You, O Lord. *Domine, exaudi vocem meam.* Lord, hear my voice.

The narrow rectangular space was lit by twelve tall white candles. The whitewashed stone walls reflected the elongated shadows of the women, who knelt one behind the other on the bare stone floor. Occasionally, when the woman in front of her managed to find a new burst of strength, a spurt of blood would spatter the one behind.

The knotted cords were carefully crafted, fashioned to a centuries-old design. The length must be from shoulder to thumb of the woman who would use it, the rope sturdy and two fingers thick. The seven knots were spaced evenly from end to end. It was called the discipline and was given to each nun on the day she made her vows as a follower of St. Francis, a Poor Clare of the Strict Observance of St. Colette.

Quoniam non est in morte qui memor sit tui . . . It is not in death that You are remembered, Lord. *In inferno autem quis confitebitur tibi* . . . In the eternal fire who will recall You?

An iron grille in the front of the cloister chapel enclosed the holy of holies, the small ornate tabernacle containing the wafers that had been consecrated in Holy Mass and were now the Body and Blood of Jesus Christ. The grille was covered by heavy curtains so those on the other side in the visitors' chapel could not see the strictly enclosed daughters of St. Clare.

In the middle of that Wednesday night only one person was present in the public section of the chapel, a man who knelt upright with his arms outstretched in the position of his crucified Lord. He could hear the soft, sighing sounds of the knotted ropes punishing soft female flesh. His shoulders twitched occasionally in response.

Antoine Pierre de Rubin Montaigne of the Friars Minor was also a follower of St. Francis, a priest of what the Church called the Seraphic Order, men who had originally vowed to own nothing and beg for their daily bread. The rule had been modified over the five centuries since Blessed Francis preached the glories of Lady Poverty, but its priests retained the humble title "Father." Rubin Montaigne was Père Antoine to all, most especially the women on the other side of the altar screen.

In the nuns' chapel the pace of the scourging had become more urgent by the time of the great cry of the Miserere: Have pity on me, Lord, for I perish. The cords flicked through the air too quickly to be seen, white blurs in the candlelit gloom.

Père Antoine, Delegate of the Franciscan Minister General in Rome, the ultimate authority for members of the order in New France, had decreed that in addition to the traditional scourging that took place every Friday before dawn, the Poor Clares of Québec would take the discipline every Monday and Wednesday after the midnight office of Matins. They would offer this special penance until the territory the British called the Ohio Country, but which had long been claimed in the name of Louis XV, was made secure, truly part of New France. When Holy Mother Church moved south to convert the native tribes, these nuns and their scars would be the jewels in her crown.

Turn Your face from my sins and all my iniquities shall be forgotten . . .

None wielded the discipline with greater vigor than Mère Marie Rose, Abbess. The shoulders of her night habit were stiff with the caked blood of past scourgings. When they buried her the garment would serve as her shroud, and she had already issued instructions that it should not be laundered. She would go to her grave with the evidence of her fervor.

Iniquitatem meum ergo cognosco . . . My sins are known to You.

For my sins, for the sins of my daughters, for the glory of God. The words filled the abbess's mind, blended with the pain, the chant uniting the two, pulsing in her blood. *Miserere* . . . Have mercy, Lord. On the king. On this New France. On our brave soldiers.

The shoulder muscles of Père Antoine were on fire. His arms felt like lead weights, but he did not allow them to drop. The pain was a kind of ecstasy and he exulted in it. For the Church. For the Order. For the conquest of the land below the *pays d'en haut* and the defeat of the heretic English.

Chapter Two

THE THREE INDIANS moved in single file along a track no wider than a moccasin. The thick virgin forest of the Ohio Country, claimed by both the French and the English but possessed by neither, shuddered as they passed, then closed around them, barely disturbed.

Quentin Hale trotted easily behind the braves. His shoulders were twice as broad and he was a head taller, but he was as noiseless and surefooted as the Indians, and as tireless. The four men jogged along the treacherous path as they had for most of the night, with no break of rhythm or purpose.

The braves Quent followed were two Seneca and a Cayuga, members of the Six Nation Confederacy that called itself *Haudenosaunee*, the People of the Longhouse. Those who hated them for their prowess in battle called them by the Algonkian word *Irinakhoiw*—snakes. In the mouths of the French—who hated them for the strength of their union, which led to power in trade, and for their alliance with the English—the word became "Iroquois." Years before, after defeating the local Shawnee and the Lenape, whom the whites called Delaware, the Great Council of the *Haudenosaunee* sent representatives of their member tribes to live among the subjugated peoples. The Iroquois in the Ohio Country had come to be known as the Mingo.

It was shortly before dawn, late May, and warm and humid. A downpour had ended a while back, but the trees still dripped moisture. The braves, naked except for breechclouts and moccasins, blended with the forest. Quent wore moccasins as well, and buckskins greasy with sweat and the smoke of many fires. A rifle was slung over his shoulder, black, with a highly polished oak stock, shiny brass trim, and a barrel nearly five feet long. The grooved bore that made the long gun stunningly accurate had been invented some twenty years earlier, but the weapons were still rare, and the few around mostly in the hands of whites.

Every once in a while the Cayuga turned his head and eyed the rifle. If there is to be a battle, he thought, and if Uko Nyakwai is to fall, Great Spirit make me the one to be beside him.

Uko Nyakwai, Red Bear in the Iroquois language. Red for his hair. Bear for his size, and the size of his courage. Sometimes his rage. The Cayuga knew he wouldn't get the long gun while Uko Nyakwai was alive.

Could it be true that this bear had once pulled a tree out of the ground with only his hands and used it to kill twelve enemies? And that he did this thing for a woman, an Ottawa squaw called Shoshanaya, but she died anyway? And after her death the Red Bear left his father's land in the country of the lakes and vowed never to return? Probably only a squaw's tale told by the fire.

The Cayuga fingered the wolf totem at his neck. His own gun, a musket known as a Brown Bess, was the ordinary type issued to British troops and colonial militia. No after-kick—the long guns had a vicious recoil—but impossible to aim. To have a long gun . . . *Ayi!* Such a thing would make him invincible.

All the Indians had tomahawks as well, and knives. So did Quent, but he also had a miniature Scottish dirk tucked into the small of his back. And his face was clean except for sweat and a stubble of red beard. The Mingo were painted for war.

Behind Quent and the braves were thirty-some soldiers of the recently formed Virginia Regiment. Like all the colonial troops they had agreed to serve for only a few months, as long as they could be spared from their farms and village shops. They were paid eight pence a day while a common laborer got three times as much. The men had enlisted because they'd been promised land somewhere along the Monongahela and Allegheny rivers after they got rid of the French.

By Quent's reckoning it would be a cold day in hell when they started plowing that land.

The soldiers thudded along the woodland path in clumsy, ill-fitting boots. Their tricornes snagged on the low-hanging branches, and their woolen jackets and trousers were saturated with rain. Every one of the poor bastards was scratching. Except for Washington.

The young officer strode at the head of what was left of the column—they'd lost at least seven to the long dark night and the twisting, narrow forest path— pretending his braided finery didn't stink and itch. Damned fool on a damned fool's errand, Quent thought. Not your worry, he reminded himself. You signed on to guide and do a bit of translating, not tell a twenty-two-year-old field- commissioned lieutenant colonel with his first command that the snakes aren't to be trusted. Least of all Tanaghrisson, the Half King. Because nothing was more dangerous than an Iroquois who'd stopped taking orders from the Great Council and decided to go his own way.

Somewhere a kingbird chattered her dawn chorus.

Quent saw the shoulders of one of the Seneca two places ahead of him move as he tongue-clicked a response. Tanaghrisson and nine more braves were running along a parallel track. The two groups had been shadowing each other for an hour.

The kingbird chattered again, fainter this time. The Seneca replied. The other party was breaking away.

Quent felt Washington's hand on his shoulder. He slowed and half turned. Both men were over six feet. Their eyes met; Washington's looked eager. Probably couldn't wait to be blooded. The Virginian had come to the Ohio Country first as a surveyor, then as a messenger sent to warn off the French. That directive had been ignored. So Washington, a young man with neither training nor experience, had been ordered back by the governor of Virginia to raise a regiment, build an English fort, and roust the Canadians, by force of arms if necessary. Bloody fools, all politicians.

"Those bird calls," Washington whispered, "that was the Mingo, wasn't it? What's happening?"

"We're almost there. Tanaghrisson and his braves are taking another route. They'll position themselves on the far side of the French encampment."

Washington nodded, keeping his face expressionless so the older man wouldn't know how much he'd hated having to ask. This Quentin Hale made him uncomfortable. That hair, for one thing. Worn unfashionably short because, he said, it made him harder to scalp. It was a flaming red flag, a constant challenge. So too the cold, ice-blue eyes.

People knew the name Uko Nyakwai as far away as Virginia. And in Virginia, where such things were important, they said Quentin Hale's mother had been a Devrey from New York City, and that his grandfather Will Devrey had made a fortune bringing black gold from Guinea to be sold in the slave market on Wall Street. They said the Devreys were sprung from a penniless Englishwoman, an apothecary come to New York back in the 1660s when it was New Amsterdam. They said she married a Dutch doctor, strangled him in his sleep, then hanged him covered in pitch from the town gallows, so the Dutch would believe it was the devil's doing. Superstitious fools, most of the Dutch.

Better bloodlines on the Hale side. Gentry, from Kent originally. Now Quentin Hale's father owned thousands of acres around the northern lakes of New York Province, a prosperous plantation called Shadowbrook.

So how had his son come to be a woodsman and sometime guide in the Ohio country rather than the landed gentleman he was born to be? God alone knew.

His legs felt heavy as millstones. Every breath was like swallowing fire. Wretched savages, would they never slow down? And Hale, did he not need to breathe like any other white man? Never mind, word was he could nick a man's right earlobe at a hundred paces with that long gun. Likely they would see something of that shooting this very morning. The notorious Red Bear and his long gun under the command of Lieutenant Colonel George Washington of Virginia. Jesus God Almighty, it was hard to believe.

They were toiling up a steep rise. Just enough light now so he could look back and scan the column. At first he couldn't see Montrose, his French-speaking civilian translator. Finally spotted the rat-faced little man at the rear with a flask to his lips. Sod the blighter. No discipline. Drunk twenty hours out of twenty-four. Ah well, not as important this day, perhaps. This time we've not come to talk with the devilish bastards. If the Half King hadn't sent word that he'd found their encampment, they'd have scouted us out and we'd have had to face them back at the Forks, at Great Meadows. With the fort still only half built and my few hundred ruffians against God knows how many French soldiers and their cannon.

He faced forward again, watching Hale, wondering how it was the man never seemed to look where he put his feet, but never stumbled.

Quent was conscious of the younger man's eyes boring into the back of his head. He couldn't remember a moment in his life when he hadn't known when he was being watched. A useful talent in a place like Shadowbrook—vital for a woodsman in the Ohio Country.

The only sounds were the breathing of the braves up ahead, the lurching soldiers behind, and the softly stirring leaves. Then the Seneca who led the file lifted his hand. The signal passed down the line and the column halted.

The French party was bivouacked in a low-lying glen between two steep hills, a site well hidden but not easy to defend. The only guard sat on a rock beside a fire, his musket gripped between his knees while his hands were busy with a mug of drink.

The colorless dawn was warming to a faint pink. A few soldiers staggered out of the bark-covered lean-tos that had sheltered them from the rain and made their way toward the fire.

A small girl stepped into the clearing. She had her back to Quent; his impression was of someone little more than a child. Young to be a whore, but what else could she be?

Quent heard Washington's sharply indrawn breath. Hard to blame him. Sweet Jesus God Almighty. Were French troops such lechers they had to bring a whore along with a search party? That's what this was, of course. A sortie to discover exactly what the Americans were doing at Great Meadows.

A man appeared and moved through the camp. The few others who were awake stepped out of his path. He was of medium height, slim and dark, wearing buckskins much like Quent's own. He kept one hand on the long rifle slung over his shoulder. His hair was tied back with a leather thong, and a jagged scar pulled the left side of his face into an unnatural grimace. Even in the half light and from a distance of fifty feet, he was unmistakable.

Washington leaned into Quent. "That's Cormac Shea, isn't it?" His voice was hoarse with disbelief.

"Yes."

Good God. The two fiercest woodsmen in North America, each a legendary shot, on opposite sides of a battle in which he was in command. Washington's throat closed, a huge lump of fear choking off what wind the long trek had left him. He tried to swallow, but he had no spit. Everyone knew it was Quentin Hale who'd held the knife that had marked Cormac Shea for life. The young lieutenant colonel put his lips close to Quent's ear. "I've never heard of Shea operating this far south. He's supposed to be in Canada."

"Looks as if he isn't."

"Why would a *coureur de bois* such as Shea be with—"

Quent held up his hand for silence, all the while keeping his eyes on the man with the scar.

Cormac Shea was a Canadian, but no French patriot. His mother was a Potawatomi squaw; his father, an Irishman who deserted the English Army, took to the north woods, and lived by trapping and trading—until he was dismembered and eaten alive by Huron who resented his selling guns to their Mohawk enemies. Despite Shea's pale skin and his Christian name, he was the scourge of French Canada. He had taken a public vow to drive every white man from the north country.

So why, Quent asked himself, was he traveling with a party of French soldiers? And dancing attendance on a white whore?

Shea had claimed a couple of mugs of drink at the fire and carried them to where the girl stood. She turned to take hers. Quent craned his neck to see her better. Someone sneezed somewhere to his right and a flight of tiny birds lifted from the forest canopy and flew off, chattering in outrage.

For long seconds the still, damp air quivered with the sound. Then the French soldiers began shouting warnings and running for their weapons. Shea knocked the mug out of the girl's hand and shoved her roughly into her shelter and out of the line of fire. At the same time he managed to start ramming powder down the barrel of his long gun.

Quent grinned. He figured he was three, maybe four seconds ahead in the loading process.

The guard had leapt up from his rock. He flung aside his mug and raised his musket to his shoulder.

Washington jumped to his feet. Quent wasted precious seconds of loading time to reach up and yank him back to the ground. The musket ball whizzed over their heads and crashed harmlessly into the forest. Meanwhile Cormac Shea had finished loading his rifle and lifted it to his shoulder. But he hadn't loosed a shot.

Quent sucked in his cheeks and whistled the throaty, three-note whoop of the northern loon. Then he sighted and fired at a French soldier on the opposite side of the clearing whose finger was just then tightening on the trigger of his musket. The man fell, jerked once, then was still.

Another musket ball hurtled out of the glen. Once more Washington jumped to his feet. This time he managed to shout, "Fire!" before Quent pulled him back down. The Virginia Regiment loosed its first volley of musket balls into the hollow.

A Brown Bess had no sight, and the Virginians were badly and inadequately trained. Still, they had the advantage of the high ground. A number of French soldiers fell. "Tell them to aim low or they'll overshoot, wound rather than kill," Quent murmured. "But don't stand up. You can holler lying down, can't you?"

Washington was quivering with excitement. Even his words shook. "Yes, yes, but, but—"

"No buts. Do it."

"Fire!" Washington yelled a second time, remaining on his belly. "Aim low!" he added, but not before another round of musket balls had peppered the hollow.

On the clifftop where the Virginians were positioned the sound was deafening. Quent knew it had to be a hundred times worse down below, booming between the pair of hills. A haze of thick and acrid smoke had formed over the glen. He could just make out a number of French soldiers running in the opposite direction from the musket fire. Futile. Tanaghrisson and his braves blocked the only other exit from the valley.

Quent squinted into the smoke but didn't find what he was looking for. Christ. He whistled the loon's cry. Nothing. He tried again. Seconds later he heard the three-note reply and breathed easier.

Four, maybe five minutes had passed since the first shot was fired. A dozen French bodies were writhing on the ground. The word was passed that the Americans had lost one man and had three wounded.

A cry echoed from the hollow below. "We have for you information only! Will you give quarter?" The English words were heavily accented.

"Yes!" Washington shouted back. "Hold your fire and we'll hold ours." He waited a moment, stood up, then looked at Hale still lying on the ground, sighting into the French camp. "I'm going down there. I want you to come."

"I'd suggest a number of your soldiers as well, Colonel. To claim your prisoners. Be about twenty of them, I reckon."

"Yes, of course."

"And Montrose to translate."

Washington looked over his shoulder. "That's hardly possible. He's some considerable distance to our rear. Sodden with rum."

"Lucky bastard," Quent said as he got up.

Eight members of the Virginia Regiment accompanied them into the valley. Holding their weapons at the ready, the ten men slithered sideways down the steep hill. By the time they reached level ground they could smell the blood and the loosened bowels of terror. Washington had to raise his voice to be heard above the moans of the wounded. "I am Lieutenant Colonel George Washington of Virginia. Who is in charge here?"

"*C'est moi.* Joseph Coulon de Villiers de Jumonville."

The man who spoke lay on the ground beside the rock that a few minutes before had provided the lone guard with a seat. Jumonville was clutching the bloody pulp that had once been his left thigh. "*Je regrette, Monsieur le Colonel, ce n'est pas possible de me mettre debout.*"

"Do you speak English, sir?"

"*Je regrette encore, Colonel Washington.* A few words only. Not enough." Jumonville turned his head toward the group of French soldiers the Americans had disarmed and were herding into the far corner of the encampment. "Sisson!" He hissed the name because he didn't have the strength to shout it.

A Frenchman, civilian by the look of him, murmured something to one of the American soldiers and stepped away from the throng of prisoners. "I am Henri Sisson, Monsieur le Colonel Washington. I am the translator official of this party." He approached the two Americans and the wounded Jumonville and bowed stiffly. Washington bowed back. Jumonville spoke a few quick words of French. Sisson translated. "There is a correspondence for you on the person of my commander. It is his wish that I to you present it. I am permitted?"

Washington nodded. Quent cocked his gun. Sisson dropped to his knees beside the wounded Jumonville, put his hand in the inside pocket of the Frenchman's jacket, withdrew a stack of correspondence, and held it out. "For you, Monsieur le Colonel."

Washington took the letters and opened the one on top. "This is in French. I do not trust myself to read accurately in that language. Hale, you speak French, do you not?"

"Some. I probably don't read it any better than you do."

Jumonville appeared to have picked up the drift of the exchange. He said something to Sisson, his voice so faint the translator had to bend close to hear. "My commander wishes me to tell you that the message of the worthy correspondence is that this is French territory, and it has come to our attention that you are erecting a fortification in the place of the river joining known as the Forks, on the flatland called Great Meadows."

Jumonville spoke again. The words came hard. Blood spurted from his wound.

"It is the duty of my commander," Sisson spoke quickly, conveying the wounded man's urgency, "to inform you that His Majesty Louis XV forbids you to continue building this fortification."

Washington began an indignant reply. Quent interrupted, speaking directly to Sisson. "Tell him I can tourniquet that leg and stop the bleeding. Keep him alive long enough to continue the argument."

Sisson translated once more, then bent his head to hear the whispered response. "My commander says he would be in your debt, monsieur."

Quent looked to Washington, got the nod, and knelt beside the wounded French Lieutenant. "Have to rip up your jacket to make a tourniquet. Unless of course"—he looked at Sisson—"that young girl I saw a while back would care to contribute a petticoat to the effort."

"Mademoiselle Nicole is—"

"Is right here, messieurs. And happy to be of assistance."

Tiny, yes, but older than he'd first thought, eighteen, maybe nineteen. And beautiful, with a few dark curls showing below her mobcap, enormous pansy-colored eyes, and skin like thick cream. Cormac Shea stepped forward when she did, Quent noted, and he didn't have his long rifle any longer. One of the Virginia soldiers had claimed it along with the rest of the French arms. Now why had Corm Shea allowed a wet-behind-the-ears excuse for a soldier to take away his gun? Because he wasn't ready to leave the scene of the battle, of course. Or the side of the exquisite little creature Sisson had called Mademoiselle Nicole. Quent looked from her to the other woodsman. For the briefest of moments Cormac looked back. Then they ignored each other.

None of the men ignored Nicole as she stepped out of her petticoat, though it didn't do them much good. She turned her back to the men and managed to get the thing off without showing so much as a glimpse of ankle. She ripped a strip from the waistband and handed it to Quent. It was still warm from her body. "Will this suit your purpose?"

"Admirably, Mademoiselle." The pale blue eyes looked her up and down with no attempt to conceal their admiration, then turned to the task he'd set himself.

Jumonville was still trying to stanch the flow of blood from his thigh with his fingers. Quent gently pushed his hand away, then applied the tourniquet, slipping a sturdy twig into the knot. There was full daylight now, and the smoke of the brief battle was entirely gone. No comfort in the feel of the rising sun on the back of his neck, or in the easy victory, though he wasn't sure why.

Quent raised his head while his hands went on tightening the tourniquet. He could see all the way across the glen to where Tanaghrisson and his dozen warriors waited. Sweet Jesus, something was definitely wrong. He could almost smell their hatred. And their impatience.

The tourniquet was doing its job; The blood had stopped pumping from Jumonville's thigh. Quent got up. Without moving his head he turned his glance from the Indians to Cormac Shea, still standing beside the woman. Quent could see the scar, a white streak that ran from Cormac's forehead to his chin and looked like war paint against his tanned skin. Quent again felt his grip on the dirk, then the surge of hot blood spurting over his fingers. They'd been boys, but each in the clutch of a man's hatred. Twenty years and he could still feel the rage. The eyes of the two men met and held a smoldering glance for perhaps a second. Then both turned away.

"Let's go over there," Quent said to Washington. He gestured to the opposite side of the glen from where the Indians were gathered. "We'll take a look at that letter of yours." They walked away from Jumonville, over to the Virginia soldiers and the twenty-one French prisoners they'd marshaled into a tight group.

Nicole began tearing what remained of her petticoat into strips that could serve as bandages.

Shea took hold of her arm and tugged her after Hale and Washington. "*Pas maintenant,*" he said quietly.

"*Mais c'est nécessaire.* I would like to help the others."

"*Pas maintenant.*" Shea was more insistent this time, and he tightened his hold on her arm. Nicole followed him because she had no choice.

Washington was inspecting the letter; he looked up when Shea and the woman reached his side. "Perhaps you can help, Mademoiselle. You are, I suspect, fluent in both French and English. This word"—a long finger tapped the page—"I take it to mean 'defend' and so does Mr. Sisson here. But Hale says—"

He never finished the thought. There was a blood-chilling yell and Tanaghrisson and his dozen Mingo braves erupted into the center of the glen, whooping and hollering and swinging their tomahawks above their heads.

Nicole gasped. "No! I cannot believe . . . What are they doing?"

"Exactly what you'd expect snakes to do," Quent said softly.

Tanaghrisson and his braves were systematically slaughtering the wounded, then flipping them on their bellies, making a shallow cut from ear to ear across the back of the neck, and peeling off their scalps. There were cries of outrage from the French prisoners. Cormac was silent. So was Quent. Washington was the man in charge. It was up to him.

The young lieutenant colonel opened his mouth, but no sound came. He half-raised one arm but let it fall instantly. The rampaging Iroquois dominated the glen and everyone in it by the sheer force of their blood lust.

By Quent's reckoning it took less than two minutes for the Indians to massacre and scalp the wounded French soldiers. All except Jumonville.

Tanaghrisson's bare tattooed chest was spattered with blood, gore, and bits of bone. He stood for a moment in the sunlit glen and lifted his face to the heavens, then went to the French commander and knelt beside him. He raised his tomahawk. *"Tu n'es pas encore mort, mon père."* The tomahawk came down and sliced off the top of Jumonville's head. Tanaghrisson plunged both his hands into the open skull and pulled out the gray matter. Then, standing so that all could see, he rubbed his palms together, washing them in the Frenchman's brains.

The whooping and screaming began again; the kill hunger of the Mingos still wasn't satisfied. A brave lopped off what remained of Jumonville's head and stuck it atop a pole. The others began hacking apart the dead bodies.

The soldiers, French and American, stared in stunned silence at the butchery. Still Washington said nothing. Quent looked for the girl. She had turned away and was retching into the bushes. He flashed another quick look at Cormac, who moved closer to Nicole. Quent took a few steps to his left, placing himself between the unarmed pair and the colonial soldiers.

The boy who had taken Cormac's long gun had it slung over his shoulder. He had his own musket held at the ready, waiting for a command to fire and put an end to the carnage taking place a few feet away. Washington remained as stiff and as silent as a statue.

Quent reached behind for his tiny dirk, palmed it, and moved closer. One deft stroke of the razor-sharp edge sliced through the long gun's leather carrying thong. Quent caught the weapon before it hit the ground and tossed it to Cormac. The Canadian snatched it one-handed out of the air. The young soldier felt the loss of his captured prize. He turned his head. "What . . ."

"Pay attention to your duty, lad," Quent said sternly. "Colonel Washington, hadn't you better . . . ?"

"Yes, yes . . ." The lieutenant colonel of the Virginia Regiment shuddered, as if he'd been bewitched and only just shaken off the spell. "Stop!" he screamed. "Stop or we'll open fire!"

Tanaghrisson looked up and saw the eight muskets pointing at him and his braves. He raised his hand. Instantly the Indians stopped their butchery and backed away. The soldiers stepped forward purposefully, as if it were not too late for them to do anything useful.

The two woodsmen slipped silently into the depths of the forest, Nicole between them. The first time she stumbled Quent picked her up and slung her over his shoulder. Then he and Cormac broke into a trot.

It was ten minutes before they came to a clearing and stopped. Quent set the young woman on the ground and turned away without a word. The two men approached each other, clasped their left hands, and held them aloft. *"Nekané,"* Quent said. The word meant "little brother" in the Potawatomi language.

"Sizé," Cormac said. Elder brother. *"Ahaw nikan."* My spirit greets you.

"Bozho nikan." And mine you.

Nicole, still dazed and shivering with the horror of what she'd witnessed, huddled where Quent had left her, understanding nothing.

Chapter Three

THE OHIO COUNTRY was mostly dense virgin forest, mixed hardwoods and conifers, but the clearing was a small bit of natural upland where the trees had thinned sufficiently to allow dappled sunshine to filter through. Quent and Corm slaked their thirst in the icy water of a rushing stream, then stood ankle deep in daisies and buttercups and let the early morning sun dry the sweat of their run. Nicole was still where Quent had left her, sitting on the ground. Her arms were wrapped around her bent legs, and her face was pressed against her knees.

Quent took a tin canteen from his belt and filled it from the stream, then carried it to the girl. She drank without looking at him and returned the empty canteen without a word of thanks.

"You under an obligation to go back to those colonials?" Cormac asked.

"Not really. Our arrangement's on a week-by-week basis, and the week ends tomorrow. Besides, Washington's done what he set out to do. He'll turn around and head back to the Forks. Tanaghrisson's sure to send a brave to show them the way."

"Washington—that the young officer who was in charge?"

"Yes."

"He appears to need a lot of showing the way."

"This is his first command. Got some growing up to do, but I reckon he'll do it fairly soon. The Ohio Country ages green wood pretty fast." Quent looked more closely at Cormac. "I said I wasn't obligated to return to him. I'm not, unless . . . you figure Washington and his farmers will make it back to Great Meadows without any more trouble?"

"None I'm aware of," Cormac said. "Far as I know, it was exactly what it looked like, a sortie to see what was happening at the Forks and suggest it better be stopped."

"And that's not your lookout? You don't have to report back to anyone?"

Cormac grinned. "I haven't joined the French army, if that's what you're asking. I've a duty, but it's not to them."

Quent saw Corm glance at the woman. She was still resting her head on her knees. "A duty to her?" he asked.

"Not the way I think you mean. Leave it for now. I'll explain later."

Quent nodded agreement. "Fine. So what are you doing here?"

"Looking for you."

"I thought that might be the case. That's why I let you know I was close by." The call of the northern loon had been their private signal since boyhood. "But it doesn't explain why."

"Because Miss Lorene asked me to."

Quent nodded. The great shame in Lorene Devrey Hale's life had been having her husband bed his Potawatomi squaw under the same roof that sheltered his wife and children. But the way it had worked out, Lorene and the squaw's son were devoted to each other. He unslung his rifle and began polishing the barrel with his sleeve. "Pity my mother sent you all this way for nothing. I've said everything I had to say to John. There's no need for any further discussion."

"I wouldn't have come if it was just about making peace between you and your brother."

"Ahaw." Somehow the Potawatomi word for "yes" seemed stronger. "You would. You'd go anywhere and do anything, as long as it was my mother did the asking."

Cormac shook his head. "John is a vicious fool and he's set to ruin Shadowbrook. I think that's something you ought to go back and fix, but it's not why I'm here."

Quent shrugged. "My father's made it clear Shadowbrook's not my lookout anymore. John's the eldest. The house, the land, everything goes to him."

"Quent, listen . . ."

Cormac's tone had changed. Quent stopped rubbing the gun's brass and looked up. "There's something behind your teeth. You'd best spit it out."

"Your father's dying. He's only got a few more months. That's why Miss Lorene asked me to find you. She said I was to tell you that afterward you could do as you liked with her blessing, but if you let your father die with the last words between you spoken in rage, she'll never forgive you. And you'll never forgive yourself."

Cormac felt better for saying it. He squatted and began attending to his own rifle, examining the severed carrying strap. Quent walked away and stood at the edge of the clearing, staring into the trees. Every once in a while Cormac lifted his head and examined the other man's rigid back.

The shade was thicker where Quent stood and the forest floor was a mass of nodding bluebells. There were no bluebells at Shadowbrook; it was too far north. There were plenty of other flowers, though. No place on earth was more beautiful. At least none he'd seen. But for him the land of the lakes would always be haunted by Shoshanaya's ghost. In the Ohio Country he was free of that, free to be his own man. And in the Ohio Country he wasn't a slave owner.

"This land be your pa's land, but it don't rightly belong to no human being," Solomon the Barrel Maker told Quentin Hale in 1732 when the boy was nine years old. Solomon had been born to a slave bought by Quentin's grandfather. He had always been Hale property, and he understood the difference between possession and ownership. "This land belong to God Almighty. It got a lot to teach you. No way you can have learned it all. Not yet."

The land known as the Hale Patent had been given to Quent's grandfather back in 1696 by King William and Queen Mary. It comprised a great swathe of upper New York wilderness that had been presented to a minor court functionary originally from the Kentish town of Lewes not because he was a noble or had any particular claim on the crown, but because he was judged foolhardy enough to take his young wife and go live there.

To the south were the Dutch families, people with names like VanSlyke and de Vlackte and Schuyler, who had settled the far reaches of Nieuw Netherland before the English took it from the Dutch in 1664. The fierce Kahniankehaka, who were part of the Iroquois Confederacy and whom the Europeans called the Mohawk lived to the west. North were the hated French. It suited the British to plant on some hundred thousand acres of the wilderness between them a colonist firmly tied to the English crown, and the English tongue, and the English way of doing and being.

By the time Ephraim Hale—born on the Patent his father had named Shadowbrook—came into his inheritance, the land had changed them all. They were English, yes, and certainly loyal to King George II. But by nature and nurture and instinct they were what the land of their birth had made them: Americans, accustomed to living beside people who were different from themselves, and to following their own rules in a place where they need want for nothing.

The Patent was a land of incredible riches, folded between the Adirondack Mountains to the west and Hudson's River to the east. It was dotted with countless lakes, most small, but a few wide enough so a man needed a day to row from side to side and a week to paddle the full length. There was more hardwood than could be cut for warmth or shelter in a dozen lifetimes. The brooks and streams teemed with fish, and there was every imaginable kind of game in the forests. The presence of the lakes and the river gentled Shadowbrook's harsh northern climate. Between them was the rich black earth of the rolling lowlands and broad alluvial flats where summer wheat grew tall and thick with seed and barley and rye and corn thrived, as did the tender hops necessary for ale.

At one of its many corners the Hale Patent rolled up to the big lake English-speaking people called Bright Fish Water, a translation of the name given it by the People of the Great River, the Mahicans, who had been scattered by the Kahniankehaka many years before. The French who lived at the distant other end of the lake knew it as the Lac du St. Sacrement. At another place the Patent folded itself around a long, curved sweep of watercourse fed by the rushing brooks and streams of the mountains. It emptied into Hudson's River which flowed south from Albany to the harbor of New York City.

By the time he was nine the land of Shadowbrook had entered Quent's blood. Then, on the frozen-in-white December day when he stood with Solomon the Barrel Maker near Tenant Mountain, near the crevasse they called Swallows Children, he saw the first thing in his young life that he neither expected nor understood.

Quent's father appeared out of the dark shadow of the snow-laden conifers that rimmed the crevasse, a treacherous wedge-shaped split in the earth, seductively narrow at the top edge with a rushing underground river below. Ephraim Hale rode a big brown gelding and a squaw sat behind him. Her arms were wrapped around his waist, and before the riders became aware of Quent and Solomon watching them, her cheek was pressed to his spine.

Ephraim saw his son and reined in his horse. He murmured something to the woman and she straightened. A small gray horse behind them stopped as well. Quent paid it no attention; he was busy examining the squaw. She didn't look to be either Kahniankehaka or Mahican. She wore leggings made of pure white skins laced tight with white thongs. The skirt of her overdress was white as well, and the thick jacket that covered the top half of her was fashioned of a sleek white fur and had a hood rimmed in long-haired white fur that might be fox, except that Quent had never seen a white fox.

"This here's my youngest boy, Quentin," Ephraim Hale said. "Goes by Quent. And that nigra with him, that's my slave. Goes by Solomon the Barrel Maker."

The squaw threw back her white fur hood and her black braid fell over her shoulder and shone in the midday sun. Her features were delicate and her black eyes enormous. She said nothing but she smiled at Quent; her teeth gleamed white against her honey-colored skin.

"This is Pohantis," Ephraim continued. "She's from Singing Snow, a Potawatomi village a ways north and west of here. She's come to stay with us for a time." He half-turned and gestured to the small figure on the gray. "That's her boy, Cormac Shea. A year younger than you. He'll be staying with us as well. Never been in these parts before. You can show him the lay of the land."

Quent looked at the other boy. He wore ordinary fawn-colored buckskins the same as Quent's. The fur of his jacket—dark brown like the boy's hair and his eyes—was probably beaver. The surprise was his skin. It was white, the same as his name. Quent felt his father's eyes watching him. Solomon's large hand exerted pressure against his back. Quent nodded in the direction of the strange boy. Cormac turned his head away and stared at his mother and Ephraim Hale.

"You'll be having your lessons together and such," Ephraim said. "Easier on everyone if you get along."

Quent would always remember that moment: his father, the squaw dressed in blindingly white fur pressed up against his back, and her son a white boy with an English name. And the easy way his father said, "And that nigra with him, that's my slave." It was the first time he'd ever heard the claim stated aloud.

He'd asked Solomon once how it was that he could be owned like a horse or a book or a bolt of cloth. " 'Cause I be bought and paid for."

"But you're a person. Like me. Can my father sell me?"

"Ain't never gonna let that happen. You be white. Ain't no white people be slaves. Only black nigra people."

"Why?"

As they talked, Solomon had been shaving the long side of a strip of oak just come from Shadowbrook's sawmill, straddling his workbench and holding the narrow plank of wood across his knees while he smoothed the adze back and forth, back and forth. When he butted that piece of oak against the next plank of the eventual barrel it would fit smoothly, and after he bound them together with leather hoops and the barrel spent a month submerged in water, that seam and all the other seams would have swollen tight shut.

"Ain't no why about it," he said without breaking the rhythm of his long, even strokes. "That's the way it is. It say in the Bible, 'Slaves, be subject to your masters.' Don't say nothin' about asking why."

Quent knew about the Bible.

One of the settlements on the Hale land was called Do Good. Maybe a dozen families lived there, and there was a small church they called a meeting house. It looked pretty much like a barn. Lorene Devrey Hale didn't hold with the services in Do Good's church. No preaching, she said. No Bible reading. No music. No flowers, not even in high summer when they were everywhere. Just the folks from Do Good sitting around and mostly not saying anything, and talking funny when they did.

Quent's mother conducted her own Sunday service in the great hall of the big house. She insisted that all twenty-six of her husband's slaves come, and of course her two sons. Most weeks the tenants who lived near enough came as well: the Davidsons, who worked the sawmill, and the Frankels, who were in charge of the gristmill and did the distilling at the sugarhouse. Sometimes even Ephraim attended. But whether or not he was present, it was Lorene who read from the Bible.

"Better suited to it," Ephraim said once when he was asked why his wife led the service. Mostly he didn't sing either. He was the only one exempt; Lorene made the others sing while she accompanied them on her dulcimer, and before Pohantis and her son Cormac came to Shadowbrook, Lorene smiled at everyone when the service was over. After their arrival there were fewer smiles.

Quent heard his parents talking soon after Pohantis and Cormac arrived, when they didn't know he was outside the half-opened door to the room where his father did his sums. "I got a fire in me for her, that's why. It's convenient having her nearby."

"You had a fire in you for me once."

"That's true, I did."

"But not since—"

"Lorene, she's a squaw and a whore. Left her people and ran off with a damn fool Irishman. Only went back to her village after he got himself eaten alive by the Huron. She's got nothing to do with you, or our life here."

"How can you say that? You brought her here. She's living under my roof."

"I decide who—"

"You'd have lost this land if it weren't for me! Don't you turn your face from me, Ephraim Hale! You know that's true. If it weren't for my dowry—"

Quent heard a crack of sound. Maybe a drawer being slammed shut. Maybe something else. Then he heard his mama crying. That scared him so he ran away.

Next day Ephraim brought Cormac to join the daily lessons Lorene gave her younger son. He was the only pupil because the two Frankel children—Elsie, eight, and her five-year-old brother, Tim—who sometimes came weren't there that day. It was the only time he had ever seen his father in the classroom.

Ephraim pushed Pohantis's boy into the seat beside Quent. "Teach him, too," Ephraim told his wife. "He speaks a fair bit of English, but he needs to learn more. And how to read and write. A little geography wouldn't hurt either."

He had always refused to let her teach the children of the slaves. Now he was bringing her a half-breed. "Why?"

"Because I promised."

Lorene's blue eyes narrowed and she nodded her head in bitter understanding. "Not her. You'd pay no mind to what you promised her. You promised the village chief, didn't you? In order to get her."

"Clever," Ephraim said softly. "Too clever for a woman. See he learns."

Cormac did learn, and quickly. And he had things to teach as well.

A few days after Cormac started coming to the classroom both boys were in the woods on a hill above the big house where they'd been sent to gather kindling. Quent spotted a rabbit standing perfectly still with his ears perked straight up and his nose twitching, seeking the danger smells in the biting winter twilight before setting out to feed. But the rabbit was sniffing in the wrong direction. He didn't pick up the human scent.

Two years before, a Scot who looked like a barrel on legs and spoke in an accent so strange Quent could barely understand him had come to visit his father. The men spent two weeks riding and rowing all over Shadowbrook. Before he left to return to what he called the "auld country" the Scot gave Quent a dirk; he'd been practicing with it ever since. Now the small dagger flew through the air in a perfect arc almost too swift to be seen. The thin, pointed blade landed in the rabbit's neck and the creature died instantly. *"Tkap iwkshe,"* Cormac murmured. Well done. It was the first time he'd spoken to Quent in the Potawatomi's Algonkian language. Quent didn't understand the words, but he could tell from the tone that they were complimentary.

Quent gathered his kill so he could bring it home to Kitchen Hannah to skin and clean and cook. She was called that to distinguish her from Corn Broom Hannah, who cleaned the big house. Quent knew names were important, that they told you things about people. "What's your Indian name?" he asked when he had bled the rabbit and tucked it into the leather bag he'd been filling with kindling.

"Don't have one."

"Why not?"

"I was named by my father. For a great warrior among his people."

"I thought the clan mothers decided the child's name."

"That's how it is with the *Irinakhoiw,* the snakes. Not with us. Potawatomi men are strong. They aren't ruled by women."

"The Kahniankehaka aren't snakes. And they're plenty strong." Quent jerked his head toward the distant hills and the land of the Mohawk. "The other *Haudenosaunee* call them the Guardians of the Eastern Door." He'd been listening to visitors to Shadowbrook tell Indian stories for as long as he could remember.

"Not as strong as we are," Cormac insisted. "The Potawatomi are the People of the Place of the Fire. Nothing's stronger than fire."

"Kahniankehaka means the people of the flint. Flint doesn't burn."

"Fire is over everything. The strongest thing of all. You wait, you'll see."

Eventually he did. But in that winter when Pohantis and Cormac came and changed his world, Quent first discovered a number of other truths. Among them, how mean his older brother John could be.

John was seventeen. Six other children had been born in the eight years between the brothers, but none lived more than a few months. Once Quent heard Kitchen Hannah say that what John liked least about his baby brother was that he lived. "That John Hale, he got himself accustomed to being mostly prized in this house simply for surviving. Not having to do nothing else to be special. Then little Quentin came along and he survived too, and John Hale, he didn't like that."

Quent guessed that was true, but he didn't worry too much about it. Mostly John ignored him. The younger boy was something to be put up with, like the flies of spring and the mosquitoes of summer and the mice that came indoors when it got cold. Quent tried to ignore John in his turn, but it wasn't always possible.

Do Good was on the northern rim of Shadowbrook's land, a couple of hours upriver from the big house. The people who lived there called themselves Friends; everyone else called them Quakers, because, it was said, they quaked before the Lord. That was maybe why they were known to be the most straight-dealing people in the colonies. Once the Quakers said it would be so—they refused to take an oath because it implied they were not always telling the truth—it was so.

Ephraim Hale allowed the Quakers to settle on his land for precisely that reason. They ran his trading post and did all Shadowbrook's business with the local Indians. The Kahniankehaka brought furs to Do Good to exchange for metal tools, woven cloth, and of course ale and spirits. Periodically the Quakers took the pelts of beaver, otter, bear, and seal to New York City and sold them. Ephraim had no part in the business side of the Do Good trading post, but he never for a moment doubted that he was getting the two-fifths part of the proceeds to which he was entitled in their agreement.

That February Ephraim sent his eldest son to Do Good to collect what Shadowbrook was owed. "Take the young ones with you."

John had yet to say Cormac Shea's name aloud. "Both of them?" he asked.

"Yes."

"Why?"

"Because I said so."

John looked quickly upstairs toward the adjoining bedrooms occupied by his mother and his father, then in the direction of the little room near the kitchen where the Potawatomi whore spent most of her time. "Maybe Mother would care for an outing," he said, looking straight at his father. "Shall I ask her?"

Ephraim didn't flinch from his eldest son's glance. "Your mother is staying here. And if you want to be allowed to do the same, you'd best do as I say."

John took Quent and Cormac with him to Do Good.

The trading post was built of split logs; it was the biggest building in the settlement and the first built. The houses and the pair of barns at either end of the single village road were made of planked wood from Shadowbrook's sawmill. The barn at the opposite end from the trading post was the Friends' meeting house and had been given a coat of whitewash. That made it the fanciest thing in the place, except maybe for the sign that said DO GOOD TRADING POST in black letters on a white board.

Inside the trading post Esther Snowberry stood at a long wooden counter. Behind her the wall was lined with shelves containing bolts of homespun, rows of tin mugs and crockery bowls, and heavy metal frying pans called spiders with three short legs so they could stand beside the hearth. One entire shelf held brown crockery jugs filled with the rum Moses Frankel distilled from the boatloads of Caribbean sugar that arrived at Shadowbrook's downriver wharf. After the sugar was offloaded the ships took on the plantation's grain and vegetables and barrels of salted pork and venison. Without those foodstuffs the Barbadian planters and their slaves would starve, since every inch of their soil was given over to cane, the king of all cash crops.

On the counter beside Esther was a pile of furs, a mix of thick brown beaver pelts and a few gray-black sealskins. She had obviously been inspecting them, but she looked up from the task the moment the Hale brothers and Cormac Shea arrived. "Welcome, John Hale. I hope all is well with thee and thine at the big house."

"Well enough. I've come for our share."

"Of course. It's put by for thee. But first thee must take a seat by the fire and have a warm drink and some food. And thy two young companions as well."

There was a large fireplace at the other side of the room, flanked by two long pine settles with high backs to keep off the drafts and broad seats that offered a place to rest and take comfort in the warmth of the hearth. The only other people in the trading post were an Indian studying a display of hunting knives at the far end of Esther's counter, and a small girl dressed exactly like Esther, in a gray dress with no trim, not even buttons or collar, and a pristine white mobcap without out a ruffle.

The girl was seated beside the fire busily stitching and pretending to take no notice of the visitors. "Judith, take thyself at once to fetch thy father and Edward Taylor. Thee is to tell them John Hale is come to collect his father's portion. And tell Prudence to bring johnnycakes and hot cider."

Quent paid the little girl no mind. He was peering into the shadows at the brave who was bent over the knives. The blue tattoos on his cheeks proclaimed him Kahniankehaka. His hair was long and black and fell free to his shoulders. Quent knew that if the brave were on the warpath he would have shaved his head, leaving only a scalp lock that challenged his enemies to take it. He'd heard plenty of stories about fierce Kahniankehaka warriors who had fought beside the English against the French back before he was born, in what his father called Queen

Ann's War, but everyone said the Kahniankehaka who lived around Shadowbrook were peaceful. Be that as it may, Quent wasn't sure what would happen if this brave knew Cormac was half Potawatomi. Corm had already told him the Potawatomi were the sworn enemies of all the *Irinakhoiw.*

John was apparently wondering the same thing. "You know my little brother Quentin, Esther. This other one's a métis, a half-Potawatomi brat. The story goes that the Huron cut out his father's heart and ate it, but they must have been too full to bother with this little something extra."

He'd said it loud enough so the brave had to hear, but the Indian didn't look up until he'd selected one of the knives. He came toward them carrying it. Cormac stared straight at him and took a couple of steps forward, so he was in front of both Quent and John. Quent's eyes darted back and forth between the Mohawk brave and Cormac Shea, whose head didn't quite come up to his shoulder. Quent moved just enough so he was closer to Corm. In case. Behind them John chuckled.

The brave ignored both children. "This knife," he said, showing his choice to Esther Snowberry. "And the cloth you have measured. And two jugs."

Esther frowned slightly, but she reached behind her and put two jugs of rum on the counter beside the cloth and the knife. The Quakers were abstemious in the matter of drink, but one of the conditions of their settlement on Ephraim Hale's land had been an agreement that their trading post would deal in Shadowbrook's rum. Few Indians would come to trade otherwise. "Thee is then fully and fairly paid for thy skins," Esther said, nodding toward the pile of pelts on the counter. "Dost thou agree?"

The Indian nodded and collected his goods. On the way out, never once having looked directly at the little boys standing shoulder-to-shoulder, he said quietly, "The hearts of those who hide behind squaws and children would not be worthy of eating. The Kahniankehaka would throw them to the dogs."

No sooner had the door closed behind the brave than it opened again. Esther's husband had arrived, bringing two other men with him. "Thee is welcome, John Hale," Martin Snowberry said. "Thee knows Edward Taylor." Martin indicated his Do Good neighbor with a nod, then turned to the third man. "This is another visitor, Daniel Willis, who comes to us from Rhode Island."

The men took seats beside the fire. Prudence arrived carrying a basket filled with still warm corncakes and a jug of sweet apple cider that steamed when she poured it into small crockery drinking bowls. The black woman served the men first, then Quent and Cormac, and finally Judith. Esther refused the refreshments and tied the skins into a neat bundle.

Edward Taylor had been summoned in his capacity as the keeper of Do Good's purse. He leaned forward and passed a soft deerskin pouch to John. "Thy father's share of the last trip to New York City is here. Seventeen pounds and eleven shillings. All good coin. Louis d'or and *daalders* and Portuguese *cruzados* and the like. Thee need not hesitate to count them if thee wishes."

John hefted the pouch in his hand and the coins inside jingled softly. He loosened the drawstring but made no further move to count the money. "What brings you to Shadowbrook, Mr. Willis?"

"There is no need to call me mister, John Hale. I'm told thee does not share our beliefs, but thee should know I seek no title of any kind."

"Very well—Daniel, then. What brings you to Shadowbrook from Rhode Island in the dead of winter? It can't have been an easy journey."

"Easy enough since it ended safely. I come on the urging of the Light Within, John Hale. To bring a message."

"Oh? What message is that?"

"It is time we stop buying and selling our fellow creatures."

John looked over at the bundle of pelts that lay on the counter. "You worried about the seals and the beaver, Daniel? We'd be overrun with the things if we didn't trap 'em."

"I speak not of animals but of people, John Hale. Negro people like Prudence here."

Quent shot a look at the black woman. She stood absolutely still and stared straight ahead, as if she did not hear what was being said. "What do you say to that, Prudence?" John asked. "You think you've been treated right?"

Prudence didn't answer.

"Thee may reply if thee wishes," Martin Snowberry said quietly. "I confess, I would hear thy answer."

"Ain't nobody in this place be's mean to me." Prudence didn't look at them and began packing the basket with the remains of the food.

"But thee is not paid for thy labor," Daniel Willis said. "Thee gets no reward for thy toil. In the Bible it says the workman is worthy of his hire."

Esther was looking from Prudence to Daniel Willis with some consternation. "In his letter to the Colossians Paul says to be fair and just in the way thee treatest slaves. Would he say that if the owning of them were contrary to God's law?"

"Dost thee not believe that the Light Within is stronger than any written word, Esther?"

"Of course I do. But we bought Prudence from a man who whipped her regularly. No one whips her here, and she is properly clothed and housed and fed. Thee must believe that it is better we bought her from a master who treated her so poorly."

Daniel Willis shook his head. "Thee canst not buy another human being."

"That would certainly surprise parliament and the king," John said. The Province of New York was the only English colony with a royal governor appointed by London; all the others had a right of self-rule written into their charters. But though no territory north of Virginia approached the number of slaves bought and sold and owned in New York, one way or another they all— north and south alike—depended on the trade for their financial health. "Nor, I suspect, would the merchants of Rhode Island be happy with the news."

"Slavery is against the will of God," Daniel Willis insisted. "Thee canst not buy and sell thy fellow human beings, nor expect them to work on thy behalf without fair recompense."

John stood up. "Not another white human being, perhaps. Nigras and Indians are different. And half-breeds, of course." John put his tricorne on. "Good day to you, gentlemen, Esther."

He and the two boys were halfway to the door when he turned and handed the deerskin pouch full of money to Cormac. "Here, carry this. You may as well be useful for something."

When they arrived at the big house, there were only sixteen pounds and five shillings in the pouch, a pound and six shillings shy of the amount Edward Taylor had said belonged to Ephraim Hale.

Quent knew instantly that John had taken the coins before he gave Cormac the money to carry. He tried to tell his father, but Ephraim wouldn't listen. And John just laughed when Quent confronted him. His mother was his last hope.

Quent found her in the little room where they stored the household linen. It was right next to the woodshed where Ephraim had taken Cormac.

"Cormac didn't do it," he blurted out. "He didn't steal Father's money, John did. He gave Corm the pouch to hold just so he could get him in trouble when we got home."

Lorene was standing with her back to him, holding a stack of carefully folded kitchen cloths to her face.

"Mama, do you hear me? Please, Mama, you've got to—"

"Hush, Quent. I hear you." Lorene turned and set the stack of cloths on the table. She was breathing with some difficulty and her cheeks were bright pink. The flush extended down her neck to the exposed skin above her breasts.

They both heard the sound of Ephraim's razor strop whistling through the air and thudding softly against flesh. Quent winced. "Mama, Cormac didn't do it."

"Tell your Father."

"I did. He won't listen."

She shook her head. "Your Father is . . . I can't tell him anything, Quentin. I'm sorry. I . . . Go away, child. I'm busy."

She was folding and unfolding the same square of cloth and her eyes were strangely shiny. The sound of the razor strop was loud in the little room but Lorene shooed him away, her eyes staring at a point somewhere over his head.

"He knew you didn't do it and John did," Quent told Corm later. "That's why he only gave you six stripes."

"If he knew I didn't do it, then it was wrong to give me any," Cormac said.

Quent agreed, but he couldn't explain Ephraim's behavior so he didn't try.

The next day John was sent to Philadelphia to stay with a Hale cousin for a year and learn something of printing, since Ephraim said he might someday want to open a print shop on the Patent.

In April four Potawatomi braves appeared and stood waiting at the edge of the long drive that led from the front door to the river landing. "They've come for Cormac," Ephraim said.

"Not for her?" Lorene asked in a flat, unnatural voice.

"Not for her," Ephraim confirmed. "She stays. Cormac spends the winter here with us learning to be white, then he goes back to Singing Snow for the summer and learns to be red." Ephraim shrugged. "The sachem said they want him to be easy in both worlds. So in the future he can speak for the Potawatomi to the Europeans."

"She stays," Lorene said.

"Yes, I told you. She stays." He stroked her cheek with one finger and smiled slightly. "There need be no interruption of our ... our mutual interests. No interruption at all."

Ephraim Hale strode out of the house to meet the Indians. An hour later they left with Cormac and took Quent along as well.

Standing in that clearing in the Ohio Country, Quent thought about that day in Do Good. He didn't know what the Quakers had decided about slaves, but the older he got the more he knew how much he hated the system. And the thing he maybe hated most was the way the slaves he knew went along with it, truly believing they were owned by another human being, and that it was the right and proper way of things.

No, maybe what he hated most, the thing that two years before had finally driven him away for good, was how John was making it worse. Blaming the slaves for the decreasing profits. Treating them like animals. Worse. Not even John was stupid enough to put his horses on half rations. But he was stupid enough—or mean enough—to ignore the fact that it wasn't lowered supply causing the financial troubles at Shadowbrook, simply less demand: cheap Pennsylvania wheat was driving the better New York product out of the market.

Quent walked back to where Corm squatted on the ground, checking the sight of his long gun. "My father's been an invalid for years. I can't remember the last time he was able to walk without sticks. But he's always been too ornery to die. What makes my mother think that's about to change?"

Cormac got to his feet and tested the repair he'd made to the long gun's carrying strap. "Good thing that dirk of yours is so sharp. You sliced this through nice and clean. Made it easy to fix."

Quent looked at the scar his dirk had made on Cormac's face. Twenty years and the pain and guilt were no less, despite the fact that a short time after it happened both boys had solemnly smoked the calumet, and the fight was truly over, forgotten and forgiven. Quent made himself ignore the scar and his feelings; it was a sin against the calumet to do otherwise. "Tell me why my mother thinks the old bastard's going to die."

"Your uncle, Caleb Devrey, Miss Lorene's brother, he's a doctor and he came and said so."

"All the way from New York City?"

"Yes. He said—"

There was a terrible noise. Nicole was rocking back and forth, making a sound of grief and pain that was like the scrape of a sharp stone on glass, so piercing it hurt the ears.

Cormac swung around. *"Est-ce que vous êtes folle? Silence!"*

The girl didn't stop wailing. "Who is she?" Quent demanded. "And why are you responsible for her?"

"It's a long story. I told you, I'll explain later. Listen, about your father, you've got to—"

Quent turned away and strode over to Nicole. "You must be quiet. We're in the middle of Iroquois country."

Her cries got louder, and she looked at him as if he were not there. Quent knew she was gazing into some terrible hell in her own mind.

He picked her up. She was limp in his grip, her arms clasped over her heart, her mouth still open, still making those terrible noises. Carring her over to the stream, he waded into the middle of it, then dropped her. She landed on her backside, and tiny though she was, made a formidable splash.

Even this late in the season the water was icy with the melting snow of the high peaks to the east. Nicole screamed and flailed around, beating the racing water with her fists, trying to get to her feet but constantly defeated by the slippery, uneven rocks that formed the streambed. Quent watched as she eventually managed to stand up. The struggle had left her soaked from head to foot. Her dress, already torn and filthy from their flight through the forest, clung to every generous curve of her small body. "You are a madman! *Un idiot!*"

"I told you, we're in Iroquois country. You were keening so's a half-dead deaf-and-blind old man could find us, let alone a few bloodthirsty braves."

She shuddered. "Those Indians, the ones back there at the glen, they will come looking for us?"

"I don't think so. That bunch has no reason to want us dead and every reason to want us alive. But that doesn't mean you should tempt fate. There are others around who have different intentions."

"I'm sorry. I didn't know I was making any sound at all." She stopped looking at him and looked down at herself. Her cheeks reddened when she saw how much the wet garments revealed. "I'm sorry," she murmured again.

"It doesn't matter," Quent said kindly. "We seem to be pretty much alone, for the moment. Ohio Country's a big place."

"What is this Ohio Country? I thought we were in the *pays d'en haut*."

"Not exactly. That's what the Canadians call the land north of us around the big lakes. As far as the Potawatomi and the Miami and the Mascoutin and the Huron are concerned, it's their land. As for this bit here, Ohio Country's as good a term as any. Which are you, by the way, French or English?"

"By birth I am both, monsieur. My father was English and my mother French. But my heart is not divided. It is entirely French."

The amount of pride in her voice made him smile.

"You are laughing at me!"

"Never."

She didn't look convinced. "I am entirely serious, monsieur. You cannot—"

"Hale. Or Quent, if you prefer. Not 'monsieur.' "

"Very well, Monsieur Hale then." Nicole tried to make for the shore, but stumbled after the first step and again fell to her knees.

This time Quent took pity on her and picked her up. "This streambed is treacherous, and you're not properly shod to navigate it. Besides, if you're going to bathe in the stream like an Indian, you should take all your clothes off to do it."

"Bathing in open water is unhealthy," she protested. "Everyone knows it." And when he'd dropped her on the grassy bank, "What is properly shod?"

"These." Quent held up his leg. His wet moccasin, ankle high and fastened with supple leather thongs, had molded itself to his foot. "They're what the Indians wear. Much better than boots in the forest. Boots"—he nodded toward hers, black leather and tightly laced to a few inches above her ankle—"have hard soles that slip and slide. The Indians make moccasin leather so it stays soft—it protects your flesh, but lets you move as if you were barefoot. You can feel the earth."

"Barefoot," Nicole said softly, "is a good thing. It's what I want to be."

Quent had no chance to ask why. Cormac had kindled a small fire. "Come over and get dry. This and the sun will do the job in no time."

Quent's legs and his moccasins dried quickly, as did Nicole's skirts. But her hard leather boots remained damp, and the top half of her was soaked through. Her nipples showed against the snug bodice of her dress. Both men tried to avoid staring at them.

"What's it to be?" Cormac turned to Quent. "What direction are you taking when we leave here?"

"My uncle Caleb, you're sure he said my father would die soon?"

"Ahaw." Yes. "He said it was dropsy. A few more months. Maybe less. I heard him myself."

Quent hesitated. He sensed no hostile force in the immediate vicinity, and even if there were, Cormac Shea would be a match for it. Corm was as good a woodsman as was ever born, and in a fight he had no equal, except maybe Quent himself. Corm and the girl didn't need him. But his mother had asked him to come. And Shadowbrook. God yes, that was the real truth of it. Shadowbrook calling him home. "I'm heading north with you, *nekané.*"

"My spirit is pleased," Cormac said softly in Potawatomi.

Chapter Four

IN NEW FRANCE, the Delegate of the Minister General of the Order of Friars Minor lived hard by the river in Québec's Lower Town, in a two-room stone hut that was little more than a hovel. The larger of his rooms was square, with one tiny window and a ceiling of rough beams darkened by countless fires, furnished with a single battered table and two straight chairs; it served Père Antoine for every purpose except sleep and worship. The other room he called his cell. It had a few straw-covered planks that did for a bed, and enough floor space so he could kneel and pray or take the discipline. It was wide enough so he could stretch out his arms in the cross prayer and not be able to touch either wall. To say Holy Mass or recite the Office in the presence of the Holy Sacrament he had to go into the street, walk a short distance, and enter the public side of the tiny chapel of the Poor Clare nuns.

However dreary his house might be, the surroundings did not diminish the force of the priest's personality. Hunched over, using the light of the only candle to study the papers spread out on the scarred table, he dominated his visitor. "This map, you're sure of it?"

"*Oui, mon Père.*"

The man, a Scot named Hamish Stewart, spoke passable French. He was the son of a minor laird from the Highlands, one of those who had clung to the True Faith since the days of the sainted Reine Marie—Mary Queen of Scots, as she was known to the English. Those who remained loyal to her these many years since her death were called Jacobites, after James II, the last Catholic king to rule over Britain and forced from the throne because of his religion. Many Jacobites smuggled their children to France to be educated, but *mon Dieu,* they never lost the Scots twist of tongue. The mutilated accent pained the priest's ears. "We will speak English, so you will not fail to understand me. This land between the lake and the river, it is exactly as you have drawn it?"

Père Antoine straightened and stepped aside. The candle flame illumined the map, the priest as well. He was of medium height, so thin as to be gaunt, and his brown hair was threaded with gray, but he still had the elegant carriage of the aristocratic family Rubin Montaigne into which he'd been born; a way of setting his shoulders and holding his head that no amount of asceticism could erase. "Exactly?" he asked again, indicating the map. "Because if there are errors—"

"Na a single error, *mon Père*. I drew the thing meself. That's the lay o' Shadowbrook's land, exactly as I saw it."

"Ah, then the question comes down to how well you see. I do not mean to be blunt, but with one eye . . ."

Hamish Stewart had left the other eye on Culloden Moor in 1746, fighting for the Bonnie Prince, Charles Edward Stuart, risking everything that a Catholic king might again rule Britain. A thousand Jacobites were slaughtered at Culloden. Thousands more were left so horribly maimed they could no longer think of themselves as men. They had been betrayed, as had happened so often before, by fellow Scots willing to sell their souls to the bloody Sassenachs, the devil-spawned English, may they choke on their God-rotting Act of Union. Blessed be the Holy Virgin and all the saints for letting him off that blood-soaked moor with na but the loss of an eye. But if he still had both—he chanced a sideways glance at the Franciscan—God's truth, he wouldna be able to stare down this mad Friar. Like burning coals in his head, those black eyes were. Were he a heretic Protestant, God's truth, he wouldna want to look into those eyes.

"The pass," Père Antoine said.

Stewart bent over the table and studied the map as if he were looking at it for the first time, his eye squinting into the light of the flickering flame. After a few seconds he straightened. "I saw this place in 1730, *mon Père*, when I still had both eyes. Ephraim Hale himself showed me the lay of the land. I dinna make a mistake."

"And tell me again why you were there."

"The clan sent me. Back then there was still a wee bit o' brass in the Highlands. There was talk o' buying a bit o' land in the New World, moving some o' the young to a place where they'd be free o' the devil Sassenachs."

"But these negotiations, they came to nothing?"

"Less than that, *mon Père*. Hale wanted too much and we had too little. And the womenfolk dinna want the young to go."

Père Antoine bent once more over the map. "Exactly like this?" he repeated.

"Aye, I swear it."

"Save your vows for the promises you make to God, my son. Here we are talking only of human intelligence."

"But for the good of Holy Church, *mon Père*. Is that na the same thing?"

"Perhaps." The black-eyed glance examined the Scot. He was a short, thick man, with straggly shoulder-length hair that was half black and half gray. His breeches and hip-length, belted coat were faded to no color and shabby with wear. "So that is why you have brought me this, Hamish Stewart, for the good of Holy Church?"

"Aye, o' course. Why else would—"

"Because you covet the Hale Patent. So it is to your advantage to break Ephraim Hale. If I send my Indians to burn his fields and he has no harvest . . ."

Your Indians, Stewart thought. Aye, that's surely the nub o' the thing. Why should I believe a Franciscan priest can say to a Huron savage "Go" and he goes, and "Come" and he comes? Lantak's a butcher by all reports, as well as a rebel. A merciless wild man his own people have banished, savages though God knows they be. But that's the way o' it. This friar and Lantak. A pair o' madmen making common cause for as long as it suits 'em. Aye, and God's truth, I've heard stranger tales. "The buildings as well, *mon Père*. It's essential that as many o' the wee out-buildings as possible are burned. The grain already harvested, that's where it'll be."

"But not his house, eh? You wish me to tell Lantak and his braves very specif-ically that they are not to put the house of Ephraim Hale to the torch."

He could na look into those eyes, however often he tried. Damn the man. Was it being a Frenchman gave him his superior airs, or his high-born family, or maybe the cloth and his holy vows? But that shouldna be. Supposed to be beggars, own nothing, go about barefoot doing good. Aye, that's what St. Francis said. He'd have wanted no part o' this French devil acting high and mighty and giving orders to a gaggle o' bloody savages. "Shadowbrook's a remarkable house, *mon Père*. None better in the province." God's truth, why was he mumbling and staring at the poxed priest's poxed feet. Sandals, not barefoot. So much for St. Francis.

"My footwear interests you, my son? You are perhaps thinking that I should be barefoot as Blessed Francis ordained?"

Sweet Jesus, the poxed man could read his mind. Stewart felt the sweat mak-ing rivulets down his back, despite the cold. Colder than the Highlands, poxed Québec was. There was a fire in the grate, but so wee and poorly fed it cast a scant shadow and less heat. "I'm thinking, *mon Père*, that it's past time I started back." Stewart nodded toward a pouch of coins on the table next to the map. "There's six hundred livres there. So I need you to tell me if it will be done."

Père Antoine put his hand over the money, but he did not pick it up. "The burning and pillaging of Ephraim Hale's Patent? That's what we're discussing, isn't it?" Because if it is done when you suggest, the priest thought—in August, just as the harvest begins—Hale will be bankrupt. Like most men of property he has land, not cash, and he has mortgaged that land to the last sou. So if I do as you ask, my one-eyed Scot, Ephraim Hale will be ruined. And his creditors will be happy to sell you his land for six of your British pence on the pound.

The Scot was standing with his hands clasped over the bulge of his belly, his single eye looking at the crucifix on the wall. Waiting for the priest's final word, a picture of patient devotion whose only aim was to serve.

You're a villain, Hamish Stewart, and you care as much for Mother Church as I care for that beetle crawling across the hearth. Less. But you will further our holy cause despite yourself. "It will be done, my son. I give you my word on it. And you in turn give me your word that afterward French troops and our Indian allies will have safe passage across this bit of portage?" The Franciscan drew one slim finger across the top of the crude map of the Hale land, from the southern tip of one long lake to the beginnings of the narrow waterway that debouched into another. Control the land between those two bodies of water and you had a straight path in any direction. The way west led directly to the French forts of the Ohio Country.

Hamish looked at the section of the land the Mohawk savages called the Great Carrying Place. "Aye, I swear it." Finally Stewart made himself look directly into the priest's God-awful eyes.

"Then you can return to New York with an easy mind, my son. I will arrange everything." The pouch of coins disappeared into the folds of the priest's habit. "Now, I will give you my blessing for the journey."

Stewart knew what was expected of him and struggled to go down on one knee. Aye, and it werena easy. Eight years since devil-cursed Culloden Moor, since he'd been in fighting trim. More belly to him now, and his thighs grown like fat hams. Time was when he could live for six months on a sack o' oats. Now he supped regularly on the incredible bounty of the New World where only the laziest fool need ever be hungry, and he feared it was making a woman of him. But if he got Shadowbrook, everything would be different. He'd be a laird, by God. He'd send to home for a young strong Scots wife and fill her belly with sons. Aye, the way a man was supposed to live. Na fighting and killing and losing, so your heart be broken along with your body. He bowed his head and waited for the priest to pray over him.

Père Antoine made the sign of the cross in the air above Stewart's bent head and murmured a Latin benediction. Possibly, he thought, the Scot's last rites. You are engaged in a perilous trade, Hamish Stewart. There are others who are much better at it, and they will squash you when and how it suits them. When that day comes, may Almighty God forgive you your greed and your venal schemes. May you be spared the fires of hell, but may you suffer in purgatory until the angels announce the Savior has come again in glory to judge the living and the dead. "Safe journey," he murmured as, the benediction finished, the other man lumbered to his feet.

"Thank you, *mon Père*. I count on your prayers to make that a certainty."

"In a few hours I shall offer Mass for that intention."

The pair went together to the door. Stewart was wrapped in a thick woolen cloak, but the priest wore only his shabby brown habit. The night was cloudless and all the colder for it. The wind rose off the river and whipped their ears, and the stars were slivers of blue ice in a black sky. Above them the massive fortifications that surrounded the settlement stood out, clear in the silver light of a three-quarter moon.

Since 1608, when Samuel de Champlain resisted the lure of Montréal with its forests and numerous waterways opening to the west and chose instead to make his great military base the natural citadel of Québec, it had been the Fortress City of New France. Built on a rock rising between two rivers, the mighty St. Lawrence and the lesser St. Charles, Québec had remained unassailable for nearly a hundred and fifty years, anchoring Canada for the French king.

Champlain had begun his building in what was now the Lower Town, the place where the priest and his visitor stood. A century and a half later it was a clutter of three- and four-story wooden houses built close together on narrow and stony streets by the waterfront, and almost always wet with the spray that came in off Québec Harbor, the broad St. Lawrence basin that could shelter a hundred ships. Over the years the settlement had climbed the cliffs behind the wharves. Now the Upper Town was surrounded by massive walls, its skyline dominated by the steeple of the cathedral. A short distance away, almost as imposing, was the steeple of the church of the mighty Society of Jesus, the Jesuits. Black-clad schemers, priests like Père Antoine himself, but more clever than St. Francis's simple sons. At least than most of us, the Franciscan thought.

The good God had made him a Friar Minor, but his brains had not been removed at ordination. The black robes had the ear of the bishop of New France and of the pope himself—some said of Louis XV, as well. *Eh bien,* Antoine would count on having the ear of God. As for this strange Jacobite, he would be made to serve Holy Church's purpose in spite of himself. "Go with God, my son." Another sign of the cross, sketched hastily in the chill air.

"Goodnight, *mon Père*."

Père Antoine watched Stewart hasten down a narrow alley between two rows of hulking cottages, listening until the ring of his boots on the cobblestones had faded. Then, despite the cold, he remained a moment longer, looking toward the charity hospital known as the Hôtel-Dieu, then letting his gaze roam upward to the redoubt outside the town walls, and the high flatland called the Plains of Abraham where a few of the locals, the *habitants,* struggled to grow crops during the desperately short growing season. Their success was limited, and not just by the endless frozen winters. Corruption riddled the Canadian economy. The few got hugely rich and the many starved, particularly the native population whose way of life had been so disrupted by the coming of the Europeans. In bad years, the priest had been told, the Indians were reduced to gnawing on the leather diapers of their children, though the infants had beshat them a thousand times. Père Antoine had seen hunger before. He believed the report to be entirely accurate.

There was no starvation for the wealthy Québécois living within the shelter of the city's mighty fortifications. They ate the best of everything and lived like kings. Europe's taste for the furs of the far north makes them rich, along with their willingness to engage in deception and thievery. They destroyed the old way of life of the Indians and made them virtual slaves, forced to trap and trade in return for the made goods they can't now do without. Cloth and metal goods, but guns mostly. And alcohol, the devil firewater. Antoine was convinced that the Jesuits, Almighty God have mercy on them, were at the center of this vicious exchange. Under their all-powerful provincial, Louis Roget, they were black spiders in the middle of an endless web. More killing and starvation and disease and death, that's what the savages got from the missionary efforts of Louis Roget.

Dear Jesus, let me show them Your holy and loving face. Let them be saved for You who thirst for souls.

A few Franciscans were with Champlain when he came. God help them, they had given up. The Jesuits filled the void, becoming the missionaries to the Indians of New France.

Allow us to return to the rich Canadian harvest, Lord. Grant us our chance to be martyrs whose blood will give You glory and insure the future of the order.

Père Antoine felt warm despite the frozen night. He stared a moment longer at the symbols of eminence in the city above his head, then turned to the hut a few doors from his own here in the Lower Town. It was bigger, but still a hovel. The Jesuits had seen to that. As if putting the Poor Clares in the humblest dwelling in the city did anything but make them more acceptable to the Savior.

The roof of the archbishop's château was halfway up the steep cliff, midway between where the priest stood and the steeples of the grand churches at the top of the city. According to the Vatican, the archbishop of Québec was responsible for the spiritual welfare of all New France, which, if the entire territory it claimed were counted, was considerably larger than Europe. New France stretched from the Atlantic coast to land yet unexplored in the far west. It encompassed the valley of the Mississippi River and the area known as the Louisiana Territory. Unlike his predecessors, the current archbishop, Henri-Marie du Breuil de Pontbriand, lived mostly in Québec.

Père Antoine made yet another sign of the cross, this one in thanksgiving. How wondrous are Your ways, Lord. For if the family de Pontbriand did not have ancient debts to the family de Ruben Montaigne, the Poor Clare Colettines would not be established in a stinking, half-rotted fisherman's cottage at the edge of the fortress city. Saving its soul. And the souls of how many savages, You alone know.

It was because of those old family ties and obligations that Pontbriand had gone against the advice of the Jesuits and allowed the nuns to make their foundation in Québec, and permitted Père Antoine to accompany them as chaplain. And it was those five nuns who would see to it that Franciscans, not black gowns, brought the Holy Gospel to the Ohio Country. Who better than the simple sons of Blessed Francis to speak to the primitive hearts and souls of the Indians?

The priest looked once more at the hovel that had become the Monastery of the Poor Clares of Québec. Much of the mortar in the stone foundation had rotted and fallen out. The bell tower, hastily erected just before the nuns came, was crooked, and barely large enough to contain a single bell. When the nuns saw it they were delighted. Just like San Damiano, they said, the ruin where Francis put Clare when she became the first nun of the Seraphic Order.

Those five women assailing heaven on behalf of the Order of Friars Minor would prevail. Nothing was more certain. They were not the first consecrated women in Québec. There were the Ursulines, who schooled girls of the best families in their large and beautiful convent on the Rue des Jardins, and the Augustines Hospitalières caring for the sick poor in the Hôtel-Dieu, as well as a breakaway group of the same congregation who had built another, grander hospital, the Hôpital Général, in the Upper Town. But women whose vows bound them to give their lives to constant prayer, fasting, and penance . . . in all the vastness of New France there was nothing to compare to his five Poor Clares. Soon to be six. Just yesterday Mère Marie Rose had said that sometime in the near future she expected a postulant to join the order. The first since they'd arrived in Canada the previous spring.

A new postulant was an omen, a sign from God that the prayers and penances of the Franciscans in Québec were accepted. Père Antoine was so sure of this he had already sent word to a house of the order two thousand miles south in Havana. They were to prepare to send him friars to be missionaries—God willing, perhaps martyrs—among the heathens in the Ohio Country.

Above his head the bells of the cathedral tolled the midnight hour. Père Antoine looked toward the hovel-turned-monastery and, as he expected, saw the tiny lights of five candles flicker past the window. The Poor Clares had interrupted the six hours of sleep they were permitted out of each twenty-four. They were on their way to chant Matins, the first prayer of the new day. After an hour they would return to their straw pallets on wooden planks and rest until four, when they would rise to chant Lauds and begin another day of fasting and prayer and labor.

Thanks be to God, the seeds were planted. They would be watered with martyrs' blood.

"*Ici*—over here."

Stewart turned toward the voice. "Glad to see you, laddie. Crossed my mind
you might o' gone."

"And why would I do that, Hamish Stewart? Did I not tell you I would wait?"

"Aye, you told me." Stewart squinted at the line looped around the bollard at
the edge of the stone dock, holding the wee boat—a dory they called 'em in these
parts—close in and steady so as he could jump aboard. Looked secure enough,
though he could never get over his suspicion o' these Canadians. Or the feeling
that in this place, wherever he went at whatever hour, he was always being
watched.

Stewart put a booted foot on the dory's gunnel. The Frenchman, Dandon,
watched the maneuver with a smile bordering on a smirk. A wave lapped the little boat and she drifted a bit seaward. Dandon slackened his grip on the line. The
gap between Stewart's legs widened. The Frenchman chuckled. "You must make
up your mind, *mon ami*, the sea or the shore." Stewart struggled to maintain his
balance, and finally, at the last second, threw his weight forward and lurched
rather than jumped into the dory. Dandon laughed again. "Not so bad, eh? Once
you take a decision."

Bastard. He could o' held the poxed boat closer in and kept her steady. Never
mind. He was aboard now.

Dandon took a lantern from between his legs and held it over the side, passing his hand over the opening in a series of signals to the sloop waiting some half
a league away. A light flashed quickly in response. "*Alors,* they are ready for us.
Take up an oar, *mon ami*. You will work off some of the fine supper the priest fed
you."

"Aye, and what supper might that be? Prayers a plenty, but na a crumb to eat."

"*Eh bien,* that is what you get for treating with the brown friars, *mon ami*. They
are committed to what they call Sister Poverty. At the black gowns you get the
finest wine in New France, and the best food."

Stewart pulled on his oar, matching the other man's strokes and settling into a
steady rhythm. "And what would the likes o' you ken o' supping with the high-
and-mighty black gowns?"

Dandon shrugged. "I have ears, no? Many things I hear."

Probably true. Why would he na hear everything that mattered, considering
that he worked for the almighty Bigot. God's truth, there was na a job in the
whole o' America better than Bigot's. The intendant o' Canada, the civil admin-

istrator o' New France. Every farthing taken in trade went through his hands, and three out o' five stuck to his fingers. But the thing about Bigot that made him different, and more successful than most villains, was that he was smart enough to share his profits wi' his friends. *La grande société,* they called themselves, and high and low belonged. Even Dandon, menial though he be, got his wee bit. That way there was none as could turn on Bigot wi'out implicating himself. A fine plan, simple but effective.

And one of Bigot's schemes was heaven-sent for the enrichment of Hamish Stewart, if he could get Shadowbrook. Bigot bought Canadian grain at prices fixed by law, five to seven livres per *minot,* milled it at government expense, and sold the flour to the Crown—that is, to himself—at the market rate of twenty or more livres per *minot.* But the way things were in Canada—inflation fueled by paper money, and the farmers hiding their grain from the representatives of the intendant so they could sell it on the black market—it was possible to do some Scots business with French Bigot. Specially for someone wi'out scruples as how he owed some kind o' loyalty to the heretic British crown. Just you be smart enough to ken the way his mind works, Hamish laddie, and the mind o' the mad priest as well, and your fortune's made.

The sloop came into view just ahead of them, her single mast and her rapier-like bowsprit showing a parade of white canvas gleaming in the moonlight. Her sails were luffing now, spilling the freshening wind of the approaching dawn, waiting for the command that would send a dozen men into the rigging to set close haul and send her speeding south.

"Ahoy!" The call was more a whisper than a shout. All seamen knew that voices carried on the water. "Who goes?"

"I'm not goin', lad. I'm comin'. And you can save your tar talk for them as is impressed wi' it. I paid for this passage. I dinna have to talk your talk as well."

The seaman let down the rope ladder. "Come aboard, Mr. Stewart. Tide's turning. Pilot said we'd sail soon as you were back."

Until they were through the shoals and reefs of La Traverse, the devilish stretch where the St. Lawrence divided between the southern tip of the long island known as the Ile d'Orléans and the mainland of Québec itself, the grizzled Canadian pilot would be God Almighty, and his words, the Eleventh Commandment. "Canna be soon enough for me, laddie." Stewart grabbed hold of the ladder and heaved himself out of the dory. "I'll be happy to see the back o' this place."

"Un moment s'il vous plaît, mon ami," Dandon whispered anxiously. "My report, what is it to be?"

"Aye, that's what it's to be. Aye and aye again. Tell *la grande société* everything will be exactly as I promised."

The man lying flat on his belly on a rotted bit of old wharf snapped his glass closed as soon as he saw a pair of seamen haul the Scot off the ladder and into the boat. He had no interest in observing Dandon row back to shore. The Scot and the overzealous Franciscan were another matter. And what about Lantak, the mad savage? His spies in the countryside had reported that Père Antoine was meeting frequently with Lantak. You forget him at your peril, Monsieur Louis Roget, priest of Almighty God and Provincial Superior of the Society of Jesus in New France, reminded himself. And the peril of Holy Mother Church.

Roget stood, gathered his black cloak around him, and began the long climb up the hill to the great fortress of the Collége des Jèsuites in the Upper Town.

Quent and Cormac and Nicole traveled by day and camped by night. The going was slow because part of the time one or the other of the men had to carry the woman. She hated that and struggled hard to keep up, but when she came to the end of her endurance and there were still hours of daylight to be utilized, Quent or Cormac picked her up and they continued.

They ate twice a day: in the morning before sunup, and in the evening after they made camp. Food and drink presented no difficulties. The men killed small game, squirrels and rabbits and the occasional partridge, and the forest was laced with streams and brooks. They lacked potherbs and saladings and it was too early in the season for berries, but once Quent found a stand of fiddlehead ferns poking aboveground. Another time Cormac contributed a couple of fistfuls of mushrooms to the evening meal.

The men took turns standing watch throughout the night. Nicole, utterly exhausted, slept. There was little time for talk. Sometimes, for a few moments before they doused the cooking fire, Quent and Cormac exchanged remembrances of the long days of summer in Singing Snow and the bitter cold of winter experienced from the safe haven of Shadowbrook. Of the present situation, of what Quent faced when he returned or Cormac's plans, they said nothing.

Nicole spoke hardly at all until the sixth night. Cormac had gone deep into the forest to relieve himself and she and Quent were alone. She was burying the bones of the quail they'd eaten, deep and carefully the way the men had shown her. She finished scuffing the earth above the bones and looked across the embers of the dying fire. "You said they had every reason to want us alive. Why?"

It took a few seconds for Quent to understand what she meant. "Tanaghrisson and his braves?"

"The Indians who . . . The murdering savages. You said they wanted us alive. Why? To torture us? Because they hate all whites?"

"Sounds like you've been listening to some stories."

"It is not true? The savages do not torture white people? Even eat them?"

"Sometimes it's true. But not just whites. They do the same things to each other. It's part of their way of life. Their religion, you might call it."

Nicole crossed herself. "You are speaking blasphemy. That is not religion. It is heathen barbarism."

Quent shrugged. "Call it what you like. It's how it is." He wasn't surprised by her papist gesture. Cormac had told him she was a Catholic on her way to Québec and that he'd taken charge of her two weeks before. Not by choice, but because he was under an obligation. Nicole had been traveling with her father, Livingston Crane, an Englishman and former army officer. They had been in Alexandria when Cormac arrived looking for Quent. Some American trappers recognized Corm, knew there was a price on his head in a dozen different places in the colonies, and laid an ambush. Livingston Crane chanced on it, warned Cormac, and insisted on fighting beside him. The Englishman took a knife wound to the heart and died in Cormac's arms. His last words were a plea that Cormac get Nicole safely to Québec. Corm had tagged along with Jumonville's party because it promised safe passage for at least part of the journey, and a few more of the creature comforts a woman required, even here on the frontier.

"If it was not to torture us or eat us," Nicole demanded, "why do you say those Iroquois want us to be alive?"

"The Half King wants witnesses."

"Why should a murderer want witnesses? And how can anyone be half a king?"

"It's an Iroquois notion. A king speaks for all his people, a half king for some of them. Tanaghrisson speaks for the Iroquois in the Ohio Country."

"You make them sound almost civilized."

"Not almost," Quent said. "Out here that's an important lesson. Not almost."

"You called them snakes."

"I never said they weren't clever. Tanaghrisson wants witnesses to tell the story of how he slaughtered Onontio. That's their name for the French governor-general. It was originally a Huron word that means 'father'; now all the Indians use it. You heard what he said before he killed Jumonville: *Tu n'es pas encore mort, mon père.*' You are not yet dead, my father. He meant Onontio, the French presence in the Ohio Country, wasn't dead." He would have said that the Half King washed his hands in Jumonville's brains for the same reason, but she was looking ill again, sickened by her memories.

"I do not understand."

"The Iroquois are English allies. They want the English to prevail in this part of America," Quent said patiently.

Cormac returned and squatted beside them. He picked up a handful of moist earth and let it sift through his fingers onto the last glowing embers of the cooking fire, extinguishing it. "Sounds like you're giving Mademoiselle Nicole a lesson in politics."

"Something like that." Quent looked from Cormac to Nicole. Was there something between them besides obligation? When it was Quent's turn to carry her through the forest he couldn't put such thoughts from his mind.

"Quent's left out some things," Cormac said. "The Iroquois aren't really English allies. They simply want dominance. That's the Iroquois way. They call it the *Kainerekowa*, the Great Peace, but it's a peace in their favor and they're willing to get it any way they can. Mostly through great war. Iroquois prey on anyone who's weaker than they are, hostile or not. From their point of view, it's only peace if they're in charge."

"You do not like them?"

"I despise them."

"I thought it was only white people you despised," she said softly. "That is what people said in Alexandria."

"They're wrong. I'm half white. I don't hate my white blood or anyone else's. I only hate what the whites are doing to the Indian way of life. If they would leave Canada to the Indians, and down here stay on the other side of those mountains behind us," he jerked his head in the direction of the Alleghenies to the east, "everything might be fine."

"Might be," Quent said. "There's no guarantee."

Cormac smiled, an odd grimace because one side of his face was frozen by the scar. "An old argument," he said for Nicole's benefit. To Quent he said, "Might be, I agree. But the way it is now's deadly for the *Anishinabeg*." He turned to Nicole. "*Anishinabeg* means 'Real People.' It's what the folks the whites call Indians call themselves. But doesn't matter what name you use—pretty soon the Real People will be wiped out. So something else has to be tried. The whites have to get out of Canada."

Nicole persisted. "Back there in the glen, when the Iroquois murdered the wounded. Is that why the American colonel allowed them to do it? Because the Iroquois are English allies?"

Quent shook his head. "Absolutely not. That would be a black mark on Washington's honor. He'd promised the French troops quarter."

"Then why—"

"It's the Indian way, to take scalps and loot after a battle. In this case Tanaghrisson wanted to prove to the other Indians in the Ohio Country, the Shawnee and Delaware who might side with the French if they thought it was in their interest, that the Iroquois are still the mightiest warriors in the area. Nothing sends that message better than leaving a pile of scalped and hacked-apart bodies to be found by the next hunting party that happens along. As for Washington, my guess is he was just too surprised and terrified to know how to stop Tanaghrisson. He's ambitious, but very young. Now that it's over, he's bound to be sick at the thought of the story getting out."

They traveled for six days and the only other human life they saw was a Mingo hunting party. Quent spotted them first; they moved off the path and hid deep in the forest, waiting while the Mingo passed. The last one in the file turned and looked over his shoulder for a long time, as if he'd heard something. Quent loosened the tomahawk at his waist. In the end the Mingo went on without stopping.

On the seventh day they neared a sprawling Shawnee camp erected beside a rapidly flowing stream.

"What do you think?" Corm asked.

"Make it a lot easier if we had a canoe." There were half a dozen beached beside the water. "I reckon we could steal one easily enough."

Cormac tapped his knapsack. He carried a rabbit and a brace of grouse shot that afternoon. "Better if we trade for one. Avoid having a war party coming after us."

Quent could feel the longing in Cormac, the need to let the Indian part of himself come to the surface. He could do that among the Shawnee, who were longtime allies of the Potawatomi. Besides, the Potawatomi were the most skilled canoeists among the *Anishinabeg*; they would make remarkably good time if they took to the waterways. Quent looked toward Nicole. She was standing a ways apart, staring at the Indian village with a look of frozen terror on her face. "What about her?"

"We take her with us. No other choice."

"I agree. But she's terrified of Indians. What's she going to make of it all?"

Cormac shrugged. "I don't rightly care. The squaws will look after her until we leave."

Chapter Five

THE WIGWAM THE Shawnee squaws used for preparing food, like the others of the encampment, was framed with saplings and covered with bark. It was longer than it was wide and tall enough to stand up in, with a rounded roof that would shed rain.

But the night was balmy, a late June evening with a bright moon rising. The squaws sat on the ground in front of the cooking wigwam, some distance from the main fire and the braves. They crowded around Nicole, touching her hair and her face, stroking her arms as they fingered the material of her dress, caressing her ankles while examining the lacings of her boots. At first she protested and tried to shoo them away; after a time she grew silent and made herself stay limp, ignoring them and concentrating instead on Quentin Hale and Cormac Shea. The two men she had traveled with for a week were gone. In their place were a pair of savages.

Monsieur Shea was naked except for a breechclout. He wore beaded bracelets above and below each elbow and on his bare legs. His hair hung loose and he had feathers pinned to the back of his head. Monsieur Hale had no feathers and no bracelets, and his hair was too short for feathers, but he had stripped to only his buckskin trousers and his chest was bare except for an amulet that hung around his neck on a leather thong.

He had told her this was a summer camp; during the winter the Shawnee divided into bands of hunters and went their separate ways, but when summer approached they came together in places like this. "It's a big three-month family reunion. Pretty much anyone's welcome long as they're not an enemy."

"And you and Monsieur Shea, you are not enemies of these Shawnee?"

"No. Corm's half Potawatomi; they're distant kin of the Shawnee. And I'm Potawatomi by adoption. Besides, I'm not an enemy of any Indian."

"Not even the Iroquois?"

"Strictly speaking, not even them."

"And if we do not speak so strictly?"

Quent didn't look at her. "I'm English. Most of the Iroquois are English allies. That's enough for the time being."

"They are your allies against the French, you mean."

"That's what I mean."

Before she could reply he'd left her in the squaw's wigwam. The women had fed her and themselves after they fed the men. The smell of roasted meats—rabbit and grouse and possum—still hung in the air. A few feet away mangy, half-tamed dogs gnawed on the discarded bones of the meal. Dusk was fading to night, and behind the men lines of fish being smoked looked like so many bats hovering near the fire.

Nicole saw Quentin Hale lean forward. The flames lit his red hair. He looked like a demon. He said something to one of the Indians and the savage put back his head and guffawed. Nearby a couple of the squaws seemed to have heard what was said because they laughed too. Nicole shivered. Dear God, what will become of me in this place? Holy Virgin, protect me.

"You are pleased to see the men of your tribe like Real People, *neya?*"

The voice whispering in her ear spoke English, but the smell—like peppermint, Nicole thought—was of squaw. Nicole turned her head and saw a woman of perhaps forty, maybe older. Her face was lined and she was missing some teeth, but her hair was still shiny black. She wore it across her shoulder in a single braid that ended with a cluster of iridescent bird feathers. The woman wore beaded bracelets that covered both arms and a short buckskin dress. She reached out and stroked Nicole's cheek. "Two strong braves. Which one do you lie with? Both maybe?"

"I don't. With neither. It's a sin to . . . Stop that! Stop poking me."

"I am saying hello, only. I forgot that white women do not touch each other." The squaw withdrew her hand. "I have been away from whites for the coming of many summers. I am Torayana. Once I was with a white man. For many summers, many years. When he died I returned to my own people."

Nicole looked from the squaw to the men sitting in a circle around the huge fire. The Indians were all as naked as Cormac, and as decorated with bracelets and feathers. The men, braves she supposed she should call them, all had long hair and wore feathers fixed to the back of their heads. A few days ago Monsieur Hale had told her that among many Indian tribes male babies had a board strapped to their heads so their skulls would flatten and make a firm place to anchor the feathers. "That's one way to tell the tribe they belong to, and the clan within the tribe, by the feathers they wear."

The night was warm and the heat of the leaping flames was fierce. All the same, she could not stop shivering.

Torayana fetched a blanket and put it around Nicole's shoulders. It smelled of Indian, musky and foreign, but Nicole was grateful for it. "Tonight," the squaw whispered, "if I were still young and good to look at, I would offer myself to Uko Nyakwai. I would lie on my back and spread my legs and ask him to cover me in the white man's way. Ayee! What a thing to have Uko Nyakwai bouncing up and down on top of me and his man part inside me. After a hundred fires my sisters would not be tired of hearing that story. Not after a thousand, *neya?*"

Torayana's face was flushed and sweat beaded her upper lip. "To be Uko Nyakwai's woman," she whispered, "that would be exciting. They say his man part is as thick as his arm and almost as long. They say that Shoshanaya nearly died of fright the first time she saw his man part. But afterward, he pleased her so much that she offered herself to him night and day. The other one"—she tossed her head toward Cormac—"he is also fine. I would offer him my back passage gladly. But he is not Uko Nyakwai, *neya?*"

"Uko Ny . . ." Nicole struggled to pronounce the words.

"Uko Nyakwai." Torayana spoke more slowly. "It is the Indian name of the man you call Hale. It means Red Bear."

"And the squaw named Shoshanaya, she was his woman?"

"His wife," Torayana said proudly. "The marrying words were said over them in a Jesus house. She was an Ottawa princess. Her father was Recumsah, a great Ottawa chief. He gave his daughter to Uko Nyakwai, and Red Bear brought her to his father's land and they were together for seven moons. Until one night when a war party of Huron came." Torayana turned her head and spat on the ground to take the taste of the enemy's name from her mouth. "When they found Shoshanaya alone in the wigwam Uko Nyakwai had built for her each of them violated her, though she did not offer herself to even one. Then, before they were done, Uko Nyakwai returned and his rage was so great he ripped a tree from the ground and used it to kill each of the Huron braves who had forced himself on Shoshanaya. But he was too late to save her. Her spirit was too shamed to stay in her body. She was carrying Uko Nyakwai's son and she took his small spirit with her and they both left this earth."

"But why did the Huron braves do such a thing?"

Torayana shrugged. "They say earlier there was some kind of fight and Uko Nyakwai killed a Huron who was stealing. They say it was the dead Huron's brothers who went to the land of Uko Nyakwai's father. They say it was for vengeance, but who knows why men do anything, *neya?* Anyway, Huron are filth." She spat again. "Look, see that brave there?" She pointed to a man who had risen and was standing beside the fire speaking. All the others were listening to him intently. "He is Pontiac, an Ottawa like Shoshanaya. He is part of her clan, the son of Recumsah's brother."

Quent could feel the women studying him. He glanced in Nicole's direction. He was pleased to see her wrapped in a blanket and chatting with one of the squaws, though he guessed they were talking about him.

No one else was paying any attention to the women; they were listening to Pontiac. "If we forget the old ways, what will become of us? We will sink deeper into the pit we dig for ourselves with the white man's weapons and his tools and his firewater. Soon we will no longer be sickened by his stink." Pontiac's tawny skin was bathed in the fire's glow, and the clan feathers pinned to his head were haloed by smoke. His hair was long like the Shawnees', and around his neck was a stone carved with the sign of the turtle. The amulet around Quent's neck was the same. Shoshanaya's father had given it to him.

"It is time to put aside our differences and remember that we are red men and that the whites are our common enemy," Pontiac said. "We must circulate no war belts against the *Anishinabeg*. We must unite to fight only those who would drive us from our lands and destroy our way of life." He turned and looked directly at Quent, still squatting beside the brave he'd been joking with a few moments before. "Look what has become of us. We allow white men to take our women. And because they are too weak to protect them, our squaws become whores for our enemies."

Quent got to his feet. He towered over the Ottawa, but he knew that did not mean the fight would be an easy one. Pontiac was known for his strength and his cunning. Quent felt the dirk against his lower spine, but he did not immediately reach for it. "Pontiac speaks like a child who steals the nuts and tells his elders he has killed the squirrel."

"I am not a child, Uko Nyakwai. And I do not mistake nuts for a squirrel." The Ottawa's head barely reached Quent's chin, but his shoulders were as wide as a bull's, and the muscles in his chest and his arms rippled when he moved. No one came armed to a talking fire like this one, but Pontiac had used his knife to cut the meat of the earlier feast. It was stuck in the ground at his feet. He bent and retrieved it.

"I smoked the calumet with Recumsah," Quent said quietly. "I cannot now fight with you over the same wrong."

"I was not at the ceremony and you did not smoke with me." Pontiac reached up and yanked the turtle amulet from around Quent's neck and flung it on the ground.

Quent had no choice now. He'd have to fight Pontiac. If he killed him, Recumsah would howl with rage and declare Quent an enemy of all the Ottawa. It was unthinkable. "I have no quarrel with you, Pontiac, son of the brother of Recumsah. Pick up the amulet and return it to me and we will put this moment on the fire and turn it to smoke."

"I have a quarrel with you, Uko Nyakwai. You do not stink like a white man, but you cannot escape your white skin. What's worse, you are English. Your kind wants more than the hearts and bodies of the *Anishinabeg,* more than our hunting skill to feed your endless hunger for skins. The English want our land and that is our soul. One less of you will be a good thing."

Quent reached behind and palmed the dirk. He felt Cormac's eyes on him and knew Corm was tensed and ready. No one would interfere with the fight until after Pontiac was dead. Then they would be furious because the visiting Ottawa had died at a Shawnee fire during a time of peace, and the Shawnee would have to pay huge reparations to Recumsah's clan in apology. As soon as that realization sank in, the Shawnee would be blind with rage and a free-for-all would begin. It would be the sixteen braves against him and Corm. Their long guns were stacked with all the other weapons some ten strides to their left. The girl was twenty strides in the opposite direction, surrounded by Shawnee squaws who could be as fierce as the braves when the need arose. Sweet Christ, what a mess.

Pontiac lunged at him. Quent feinted. He brought the dirk up in his clenched fist and the tip grazed the Indian's shoulder and drew blood.

"Stop!" The voice of the brave called Teconsala was not loud, but all heard it. "Stop," he said again, and Quent and Pontiac backed a few steps away from each other. Neither man was breathing hard, but blood trickled down Pontiac's naked torso from the wound on his right shoulder.

"This is a fire of summer peace and none here have any quarrel with Pontiac or Uko Nyakwai," Teconsala said. "You will settle your differences in another time and place. Not here."

Teconsala was not a full chief, but he was the senior brave present at the camp. And apparently the coolest head. The others nodded and murmured agreement. The pleasure of watching a death fight between two such warriors had to be weighed against the size of the reparations required if Pontiac should be the one killed. Teconsala gave good counsel.

"I have lost blood," Pontiac said, gesturing toward his shoulder. "I am due payment."

"This is true." Teconsala looked at the white man whom the Potawatomi had adopted. Let us see if your courage is really that of the bear they call you, man of the red hair. "Pontiac is entitled to one cut in return. It can be anywhere he chooses." He could have restricted the area for the vengeance cut, said it must not be a death thrust or a cut that took away Uko Nyakwai's manhood. He had set no such limit. Now the Red Bear was wholly at Pontiac's mercy. "You agree, Uko Nyakwai?"

"Teconsala speaks fairly and with wisdom. I agree." Quent opened his hand and let the dirk fall to the ground. He stood where he was with his legs spread, arms hanging loose at his side, and stared straight ahead.

Pontiac took a step toward him. His knife was a honed piece of flint, and it was sharpened to an edge that could slice easily through aged leather. He held it in his right hand to show that he cared nothing for the pain of the wound in his shoulder. Pontiac aimed his weapon at Quent's heart.

Quent looked past the Indian into the fire. He opened himself and allowed his spirit to leave his body and fly far. In his head he sang the death song he had composed as a boy, under the guidance of Bishkek, his manhood father, the old brave who had helped him become a Potawatomi and a man. Whiteness. Snow covering the earth. A spirit soaring free.

Pontiac waited, studying Red Bear's face, trying to engage his eyes but failing. The only sound was the crackling of burning logs.

Pontiac did not strike. He dropped his knife until it no longer pointed at his enemy's heart but at his groin.

Castration. A fitting punishment for a man who could not protect his Ottawa squaw and allowed the Huron to defile her. Quent did not move. Whiteness and a free spirit.

Pontiac shifted his weight forward and slashed. At the last second he moved the blade so it merely grazed the hard muscled flesh of Quent's side. Deep enough to draw blood, but nothing more. Pontiac wiped the flint on his wounded shoulder, signifying that he was repaid for the loss of his own blood, then sheathed it at his waist. He bent down and retrieved the turtle amulet and the dirk and handed both to Quent. "These are yours, Uko Nyakwai. I heard your death song as it was in the air between us. It was a good song, like the softest snow is good. Perhaps I will kill you one day to avenge Shoshanaya, but not here and not like this."

Quent drew a long deep breath and slowly, with pain, his spirit returned to his body.

The others watched and waited, knowing that Uko Nyakwai had faced certain death and that he must be given time to recover. After a few seconds a shudder passed through him. Teconsala saw and nodded to the drummers and the dancing began.

The feet of the men shuffled slowly at first, then the beat of the drums became faster and the dance quickened. A singer, a young boy, added his voice and at various times the braves sang with him. Quent sang too. The beat of the drums entered his blood, making his heart beat with their rhythm.

The squaws got to their feet and began to sway in time to the music and the dance. Torayana pulled Nicole up beside her. "It is a mark of disrespect to stay on the ground when the dance begins. Now," she whispered urgently, "you must choose."

"What do you mean? I—"

"Who will you have, a Shawnee brave or one of the two you came with? If you do not choose, it means you will accept only a chief. Tonight that would mean you belonged to Teconsala. Or if he wanted, he could give you as a gift to Pontiac. By not choosing for yourself you will give him that right."

The dance was a whir of speed now and the singing was a high-pitched frenzy that to Nicole sounded only like a wail. "You are mad. I will not lie with any man. I have made a vow."

Torayana's dark eyes widened. "You are a virgin. Ayee! What a prize!"

Nicole tried to duck back into the protection of the wigwam, but Torayana grabbed her arm and held it so tightly she could not get away. "No! That means only that you invite Teconsala."

Quent saw the scuffle from the corner of his eye, but he didn't focus on what it might mean. His entire being was one with the music and the dance. His life had been returned to him and his body sang with the joy and the desire and the need of the drums. The first time he'd danced he'd been thirteen years old, newly made a Potawatomi man because he had earned the right. That time he'd been embarrassed by the reaction the drums and the dance produced until he saw that all the dancing braves had the same response. And in moments a squaw had chosen him—an older woman whose breasts sagged and who had few teeth. She led him away to the woods and squatted for him, showing him how to mount her from the rear. He'd lost his virginity in a howl of excitement and triumph. Next time, she'd told him, he could have a young and beautiful squaw, and not shame himself by not knowing what to do.

The first of the squaws to break from the cluster of women in front of the Shawnee wigwam went to Pontiac and touched his shoulder. He followed her into the woods.

"Quick," Torayana whispered, "if you want Uko Nyakwai choose now. Otherwise one of the others will pick him." Her advice came too late. One of the squaws, the youngest and prettiest of them, darted forward and touched Quent's shoulder. He followed her into the trees without once looking back toward Nicole.

Torayana saw the terrified look on the white girl's face. She waited a second or two more until Cormac was in their direct line of sight, then gave Nicole a huge shove toward him. The girl stumbled into Cormac's dancing body. He grabbed her to keep her from falling, then picked her up and carried her away.

Chapter Six

THE SEVEN MEN sat in a circle in a clearing hard by a small trading post known as Gist's Settlement. Washington and his civilian quartermaster, an Irishman transplanted to Virginia named George Croghan, were the only whites. The others were Tanaghrisson the Half King, a Delaware, two Mingo, and a Shawnee. According to Tanaghrisson, they were all war chiefs. So far they hadn't shown any stomach for the fight Washington urged.

The Virginian's foothold in the territory, the fort he'd erected on Great Meadows, was six leagues east. He'd left a hundred troops behind to guard it. The French were twelve leagues west at Fort Duquesne.

If he turned his head Washington could see the three hundred militiamen he'd brought with him. They were strung out in clumps of twenty or so, each working party with a distinct job: felling trees, hauling them out of the way, leveling the path, beating the raw earth into some semblance of a surface hard enough not to ensnare the broad wooden wheels of their transport. It was slogging, backbreaking, thankless work, and the men cursed and sweat and stank their way through it. All with one aim, to complete the road that would take them the rest of the way to the French fort. They had been about that same task for two weeks of hard days and exhausted nights with never enough time to sleep, inching through the forest with their supply wagons and their big swivel guns. Never mind, Washington told himself, success was assured. The men would thank him for it in the end and they would thank Almighty God they'd been privileged to serve with George Washington. There was glory in him; he could feel it in his bones. Bloody damn, he could taste it. But right now he needed to concentrate on the Indians.

Bloody savages all of them, and Tanaghrisson the worst. An animal who washed his hands in another man's brains. In Christ's name . . . Best not to think about it. Nearly a month now and no repercussions. No surprise from anyone when he reported that the Virginian musketry killed ten that day, including Jumonville, and afterwards the Indians scalped the dead. Everyone knows they do that. As for the French prisoners, they're spies and lie about everything. Any right-thinking person would take the word of George Washington of Virginia over a lying Frenchman. Put it out of mind. Concentrate on what's happening right now. Tanaghrisson is right; it won't hurt to have the hatchets of these savages and their warriors on our side. Put the fear of the Almighty in the French. But God help me, it's a strange business to listen to a painted savage go on for over a quarter of an hour and not understand a word he's saying.

Tishcohantin, the Delaware, was doing most of the talking, pacing back and forth in the middle of the circle holding a string of wampum in his left hand. Croghan said they did that to give their words weight; the number of times the speaker twisted the wampum around his wrist indicated the importance of what he had to say. Also, at least according to the Irishman, the reason the Delaware had that squirrelskin tobacco bag with the pipe sticking out hanging around his neck was to show himself a man of peace. Peace be damned. Not now. Not yet. Peace has to be earned. And you, you blighted heathen, had best say soon if you're for us or against us. I shan't tolerate that icy stare much longer.

Tishcohantin of the Lenape—whom the whites, the *Cmokmanuk,* called Delaware—had made four loops of wampum around his left wrist. Now he spoke slowly, with no outward emotion, and his steady gaze never left the face of the young Virginian. "Last winter I warned your people, and the winter before that. Still you English did nothing. For two winters Onontio has come and built his forts in this valley, and you did not listen when I told you what that meant. Now, after you have spent the strength of your warriors coming to this place and divided your forces, three hundred of them here and another hundred left back at your new fort . . ." Tishcohantin looked at Croghan, then at Tanaghrisson.

Those two understand my words, but not this young one who is supposed to be the leader, the war sachem. No matter. The others will tell him I have taken his measure. Four hundred men altogether. They say more are on the way, but if they come—and knowing these English, they may not—where will he put them? That pissing hole he calls Fort Necessity, which is now a hard journey behind him? If he meant to make a stand at Great Meadows he should have stayed there. Getting this far on the way to his enemy has wrecked his wagons, and they and his heavy guns have made bad paths worse. I know every stupid thing he has done and still he wants me to take up the hatchet to fight for the English against the French. Why should I do that? Why should any of us?

Washington stared back, uncomprehending of anything except the question in the red man's eyes. He leaned toward Tanaghrisson. "Tell him it is my intention to march on and take Fort Duquesne. Tell him we'll rout all the French, all Onon-tio's soldiers, from this valley. If the Delaware and the others will fight with us, together we will become stronger than before and all can live in peace."

Tishcohantin began speaking again, before the snake Half King could say any-thing. Before the boy who wanted to be a war sachem realized that Tishcohantin the Lenape understood his language, though he refused to speak it. "If you English and the French are going to fight here, this valley will not be safe for our families. We will have to move them to your settlements in the places you call Pennsylvania and Virginia." He spun around so he was facing the Mingo and the Shawnee. "And what would our women and children be in those places, those white shitholes where men and women separate themselves from the feel and the smell of the world the Great Spirit made and lose touch with all reality? They will be refugees, strangers with-out respect. And do these English know anything about hospitality? You all know well that they do not." Tishcohantin paused for the length of one long breath.

"Once there were *Anishinabeg* in those places where now only the *Cmokmanuk* live. It is impossible for Real People and English to live side by side. Little by lit-tle they are squeezing the life out of us. They have a sickness these people, a hunger for land. They think they can take possession of the very earth beneath our feet. The French come and trade—sometimes, I admit, they fight and try to kill us—but eventually they go away. The English bring their women and children and they remain. They bring only ruin. Are we to take up the hatchet for them, commit our braves to fight and die, so that afterward they can overrun us? This is a plan without wisdom."

The face of the Half King remained impassive, but he read the decision of the others in their eyes. Tishcohantin the Lenape had convinced them. *Ayi!* Not only would they not fight with Washington, they would most likely take up the hatchet for Onontio, who was not dead after all, however hard he, the mighty Tanaghris-son, had tried to kill him.

The Half King flicked a quick glance at Croghan, the Irishman. He knew it as well. It was plain on his face. Would he tell Washington? Maybe. Maybe not. But it did not matter whether or not the Virginia sachem knew. It was over. The great plan for removing Onontio from the Ohio Country had failed. Tanaghrisson felt a little shiver deep in his belly, a knowing that was coming to lodge in his gut. It would probably kill him, this knowing. But first he and his would suffer more. May the Great Spirit curse all *Cmokmanuk,* and forgive us for ever thinking we could live with them in this place.

"Why do you return alone?" Tanaghrisson's wife asked. "Where are the soldiers and the others who left with you?"

"They are not here."

"I can see that. Do you think something has happened to my eyes?"

"You have a squirrel's tongue. Click-clack, click-clack and you say nothing. It makes me tired to listen to you. Get everything ready, we are leaving."

"All of us?" Her husband had brought eighty people here, twelve of them braves, the rest women and children and old people.

"All," he said.

"A far distance?"

Tanaghrisson shrugged and she knew that meant probably yes.

So. Another journey with cranky children, exhausted elders, no proper cooking fires, and all the other discomforts that went with such treks. At least four of the women with full bellies would have to deliver on the trail, without a proper birthing lodge. Men were stupid, but it was never any different. "Perhaps you will take just the braves," she urged, "leave the rest of us behind to follow some other time."

"I said *all*. Can you not understand plain speech?"

Ayi! There was no hope for it now. "Where are we going?"

He wasn't sure. Aughwick, Croghan's trading post, perhaps. Three days' journey east. Maybe four with the squaws and the children. "When we get there, you will know where we are. Pack."

Tanaghrisson turned away and looked at the death trap Washington called Fort Necessity. This little thing on the meadow should have told him he'd made a bad bargain as soon as it was built. The notion of a pact with the English to defeat Onontio and make him, Tanaghrisson, the lord of all the war chiefs in the Ohio Country required battle-seasoned allies. Instead he'd associated himself with a few ill-trained soldiers in a stockade with split-log walls just a little taller than the Virginia sachem himself. The space within it was hardly big enough to shelter some weapons and a few tents. A man could walk the whole circle in forty strides.

The runner he'd sent out had brought word a short time before. Five hundred of Onontio's heavily armed soldiers had left Fort Duquesne. And as he'd feared, a hundred Lenape and Mingo marched with them. If Onontio met the Americans in the forest, Washington and his men would all die swiftly. If the French came here they would place themselves in the hills that surrounded this meadow and easily kill the fort's defenders one by one. Tanaghrisson sighed. The sense of disaster was a physical thing. It shivered in his belly now as it had a few days ago back at Gist's trading post. "Pack," he said again. "I will tell the others."

His wife looked at him shrewdly. "You have lost everything you wagered. How did this happen?"

"This Washington is a good-natured boy who will someday be a good man, but he has no experience." Tanaghrisson glanced again at the ill-sited fort with its paltry defenses. "Worse, he will not listen to those who have."

Two days later Washington got word that Tanaghrisson and his followers—including his dozen braves—had left Great Meadows. He sent a messenger to try and get the Half King to return, but didn't have much hope of success. There were only a couple of Indians with them now, malcontents who preferred to stay rather than leave with their companions, and they were not to be trusted. For all intents and purposes, he and his men were marching on alone. It was hard not to give in to a certain despair. No, he told himself, despair had no place in a heroic life. He was meant for greatness. He had been ordered to rid the Ohio Country of the French and he would do so. But without substantial numbers of Indians to swell his numbers he dare not attack Fort Duquesne. Very well, they would wait for reinforcements from Virginia and Pennsylvania, but not here at Gist's. Exhausted as they were, he would somehow drive the men another six leagues to the trading post at Red Stone Creek, or Red Stone Fort, as some called it. It was sure to be a better place to take a stand.

Only his determination built the additional six leagues of God-rotting road. And when they got to Red Stone Creek—not a fort after all, just a single fortified building called a blockhouse—it was his will that got the trenches dug to defend their position. He was a madman, compelling the world and everyone in it to do his will, and miraculously perhaps, they obeyed. Two days later everything changed.

"Scout's returned, sir." The lieutenant jerked his head back toward the Mingo standing a short distance away examining the preparations for battle that had been made in his absence. He did not look impressed.

"Bring him to me."

The news was straightforward. Six hundred armed men had left Fort Duquesne—five hundred French infantry and a hundred Indians. The Virginians were outnumbered three to two. "What kind of a force?" Washington demanded. "Do they look as if they're just exploring?"

"They come to fight." The Mingo's gaze kept traveling the perimeter of the encampment, taking in the shallow trenches and the spent men. "Soldiers and braves all with many scalps at their belt. And big guns. Bigger than those." He gestured toward the swivel guns the Virginians had brought with them at such cost. "Much bigger."

Washington turned away so neither the officer nor the savage would see his struggle. He'd proved he had the potential for greatness simply by getting this far. But force of will could not deflect grape and chain. It would not turn away cannonballs, or shield men from musket fire. When Washington turned back, the

Mingo was walking away, planning to disappear into the forest most likely, but the lieutenant was still awaiting his orders. "Tell the men to prepare to leave. We are returning to Fort Necessity."

"Now, sir? The boys are very tired, they—"

"They are alive. I intend they should remain that way. Now, Lieutenant. In fact, sooner."

Back at Great Meadows Washington assembled his men in the open fields and waited to engage the enemy. When the French arrived they dispersed themselves in the surrounding trees and raked his lines with musket fire. The Virginians retreated to the shallow trenches surrounding Fort Necessity. And then, sweet Christ Jesus, it poured down with rain. Sheets of it. The trenches filled with water and the enfilading fire never let up.

Some ten hours after the engagement began a boy—he was barely fifteen—whom Washington had made a corporal a few days before crawled on his belly through the mud to the trench where the colonel had positioned himself. "The troops, sir. They got into the rum. A good number's pretty drunk."

"I can suggest no immediate remedy for inebriation, Corporal. And under the circumstances there's nothing we can do to point out the error of their ways, but they will be disciplined when this is over." Bloody hard to blame them for wanting liquor to ease the terror, but there would be a few hours respite fairly soon. Washington's eyes raked the horizon. It was eight o'clock and the dusk was thickening; soon it would be too dark for shooting. And with sunrise, who knew . . . maybe the rain would stop. Maybe the reinforcements would come.

"Yes, sir. But it's the bloody rain, sir. The boys' muskets is soaked; they won't fire. Not if they ain't dried and cleaned. And the screw that cleans 'em, sir, we've only two of those between all of us."

"There's little I can—"

"Monsieur le Colonel Washington!" The voice from the trees thundered over the sodden meadow like the summons of the Archangel Gabriel. "Monsieur le Colonel, can you hear me?"

Bloody hell! If he stood up he'd be a sure target. But glory demanded action. Washington got to his feet. The young corporal grabbed at his sleeve and tried to haul him back down. "No, sir! Don't! It's not full dark. They can still see you, sir."

Washington shook him off. "I am in command of the Virginia Regiment, Corporal. I quite mean for them to see me." Then he stood as tall as his more than six feet allowed, with both hands cupped to his mouth so they'd be sure to know exactly the direction of the shout. "I am right here, sir! And I can hear you quite plainly."

"*Eh bien, mon Colonel.* Do you wish perhaps to negotiate?"

Sweet Christ Jesus. Maybe they wouldn't all die in this Godforsaken mud.

"His name is Captain de Villiers, Colonel Washington. He says he is the brother of the French lieutenant. The one who was— The one who died last month in the glen. Joseph Coulon de Villiers de Jumonville."

"Yes, I remember his name quite well." The storeroom was the driest place in the stockade, but it leaked like a sieve. And there was only one flickering candle to read by. "This bit here," Washington thrust the document closer to the French-speaking captain he'd sent to do the negotiating. "What does this mean?"

"Those are the terms, Colonel. We are offered the honors of war. We can leave with our arms if we agree to withdraw from the Ohio Country and pledge not to return within a year. We have to repatriate their prisoners, sir, and leave two officers as hostages at Fort Duquesne. I'll stay behind, sir. And I'm sure there's another—"

"Why such generous terms, Captain? Have you any idea?" Blast and damnation. Did this de Villiers know something he did not?

"I can't rightly say, sir. They look pretty well dug in up there in the trees. They're all around us, sir. And—"

"I know they're all around us." The fusillades had been pouring down on them from every direction for hours. "What about ammunition? Supplies? Perhaps they're running low."

"Perhaps, sir. I couldn't say. No way to tell. But Villiers . . ."

"Yes?"

"He says he came to avenge his brother's death, sir. And he considers that he's done that."

Yes, by Christ Jesus, he had. They'd brought him the reckoning a few moments before. Thirty of his men were dead and seventy wounded, and the surgeon didn't think he could save many of those. There was not a mule or a horse or a pig alive in the stockade. They were not only without four-legged transportation, they were without a steady supply of meat. Washington stabbed at the paper containing the Articles of Capitulation. "Jumonville's mur— His brother's passing, Captain, is there anything in here about that?"

"A few words, sir, nothing important." What bloody else could he say? De Villiers had written the damned thing on his knee. The bloody document was all but illegible. He had thought there was something in there about Washington accepting responsibility for Jumonville's assassination, but he couldn't find it when he looked again. Maybe he'd been mistaken. He was offering himself as a hostage so the men could live; what in hell's name else could be wanted of him? Wasn't him who should have given the command to stop the massacre back in the glen. "I don't think there's anything that matters, sir. About Jumonville, I mean. But there's one other thing . . ."

"Yes?"

"The Indians fighting with them, Colonel Washington, I expected it would be the usual French allies, sir. Ottawa and Huron. It's not."

Washington knew almost without having to ask, but he wanted to hear the words. "Very well, Captain. Which Indians, then?"

"Ours, sir. At least the ones supposed to be ours. Mingo and Shawnee and Delaware."

Washington reached for his quill. "Pray God this ink is not too full of water to be readable, Captain." He signed his name with his usual flourish.

The Virginians, Washington leading, left Fort Necessity the following morning, the fourth of July 1754. Most of the men were barefoot, and there wasn't a complete uniform between any ten of them. They carried their muskets pointing downward, as custom demanded of surrendering troops.

De Villiers had lost three men of his six hundred; a few more had sustained light wounds. The victors watched the militiamen leave, then destroyed Fort Necessity before heading west. On their way back to Fort Duquesne, traveling the road the Virginian troops had built, the French burned to the ground Gist's trading post and Red Stone Fort. The Ohio Country was once again safe for New France.

Chapter Seven

THE MAN, A *habitant* wearing leather breeches and a belted hunting shirt and a broad-brimmed hat pulled down over his forehead, made his way across the Place d'Armes, the ceremonial heart of the Upper Town, and headed toward the Porte du Palais. There was a guard at the gate, a Canadian wearing the uniform of the colonial *troupes franches de la marine.* He glanced at the basket fixed to back of the *habitant.* "You go for firewood?"

"*Bien sûr, mon ami.* How else can my family eat?"

The guard waved him on. The man shuffled forward, not stopping to glance at the great château on the banks of the River St. Charles that was home to Intendant Bigot. It was said that Bigot could lose thousands of livres at gaming tables in his great ballroom and never count the cost. Nothing to do with a man who must gather firewood in the forest to survive.

The woods thickened when he was out of sight of the château's wooden palisade and its cannon. Now Louis Roget did not feel the need to stoop so markedly; he walked with a bit more ease, enjoying the tall pines and fir trees and the feel of their needles beneath his feet, glad of the shade and the breeze off the river. Except for the nature of his errand, the Provincial Superior of the Society of Jesus would have found this a pleasant stroll in the country.

"*Vous! Ici!*"

The savage was covered from head to foot in blue tattoos. Both cheeks were scarred with knife cuts that ran from ear to mouth, precise enough so it was obvious they were ceremonial marks, not battle scars. He wore feathers in his long black hair, a breechclout, and little else besides an array of bracelets on his arms and legs. A large medicine bag made of the whole skin of an otter hung round his neck, marking him as a member of the powerful Midewiwin priesthood. The

Jesuit suppressed a sigh. Dear Lord, that You have sent us to such a place as this to deal with such men as these.

"*Tu n'as pas de savoir-vivre, mon fils.*" Roget spoke slowly and with more than usual care. He was never certain how much French these savages understood. "You forget your manners, my son. Remember to whom you speak and adjust your tone."

The Indian shrugged. "We are both priests, is that not so? Do you think you are higher than me?"

"I am a priest of the one Great Spirit that rules the heaven and the earth."

The sun was directly overhead now. The red man had been waiting in these woods since it was only a quarter way above the horizon and he had eaten not long before; he belched loudly, then squatted. In his own language he was a Twightwee, a crane person. The Europeans had adopted the Ojibwe word and called them Miami. By whatever name, his people had inhabited the land the French called the *pays d'en haut* since long before the *Cmokmanuk* arrived. Still more important, he was a priest of the Midewiwin, a member of one of the most powerful lodges, and a holy man who could speak with the spirits. He had little use for these Europeans no matter what tribe they belonged to, French or English, but he had learned to make choices between bad and worse.

The French made trade, they gave gifts, they showed respect—at least most of them did, this haughty black robe was an exception—and there were not so many of them. The English multiplied like grasshoppers and devoured the land the way swarms of insects devoured leaves. When the English came, the hunting grounds were destroyed and the *Anishinabeg* had to leave their homes and the bones of their ancestors and search for new places to live. "Since we agree that there is but one Great Spirit," the Indian said, "all his priests must be equal."

Roget had not come into the woods to argue theology with a savage. He remained standing, but he removed a small chamois bag full of coins from beneath his shirt and held it in plain view. "I was told you had important things to say. I am listening, but I hear only small words."

The Midè priest looked up, thinking that he would like to cut out the heart of this arrogant European, and that if he did he would not eat it but feed it to the dogs in his village. But the bag of coins would buy a large quantity of firewater. His mouth was dry with his need for it, and sour with the taste of betrayal. He licked his lips. "I speak big words, black robe, important words. I am offering you more power over the red men than you can believe possible. I will make you king of all the *Anishinabeg*. You will be able to summon them to fight for Onontio and defeat the English once and for all."

"I am not interested in your spells and incantations. You must offer me more than just words."

The Indian summoned the spittle for speech and tried to ignore the sick feeling in his belly. "Memetosia, an old and wise Miami chief, is in Albany now. He makes powwow with the English who would overthrow Onontio."

"It is three years, many moons, since the Miami turned their back on their father Onontio and chose to listen to the lies of the English. It is not a surprise that they attend a powwow with Onontio's enemies."

Ayi! Half of him hoped this dog turd would refuse the bargain and try to walk away. Then he would kill him and take the money and have no need to betray Memetosia. But he was sure to have brought only a part of the payment. If he killed the black robe now he would never get the rest. "Do you tell me you are not interested in what happens between Memetosia and the English in Albany?"

"I am interested in the glory of the One True God and His Church. The English separated themselves from that Church. They are in mortal sin and doomed to hellfire."

Impossible to deal with men who thought they knew everything. The priest felt a fart coming on and rose slightly on his haunches and freed it, laughing inwardly at the flicker of distaste he saw on the face of the black robe. "If you do not like the English, then you must agree my words are big words."

"If they concern the enemies of Almighty God, yes," Louis Roget said, finally squatting beside the Indian, "they are big words. And I am listening with both my ears."

"How much do you have there?"

So, now we come to the heart of the matter, the Jesuit thought. The servant asks and the master pays. "One hundred livres." It was a third of what had been stipulated.

The Miami spat on the ground in disgust. "It is not enough."

"It is a first payment only. One hundred now. Two hundred more when you accomplish 'the great good thing' you have promised."

The Miami hesitated a moment, thinking about how much firewater he could purchase with three hundred livres, of the hunger that never left of his belly, and of his great need. Finally he took up a twig and scratched a series of symbols in the earth. "*Papankamwa,* the fox." He tapped the first mark, then indicated the others in turn. "*Eehsipana,* the raccoon. *Ayaapia,* the elk buck. *Anseepikwa,* the spider. *Eeyeelia,* possum. *Pileewa,* turkey." After each pronouncement he looked up to be sure the black robe was paying attention.

Roget waited until the recitation was complete before speaking. "I told you I would not pay for your charms and incantations."

The Midè priest felt such a need to cut out this one's tongue that it almost overcame all else, but his great thirst reminded him that it did not. "When you speak words over the bread and the firewater in your Mass, do they not change?"

"Yes, but—"

"So we are agreed that words can be very powerful." Then, before the black robe could find another argument: "Your bread and firewater look the same after you speak your words, yet you say they have become different. I speak of something you can touch and see. Ancient stones, black robe, magic more powerful than the words of your Mass. *Papankamwa, eehsipana, ayaapia, anseepikwa, eeyeelia, pileewa.* My words will make you a king."

MONDAY, JULY 13, 1754
NEW YORK PROVINCE

The reeds that grew beside this stretch of Hudson's River were taller than Nicole's head, taller than either of the men. They parted with soft, sighing sounds as the party of three moved through them, then closed as if they had never been disturbed.

It had been three weeks since the night beside the Shawnee fire. The journey by canoe had been infinitely easier for Nicole, but the boat had been abandoned the day before and left well hidden on the riverbank.

"Not a good idea for us to announce our arrival by paddling alongside the Albany town wharves," Quent said. When Nicole asked why, he hesitated, then grinned. She liked his grin. It made him look like a mischievous small boy. "Can't say I'm certain of the answer to that," he admitted. "But it's not the way Corm and I do things."

She understood what he was saying. Stealth was bred into them; it was how they survived. Anyway, she didn't mind giving up the canoe as much as she'd thought she might. The paths here were well marked and a bit wider than in the Ohio Country. The trek had been easier than she'd expected until they got to these dreadful reeds.

She was in her usual place, between the two men. The sun was not yet directly overhead, but already perspiration poured off her and the buckskins of the men were dark with sweat. She could smell their ripe, musky odor mixing with the fetid heat rising off the marsh. When evening came all three of them would strip off their clothes and bathe in the river, then eat and sleep. It was the prize, the goal that made her able to put one foot in front of the other.

A reed swiped her cheek and Nicole knew from the sting that she had been cut. She wiped away the blood and the sweat with a corner of her torn and shabby skirt. Then Monsieur Shea, who was in the lead, stopped walking and Monsieur Hale put a hand on her shoulder. They waited like that for a few heartbeats. By now she knew better than to ask what or why. Nicole held her breath.

Another man appeared, an Indian, dark-skinned and flat-faced, with flared nostrils. He wore buckskins and had a tomahawk at his waist. His hair was black and coarse and worn loose to his shoulders. What looked to be the tail feathers of some bird hung from his ears, and his face was covered with the strange markings Nicole had been told were called tattoos. She had become adept at reading the reactions of her two companions. She knew at once the newcomer was not an enemy.

The three men spoke for a moment or two in that rapid, guttural language she didn't understand. The Indian kept staring at Nicole and jerking his head to indicate a spot somewhere to his right. Eventually Cormac Shea and the stranger took a few steps in that direction, disappearing into the all-concealing reeds.

"He doesn't like speaking of important things in front of a squaw," Quent said.

"But I do not understand a word of his language."

Quent shrugged. "He doesn't know that. Wait here. If you don't want to be lost in these reeds forever, don't take a step in any direction." He followed after the other two. Nicole had no idea where they had gone. The tall reeds had an eerie way of distorting any sense of direction. She could, however, hear the low murmur of their voices.

A few moments later Quent reappeared at her side. He was alone. "We're going on. Cormac has to see someone. He'll catch up with us later."

"I wouldn't have been lost forever if I'd moved," she said. "You'd have found me."

"I expect so."

"Then why did you say it?"

"To make you behave."

"I am not a child. You must stop treating me as if I have no understanding and no intelligence."

"You're right. I won't do it anymore. This journey," he added, "it can't have been easy for a white woman who's never been in the wilderness. You've done well."

Nicole blushed at his praise and managed a prim nod. "Where has Monsieur Shea gone? Who was that man?"

"His name is Mikamayalo. He's a Twightwee, what whites call Miami."

"How did he find us here, in these . . . these abominations." She pushed the reeds away from her as she spoke, staying close to Hale's back and the path he cut for her through the whiplike vegetation.

"Indians are used to seeing things," Quent spoke in an easy, normal voice, not the hushed tones of exaggerated caution. "Mikamayalo had word we were coming."

"How? Who could have told him?"

"Other Indians. They have many ways of communicating." He didn't add that a brave or two moving on their own, without a woman, would have left them behind long since. "Mikamayalo had a message for Corm. An old friend in the town wants to see him."

"Who is he, this old friend?"

"Not a he, a she."

"A woman?"

He chuckled. "Mostly if you're a she, you're a woman, right?"

"Do not make fun of me."

"Don't take well to a bit of teasing, do you?" He kept his tone light, but there was a small knot of anger in his belly. How come she cared so much where Corm went and what he did? "Listen, if you'll just stop talking and keep walking we'll be out of these reeds in less than an hour."

"And then?"

"Then we'll be in Albany. Or near enough as makes no difference."

In the days when the Dutch ruled Nieuw Netherland, the outpost some hundred and sixty miles up Hudson's River from Nieuw Amsterdam was called Fort Orange and was largely a trading post dealing with local Indians. The settlement that grew up around it was known as Beverwyck. In 1664, when the English took control of Nieuw Netherland, Nieuw Amsterdam became New York, and Fort Orange and Beverwyck became Albany. A palisade of rough-cut logs still surrounded the city, which was little more than three hundred or so wooden dwellings tightly wedged on a grid of about a dozen streets—only two of them of any width—and many narrow, crooked lanes, most butting up to the shoreline of Hudson's River. Fort Orange had been constructed of logs and positioned close to the river; it had fallen into ruin. The redcoats were garrisoned at the newly built Fort Frederick, a stone redoubt two thirds of the way up the city's highest hill. The inns and drinking houses were well below the fort, concentrated as they had always been around the intersections of Green and Beaver streets with the broad road known as Market Street that fronted on the river.

A dozen ships—cutters and sloops and schooners—rode at anchor a short distance from the riverbank. "So many boats," Nicole said, looking back over her shoulder as Quent led her toward a taproom with a sign that pictured a horse's head, "for this place."

"Don't be so sniffy. This place, as you call it, is breadbasket to the sugar plantations of the Caribbean. At least the farms around it are. Without what we grow in this part of the world the Islands would starve. Without the river, how would the crops get to the buyers?"

Nicole wrinkled her nose. "Even so, it smells."

"That's not the river, it's the town. And only because it's high summer," Quent said, laughing. "Anyway, we won't be here long."

She smelled like the woods. He was astounded at the changes the six weeks of their journey had produced in her. She'd taken to washing herself in the brooks and streams the way he and Corm did, insisting they stand guard with their backs to her. He couldn't imagine another white woman doing that. And she'd begun rubbing her body with wild herbs, squaw-fashion. How else would she smell of peppermint and thyme the way she did? Like Shoshanaya.

He wondered if the Shawnee women had shown her how to bathe and perfume herself, and if she did it because she was now Corm's woman. He'd seen them come back from the woods together the night of the Shawnee dance. Nicole and Corm had spent little time alone together since. Soon it might be different.

The big house on North Pearl Street was sturdily built of stone and white pine shingles, as befit the wealth and station of the man called John Lydius. It had been erected gable end to the street, in the old Dutch fashion. A few steps above ground level there was a deep front porch with long benches built on either side. Cormac Shea had been to the Lydius house many times, and this was the first occasion on which he found it guarded by Miami braves who stood rigid either side of the front door.

Mikamayalo stepped forward and spoke a few words. Ceremony, the proper way of doing things, was of great importance to the Miami. Corm knew that. He waited respectfully, asking no questions, taking his cue from the braves. After a moment one of them opened the door and motioned Corm and Mikamayalo inside.

Another brave in the wide front hall demanded Corm's weapons. Unhesitatingly Corm slipped the long gun off his shoulder and stood it against the wall. The brave waited. Corm took his tomahawk from his waist and lay it on the table. "*Maalhsi,*" the brave said, using the Miami word for knife. Corm slipped his from his belt and left it with the other things. Satisfied, the brave nodded and motioned Corm deeper into the house. This time he went alone. Mikamayalo murmured something to the guard and slipped back out the door. Corm didn't catch what had been said. The Miami language was very close to Potawatomi, Shawnee, and the other Algonkian tongues of the *pays d'en haut*. Too close. Corm could understand most of it without effort so he had never taken the time to learn it properly.

He felt naked without his weapons, but he had guessed it would be like this. No one treated their chiefs with more deference than the Crane People. To enter the presence of one of them bearing arms of any sort would be a gross discourtesy. Moreover, if Mikamayalo's story was accurate, he had been sent for by none other than Memetosia, grandfather of the mighty war sachem Memeskia. It was Memeskia who in recent years had renounced exclusive trading agreements with the French, forged alliances with Britain, and invited other tribes living below the lakes of the *pays d'en haut* to join him. The French saw Memeskia's action as a threat to their claims on the Ohio Country. Two years ago they and their Ottawa and Ojibwe allies had attacked Memeskia's village of Pickawillany, completely destroying it and slaughtering or capturing every inhabitant.

Among Memeskia's clan the wounds would still be raw, and the Potawatomi were brothers to the Ottawa and the Ojibwe. Once all three had been known as the Fire Nation. So why send for Cormac Shea? More important, why would an old chief like Memetosia, who should have been waiting out his time to die in some peaceful village of his own people, have come to Albany in the first place? If he hadn't, if Mikamayalo was lying, Corm was walking into a trap. He never remembered this house being so dark or so silent.

Genevieve Lydius was a métisse like himself, half French and half Piankashaw Indian. Her husband, John, was French speaking, but of Walloon descent and a Protestant. When he was banished from New France it was on the charge of being a British spy. Corm had no idea if that was true, but Lydius had become one of Albany's wealthiest traders. He'd had frequent dealings with Ephraim Hale, and maintained a trading post with the Indians on land he rented from Ephraim up in the part of the Patent known as the Great Carrying Place. Cormac knew Lydius used it for smuggling guns to the Indians in Canada; so did Ephraim, but he preferred to turn a blind eye. When Cormac was a boy, John and Genevieve Lydius had been regular visitors to Shadowbrook. *"Alors,"* she'd said one day when she came upon Corm heading for the realm of Kitchen Hannah and her fresh-baked gingerbread, *"le petit métis."* The little half-breed. *"Moi, je suis la grande métisse. You must come and see me when you are next in the town."*

He'd be grateful to see her now. It would convince him he wasn't about to plunge into a bear pit.

The house was big and sprawling. John and Genevieve had eight children and at least twice as many grandchildren. Usually you heard young voices and innocent laughter the moment you walked in the door; today there was only silence. He walked on a few steps, his heart beating a bit faster as the darkness became more intense. Damn fool he'd been. He should have insisted on keeping at least his knife.

"Cormac. *Ici.*" The words were a soft whisper, but he recognized Genevieve's voice and turned in the direction it had come from. He could just make her out in the gloom. She was standing in front of a pair of heavily carved double doors.

Genevieve Lydius was a big woman, stately, with no sign of gray in her black hair. Flanked by two Miami braves, she might easily have been a queen.

Cormac's eyes had grown accustomed to the dimness and he could see that both braves carried muskets. That made at least five armed Miami in the house. What if instead of being here to protect their chief, they'd taken Genevieve captive for some reason? His mind was racing faster than his heart. His long gun was equal to five muskets, but it was three rooms away, guarded by yet another Miami. Then Genevieve came forward and greeted him with a kiss on both cheeks and Corm felt his tension drain away. He would have smelled fear on her and there was none. She would not willingly conspire against him. Genevieve would never be his enemy.

"I am glad you have come at last, Cormac. Memetosia is very ill. There may not be much time." She nodded toward the pair of doors.

"It's true then? He is here? The house was so quiet, so dark. I was worried. The children—"

"We have sent them all away. Memetosia is too ill for the noise."

Cormac glanced at the braves guarding the double doors. They stared straight ahead, seemingly uninterested in the conversation. Cormac knew that at least one of them would be listening carefully to every word. "Why is the honored Miami chief in Albany?"

"There was a meeting. Governor De Lancey from New York City and many other important men. They called it the Albany Congress."

"White men. *Cmokmanuk,*" Corm said, not quite believing that a congress in Albany was an explanation for Memetosia's presence.

"Yes, but a number of the chiefs as well. My revered uncle, even Thoyanoguen of the Kahniankehaka." What she didn't say was that they were there because there was a scheme to sell land some ways to the west. The Iroquois who ruled in the Ohio Country had long before given the areas known as Wyomink and Shamokin to the Delaware, but just this week at Albany they had sold that same land to the British. John wasn't in Albany now because he was trying to get control of that land on the Susquehanna River on behalf of businessmen from Connecticut. She would tell Cormac nothing of those dealings. It would only anger him. "Mr. Franklin of Philadelphia proposed a way for the colonies to band together to protect themselves. A Plan of Union."

"A union of English whites to protect themselves from French whites." For over a hundred years the various tribes had been trying to survive by playing off one group of white men against the other and finding a place for themselves in the space between. Still the numbers of Real People grew ever smaller, and their way of life ever more threatened.

Genevieve shrugged. "Of course from the French. They are the enemy of the moment. At least here in Albany. Anyway, it does not matter. The assemblies in each colony must approve this so-called Plan of Union. It will come to nothing."

Men's inconsistencies did not trouble her overmuch. She was married to a man who called himself English when it suited him and French when it did not. Half French she might be, and half Indian, but her job was to protect her family and her blood kin. "Memetosia is so old and so revered he can do as he likes. He wanted to come, so he came."

"It won't help them. Not any of the tribes," Cormac said glumly. "In the end it doesn't matter whether they side with the French or the English, the Real People are doomed unless—"

"Cormac, I know what you think. And you know my opinion." Genevieve stifled an impatient sigh. How often had she heard him say that the *Anishinabeg* must find a way to preserve their way of life, but be at peace with the whites? All the while he was growing up he'd been telling her the same thing, and she'd given him the same answer: *You are filled with elaborate plans for the whole world. Better to make a plan for yourself. We cannot win this fight, Cormac Shea. The Real People cannot win. We are too busy fighting among ourselves to fight the whites. Find a way to survive and prosper. Let the white half of you take command and let the rest of it go.*

Genevieve had done exactly that. She looked as the wife of prosperous John Lydius should look. Black hair twisted in a neat knot; a fine dark red dress trimmed with lace, the skirt fashionably wide, swishing when she walked; a shawl made of soft blue wool. But half her blood was Piankashaw; her mother's people were a sister tribe of the Miami. Chief Memetosia had come to Albany for reasons of his own that Genevieve did not pretend to fully understand. But no man, not even an honored Miami chief, could change his fate. The old man had become ill in Albany; it was entirely proper that he rest and recuperate in the home of a daughter of his people. Besides, keeping everyone happy was good for trade; French livres and English pounds enriched the Lydius accounts equally.

"In here," she said, taking Cormac's hand and leading him forward. The armed braves continued to stare straight ahead, but they stepped aside. "You understand the Miami ways? Memetosia is a full chief, remember."

"Yes, I know how to behave."

She seemed satisfied. "We keep the room very dark because the light hurts his eyes, but he can see us quite plainly. And there is nothing wrong with his hearing." Genevieve opened the door. *"Teepi nko hka neewaki,"* she murmured, bowing low. I beg to be admitted to your presence.

There was no reply, but the old man raised a hand from a sofa piled high with cushions and blankets against the wall near the fireplace. Mostly white man's furnishings, but the blanket wrapped around the chief's shoulders had been woven by a Miami squaw. Even at this distance Cormac could make out the crane symbols.

"I have brought you Cormac Shea, revered Uncle," Genevieve said. "He is the Potawatomi brave you asked to see."

Cormac took a few steps closer to the sofa and squatted, waiting for Memetosia to acknowledge his presence. After some seconds the chief waved a carved stick that ended in a sheaf of crane feathers in the direction of each of Cormac's shoulders. "*Teepahki neeyolaani.*" It is good to see you. Corm stood up. "Now," Memetosia said, "send the squaw away and we will talk."

Cormac turned to Genevieve, who was already backing out of the room.

Memetosia coughed. Cormac made a move to help him, but the old man waved him off. Memetosia spat repeatedly into a bowl beside the sofa; finally the fit passed. "You must forgive me if I do not speak of the things that should come first, but I am ill and soon I must sing my death song." He was apologizing for not asking about the last time Cormac had hunted and how things were in his village, the common courtesies that should begin any conversation among *Anishinabeg* who met in friendship. "There are things I must say quickly, while I still have the strength. I am told, Cormac Shea, that you met with the Ottawa, Pontiac, and that your brother who marked your face was with you. I am told that either he would have killed Pontiac or Pontiac would have killed him if wiser men had not stopped them."

"Memetosia hears all that happens in our world, as is fitting. But it was not Uko Nyakwai's choice to fight Pontiac, revered Chief. Pontiac questioned Uko Nyakwai's right to the totem given him by the great Ottawa chief Recumsah."

Cormac was puzzled by the lack of anger with which the old man talked about the Ottawa. It was the Ottawa who, after everything else in Pickawillany was destroyed, had killed and eaten the old man's grandson, Memeskia.

Cormac's eyes had adjusted to the near-dark of the room. He could see the chief clearly now. Despite Memeskia's fierceness in battle the French had called him *La Demoiselle,* the Young Woman, because of the delicacy of his features. Memetosia had the same small nose and large eyes and thin face as his grandson. In his youth he, too, would probably have made a pretty girl. Now he looked gaunt and gray with illness, and beneath his many tattoos his cheeks were covered with the marks that showed that sometime in the past he had survived the great sickness, the smallpox, that had slaughtered so many of the Miami.

The rheumy old eyes studied Cormac. He seemed to know what the younger man was thinking. He made an impatient gesture, as if he did not wish to discuss the wrongs he and his clan had suffered at the hands of the Ottawa, who were brothers to the Potawatomi. "You call Uko Nyakwai by a name that makes him a Real Person," Memetosia said, "but he is white."

"He walked through the Potawatomi fire, revered Chief."

Cormac let the words hang in the air between them. Memetosia knew this to be so; it meant that Quent was Potawatomi by adoption and despite his white skin he was truly *Anishinabeg*. That could never be undone, not even by a full Miami chief.

"*Ayi!*" the old man grunted. "Do not tell me things I know. You waste my time!"

Cormac quickly bowed his head low. "I beg your forgiveness, revered Chief."

The crane-feather stick was waved over his head, dismissing his impertinence and accepting his apology. "They say that you are wise in the two worlds, that you do not give yourself to one at the expense of the other. From many people I have heard this. It is true?"

"It is as true as I can make it, revered Chief."

Memetosia started to say something, but another fit of coughing stalled his words. Cormac looked around, spotted a tankard, and sniffed it. Water. "Will this help you, revered Chief?"

The old man sipped the water, letting Corm hold the tankard for him. He spoke again. "There are others who are like you and the Piankashaw squaw." The old man nodded in the direction of the double doors where he knew Genevieve waited. "Others who have the blood of both the whites and the Real People. This is true, is it not?"

"There are many of us, revered Chief. Some call us métis."

Memetosia nodded agreement. "That is true. The one called Charles Langlade, he too is a métis, is he not?"

Langlade, who had led the raid on Pickawillany, was half French and half Ottawa. Cormac had heard it was Langlade who threw Memeskia into the pot. *Ayi!* How could he be so stupid as to have forgotten that. "He is, revered Chief, but—"

Memetosia cut him off with another wave of the crane feathers. "A man can be good or evil and be all *Anishinabeg* or all white. Why should a mix be any different? Tell me something else—Lantak, the outlaw who no longer obeys his own chiefs, you know him?"

Cormac tried hard not to show his shock. Memetosia seemed to be implying that Lantak was also a métis. He'd never heard that before. "I have seen Lantak, revered Chief, but only down the barrel of my long gun."

"It is a pity you never shot him. He is a danger to Real People and whites alike."

"I agree."

"So will you shoot him now?"

Cormac had no idea where this conversation was going, or what was truly being said. "If I find him in my sights, I will shoot him. It is as you say, Lantak cannot be trusted by either side. And he preys on squaws and children."

The old man nodded. "Yes. That is all true. But usually white squaws and white children. They are our enemies, too, are they not?"

Cormac spoke slowly, choosing his words. "I have much reverence for your great age and wisdom, Memetosia, Chief of the Miami. But I have also spent many moons thinking of this thing that has come to the lands of the *Anishinabeg.*"

The old man's gaze became more intent. Perhaps everything he had heard about this young man was correct. "Your skin is white, Cormac Shea. But they say you are truly of the *Anishinabeg.*"

"I am truly red and truly white, Revered Chief. When the white men came to our land they created some like me who have inside them the blood of two worlds."

Memetosia nodded, encouraging the younger man with his eyes. He waved the stick of crane feathers in a gesture of agreement.

"I take neither one side nor the other when I say that if the *Anishinabeg* continue trying to fight the white men, the *Anishinabeg* will lose. Eventually there will be no Real People left in the woods beside the salt waters, or the great waters without salt, or even in the high hills." Passion rose in Cormac as he spoke and his white skin no longer mattered. He was truly Indian. "We are no longer happy simply with knives of flint and tomahawks of stone. We want their iron weapons. We want their cloths and their ornaments. We have killed nearly every beaver in our lands attempting to satisfy their hunger for skins, and ours for what they have. But our hunger is never satisfied and we are always at their mercy. We get guns and they come with bigger guns. And there are many more of them than of us. They enslave us with their firewater and sicken us with their diseases. We must find a way to live in peace with the *Cmokmanuk,* and at the same time remain who we are: Miami and Potawatomi and Fox and Ojibwe, even *Irinakhoiw.*"

"Even *Irinakhoiw* were put in this world by the Great Spirit," the old man agreed softly. "I have heard what you said. And I take it you do not believe what Pontiac says. That we must band together to fight the whites if the *Anishinabeg* are to survive."

"It may be true, revered Chief. But I do not think it can ever happen. For Pontiac's plan to work, all the Real People would have to forget all their ancient grievances and fight side by side."

Memetosia made a sound in his throat. "To fight beside the *Irinakhoiw,* the snakes . . . The sun will fall out of the sky before that will happen."

"Yes, I think so, too. That is why Pontiac's way cannot come to pass."

"The squaw out there," he nodded toward the part of the house beyond the double doors where Genevieve waited, "she tells me you have another plan."

At last Cormac understood what he was doing here: Genevieve had told Memetosia of his dream. And if Memetosia had summoned him to his deathbed to discuss it, then the old man must believe that it could be effective. "Revered Chief," he said eagerly, "I believe we and the whites must divide the land. They will stay in one part and we will stay in the other. We will take the land of cold and snow because we are the great hunters. They will take the rest, the land where the sun shines in every moon, because their crops will grow there. We will trade when it suits us and suits them, but we will have no need to spill blood over the land."

"And on which side will you be, Cormac Shea? With the *Anishinabeg* or with the whites?"

"I cannot change my destiny, revered Chief. I and those like me will always move between two worlds."

The old man nodded. "Yes, that is so. But it is also true that no one can own land. It belongs to the Great Spirit who created it."

"I know. But people can divide the land according to how it is to be used, and who may be permitted to make their villages and live in peace."

"That is the question," Memetosia said softly, speaking it seemed more to himself than to Cormac. "Can the whites ever be made into Real People? Can they be trusted to give their word and keep it?"

"Some of them can."

The chief nodded. "So you say. So others say. Tell me, my son," it was the first time he had used that form of familiar affection with Cormac, "did your totem reveal this plan to you in a dream?"

Cormac lowered his head, thinking deeply about his answer. A plan revealed in a sleeping dream would carry much more authority, but to lie about such a thing . . . He could not hope for success if he made a mockery of everything he'd learned at the fires of Singing Snow. If he allowed himself to be more white than Potawatomi, he would no longer be a bridge and nothing he hoped for could come to pass.

"The way was not shown to me in sleep, revered Chief. It was revealed slowly. Many times in my village, as a boy and later as a man, I would go to the cleansing place, and after I was purified I would open my mind and let the Spirit show me truth. It was in this manner that the way for the two worlds to live in peace was revealed to me. After a long time and much purification."

Memetosia nodded, slowly and with much gravity. "Sometimes that is how the Spirit speaks. Yes. I, too, have opened my mind to my totem in these last days of my time here." He reached beneath the blankets and came up clutching a medicine bag. "I came here to this place, even though I knew I was beginning to let go of my spirit, to speak with the white chiefs," Memetosia murmured. "I thought I must try one more time . . ."

"Try what, revered Chief?"

"It doesn't matter. They are more concerned with each other now than with us." The rasping whisper was weaker now and Cormac had to bend close to hear the words. "There is going to be war between the French and the British."

"There is always war between the French and the British."

"Yes. But with every sunrise the drums grow louder in their ears. There was a fort made by the ones who call themselves Virginians, where the two rivers meet in the country of the snakes called Mingo."

"Fort Necessity," Cormac said. "Uko Nyakwai told me about it. The young man who is called Washington, he—"

"He was surrounded by the French and their big guns, and they killed all his horses and mules and oxen and he surrendered. The French were fools and let their enemies walk away, so they must fight them again, but someday—soon I think—one will truly win and the other will truly lose. When that happens the winner will be strong enough to crush the Real People entirely. We must protect ourselves against that day. Perhaps by Pontiac's way, perhaps by yours. But some method must be found. If we go on as we are, they will eat our flesh and throw our bones into the fire."

"Memetosia speaks wisdom." Cormac could smell the sourness of the old man's breath, the unhealthy reek of his ebbing life.

The hand holding the medicine bag snaked toward Cormac. "Take this, Cormac Shea who is both white and *Anishinabeg*. It is the most precious gift I can give. Take it and when the time is right, use it."

"Revered Chief, how will I know—"

The old man had closed his eyes. He turned his face away and made a languid, dismissive gesture with the crane feathers. There would be no more talk.

The medicine bag was a pouch smaller than the palm of Cormac's hand and made of fine, very soft deerskin, pure white and decorated with red and black crane symbols, tied tightly with a long deerskin thong fashioned into a large loop. Corm fingered it cautiously. There were a number of hard, uneven objects inside, not flat like coins or small and tubular like wampum.

On the sofa Memetosia sighed loudly. The old hawk clearly didn't want Cormac to examine his gift in his presence and wasn't going to explain its significance. Corm slipped the looped thong over his neck and tucked the medicine bag inside his shirt where it didn't show, then backed out of the room.

There was only one brave guarding the door. Cormac wondered where the other had gone, but before he had time to worry, Genevieve walked toward him. She seemed to be studying his face. "Well?"

"He's resting. No worse than when you saw him." Her piercing glance was unnerving. He did not really think it was the condition of the aged chief that was causing her such anxiety, but what else? And was it his imagination that she was staring at the thong around his neck?

"You look so tired, Cormac." Now she sounded more like herself, motherly as she'd always been with him. She touched his cheek and started to trace the puckered skin of his scar, even though she knew he hated for anyone to do that. He pulled away. "Sorry," she murmured. "But—" She broke off, her tone and her look changing. "Come with me," she said firmly. "I've something to show you."

He glanced at the Miami still guarding the doors to the room where Memetosia lay dying. The brave's face betrayed nothing. He felt naked without his weapons; presumably they were still in the front hall. But the mystery of the medicine bag was more compelling. He hurried after Genevieve.

There was a Miami squaw in the kitchen, kneeling beside the fire stirring something in a big pot. Cormac smelled the familiar reek of rancid bear fat and parched corn, probably the special white corn grown only by the Miami. The Lydius house had become a Miami village. "This way." Genevieve hurried him through the stone-lined dairy behind the kitchen, and the herb-drying room beyond that, through the kitchen garden, past rows of potherbs, and squash and beans and pumpkins ripening in the high summer heat. In a few strides they reached the woods that covered much of the Lydius land. Cormac was grateful for the shade. "Where are we going?"

"You'll see. It's just there. Look."

They had reached the banks of a small stream that cut across the edge of the property. Beside it was a newly made clearing, the stumps of the cut trees still creamy and fresh. A space had been made that was big enough to accommodate a small wigwam formed from willow saplings stuck in the ground in a circle and tied together at the top and covered in skins. There wasn't any chimney opening that Cormac could see, but he spotted a fire pit for heated stones just inside the flap that served as a door. It was a sweat lodge; he could feel the heat from where he was standing. Another Miami, almost as old as Memetosia from the look of him, was moving between the wigwam and a second fire, this one with a lively blaze that was being used to heat the stones for the pit inside the lodge.

"I knew as soon as I saw you this morning that you needed this," Genevieve said. "I asked Takito to make everything ready for you. As an honored guest." While she spoke the old man squatted beside the fire pit at the door of the lodge and used two forked sticks to probe the heated stones.

It was unthinkable for Cormac to refuse the high hospitality of the sweat lodge; the steam bath was both a religious ritual and a mark of affection and esteem. "I do not deserve such an honor," he murmured.

"Nonsense. We made it for Memetosia, to soothe his old bones and help him prepare for death. Now you must use it to prepare for life, for what you must do."

Corm's mind was racing, trying to sort out the remarkable events of the past few hours. He'd already decided Genevieve must have played a part in events of the day. How else would Memetosia have known that Cormac had a plan for the survival of the *Anishinabeg*? Maybe she also knew the old chief had given him a gift. Maybe she knew what it was. If so, she knew more than he did.

He could feel the deerskin pouch resting against his chest. It seemed to generate its own heat. He sensed Genevieve waiting for him to mention it, but she didn't say anything. Instead she called to the old man tending the fire of the sweat lodge. "Takito, I have brought you the brave called Cormac Shea. He is of the Potawatomi people from the village of Singing Snow."

The old man put down his sticks and got to his feet. He moved slowly, and his body, naked except for a breechclout, was ropy with age. One leg was shorter than the other and his gait had a distinctive leftward lurch. "*Kihkeelimaahsiiwaki*," he murmured. I do not know him. "But I have heard of his deeds and his skill with the long gun."

Cormac was startled to see a whole-skin otter medicine bag around his neck. He lifted his hand in greeting, then realized Takito was blind; there were rough scars where his eyes should have been. The tattoos on his cheeks and forearms were distinctive and confirmed the message conveyed by the medicine bag. "I am honored to meet a priest of the Midewiwin," Cormac said. "I am not deserving that such an esteemed healer should prepare the sweat lodge for me."

The Midewiwin priesthood was active among the Potawatomi as well as the Miami and Ojibwe and Ottawa. When they were formed, the Great Spirit had chosen to communicate with them through means of an otter who helped a brave whose leg had been crushed in an accident (a Potawatomi, according to the way Cormac had heard the story). The otter told that first Midè priest that in exchange for the loss of his leg he and those who joined him would be given means to protect the *Anishinabeg*. After that it became common for many members of the Midewiwin to sacrifice a part of their own bodies at the sacred festival that conferred priesthood. It was possible that Takito had gouged out his own eyes.

The priest pointed at the sweat lodge. "Everything is ready. Come."

Cormac looked around for Genevieve, but she was gone. "With your permission, esteemed priest, I will prepare myself for this great honor."

There was a place at the edge of the clearing where three tall pines formed a natural curtain around a flat rock ledge at the edge of the stream. Custom demanded that Cormac enter the rebirth of the steam lodge as he had entered the world at the time of his first birth, entirely naked, without even a totem or a medicine bag of any sort. He took off his moccasins and trousers first, folding them neatly, stalling before he must remove his shirt, trying to sense any prying eyes.

Instinct told him he was alone except for the old priest squatting beside the fire pit, chanting.

"*Haya, haya, ahseni . . .*" The sound was low, soothing, luring him back to the pleasures of the steam. What did it matter where he left Memetosia's gift? They were alone and Takito was blind. He could leave the pouch tucked unobtrusively under his clothes and it would be there when he returned to dress . . . *Ayi!* The steam had already turned his thoughts to smoke. "The most precious thing I have," the old chief had said.

The chanting stopped and the priest called him, "Cormac Shea of the People of the Fire, come. These stones are waiting for you."

"I am preparing myself, esteemed Priest. Only a few breaths more."

A short distance from the rock was a maple tree that had been three-quarters felled, probably by lightning. Most of the trunk lay along the ground, leafless and withered. A shadow-tree remained upright, a single piece of the trunk that was still struggling to grow. Its leaves were yellow and curled in on themselves. Only one branch at the very top was still green and full of life.

Cormac grasped the skinny remains of the tree with his knees and began to shimmy up the ghost trunk. It swayed and bent toward the earth. The rough and splintered bark tore at his naked legs, but he ignored the pain. The single live branch stuck out of one side and hung almost over the stream. Cormac tested it gingerly.

"*Haya, haya, ahseni . . .*" The chant had started again. People said that a Midewiwin priest could see with his eyes closed. Maybe Takito could see with no eyes at all. But what did it matter? Takito was not his enemy. There had been trouble between the hereditary chiefs and the Midè priests since the chiefs had been unable to cope with the devastation caused by the white man's diseases. That had allowed the Midewiwin to become more powerful, and in many of the tribes they struggled with the chiefs for power. But if Takito wasn't loyal to the old man dying a short ways away in Genevieve's parlor he wouldn't be here.

"*Haya, haya, ahseni. Haya, haya, ahseni.*"

The single live branch of the maple tree dipped perilously close to the water. *Ayi!* He was going to fall in and make a fool of himself. He moved back a couple of inches and the branch stopped swaying. He glanced over at the steam lodge one last time. Takito's back was to him. Cormac reached up with one hand and slipped the deerskin medicine bag from around his neck, wound it securely around the single living branch of the dying maple, and shimmied carefully back down the branch. When he was on the ground he saw that the green leaves entirely hid the treasure.

Utterly naked, at last he approached the lodge. Takito stopped chanting and stood up. He rubbed Cormac from head to toe with bear grease, then he held open the flap of the small wigwam and waited.

Cormac had to stoop to get inside and once there he couldn't stand upright; the wigwam had not been built for standing. On the floor was a frame of laced-together saplings that stood about two hands high and supported a woven lattice of hide thongs. When he lay down on it Cormac felt as if he were floating. The air was already thick with moisture, but he heard the sound of liquid splashing on the rocks in the fire pit and more clouds of steam filled the little lodge. The moist heat surrounded him, entered his muscles, and began its work. He gave himself up to the healing magic of the Midewiwin.

Chapter Eight

HAMISH STEWART DID not like cities in general, and Albany, for all he'd lived here going on a twelvemonth, he considered the least likable of all. Nothing to inspire a man to awe or even admiration, only squat wooden buildings, na the fine red stone o' Edinburgh ni the impressive gray granite o' Glasgow. Wi' a wooden stockade around the bits that mattered, the fort and such, there were too many people crammed together in too little space, and the men all haggling and cursing and spitting and pissing at the same time into the same wee drainage ditches as ran down the dirt roads and emptied their filth into the river. The decent God-fearing sort of women turned their pinched faces away and pretended they dinna see or hear the goings-on. The wenches as lifted their petticoats out behind one or t'other o' the town's taverns or grog shops and bent over for any as had five copper pennies to pay for a straightforward fucking—or a bit more for something fancy—those sorts o' lassies dinna care.

There were plenty o' that sort in this place. The taproom belonged to a Dutchman, Peter Groesbeck, and as in the rest of Albany, you were as likely to hear under its roof the Frankish speech of Holland and the other Low Countries as the bloody king's English. Groesbeck, like most, spoke both tongues. What set him apart was that he let the whores do as much business as they liked out o' his establishment at the Sign of the Nag's Head, long as they paid him his share at end o' day. Hamish had no quarrel wi' that. You survived how best you could. What bothered him about Groesbeck's taproom was that geneva could be had for a ha'penny the glass and rum for a penny, but you couldna get a dram o' real whiskey at any price. None to be had anywhere in the town. A pox on Albany. Once Shadowbrook was his he wouldna come again to this miserable excuse for a town. He'd send his slaves to do whatever business he had with Albany.

Hamish finished his rum and called for a refill. Old man Groesbeck himself brought the jug and filled the Scot's glass. Hamish put a wooden penny on the table and the Dutchman took it and went away.

Slaves. God's truth, it was a mighty strange notion. He dinna think he'd ever be really comfortable with it. Men and women running about doing whatever they were bid for no pay, and no reason for it other than that the slaves had black skin and the masters had white. Could be this whole slave business was a heretic Protestant notion. On t'other hand, St. Paul himself said that slaves should be obedient to their masters. Besides, slaves and Shadowbrook went together. First time he'd seen the one was first time he saw t'other. And God's truth, Shadowbrook was meant to be his.

He'd known that back when he still had two eyes, the first time he saw that glorious piece of God's creation called the Hale Patent. Shadowbrook was his destiny. That's why the Almighty had let him live through the sinkhole o' death that was Culloden Moor. It was why he'd survived the bloody slaughter o' the hunt the Sassenachs mounted after the battle ended, pursuing the Highlanders up every *brae* and down every *ben,* killing them wherever they could be found. After Culloden the Highlanders were na permitted e'en to wear the plaid, God help them all. But Hamish Stewart still had his plaid, woven for him by his own grandmother in the soft blues and rose reds o' the tartan o' the Stewarts o' Appin. He would wear it again, by God, when he was laird o' Shadowbrook.

His destiny, Hamish reminded himself, and pushed away the faint unease he felt each time he thought o' how it was he'd gotten enough brass to make it all happen. By Christ, had he gone to London and paid the ass-licking court flunky as was supposed to get it, what would ha' happened then? Nothing. Whatever the wee favor the Sassenach was supposed to do for the poor bedeviled crofters who dispatched Hamish Stewart to pay the Englishman their life's savings, he would na ha' done it. No Sassenach can be trusted. Ach, what was the point o' thinking on all that now. "Landlord! Another rum. A man can be dead o' thirst in this place and you'd not notice."

"And will you treat me to one as well?" a woman's voice asked from somewhere over his shoulder.

"Aye, glad I'll be to do it, Annie. If you'll sit yourself down and talk a wee while."

"The talk's easy enough, Hamish. But the sitting is another matter." Annie Crotchett was on the wrong side of twenty-five. She was missing two front teeth and her skin was beginning to look like badly tanned hide. Aye, but her breasts were still fine things. They rose above her bodice like a pair o' ships in full sail. Hamish had heard she charged tuppence extra to unlace her dress and let a man suckle. He couldna say for sure because he'd never gone with Annie out behind the Nag's Head. A man shouldna shit in the same place he ate, a lesson he'd learned early on. Annie was a matter o' business.

She sat gingerly on the bench beside Hamish, keeping her weight more or less on one cheek. "I keep telling meself it's not worth letting a man ram his cock up yer arse for a guinea, much less a shilling," she sighed, "but I give in every time." Groesbeck appeared and gave them each a tot of rum. Hamish put tuppence on the table and the landlord scooped it up and turned to go. "Hold on." Annie reached between her breasts and extracted three sixpences. "Here's your share of me day's earnings, Peter. I'm done work until tomorrow. Got to give me poor bottom a bit of rest or they'll be burying the whole of me by week's end."

Hamish waited until the landlord had left them before asking, "What about John Hale? Does he like to ram it up your backside, as well?"

Annie laughed. "Lord no. Wish he did; I'd hold my shit for a month if I thought I could bury that bastard's cock in it. It's other things John Hale likes."

"What things?"

"None of yer business. I told ye afore I took yer poxed money, I'll tell you anything he says, not what he does." She was too ashamed to tell what Hale made her do the two or three times a month he came to see her. The Scot had offered her a golden guinea to loosen her tongue, but no amount of money would make her. " 'Sides, I ain't seen John Hale at all this past fortnight." And glad she was of it, much as she missed the shilling Hale paid her for each visit.

"When you did see him last, was he talking about the harvest? Did he say how—" Hamish stopped speaking. Nearly everyone in the taproom stopped speaking.

A huge redheaded man had walked in. There was a lassie with him, a wee scrap o' a thing. Half undressed, she seemed, so tattered was her frock. The man sat at a table near the door and called loudly for a pint o' ale for himself and a glass o' Rhenish wine for the lady; if he noticed how quiet the taproom had become, he dinna let on. Hamish felt a cold hand grip his bowels and clamped his teeth tight shut to keep from groaning aloud.

"Only drinks wine." Annie didn't seem to have noticed Hamish's distress. "Lady is she? Don't look like it to me."

Hamish wasn't interested in who or what the lassie might be. "That's Quentin Hale, isn't it?"

"That's him," Annie confirmed.

People had started speaking again, rather more loudly than was normal. And making a point of not looking at the newcomer or his companion. "The Red Bear. That's what they call him, isn't it?"

"Uko Nyakwai, the savages say. Practically one of 'em hisself, if the truth be told. Married a squaw, and in a proper Christian church, if you don't mind. And when—"

"I thought he was gone. I heard after the squaw died, Quentin Hale left Shadowbrook for good and went to the Ohio Country." To Hamish's ears his voice sounded hoarse and unnatural.

"Not right away. Stayed up there on the Patent for maybe a year, then he had a huge fight with his pa and left. Doesn't matter anyway. Shadowbrook was never going to be his. John's the elder brother. That's how rich folks do things, isn't it? The first one gets the best of whatever there is, and the rest are left to squabble over the leavings."

"That's how it happens sometimes," Hamish said.

God-rotting hell! He'd been sure he wouldna have to deal with Quentin Hale. Leastwise not until long after everything was settled and he had the law and possession on his side. God-rotting hell, but sometimes a man's destiny was a hard thing to live with.

Nicole was glad to leave Albany. The women of the town had looked at her in surprise, then quickly looked away in disapproval. Her dark hair hung in a plait down her back like a squaw's, because she had lost all her pins. She had no petticoats and no chemise, and her dress was little more than rags. The lingering glances of the men were worse. She could tell what they were thinking. If Quentin Hale wasn't with her she'd have been mauled like a common whore. "Where are we going now?" she demanded when they quit the town. "Where is Monsieur Shea? You said he would rejoin us."

"He will, when he can." She'd have to stop asking so many questions if she was going to be Cormac Shea's woman. Not his worry, Quent reminded himself. Corm had claimed her; it was up to him to break her to his ways. "We're going the same place we've been going right along," he said. "Shadowbrook. We'll be there before midday tomorrow if you'll stop talking so much and keep walking."

"That's your family's home, isn't it? I have heard you and Monsieur Shea talking about it."

"That's right." He said no more and they walked in silence for what remained of the day.

At dusk they descended a steep hill to a shallow cove beside the broad river. There was a narrow strip of sandy beach that ended in an outcropping of rocks, the whole protected by a half circle of willow trees growing at the foot of the cliff. Quent waited and kept watch while Nicole bathed. "Stay this side of the rocks," he told her. "There's an undertow." When she came out, refreshed and ravenous, he had already stripped to the waist and taken off his moccasins. "I'll bring back supper," he called over his shoulder as he moved off. He dropped his breeches, stepping out of them, and bent forward to gather them up. Nicole's cheeks grew hot and she quickly turned her head. By the time she turned back, the bare backside of the Red Bear was nowhere in sight.

Nicole wondered why he hadn't made a fire for her to cook the fish he clearly intended to catch, but when Quent returned he was carrying a basket woven of willow reeds. He came clambering over the rocks, wearing his breeches, droplets of water still clinging to his shoulders and chest and red hair. "Supper," he said, depositing the basket at her feet. It was full of rough-shelled oysters, each almost as big as her palm. "Biggest and sweetest you've ever tasted," he promised. He bent over to reclaim his dirk from the things he'd left on the shore, pried open the first mollusk, and handed it to her.

Nicole downed the shimmering oyster. "Delicious," she agreed. "I love oysters. Maman did not approve. Not fit food for a lady, she said. Only for common folk."

"What would your maman say if she saw you now?" Quent asked, slurping down two oysters and opening two more for her.

"She would wag her finger," Nicole admitted. "But she would understand after I explained that it was oysters or nothing, and that I am very hungry. Where did you get that?" She nodded toward the willow-reed basket, grayed with age and long soaking.

"There's a cave beneath those rocks. The entrance is underwater and it's hard to find unless you know where to look. The basket was in there."

"You knew where to look."

"Yes. We're on Shadowbrook land now. I've been swimming here since I was a boy."

"You and Monsieur Shea?"

"That's right." Damn the woman. Every conversation he had with her ended with Cormac Shea.

In the morning they left the riverbank and cut inland. "Straight up the bank would get us there faster," Quent said, "but there's a stretch of marshland between here and the house where the mosquitoes are the size of your fist. Better if we avoid that."

Nicole was grateful for the shade of the woodland route, and Monsieur Hale seemed to enjoy pointing out various landmarks and features of the Patent as they came into view. More for himself than her, Nicole thought, as if he needed reminding.

"That road there leads to the sawmill. Used to be only half as wide, but we broadened it some years back. This is the back road to the mill. Round the other side there's what we call the big road, the one my grandfather built when he first got here." Quent squatted and studied the rutted track. "Doesn't seem to have been scraped or graded for the last couple of seasons."

A league or so further on there was another break in the trees, and another path wide enough for a horse and wagon. "That's the back way to the gristmill and the sugarhouse," he said. "But if you're not driving a wagon, quickest way's to take the cutoff by a pair of white pines. Takes you by way of Big Two."

"What is made at a sugarhouse? And what is Big Two?"

"Sugar's how you make rum."

"And Big Two?"

"Pair of hills." He didn't explain that the hills had gotten their name because of their resemblance to a woman's breasts.

A bit farther on they climbed a rise that gave them a view over what appeared to be an inland sea, or perhaps a lake. Only when she looked more closely did Nicole realize it was a field of wheat, the tall stalks rippling in the early morning breeze.

They stood for a time while Quent shaded his eyes with his hand and gazed at the crop. "Almost ripe by the smell of it," he said after a few seconds. "But there's far too many weeds been allowed to take root. Can't think why—" He broke off.

"Why what?"

"Nothing." No point in telling her that it was perishing strange that the sun had been up for nearly four hours and there were no slaves pulling the weeds from the field. He didn't look forward to telling Nicole about Shadowbrook's slaves.

It disturbed him that he'd seen no one on the sawmill road, or heading to or from the sugarhouse or the gristmill. More than fifty people lived in this southern part of the Patent; if you counted the folks up north at Do Good, there were close to three times that many on the place. But they hadn't passed another human being since they set foot on Shadowbrook's land. The hairs on the back of his neck were prickling. Quent took his gun from his shoulder and began pouring powder down the muzzle while they walked.

Nicole watched him, her dark eyes nearly black with concern. Quent said nothing, and for once she didn't ask any questions.

An hour or so later, when the sun was directly overhead, the house appeared. "That's Shadowbrook," Quent said softly.

Because of the detour they'd taken to avoid the marsh, they approached the house from the side, but that wasn't much of a disadvantage. Like most houses she'd seen here in the New World, it appeared foursquare, planted solidly atop a rise and fronting on the river. As far as she could see, Shadowbrook was without wings, though it seemed to sprawl out the back for some ways, as if bits had been added on year by year. It was built of wood and gleamed white beneath a slate roof, with shutters the same dusky blue-gray color. She counted four chimneys, though she expected there were more. "It looks to be a fine house," she said.

He heard her voice as if it came from a far distance and raised his hand to silence her. Quent listened hard, trying to hear the danger. He knew it was there—the hot July breeze carried the stink of fear along with the smell of the river and of rampant summer growth. He heard nothing but silence at first, then a shift in the currents of air brought a whisper of something that sounded like moaning.

For a moment he wondered if his father had died, if he was hearing Ephraim Hale's mourning song. No, if it were, everyone would be up by the burying place at Squirrel Oaks. This sound came from the vicinity of the house.

The sound grew louder. It was a keening, a collective misery. Now Nicole heard it, too. "*Mon Dieu,* what is that?" She made a hurried sign of the cross.

"I'm not sure. Could be—" He stopped because there was another sound, a whooshing and cracking, and a second immediately after. "Sweet Jesus Christ! Sweet Jesus! Stay here. *Don't move.*" He took off, his long strides burning the distance between himself and the house.

Nicole watched him for a moment, felt the loneliness of the woods at her back; then, ignoring his words, she went after him.

The grass around the house was usually close cut and bright green. Now it was browned and brittle and long enough to flatten as Quent ran across it. The moaning had stopped; and he heard only the whoosh and crack.

There was a flat piece of earth on the far side of the house; they called it the Frolic Ground. It got its name after Quentin Hale survived to see his first birthday. His father gave a great dinner, a frolic, to celebrate.

The Frolic Ground was a hundred fathoms long—it would take a tall man two hundred strides to cover its length—and nearly as wide. It was surrounded by ornamental posts from which lanterns could be strung to light the darkness. There was an enormous fire pit to one side, big enough to roast a couple of oxen and many, many fowl, as Ephraim had done on Quent's first birthday. Over a hundred local Indians were there that day, along with every single soul who lived and worked on the Patent, whatever their color or religious persuasion. Even the Quakers of Do Good came, standing primly to one side and not joining in the dancing or whooping and hollering that marked the occasion.

A seventh whoosh and cracking cut through the midday summer silence. Quent winced. In a moment he had covered the last twenty strides.

Fifty men and women huddled together in the Frolic Ground, black slaves and the white tenant farmers who worked on the Patent. They stood in a semicircle around one of the big wagons used to haul felled trees to the sawmill. The wagon's traces were empty and staked to the ground, and guylines had been fixed either side to keep the whole thing steady. The wagon wheels were nearly as tall as Quent himself, sturdy enough to carry the weight of four or five massive tree trunks. Plenty strong enough to support even the huge man who was tied to one of them.

The man was spread-eagled and roped in place, belly to the hub, arms and legs splayed against the spokes, and naked from the waist up. His broad ebony back was welted with the stripes he'd received since Quent had heard the first crack of the whip moments before. His huge bald head was turned away from the Ground's entrance, but Quent knew the man tied to the wagon wheel was Solomon the Barrel Maker.

The crowd was silent, their attention riveted on the man with the whip.

Quent raised the long gun to his shoulder, his finger tightening on the trigger. "Use that thing again and I'll blow your head off."

The crowd swiveled toward him as if it were a single creature. "Master Quent," someone muttered. "Master Quent be home."

"How in bloody hell did you get here?" John Hale stepped from the far side of the wagon to the empty space between it and the onlookers. The hand hanging at his side held a pistol. "Whipper, pay him no mind. Do your duty."

The whipper looked first at the tall redhead wearing buckskins and pointing a deadly long gun directly at him, then at the much shorter dark man dressed in black breeches and a white linen shirt, coatless in deference to the hot sun.

"If he wants to stay alive, he'd better not," Quent called out. "And whatever you call this business, it's got nothing to do with duty. There's not been a public whipping on Shadowbrook since Grandfather's day. Father forbade it."

"Father is ill. I'm running things now. The Barrel Maker told me an untruth." John raised the hand holding the pistol and cocked it. He aimed it straight at his brother. "Put down the long gun or I'll shoot."

"Don't be a jackass," Quent said. "You can't shoot faster than I can and you know it. You there, whipper, I said put it down. This is the last time I'm telling you. Next time I'll shoot your hand off."

"Don't—" John began, but the man had already dropped the whip.

"Good," Quent said. "Now, kick it over toward me. Good." Quent addressed the crowd without taking his eyes off his brother. "Big Jacob, you there?" He'd seen the old man in the crowd as soon as he approached the Frolic Ground. Big Jacob lived at the sugarhouse and looked after the young horses kept in a paddock on that part of the Patent.

"I be here, Master Quent. And mighty glad to be seeing you."

"Glad to be here, Jacob. Now, kindly come forward and untie Solomon."

John whirled around and pointed the pistol in the direction of the slave. "Stay where you are."

"John, if you discharge that pistol in any direction, I will blow you to kingdom come. You have my word on it. Do as I say, Jacob."

For a moment no one moved. Quent heard a woman whisper; he was pretty sure the speaker was Clemency the Washerwoman. Clemency carried a lot of weight among the slaves, in every sense. She was as wide as most doorways, though a good deal shorter. He looked into the crowd for her and spotted Six-Finger Sam, who looked after the kitchen garden and did odd jobs around the big house. In apple season Sam ran the press that made their cider, and was in charge of the huge cauldrons in which they cooked apple butter and of drying some part of the crop, so one way or another they'd have a taste of fruit throughout the winter. Six-Finger Sam almost never spoke. On the other hand, Clemency, was the storyteller among the Patent Negroes. "Clemency, she be the one keeps our yesterday," Kitchen Hannah had told Quent years before. "The Washerwoman, she knows who be who and what be what, and how they came to be the way they be. Clemency, she keep the inside-free alive in us slaved folks."

Quent knew about the inside-free. "That be the real difference between white peoples and nigra peoples, little master." Solomon had told him. "We nigra peoples got to rely on the inside-free."

"Jacob!" Quent called again. "Do as I say. No one will hurt you."

"Stay where you are!" John's voice was edged with panic. His extended arm trembled. "I'm the master here!" It was a shrill shriek, almost like a woman's. "You do what I say."

"No, that's not exactly true just yet." A new voice spoke, one that was infirm and shook with illness, but that still carried authority in a way that John's never would. Ephraim Hale stood just inside the gate of the Frolic Ground. Quent took his eyes off John long enough for one quick look at his father. Ephraim was bent over a pair of waist-high sticks, leaning heavily on them, but his voice grew firmer and more sure as he spoke: "I am the master here as long as I'm alive. John, Quent, both of you put down your weapons. Jacob, do as Master Quentin instructed. Release Solomon from the wheel."

Quent felt a flood of relief. He would not have to kill his brother. At least not yet. But John's outstretched hand was shaking noticeably now. Nothing was more unreliable than a pistol; this one could go off and do considerable damage. "Both of us at the same time, John," Quent said easily. "As Father wishes. On the count of three. One, two . . ."

Then the guns were on the ground and Jacob was untying Solomon the Barrel Maker. And in a flurry of petticoats and purpose, Lorene Devrey Hale arrived to take charge of her household.

Cormac knew that time had passed, but he had no idea how much. He was enveloped not just by steam, but by a strange fragrance, sharp and at the same time sweet, like nothing he'd ever smelled before. It entered through his nose and filled his entire being. It was wonderful. He opened his mouth and swallowed the scent. He hungered for it, wanted as much of it as he could devour. The magic went straight to his crotch. He was enormous, filled with a sweet hot pressure that must be satisfied. He thought of Nicole. At least once he whispered her name aloud.

He wasn't sure if he was awake or asleep when he felt himself swallowed and sucked dry. He had only a vague impression of thick dark hair and pale, naked flesh, somehow cool despite the heat of the sweat lodge. The steam was too thick to allow him to see anything, but he didn't care. He shuddered with pleasure, gave himself up to bliss, and then to deeper sleep.

The next thing he knew someone was calling his name. He recognized Takito's voice. "Roll over, my son. I will finish what the steam has begun."

There was no resistance in Cormac and no questioning; the steam had melted both away. He turned on his belly and the powerful touch of the curing priest began at the nape of his neck and traveled rapidly to the base of his spine, probing every muscle, every old scar, missing nothing. Takito, he knew, was using his fingertips to read not just his body, but his mind.

After a time the touch changed. It became somehow stronger, more insistent. And it did not soothe as it had. The fingers felt less skilled, more bruising. Takito wasn't a tall man, but Cormac sensed the priest crouching in the low-ceilinged wigwam. He was aware of the priest moving around to the other side of the pallet, swiftly and smoothly. There was no lurching movement, no indication that he dragged one foot.

Cormac didn't move, unwilling to show that he was now totally awake and no longer drunk with steam and the powerful herbal magic of the Midewiwin. The man's fingers attempted to reach under him—it was not Takito anymore, he was sure of that.

"Ayi!" Cormac rolled toward the imposter, using his full body weight to drive both himself and whoever had replaced the blind priest to the ground. The man uttered a surprised grunt, but in the time it took to draw one breath Cormac knew his adversary was a skilled wrestler. He fought off the attempts to imprison his leg. The only sounds were their struggles for breath as both men grappled for control. The imposter was stronger and every movement brought him closer to dominance. The only thing that saved Cormac from being immediately overwhelmed was what remained of the coating of bear grease. He was still too slick to grab, but it was only a matter of time before the other man's strength would overpower him.

The assailant gave up trying to capture a leg in the classic hold and rose to a crouch, dragging the half Potawatomi brave with him. In a swift movement he wrapped both arms around the chest of the powerful métis and squeezed. *Ayi!* He had heard this one was a fighter from the land of the clouds, a *kapi* who had come from the world beyond, where the redheaded warriors of his father's people hunted beside the fearless *Anishinabeg* braves of the old days. Still, after the priest's special attentions, he had not expected such a struggle.

Cormac felt the life being crushed out of him. His opponent's arms were iron bands tightening around his chest. He made his mind a blank and saw only the Sacred Fire of the Potawatomi. He saw the glowing red coal of his manhood ceremony; he felt himself grasp it and find it cool as ice in his hand. Strength rose from his belly and filled him. He reached up and clasped his hands around the other man's neck. It was like a tree trunk, thick and unbending. The arms that imprisoned him hugged him still tighter. Nothing he did freed him from the increasing pressure on his chest. He couldn't breathe and he wasn't strong enough to pull his opponent over his head. Soon he would lose his spirit. No, by the Sacred Fire, he would not. He was not meant to free his death song in a dark sweat lodge, crouched over like an animal.

With one last, enormous effort the tree trunk bent. The imposter's chin was almost touching his shoulder. Close, closer, finally close enough so Corm could turn and sink his teeth into flesh. The man screamed.

Cormac tasted the brave's blood and did not relax his jaws until he had torn away a chunk of flesh. The other man screamed again and Cormac increased the pressure on the powerful neck until finally he heard it snap and felt the sagging weight of death.

For a moment he stayed where he was, gasping for air, then he realized that his jaws were still locked around a piece of the cheek of his enemy. He shuddered. This was the one way in which he was not truly even half a Real Person; he had been infected with the white man's horror of human meat. He spat out his enemy's flesh and staggered out of the wigwam. If the priest were still there he would kill him, too. Cormac's eyes were having difficulty adjusting to the light after so long in the dark, but he was sure the clearing was empty. Both the fires had been put out and it was dusk, the relative cool of evening descending. He must have been five or six hours in the sweat lodge.

He thought of the medicine bag hidden in the dying maple tree. *Ayi!* Great Spirit, let it still be there. It had to be; if they had found the deerskin pouch, why would they have sent someone to search him? And that had to have been what the assailant was trying to do. Otherwise he would have simply slit Cormac's throat in the first moments of the attack.

He was still pouring sweat and his heart was beating like a war drum. Whatever had happened to Memetosia's treasure couldn't be changed now. The immediate task was to clear his head so he could decide what to do next. Cormac took a couple of unsteady steps toward the stream and plunged in.

The first shock of the icy water on his overheated skin stole his breath, and he sucked in great gulps of air. Then the cool water soothed him, calming his heart and restoring strength to his muscles. When he got out of the stream he was himself again.

He stood for a moment, listening with his body as well as his ears, totally *Anishinabeg* for the few heartbeats that could spell life or death. There was no immediate danger. He was alone.

His buckskins were no longer neatly folded on the flat rock where he had put them. They had been shaken out and examined. After he was dressed he climbed what remained of the dying maple tree. When he reached the branch hanging out over the water he paused for a moment, preparing himself for whatever he must find. He shimmied forward and stretched out his hand; his fingers touched the leather thong of Memetosia's medicine bag. Cormac reached for the pouch, clutching it tightly as he unwound the thong. Whatever was inside was still there. He could feel it. He breathed a prayer of thanksgiving to the Great Spirit of the Sacred Fire, then, thinking of the many Sunday mornings in the front room of Shadowbrook, one to Miss Lorene's Jesus God as well.

He spent a few more moments at the sweat lodge, then made his way back to the house. It was dark, but he could see no shimmer of candlelight behind any of the windows. The Lydius house loomed like a black smudge in the night. Cormac tried the back door. It was open. Cautiously he let himself in and went from room to room. The house was empty; even the kitchen fireplace was cold. There was no sign of Genevieve or any of the Lydius family, much less of the Miami chief and his entourage. The only proof that Memetosia and his braves had been there, that Cormac had not somehow dreamed the whole thing, was the medicine bag around his neck and the faint, lingering scent of bear grease in the kitchen.

His tomahawk and his knife were where he'd left them in the front hall. His long gun was gone.

THURSDAY, JULY 16, 1754
SHADOWBROOK, THE HALE PATENT

Nicole had not realized how much she longed for food that was not meat. There were bright orange carrots on the table, short and stubby and slathered in honey and butter; potatoes that were hashed with cream, and turnips that had been cooked in the dripping pan below spit-roasted small birds and bathed with their juices. The birds were crisped to a fine golden brown and had been brought to the table skewered on spits that stood upright in a special holder, quail, perhaps, or maybe very young pigeons. Nicole wasn't sure and she didn't care much. The large pie filled with spiced venison appealed to her much more, but not as much as the produce of the gardens she'd seen out behind the house earlier, or the biscuits made from the wheat flour they said was milled a short distance away.

"Mostly squirrels and birds, and once we took to the rivers, fish." Monsieur Hale might have been reading her mind, but he was simply responding to a question from his mother. "And rabbits. Plenty of those. But no potherbs or saladings and no biscuits or johnnycakes. That's what you miss most in the wilderness." He helped himself to another couple of biscuits as he spoke.

"Then perhaps"—Lorene Devrey Hale had a beautiful speaking voice, low and clear and like the rustle of silk—"given the quality of the fine potherbs here at Shadowbrook, and our excellent wheat, you will not again stay so long away in the wilderness." She wasn't looking at Quent when she spoke. She was studying her firstborn. John did not return her glance, but stayed concentrated on eating, ripping apart a pigeon with his hands and his teeth.

Nicole watched him as well. He ate with anger, as he seemed to do most things. Her companions of the journey were both easier in their skin than was this John Hale, and he did not make her feel easy in hers.

Yesterday Madame Hale had appeared while they were all still in the place they called the Frolic Ground. She had been very white, with two spots of high color on her cheeks, but she had created order out of chaos. Clearly she knew it was a miracle that both her children were not dead. Her eyes kept flicking from one son to the other. Lingering longest on the younger, Nicole thought.

Madame's instructions had been quickly obeyed. Two of the slaves made a carrying seat of their clasped hands and gently lifted Ephraim Hale as if he weighed nothing and took him away. Nicole had never seen a black-skinned person until she and Papa landed in Virginia. Once there she had seen many. Every one, she discovered, was owned by a white person. The mistress of the boardinghouse where Nicole and her papa stayed explained: "Says in the Bible that's how it's to be, child. Noah cursed his son Ham. And Ham went to Africa and turned into a darky, and he and his descendants have always to be slaves. That's the will of God Almighty, child. It's right and proper that black heathens work for good Christian white folks. Long as they do what they're told and don't make any trouble, they're taken care of."

Oui, as the big black man with the bald head had been taken care of. Nicole watched two of the slave women help him walk away from the scene of the whipping.

Madame Hale, too, had watched them go, then she turned to the crowd. "Now you must all return to your work. This affair is over and done with." She turned to her younger son. "And you, Quentin, your business, at least for the moment, is to tell me who this is." That's when she'd looked directly at Nicole for the first time.

And that's when Quentin Hale realized she was there. "I thought I told you to wait where I left you."

"I chose to follow you."

"So I see." He didn't say more because his mother was waiting. "May I present Mademoiselle Nicole Crane. She was traveling with Cormac when he found me. We couldn't leave her in the woods, so we brought her along. Mademoiselle, this is my mother."

"*Enchantée, madame.*" Nicole had known what she looked like, but she pretended she was in Papa's drawing room being presented to a general or diplomat. She dropped a deep and graceful curtsy.

Lorene's eyes had narrowed; she nodded and murmured some politeness in response to the greeting. Nicole wished she knew what the other woman was thinking, and the meaning of the quick but studied glance she directed at her youngest son. But all she said was, "You look like a savage, Quentin, and you smell worse. Where is Cormac?"

"He had someone to see in Albany. He'll be along."

"Very well. Go and make yourself presentable. I will take charge of our guest. Come along, my dear," and she'd reached out her hand. Nicole had had no choice but to put hers in the older woman's, acutely conscious that she had been without any creme or lotion for months and her skin felt like tree bark.

Lorene made no mention of the girl's roughened hands. She took Nicole to one of Shadowbrook's large bedrooms and had a slave called Runsabout—"Her real name is Ruth, but when Quentin was little he called her Runsabout, because Kitchen Hannah was always sending her on errands"—bring a large copper tub and buckets of hot water. "You'll be wanting a bath, mademoiselle. And some clothes. I will have someone bring you some dresses of mine if you would not mind borrowing them."

"I would be honored, madame. You are so very kind." Nicole wondered what Quent's mother would say if she knew of the many times Nicole had bathed naked in forest streams, with Quent and Cormac keeping guard. Whenever she looked their backs were to her, but she'd never been entirely sure they hadn't peeked.

"It is my pleasure," the older woman had assured her. "And I'll send a seamstress to make some quick adjustments." Quentin's mother was at least a head taller than Nicole. "Such a dainty one you are, mademoiselle. My son looks like a giant beside you."

"Your son is a giant, madame."

Madame Hale had simply smiled and said that in light of everything that had happened, she had decided to cancel the midafternoon dinner for that day.

When Runsabout arrived with the clothes, she also brought a basket filled with various unguents. "All made right here on the Patent for mistress they be. It's Sally Robin what makes most of 'em. That's cause they got honey in 'em and Sally Robin, she got the gift, she does. Them bees just love to have her come and take their honey. She sings to 'em while she does it and they don't think nothin' 'bout stingin' nobody. But this here Hungary water"—Runsabout picked out a small flagon from the bottom of the basket—"this be coming upriver all the way from New York City." Runsabout spoke the name of the town as if it were on the other side of the earth. "Smells as sweet as ever it can smell, missy. You just bound to like Hungary water." Nicole did not tell her that her own mother had favored the scent.

After her bath and the fittings, Madame Hale sent food to Nicole's room—a slice of cold pork pie and some of the flat, yellowish johnnycakes made of the Indian meal of which all in America seemed so fond, and a mug of ale. Apparently the others in the house ate alone as well. Once, Nicole stepped out into the hallway and peered down the stairs, but she heard nothing except the quiet background hum of the household servants going about their work. Eventually she went to bed, marveling that after so much time sleeping outdoors, she found it a bit difficult to get comfortable in the soft feather bed.

Since '45, when she was nine years old, Nicole had feared her dreams. In the wilderness, with the two men close beside her, she did not once wake screaming and shaking as she had so often before, perhaps because there were other, more immediate fears. The first night she slept under Shadowbrook's roof she dreamed a different sort of dream.

She was five years old and Maman had prepared a feast to be eaten outside under the trees, sitting on the grass, with no servants or proper cutlery. Nicole remembered wearing a white dress with a long blue sash, and when she ran after the butterflies, trying to catch them in her pudgy, little-girl hands, the tails of the sash sailed out behind her in the breeze, and Papa laughed and called her his bluebird. But when she turned back to her parents, breathless with the futile chase and full of laughter, they did not at once notice her because they were kissing, lips pressed together, hands clasped. "Maman! Papa! Look at me!" And they did, and opened their arms to her. She ran to them and tumbled into their embrace, but she felt nonetheless a pang of intense jealousy, because she knew that for a few moments they had been more interested in each other than in her. Perhaps, Nicole thought when she woke, the memory was wakened by the scent of the Hungary water.

Today, her second at Shadowbrook and three days since she'd actually been on the land of the Patent, was the first time she had seen the family gathered together in a normal way. All except the elder Monsieur Hale, who was too ill to leave his bed.

Nicole slowly chewed on a carrot, savoring the sweetness. How extraordinary to see Quentin Hale—the woodsman who danced to Indian drums—wearing breeches and a fine white linen shirt with ruffles in the front and full sleeves. He could be any gentleman in Paris or London. But what did she expect? That he would appear at his mother's table wearing buckskins? He seemed a bit stiff, and in truth, so was she. She had not sat at a meal like this in a setting such as this since she and Papa left England. No, before that. Since 1750, when Maman had died.

The older brother, John, was looking at her. There was anger in his eyes. He finished stripping the flesh from a pigeon and tossed the tiny bones over his shoulder toward the fireplace. It was too hot for a fire. The bones lay on the bare hearth waiting to be cleared away later by the servants. John reached across her for a piece of the venison pie. He did not, Nicole realized, make a serious attempt to keep his arm from brushing by her breasts. Her cheeks flushed. He thought she was a whore. Why not? Consider the way he'd first seen her, half naked and browned by the sun, her hair braided like a savage's.

Madame Hale had given her pins along with everything else a lady needed. Today she was wearing a dress of pale lavender silk trimmed with white lace, with proper petticoats and a corset. Runsabout had helped her dress. "There now," she'd said, giving the laces a final tug and tying them firmly, "now you got a waist so tiny Mister Quent could maybe put his big hands around it." Nicole knew it was a sin of pride, but she was glad of her tiny waist. Only now, at the dinner table, she wished the corset weren't quite so tight. It was nearly impossible to eat enough to satisfy her hunger.

The table overflowed with food, savories and sweetmeats all served together in the local fashion. Maman liked the service to be a few things at a time in the French manner, but she would have approved the pretty serving dishes, some glazed dark yellow and some a creamy blue. The table, too. It was long and made of golden oak polished to a high shine. Three pewter chandeliers hung above it, each containing a dozen or more candles, but none were lighted. It was midafternoon and the sun was still high, streaming in the windows that looked toward the long, broad path that led to the river. The white walls of the large square room were marked by waist-high moldings picked out in gold leaf, and just below the ceiling was a plaster and gilt frieze of fruits and flowers. She couldn't help noticing that everything could do with a fresh coat of paint, but it was still one of the prettiest rooms she'd seen in America.

Kitchen Hannah appeared carrying an enormous platter of ears of corn, the outer leaves folded back up to protect the kernels from the heat of the fire. "First of the season these be," she announced. "Growed 'em myself, I did. Out behind the necessary, in that little patch what catches the sun nearly the whole day long." The cobs were no longer than Nicole's hand, the kernels a yellow so pale it was almost white. The platter passed her way and Nicole took an ear quickly, with just the tips of her fingers, because it was still almost too hot to hold, and laid it on the side of her plate.

Quentin Hale did not seem to mind the heat of the toasted corn. He bit into it eagerly, watching her all the while. He had been watching her since they sat down. In this fine house, in his fine clothes, with his mother and his brother and all the anger that buzzed just below the surface dancing in the air beside the tiny dust motes illuminated by the high-summer sun, he seemed again a stranger. It was impossible to imagine that this was the same man she had seen dance half naked among the savages, then disappear into the woods to rut with one of the squaws as if they were both animals without shame.

The thought made her breath come hard and Nicole busied herself with the ear of corn.

"You have not spoken of Cormac." Lorene Hale addressed herself to her younger son. "Someone to see in Albany, you said. Should he not have come by now?"

"I'm sure he'll come as soon as he can. He and Mademoiselle Crane are on their way north."

Lorene looked down at her plate, as if he'd said something that displeased her.

"Crane is not a French name." John's eyes were fixed not on Nicole's face, but on her breasts, pushed high above the lace trim of the bodice of her dress. He made no effort to conceal his gaze.

"I had a French mother and an English father." Nicole pretended to ignore his insolence.

"And you're on your way . . . north." He made it sound as if she had announced that she was on her way to hell.

"Oui, monsieur. To Québec."

"I see. And just what is it that you have to do in Québec?"

Quent answered before she could. "That's not any of your—"

"Non, non," Nicole said softly, then quickly to John Hale, "I have family business to see to in Québec, monsieur."

"Take care, mademoiselle, lest someone take you for a French spy." John spoke as if he were making a joke, but there was no laughter in his eyes.

After the meal Nicole and Quent sat on a wooden seat that had been built round a massive chestnut tree midway between the river and the house, enjoying the cooling of dusk and the faint breeze. "A French spy," Quent said, "why didn't that occur to me?"

"Because you know it is ridiculous."

"Yes. So does my damn fool brother. He only said it to make you angry. I think he imagines it to be a form of courtship."

She did not want to talk about John Hale, much less be courted by him. "When do you think Monsieur Shea will be here?"

Quentin had been wondering the same thing. It seemed unlikely that whatever business Genevieve Lydius and the Miami brave Mikamayalo had with Corm would take this long. But he wasn't yet worried enough to go back down to Albany and look for him. Corm could take care of himself. Besides, he was in no hurry for Corm to see Nicole the way she looked now. He wanted to keep the pleasure of that transformation for himself, at least for a time. "I don't know when he'll be here. When he can."

Damn! Couldn't he at least try not to show his feelings every time she made it clear she preferred Cormac? Sweet Jesus, what that dress did for the color of her eyes, not to mention her breasts. The dark curls pinned up like that were elegant, but he liked her better when her hair was loose down her back. Or plaited like a squaw's. Seeing her like this, looking the lady she really was, that made him feel . . . he wasn't sure what. Different. She was different at Shadowbrook and so was he.

Still later, when the candles had been lit and then extinguished, and the women had gone to bed, Quent found his brother pouring himself a final glass of rum to carry upstairs. "She's not what you think," Quent said. "Her father was an English officer, a hero of Culloden Moor. Her mother was the granddaughter of a French marquis."

"I'm delighted to hear the lady's lineage, Quent. Is she on offer, then?"

"I'm telling you so you'll know how to behave. And there's something else . . . I think you're dead wrong to whip any slave on the Patent, much less a fine man like Solomon, but I'm sorry about what happened yesterday. I realize with Father so ill, you're in charge here."

"After he's gone, as well." John held the rum up to the light of a candle set in a wall sconce, studying the color. It was pale gold with a hint of amber, the best they made on the Patent. The rum they traded to the local Indians in return for pelts was cloudy, and the proof was so high it did little more than burn a man's mouth and throat, not to mention his gut. "Shadowbrook will be mine after Father's dead."

"I know that. It's why I'm giving you fair warning to restrain yourself until after I'm gone. It won't be long. I can promise you that." Shadowbrook had claimed him again the moment he set foot on the Patent. The brooks and the trees and the hills whispered that he belonged to this place more than it could ever belong to him or to anyone else. But he was the second son and it would never be his. The sooner he got away again and broke the Patent's hold on his heart and soul the better it would be. "Just be clever," he said to his brother. "Keep your bloody whipper on a tether while I'm here. I wouldn't want to kill you, John. Not in this place, not while Mother and Father are alive."

"And afterward?" John asked, tossing back the rum and pouring another. "Will you try to kill me after they are gone?"

"I hope it isn't necessary," Quent said.

"Ah, but that's the only way you'll get Shadowbrook, isn't it?"

Quent's bedroom was in the east corner of the second floor. The purple flowered vine that grew up that corner of the house had been there as long as he could remember; the main stem was as thick as a tree trunk. The flowers appeared in June most years, sometimes in May. He'd always made a point of keeping his windows open when the vine bloomed. The perfume was faint but intoxicating, even to a small boy.

Now it was well into July and the vine had finished flowering. He had no memory of leaving the window open, but when he went into his room, moonlight spilled across the rag rug between his bed and the unused fireplace and Corm was sitting at a small round table beside the empty grate. "Something wrong with the front door?" Quent asked.

"I needed to speak with you before I saw any of the others. How's your father?"

"Very ill. Fading fast."

"But still alive? You had a chance to talk to him?"

"Yes to both questions. What peace could be made between us was made. You did what my mother asked, no need to worry about that. What's that you're hanging on to?" Corm's hand was covering something lying on the table. "A medicine bag? Where'd it come from?"

"I'll tell you in a moment. First you tell me something. What day is this?"

"Thursday. What day could it be?"

"It was Monday when Mikamayalo found us in the reeds." The hand holding the medicine bag squeezed it tight. Corm's knuckles whitened with tension. "So it has to have been three days, not six hours. That explains a great deal."

"Not to me."

"*Co.*" Corm used the Potawatomi negative. "No, I know it doesn't make sense to you yet. Sit down. I'll tell you what happened."

"Any reason we shouldn't have some light first?"

Cormac glanced toward the window. "None I know of."

The question had not been meant seriously. There had been no hostiles on the Patent for fifty years. Corm's glance betrayed a sense of caution that didn't seem appropriate, but Quent trusted it. He went to the mantel, all the while figuring how many strides he'd need to get his long gun from the cupboard where he'd stored it. Three, he decided, then realized that Corm didn't have his gun. He struck a spark from the tinderbox and lit the pair of candles on the table, then sat down. Habit made both men stretch their long legs toward the empty fireplace. The silver buckles on Quent's leather shoes gleamed in the candlelight, a contrast to Corm's well-worn moccasins. "Talk," Quent said. "I'm listening."

"The old Miami chief Memetosia was at the Lydius house, just as Mikamayalo told us. Genevieve was there, too. Not John, or the rest of the family. I saw four braves in addition to Mikamayalo, a squaw in the kitchen preparing food, and a Midè priest called Takito."

Corm told the story of everything that had happened. Quent listened without comment. "And you thought you'd only been in the sweat lodge six or seven hours?"

"At first. Then, when I was on my way here, I realized I was famished, weak with hunger. I had to stop and find food before I could go on. That's what made me think it was longer. It's taken me the better part of a day and a night to get here, so if this is Thursday, I've been gone four days and I was in the lodge for almost three of them."

"Takito must have been using pretty powerful herbs in that steam."

"Apparently so." Cormac remembered the young woman who had pleasured him with her mouth, the one he had imagined to be Nicole Crane, though he knew that wasn't possible. Could be there hadn't been any young woman at all. Could be the whole experience was Midewiwin magic. "Very strong herbs. Like nothing I've ever known."

Quent didn't want to push Corm to describe what had happened in the sweat lodge. The priests, particularly the Midewiwin, had many ways of bridging the distance between this world and the next; the sweat lodge was one of the most effective. He'd participated in the ritual four times, never for more than an hour or two. Each time the experience affected him profoundly and he emerged slightly changed. "The brave you killed was Miami?"

"No, that's the strangest thing of all. Huron."

Quent sucked in his breath. "Huron." The Huron were bitter enemies of the Miami. "Listen, maybe there was trouble. Maybe the Huron sent a war party to the Lydius house and—"

"The Huron wouldn't send a war party to the center of Albany. And there was no evidence of any kind of fight. The house was empty, but nothing inside was disturbed." Corm didn't mention that his knife and tomahawk had been exactly where he left them, something that would not have happened if there had been a war party rampaging through the Lydius house. If he told Quent that, he'd have to tell him about his long gun being stolen. "Whenever Genevieve and the Miami left, they did it peacefully."

"It doesn't make sense."

"None at all. Neither does this." Corm released his grip on the medicine bag and pushed it toward the light of the candles. The fine white deerskin and the red and black crane symbols shone in the glow. "At least my having it doesn't make sense."

"This is what Memetosia gave you?"

"Yes."

Quent was intensely curious about what was inside, but it was up to Corm to decide when to open the pouch. "Where did you leave the Huron's body?"

"In the stream." Cormac had been unwilling to grant the Huron the dignity of a burial. That was an honor due a worthy enemy, not one who sneaked up on a man drunk with magic. He took the scalp before he'd kicked the corpse into the water, and left it in the Lydius's front hall, in the place where his stolen long gun should have been.

Cormac fingered the medicine bag. It was miraculous that it hadn't been found and stolen while he was under Takito's spells. The Spirit of the Sacred Fire had protected the medicine bag because Corm was meant to have it and do something with it. Only he had no idea what.

He pushed the pouch toward Quent. "Take a look. It's six shells. Wampum but like nothing you've ever seen."

Quent closed his eyes and breathed deeply. Only when he felt himself calmed and ready did he loosen the thong and carefully, with great respect, withdraw the contents and spread them on the table.

Each shell was about the size of Quent's thumbnail. He'd never seen wampum that big before. In the days before the Europeans came the *Anishinabeg* used stone drills to bore holes in shells so they could be sewn onto belts and bands. The position of the wampum on the belts carried the messages they sent one another on the most solemn occasions. Nowadays a skilled wampum carver using metal drills could craft smaller pieces, but ordinary wampum had nothing in common with Memetosia's gift. Wampum was always white and tubular. These were flat beads made from the purple-black shells of the big clams called quahogs. Individually they were called *Súki* beads, collectively *Suckáuhock*. "How old do you figure these are?" Quent asked softly.

"I've been wondering about that since I opened the bag." Corm had examined the treasure yesterday, after he was well beyond Albany. He'd finally given in to his hunger and stopped to fish, and torn into the raw flesh of the fat walleyed pike with his teeth. It was not the mark of a true brave to eat uncooked food, but he didn't want to risk a fire, and couldn't wait to get the taste of Huron flesh out of his mouth. After he'd eaten, he had examined Memetosia's gift. "I figure they're at least a couple of hundred years old. Could be more."

"Maybe a lot more," Quent said.

"Maybe."

"The carving is marvelous. I've never seen anything like it."

Each of Memetosia's treasures was a complex picture, the shell punched through in some places, deeply engraved in others. In the tiny space available, the ancient artist had depicted signs that stood for various animals and surrounded them with a whole raft of other, more mysterious symbols. Quent recognized the turkey, the spider, and the possum. "What are these?" He gently pushed three of the beads toward Cormac.

"That's *papankamwa*, the fox. This is *eehsipana*, the raccoon. I'm not sure about this one. It's an elk, but I don't know if it's *ayaapia*, the buck, or *apeehsia*, the fawn."

"There are six Miami nations, aren't there?"

"Yes. The Miami themselves, plus the Kilatika, the Mengkonkia, the Pepikokia, the Wea, and the Piankashaw."

"You think the stones represent the six nations?"

"That's my guess, but I don't know which symbol represents which tribe, or what any of it means. Or what Memetosia meant me to do with them."

"And after you got out of the sweat lodge, he was gone?"

"They were all gone. Even Genevieve."

"You think she was working with whoever tried to kill you?"

"I don't know what to think. She's always been—" He broke off. It was as hard to imagine Genevieve plotting to murder him as it was to think of Miss Lorene wanting him dead. His own mother had considered him a burden and an embarrassment, but two women, one white, one a métisse had given him the affection Pohantis refused. "Genevieve's half Piankashaw. That's why Memetosia was taken to her house."

"When he spoke to you, he didn't say anything that would give you some notion of what he was—"

"I told you—mostly he talked about the danger the whites are to the *Anishinabeg*, and predicted more war between the French and the English. And oh, yes. That young officer you were with, Washington? Seems he surrendered his Fort Necessity to the French and went back to Virginia with his tail between his legs."

Quent shrugged. "I saw something about that in one of Father's newspapers. The reinforcements never got there. Wouldn't have been much good anyway. Story was, all they had by way of munitions was one barrel of spoiled gunpowder. The North Carolina troops were promised three shillings a day. When word went out it was to be reduced, they disbanded and went home. Besides, that so-called fort the Virginians built at the forks wasn't going to withstand well-trained French regulars. Paper said it was Jumonville's brother who led the French attack."

"Jumonville? The one Tanaghrisson . . ."

Quent nodded and both men were silent for a moment. Quent was the first to speak. "Listen, you think it was Genevieve who told Memetosia about your notion that Canada can be the home of the *Anishinabeg* if the French will just get the hell out?"

"Has to have been. Except that Memetosia knows as well as I do that the French won't just get out. Someone's got to make them go."

Quent looked at the stones. "These six tribes?"

Corm shrugged. He could hear the doubt in Quent's voice; he felt the same. The Miami union wasn't mighty enough to battle the French and win. They might have been once, but since the coming of the Europeans they, like so many of the tribes, were a pale shadow of their old glory. "Maybe the British will do it."

"Doesn't look that way. Not if they keep sending boys to do the job of men. But even if the British were to drive the French out of Canada, it's not likely they'd hand the place over to the red men, is it?"

"Not likely," Corm agreed. "Not unless they're made to."

"Which brings us back to the same question," Quent said. "Who's going to make them?"

The exquisitely carved Suckáuhock winked in the candlelight. Cormac gathered up the beads and returned them to the deerskin pouch.

"You still hungry?" Quent asked.

"I wouldn't refuse some food."

"C'mon, let's go down to the kitchen and see what we can find."

Most of the big-house slaves slept on corncob mattresses, tucked in below the roof rafters. They called it the long room, though it wasn't really a room at all, just half an attic, a space between the house and the sky. Kitchen Hannah's corncob mattress was downstairs, on the floor in an alcove behind the cooking fireplace, close enough to her domain so she heard the sounds of her larder being rifled. By two peoples, from the sound of it, she thought, men peoples. Not Master John. He wanted something to eat in the middle of the night, he'd wake her up and make her get it for him. Had to be Master Quentin, and Cormac most likely. She'd heard those two down there plenty of times before. Kitchen Hannah knew there wouldn't be a johnnycake left in her stores come morning, and could be a good part of the honey would be gone as well. She smiled her toothless smile and rolled over and went to sleep.

Normally Cormac had no difficulty sleeping. "Whatever troubles you will await a solution in the sun-coming time," Bishkek, the wise old one who was manhood father to both he and Quent, had told him. "The time of dark is for rest, to invite the spirits who speak in our dreams. Difficulties are to be fixed when the Great Spirit sends the sun." It was a notion Cormac held close and tried to honor. It was one of the things that kept the Potawatomi half of him alive here in Shadowbrook where the white half had come to rule. But tonight Bishkek's wisdom could not soothe him.

He'd been sleeping in this same bed since he first came to this place. It suited him that it was just wide enough for one person, and that his bedroom was a small space under the eaves, a cubby hole next to the attic long room. That first winter, after he'd been at Shadowbrook maybe a month, Miss Lorene had tried to move him to a bigger bedroom across from Quent's on the second floor. Cormac had refused to go. "You are not a servant in this house," she had told him. "You do not have to sleep in the attic." Back then he hadn't understood why she spoke with so much urgency or looked at him as if she were sorry for many things he had no idea about.

"I want to stay where I am."

"Prefer," Miss Lorene had corrected automatically. "It is more gracious to say 'I prefer to stay where I am.' And don't forget to say 'ma'am.' "

"Yes, ma'am. Like I said, that's what I want. To stay where I am." It was the white way to speak to a squaw as if she were an equal, even sometimes a superior. He had learned that, along with many other things, since coming to Shadowbrook a few short weeks before. But he wasn't ready to give in to every white notion of how things should be done. Sometimes, during the night, he snuck out of the house and slept in touch with the earth, the way he had every night of his first eight years. He only did it when he was sick with longing for Singing Snow, but if he were across from Quent he'd be found out.

Now, twenty-two years later, Cormac lay in the familiar bed in the attic and held on to Memetosia's remarkable gift, tormented by questions he could not answer. *When the time is right, use them.* How? For what? How would he know the right time? Why was a Miami Midewiwin priest in league with a Huron enemy? And why had Genevieve Lydius, who had been a friend all his life, betrayed him? Finally he slept. And the *Anishinabeg* part of himself dreamed.

A field of snow, utterly white with no mark upon it anywhere, and soaring above the snow a hawk, silent and beautiful. Very high. Then blood appeared on the snow, a river of crimson cutting a jagged path across the pure white. The hawk followed the river of blood until it led to a vast group of birds that remained on the ground, in a patch of snow untouched by the crimson stain, sheltering their heads beneath their wings. A bear as white as the snow appeared on the horizon and loped toward the birds. The hawk plummeted downward like a streak of lightning, talons extended. The birds rose into the sky in a great fluttering of wings and cries as the hawk attacked the bear, tearing at it with its beak and claws. The other birds hovered above the bear's head and waited. Then a white wolf emerged from the trees and approached them.

One moment Quent was asleep, the next he was awake. He did not move and the sound of his breathing did not change. He merely came to immediate consciousness with the knowledge that he was not alone. Slowly, with great care, he opened his eyes.

The light had changed. He had not drawn the heavy curtains across the open window and the blackness of night was paling to a gray false dawn. Quent moved one hand slowly beneath the sheet that was his only covering and found the dirk beneath his pillow. He heard nothing, but he knew the intruder was coming closer. Fine, he was ready.

"Quent, it's me. I know you're awake."

"Well, I wasn't, but I am now." He saw Corm's tall, spare frame move past the window and approach the foot of the bed. "What's the matter?"

"I have to leave."

"But you just got here. Where are you going?"

"North. To Singing Snow. I have to go right away."

"You had a dream." Nothing else could have happened in the few hours since they'd parted. Cormac admitted that was so, and told him the events of the dream. "And you're the *wabnum,* the white wolf," Quent said. He had spent too long with the Potawatomi not to understand.

"I think so, since it's my totem."

"Your dream, too. But my totem's *wabnum,* as well. You want me to go with you? If something's wrong at Singing Snow I—"

"No, not now. Your place is here for as much time as your father has left. If I need you, I'll send word. But there is something . . ."

"What?"

"I want you to take care of Nicole."

"Of course." His belly knotted; by giving her into his care Corm had made it impossible for him to compete for her affection.

"Not just look after her," Corm insisted. "I need you to take on my promise."

Quent got out of the bed and reached for the dressing gown Corn Broom Hannah had spread in readiness on the chair. The silk felt cool against his skin, but it did not soothe him. "Just what kind of promise did you make her that you mean me to take on?"

"Not her. Her father's death wish was that I take her to Québec."

"As you wish. When I can leave. After my father—"

"Ahaw." The Potawatomi word for agreement. "That's fine. I don't have the impression it matters much when she gets there. Only that she arrives safe."

The sky was rapidly turning pink, promising fierce heat. Quent could see Corm clearly now; he was wearing buckskins. Quent had gone to sleep wondering if Corm would come to breakfast in his home clothes and what Nicole would make of him when she saw him like that, more white than red. "You leaving now? Before breakfast?"

"Yes. I must. I just wanted to say goodbye, and ask you to look after Nicole."

Both men knew there had never been any doubt about Quent's reply to Corm's request. "You're missing something," Quent said, eyeing the tomahawk and knife at Corm's waist.

Cormac didn't answer. Quent went to the cupboard in the corner, picked up the long gun leaning against it, and tossed it in Corm's direction. Corm caught it with one hand, but he didn't put it over his shoulder. "I had to leave my weapons in the front hall when I went to see Memetosia. By the time I was in that hall again my gun was gone."

"But not your tomahawk or your knife."

"No, not those."

"Doesn't make much sense." For a Miami to steal a weapon that had been left behind to do honor to one of his chiefs was unthinkable.

"No, I know it doesn't. Not much of what happened there makes any sense. But the dream was clear." Corm held out the long gun. "Here. Thanks, but I can't take this."

"You can't go off to fight a hawk and a bear without it. Besides, there are no hostiles at Shadowbrook." Both men thought of John and smiled. "Least, not the same kind you're after," Quent added. "Don't worry, I know where I can get another."

Corm's face grew grave. "Do it. Right away. There's something . . ."

"What? You dream something else? Something about Shadowbrook?"

Corm shook his head. "No, nothing. But—"

"I told you, don't worry."

Corm raised his left hand and Quent put his palm against it. Because he was the older brother, he spoke first. *"Pama kowabtemin mine,"* he said. We will see each other again. "Be safe. The bear is a fierce enemy."

"Wabnum is a mighty foe. *Pama mine,"* Corm repeated. "Tell Nicole I'm sorry I couldn't say goodbye."

Quent didn't have to ask if Cormac was taking the Miami Suckáuhock with him. He could see the thong of the medicine bag around Corm's neck.

Chapter Nine

"HAD TO GET ME old bones up real early and make these johnnycakes for breakfast," Kitchen Hannah said. " 'Fore even the sun come up I was stoking up that kitchen fire and getting that griddlestone hot, and mixing up my Indian meal and a tiny bit o' 'lasses and some o' my special water from the spring up by the still—what poor Deliciousness May has to carry to me all the way from the sugarhouse and now I ain't got none left—and making these here johnnycakes for breakfast. 'Cause there wouldn't be none otherwise. Seeing as how all my stores was raided in the black of night, when proper folks ought to be asleep in their beds."

She put three fresh johnnycakes on the plate in front of Quent while she spoke, then, after a slight hesitation, added a fourth. "Some folks just are never filled up, no matter what you puts inside 'em."

Nicole had difficulty understanding the speech of the Patent slaves, though she liked the music of their accent. This morning it was easy enough to tell that Kitchen Hannah was scolding Quentin, that she didn't mean a word of what she said, and was intensely pleased at his return.

"Thing is," the old woman continued, "I could have sworn there was two peoples eating up my store of johnnycakes. You got any idea who the second people might be, Master Quent?" She glanced up toward the attic above their heads. "You think I be having to save some of these nice fresh johnnycakes for whoever might be presenting hisself to eat 'em?"

"No, Hannah. I don't think that's necessary." He could tell from the surprise with which his mother and the old slave looked at him that Kitchen Hannah had already told her mistress Corm had arrived. "There's no one here planning a late breakfast as far as I know."

"But Hannah said—" Lorene broke off and waited for her son to explain.

"Corm did come during the night, but just to give me a message." Quent was afraid to look at Nicole. Too much of what he was feeling might show in his face. Damn her, she made him forget everything he'd ever learned. "He was sorry not to see either of you," he nodded toward his mother and Nicole, "but he had to leave right away."

"And when will he be back?" Nicole seemed to be trying as hard as he was to maintain some dignity. "Did he say when—"

"He didn't know."

"But he promised! Monsieur Shea promised me, and he promised Papa—"

"I know. We talked about that. Corm asked me to take you north to Québec and I said I would."

"But he—"

She stopped speaking and Quent wondered what other promises Corm had made.

"More drink, my dear. It's good for you." Lorene refilled Nicole's tankard from the pitcher of frothy brown ale cut with heated milk. She was sorry not to see Cormac, but he had been like that since he was grown, coming and going according to his own thoughts and fancies and explaining little. Besides, she was glad to have the girl here a bit longer. The blue frock suited her even better than the lavender had. Lorene told herself she'd have to look for the remains of that blue cloth before the mantua maker called again next week. It had been a very dear bolt, come all the way from London, and she had thought to have a cloak made of what she had left. But just now that blue cloth could be thought of as an investment.

John appeared and took his place, waiting for Kitchen Hannah to serve him. He'd been out on the land for some hours already and had heard the news of Cormac's arrival. "Ah, I was expecting our tame savage to be here." He spoke to no one in particular. "It's always interesting to see if he'll show up in breechclout and feathers or done up in his fancy white-man costume."

Quent did not rise to the bait, though he saw the distress of both the women and hastened to change the subject. "Corm stopped by, but he had business in the north. He's already gone. How's the harvest looking?"

"Good—excellent, in fact. Best in years. Takes a strong hand to get the niggers to do anything, but once they understand that slacking won't be permitted, they fall into line."

Quent made a noncommital sound, then asked, "Exactly what is it you've got planned for them today?"

John stopped eating and stared at his brother. "And just why should you care? Gone for three years, then back and asking for explanations?"

"I was wondering, is all. And about that wheat, the field down near the sugar-house road's gotten itself full of weeds. Going to be a huge amount to winnow if they're not pulled soon."

"Don't tell me how to run Shadowbrook." John's words were spit out through clenched teeth.

"Wouldn't dream of it. Just happened to notice that field when we walked in and thought I'd mention it. Considering what we were speaking of last night. I'm sure you remember our conversation."

Nicole hardly registered what they were saying, or the animosity between them, or the way Madame Hale was looking from one son to the other. She was too absorbed in her own distress.

Lorene searched for a way to relieve the tension. "There will be a prayer serv-ice in the great hall on Sunday, mademoiselle. Perhaps you—"

"Mademoiselle Crane is a Catholic." Quent spoke the words with no particu-lar emphasis, as if he didn't know how distasteful that idea would be to his mother.

Lorene, however, didn't look surprised. "Yes, I presumed so. I just thought—"

"Thank you for inviting me, Madame Hale. It is most gracious. But if you don't mind, on Sunday I will simply stay in my room and say my prayers."

"Yes, of course." Lorene rose from the table and both her sons quickly got to their feet.

The two men waited until she'd left the room, then took their seats again on either side of Nicole. It was obvious that neither would leave the room until she did. Nicole waited a few moments, then got up and made her escape.

Quent and Nicole again sat on the circular bench that surrounded the chestnut tree on the front lawn. "He promised," she told Quent. "Monsieur Shea promised. He has broken his word."

"No, he has not. He has given me the charge, and that's the same thing as doing it himself. I'll take you the rest of the way. As soon as I can." Small wonder she was upset. After claiming her the way he had, Corm had left her behind without a word. Hard for any white woman to understand, particularly one like Nicole. Probably she'd been a virgin until that night in the woods. Shoshanaya had come to him a proud Ottawa squaw, knowing and aware. Nicole had probably never been with anyone before her first night with Corm. She would— Sweet Christ, he was a bloody fool, and worse, a disloyal friend.

"You defend him," Nicole said with some bitterness. "But a gentleman would not do such a thing. Not go back on the word he gave to a dying man."

"Look, Corm's not like us, exactly. He's half Potawatomi. Their ways are different from what you're used to. You had to have known it before you let yourself become—" He broke off.

"Become what?" she demanded. "Please, Monsieur Hale, I would like to know what you are thinking. Before I became what?"

"His . . . Corm's woman. That night with the Shawnee, when you chose—"

"I did not choose anything that night, Monsieur Hale. The squaw, the one who called herself Torayana, she told me I had to pick one of the men, but I refused. She pushed me at Monsieur Shea. I did not choose."

Quent shrugged her words away. "Doesn't matter. What's done is done."

She felt her cheeks redden with anger. "Nothing is done, Monsieur Hale! Nothing of what you mean! I am not a squaw, not some savage who—"

Quent looked at her, saw the rage. "Wait a minute, you're telling me— Are you saying you and Corm didn't— You didn't promise—"

"We did nothing. And I promised Monsieur Shea nothing. Except for my undying gratitude and a lifetime of prayer in return for his bringing me to Québec. I have taken a vow, monsieur. I mean to give myself to God and become a bride of Christ. A nun. It is a sacred and solemn duty and—"

"But with the Shawnee . . . You and Corm, you spent the night in the woods. I saw you come back the next morning."

She looked at him, some of the fire turning to ice. "I spent many nights in the woods with both of you, monsieur, and many days. Was my conduct on those occasions not appropriate for a lady? And did I have a choice to do something else?"

"No, but that was different. The drums—"

"Some of us do not become animals just because we are in the forest, Monsieur Hale."

His heart was pounding against his ribs. He wanted to whoop but he didn't dare. "Listen, I'm going to do what you want, I'll take you to Québec. I gave my word and that's that. But there's one thing you have to do. Now. Otherwise all promises are canceled."

"What thing, Monsieur Hale?"

"That's it exactly. Stop calling me Monsieur Hale. My name's Quent. Call me Quent. Promise?"

She stared at him, then nodded. The look in his eyes was remarkable. It was almost . . . triumph. The way men looked when they won a battle, or did some remarkably dangerous thing and survived. Papa and the other military men she had known since childhood, they had looked like that sometimes. She shivered, then got up to go.

Quent clenched his hands into fists. In a few weeks, a month perhaps, they would be in the woods again. But this time there would be just the two of them. Corm had staked no claim and she had given no promise.

Lorene Hale watched Nicole walk back to the house, then dropped the curtain. Quentin, she noted, had remained where he was, staring after the girl. "I think Quent is quite smitten with that young mademoiselle, Ephraim. Have you seen her? She is very beautiful. And she has exquisite manners."

She turned to her husband. These days, even in the summer heat, he was always cold, and his mind was not what it had been. The newspapers he had delivered each month when the mail packet reached Albany, the *Weekly Post-Boy* from Boston and the *Gazette* from New York City, were stacked on the table by the window, untouched unless Quent or John read them. Ephraim did not ask about the progress of the crops or the reports from the trading station at Do Good as avidly as he once had. Her husband was receding from her and from this world while he prepared for the next. He was sitting up in a chair today, but he had two blankets piled on his knees and clutched a woolen shawl around his shoulders. "Are you still chilled, Ephraim? I can get—"

"She's white, is she?"

"Who, Mademoiselle Nicole? Of course she's white. Her mother was French and her father English. An officer."

"Never thought Quentin would be interested in a white woman, not after—"

"Shoshanaya's dead, Ephraim. Quentin is here and there's a young woman with him and she is eminently suitable for . . ."

"What? Finish what you were going to say. Suitable to be mistress of Shadow-brook. That's what you mean, isn't it?"

Lorene nodded.

"John's the elder."

"Quent noticed that the wheat in the sugarhouse fields is thick with weeds. He told John about it at breakfast this morning. I think John forgot all about those fields."

Hale was seized by a coughing fit so severe it left cold sweat running down his face. When he'd taken a few sips of ale and could breathe, he said, "John's the elder. And Quent has a taste for red women."

"So had you once." She drew her breath in sharply, surprised at the words she hadn't planned to say.

"And you," her husband said softly. "And you."

Lorene turned away. "In the past, Ephraim, all of it." It wasn't like her to call up those memories like this. "It's Shadowbrook that concerns me, that must concern us both." She'd been sixteen years old when she married him and he brought her here from New York City. She was fifty now. She'd spent the better part of her life on the Patent. "You're doing the wrong thing," she said. "Quentin will look after the land and everyone on it. You must—"

"I'm tired," Hale interrupted. "Go. And send someone to put me to bed."

"Ephraim—"

"Go, I said!" Then, before she was out the door: "Later, after I've had my dinner maybe, bring that Mademoiselle whoever up here. Let me get a look at her."

SUNDAY, JULY 26, 1754
QUÉBEC, NEW FRANCE

There were plenty of mean streets in the lower part of the city of Québec where Père Antoine spent most of his time, but nothing to compare with the bleakness of the little settlement of St. Pierre on the Ile d'Orléans. The church where he was celebrating Holy Mass in honor of Ste. Anne, the mother of the Blessed Virgin, was the finest structure in the settlement, and it was little more than a rough shack, devoid of ornament and hot and airless though the front door was open.

"*Introibo ad altare Dei,*" the priest said softly. I will go unto the altar of God.

"*Ad Deum qui laetificat juventutem meam.*" The boy who was acting as server reminded him that God gave joy to youth.

Antoine sweat profusely under his heavy green satin chasuble, the top garment that since medieval times a priest must wear when offering the sacrifice. Beneath it he had on a long white garment called an alb and the rope tie known as a girdle, a green maniple draped over his left arm, and a green satin stole around his neck. And underneath all of that his brown habit. Dear Lord, this Canada was a place of penance. Most of the year it was frozen solid, but for a few days in summer it baked as if the fires of hell had broken through the earth. "*Gaudeamos omnes in Domino.*" Rejoice we all in the Lord.

Père Antoine's back was to his congregation, but he knew who was there. He had confessed each of them before Mass began. There were twenty people in all: nine Catholic Hurons—five squaws and four braves—and five French farmers with their wives, plus three Frenchwomen whose husbands were either dead or confirmed in sin and unwilling to be shriven. All the white women had come from France years before as part of a program said to have been devised by Louis XV himself to increase the population: Single women without dowries, who couldn't expect to find a husband in their homeland, were sent as brides to New France.

Only *le bon Dieu* knew how hard the white women of St. Pierre had tried to satisfy His Majesty's hopes for this northern part of New France. These eight had probably had forty or fifty children between them and it was the same everywhere else. Some seventy-thousand white people, good Catholics of French descent, called this place home. Fewer than fifteen thousand lived in the three

cities on the St. Lawrence—Québec, Trois Rivières, and Montréal; the rest occupied farms in little villages and missions and seigneuries, trying their best to do
what the king—and indeed, Almighty God—asked of them: increase and multi-
ply. But the land was so vast, and most of it so inhospitable, that no matter how
many were born and how many the mothers managed to nurse to survival, much
of the territory remained a frozen wilderness empty of any but heathen savages.

Holy Mass continued until finally the Franciscan bent low over the altar, fixing his concentration on the flat wheaten wafers and goblet of thin, sour wine.
*"Sacrificiis praesentibus quaesumus, Domine, placatus intende: ut per interces-
sionem beatae Annae . . ."* Look favorably, Lord, upon these dedicated offerings,
so that by the intercession of blessed Anne . . . For some obscure historical reason it was called the Secret Prayer and not spoken aloud. Not that it mattered; all
the words of the Mass were a secret to this congregation. Not one could understand the Latin, and probably none could have read a translation in their own
language if such existed.

No matter, Père Antoine felt their devotion, and never more intently than
when he intoned, *"Hoc est enim corpus meum,"* and lifted the sacred host above
his head. A few seconds later he had, by the awesome power of Almighty God,
turned the wine into the Blood of Jesus Christ. *"Hic est enim calix sanguinis mei."*
Blood shed to save. Lord, look favorably upon my desire to give You glory. Let it
all happen as I have planned.

He moved along the altar rail, distributing the Body and Blood of Jesus Christ.
The men opening their mouths to receive the Sacred Host, red and white alike,
were past warrior age. The Franciscan had come seeking warriors, but he didn't
expect to find them in St. Pierre.

At length the service ended. The villagers left the church and Père Antoine
soon followed them. His way back to the river and the boat waiting to return him
to Québec led through the woods, silent except for the occasional burst of birdsong and the noise his sandals made as he walked. He was grateful to at last be
wearing only his threadbare brown habit. And for the deep forest shade.

The priest slowed as he approached a large rock with a flat, tablelike top. An
Indian appeared in front of him as if he'd been conjured from the air. A Huron,
but not one of those who had been at Mass. This one had a musket over his
shoulder and a tomahawk in his hand. The Franciscan nodded toward the tomahawk. "You can put that away. I'm the man you are expecting."

The Huron didn't acknowledge the words, just used the tomahawk to point to
a small, half-hidden path that cut off the main one the priest had been on. "Very
well. I will follow you." It was exactly what he had arranged. And prayed for.

A few minutes later he was sitting on the ground across from the renegade
Lantak. The Huron said nothing, waiting for the priest to speak. "I am glad you

could meet me here," Père Antoine began. "It is good to see you again, Lantak. Have you thought about what we discussed last time we spoke?"

"Your words are like the snow, priest. When it falls it seems heavy, but as soon as the sun comes it melts and disappears."

"Jesus Christ does not disappear, my son. He is with His followers always. Here." The priest touched his heart. "In the Mass He gives us His Body and Blood to eat, food that will never fail."

"Two winters past, in the mission of Ste. Charité, twenty-seven Huron died of disease and starvation. The black robes who lived with them died as well."

"Ah, but Lantak thinks in terms of this life only. Our time on earth is short. It is important only because it is a test, an opportunity to give ourselves to the love of Jesus Christ. When it ends we rejoice with Him in heaven. If . . ."—the priest paused for effect—". . . we have not failed the test."

Lantak spat on the ground. "Your words make an ugly taste in my mouth. Perhaps I should wash it away in your blood."

Père Antoine felt a pleasurable trembling deep in his belly, the same unbidden ecstasy that sometimes came to him at night when he was sleeping and could not control . . . No, no. He could not expect this. It was too easy. To be martyred here and now, on the feast of the mother of the Blessed Virgin, shortly after offering Holy Mass. To go straight to heaven this very day. Thank you, Lord, but I do not yet ask for such an honor. I still have much to do for Your Church. "I do not think that is what you want, my son. I am useful to you, am I not?"

Père Antoine took a pouch of coins from a pocket in his habit and put it on the ground between them. Would it count as martyrdom to be murdered for money? And blood money at that. But the answer need not concern him. Lantak was smart enough to understand that once you wrung the neck of the gander, there could be no more golden eggs. "Two hundred now," the priest said. "Two hundred more when the deed is done." He had made an offering of a third of Hamish Stewart's original six hundred livres to the upkeep of the Poor Clares. Their prayers might keep the Scot from eternal hellfire.

For a few heartbeats Lantak did not answer. The priest watched him and waited. It was said that though Lantak had been born in the Longhouse, he had a white father. If it were true, it did not show on his face. His bronze skin was stretched over prominent cheekbones, and his nose was beaked in that manner peculiar to many of the Huron. His straight black hair fell almost to his shoulders, and he wore a single white feather pointing down toward his right shoulder. The feather and his tattoos contrasted with the rest of his appearance. He had on neither the breechclout of the Longhouse nor the linen smock and loose trousers of the Jesuit missions. Lantak wore the buckskins of a *coureur de bois*. Probably stolen from one of the many people he had murdered. A long gun lay on the ground a short distance from his hand. Doubtless he'd gotten that the same way.

Finally the Indian spoke. "Sometimes, yes, you are useful." Père Antoine knew he would not be a martyr this day. "Why did you want to see me?"

"Shadowbrook," the priest said quietly. "I wish to speak to you about a place many leagues south of here called Shadowbrook." *Then Jesus said, "I come to cast fire upon the earth and what will I but that it be enkindled?"* Blood shed to save.

The way to the sugarhouse was through a dense and deeply shadowed wood. Mostly mixed oaks and elms and maples, Quent explained, with some conifers, pine and blue spruce. They were great trees; Nicole could not wrap her arms around them. It had been the same in the Ohio Country. "In the Old World," she murmured as they walked the narrow path, Monsieur Quent ahead of her as always, showing the way, "I have never seen trees of such girth."

"That's because white folks have been cutting down the trees in the Old World a lot longer. The Indians never do such a thing, and we whites haven't been here long enough to spoil the New. My guess is we will soon enough. Mind how you go here," he added. "The path narrows."

One moccasin wide, he'd explained, was how red men made a forest path. It was all they needed, so they chose not to disturb the woods more than necessary. She too wore moccasins, white ones made from the hide of a white bear, but still it seemed to Nicole as if there were no path at all. Only Monsieur Hale who . . . No, not monsieur. He wanted her to call him Quent, and he was a man accustomed to getting his way.

The size of him blotted out much else. How many times now had she walked behind that broad back? More than she could count, but she remembered each one. Or thought she did.

"Moccasins still comfortable?" he asked.

"They are wonderful." It was true. Quent—it was easy to think of him by that familiar name, but not so easy to speak it aloud—had waited until they were out of sight of the house before giving them to her. "Take off your boots," he'd said, indicating a log she could sit on, "and your stockings as well. You need to be barefoot for moccasins to grip properly. I've been thinking of giving this pair to you for some time. I figure they're about the right size."

He was gentleman enough to turn away while she removed her boots and hose. As if he hadn't already seen her ankles and even her legs many times. "I am ready," she said finally. "Please, give them to me."

He turned back to face her and knelt beside the log. "Let me do it. They have to go on just so, with the drawstring adjusted to make the fit perfect."

She was embarrassed by his touch, and by a feeling to which she'd chosen to give no name. It was somehow more intimate than all the many times he'd carried her through the forest. His big hands had cradled her feet as he slipped on first one moccasin, then the other, and tightened the lacings and molded them to her instep. His hands were remarkably gentle. She had wanted to ask if the moccasins had belonged to his wife, but he'd given her no opportunity, just tied the laces of the boots together and put them around his neck. "I'll carry these for you. You'll need them later."

"Later" had apparently arrived. "We're almost there. You'd better put the boots back on." Quent swung them off his shoulders and gave them to her, and Nicole again sat on a log and changed her footwear. This time he didn't help, just turned his back to once more give her a bit of privacy. For the hundredth time she wondered if he'd ever peeked while she was bathing naked in the forest streams. A tiny corner of her mind told her that she wished he had, and her cheeks reddened and her breath came fast. Nicole laced the boots so tight they hurt, to remind herself of who she was and where she was going. "Very well. I am ready."

He turned back. "You want me to take those?" He nodded toward the moccasins she held in her hands.

"I can put them in my pockets."

"Fine. They're yours now. You can do as you like. We'd best get going." He started walking again, leaving her to follow.

"The moccasins," she blurted out, "were they Shoshanaya's?"

He stopped walking for just a moment—a half step lost, then quickly regained—and he didn't turn around. "What do you know about Shoshanaya?"

"Only that she was an Ottawa princess, and your wife, and that she died. I offer my sympathies for your loss," she added. It was difficult to walk in the hard-soled boots now that she had become used to the way the moccasins glided over the woodland path. Besides, she'd made the laces so tight they were truly painful. She slipped and slid as she struggled to keep up. "I heard that Shoshanaya was very beautiful."

"She was." He slowed and Nicole wasn't sure if it was because he sensed her difficulty or if it was the heaviness of his thoughts that checked his pace. "Did my mother tell you about Shoshanaya?"

"No, Madame Hale has not mentioned her. It was Torayana, the Shawnee squaw, the night of the drums."

"Seems like there was a lot that got itself done or told about that night."

"I am sorry if I have offended you, Mons—Quent. I only wanted to know."

"The moccasins are Potawatomi, not Ottawa. You can tell by the way they're made, and the fact that there is no beading. They're white bearhide. That's unusual. They belonged to Pohantis, Corm's mother. She had a liking for white skins, and she knew how to get them. Pohantis died a long time ago. She's buried up by Squirrel Oaks, the Shadowbrook burying place, but some of her things are still around. All Shoshanaya's things were sent back to her people, after she was gone. To honor her."

Nicole wanted to ask why, if that was the way Indians honored their dead, the same had not been done for Pohantis, but she had become adept at reading his back. Now it cautioned her to silence.

"Almost there," he said after a little time. "You'll see the road just as soon as we get past that stand of oak up ahead."

The light was changing, the shade brightening. Soon sunshine burst upon them and they were on one of the wide roads he'd pointed out the day they first walked onto the Patent. The heat of the road was devastating after the woodland cool. Fortunately they did not have far to go. "There's the sugarhouse." Quent pointed to a large building made of logs, with a steeply pitched roof and one enormous brick chimney. "And there's Deliciousness May, waiting for us."

The black woman had white hair and her face was deeply lined. She was older even than Kitchen Hannah, Nicole decided, but Quent was every bit as fond of her. He picked her up and swung her around in greeting and Deliciousness May giggled like a young girl. " 'Bout time you got yerself home, Master Quent. And how come it took you better 'n a whole week to come see Deliciousness? Never you mind, I got a pair of hares all sweetened up with a bit o' syrup from last winter, the way you likes, and two peach pies ready to go in the oven. Lilac! You hear me, girl? You waitin' there like I told you?" All the while she was speaking the black woman was eyeing Nicole up and down, never once letting on that she was doing it. *Grace á Dieu,* the moccasins were in her pocket, not on her feet.

A little girl jumped out from behind a large elm. Perhaps four, Nicole thought, with black curly hair that was parted in the middle and tightly gathered over each ear, and surprisingly light skin. "This be one half o' what my Runsabout popped out year before you went away. You remember that, Master Quent?"

"I surely do, Deliciousness. The other one's a boy, isn't he? Willie?"

"Sugar Willie he be now," the woman said with some pride. "Moves the sugar faster than any mule ever been seen around here." Deliciousness May nodded toward the sugarhouse at the same time that she gave Lilac a shove in the opposite direction. "You go on home, girl, tell Mistress Sarah that Master Quent and his visitor be here. Go on! And you help Mistress put them peach pies in the oven. The heat be just about perfect now."

Quent showed Nicole the inside of the sugarhouse before they went on. It was a huge open space with an elaborate still in one corner. The smell was sickly sweet, almost overpowering. Nicole felt ill, but Quent didn't seem to notice. "The sugar comes from the islands, in the ships that take back our flour and vegetables," he said, "and—"

"I didn't know Runsabout had a husband and children."

"No husband. Just the twins."

"But they are here at the sugarhouse and she is—"

"Everyone goes where their work is needed. Besides, Deliciousness May is Runsabout's mother, and Lilac and Willie's grandmother. Her husband, their grandfather, is Big Jacob. He lives here at the sugarhouse most of the time, too. His main job's to look after the young horses. The paddock's not far from here."

"That day . . . when you stopped the whipping, Big Jacob's the one you called to untie—"

"That's right." He hated that the abomination in the Frolic Ground had been the first thing she saw of Shadowbrook. "The Frankels, the people who run the gristmill and the sugarhouse, treat the slaves fairly. You'll see."

Nicole nodded. "I already see," she said. "This place, your Shadowbrook, it is a great enterprise."

"It is. In the sugarhouse, for instance, we make rum not just for ourselves, but to trade with the Indians. I'll take you up to Do Good sometime. You can meet—"

"I must go north, Quent. To Québec. You promised."

"Do Good's north. Three hours distant by wagon. Road's somewhat round-about because it skirts the hills. If you don't mind a bit of climbing you can walk. It's a shorter distance. Either way, don't worry, I won't forget my promise."

All the time they'd been on the trail he had been so reserved. Now . . . The look he was giving her was more than she could bear. It hurt her heart. Two people, a man and a woman, kissing in the sunlight, a unit so tightly forged, so at one, that even their own child could not know its depths. Nicole dismissed the memory. "You were explaining about the sugar."

"Yes, we get it up here from the river in those carts."

He indicated three large, open wooden chests, each with a pair of wooden wheels, and short traces that finished in a harness. "By mule?" she asked.

"Sometimes." He looked uncomfortable. For a moment she didn't understand, then she realized that the boy they called Sugar Willie had that name because his job was to be harnessed to the heavy wooden cart and pull it fully laden from the river to the sugarhouse. How far was that? A league at least.

They went outside. Deliciousness May was gone, and Quent led Nicole on a path through the woods to the house where a white woman was waiting for them. Tall and thin, with hunched shoulders and an unfortunately long nose, her narrow features all seemed crowded in the center of her face. "This is Sarah Frankel," Quent said, "she and her husband are in charge of the sugarhouse."

Sarah's wide smile turned her homely face into something almost attractive.

She was less effusive than Deliciousness May had been, but she seemed every bit as glad to see Quent, and as curious about the young woman with him. Nicole was glad that the dark taffeta dress she'd chosen for this excursion didn't show any dirt from the shortcut through the woods, and that the moccasins were in her pockets and not on her feet.

They were nine at the dinner table. As well as Quent and Nicole there were Sarah and her husband, Moses, a large red-faced man with the shortest, pudgiest fingers Nicole had ever seen. They looked out of place on his big hands, as if they belonged to someone else. Tim, the son of the house, was quiet and withdrawn and appeared to have no wife.

"Ellie and Tim and I pretty much grew up of a piece. We used to have lessons together at the big house," Quent said, clearly trying to make her feel part of this group who had known each other so well for so long.

"And Monsieur Shea?" she asked. "He had lessons with you as well?"

"Corm, too." Quent looked at her only briefly, but his blue eyes were dark, and for a moment fierce.

If a man delights you, ma petite, *it is always wise to keep him the tiniest bit jealous.* Maman had said such things before she knew Nicole was to be a nun. It was sinful to think of them now. Worse to actually put the advice into practice. She would say two entire rosaries in penance. All fifteen decades each time.

And she would distract herself from wicked thoughts by paying attention to the others, not to Quent. Ellie—she had been introduced as Mistress Bleecker—did not have the puckered prune face of her mother, or the spare, narrow form. She was a big blowsy woman and her children, two girls and a boy, looked set to take after her. They sat silent at the foot of the table and pushed food into their mouths as if they had never eaten before, despite being repeatedly told by their mother and grandmother to mind their manners. There was no father to make them behave.

"My husband went logging last winter." Ellie's voice was so emotionless, she might have been asking for another hot biscuit. "Lost his footing and got crushed in the white water."

"I am so sorry, madame." Ellie shrugged, and Nicole leaned close enough to catch a whiff of the musky smell her brown kersey frock had acquired after *le bon Dieu* alone knew how much wear. She put her hand over Ellie's, then quickly withdrew it, offering both sympathy and dignity in the space of three breaths.

"You were good with them," Quent said after they left. "They liked you."

Shoshanaya had never had much to do with the tenants. He hadn't expected it of her, and they wouldn't have accepted her in any case. He'd told himself it didn't matter. It still didn't. He was never going to be master of Shadowbrook. All the same, Nicole was different. But it was foolish to think of such things. The situation was no different than it had been. John was still the elder and the heir.

Chapter Ten

MONDAY, AUGUST 3, 1754
LORETTE, NEW FRANCE

IN 1535 JACQUES Cartier explored the St. Lawrence River and claimed for France the Gaspé Peninsula. At that time the Iroquoian-speaking *Anishinabeg* known as Wyandot occupied their ancestral lands near what the French first called the Great Freshwater Sea. The Wyandot called their land Ouendake. The French renamed them ruffians, Huré, which became Huron. The sea was eventually known as Lake Huron and the Wyandot land was called Huronia.

The Huron were skilled farmers; no one knew better how to grow squash and beans and corn and insure that there would never be famine, but to ease their grief they made war. It had been so since the beginning of the *Haudenosaunee*, in the first Longhouse built on the turtle's back where Sky Woman wept for her dead father.

When a family had suffered a loss, whether through illness or accident or a tribal raid, the lamenting survivors would for ten days be excused from all community duties, and even the most intimate obligations of bathing and dressing. For a year after that they would continue to neglect their personal appearance, while gradually resuming some part in village life. But if the women's tears still did not cease, then only the replacement of their dead relative by a war captive would ease their pain. If the young men related to the survivors did not mount a raid to bring back those who might be adopted into the bereaved family, the women publicly accused them of cowardice and the braves were shamed before the whole people.

So the braves would form a war party and go to take captives from among their traditional enemies—sometimes other Iroquois speakers and sometimes those belonging to the Algonkian nations—and bring them back to the warriors' home village. There the women devised many tests to see who among the prisoners could withstand the greatest amount of pain and thus be worthy of adoption.

A captive judged unworthy was slated for death. But first such a one was addressed as uncle or nephew and ceremonially painted for a death feast at which he was allowed to recite his war honors and receive the homage of the entire village. Then he was tied to a stake with a short rope, and the villagers, including the smallest children and the oldest squaws, used firebrands to burn him. They did so artfully and with imagination, working slowly from the feet up, all the while speaking in formal terms of the caresses they were bestowing. Before he died the prisoner was scalped and hot sand was thrown onto his bare skull. In this way he was allowed to prove his bravery and enter the next life covered with glory. Finally a knife or a hatchet ended his life. Then the women dismembered the corpse and threw it into cooking kettles from which the whole village feasted—including the chosen adoptees who were now considered to be truly Huron.

So the wound in the spirits of the bereaved was healed, and the empty place at their hearth in the Longhouse was filled. Always, for all the tribes since the beginning of time, there had been such wars of mourning. Until, in the words of the storytellers of the Longhouse, "Everywhere there was peril and everywhere mourning." Seeing this endless river of tears, the Great Spirit whispered wisdom to the chiefs of five of the Iroquoian-speaking nations and they formed themselves into the Great League of Peace and Power. But the Huron had many years before formed a confederacy with some of the other Iroquoian-speaking tribes. They did not join this new league. So its members set upon them and drove them from Huronia. They said it was to bring them an end of mourning wars and to give them the *Kainerekowa,* the Great Peace.

When Cartier had first met those he called Huron there were forty thousand of them. A hundred years later, after the diseases brought by the Europeans and the wars made by the Five Nations of the Great League, there were perhaps a thousand left alive. The remnant of that thousand was driven from Huronia to take refuge in a village just north of Québec, called Lorette by the French. They numbered fewer than three hundred men, women, and children. Many of these had become Christians, but others had not and lived separately from the converts.

On a hot and humid morning in early August, Monsieur Philippe Faucon of the Society of Jesus ducked his head to enter the largest of the longhouses outside Lorette, then stood and blinked his eyes a few times to clear them of the smoke of the five fires that formed a single column marching from one end of the dwelling to the other. The total length of the structure was fifteen fathoms, thirty of a tall man's strides. It was formed of saplings covered by bark, with a curved roof pierced in a number of places to allow the smoke of the many fires to escape. Family apartments were built along both sides. Each was constructed on a platform built knee-high above the ground, separated by curtains of bark, and deep enough and high enough so even a man of the Jesuit's considerable height could easily stretch or stand his full length inside, and wide enough so that even this big longhouse could contain only eight down each side. "The peace of Jesus Christ be upon this place."

A number of squaws were tending pots suspended over the various fires. Some looked up at him, then looked away. Since they were not Christians they did not hold him in any particular reverence, but neither was he an enemy. The hot sun combined with the heat of the cooking fires made the longhouse uncomfortable. No braves were present, and no children. Only the cooks, and one old man puffing on a pipe. He was so thin his bones showed and he found the heat a comfort. After a few seconds the old one struggled to his feet. "Ah, Magic Shadows. Welcome to my hearth."

"You sent for me, Geechkah. I am honored to come."

"Yes, yes . . . You brought your medicine with you?"

"Right here." The Jesuit held up a deerskin envelope that contained his sketch pad, sheets of bark, and his quills and bits of charcoal. The Huron were awestruck by the ability to draw. It seemed that no one among them had ever attempted to recreate what he saw with any degree of realism or proportion. Their language had no alphabet in the way of European tongues. In that sense neither they nor any of the red men of whom the priest was aware wrote words, but Faucon had been long enough among them to know that strips of cured hide called belts were frequently circulated among the tribes. The belts carried complex messages in the form of wampum embroidery and symbols cut into the leather. The savages could read the belts as readily as an educated white man could read a book. Even tribes that did not speak the same tongue could communicate by way of the belts because the markings, pictures of a stylized and symbolic sort, had been regularized for as long as anyone could remember. But as remarkable as that feat might be, the lifelike drawings of the Jesuit inspired wonder in the Huron. "I have my tools with me, Geechkah. I knew you would want me to bring them."

The old Indian looked at the deerskin envelope and nodded with approval, then led his guest out of the longhouse and past fields where the corn plants were as high as the Jesuit's waist and heavy with ripening ears. Vining beans planted at their base used the thick cornstalks for support, and squash sprawled among them, luxuriating in the protection offered by the taller plants. Lines of fish had been hung to dry in the sun, strung between the longhouses like banners decorating the masts of mighty ships. Some distance away a group of young men were hacking apart the carcass of a deer. It would be dressed with the boiled-down sap of the maple trees and smoked over a fire of balsam branches before being set aside as provision for the winter. "The Great Spirit has taught the Huron how to make good use of the land and all that is on it." Faucon spoke the words to the old man's back. Geechkah continued leading the priest through the village while Faucon talked. "Now the Spirit has sent the black robes to tell the Huron of the great Lord of All, Jesus Christ, and the truths that will offer eternal life to—"

Still without turning around Geechkah held up his hand. "Your words make me weary, Magic Shadows. We have discussed these things many times before. We do not have to talk of them again today."

"But it is because I respect your great age and wisdom that I—"

"Enough. Look, this is one reason I brought you here." They had come to a corner of the village where a squaw sat nursing a papoose. "My daughter's daughter has given birth. I learned in a dream that her son will be a great chief. Make the child's face appear on your magic bark."

The bark was ordinary white birch and the quick sketch of mother and child was drawn with charcoal in a style that had been popular in Europe for hundreds of years. Still, when Faucon gave it to Geechkah the old man looked at in wonder, repeatedly turning his head to compare the subject and the drawing. "What I see on this bark is truly what my eyes see, but it will stay when the squaw goes," he said in a tone of awe. "This is strong magic," he added after another few moments. "This shadow that does not move will protect the boy until he grows to meet his destiny."

"I can give the child better magic than that. If you allow me to baptize him and send him to a mission school, he will—"

Geechkah again held up his hand. "Come. There is something else."

Faucon followed the old Indian. He hadn't really expected to be allowed to baptize the infant and send him to live in one of the missions and be taught the Catholic faith that would save his soul. Given how important Geechkah believed the child's future to be, it was impossible. But the priest always made some effort at conversion when he came to a longhouse. Otherwise he would not be able to honestly divert the criticism of his Provincial Superior; Louis Roget had little use for the meticulous drawings of local plants that were Philippe Faucon's overwhelming preoccupation.

Philippe's family—for generations keepers and trainers of the royal hawks—had made him a Jesuit priest; Almighty God had made him an artist, one with a small gift for portraiture, but a true passion for documenting the native flora of Canada. His drawings were said to be the delight of the king himself. Philippe was of the opinion that since Louis XV was known to be interested only in food and sex, it had to be his mistress, the powerful Madame de Pompadour, who made so much of the sketches of the Jesuit missionary, and arranged that the seeds he sent to Versailles were carefully planted and nurtured in the *jardins des roi*. No matter. Given that Monsieur le Provincial believed the king of France, and certainly his official concubine, were both of considerably lesser importance than a Jesuit Superior, Faucon had always to be on his guard.

"What is it, Geechkah? What have you found for me?"

"That plant I told you about, the one that only makes flowers in this moon. I think I have found it."

"Alpine campion," Faucon murmured. His heart beat faster with excitement. In Europe horticulturalists believed that *Lychnis alpinus* grew only in the Alps of Switzerland, but the plant Geechkah described could be nothing else. The priest couldn't be certain until he saw it in bloom. Then he must confirm the identification, and sketch the flower. And, of course, make provision to gather seed. If this were true it would be—

"Wait." Geechkah abruptly stopped walking. They were at the top of a ridge at the far edge of the village. The old man held up a hand for silence, then dropped to his belly in the tall grass and indicated that the priest should do the same. He pointed to the valley below. "Look there." His voice was a faint murmur that carefully avoided any echo from the gorge. "Use your seeing-big glass. This too is a sight not often seen."

A line of Indians on horseback was riding through the valley. Even at this distance and with the naked eye it was apparent that they were alert and ready for any danger that might come from the surrounding hills. The Jesuit fumbled at his waist for his glass, extended it to its full length, and squinted through one eye at the men below. There were nine altogether. Five were in the traditional black and red breechclouts of the Huron, the other four wore thin-legged buckskin trousers. All were heavily painted in red and black, and each of the braves had shaved off all his hair except for a single tuft that extended from forehead to the nape of the neck. "Scalp locks," the priest said softly.

"Yes."

Faucon snapped the glass closed. "They are a war party."

Geechkah nodded. So this was the real reason the old man had sent for him. Somehow he'd known that the war party, whoever they were, would be passing this way at this time. And he'd brought Philippe up to the ridge so he'd be sure to see them.

Geechkah scurried back from the edge. Philippe followed, sliding backward on his belly so he never presented a black outline on the horizon for any scalp-locked brave who happened to look up. "They're Huron," he whispered urgently. "Why would the Huron make war on Québec when—"

"Those men you saw, they are Lantak and his renegades. They belong to no hearth in any Longhouse." It was a solemn denial of kinship. To be without a connection to the Longhouse was to be forever outcast. "And they do not go to Québec."

"Where then? How do you know all this?"

"Among us when an arm is cut off from the body, whether by accident or by an enemy, it is buried near the hearth of the brave to whom it belonged, so that the brave or his relatives can listen to the earth above it and always know what the arm is doing. Once my hearth was Lantak's. I listen to the earth around him and I know what he is doing. As to where he is going . . . It is a very long way away, a distance of many sunrises. I do not know the place, but I know that the brown robe paid hundreds of livres to send Lantak on this long warpath."

Some hours later, in the oak-lined reception chamber of his private apartment in the Provincial House of Québec, the Provincial Superior of the Society of Jesus in New France listened in silence to this tale. When at last he spoke there was sorrow in his tone, a clear indication that the younger man had disappointed him. "It is difficult—no, impossible—to believe that Père Antoine would pay Indians to commit murder. Any Indians, much less the renegade Lantak and his followers." Louis Roget rose from behind his writing table and stood looking at the distraught priest whose immortal soul had been given into his care. "You speak slander, my son. It is a grave sin."

"As Almighty God is my judge, I wish no ill to any man, least of all the Franciscan. He is, after all, a priest of God."

"Exactly," Roget agreed. The younger man towered over him, but in every other way there was no doubt about who carried the burden of authority. Faucon was sweating, mopping his brow repeatedly despite the fact that the dim, high-ceilinged room was relatively cool for an August evening. The Provincial was calm, untroubled by the summer heat, and the longer he spoke the more icy his words became. "And you took the word of a savage for this calumny, Philippe. Do you not think—"

"With respect, Monsieur le Provincial, Geechkah is a wise old man. And a peaceful one. He has no reason to stir up trouble unless—"

"Unless the devil is struggling with you for his soul, Philippe. Have you made any progress toward converting your friend Geechkah?"

"Not yet, Monsieur le Provincial, but—"

"But he speaks to you of those little leaves and twigs that so fascinate you, eh? And the doings of renegade Huron braves. Does it not strike you as strange, Philippe, that a Huron who remains a pagan would take you into his confidence?"

"I think he was hoping to prevent unnecessary bloodshed, Monsieur le Provincial."

Roget sat down again, leaning back and folding his hands over his long black soutane. "Bloodshed. Yes, there is plenty of that when Lantak is involved. A few years ago I saw what was left of a pair of his victims. One, an old man, had been staked to the earth and a hundred or more shallow cuts administered to his body.

Then rats were loosed upon him; they ate him alive. I was told it took some hours. You look faint, my dear Philippe. Perhaps you should sit down. The other was a young woman. Whatever Lantak and his braves did to her while she was alive cannot have been worse than her death. They impaled her on a stake, through the anus, I believe, and carried her with them as a kind of standard for as many days as it took her to die. There are numerous such tales, each more gruesome than the one before. Père Antoine has not been long in Québec, but he is bound to have heard about Lantak. Do you really think he would make common cause with such a heathen devil?"

Faucon mopped his brow again, and fought to swallow his vomit. "I do not know, Monsieur le Provincial. Only that I saw them. With scalp locks and war paint, so—"

"So they meant no good for someone. I do not doubt that, my son. It is Lantak's way. But to accuse a priest of Holy Church of being complicit in such acts ... Perhaps you would like to go to the chapel now and ask Our Blessed Lord for right thinking in the matter of your superiors and your brother priests. It will not be necessary to come to the refectory for the evening collation, or to go to your bed tonight."

Louis Roget waited until the young man had gone, then went to one of the ornately carved oaken panels in the south wall of the room and touched a particular leaf. The panel swung open to reveal a view of the Lower Town. It was heavy dusk, soon to be dark, but the Jesuit readily picked out the roof of the monastery where Mère Marie Rose and her Poor Clares lived their lives of cloistered penance, and that of the nearby hovel he had arranged to be home to the Delegate of the Minister General of the Order of Friars Minor. "So, *mon Père,* the mad dog you have so carefully cultivated now attacks at your bidding. And you have sent him a long distance to the south," Roget whispered aloud. "Across the border into the English colonies, I'm quite certain. Nothing else would be worth hundreds of livres."

If only the Blessed Virgin would enlighten him as to the object of the attack, and its purpose. Then he would be in a position to use his knowledge for the good of the Society, which was the same thing as saying the good of Holy Mother Church. Perhaps he would join the feckless Monsieur Faucon in a night of prayer and penance. After he had read the prayers of Compline, the Jesuit who ruled in New France decided. And after he had shared in the evening collation.

WEDNESDAY, AUGUST 5, 1754
ALBANY, NEW YORK PROVINCE

Quent rode into Albany alone. He had an excellent reason for the journey, to secure a long gun to replace the one he'd given Cormac—which also gave him a fine excuse to visit the Lydius household. John Lydius was the best source of munitions in the province and had been for dozens of years. Selling arms to whoever could pay for them remained the major source of the Lydius fortune.

The house on North Pearl Street looked as it always had, sturdy and impressive. It stood out among the humbler dwellings behind the town wall. John was at home. Genevieve as well, and a number of the Lydius children and grandchildren. No sign of any Miami.

The Lydius family greeted him warmly. John said he was pretty sure he could put his hands on a long gun, seeing as how it was for Uko Nyakwai, a legendary shot as well as the son of one of Lydius's oldest friends. "How's your father these days, Quent?"

"Not well. My mother thinks he won't be long with us, and I fear she is correct."

Lydius had lost an eye in some long-ago battle. He wore a black patch over the empty socket and had a way of cocking his head when he looked at you, bringing you into his limited focus. "Sorry to hear that. I'm told John's in charge of Shadowbrook now."

"That's right."

"I always thought . . ." Lydius shrugged. "Ah well, no point in wasting time on foolishness, is there?"

"None. About that gun . . ."

"Yes, of course. Take me about a day to get my hands on something that will suit your needs. Shall we say tomorrow afternoon? About this hour?"

"Suits me." Quent started to leave, but Genevieve stopped him before he reached the door.

"I heard John say your business will bring you back tomorrow. You'll have to stay in town the night in that case. Rest with us, Quent. There's always a bed free for you, you know that."

"I was figuring on old man Groesbeck's place. I wouldn't want to put you out."

"You're not putting us out. And the sheets here smell a great deal sweeter than those provided by Peter Groesbeck, I warrant."

"So do I," Quent agreed with a smile. "Thank you. I'll be glad of your hospitality."

And so he was, but though he prowled the property thoroughly during the night—something he'd have returned to do even if he'd slept at Groesbeck's Sign of the Nag's Head—he found nothing of the sweat lodge, nor any indication of the strange happenings Corm had described. He tried once more after breakfast when he managed to get Genevieve on her own in the kitchen. She was giving instructions to one of the household slaves, and he waited his opportunity, then said, "I hear you had an important guest a while back. Chief Memetosia of the Miami."

"Yes. He stayed for a time after the Conference, in June. You heard about that,

I suppose. All those important people arguing and coming up with their probably useless Plan of Union."

"Cormac mentioned it." He searched her face for any reaction to Corm's name,
but there was none. "Memetosia was ill after the conference, wasn't he? Practically
on his deathbed."

"So it seemed when he came here. But he's a tough old bird. He rallied and—
Oh no, Jess! Not like that. I told you, Master Lydius likes his pie made with just a
little salt, not a whole handful." Then, turning to her guest: "You must excuse me,
Quent. I bought this one not long ago when our old cook died, and she has no
idea how we like things done. If you don't mind . . ."

He had no choice but to leave. The visit to the kitchen wasn't, however, an
entirely wasted exercise. There was a bench by the rear door heaped with baskets
of various shapes and sizes, and he spotted one with a few kernels of the parched
white corn that was a specialty of the Miami.

In the afternoon, as promised, John Lydius produced the long gun. It appeared
to be a fine weapon. The stock was made of curly maple the color of dark honey,
and when he stood it next to himself the gun was almost as tall. Quent inserted a
finger into the barrel. The grooving felt as it should, defined and regular. He
swung the rifle around—the balance of the thing was a wonder—and squinted
down the brass sight. A candlestick on the mantel came into clear focus. "Seems
right." He kept his tone neutral, careful not to betray his pleasure in the weapon.
"Where was it made?"

"Right here in the colonies."

He'd thought as much. Because of the use of maple. Oak was the wood of
choice for the stock of a gun made in England, where the instructions for the
rifling of the weapons were kept locked in the Tower of London along with other
treasures of state. "Pennsylvania," he guessed. It was widely held that the best gun-
smiths in the colonies were from Pennsylvania.

"New Hampshire," Lydius said. "By a reclusive genius who turns out maybe
one such gun a year."

"How much you asking for it?"

The eye not covered with the black patch studied him without blinking. "Forty
golden guineas, and cheap at the price."

It was a fortune. A man could set up a homestead with little more. "I'll need
to test it."

"Of course." Lydius was seated at a writing table in the private chamber where
he conducted business. He swung around and reached a powder horn and a box
of shot from the chest behind him. "Here you go."

"Thanks. To be safe I'll take it off the property. Back in an hour or two with
my answer."

"Agreed," Lydius said with a smile. "You'll return happy. I'm sure of it."

Quent was sure of it as well. Hellfire, he was happy already. He slung the gun over his shoulder and made his way to the end of North Pearl Street, to the broad hill road that had the old Dutch church at the bottom end and the newer English church at the top. Beyond that was the fort and finally the crest of the hill. On the other side was woodland.

He spent less than an hour testing the long gun. When he headed back to the town the barrel was warm with many firings, and the powder horn nearly empty. Lydius was right, it was a superb weapon. Quent didn't return by way of the fort but stayed outside the town until he was level with Market Street, then entered through a narrow gate and approached the Lydius property from the rear. He spotted the flat-topped rock and the half-felled tree with the single tuft of greenery where Corm had hidden Memetosia's medicine bag, and in the daylight he was able to make out two charred places in the earth where the fires had been, just as Corm described them. There was no sign of the sweat lodge, much less a Midewiwin priest or a dead Huron brave.

THURSDAY, AUGUST 6, 1754
SHADOWBROOK

Nicole was restless. The heat perhaps. And the fact that Quent had been gone four days. She wished she had gone with him, but that was impossible. While she remained a guest in the Hale household she couldn't march off on a trek to Albany with a man to whom she was not related. But when the time came to go north, she would no longer feel constrained by such mannerly concerns. Some obligations were more urgent than the requirement to, as Maman would have said, comport herself always as a lady.

Had Maman always been a lady? Alone with Papa, doing whatever it was married ladies did with their husbands, was she as reserved and elegant as usual, or did she fling herself at him the way the squaws did when the savage drums pounded out their blood rhythms? That day when she was little, when she saw her parents kiss, were they—

"Ah, Nicole. There you are. Matilda Davidson's time has come. She's been huge these past few months. Twins, I'll warrant. And her first birth. I'm afraid it won't be easy. I thought you might come with me to lend a hand down at the sawmill."

"But of course, Madame Hale." In this world, as in the one she had left behind, such an errand was a duty of the squire's wife. Nicole knew that she was, for whatever reason, being treated as a daughter of the house. "I would be glad to be of any assistance."

"Thank you, my dear. I'm getting some things together from Kitchen Hannah's stores. You've seen the little room where we keep the linens? Good. Perhaps you'd be kind enough to go there and fill this basket with some clean cloths. We'll be needing an ample supply."

She found the Indian things in a small chest in the linen room. Nicole had already filled the basket with cloths; when she opened the chest she was clearly prying. She knew it was wrong, but she had no shame. The chest was made of wood painted a dark, blackish green, and put carefully aside under a table beside the window where pins and thread and other sewing things were kept. It drew her like a magnet. She dropped to her knees, pulled it forward, and flipped up the cover with an excited sense that some of the questions she had been harboring since she arrived were about to be answered.

In a manner of speaking, they were. The clothes were folded neatly and she shook them out with eager hands. A tunic, leggings, a few headbands. Everything made of snow-white bearhide, beautifully cured and remarkably soft. No moccasins; she already had those.

"Mademoiselle Nicole, are you in there? Are you ready?"

She shoved the clothes back in the chest and, picking up the basket of cloths, ran out to the hallway. "I am ready, madame."

They traveled in a wagon drawn by one horse. A stable boy called Little George helped them up to the high front bench and stowed their things behind them. When everything was ready, he handed the reins to his mistress and Lorene Hale expertly clucked the horse into motion. "No need to take any of the others away from their work just now," she said. "Harvest is coming, and there's much to do. And I can handle any wagon as well as a man. Does that shock you, my dear?"

Ah, a test. "Not at all, madame. Maman always said one of the marks of a true lady was to do whatever was required—but with as much grace and elegance as she could manage. You drive the wagon with great charm, Madame Hale. I hope you do not think me too forward for saying so."

"Not at all. I am flattered. And your maman sounds very wise. I'm sure she was beautiful as well."

"*Oui, madame.* Very, very beautiful." She had at least passed the first part of the test. That emboldened her. They were out of sight of Shadowbrook now, moving along the wide road Quent had told her had been laid out by his grandfather before even the building of the big house began. "Please, Madame Hale, both Monsieur Quent and Monsieur Cormac have been so kind to me, protected me so well . . ."

"Yes? You have a question, might as well ask it." Lorene held the reins effortlessly and the horse seemed to know his way with no guidance. She turned to the younger woman and her eyes smiled encouragement.

"Monsieur Cormac's mother, I believe she was called Pohantis, when did she die?"

The eyes of Quent's mother were the same pale blue as his own, but Nicole had never seen Quent's eyes go cold in that way. Not when he looked at her. Madame Hale only turned the icy glance on her for a moment, then she looked away. "Who talked to you about Pohantis?"

"Monsieur Quent. But he said only that she died. And that she was buried here in the cemetery of Shadowbrook. I wondered why—"

"She's been gone for almost twenty years, I think. C'mon, you old nag!" Lorene tightened her grip on the reins and became very busy urging the horse forward. "We do not wish to arrive at the sawmill too late to be of any use."

Matilda Kip Davidson—wife of Hank Davidson, who was the son of the sawyer Ely Davidson—produced a son shortly before the following dawn, after a labor that involved much blood and pain, but enormous courage and very few screams. "A boy, Madame Davidson," Nicole said, looking into the new mother's worried eyes. "A very big strong boy, which is why you had so much labor to bring him into the world."

"He is healthy?

"He is perfect, wonderful. And so is his maman." Nicole sponged the new mother's face while Lorene swaddled the infant.

"And you," Lorene murmured, smiling fondly at Nicole. "You too are wonderful."

Eh bien, she had passed another test. But what did it matter? She was going to Québec to hide herself in the monastery of one of the strictest and most penitential orders of the Church. She had made a vow to God; there could be no turning back. Still, after making the faux pas about Pohantis and discovering how icy cold those blue eyes could be, she was glad to be again smiled upon by Madame Hale.

They left the sawmill after Nicole had been formally presented to the three other slaves who worked there, hauling logs and feeding them into the numerous water-powered saws that terrified Nicole the moment she saw them. The three were brothers, little more than boys, named Sampson, Westerly, and Josiah, and they looked so much alike Nicole knew she would never be able to tell them apart. But she did not need to. She would be at Shadowbrook another few weeks, perhaps less. Just until poor Monsieur Hale recovered, or most likely died.

Sitting in the wagon thinking of the impending death of Quent's father, Nicole made a furtive sign of the cross. She saw Madame Hale purposefully avert her eyes. Nicole being a Catholic—*merci á le bon Dieu*—was something the other woman chose to ignore. Since Nicole's refusal of her first invitation there had been no further request that she appear at madame's Sunday morning services.

Of course Nicole would never participate in heretic worship. Madame Hale had to know that, but if it bothered her she did not show it. That was another part of the strange dance they were dancing. A step forward, a step back, and always, Nicole knew, Madame Hale calling the tune. Like the leaders of the Virginia Reel she had seen in Alexandria. Everyone dipping and twisting and turning, and winding up exactly where they were when the dance began.

It was mid-morning and a copper-colored sun burned in a cloudless blue sky. "You are tired, madame—perhaps I could drive the wagon."

"You have done it before?"

"Never, but— *Mon Dieu,* what is that?"

Lorene reined in the horse, clucking softly and murmuring approval when it stopped and patiently waited for her next command. There came the sound of a low singing in the windless air, a tune that rose and fell and rose again. "Sally Robin," Lorene said. "I thought that's what it had to be."

It had been an exhausting night, and Lorene was tired in her very bones— more weary inside herself than this girl-child, on whom she pinned so much of her hope for the future and her chance to redeem the past, could ever know. But she mustn't let that interfere with her grand scheme. All these years, so many mistakes, so much shame . . . If she could leave the Patent in good hands, in Quentin's hands; if something of what they had been given charge of here could grow and go on and be protected, perhaps then it would not all have been for nothing. "You must meet Sally Robin, mademoiselle. She is one of the marvels of Shadowbrook."

They left the wagon where it was and the horse untethered in the middle of the road. "They're not going anywhere, and neither is anyone likely to be coming in the other direction," Lorene said, clambering down and leading Nicole into the bordering woods.

The song was all around them now. It filled the air and quivered in the trees and trembled in the leaves. The ground under their feet soaked it up and gave it back. Nicole wanted to say that she had never heard such music, but what she saw in the clearing they soon came to silenced even her wonder.

Nicole at once recognized the domed woven straw beehives known as skeps. When she was a child she and Maman had spent summers with Grandmère, at her country house outside Paris. There were skeps there as well, and a beekeeper to tend them and gather the honey. But when he worked with the bees, Grandmère's keeper wore heavy gloves and a wide-brimmed hat from which hung a long veil, and of necessity he destroyed the hive in the process. The black woman collecting honey from the skeps near the sawmill used her bare hands to reach inside the hive and detach the waxy combs laden with the golden treasure. She wore no protective clothing of any sort, and she didn't seem in any kind of hurry.

She examined each comb to see if it was full of honey before putting it in her basket. Those not quite ready were returned to the hive. And all the while what seemed like thousands of bees surrounded her, circling lazily, buzzing softly in what seemed a counterpoint to her melody.

When Sally Robin was finished she picked up her basket and walked toward them, still surrounded by the cloud of bees. Nicole instinctively pulled back. The woman chuckled. "Don't you mind yourself, missy. Don't you never mind. These be my friends and they don't be fussing you none long as I'm here." She sang a few notes, different from the earlier tune, and the swarm veered off in the direction of the skeps.

"*Incroyable.* I have never seen such a thing."

"Nor, I think, has anyone else," Lorene murmured. "Sally Robin is unique."

The beekeeper was taller than any of the Shadowbrook blacks Nicole had met so far. She was a thin woman with skin the color of milky coffee and an unusually long neck, and prominent cheekbones that defined her face. Her hair was cut short, a cap of black fuzz that barely covered her scalp. It was impossible to tell her age. "Mr. Hale bought her at the slave market in New York City the morning of our wedding," Lorene said. "Sally Robin and I came to the Patent together, didn't we, Sally?"

"That be entirely true, mistress. Long time now."

"Nearly thirty-four years. And when he bought her, my husband had no idea of what she could do. We didn't know what a treasure we were getting, only that she was a seasoned slave from the Islands. But Mr. Hale, he looked in her eyes and said he thought she might be useful."

"Don't know about treasure, mistress. I do what I can. Long as . . ."

Her words trailed off, and Nicole was conscious of a tension between the black woman and her mistress that neither seemed to want to address. It was almost as if Madame Hale were embarrassed and the slave were angry.

"How's Solomon the Barrel Maker, Sally Robin?" Lorene asked finally. It seemed to Nicole that whatever had transpired between the two women, it was the mistress who had given in.

"He be bettering. I be looking after him."

It occurred to Nicole that she had not seen Sally Robin that day in the Frolic Ground. She'd have been bound to notice a woman so tall and extraordinary looking. But she remembered clearly the name of the man being whipped. Solomon the Barrel Maker. And she had not seen him since, though nearly a month had gone by.

"Solomon be bettering quickly in his skin," Sally Robin added. "It be his spirit that's still poorly. He never told no lie to Master John. He—"

"I'll send Master Quent to visit Solomon." Lorene cut off the complaint as soon as it got started. However much a fool John might be, she could not be put in the position of having to take sides between her son and a slave. "As soon as he gets back from Albany I'll ask Master Quent to ride down here for a visit."

"Solomon be liking that, mistress." Sally Robin appeared to have thought better about her audacity. "And I be looking after Mistress Matilda now that the birthing be done. Don't you worry your mind about her."

"I shan't, Sally Robin. Not for a moment."

Lorene and Nicole returned to the wagon and began the long journey back to Shadowbrook, and not until they neared the big house did Lorene break the weary silence she'd maintained for two hours. "As I said, Sally Robin came from the Islands. A seasoned slave."

"When you buy them, you know their history?" Like the pedigree of a horse or the breed of a cow, Nicole wanted to say, but thought better of it.

"Most folks try to find out something besides the auctioneer's patter. It was easy for us. My papa owned a piece of the slave market on Wall Street in New York City, and a fleet of Guinea ships, the boats that sail to Africa and bring back the nigras. Will Devrey always knew everything about the merchandise going on the auction block. Sally Robin's a skilled healer as well as a beekeeper, makes all our unguents and lotions here on the Patent. But she never attends a birthing. Won't go near the new mother until it's over. Clemency the Washerwoman tells me it's because Sally Robin's barren. She's been with Solomon almost from the day she arrived at Shadowbrook, but she's never had a child. Clemency advised against my insisting on Sally Robin's attendance at childbirth. She's a very wise old woman, is Clemency. The other slaves look to her for guidance in many things. You'd do well always to—"

Dear God, what was she thinking of? She must not speak as if Nicole were already her daughter-in-law. Ephraim hadn't yet agreed, and as far as she knew, Quent and this young woman hadn't made any plans. But the girl was considering it. Dreaming of it, perhaps. Oh yes. Just look at how pink your cheeks are right now. You are thinking much the same things that I am thinking, little Mademoiselle Nicole. Oh yes.

The long gun with the maple stock felt right slung over his shoulder. Quent had not realized how naked he was without his weapon until he replaced it. Still, he was glad to have given the other gun to Corm. Crazy to go riding off looking for God knows what kind of enemy without one. Crazier still the way Corm's own gun had disappeared. Genevieve hadn't acted as if she had anything to hide. She'd even urged him to stay longer. *Spend another night with us, Quent. The children never tire of your stories.* He'd begged off, using his father's ill health as an excuse, and left the Lydius house soon after noon. It still wasn't quite the dinner hour, but he didn't plan to set off on the trek to Shadowbrook with an empty belly.

The taproom at the Sign of the Nag's Head was about three-quarters full. It smelled of men and animals and old ale and nearly raw spirits, but above everything was the aroma of some kind of rich stew. Venison, Quent guessed. The notice over the ale barrels by the entrance proved him right. "TODAY ONLY," it read, "JENZY'S VENISON JAMBALAYA."

"Who's Jenzy and what's jambalaya?" Quent asked.

Old man Groesbeck was preparing to tap a keg. He paused with the mallet in his hand only long enough to identify the questioner. "Oh, it be you. Should have guessed. Don't be many folks around here not be knowing Jenzy. She be marrying my boy two years past. Found her down near New Orleans, he did. A jambalaya be what we call a stew. Only it be different when she makes it in the way of her people down there in the French country."

"The same but different, is that it?"

"*Ja*, pretty much. Got some squirrel pie, too, if you'd rather have that. Jenzy make that my old woman's way. Or oysters fresh this morning. Six wooden pennies for a dozen. Five if you pay with coppers."

Someone called out that he was perishing with thirst and Groesbeck should stop talking and get on with tapping the keg. "Two dozen of the biggest oysters," Quent said. "And a glass of your best ale to wash them down. I'll be over there waiting." He took a seat on the bench that ran along the taproom's west wall. It gave him a good vantage point for surveying the scene.

The last time he'd been in here—when he'd brought Nicole because she was desperate for food and drink and a place to sit down out of the sun—it had been later in the day. The taproom had been too crowded for him to identify who was who in the throng. Now he could clearly see a pair of whores drinking at a table at the far end. The trappers with them looked as if they were already too drunk to be able to use the services they were paying for. There were a number of local craftsmen and laborers as well, and four or five tars in their distinctive short jackets and striped shirts and oiled breeches.

"Two dozen oysters," the barmaid said as she put the plate in front of him. "Opened 'em meself, I did. Seeing as how they were for Uko Nyakwai. Might open something else if you asked me nicely."

Quent laughed and flipped her a wooden shilling and she caught it expertly before it could fall to the sawdust-covered floor. "That one's for old man Groesbeck. There's another meant just for you if you tell me if you've seen any strangers around here in the past week or two."

"Always be strangers in Albany. What with them boats coming and going every day the way they do. Be even more now that it's almost harvest time."

"Yes, I know about the tars and the traders. I was thinking more about Indians."

"Old Groesbeck don't encourage Indians. They drink too much too fast, then they make trouble. Ain't too many slop shops or taverns in Albany as welcomes savages. Best if they come into town, do their trades, and get a jug to take with 'em."

"All right, what about just walking around the town, then. Someone you've not seen before. A Huron perhaps."

"Ain't never seen no—"

"Stop your jawing, girl!" Groesbeck's yell cut through the hum of voices in the taproom. "Ye be coming back to work sometime this day, or do I gotta be floggin' the skin off yer lazy back?"

The girl shot a quick look at the landlord. And thought of the shilling the Red Bear had promised. "Hold yer water, ye poxed old man! I be coming." Then, to Quent, "Only stranger like what you mean that I be seein' round here be the Scot what's living above the gristmill. The Widow Kreiger rented him a room nearly a year past, but he still talks like his tongue's got a knot in it. Can't hardly understand him meself. Though there be some as talk to him often as you like. Even giving up the chance of a few coppers out back in order to do it."

"One of the whores, you mean. A Scot comes in here and talks to one of the whores regularly. Is that it?"

"That's it. What about that shilling then?"

"Which one of the whores?"

"Annie." The girl turned and craned her neck to see over the heads of the crowd. "Don't see her just now. Not the Scot neither, but if you come back a bit later, I bet he'll be—"

"You be heading for a flogging, girl! Ain't bein' no doubt about it."

Quent flipped her the coin. "Here. And tell Groesbeck I kept you. And that if he takes a whip to you, I'll return the favor."

The girl caught the coin and opened her mouth wide in a burst of laughter so strong it jiggled her full breasts. Three of her top teeth were black with rot and most of the bottom row were missing. "Don't ye bother yerself none about that. The old fool's been promising to flog me since he bought me indenture. Never has and never will. Can't stand the sight of blood, old Groesbeck. Can't even stick a pig without weeping. You come back later, Uko Nyakwai. I'll point 'em both out, the Scot and Annie. And ye can have anything else ye likes while we're about it."

"I'll be looking forward to it." God protect him from ever being that desperate for a woman.

Quent ate and left the taproom, considering his options. He could look for the

Scot over at the gristmill, or hang about and come back to the Nag's Head in hopes of finding him there later. But there was no Scot in any part of Corm's tale, and no reason to think this one—whoever he might be—had any role in the business of the sweat lodge and the Midewiwin priest and the dead Huron. Besides, he was anxious to return to Shadowbrook. His father's health, of course, as he'd said to Genevieve. But also, or perhaps first, Nicole.

SATURDAY, AUGUST 15, 1754
THE LAKE CHAMPLAIN–HUDSON RIVER CORRIDOR

In the days when the Kahniankehaka, the Keepers of the Eastern Door, truly ruled these lands, a Huron war party would move with more stealth than Lantak and his eight braves practiced now. Before the white stink covered the land and the testicles of red men shrank like those of boy children in a cold wind, Lantak would have been a mighty war chief; not an outlaw driven from the Longhouse by chiefs who had the hearts of squaws, and ran from their enemies like chattering squirrels fleeing a hawk.

In the past he would have been at the head of thousands of warriors, coming to engage other *Haudenosaunee,* the braves of the Five Nations who had bound themselves to observe the *Kayanashakowa,* the great law of the union that had set itself against the more ancient Huron Confederacy. Theirs would have been a war of red men against red men, true warriors against a worthy enemy. Instead he moved through a land of all but empty forests and rivers. He saw none of the wooden boats made by the whites, but no birch canoes either. Lantak and his braves were alone on the water they called Oswegatchie and that the French had named Lake Champlain. Their two canoes traveled in the sun-coming direction, in a world of silence broken only by the soft, slapping noises of their perfectly synchronized paddles.

The *Haudenosaunee* had been put on this land by the Great Spirit, but they had allowed the others to come and make them slaves and squaws. Their lands were infested by vermin and they did nothing. They had shriveled like dog turds in the sun, all their life juices dried up and gone. When he thought these things, the burning began inside Lantak, and the fire that would not die roared in his belly and he yearned for release.

The sun was dropping behind them, going into the center of the earth to rest. Already the three-parts-round moon could be seen in the sky above the trees to their left. Lantak smelled the approaching dark, and the stench of white men. The French were not far off. Fort St. Frédéric, the place the English called Crown Point, was only three days' journey ahead. The French patrols might easily come this far. When the sun returned, he decided, the war party must leave the water and travel through the forest, take the long way to their destination to avoid the fort. So be it. A wise war sachem chose his battles; he did not allow them to choose him.

He raised his hand and pointed at a cove with a shallow beach, and both canoes turned effortlessly and headed for land. "We will camp here tonight," Lantak said when the canoes had been brought on land and carefully hidden. "Tomorrow we journey by foot. If we find horses we will take them. If we do not it does not matter. When the sun comes back no more than this many times," Lantak held up the ten fingers of his two hands, "we will be on the land of our enemy and there are horses there. We will take them, and many scalps, and some white captives to caress." Then the fire in his belly would be quieted. The screams would calm it and the blaze would leave him in peace for a time.

Tuesday, August 25, 1754
Shadowbrook

"Look, Ephraim." Lorene spun the chair that Solomon the Barrel Maker had fashioned for his master when Ephraim first took ill. Where its rear legs should have been were big, barrel-stave wheels. If you tilted the chair slightly backward, it made moving Ephraim a thing of ease. She was adept at using the chair and she was able to quickly adjust his position so he was facing the window. "Quent. And the girl, Mademoiselle Crane. See how he lifts her into the wagon? I told you. He's smitten with her."

"Because he assists her up onto something too high for her to reach by herself? What does that mean?"

Dear God, but men were obtuse. And blind. "It's the way he does it, Ephraim. And look how he waits before driving off. Asking her if she's comfortable, I'm sure."

"So it's Quent's good manners I'm supposed to be impressed by. I don't think—"

"That's it exactly. You don't think. You're being a stubborn fool, Ephraim. And you're putting the Patent in harm's way."

He was mostly too ill to laugh. Not enough breath for it, and the belly pain that was always with him was worsened by laughter. This time he allowed himself a small chuckle. "How easy it is to tease you, Lorene. And after all these years you still blush at my words." It had been remarkable the way he'd burned for her the first time he'd seen her. Just a girl of sixteen, younger even than this little French half-breed that had turned his household around. Lorene had brought some sunshine to the place too, back then. And some hope. He'd made the decision he had to make and never let on how it pained him, but it had been a black and bitter thing to think of John taking over Shadowbrook. "Look," he repeated with another small laugh, "the flush is on you even now."

Lorene glanced down at the pink suffusing her breasts where the corset pushed them above her bodice, and felt the heat of it on her neck and cheeks. "We're not talking about me, Ephraim. I'm trying to tell you that—"

"Quent is the man to take on the Patent. I know."

"Yes, and that this Mademoiselle Nicole Crane will make a perfect wife for him. She's good for the place, Ephraim. Even Sally Robin looked at her with approval."

"Sally Robin, eh?" The slaves said Sally had the gift of sight. He'd never been sure about that, but these days massage with one of her creams gave him what little ease he could find. He'd be grateful for that right now. His joints were aching something fierce. He was too tired to go on talking. "I need to go to bed, Lorene. Send Runsabout to help me. She gives my poor legs more comfort than any of the men. Better hands for it."

"I will, Ephraim. In a moment. But if you'd just consider how much better Quent would—"

"Lorene." He was gentle with her, his voice steady and soft. The time for teasing was past, probably forever. "I told you. I know."

"But I thought you meant to . . ."

He nodded toward the small wooden chest with the inclined top that he used to facilitate writing when he was in bed. The cover lifted and there was a place to store those few papers that these days he considered important. Not many now. Life, he'd learned, was stripped to bare essentials at its end. "In there. I wrote it all out. My instructions for after I'm gone. Quent is to have Shadowbrook."

"Oh, Ephraim! Thank heaven! I can't tell you—"

He held up a forestalling hand. "It's Quent who shouldn't be told. Not just yet." He had to stop for a moment because a surge of pain took his breath away. "Lorene, I truly need to—"

"Go to bed. Yes, my dear." Lorene half stood. "I could help you, Ephraim, if you'd permit me." He weighed so little these days. She could easily put him to bed herself.

Ephraim's face got hard and he shook his head. He would never allow her to do for him as if he were a child. Not Lorene. Not after all the times she'd been soft and pliant beneath him and he'd been the master of her body as well as of all else. "Send Runsabout." He had never expected the slaves to spread their legs for him. Damn fool thing to do, he'd always thought. Gave them entirely too much of a hold over their master, to have gazed up at a face contorted with passion. As for the children that might come from such trifling . . . A damn fool thing. No telling John that, though. No telling his oldest boy anything. He'd even considered naming Cormac, back when he thought Quent beyond his reach. But that would have been a hundred times worse. "Lorene, I perish with fatigue."

"Yes, of course." She stood and gathered her embroidery hoop and the little spools of many colored cottons that had been spread in her lap. "I'll send Runsabout, and Jeremiah to help her." Jeremiah was the stable master. He had long experience of rubbing unguent into sore limbs.

"Don't say anything to Quent. Not yet," Ephraim repeated. He wanted to add that whatever was going to be between his younger son and the small but he thought very independent women who had stumbled into their lives, it should develop naturally, with no false pressure put on by notions of inheritance. He hadn't the strength to explain. "Not yet," he repeated.

"As you wish, Ephraim. You have my word on it." Lorene glanced out the window once more as she left the room. The wagon was gone. Quent and Nicole were on their way to the sawmill to see Solomon the Barrel Maker. As she'd promised. It had been her suggestion that Nicole go along—she'd given her some things for the newborn to take to Matilda—but it was obvious that Quent would have invited the girl even without his mother's manipulations. Lorene thought of the long journey to the sawmill and back. Just the pair of them. She smiled.

If he'd taken a horse, Quent could have covered the distance in an hour; with a wagon it took two. His original excuse had been that he was taking some kegs of ale to the Davidsons, their quarterly supply according to the tenancy terms. *Might as well come along,* he'd planned to say to her. *Since I'm taking the wagon.*

She rode, he knew. They'd talked about it once. But Lorene never had, and Jeremiah had informed them there were no sidesaddles in the Shadowbrook stables. "Pohantis and Mistress Shoshanaya, they be the only womans ever rode a horse on this place, Master Quent."

Both Pohantis and Shoshanaya had ridden bareback and astride, like all squaws. Next time he was in Albany, Quent promised himself, he'd order a sidesaddle made for Nicole. Should have thought of it this last visit, except he'd been too fixed on Corm's story and finding out what he could. Less than nothing, as it turned out.

"What are you thinking?" Nicole asked.

"Nothing much."

"But we have been traveling for some time and you haven't said a word."

He glanced around and realized they were almost at the sugarhouse. "Sorry. Lost in my thoughts, I guess." He had no intention of mentioning Cormac to

Nicole. Even after what she'd told him, he couldn't bear to remember the two of them together. "We could stop at the sugarhouse. It's on the way. If we do, we can bring some jugs of rum to the Davidsons. Maybe one for Solomon while we're at it."

"Are the slaves permitted rum in this place?"

"Far as I'm concerned, the slaves can do as they like, long as the work's done."

"Your brother doesn't seem to share that opinion."

"My brother is a fool, and cruel with it." He pulled gently on the reins and the horse obediently made the turn onto the spur road that led to the sugarhouse.

"I've three pies here." Nicole looked into the basket that had been packed for her by Kitchen Hannah. "We could give one to Mistress Frankel if you've a mind."

"Women's business," he said. "Do as you think best."

"One for Sarah Frankel, then," she said, lifting out the top pie. "From your maman."

It was just the sort of thing his mother would have done. And like her, Nicole did it instinctively.

The sugarhouse was idle. "All the sugar from last year's used up," Moses Frankel told him.

"More soon," Quent said. He nodded toward the gristmill down the hill, idle too. "Everything ready?"

"Ready as ever it can be."

Frankel was the miller, as well as in charge of the distilling. When the wheat harvest started coming in he would open the dams that allowed the race that powered the gristmill to fill and roar down the sluices. The great wheel would turn and set the huge stones to grinding, and the wheat would become flour to fill the bellies of the poor black bastards who were enslaved to the cane. Maybe not fill their bellies, exactly. Ward off starvation, more like. All the same, the Carribean plantations required every bushel of flour Shadowbrook could produce above what they needed for themselves. Last time Quent heard the count there were better than sixty thousand African slaves in the Leewards alone. And that didn't include Jamaica or Barbados.

The boats that ran the trade, were each owned by a consortium of merchants dependent on the captain to make them a profit by finding the best deals. They were even now headed for Albany. He'd heard talk of little else when he was in the town. The two-masted brigs would arrive and cast anchor in the deep middle of the river, riding low, heavy with sugar. Smaller craft—a couple of sleek sloops spreading yards of canvas, and countless little boats propelled by a determined tar and a single sail run up a sturdy pole—would leave their moorings at the town wharves and hurry to take aboard the rich, dark product of the cane, the single greatest cash crop the world had ever seen. Much would go to the sugarhouses where rum was made to supply the grog shops and taverns of Albany. Still more would head downriver to settlements at the Manor of Livingston, the Great Hardenburgh Patent, and the Patent of the Nine Partners. A goodly share would come upriver to Shadowbrook, and the boats that brought it would ferry the produce of the Hale Patent back to the brigs. There was no better flour to be had anywhere in the valley. The big ships would remain moored in Albany—square sails furled, most of the crew riotously ashore, filling the town's coffers—until the Hale harvest ended and they'd laded all they could carry.

The harvest was almost upon them. At Shadowbrook they would begin bringing in the wheat in a couple of weeks' time. They were already making hay. And Quent had seen small farmers closer to the town gathering corn and potherbs in plenty. "Looks to be a good year."

"God willing," Frankel added piously. Then for good measure spat to the north, into the devil's face, as the old saying had it.

The women were coming out of the house, heading for where the men stood by the wagon. They sounded like a flock of small birds. Ellie Bleecker kissed Nicole farewell, and Sarah shook her hand warmly. Even Deliciousness May beamed at her.

"The Frankels like you," he said when they were once more on the way to the sawmill.

"I like them. I was sorry not to see the little ones again. Lilac and Willie."

"Where were they?"

"Helping with the haying, according to Deliciousness May. Seems they're gone until late at night."

He heard the distress in her tone. "It's not always like that. There's much of pleasure for young folks on the Patent."

"You think it a good place for children, then?"

He glanced at her. There seemed to be no special meaning behind her words. "It can be." When the harvest began in earnest Lilac and Sugar Willie would work twenty-two hours out of twenty-four for weeks on end. To be fair, Ellie's children would work almost as hard, but in the winter when there was less to be done they'd be sent to the big house to learn to read and write. Anyone who tried to teach those skills to Runsabout's twins would suffer mightily. Particularly if John had anything to say about it. Quent had always been fairly certain it was his brother who had fathered those babes on Runsabout, but that didn't change his brother's feelings toward the youngest slaves.

"The slaves, what is to prevent there being a small wage paid them?" Nicole did not realize she was going to ask until the question was out of her mouth.

"Far as I can see, only money." Quent's tone gave away nothing of the fact that lately he had been thinking on that same equation. Could the Patent be made to show a profit and at the same time pay the slaves something for their efforts? So they wouldn't, strictly speaking, be slaves. *The workman is worthy of his hire,* said the Rhode Island Quaker he'd met at Do Good all those years ago.

"We are almost there, are we not?" Nicole's voice interrupted his reverie. "That little path between the two rowans, I remember it from last week when I came with Madame Hale."

"Rowans," Quent said, repeating the name she'd used. "In these parts we call them mountain ash." The two small trees were heavy with bright orange berries. Shoshanaya had said they were talking trees, because when the berries were thick on the branch the way they were now, you knew it would be a hard winter, with much snow. "Did my mother take you down that path?"

"No. We drove right past it." Nicole noted something odd about the set of his jaw, a kind of hardness that she did not remember seeing before.

Quent reined in the horse and stopped the wagon. "I want to show you something, but we'll have to go by foot. Path's not wide enough for the wagon."

"Very well." Nicole reached into her pocket and brought out the white moccasins. "I have these. May I take the time to put them on?"

"Good idea," he said, and turned away while she unlaced her boots. When he turned back, she had on Pohantis's moccasins and was holding out her arms for him to lift her down.

Nicole felt his hands on her waist as he swung her to the earth and begged forgiveness of the Virgin. She could easily have jumped to the ground.

"This way," Quent said.

And once more she was following him into the woods.

Chapter Eleven

NICOLE ESTIMATED THEY had walked for half a league, most of it uphill, before he stopped. The sun had disappeared and the sky was grayed over with heavy clouds, but still there was no breath of air and she was glad of the opportunity to catch her breath. She looked around, eager to see what it was he'd brought her to see. All around were tall oaks and elms, their thick black trunks interrupted here and there by the white of birch and the dark green of pine. Where trees had been felled, perhaps by the fierce rainstorms that had so astonished her in this New World, or by men needing them for the sawmill, saplings grew. Neither the small woodlots of France nor the neat fields and broad hedgerows of England had prepared her for this unspoiled land. "It is very beautiful. And so peaceful." She looked at the weapon slung over his shoulder. "Why did you bring your gun?"

He paused, turned back to her. "I don't know," he said after a few moments, with that half smile that was her favorite of all his expressions. "Just habit."

A habit of guns. She need only close her eyes to see the burning and the blood that day in the Ohio Country, and before that . . . No, she mustn't. She had promised herself she would not. Nicole opened her eyes. She trembled, only a little and only for a moment, but he saw.

"What's wrong?"

She shook her head. "Nothing."

He wanted to put his arms around her, to promise her that she had nothing to fear, that he would always protect her, but he couldn't. Once before he'd made such a promise when a woman feared his world because it was different from hers and had been unable to keep it. "Say my name." He bit out the words. "Say it."

"What . . . I don't—"

"You promised you'd say my name."

"Quent."

He exhaled loudly, the demons banished by the sound of her voice. "Thank you." He put out his hand. "Come, it's only a short distance farther on."

Nicole kept hold of his hand and let him draw her deeper into the forest. They'd gone only a short distance when she heard the sound of rushing water. "You're taking me to see a falls."

"The falls are part of what I want to show you."

For a time they said nothing more, but the sound of the falls grew louder. They climbed a steep rise and suddenly, without warning, they were in a small clearing the shape of a half moon surrounded by a birchwood. There was a rushing stream, and a few willows grew close by the water. In the places where the shade was deepest, the ground was covered with dark green moss. A path of flat stones meandered through the trees and disappeared. She could hear the laughing falls, but not see them. "It is magic," she whispered. "An enchanted kingdom."

"I made this clearing. I brought Shoshanaya here after we were married." He tugged her toward the stepping stones.

"Did you make this path as well?"

"No, Shoshanaya did that. She . . ." He paused, and put up his free hand to signal silence. They waited a few moments, then he shrugged and moved forward again.

"What did you think you heard?"

"The wings of Shoshanaya's eagle. Handsomest bird you've ever seen, with a beak that could rip out a man's throat. She tamed him back on the Ottawa lands when she was a little girl. Taught him to eat out of her hand. When I brought her here, the bird followed. He used to come every few days and sit on her out-stretched arm and she'd feed him parched corn, then he'd rub the top of his head against her cheek before he flew away."

"And now?"

"I don't know. After she . . . After we buried her the bird stopped coming. I hung around a whole year waiting for the danged thing, but it never came back."

Truly it was an enchanted kingdom, and Shoshanaya was its princess.

They came to the end of the stepping stones. "Just here," Quent said, pulling her around a great oak. "Look."

The falls were neither very wide nor very deep, simply a drop down a shallow rock face, maybe twice as tall as she was. Even this close they were no louder than a tinkling melody. Quent pointed to a small wooden platform cantilevered out over the water. "I made that as well. Indians usually have more than one name; Shoshanaya's woman-name was Laughing Brook. Soon as she told me that, I knew I wanted to bring her here. We had a cabin in that clearing back there, but we used to come sit here lots of days. Some nights as well."

"What happened to the cabin?"

"I took it down."

Something cold and hard formed inside Nicole. A little knot of . . . what? Rage? How could she be angry with a woman who had been raped and murdered? Because Quent had loved her, adored her, the way papa did maman. Nicole felt Shoshanaya's spirit was in this place. "You still miss her," she said.

"I did. Come over here and sit by the falls. The water's not so cold this time of year, but it's still a comfort from the heat of the day."

"Why do you say 'did'? As if what you felt was in the past."

"Because it is. That's why I brought you here. I wanted you to know that. Shoshanaya's gone. I can't bring her back, and I've come to accept that."

"Since when?"

"Since I met you." He hadn't expected to be so open with any woman ever again. He turned away, afraid of what she could read in his face.

Why didn't she believe him? Because she could still feel the Ottawa squaw, the honey-skinned princess who had loved him and lay with him and had been about to bear him a son, looking down at her. Shoshanaya was laughing. As if she knew that death had given her the ultimate power. She would never grow old and in memory she would always be perfect.

The platform was still sturdy; they both sat.

"This water is in a great hurry," Nicole said. "Where is it going?"

"To Hudson's River, eventually. But first, down into the valley where we left the wagon. Then it joins up with a couple of other streams, and by the time it reaches the mill it's strong enough to power the saws."

She touched the smooth boards on which they were sitting. "These came from there? From the sawmill?"

"Yes."

The way in wasn't wide enough for a wagon. He must have carried the planks through the woods to build this throne for his princess.

"You look warm." Quent reached up and moved a stray curl from her cheek. Nicole's eyes grew shiny with unshed tears. "If you take off the moccasins," he said softly, "you can put your feet in the stream."

"*Oui.*" The word came unbidden, a whisper of consent. But she did not move. Quent reached down and took off the white moccasins.

He allowed his fingers to linger on her ankle. He could not keep his palm from sliding a ways up her calf.

Such a light touch. Perhaps she was merely dreaming it. Perhaps everything was a dream. Everything. She lay back and closed her eyes, and when she felt his mouth on hers Nicole parted her lips to receive him.

There had been plenty of rain in the spring, followed by bright sun for much of July and all of August. The grasses were lush, the fronds so heavy with seed they bent with their own weight. The hay made from such grass would be excellent, full of nourishment that would keep the horses and cattle healthy throughout the long snowbound winter that was sure to come. Every hand not doing other vital work had been put to the haying: all the slaves from the sawmill and a number from the gristmill and the sugarhouse. The twins, Lilac and Sugar Willie, were too small to swing scythes, but they ran to and fro gathering the cut grass and helping to build the haystacks that dotted the fields.

The first flaming arrow landed in a haystack right near eleven-year-old Westerly, the youngest of the three slave brothers who worked the sawmill. The boy beat at the flames with his hands and tried to tear the burning hay away from the stack itself. "Sampson! Sampson! You over there? I needs you to—" Another arrow caught him in the throat and cut off his words. Six more fire arrows were launched at the field. The flames licked at the ripe grass and crackled across the ground, and a few plumes of smoke rose into the overcast sky.

Sally Robin was bent over, sweeping the hay into a pile for Sugar Willie to carry away, when she saw the child caught up by a tall brave with a red- and black-painted face. A knife slit Willie's throat and scalped him before she could draw a breath. Then the savage grabbed a hatchet from his waist and Sugar Willie's naked skull flew in one direction while his body was hurled in another, into the flames leaping up around them. Sally Robin composed herself, waiting to die. A song rose in her and she let it loose. The tall Indian stood over her and she saw his knife red with Sugar Willie's blood, and how the blood dripped down the front of his buckskins. The field was full of screams and war whoops and the sound of fire. Sally Robin's song couldn't compete with all that bitter noise, but still it wanted to sing itself and she allowed it to do so.

Lantak stared at the woman who was singing in the face of certain death and realized she was a witch, and a great danger to him. He turned away just in time to avoid the thrust of the pitchfork carried by a huge man hurling himself forward. Lantak's hatchet cut the air between them and the man fell. The witch stopped her singing just long enough to scream "Solomon!"

His tongue traced her teeth; she was as sweet as he'd known she'd be. Her hair started to come loose and Quent let his blunt fingers play with the strands the way he'd longed to do for so many weeks. Nicole breathed a sigh into his mouth and arched toward him; her small, perfect breasts pressed against his chest. He wanted to know all of her. He kissed her eyes and her nose and her cheeks and tasted salt. Her tears or his? He wasn't sure and it didn't matter.

Her skirts had worked themselves up above her bare legs to her waist. He let a tentative hand stroke the inside of her thigh and Nicole uttered a little cry that thrilled him, filled with both desire and innocence. He would teach her everything, show her everything, and she would be his forever. "I want you," he whispered. "Now." She did not pull away.

The platform he had made to sit above the laughing water with Shoshanaya was made of elmwood. He'd given the planks their final smoothing with his own hands. It was hard and unyielding beneath them and he gathered Nicole close, intending to lift her to the softer, moss-covered earth. "No," she whispered. "Here."

He was large with wanting, but he did not hurry. Nicole had contrived to release the laces of her bodice and he bent his head to her breasts and lost himself in the incredibly sweet smell of the skin between them.

Here, she had told him, because it was Shoshanaya's place. Nicole could feel the presence of the woman he had loved before her, but she knew she would triumph. I am alive and you are dead. I can satisfy the fire in him, but you cannot. I will give him live sons. Yours is nothing but bones in the ground.

"Here," she whispered again. Her hand sought his and she guided it to her breast.

Quent felt her nipple swell with desire beneath the palm of his hand. He took her mouth again, more eagerly this time, his tongue more demanding, sucking her breath, her life force, into himself. He stretched full length over her, pressing her into the boards. She belonged to him, was his to— There was the sound of someone running, crashing through the woods.

Quent rolled off her. He'd left his gun back in the clearing and the only weapon he had was his dirk. It was in his hand before his feet touched the earth.

"Master Quent! Praise God, it do be Master Quent!"

"Sampson?" What in Christ's name was the sawmill slave doing here when he should have been haying with the others? For as long as Quent could remember the haymaking at Shadowbrook had begun at the western edge of the Patent, with the fields beyond the topmost sluice that fed the millrace.

"They be burning up everything, master. And one of 'em, he killed Westerly. Little Sugar Willie, he be dead too. Got his head chopped right off. I didn't wait to—"

"Who? French soldiers?" Fort Frédéric was the nearest hostile sanctuary. But it made no sense for—

"Not no soldiers." The boy was weeping. "I saw what happened to Sugar Willie and I figured best thing I could do was run and tell."

"Who? Damn it, Sampson, make some sense! Who's attacking Shadowbrook?"

"Savages, Master Quent. With painted faces and their hair all standing up in the middle of their heads like this." He ran his hand from his forehead to the nape of his neck to signify a scalp lock. "Them Indians be screaming and burning and killing and—"

Quent heard a small gasp and turned. Nicole was standing behind him; she'd made no attempt to adjust her clothing. She was staring at Sampson and the look on her face was of pure anguish. Quent grabbed her arm and pulled her back toward the stream. "Don't move," he shouted to Sampson. "Stay right there till I come back."

As Quent dragged Nicole across the clearing, the small stones and twigs cut her flesh and lacerated her feet. She felt nothing except the thoughts that pummeled her. My fault. My fault. My fault. Death everywhere. My fault.

Quent snatched her into his arms and waded with her into the center where the stream was deepest. "Hold your breath." Nicole looked at him as if she hadn't heard, as if she had no idea who he was or what they were doing there. "Nicole! Do as I say. Take a deep breath and hold it."

He saw her chest move and plunged them both below the water. Holding her with one arm, he swam toward the falls with the other. The entrance to the cave was behind the wall of falling water, entirely hidden by a fold in the cliff face. Solomon the Barrel Maker had shown him this cave, back when Quent was six years old. He had no memory of learning to swim. It seemed like something he had always known, but the cave . . . He remembered how it was when he'd first seen that. Solomon watching and laughing, delighted with a little boy's wonder.

A pale aqueous light filtered through the falls. Fresh air came in from an opening some distance to the rear that led deep into another part of the forest. The walls were glass smooth, except where things had been drawn by people so ancient they were beyond memory, a few faint symbols etched into the rock that meant nothing now but had once meant everything to the artists. "Way I figure, Master Quent, the folks who lived here before, they left these marks to sort of say hello. I can't rightly figure what they were saying. Maybe when you grow up, you'll know what the signs mean. Till then, I figure this place has to be our secret, yours and mine."

There was a chance that someone who didn't know about either opening could stumble into this cave, but it was a small one. Quent had no choice but to take it. "Nicole, listen to me. I have to go, but you must stay. You'll be safe here."

She made no sign that she'd heard, and he put his hands on her shoulders and shook her. "Nicole! This time you have to do what I say. Your life depends on it. Promise you'll stay here."

"I promise."

Her whisper was so quiet he read her lips more than heard her voice. And she was still staring beyond him, into terrors he could only imagine. "I love you," he said. "I brought you to the clearing to tell you that. I have to leave now, but I will come back for you. Do you understand me, Nicole? You will be safe here and I will come back for you. I swear it."

She put up a hand and touched his cheek. "Be careful. Do not—"

He clasped her small hand in his. "Nothing is going to happen to me. I will return, Nicole. I will always return for you. If you know nothing else, know that. Wait for me." He leaned forward and kissed her gently. Then he was gone.

There was no point in heading back to the big road. The shortcut that had brought Sampson to the clearing would get them to the sawmill faster.

Quent ran along the track trying to unravel the puzzle. There hadn't been an Indian attack on Shadowbrook in half a century at least, perhaps more. A scalp lock in these parts likely meant Iroquois, and around here that meant Mohawk, Kahniankehaka. But they had been English allies for years. All the same, Sampson was adamant. He kept insisting, "I seen 'em, Master Quent. I seen them savages. They was—"

"Stop your wailing, Sampson. I believe you. Save your breath for running. We'll be at the sawmill soon."

Quent smelled the blaze before he saw it. There was no wind and the smoke from the burning buildings rose straight up into the sky. He saw Matilda Davidson's body first, an arrow in her chest and her ten-day-old child still in her arms. They'd both been scalped. Sampson reached for the infant. It uttered a single cry and died. Quent took the tiny corpse away from the boy and lay it back on its mother's breast. "There's no time now. This way." He'd spotted Hank's body as well. Matilda's husband had been brought down a short distance farther on. There was no sign of Ely. And no way Quent and Sampson could put out the flames that were devouring the mill.

A nearby maple was the tallest of the trees beyond the screen of smoke. Quent scaled it quickly. The heat from the flames of the burning sawmill was stronger the higher he climbed. Sparks flew with sudden bursts of vigor as they consumed the moist, fresh lumber waiting to be dressed.

Quent shaded his eyes, blinking them clear of the soot flying everywhere, and peered across the horizon. Dark as the afternoon had become, the smoke made a darker smudge in the sky revealing the destruction. It was a thought-out burning, Quent thought; the wheat fields are the target. All the same, the woods will go as well if a wind comes . . . Thank Christ for the day's stillness. Feels almost unnatural, but I'll take the devil if he's the only ally available.

"Master Quent! Look here, Master Quent!"

Sampson had found Ely Davidson. The boy was propping the old man up with an arm around his waist. Still, the sawyer was alive and standing on his own two legs, and his scalp was intact.

Quent came down the tree faster than he'd gone up. Ely looked dazed but unharmed, except for an ugly gash on his forehead. A long gun was slung over his shoulder. The barrel was clean and the ramming rod in place. It did not appear to have been fired. "What happened? Are you all right?"

"I'm not exactly sure." Ely's voice shook. He was staring at the bodies of his son and his daughter-in-law and his tiny grandson. "I'd gone up to the 'race to check the dams. I heard a commotion down here, started back, and—"

"What kind of commotion?"

"Couldn't tell at first. Then I saw smoke and figured it meant fire. Panicked me, I guess. Didn't look where I was goin'. Damned stupid after all these years. Ran so damned fast a branch caught me in the head and knocked me out. By the time I got here they was leaving. And"—he gestured to the three corpses—"it was too late to do any good. Never got off a shot."

"Just as well. You'd be dead too if you had." Quent put a hand on the older man's shoulder. "They're burning the wheat fields. Did the ones you saw have horses?"

Ely shook his head. There was another shower of sparks and the flames roared. "Didn't see no horses."

No matter, the war party wouldn't be on foot for long. There was a paddock between the sawmill and the sugarhouse. Sweet Jesus, at least a dozen animals were there for the taking. Quent turned to go. "We can head them off if we take the path around Big Two." The sawyer didn't move. "Ely," Quent's voice softened. "I need you." The old man continued to stare at the corpses of his family. "There's no time to bury them now, Ely." Once they had horses, the braves could get from the sugarhouse to the big house in under half an hour.

Davidson hesitated half a moment more, then took his gun from his shoulder and began ramming powder into the barrel. "Sampson, you come with us!" he called.

"I be coming, Master Ely. Just getting me something to bring along." Sampson had spotted Hank Davidson's musket, just a corner of the stock showing beneath the dead man's shoulder. The boy dragged the musket free and ran into the woods after the two men.

Quent turned his head and spoke over his shoulder. "The ones you saw, Ely, were they Kahniankehaka? Mohawk?"

"No. Wrong war paint. Not blue. Red and black."

It sounded like Huron. Quent felt a chill start in his belly. "Red and black? You're sure?"

"I'm sure."

The path of the shortcut that skirted Big Two bent in opposite directions a ways farther on. Quent had to decide. If the attack was purposeful, as it appeared to be, the war party had knowledge of the Patent. If someone has told them to fire the wheat fields and sent them here on foot, that someone will also have told them where to find horses so they can finish the job. Where should we turn? To the sugarhouse—if the Frankels and the others are still alive, two more guns might keep them that way—or the paddock?

"Moses and Tim Frankel's bound to have figured out what's going on." Ely was past the age when running was easy, but his voice didn't waiver. Determination supplied his breath. "Thing is, they've only got muskets up at the sugarhouse. They'll be right glad of—"

"This way," Quent said, veering to his left.

"But the sugarhouse is—"

"This way. The braves will head for the paddock first. They need horses and they'll know where to find them." Christ help them all if he was wrong.

"Savages don't need horses to get scalps. We need to—"

"Stop talking, Ely. Save your strength for shooting." He could feel the older man's disapproval boring into his back. And young Sampson's terror.

John spotted the gray smudge on the horizon when it was nearing two o'clock, a good hour before dinner. He had intended to ride out and check on the progress of the haying after his meal. Instead he forgot his empty belly and rushed toward the stables shouting for a horse. "There's a fire. Hurry up with that saddle, damn you, or I'll have you flayed alive!"

Little George gave the straps a final tug even as John mounted. "Get a wagon," John told him. "Load it up with buckets. Find Jeremiah and Six-Finger Sam and come after me." There were dug wells all over the Patent. The only prayer for fighting a fire was if one of them, or better yet a brook or a stream, turned out to be near enough to the flames to do some good. If that were the case, they'd need every available hand to form a bucket chain. "Bring Runsabout, as well. And Corn Broom Hannah." Kitchen Hannah was too old to be of any use.

"John! John! Did you see?" Lorene raced out of the house, holding up her skirts. "It looks like fire!"

"I know." John's horse sensed his urgency and pawed the earth. "I've told the others to come by wagon."

"I'll come too. I can—"

"No, you stay here. I'm taking everyone but Kitchen Hannah. Father shouldn't be alone."

She protested, but with only half a heart. For once John was right. Lorene watched him ride out, then supervised the readying of the wagon that went after him. When it left, she stood in the stable yard, hands hanging by her side clenched into fists. She was alone with Ephraim and Kitchen Hannah, helpless to do anything useful, and the smudge of smoke on the horizon grew bigger and blacker by the moment. Dear God. Dear God. A crack of heat lightening thundered overhead. Dear God, let it rain. Don't let it be just a dry storm.

"Lorene!"

She looked up. Ephraim was at his window gesturing toward the horizon. "Fire, Lorene!"

"I know. John's gone and taken the slaves with him. They'll see to it, Ephraim. I'm coming up. Don't fret yourself."

Quent and Ely and Sampson came out of the woods onto a piece of upland in a natural clearing. The paddock was within view.

Quent pointed to a large oak with a trunk substantially wider than the sawyer. "Ely, you stay here. Keep your eyes open. Don't fire until after I do. Sampson, follow me."

He led the boy some twenty strides farther on, then gestured to the musket. "You know how to fire that thing?"

Sampson grinned. "I surely do, Master Quent."

It was against the law of New York Province to give a slave a weapon. They pretty much made their own laws on the Patent, but John would have flogged the hide off Sampson if he'd caught him with a musket. "You got any shot? Any powder?" The boy held up the ammunition he'd taken from Hank Davidson's body. "Fine. You stay here, behind this tree. After you hear two shots, mine and Master Ely's, you fire your musket, then reload as fast as you can. Soon as you've done that, fire again."

"I can climb up the tree, Master Quent. That way I—"

"No. Do exactly what I say. You got that?"

"I gots it."

He needed all the shots to come from ground level; it was the only way they'd create the impression of a surrounding force. Quent shaded his eyes and looked down the main path leading to the paddock. It was empty. He knelt and put his ear to the ground. Nothing. If he'd guessed wrong, the braves would already be at the sugarhouse and the burning and killing would be under way. Too late for second thoughts. He was committed.

Quent made his way to a stand of elms halfway across the clearing from the paddock, on the opposite side to the tree hiding Ely. The sky was darker than ever and there was still no wind, but the smell of smoke drifted toward them, carried on the high currents of air that sometimes moved the clouds when not a leaf stirred on earth. The horses smelled it, too. They were beginning to paw the earth and make soft whinnying sounds of distress. There was another sound, barely audible, but growing louder by the moment, moccasins pounding swiftly on the earth. Quent raised the gun to his shoulder and fixed his sights on the place where the main path ended and the clearing began.

The brown robe had drawn on the ground with a stick, showing Lantak the things he needed to know. So far everything had been exactly as the priest said. Lantak heard the sounds of horses and grunted softly with satisfaction. He held up his hand to signal those behind him to pause, then signaled to the men behind him. Three braves broke off and made their way through the trees to Lantak's right. Three more went to the left. Lantak waited. Until now there had been no organized resistance, but a wise war sachem never assumed that his enemy was stupid. And surprise was a weapon that could be used only once.

The silence told Quent the braves were dividing. If there were enough of them to fully encircle the clearing they'd come on Sampson and Ely and the game was over, he was betting there were not. Indians fought with stealth, in small raiding parties. Besides, a group of Huron large enough to deploy all the way around the paddock would have been bound to attract attention before they got there. There were probably fewer than a dozen, and some would enter the clearing from the main path. At the spot he had firmly fixed in his sights.

A few leaves moved.

Sweet holy Jesus. Huron war paint all right, and a scalp lock exactly as Sampson had described. But this brave wore buckskins. Not many Huron wore . . . Holy Christ. He squinted into the unnatural dark of the afternoon, forced to accept that he was looking at Lantak, the most feared renegade in all of New France. A man so crazed with hate that his own longhouse wanted no part of him. If he found Nicole . . . Quent's heart thudded in his chest, probably loud enough for the murdering bloody bastards to hear. Except that the horses were making enough noise to give him cover. They had picked up the scent of the Indians and were truly agitated now, stomping and snorting.

Lantak and the two braves with him headed for the paddock. Quent's finger tightened on the trigger, but he didn't shoot. He knew there were others and he wanted them in the open when the fight began, not hiding in the woods.

The braves had to cross six fathoms of open field to reach the horses. Quent kept Lantak in his sights, while he registered the silent arrival of six more Huron. He waited for the space of another few heartbeats. No more Indians appeared. There were nine in all; Lantak and two others had long guns, the rest muskets. If the man across from him were Cormac rather than old Ely Davidson, he'd figure they could take the lot in a couple of minutes.

"Stop right there, you thieving savages!" Big Jacob burst out of the woods and his voice rang out in the clearing. "You ain't having these horses. These be—"

Quent fired at the same instant that Lantak spun to his left and loosed his tomahawk. The head of the brave who had been behind the leader exploded in a shower of blood and bone. Ely Davidson took down another of the Indians. A third brave took Sampson's musket ball in the shoulder and staggered before falling to his knees. By the time Quent reloaded and was ready to fire again, he couldn't find a target. The raiders had all dropped to the ground and were rolling toward the woods.

Big Jacob lay on the ground, Lantak's tomahawk buried in his forehead. The stink of gunfire hung in the unmoving air along with the musk of men. The only sound was the frightened whinnying of the horses. A long gun erupted. Quent figured it for Ely's, but the shot, connected with nothing. Quent saw the brave closest to the paddock begin crawling toward the gate. If he loosed the horses, every Indian except maybe the one who was wounded would be astride in a heartbeat. Quent as well. But not likely Sampson or Ely. It would be just him chasing half a dozen murdering Huron. He tried to fix the crawling Indian in his sights.

A musket shot rang out, Sampson's probably. Quent heard the ball crash in the woods. There was no answering fire. The Indians were battle shrewd, unlikely to waste ammunition on targets they couldn't see. The brave trying to reach the paddock was almost there. He rose up slightly and stretched his arm toward the gate. It was enough. Quent's shot took off the top of his head. A roan smelled the blood and screamed in terror.

A crack of lightning ripped across the blackened sky and the paddock was bathed in a strange blue light. The neighing and whinnying grew deafening. An Indian rose to his knees and another streak of light cut through the heavy air. This one was a flaming arrow that landed in the center of the paddock. One horse bellowed in agony. The others hurled themselves against the paddock fence and it gave beneath their combined weight. The horses were loose.

Quent threw himself forward and grabbed the mane of the first horse he could touch, a gray mare. She tried to shake free of him but he hauled himself up on her back, then swung his body to the side so her flanks gave him protection. No way he could load and sight. The only weapon of any use was his dirk. And once he threw it, it was gone.

As he'd expected, every Huron still alive had managed to grab and mount a horse. There were six of them pounding across the clearing toward the main path. Lantak turned and his knife cut through the air, aimed straight for the forehead of Quent's mare. Quent crouched, knowing his size made a target of him even so, and yanked the horse's head down. The knife sailed over both of them.

He saw Lantak sprawl low over his horse, becoming almost one with the animal, and he knew the Huron's knees were pressing into the animal's sides, because he saw it leap forward. Behind them the paddock was starting to burn in earnest, the fire first creeping across the short, well-grazed grass, then fueling itself on the split logs of the fence and racing onward. Another flash of lightning split the sky. Quent saw Sampson start toward him across the clearing. "Head for the big house!" he shouted. "Tell Master John!"

Those few moments gave the Indians the advantage. They were well ahead of him now, thundering along the path. Quent rode after them. The rearmost brave had turned himself around, riding sightless, trusting the horse to follow the others. He fixed an arrow in his bow and let it fly. Quent rolled to the side. Two more arrows came in swift succession. Quent dodged them both. Before the brave could loose another, a low-hanging branch connected with his head and shoulders and knocked him off his horse. The horse reared up, startled by the sudden loss of the weight on its back. The brave rolled to avoid being trampled, and rose to his knees. Quent's dirk caught him in the throat and he shuddered, then fell. Quent slung himself off the side of the mare, hanging on by the grip of his knees and one hand tangled in the horse's mane. He drew level with the dead brave and retrieved his dirk, then righted himself and rode on.

The riderless horse was the roan gelding. Now it was between him and Lantak and his braves, all of them still well ahead. Five God-rotting murdering bastards too many. God curse them all to hell. Quent dug his heels into the mare's sides, slapping her flanks with the palm of one hand. "C'mon, you she-witch! Run, damn you! Run!"

The path had been made wide enough for a small wagon so Big Jacob could break some of the horses to the harness and give them more training than the paddock clearing allowed. Now Big Jacob was dead at the hands of the most notorious Huron in Canada. How in Christ's name had Lantak come to attack Shadowbrook? He'd told Sampson to find John. But perhaps John already knew.

Sped on by Quent's ceaseless demands, the mare had finally drawn level with the riderless gelding. Quent reached out and grabbed the mane of the second horse. For a few seconds he controlled both horses with nothing but his bare hands, then he hurled himself onto the gelding's back, lying low over its head and urging it forward. "Go, you confounded bloody beast! Go!"

The five braves had opened still more distance between Quent and themselves and were approaching the place where the path intersected the big road. Quent could see them and he was near enough to get off a shot, but he'd lose more precious time reloading, and the brave nearest him wasn't wearing buckskins. If he couldn't be sure of getting Lantak himself—on the first try—it was better to wait. Now everything depended on which direction the raiders chose when they reached the big road. If they went right they were heading for the big house. Left meant they'd decided to retrace their steps.

The war party came to the end of the path and turned left. They were heading back the way they came, probably leaving the Patent for reasons as mysterious as those that had brought them here. God alone knew what was happening at the big house. Christ, maybe there was more than one war party and Shadowbrook was already in flames. He should get back there, back to his mother and his almost dead father, to a brother possibly more treacherous and evil than he had ever imagined.

Fear rose in him uncontrollably. Lantak was a butcher, a bloodthirsty madman. He told himself there was no way Lantak could suspect that Nicole was hidden in the cave behind the waterfall, and no reason for the Huron to care. But nothing else that had happened this day made any sense. Once before, he'd left the woman he loved alone in that same God-cursed clearing and she died before he could save her. Not this time, by Christ. Not this time.

Quent turned the gelding's big head left and galloped away from the big house and after the braves. There was a rumble of thunder that sounded as if it rose from the bowels of the earth. Sweet Christ, if only it would rain. He turned his face up, praying to feel a drop or two, but the only moisture he felt was his sweat. Ahead of him Lantak and his renegades sped on, the wind of their passage the only movement in the heavy air. Quent urged his horse on, but the distance between himself and the Indians continued to widen. He was twice as big as any of the Huron; the gelding was willing, a big-hearted horse, but he simply had more to carry. Quent took his long gun from his shoulder and held it at the ready, even though he knew that by raising his body and moving he slowed his passage still more. If he was going to lose them anyway, maybe he could get off a single shot and make it count.

John rode along the perimeter of the blaze, and dismounted a quarter league southwest of the sugarhouse. There was fire as far as he could see, a line of flames that filled the space between the horizon and where he stood. Jesus God Almighty. They were ruined. He was ruined.

He thought of his merchant backers in New York City and a cold hand gripped his bowels and twisted. Nothing had been signed of course; he couldn't sign anything as long as his father was alive. But there was an understanding. He'd given his word: the proceeds of this year's harvest pledged as the down payment on the land in St. Kitts. Not just land, Goddamn it. Sugar land.

How many years had he argued with his father about it? You didn't have to live in the God-blighted Caribbean to profit from sugar. The islands were a living hell ruled by the lash and burnt by the sun, a place where no white man could thrive, much less a white woman. No one but an African could tend and harvest cane in the remorseless heat of the bug-ridden islands, and even they only did it under the whip. But these days the plantation owners lived in the colonies or in London and left agents in charge of their business. As for the trade between the cane lands and the northern suppliers of the produce that fed everyone in the Caribbean, it was controlled by the ship's captains who ferried the exchange. But if a man owned both, the cane land and the land that produced the food, that man was set for a fortune. But most of those around him were either too stupid to see the opportunity or too land-poor to seize it. Even, God help them, Ephraim Hale. "Morris does it," John had told his father repeatedly. "So can we."

Ephraim always gave the same answer: "Cane's a filthy business. I want no part of it." Never mind that without the sugar plantations to buy his flour and his vegetables and his beef, he'd be just one more farmer with dirt under his nails eking out a subsistence living.

John Hale did not intend to be that kind of farmer. And by Christ he wouldn't doff his cap to the New York City lords, to the Morrises and the Livingstons and the Van Cortlandts and the like, with their education at Yale or Princeton and their fancy houses and besatined women. Money was the great equalizer. With enough of it a man could be as important as any other, whatever his name or his education. With land that produced cane as well as land that produced wheat, he would be . . . No, he would not. Not now. John shaded his eyes and gazed into the flames that were destroying all his dreams.

"Master John!" Six-Finger Sam had run the full distance from the gristmill. He was soaked in sweat and his no-longer-young legs were trembling with the effort. "Master Moses, he be sending me." The slave was breathless and these were more words than he'd spoken together in as long as he could remember. But this was a perilous day. A bad, bad day. "Master Moses, he say to tell you we be soaking the mill and the sugarhouse and the rest until they can't be holding any more water. He say maybe we should cut—"

John turned, and his hand cracked Sam's cheek so hard he felt the shudder up to his own shoulder. "I'm not interested in what Moses Frankel thinks we should do, you God-blighted fool. I told you to stay put and make sure those buildings were safe." His hand hurt, but he felt better. John started to loosen his belt. "I'll teach you to dis—"

Lightning crackled overhead, followed by a huge boom of thunder. The skies opened and blinding rain—salvation—poured from the heavens.

If the brown robe tried to tell Lantak he would not get his second payment of two hundred livres because the rain put out the fires, he would kill him. Better, he would kill him anyway. Best would have been to kill Uko Nyakwai. By the time he realized who it was who had set the trap for him in the paddock, it was too late to get a clear path for his gun or his tomahawk. Now—Lantak glanced quickly back over his shoulder—he could no longer see the horse carrying the Red Bear. The rain was so heavy he could see little beyond the length of his arm. And the horses were tiring. If more whites came after them on fresh horses it would be bad.

These thoughts were so much in Lantak's mind that he did not see what was ahead of them until one of the other braves drew level and spoke. "There, beside the road." He pointed a short distance ahead. "Two blacks, a squaw and a man. I will get their scalps."

The brave started to turn his horse toward the man and woman kneeling in the bordering woodland. Lantak watched, uninterested. Then, after a few more strides, he saw who the woman was and he remembered the singing. "Wait!" he called out. "Do not touch the squaw. She has a spirit." He glanced up at the sky. Perhaps it was she who had sung the rain into being. "Kill the man if— No, don't kill him. Take him captive." It was this man or no one. Despite the presence of the squaw who had the spirit, Lantak's need drove him. "He is big. He will endure many caresses." The brave didn't turn around, but he raised his hand to signal that he had heard.

Quent had started to slow the roan some ways back, well before Lantak and his renegades drew level with the pair of mountain ash that marked the path to the glade. By the time he made the turn that led to the clearing and falls, the Indians were too far ahead to see where he went.

He thundered forward, urging the horse to go as fast as it could on the narrow path, but he was still short of the clearing when he slid off the animal's back. Quent turned the roan around. "Go on, boy. Go on home. You've earned it." More than likely the gelding would find his way back to the paddock, or whoever John sent to round up the animals would find him between here and there. John . . .

Sweet Christ, it wasn't possible. When he thought of all the destruction that had been wrought on this day, Quent felt sick. To imagine that John would have caused such havoc made no more sense now than it had earlier.

Nicole was safe, though. There was no sign of any hostile's passage on the path to the glade, and when he got to the clearing it looked exactly as he'd left it. His eyes examined every tree and every square of moss before he left the protection of the encircling trees. Thank God for the empty glade. Thank God for the rain. There had been no trouble here. At least not this day.

Quent wasn't sure what had driven him to bring Nicole here. It had seemed so important, but now he couldn't rightly say why. He'd lost one love in this glade, and almost lost another. There was a spirit here. Shoshanaya had called it a *nawa*, a ruling spirit. She said it was benign and wished them no ill. She was wrong. I'm done with you, *nawa*. You're a deceitful witch. This place looks like paradise on earth, but it lies.

He made his way to the stream, seeing nothing that caused alarm. He was so wet from the downpour he didn't feel the water of the stream as he waded to the center, only the slight resistance of the swiftly moving flow. He checked the clearing and the surrounding forest one last time before he drew a deep breath and sank beneath the surface. It took some effort to swim against the current, but not a great deal. Another, stronger effort was required when he breached the falls, then he was at the mouth of the cave.

He used both hands to give himself purchase on the cave's edge and pulled his body inside. "Nicole. Don't be frightened. It's me." There was no answer. "Nicole. It's Quent. Where are you?"

He blinked the water out of his eyes and pushed his hair off his forehead. "Nicole . . ." He could see plainly now. The cave was empty. It couldn't be—she'd promised—but she was not there. "Nicole!" This time he shouted, and his voice echoed back to him from the depths of the underground passage. He hesitated, unsure whether to go back to the glade or deeper into the cave. Without light it would be pointless to try and track her in the endless blackness of the passage ahead, but she could be nowhere else. Nicole couldn't swim. She paddled a bit, but not well enough to get herself out of the cave and through the falls and into the clearing. She had to have gone deeper into the tunnel. But why? God-rotting hell, who knew why women did anything?

Quent battled his feelings of foreboding, his terror that the *nawa* had won again and taken from him the most precious thing he had. Rage boiled up inside him. What are you angry at, fool? He asked himself. A spirit? You can't outwit spirits. Deal with what you can control. Nicole was frightened. You weren't here. She couldn't swim well enough to get out through the falls so she walked into the depths of the cave. But a few feet in that direction it was black as pitch. Blacker.

Quent looked around, studying the rock walls. Years ago he and Shoshanaya had hidden tinder, and a lantern here, behind a stone. Which one?

Quent thought for a moment. So much of that time had become a blank to him. He'd made it so, otherwise the grief would have killed him. Ah yes, the one that was shaped like a tepee. It was loose, and if you pried at it a bit . . . He used his dirk and the stone came forward. There was a small opening behind it, and in it the lantern and flint and tinder box he and Shoshanaya had put there a lifetime before.

He struck a spark and coaxed the wick to kindle. There wasn't much oil. Enough for perhaps a quarter of an hour. Sometimes they'd made love in this cave, and lingered until it grew dark outside. That's what the lantern had been for, so he could see her smile when she stretched out her arms to him.

"Nicole." He called her name again and waited. There was no reply. Quent strode forward. In moments the lantern was the only light and everything behind him was darkness.

Before he'd gone a quarter of the way in the tunnel, he found Nicole kneeling on the rock floor, upright, eyes closed and arms loose at her side. She didn't react to the light of the lantern. "Nicole! Thank God. I was— Why didn't you answer? Nicole . . ."

She did not seem to hear him. Quent put down the lantern and went toward her. When he touched her she shuddered, and finally opened her eyes. He drew her upright into his arms and she made no protest, but she did not melt against him the way she had earlier. "I was so worried," he scolded, stroking her hair. "Didn't you hear me calling you? I told you to stay where I left you. Why did you come into the tunnel?"

"I was following the light."

"There is no light. Not until you've gone a league and a half, and then you're out by Swallows Children. It's very dangerous if you don't know— Nicole, I was so . . . I thought I'd lost you."

He gave up being angry and murmured the last words against the top of her head. She made no reply, unmoving in his arms. He decided it was the shock that had made her forget that back there, in the glade, before Sampson came crashing through, everything had changed between them. No matter; later, when things were normal again, he'd remind her. "It's all right now," he soothed. "It's raining, pouring in fact. The fires are out and the Indians rode off the way they came. We've got to get back to the big house. I'll be needed."

"I followed the light," she repeated. Quent pretended not to hear.

"Some half part of the wheat crop is destroyed." Ephraim avoided meeting the eyes of the forty or so people looking at him. "And all the hay. The sawmill is burned to the ground. Most of the saws are completely useless; one, High Josiah, may be salvageable." All the saws had come from England with his father and all had names. High Josiah was the pendulum saw that hung on leather thongs from the topmost rafters of the mill. There were no blades anywhere in the colonies to equal those that had been ruined. He'd have to send to London for replacements, and build a new sawmill to house them. It would take upwards of a year before they were back to the place they'd been just this morning, before the disaster of this day. And all these poor devils, white and black alike, gathered here in the great hall of the big house as if it were the church Lorene tried to make it Sunday mornings, they were all staring at him as if they expected some pronouncement that would make the horror of it disappear.

God-cursed savages. May they burn in eternal hellfire. Every one of them. Even the one he'd thought he couldn't do without. Mostly her. He thought of her dainty bones, picked clean of flesh long since, lying in the earth up there at Squirrel Oaks. It was Lorene who had insisted a Potawatomi whore be buried with the dead of the Patent. For Cormac's sake. And by then it was Lorene who truly grieved for her. Not him, not then and not now. He hated her.

It was because of Pohantis that his youngest son, the best he'd produced, was someone other than the man he'd been born to be. If it hadn't been for her, for the fire she kindled in both of them, him and Lorene, Quent wouldn't have been sent to live with the Indians every summer during his boyhood, wouldn't have turned out more red than white. Ephraim tried to push the thoughts away. The household, men and women, slaves and tenants, his flesh and blood, all of them were waiting for him to say something that would give this terrible day some meaning, make it something they could understand.

This ought to be the moment when I tell them Quent's in charge, that he'll take over the Patent when I'm gone and they'll all be out from under John's stupid, bloody fist. They respect Quent. Hellfire, most of them love him. He could say it right now, but God help him, he dare not. No matter what Lorene said, he could not be sure that Quent had changed.

Damn the past. Damn the Potawatomi for making Quent more like them than his own kind. Look at him, standing over there in the shadows. Talking to one of the slaves as if she were an equal. Granted, it's Sally Robin and she's the equal of any woman ever born. Hell, the better of most. But I would never allow her to know I think that. Quent lets it show. As if the coloreds, red or black, are the same as whites. Stupid to blame the Indians. It's my doing. Because of Pohantis, and Lorene, the way we all were back then. Damn the past, bury it in everlasting hell. It's now that counts. Quent's wearing buckskins again; he's got his long gun and his tomahawk. Could be he's simply prepared for more trouble . . . But I know he's bloody well planning something, and that it's not good for the Patent. Or at least, that the Patent doesn't come first.

Ephraim shifted his focus to John, who was sneaking curious glances at his brother when he thought no one would notice. Ephraim caught something in John's eyes. Pure hatred. He felt the weight of it all. So much loss and grief. So many wrong turnings. And God help him, standing here this long was killing him. His arms were on fire and the two sticks felt as if they might be flaming swords. He didn't have much longer, he knew that. This business would likely speed the end. No bad thing that; he was tired, ready to go. And the sticks weren't going to hold him up much longer. He'd best get on with it.

"Ephraim," Lorene appeared at his shoulder. Her voice was a murmur, loud enough only for him. "Let me tell them to bring you a chair."

"No. I'm fine. Go on with your business."

Lorene and the big house slaves were busy. As if doing would keep them from feeling. Kitchen Hannah had stirred up her fire hours before, the moment she knew there was trouble. Now there were bannocks and biscuits and salt-rising bread hot from the bake oven built into the wall beside the hearth. Stacks of johnnycakes had come off the griddle stone. Lorene was overseeing the passing of the food along with mugs of ale. "Johnnycakes for the slaves as well," she'd told Runsabout a few minutes before. "And ale if they like. Buttermilk if they prefer." The blacks were as soot-blackened and blaze-weary as the rest.

They were all there, Lorene noted, everyone who lived on the Patent except for the Quakers up at Do Good, who were too far away and doubtless didn't yet know what had happened. The whites sat up front and the slaves were crowded into the back of the room the way they were most Sundays when she conducted services. But everyone was watching Ephraim with a look they never turned on her—as if he held the answers to the meaning of the senseless slaughter, the devastation. Not all. Ely Davidson was staring straight ahead. Lorene moved to him and put a hand on his shoulder. "How's that bandage keeping, Ely?"

He nodded a wordless reply. Lorene lay a finger on the forehead wound; it was cool to her touch. She'd used one of Sally Robin's unguents meant to ward off pustulating eruptions. Sally was off in a corner speaking urgently to Quent. Lorene considered working her way over toward them, but Ephraim's voice stopped her.

"Eight horses are missing." He continued his litany of destruction. "Two were badly burned and had to be put down. The rest, I fear, are gone for good. Seven slaves are dead. That's a quarter part of the stock. Two were mere children. Lilac and Sugar Willie had a lifetime of labor left." Lorene heard a choked sob behind her. Ephraim seemed to have forgotten that Runsabout was the mother of the twins. "And then there is the personal loss," he said, clearly excluding Runsabout and the other slaves from such delicacy of feeling. "The sawyer's entire family. You have our deepest sympathy, Ely."

Ephraim paused while Moses Frankel and his kin nodded in the direction of Davidson. They looked embarrassed to have been the lucky ones, Ephraim thought. The sugarhouse and the gristmill were unharmed and every one of the Frankels was alive. They'd lost a few of their best workers; Big Jacob was a particularly terrible loss. Not a black or a white anywhere who knew more about horseflesh than Big Jacob. That white-haired slave over there pouring an ale for John, that was Deliciousness May as he recalled. Considered herself married to Big Jacob. Ephraim was never quite sure what that meant among the blacks. Still . . . "How did this happen?" he asked. "How did this abomination come upon us?" They were all waiting for him to answer his own question. Damned fools. If he knew the answer he'd be doing something about it, not just standing here counting the cost. But he couldn't go on standing. Not even his iron will could supply the strength for that. "You," he pointed to Little George, "get me a chair."

John stood up and offered his. In the few moments while Little George took it to the front of the room and helped Ephraim to sit down, his eldest son spoke. "You ask how all this happened, Father. But we know the answer to that. It was Indians. Savages. If we go to the Mohawk village we'll probably find—"

"It wasn't Mohawk that attacked us." Quent's voice cut him off.

"You can't know that for su—"

"Yes, I can and I do. I saw them, John. So did Ely. You did not. They were Huron, a band of renegades who have been banished from the longhouses of their birth. The brave leading them is a notorious killer called Lantak."

Ephraim was startled. Sweet Christ. Huron this far south. The first time they'd come to the Patent they'd intended to take something irreplaceable from the legend they called Uko Nyakwai. And they had. What motive did Huron renegades have to attack Shadowbrook this time? "You recognized this Lantak?" Ephraim asked. He leaned forward and studied his younger son.

"I did."

"So you got close enough to tell one savage from another," John said, "but I don't imagine this Lantak's dead, or you'd have said so."

"He got away." There was a murmur of surprise around the room. No one was supposed to get away when he was in Uko Nyakwai's sights. Quent ignored the hum of disappointment. "According to what Sally Robin here's been telling me, it's worse still. Lantak took Solomon the Barrel Maker with him."

"Solomon, he be dead." It was Sampson, speaking up from the back. "Right away when it all started, when we was haying, Mr. Quent. 'Fore I ran away and happened on you. Solomon, he went after that savage with a pitchfork, and the savage he threw a hatchet at him, and Solomon, he fell down. I saw."

"Solomon don't be dead. Least he wasn't." Sally Robin closed her eyes when she spoke, as if she were seeing it all again. "That tomahawk just hurt Solomon in his shoulder. He bled mightily, but I was with him and we walked right out of that field what was on fire, to the big road. We couldn't go fast—Solomon was too weak for that—but we walked a goodly ways."

"Where were you going?" It was John who asked the question. "And how come the savages didn't take you as well?"

"I don't rightly know the answer to either of them questions, Master John. Only that we was going in the opposite way to the fire and the savages, but they caught up with us anyway. They was on horses, and one of 'em, he rode right up to where we was and he dragged Solomon up on his horse and rode away."

"And left you behind."

"Yes. I sang my I-ain't-feared song and them savages heard it and left me be. Only my song don't be big enough to protect Solomon same as me." Two big tears were rolling down Sally Robin's cheeks. Quent wasn't sure she knew she was crying. She started to hum, very softly.

"I'm going after Lantak," Quent said.

Ephraim sighed. It was time to find out if things were as they had always been, if Quent were more Indian than white, or if, as Lorene insisted, their youngest boy had changed. "No, you are not," he said quietly. "We need you here, Quentin. Shadowbrook needs you here."

"I have to go, Father. If Lantak—"

Ephraim had propped his sticks against the hearth. Now he reached for them and struggled to his feet. "I don't give a damn about Lantak. I care about the Patent. Bringing the punishment he deserves to this renegade Huron may make you feel considerably better, Quentin. It may serve your sense of honor, and add to your reputation among the savages, and console you for letting him get away in the first place. It will not put one more sack of wheat aboard one more ship. Our survival depends on how clever we are in the next few weeks, and how hard we work. Whatever code you may have learned in all the time you've spent with the Indians, it's useless here among civilized men. We have a living to make and a holding to protect. The Patent comes before anything else."

"It's nothing to do with revenge." At that moment, more than anything else in the world, he wanted his father to understand.

"With what then?"

It was as if father and son were alone, Lorene realized. They were finally saying what they had not said for years. She looked about for Nicole, but couldn't see her now. If she was correct, Nicole was the tether that would hold Quent on the land. But she had to be present.

Sally Robin was still humming so quietly Quent thought he might be the only one who heard. He knew if he explained about Solomon and Lantak and why he had to go, she would suffer more. But if he did not, his father would never understand. "Lantak won't just kill Solomon. And he won't hold him for ransom. He will . . ." His parents and his brother were all looking at him, waiting. "Lantak will torture Solomon to death. Very slowly, over a very long time." Sally Robin hummed a little louder, a little faster. Quent couldn't look at her.

Ephraim took a moment or two to absorb the words. "That's a filthy business," he said finally. "I regret that it is so. But it changes nothing."

"It changes everything. I can't let Solomon be—"

"He is property, Quentin. We have lost much valuable property this day. As I said, I regret it all."

"Solomon is a man, damn it! A human being."

"I bought him. Do you not think that I—"

"You bought his labor. Good God, Father, you cannot—"

"Quentin." Ephraim stared at his son, at the Patent's best chance for a future, maybe the only chance. "Until now I have not pointed out that once before, Huron came here and did terrible things. That was all to do with you and yours and no one asked you for any explanation. I am asking for none now. I am only stating an irrefutable fact. You are needed here on the Patent. At Shadowbrook. Are you staying?"

It was the final question, and the only one that mattered. Quent looked for Nicole and couldn't find her. The pain of leaving without seeing her one more time, without explaining, was a truly physical thing. He could feel it in his heart. No matter, she would be safe here. Whatever Lorene thought of him, however angry she was about his leaving, she would take care of Nicole.

His mother was in fact staring at him as intently as if she were trying to see into his soul. John, too. They had different goals and different expectations, but both realized what was at stake as well as he did. He'd planned to talk to his father again, say he would stay if. . . . His birthright, the Hale Patent and everything he had loved best almost from the first breath he drew was at risk. Nicole might wait for him; nothing else would. No matter, he had to go. Quent turned and walked away.

Book 2

The World That Came from the Belly of the Fish

1754–1756

Chapter Twelve

THE TELLING OF THE GREAT HEAT MOON
THE VILLAGE OF SINGING SNOW

"HAYA, HAYA . . . At that time we Potawatomi and the Ojibwe and the Ottawa were one people, one Fire Nation." Ixtu the Teller chanted the words in the same tone as had every Teller in the long line that preceded him.

"*Haya, haya, jayek,*" the listeners chanted in response. So, so, all of us together.

It was evening, and the hard, dry earth gave back the relentless heat it had absorbed during the day. Sweat ran down the faces of the people of the village of Singing Snow. Their bodies glistened with it, old men and braves and squaws and children. "*Haya, haya, jayek.*" So, so, all of us together. In the Circle of Telling.

"At that time," Ixtu told, "each morning when the sun returned, we were the first *Anishinabeg* he saw. Then the sun grew tired of looking at us and he came less and less often, and the world grew cold and our braves could find no game and our squaws could find no fish and no berries, and there was only grass to eat. Then we and our brothers the Ojibwe and the Ottawa said, 'When the sun comes next, let us follow it.' And so we did. The Fire Nation followed the sun."

"*Haya, haya, jayek.*"

The rhythm of the response, like the rhythm of the Telling, had become part of Cormac. Some days before, he had exchanged his buckskins for a breechclout made of deerskin and decorated with the porcupine symbols that identified him as a Potawatomi warrior. His body was tanned a dark bronze. He wore beaded bracelets on his wrists and ankles, and three eagle feathers in hair that hung free, not tied behind the way he wore it when he was in the white world. "*Haya, haya, jayek.*" His blood pulsed to the rhythm of the chant and the Telling, matching the blood rhythms of the others. "*Haya, haya, jayek.*" So, so, all of us together.

Ixtu had begun his story at sundown. Before that he had picked up an ember from the Sacred Fire that came from the First Fire, and carried the smoldering piece of wood in his bare hand to the place he'd chosen for this Telling. Then he built the New Moon Fire from the old, and the people of Singing Snow gathered around it and listened to the history of the world.

As always the Teller began with how Shkotensi, the Great Spirit, created fire in the belly of Abigigos, the first fish, and how Abigigos swam until he came to the end of the ocean and fell to the earth. There he opened his mouth and the fire came out, and after it the People of the Fire. Now the new moon was high overhead and Ixtu had come to the part of the story that told what happened when the Fire Nation left their traditional homeland near the Great Salt Water and began their migration west, or in the story words, in the sun-going direction.

Ixtu paused to gather his thoughts. He always paused at just this place.

"*Haya, haya, jayek,*" the listeners chanted. So, so, all of us together.

Now a kind of humming was added to the affirmation and the people in the circle began to sway side to side, everyone keeping to the same rhythm. Cormac gave himself entirely to the music and the movement and the story that was told at every New Moon. He had heard it many times before, spoken in exactly the same way, using exactly the same words, but that did not matter. It was always the first time. He had no thoughts in his head that were not also the thoughts of the others humming and swaying either side of him, and no questions Ixtu could not answer.

A woman began beating a small storytelling drum. When he heard the drum Ixtu began to speak again. He told how the Potawatomi separated themselves from the Ottawa and the Ojibwe, and how the Fire Nation became three brother nations. He told how the Potawatomi, who were called the People of the Place of the Fire, learned to put seeds in the earth and make things grow so they would not starve even when there was no meat and no fish and no berries. He told how the *Cmokmanuk,* the whites, came, and how at first the Potawatomi hid themselves and did not look at them, but eventually they did. And when the *Cmokmanuk* asked for beaver skins and offered to trade for them, the Potawatomi, like the other tribes, used their great hunting prowess to get beaver skins, and how they came to cherish the *Cmokmanuk* things they got in exchange. But the *Cmokmanuk* never had enough. They demanded more and more skins. And the *Anishinabeg,* too, wanted more and more trade, until almost no beaver could be found and the Real People made war on each other over what was left.

"*Haya, haya, jayek.*" So, so, all of us together.

Next Ixtu told how those not killed by their traditional enemies were killed by the *Cmokmanuk* sicknesses. By then there were three drums, all beating to the rhythm of the group's collective heart.

From the moment when the Telling began, Ixtu had sat cross-legged on the ground, his voice doing all the moving, his body still. Now he staggered to his feet.

His old legs trembled with the pain of standing after such a long time in one position, but they held him. "At that time, Insigison the wise chief took a band of the Potawatomi away from the fighting and the sickness. They traveled in the suncoming direction until they returned to the land they had left long before. So Insigison brought the fire and the People of the Place of the Fire to this place."

"*Haya, haya, jayek. Haya, haya, jayek.*"

The drums beat faster. Cormac's heart kept pace with them and he could feel the heartbeats of the others doing the same. "At that time, when Insigison and the braves and the squaws who had followed him arrived here, it was during the Long Night Moon. The ground was covered with snow and Insigison could not see if this was a place where the seeds would grow to make food that would prevent famine, or if the hunting would be good, or if there were fish swimming in streams or bushes with berries. None of them could see anything but snow and Insigison was not sure he was in the right place. At that time, the father of my father's father's father, Axtu, was the Teller. And he said, 'This is the place we are meant to be. There is no doubt.' And Insigison questioned the wisdom of old Axtu. 'How do you know that?' he asked. 'I know it,' Axtu said, 'because I can hear the snow singing.' So even though they were many, many sun's journey from any others of the Fire Nation, Insigison and his people let the fire they had brought with them burn in this place. And it was our fifth fire, the fifth home-place of the journey that began when the three peoples were one. And in honor of Axtu they named the place Singing Snow."

The hours passed and Ixtu continued the Telling, reciting the happy stories of many successful hunts that set out from this village, and many bountiful crops, and of times of weeping when many braves were killed on the hunt or in raids made by their enemies or raids they made, and when there was drought and the crops did not grow and the people, all but the strongest of them, starved, the youngest children, of course, dying first. Until finally when it seemed he must be too exhausted to speak another word and it was almost morning, he told the tale of Thunder Moon, the moon before this Great Heat Moon. "At that time the squaw Sohantes gave birth to three children, all at the same time and all sons."

"*Haya, haya, jayek.*" So, so, all of us together. "*Haya, haya, jayek.*"

Sohantes sat across the circle from the Teller, her three infants strapped to her back in a carrier specially made for her because nothing like this had ever happened in the village before, and chanted with the rest.

All of us together, she thought, but this is my part of the story. Forever.

"And Sohantes was the wife of the chief Kekomoson," Ixtu intoned. "And he had no other wife but her, and he had promised not to take her sister as another wife as long as Sohantes lived. When the other women told him what had happened in the birthing house, Kekomoson went out and found a fat buck standing alone on the top of a hill, and Kekomoson killed it with one arrow so perfectly shot it went directly to the killing spot between the buck's eyes. Then Kekomoson gave a great feast to celebrate this thing that no one remembered seeing before, three sons all born together."

"*Haya, haya, jayek. Haya, haya, jayek.*"

Kekomoson sat beside the Teller, in the place of honor because he was the chief. He did not let his face show how pleased he was to have found a place in the Telling.

"*Haya, haya, jayek.*"

Ixtu was coming to the end. He looked once at the sky. Still gray, but lighter than before. Soon he would know if he had correctly performed the Teller's most important duty. If he had failed he would walk away into the wilderness, taking nothing with him and eating nothing and drinking nothing, and when he could walk no more he would sit down and wait to die. Great Spirit, grant that I may die beside the fire with my brothers, not alone, parched and starving in a far place.

"And that is the story of the Real People of Singing Snow. Until the time of this Great Heat Moon."

"*Haya, haya, jayek.*" So, so, all of us together.

The humming ended and the drums stopped. The sky was streaked with pink now, and the sliver of new moon had disappeared behind the encircling hills. The people waited. Each New Moon Circle of Telling was held in a slightly different place and the sacred fire was set to burn where the Teller said it was to be. Only at the end of the night did the people know if the place had been chosen wisely, if the New Moon would bring them safety and prosperity, or if the Teller had failed them and they were cursed. At last, the red-orange sun peeked over the horizon. The people held their collective breath and waited.

The first low-angled rays of the sun reached the earth and touched the Sacred Fire of Shkotensi, the Fifth Fire of the Potawatomi of Singing Snow. Happiness rippled around the Circle of Telling. *Ayi! Ayi!* Ixtu thought. It is good. If I die before the next Telling it will be here, on soft skins, with water to drink and, if I want it, corn to eat. Or even meat. *Ahaw,* yes, the Great Spirit is good.

"*Haya, haya, jayek.*" All was well. "*Haya, haya, jayek.*" So, so, all of us together.

Only one thing remained to be done. At every New Moon Telling, Ixtu added words to the story. They would become sacred words, never to be changed, always to be repeated. The people waited, humming softly, and after a time Ixtu spoke again. "And at that time, the Telling of the Great Heat Moon," he turned his bent old body so he was facing Cormac, "the people were happy because the bridge person, who was called by the name of the mighty warrior of his father's people and by no other name, to signify that he is different from all others, the bridge person, returned to Singing Snow after being long away. And the bridge person was present at the Telling, and he listened with respect and his heart beat with the others. So the people knew he was truly their son and their brother."

"*Haya, haya, jayek.*"

It was done.

"So nothing important happened this moon and you got a place in the Telling," Bishkek, Cormac's manhood father, told him later. "Don't let your head grow to fit a warbonnet because of that. You have been too long away and I am shamed that you forget your home village and your old father."

"I have never forgotten you, Father, and Singing Snow is always in my heart. But much has been happening in the white world. I could not get away as soon as I liked."

"And what about my other white-face son, your brother? Why does he not come to see me? Does he, too, forget me?"

"I am sure he does not, Father. But his birth father is dying and he must stay with him until the spirit leaves the old man's body."

Bishkek nodded. "That is the correct thing to do. But when it's over he must come at once and pay his respect to his manhood father. That too is correct. Does my other white son know this?"

"I believe he does, Father. He will come. When it is over." Cormac paused. "If he can."

"And why could he not?" Bishkek knew that Cormac spoke with purpose and he asked the questions he hoped would help the younger man say what he wanted to say. "Is my other white son suddenly stupid in his head so he cannot do his duty? Are his legs no longer able to carry him? Has he forgotten how to find his way through the woods and across the rivers and streams that separate us?"

"None of those things have happened, Father. But there is talk of war."

"Not among us," Bishkek said sadly. "The *Anishinabeg* are no longer strong enough to make war on each other. Not real war. They fight like they fart, without warning and with no plan, except maybe to make a little stink. Worse, they allow themselves to be hired killers for the whites. So who makes war? The English? War on Onontio?" Bishkek spat on the ground to take the taste away.

"Yes. At least I think they are going to. Very soon now the English and the French will fight. To the death, probably. And if such a war is to start, it is possible that Kwashko"—he used Quent's manhood name of Jumps Over Fire—"will not be able to come to Canada, because he is English, but—"

Bishkek snorted. "That is nonsense. Kwashko is Uko Nyakwai, is he not? How can a red bear be unable to come here? Disgusting name," he added under his breath. "How can my son permit they call him that?"

The Potawatomi hated bears. Once, according to the storytellers, a bear had killed the son of a Potawatomi chief and neither ate him nor left him where he fell so he could be buried with dignity. Instead the bear pulled the body of the young brave apart and left the pieces scattered everywhere. Such an insult demanded vengeance and to this day the Potawatomi killed any bear they could capture, slowly, painfully, and with much taunting. That Kwashko, who was a true Potawatomi and truly Bishkek's son, should be called a bear—and in the tongue of the snakes, to boot—was something the old man could never accept.

Cormac knew Bishkek's thoughts on the subject; it was an argument for another day. "Father, *giyabwe*." I had a dream.

Ayi! At last they were getting somewhere. "And it is this dream that brought you home?" Bishkek picked up a stick and began idly drawing lines and swirls on the ground. There had been little rain all summer and the earth was covered with a thick layer of dust.

"*Ahaw*." Yes. Cormac was ashamed to admit any motive other than a desire to see his village and his manhood father, but he would not lie.

"Then it was a good dream," Bishkek said mildly, for once not chiding him.

"*Co*." Cormac shook his head. "I do not think it was."

"*Ktakagikto*." Tell me.

"*Sheyoshke. Penshiyuk. Mskwe*, everywhere *mskwe*," Cormac said. A bird flying fast, a hawk. And little birds. And blood. Everywhere blood. "In the end," he added, *wapshkayakmko*." A white bear.

Bishkek stopped what he was doing with the stick and looked directly at Cormac. "*Neni*. Your mother."

Cormac shook his head. "*Co! Cozhena neneyum!*" I never dream of her.

Again Bishkek spat on the ground. "That is *Cmokmanuk* talk, the words of white men who know no better. A dream comes to you. You do not invite it. It is not for you to decide what it will be. Your mother was she of the white bearskins. Always. Tell me more of the dream."

Cormac explained about the hawk and the birds and the river of blood. "Then the white bear came and the hawk flew away. The bear was somehow protecting the birds."

Bishkek made a sound in his throat. "*Ahaw*," he agreed. "Then perhaps it was not your mother." In her whole life Pohantis had never protected anyone but herself. She was a whore, giving herself to anyone who wanted her, not because she admired them or cared for them, only to get what she wanted. Since she was a child she'd never been any different. Like the women of the snakes. Such behavior was unacceptable among the Potawatomi. The only reason Singing Snow had taken her back after she ran away with the white gun trader was because she brought them a bridge person, a son who was half white and half Potawatomi, and the elders thought that such a person would be useful. *Ahaw*. That was a good decision. Better still was the decision to give Pohantis to the other white man who wanted her, and that way get white training into the head of my half-white manhood son. Now Cormac is truly a red man in a white skin. Surely the future must belong to such men as him. He listened very carefully as his son told him the last of the dream. A white wolf, *wabnum,* loped out of the forest and toward the bear.

"That part is easy. You are *wabnum.*"

"Yes, I know. But I woke up before the wolf attacked." Cormac lowered his gaze and did not ask the final question—who would win, the wolf or the bear? He felt Bishkek's eyes studying him and he wondered if the old man had any more idea than he did of what the dream meant. It had seemed so important to come here and tell his story. *Ahaw,* but now that he was here, what had he accomplished? His manhood father offered no explanations, just stared at him. He seemed to be looking at the place where Cormac had hidden Memetosia's gift, strapped to his thigh and hidden by his breechclout.

It was not for Cormac to break the silence and for a long time Bishkek didn't speak. Around them people moved slowly in the growing heat of the morning. Because of the New Moon Telling no one had slept the previous night. Now it was too warm and airless to go into the wickiups, the dome-shaped houses built of bent sapling frames covered with bark. Most of the braves and squaws snored softly under whatever shade they could find. One woman nursed an infant and another sat watching a group of sleeping children and grinding corn in a huge bowl made of a single maple tree burl, using a rounded stone. It was a peaceful scene, but neither man had any difficulty imagining it engulfed in a river of blood. Both knew too much of the history of the *Anishinabeg.*

"Is that all?" Bishkek asked finally. "There is nothing more to tell of this dream?"

"That's all of the dream. But there was something else. Something that happened while I was not exactly awake, but not sleeping either."

"*Ktakagikto.*" Tell me.

Cormac repeated what the Miami chief Memetosia had told him, and told of the blind Midè priest Takito, and the sweat lodge, and all that had happened after he went inside. Bishkek listened in silence. When Cormac finished, Bishkek took up the stick again and drew lines and swirls in the dust. "There is something you are not telling me. And something hidden there beneath your breechclout. That is not the bulge of your manhood I am seeing."

"Bishkek is wise as always."

"And my bridge person son does not lie. So what is this unsaid thing between us?"

"A gift, Father. From Memetosia." He lay his hand over his thigh. "It is a great mystery to me. I do not know what the gift means or what I am to do with it. A medicine bag containing the black wampum called Suckáuhock."

Bishkek's eyes opened very wide. "Such a gift must be very ancient."

"*Ahaw*, it is." Cormac looked around. No one seemed to be paying them any attention. He started to reach beneath his breechclout, but Bishkek held up his hand.

"*Co*. I do not wish to see this thing. It is better not to look on mysteries. Memetosia gave the Suckáuhock to you, not to me. I do not have to burden my eyes with it. The Midè priest, you are sure he was called Takito?"

"That's what my friend the Piankashaw métisse called him."

"And it was in the home of this so-called friend that your gun was stolen after you left it as a sign of respect, and a Huron arrived from nowhere to try and kill you?"

"It wasn't Genevieve's fault," Cormac said stubbornly. "I don't believe she had anything to do with it."

Bishkek nodded and wrapped his arms around himself and rocked back and forth for a time. "Let me think on this thing, the dream and everything else," he said finally. "Go and sleep."

Cormac found a place in the shadow of a spruce that had been bent to the direction of the prevailing wind. The shade beneath it was deep; he lay down and felt comforted by the pungent familiar smell of the resin that was used in the making of the Potawatomi canoes, which were the best to be had in both the white world and the red. He fell asleep the moment he closed his eyes. When he opened them a squaw, her face entirely covered with tattoos, was staring down at him, holding a knife with the sharp point aimed directly at his heart.

"Do not move," Bishkek's voice said. "Not even a single eyelash."

Cormac knew beyond any doubt that his manhood father would never betray him, so he did exactly as he was told. The woman holding the knife moved it in slow circles, the sharp point aimed always at Cormac's heart. After a time she changed her position and the whole-skin otter medicine bag she wore around her neck came into view. Another Midè priest putting Midewiwin magic into him. It was supposed to be a healing thing, but he'd known nothing but unease since he met Takito. Cormac wanted this squaw priest to stop doing what she was doing, and he was on the verge of saying so when the priest began her chant. *Wa hi, hi, hi . . . Haya, haya, ahseni. . .* That was the chant he remembered from the sweat lodge. *Haya, haya, ahseni . . .*

After a time the priest stood up and murmured something to Bishkek, who listened, then said, "Get up, my son. This part of the ceremony is finished."

Cormac struggled to his feet. He was still tired. And his head felt stuffed with wool. Most of the village was yet asleep, so not too much time could have gone by. Where had Bishkek found a Midè priest so quickly? None had been at the ceremony the night before.

"This priest is called Shabnokis. She lives alone near here and comes when we need her." As usual Bishkek had anticipated the questions in Cormac's mind. Always *Cmokmanuk* questions. Why? How? Which happened first? Which later? Why that way and not some other way? It was the white part of this son that made him ask such things. Shabnokis is here. What does it matter how she came to be here? It matters not at all to me or to other Anishinabeg, but to this bridge person, yes, it matters. He cannot help it. He is as he is. "I went and asked her to come," Bishkek explained. "Because of what you told me."

Cormac said nothing. A Midè priest was involved in all the trouble. Another Midè priest might be able to explain why.

"This Takito, I know of him," Shabnokis said. "But I have never met him. He is very old and we are from different lodges."

"Why would he send someone to kill my bridge person son who had done him no harm?" Bishkek asked.

"I do not know that."

This priest was missing three fingers of her right hand, Cormac noted. Maybe less was demanded of the squaw priests of the Midewiwin. "I'm told there are many differences in your lodges."

"Not differences in our magic or our cures. But other things, yes, they are different."

"Why did you point your knife at me?"

Bishkek made a sound in his throat. *Ayi!* This son will offend the priest with his *Cmokmanuk* questions. Then where will we be? "You say 'why' too often," he scolded. "The priest is wise, listen to her."

Cormac understood his manhood father's annoyance. Bishkek had asked a question to which he had no answer while he, Cormac, questioned the actions and decisions of the priest. The first was acceptable, the second was not. All the same, it was important to him to know, and Bishkek understood that the point of a bridge was to travel in two directions. Whether the squaw priest did or not didn't matter. "Your knife," he repeated, ignoring Bishkek's reprimand, "why were you holding it over me?"

The woman crouched down and spat on the ground, then drew her finger through the spittle, making symbols only she understood. "If this Takito put bad magic into you, I would draw it out. With my knife. Otherwise, if I was not strong enough, the knife would be sucked into your heart."

"By the bad magic?"

The woman nodded. *"Ahaw."*

"That's a poor bargain."

"You are still alive," she said, smiling.

"But am I alive because your magic was stronger than Takito's, or because—"

"There was no bad magic in you. Or at least very little. It was not difficult to keep the knife away from you."

"In that case," Bishkek said, "this Takito meant my son no harm. What of the Huron who tried to kill him?"

"You have not told me why your son thinks that happened."

"It happened," Bishkek said. "It is for the priests to tell us why."

"I think," Shabnokis said, "that because the leaves of a tree turn red in the time of the Great Heat moon does not always mean the tree is a sumac." She gestured with her head to the place where a number of the stubby sumac trees grew. Leaf-falling time was two months away for other trees, still some weeks away for the sumac, but the leaves were already scarlet. Fair enough, but what possible connection could there be between sumac trees and what had happened in the sweat lodge?

"Red leaves can be found in many places," Shabnokis said. Then she stood up and walked away.

WEDNESDAY, AUGUST 26, 1754
SHADOWBROOK

Quent had known for some time that he was being watched; since he left the big house in fact. It wasn't Lantak or one of his renegade butchers. They were still far ahead of him. Besides, if it had been, the attack would have come long since. He'd had enough of vigilance and waiting; it was time to lure whoever it was into the open.

He knelt beside the stream he'd been following at a brisk trot and washed his face, then dipped his leather-covered tin flask into the water. While it filled, he carefully looked around. Yes, over there on the left. Whoever it was, was crouched behind that low stand of juniper. It was the stream, Quent realized, that was the attraction. His stalker was thirsty, really thirsty, with that lust for water that pretty much overcomes everything else. Even caution, and the fear of Uko Nyakwai's long gun.

The bubbles stopped rising from the mouth of the flask. Quent lifted it out of the water, conscious of the fact that the sounds he was making would inflame the stalker's thirst even more, and carefully, taking his time, bunged the cork stopper into position. He left the canteen under a tree—a thick-trunked old elm on the other side of the clearing from the juniper, then made a great show of stretching and yawning. Quent reached for the drawstring that held up his trousers, untying it as he moved off away from the stalker and the stream to relieve himself.

The surrounding forest was the usual mix of hardwood and conifers. The needles of the evergreens made a thick carpet covering the earth, soundless beneath his moccasins. He circled around and approached the stream from the right. And saw exactly what he expected to see. Someone was kneeling beside the wat— Sweet Jesus. He was looking at a ghost.

For a moment he couldn't focus. Quent rubbed his eyes, trying to clear away the shock-induced fog. Pohantis was dead. He'd stood next to the grave when they lowered her body into it and helped shovel in the dirt. He'd told Cormac that he was glad she was gone because she was a whore. And all the time he'd been sobbing inside, thinking not of his father but of his mother, and the way, when she thought no one could see, she would slip her hand into Pohantis's, and Pohantis would raise that hand to her breast. Then he and Corm had fought, and Quent had scarred his brother's face for life and— Pohantis was dead. It wasn't she kneeling here by the stream, dressed in white bearskin scooping water into her mouth as if she'd die if she didn't get enough.

Quent raised his gun to his shoulder and released the hammer. "Get up real slow and turn around." He spoke in English, then repeated the words in Mohawk Iroquois. Because, God blast it, the squaw couldn't be Pohantis, and this was Mohawk country. "*Desatga hade nyah.*"

Nicole stopped with her cupped hands halfway to her mouth. She allowed the water they held to trickle back into the stream, then got to her feet and turned around. "Don't shoot me, please."

Quent lowered his gun, but he moved no closer to where she stood. "In God's name . . . How did you get here?"

"I followed you. As soon as you changed back into your buckskins, I knew you meant to leave and go after the savages who attacked the Patent. But you made me a promise and you must keep it. You must, Quent." She wasn't pleading, she was stating a fact. "You must take me north. I cannot go without you, and it is imperative that I get to Québec at once."

"What do you mean you followed me? Are you saying you're the one who's been tracking me since last night? Since I left the house?" She nodded and he had no choice but to believe her.

Sweet Jesus. Twelve hours at least, and he'd kept up a steady trot, without a break. He'd never have imagined she could maintain such a pace. "What about those clothes?" he demanded. "Where did you get them?"

"I found the clothes some time ago, in the room where your maman keeps the household linens. I think you must have known they were there, since you gave me the moccasins."

"Yes, I knew. But—"

"I had to take them," she interrupted. "I left a note for Madame Hale, to apologize. But I could not go off with you, wearing one of the beautiful dresses she gave me. I thought you would take a horse. I would need—" She glanced down at Pohantis's leggings.

"You can't ride a horse in woods like these." He nodded toward the thick forest all around them. "The Indians will take a different route, but I know where they're headed. I'll get there faster on foot."

"All the same, to go with you these are better clothes."

"You cannot go with me whatever you're wearing. Do you have any idea what I'm about to— No, of course you don't. But that doesn't matter either. You have to return to the house, Nicole. We're still on the Patent. It's safe enough."

"I do not know my way back. I told you, I followed you; I didn't pay attention to the trail. And how safe can it be if a band of murdering savages attacked us?"

"You can't come with me. It's out of the question."

"I kept up with you all night and most of this morning. And you didn't know I was there." She couldn't keep the pride from her voice. She had kept up with Uko Nyakwai, the Red Bear. She'd driven herself to the point of almost total exhaustion, to where she thought she couldn't take another step, and then she'd taken ten more. And not once had she forgotten the woods lore she had learned from Quent and Monsieur Shea in six weeks of trekking with them. How to be silent, how to stay close enough to see but not be seen. "I kept up."

"Yes, you did." He had to admit his admiration for what she'd done. Wrong and pointless though it was, it was remarkable, and she was indeed what he'd suspected from the first moment he saw her up close, ripping up her petticoat to stanch the blood of a wounded soldier. Much woman. Very much woman.

"And you didn't know I was there."

He couldn't let her continue to believe that. Not because of his pride but because to overestimate your strength is to be weak. "I knew someone was there. Only not that it was you." Still, she deserved to know how well she'd done. "I thought it was a man."

She needed to sit down. The water had helped, but she had eaten only the few mouthfuls she could grab as they passed by some highbush blueberries. She needed desperately to rest, but she couldn't give in to her need until she was sure he would take her north. "Then it's settled. You will take me to Québec. That's the direction you're going, isn't it? You're heading north." She'd remembered what he and Monsieur Shea always said, the thickest bark and the heaviest concentration of moss were on the northern side of the trunk.

"Yes, I am. But . . . Confound it, Nicole, look at you." Her face was as white as her clothes, and her legs, were trembling with fatigue. "You're half dead with thirst and exhaustion, and we're nowhere near where we have to go."

"I came all through the Ohio Country, didn't I? With you and Monsieur Shea. And you never heard me complain, or—"

"Exactly. With me and Corm. We could take turns helping you, and we weren't in that much of a hurry. But now there's a man's life at—"

"You must take me north, Quent." She would not listen to his explanations. "I must go and if you will not take me, I will go alone." She would probably die in these woods, but surely *le bon Dieu* would accept that sacrifice.

Quent watched the play of emotion on her beautiful face. He took a step in her direction and reached out for her. Nicole backed away. "Don't," she whispered. "I am sorry. Truly. But you must not."

She sounded the way she had when he'd found her in the cave behind the waterfall. He let his arms drop to his sides. "Nicole, you have to trust me. If there's to be anything real between us, anything that lasts, you have to believe that I know what's best. I can't talk about it now. Whatever the problem is, whatever you've become afraid of, I can't address it until I have gone where I have to go and done what I have to do. You must return to the house and wait for me there."

"I cannot," she repeated. "I do not know the way. I swear by Almighty God that is the truth." She made the sign of the cross to attest to her oath.

He hated the popery, and hated that she was dressed in a whore's white buckskins. "You can't go with me. I told you, it's out of the question."

"I don't want to go wherever you are going. I want you to take me north, as you promised. To Québec. Monsieur Shea made a vow. He passed the responsibility to you, and you told me it was a sacred trust, the same as if he were doing it himself. Now I am asking that you keep your word."

He was torn between wanting to spank her because she was acting like a stubborn child, and wanting to smother her with kisses. Worse, he was wasting precious minutes while Solomon . . . A solution to the stand-off came to him in a flash. Not ideal, but better than any alternative. "Very well." There would be more remonstrations he knew and probably tears, but he'd deal with them when they happened. "We'll sleep for an hour first. Then we'll go on."

She sighed, and having won, gave in to the needs of her body. The trembling spread from her legs to the rest of her, and she sank to her knees. "Quent, is it possible . . . Could we eat something before we rest?"

Christ, she must be starving. "Here, chew on this." He took a piece of dried beef from his haversack and gave it to her. "Kitchen Hannah's best jerky. Have you tried it before?"

She shook her head, concentrating on chewing. Her eagerness made him smile, and while she ate he swept pine needles into a pile to make a bed.

The jerky disappeared quickly. He had more and she was probably still hungry, but he didn't offer her another piece. Better if she didn't get too comfortable. She had to remember how difficult even this, the easiest part of the journey, had been. Later, when she was as furious with him as he knew she would be, she had to remember what it felt like when hunger gnawed at her belly and she had been parched with thirst and tired blind. He mustn't push her too far, though from the look of her she was ready for whatever he asked.

Quent felt tenderness rising like a river inside him, tempting him to take her in his arms; to turn and run back to the house and make his peace with Ephraim and claim what could be his and hers. He'd guessed his mother's scheming all along and seen the changed way his father looked at him. He pushed such thoughts away. For both their sakes. They could have no future built on the agony of Solomon the Barrel Maker, or on him turning his back on what he knew to be his duty. "Sleep now." He nodded toward the heap of pine needles. "I'll wake you in an hour and we'll go on."

"You always wake up when you tell yourself to," she said softly, remembering what he'd told her back in the Ohio Country.

"Yes, I do." He'd thought to rest a short distance away from her, leaning against the gnarled old elm. Not letting himself get too comfortable was one way he controlled the amount of time he slept. But watching her stretch out on the pine needles, with a sigh, he was suddenly hungry for her again, with the same overwhelming need he'd felt the day before in Shoshanaya's glade. Christ, had it been less than twenty-four hours? Maybe if they made love now, finished what hadn't been finished yesterday, she would know how truly she was his. Maybe it would make what was going to happen later today a little easier for her to bear. He knew he was only finding excuses to do what he wanted to do, but he couldn't stop.

Quent knelt beside her, placed his hand beside her cheek. "Nicole . . ."

She looked at him but didn't move to push him away. "No. I am sorry, but no."

"Nicole, yesterday—"

She reached up and moved his hand away from her face. "No," she repeated. "It is no longer yesterday. I am sorry."

Damn her! If she didn't want him as much as he wanted her, then so be it. He wouldn't— Ah, he wasn't being fair. She hadn't been brought up to this life—she was white, not Indian. There were conventions he couldn't expect her to overcome. At least not twice. Later, when they were married, it would be different.

He went to the elm and sat beneath it, leaning against the hard, unyielding trunk. And because he knew how much his body needed it, he closed his eyes and allowed himself the one hour's sleep he had decided was justified.

"What is this place?"

"Do Good; it's the Shadowbrook trading post. I told you about it, remember? The folks who live here are Quakers." It was the first question she'd asked since they woke and started walking again, and more words than he'd spoken since she had refused to let him touch her.

He hadn't intended to go through Do Good, but it wasn't far out of his way, and it occurred to him that Lantak and his band might have caused trouble here as well. But Do Good looked as it always did. Neat, clean. The black-on-white sign, the whitewashed meeting house, the weathered gray barns and houses: everything was exactly the same as always.

Quent pushed open the double swinging doors of the split-log trading post and walked inside. Esther Snowberry was standing behind the counter. "Good afternoon, Esther. I hoped I'd find you here." He hadn't seen Esther for five years. Her hair was entirely white now, and her face was lined.

Esther turned to him with a broad smile. "Good afternoon to thee, Quentin Hale. Of course I am here. And thee is most mightily welcome. We'd had word that thee had returned to Shadowbrook and I was hoping thee would visit us soon. Sit down and rest thyself. Thee must—" She caught sight of the woman behind him, wearing white bearskins. Long ago there had been a squaw on the Patent who wore such things, but she'd thought . . . No, this woman was young, and white, not Indian. "Perhaps thee can introduce me to thy guest, Quentin."

"This is Mademoiselle Nicole Crane," Quentin said. "I must ask permission to leave her with you, Esther. Until someone from Do Good can find the time to take her back to the big house."

Nicole whirled on him. "No! You promised, Quent! You promised!" This betrayal after he had given his word was too much, too cruel. She could not entirely choke back the tears of fury and frustration. The white-haired woman was looking at her. No doubt she believed the problem to be that Quentin Hale did not want her. As if she had thrown herself at him and he— *Mon Dieu*, forgive me. Forgive my pride. *Sainte Vierge*, help me. "Please forgive me, madame. I do not wish to be rude, but—"

"I need no title, child. I am called Esther Snowberry. And thee must not excite thyself so." The girl was distraught. There were blue circles beneath her eyes and her cheeks were sunken with fatigue. "It is no trouble to us to have thee here. My son-in-law will happily drive thee to Shadowbrook tomorrow. He will take the wagon and bring back a fresh cask of rum for our stocks here, so the journey will be as useful for us as for thee."

Nicole started to say something, but Quent cut her off as if she were a disobedient child. "I've not got a lot of time for explanations, Esther. There's been an Indian attack on the Patent, Huron renegades." He ignored her gasp of shock and went on. "They did much damage. It well may be there's no rum ready for you. But in any case Mademoiselle Crane must be returned safely to my mother's care, and I cannot take her."

"You promised," Nicole whispered. "You made a sacred vow."

"Later," he snapped, turning his head and speaking directly to Nicole. "I told you. I'll take you north later."

"Thee can settle thy business after thee has rested and eaten," Esther Snowberry said. "It is not possible to make wise decisions when thee is hungry and thirsty and without ease. Come, sit over here." She indicated the pair of benches that flanked the big fireplace. "I will send for food."

Quent started for the door, pretending to believe her words had been meant only for Nicole. "Quentin Hale." Esther's voice stopped him. "Thee can make far better time wherever thee is going with a bit of proper food in thy stomach. And it will be quicker to have it here than to find it and kill it and cook it in the woods."

Her tone did not permit defiance. He walked to the bench and sat down. The fire was banked because of the August heat, but smoldering enough so it could be revived if it were needed. Nicole sat opposite him. She did not speak. He expected her to argue further, tell him what a scoundrel he'd been, say he'd lied to her—he hadn't lied, just hadn't told her all the truth—but she only looked at him as if he were a dog turd, blast her. There was no denying that's exactly what he felt like.

"Hepsibah Jane," Esther called. A child appeared from the shadows where she'd retreated when the shouting began. "This is my Judith's girl," Esther said. Hepsibah Jane looked to be about five. She had a wooden sampler frame and a needle still in her hands, though judging from the big-eyed stare she fixed on the strangers it was a safe bet she hadn't taken a stitch for some minutes. "Go find thy mother, child. Quickly. Tell her Quentin Hale is here from the big house. With a guest. They are needing to be fed."

After the little girl left not a word was spoken by any of them. Quent and Nicole sat and tried not to look at each other. Esther busied herself among the trade goods behind the long wooden counter. When she turned back to them she held a stack of clothing. "Perhaps thee would care to try these things, Nicole Crane. If thee does not wish to wear a squaw's clothing for whatever part of thy journey lies ahead. There is a small room behind, where thee might see if these would accommodate thy needs."

Yes, that was sensible. Whatever Quent said, she had not given up. She was going to Québec, not Shadowbrook, and for what waited at the end of her journey, the white bearskins of an Indian squaw were certainly not suitable. Nicole nodded her thanks and stood up.

Esther led her toward the small storeroom in the rear. Quent rose. "Judith will come quickly, Quentin," Esther said without turning around. "Thee need not rush away thinking thee will be much delayed." He settled back on the bench.

Five minutes later Judith hurried in, carrying a basket filled to overflowing. "Thee is most welcome, Quentin Hale. It is good to see thee again."

"And you, Judith." She was expecting another child, and glowing with the prospect. "I had thought to see your slave—Prudence, as I recall. But I'm glad for the chance to say hello to you."

"Prudence is here, but she is no longer a slave," Judith explained as she unloaded the basket. "She has a house of her own and makes those calico bags." She nodded to a stack of yellow and blue drawstring bags piled high on the counter. "The Indians quite like them as trading goods."

"Not a slave?" Quent said quietly. "I'm not entirely surprised."

"It was the decision of the entire community. Many Friends are so thinking these days. We discussed it at Yearly Meeting three years past and it was agreed there would be no more slaves in Do Good. Thy father had no quarrel and no rea son to complain, since the business here is done the same as always, with or without them." She removed two large slices of meat pie from her basket as she spoke, and a pile of biscuits spread with butter. "Hepsibah said there was someone with thee. I brought enough for two now and something for thy journey so—"

"I brought a young woman, a guest of my mother. She has gone with your mother to see if some proper clothes can be found for her."

Judith looked puzzled, but Esther Snowberry appeared before her daughter found a way to voice a tactful question.

The older woman beckoned him to the back of the trading post. "Quentin, I beg thy indulgence."

He murmured, "Excuse me," to Judith, then got up and went to where Esther stood waiting.

"I apologize for discussing that of which I have no knowledge," she began, "but among us it is a good thing to speak plainly, as thee knows."

"I know. Speak your piece, Esther. I'm listening."

"That young woman is sorely tried, Quentin. She is in great need of understanding, and I fear it can come only from thee. Thee must examine thy conscience and see if there is any way thou has not dealt fairly and respectfully with her."

God help them, Esther thought he had taken advantage of Nicole, and that he was deserting her. He had no time to explain. Every moment that passed he chafed to be on the trail, prayed that Solomon would survive until he caught up with Lantak and the others. "Esther, I give you my word, I didn't— I mean there was nothing— Confound it! I've no idea how to explain."

"Thee owes no explanation to me, Quentin Hale. It is that young woman who is beside herself with dismay." She nodded toward the room behind her.

"I haven't got time right now. There's trouble, Esther. I told you—"

"Thee alone can decide where thy obligations lie, Quentin. Thee owes no explanations to me."

What was his obligation, as Esther put it? Damn! What difference did obligation make? He loved her. He wanted to marry her, but for the moment Solomon needed him a hundred times more. Nicole was an innocent, a virgin. He knew that now, and . . . Sweet Christ! How could he have been so blind? She was indeed a total innocent. And she thought that what had happened was all there was, that merely by kissing her and fondling her he had . . .

He glanced back at Judith, neatly laying out the food and pretending that nothing unusual was taking place. She looked as if she would foal any day, but she moved in a permanent, joyful glow because she had a husband and a respected place in the community. What if Nicole was worried that she might have conceived a child as a result of the caresses they had shared? What if she thought he was going off and leaving her alone with some terrible shame? It was an unbearable notion.

"Give me a moment alone with her, Esther. I'd appreciate it."

Esther Snowberry stepped aside and nodded toward the door of the small storeroom where she'd taken the girl to change her clothes.

Nicole was standing beside the window, wearing a plain gray Quaker frock. A pile of bright-colored trade goods, the homespun smocks that had been dyed red and yellow and green as the Indian women preferred, were stacked on the chair beside her. Her back was to him, and he could see that beneath an austere mobcap without so much as a ribbon or a ruffle, her hair was still in a single plait hanging down between her shoulders. "Look at me," he said. "I have to speak and there isn't much time."

She turned her lovely face to him and he wondered if he could be wrong. Her expression and bearing weren't those of a frightened young woman who thought she'd been taken advantage of, they were those of a queen. "You gave your word," she said, "and you are breaking it."

"Damn it! I'm not! Can't you understand? I'll come back and we'll be the way we were yesterday by the waterfall. I love you, Nicole. I want to marry you."

"I cannot ma—"

"Ssh. Don't say anything. Just listen to me." He took a step closer and put his hands on her shoulders. This time she didn't push him away. "Nothing happened between us yesterday that should not have happened, Nicole. I give you my word it did not. You are in no danger of—"

"Your word is not worth having. You have proved that." She regretted the statement as soon as she made it. She saw first the hot rage in his eyes, then the coldness. "Quent, I did not mean that. I have not explained very well. Please, let me try."

His anger died as quickly as it had been born. "Ah, my love, I need no explanations." He put his hand beside her cheek and she allowed it to remain. "We'll be married," he said softly. "As soon as I deal with the renegades and bring Solomon back to the Patent. Then I'll show you what truly happens between a man and a woman. What happened yesterday, my love, in the glen, that was only the beginning. Nothing we did can cause—"

"I cannot marry you, Quent." She reached up and removed his hand from her cheek. "I have sworn to be a nun."

"A nun! Good Chr— That was no nun with me beside the waterfall yesterday. What kind of an insane—"

"Yesterday I almost forgot a vow I made to Almighty God kneeling before the Blessed Sacrament, and again at the bed of my dying maman. Yesterday is one more terrible thing for which I must do penance the rest of my life."

"Penance . . . Nicole, I don't pretend to understand your religion, but surely not even popish priests would teach that the natural way of things between a man and woman is cause for penance."

Nicole glanced at the door. It was shut, but heaven knows what these people must think of what was happening inside. "Ssh," she said. "We give scandal. I do not speak of what we did in—"

"Almost did," he corrected in a harsh whisper. "I told you, nothing happened that is reserved for a husband and wife."

"I know." She didn't, not really, but she had no reason to doubt his word about such things. "I am trying to tell you something much worse than anything you are thinking. The little twins, Lilac and Sugar Willie . . ." She took a step backward, away from him. "They are dead because of me."

"That's insane as well. They and the others are dead because a vicious Huron renegade named Lantak attacked the Patent. It has nothing to do with you."

"How many others?" And when he didn't answer: "You must tell me! How many?"

Ephraim counted blacks and whites separately. Quent didn't look at things that way. "Eleven, not counting Solomon the Barrel Maker. He's been captured, but I am sure he's alive." For a time at least. But if he didn't get to him quickly, Solomon would be praying for death.

"Eleven dead," she whispered, making the sign of the cross. *"Tiens pitié, mon Dieu.* And the rest? There was more destruction, I know there was, I saw it."

"Eight horses, stolen or so badly wounded they had to be put down. Almost half the wheat crop burned. And the sawmill is totally destroyed. What do you mean, you saw it? You were in the cave behind the waterfall."

"I saw it," she repeated. *"Le bon Dieu* showed me what I was causing by my willfulness, my refusal to honor my vow, my sin of disobedience." She hesitated.

"And what I almost did—what I wanted to do—with you." She stared at the floor. Her voice was so low he could barely make out what she was saying.

"We love each other. What kind of God would begrudge us that?" Even as he said the words he knew it was hopeless. She barely reached his shoulder but she was a tower of determination. By Christ, what a woman! And he was going to lose her to a nunnery, a swamp of popish superstition. It was an abomination.

"I have no right to love you." Nicole raised her face. She was still very pale, but there were no more tears. "Long before I met you, I had already given myself as an offering to Jesus Christ. In reparation."

"Reparation for what? What can you have done?"

"For myself, I did nothing. I do not have that on my conscience. But I watched what others did. What my own father did. You have heard of the Jacobite Rebellion, the forty-five in Scotland? Of Culloden Moor?"

The stories of Culloden Moor had reached as far as America. It had been a field of slaughter, terrible carnage. What could such things have to do with Nicole? "There is no joining between—"

She shook her head, impatient with his disbelief. "There is every joining. I was there. I saw it. No, don't look like that. I do not mean I was shown a vision. I saw it with my own eyes, just as I am looking at you now. I was ten and Maman and I were living in a little house near the barracks at Ruthven, in the Scottish Highlands. Many of the other wives and children had already been sent home to England. But Maman said we would not go because so many doubted the loyalty of my papa, since his wife was French and a Catholic. And the day after the battle we were taken to see the scene of the great English victory. The dead and the dying were everywhere. The king's soldiers, even Papa, walking among them, cutting the heads off the wounded. They scoured the countryside for any who might be hiding. When they were found, they were hacked apart and the place that had sheltered them burned to the ground. I saw everything and I made a vow that I would be a nun to save the soul of my beloved papa. *Le bon Dieu* is kind. After he was retired from the army, Papa renounced his Protestant heresy and was received into the True Church. I did not know what convent I was meant to enter until, by chance, I heard of the Poor Clares of Québec, the smallest, humblest monastery of the order. Papa had business in Virginia, so he took me with him." She managed a smile, as if everything was now explained.

Quent stretched out his hand, but she backed away. Nothing he could do, nothing he could say, would alter her decision. All the same, he had to try. "Nicole . . ."

"There is no more time for words, Quent. I must go to Québec."

He had lost. He had only to look at her to know that. "Very well. If you insist this is what you want, I will take you to your convent."

Merci, mon Dieu. Since the terrible visions that had come to her in the cave behind the waterfall, the pain in her heart had been intense, a misery of sorrow and regret. Now her grief eased. "I will always pray for you. You will never—"

"I'll take you as soon as I've brought Solomon home. Meanwhile you have to go back to Shadowbrook."

"No! Quent, you cannot—"

He turned and walked back to the main trading hall.

Judith held out the parcel of food for him. He took it and stowed it in his haversack. Esther said nothing, but her glance darted between Quent and the girl who stood in the open doorway staring at him, looking as if her world were totally destroyed.

"Take her to the big house," Quent said as he strode toward the door. "Kindly tell my mother I'll return as soon as I can. Then I'll take Mademoiselle Crane wherever she wishes to go."

The doors of the trading post swung open before he reached them. The man who came in wore a blue jacket trimmed with an officer's gold braid, a ruffled shirt, and an officer's tricorne. Beneath it his long hair was pure white, tied at the back of his neck with a grosgrain ribbon. His face was marked by the ritual tattoos and scars of a Kahniankehaka chief. "They told me I would find you here, Uko Nyakwai. *Skennenteron.*" Peace to this house.

"*Skennenise,*" Peace to you. It had been many years since Quent had seen Thoyanoguin, the Mohawk chief the whites called King Hendrick. He had changed little, as wizened and wrinkled now as when Quent was a boy. But his eyes, usually pools of calm, were troubled. "Why does the great Lord of the Kahniankehaka look for Uko Nyakwai?" Quent asked.

"*Teiononhkeri,* Red Bear." Things have gone wrong.

"What things?"

"There are five dead horses by Bright Fish Water. Killed not for food or for mercy, only for spite."

Bright Fish Water was the northernmost boundary of the Patent, but only half on Hale land. It took a long day to paddle a canoe from one end of Bright Fish Water to the other, and when you arrived at the far shore you were in Canada, in what the French claimed as New France, on what they called the Lac du St. Sacrament. "Does Thoyanoguin know if the horses belonged to my father?"

"They were stolen by Lantak in the raid."

No surprise there. Thoyanoguin had probably known that Lantak and his renegades were on their way well before the murdering bastards appeared. But as long as they went after whites, not Mohawk, the old chief was content to let things take their course. He'd not have come to warn Ephraim Hale unless there was some immediate gain for him in it, and obviously he'd seen none. But why come to Quent with this news now? He didn't ask the question outright. No one put a higher value on negotiation and subtlety than a member of the Iroquois Federation, and no one was better at it then Thoyanoguin. "Did the Huron renegades slaughter their horses because they had a canoe? Since they are so far from their homelands, where would they get such a thing?"

Thoyanoguin shrugged. "Canoes can be found, or even stolen."

You're lying, you clever old fox. Quent thought. You don't give a blacksmith's cuss for what Lantak and his men did on Shadowbrook. Hell, you sold them the bloody canoe to make sure they got away. And one of the things that's made you decide to come and tell me about it is that instead of turning the Hale horses loose and giving you a chance to round them up, they killed the poor animals just so you wouldn't have them. "The renegades took a captive from my father's lands, wise Chief. Only one. Did you see him?"

"I told you, I saw nothing. If I had been there I would have demanded an explanation of all their evil deeds and brought them to your respected father for justice. But two of my braves saw Lantak and they told me of the captive. A black man. One of the ones you call slaves." Thoyanoguin's disgust showed in his tone. "The black man's blood was on the ground near where the canoe set out on the water. My braves tell me that it was the same color red as yours or mine."

"I know that, wise Chief. Red or white or black, the same color blood." Quent suppressed the sense of urgency that was making his skin crawl. "The captive's name is Solomon. He is a good man. Is he near death. . . *tehokonhentonsken?*"

"He is not yet dead. Not even dying." Thoyanoguin's glance had fixed on Nicole, standing in the shadows by the storeroom. The Mohawk kept looking at her even as he spoke to Quent. "But now this Solomon, he sees singly." He raised his fist to his face and made a gesture indicating a knife gouging out an eye.

He'd hoped Lantak might wait till he was back on his own ground before. . . Sweet Jesus Christ. "The Huron, Thoyanoguin, *to nihati?*" How many did you see?

"I told you. These old eyes saw nothing. My braves tell me there were five pieces of Huron dung stinking up the place. Uko Nyakwai . . . there is something . . ."

It was coming at last. "I am listening with both my ears, wise Chief."

"Last night, before the horses were killed and before my braves saw these Huron dog turds, I had a dream. I saw a red bear."

Quent clenched his fists, but left his arms hanging loose at his sides. He mustn't in any way betray his impatience. But the total trust in dreams that Indians had escaped him. He never had felt the same. *If my white son does not trust the spirits that come when he sleeps, soon they will not bother coming.* Bishkek, his manhood father, had told him that long ago. And when Bishkek was teaching him to fashion his death song, Quent did indeed have one dream that helped him. He must have interpreted it correctly, because his song was good and powerful. That had been proven the day in the Shawnee camp when Pontiac could have killed him, but didn't. "I was the red bear in Thoyanoguin's dream?"

"*Hanio!* Who else could it be? But until now I did not know the identity of the *raon,* the tiny bird that beats its wings so fast they cannot be seen, so it seems still when it is moving. Now I know."

The Mohawk continued to stare at Nicole. She was the hummingbird in Thoyanoguin's dream, Quent realized. "What happened to the *raon?*"

"A hawk came and tried to capture it, but the little bird escaped. Still the hawk flew after it, and when the little bird grew tired of beating its wings so fast, it landed on the back of a red bear and asked the bear to carry it to safety. But even though the bird was very tiny and the bear very big, the bear said it could not and rose up on its back legs and shook the little bird off its back. Then the hawk swooped down and killed the *raon.* And the blood from that one tiny bird covered the village of Thoyanoguin and many other villages. And all the Kahniankehaka were drowned in it."

Nicole was aware of the currents, if not the meaning of the words. "He told you something about me, didn't he?" she whispered to Quent. "What did he say?"

You tell me, my white son, that Christians believe in Shkotensi, the Great Spirit, that they know that all of us were put here to play our part in the Telling being told by the Great Spirit. But how can we know what Shkotensi says if we do not listen when he speaks? He'd had no answer for Bishkek then and he had none for Thoyanoguin now. A river of blood. Cormac had seen that, too. And many little birds protected by a bear. Here, now, there was only one little bird.

Quent found his voice and spoke to her, not to Thoyanoguin. "You said you expected me to take a horse when I left Shadowbrook, that the reason you took Pohantis's clothes was so you could ride. But there's no—"

Nicole interrupted him. "No sidesaddle fit for a lady in your stable. I know, Little George told me that weeks ago. It doesn't matter. When we lived in Ruthven, near the barracks, the soldiers amused themselves by teaching me. I can ride astride like a man, even bareback."

Not in a Quaker frock she couldn't. "Then go change. Hurry." Then, to Esther: "I need two horses." There was a wide and decent path between here and Bright Fish Water, and much as he would like the feel of her mounted behind him, two horses carrying single loads would make far better time. "I did not bring money, but I will pay when I return."

"Thee can have whatever thee needs from this place and welcome, Quentin Hale."

He turned to Thoyanoguin. "When I get to Bright Fish Water I will need a canoe."

"It is waiting for you already. *Ahkwesahsne*." In the place where the partridge drums. "*Tyientaneken kanehsatake*." Two logs side by side on the crusty sands. "Follow in the direction they point. The canoe is well hidden, but because you know it is there, you will find it. And there are two paddles," Thoyanoguin added, nodding toward Nicole with satisfaction.

Chapter Thirteen

TO PAD ALONG a rough stone floor in your bare feet was not much of a penance in September, even in New France. When she was a child, a little girl in the great château on the banks of the Loire, Mère Marie Rose used to get up in the middle of a winter's night and test her fortitude by walking barefoot through the icy corridors and halls, always careful to avoid the rugs. Once, in February, she went outside and challenged herself to do the same along the frozen riverbank. Petí, her beloved *bonne d'enfant*, caught her that time, and there was no *goûter* for a week. Mère Rose smiled slightly remembering Petí, who always smelled of powder and cloves, and the afternoon snacks of childhood, warm milk with honey and buns topped with fresh butter or sweet preserves.

It was twenty-two years since she had tasted such things, since she was fifteen and the cloister door of the Poor Clares of Montargis was closed and locked behind her. *At least the Ursulines, her mother had begged. Or the Benedictines. If you insist on pursuing this madness, choose a convent where you need not endure so much.* But her mother would surely have agreed that the stone floor of the tiny monastery in Québec Lower Town presented no hardship in the middle of a September night. Besides, there was never very far to walk in this hovel of a monastery.

Summer and winter alike, moments after every midnight of the year, after they had slept for three hours, the abbess of the Poor Clare Colettines of Québec woke her daughters and led them to prayer. They reached the door of the chapel, wheree Mère Marie Rose paused and dipped her right forefinger in the holy water stoup and made the sign of the cross. In winter when the holy water froze and not a drop adhered to her finger she made the gesture anyway, and each of the four nuns behind her did the same.

The nuns entered the chapel in single file, each pausing to bow deeply from the waist in front of the tabernacle before taking her place in the facing rows of wooden boxes called choir stalls. Since they were five altogether, there were two nuns on one side, three on the other. The asymmetry disturbed Mère Marie Rose.

Le bon Dieu had promised her a postulant. He had spoken to her as plainly as anyone could wish. *I am sending you another daughter to be consumed in the flames of my love.* She had even shared the joyous news with the community and with Père Antoine. Where was she, this sixth offering of prayer and penance?

"O Lord, open my lips and my mouth shall declare Your praise." Soeur Marie Joseph, the cantor, had a lovely voice. She intoned the great antiphon of Matins, the First Hour of the new day, and the assembled nuns answered with the opening psalm, *"Confitebor tibi quia terribiliter magnificatus es . . ."* I will praise You for You are terrible and magnificent . . .

Their chant was tremulous in the candlelit dark. Only Joseph could truly sing, and Mère Rose and her nuns did not spend hours in practice, like the proud Benedictines for whom the perfection of each note was a sacred duty. But all of them knew their chant rose from their hearts to heaven on a direct course. *"Nonne qui oderunt te Domine oderam?"* Have I not hated them that hated You?

Midway through the third psalm of the Matins office a red haze obscured the words on the page of Mère Rose's Psalter. The abbess closed her eyes and continued to chant from memory. She plunged into the haze, offering herself to appease God's wrath. Flames. A river of blood. What did they signify? Tell me, my good God. Tell me what I must know. There was no answer, only the chants of Matins: Taste and see that the Lord is sweet. Magnify His name with me.

The visions had begun when she was a little girl. She had only to close her eyes to see twisting, writhing souls in torment surrounded by slavering demons. And holding back the demons, a circle of women wearing black veils that fell in soft folds to their shoulders, and rough gray robes tied with knotted white cords, and nothing on their feet. But the women could not join hands to close the circle and release the souls from their agony. They stretched as far toward each other as they could, but one person was missing. The little girl who would grow up to be Mère Rose had always known the brown-clad nuns were waiting for her.

These days she saw other things. Red men, savages who did not know Jesus Christ and His Church and who were therefore unable to enter heaven, who must remain in emptiness and nothingness for all eternity. Their sadness and loss overwhelmed her. Their ignorance appeared to her as a great boulder blocking the mouth of a cave, preventing the light from entering. Oh my God . . . only one more. One more. To roll back the great stone of unbelief, just one more woman was needed. Preferably young and beautiful and pure, and willing to offer herself in total sacrifice.

Half an hour later the prayers of Matins ended. The nuns knelt in their stalls, waiting for the abbess to give the signal for them to rise. It did not come. Soeur Marie Celeste was vicaress, Mère Rose's second in command. She glanced at the abbess and saw that her eyes were still tightly shut, as they had been for much of the Office. Celeste waited a few moments more. It was the abbess who should lead them from the chapel back to their cells, to the three hours' sleep that comprised the second part of the night's rest for Poor Clares of the strict observance. The abbess did not move. *Eh bien,* such things were common with *la bonne Mère.* She was a chosen soul. Celeste stepped out of her choir stall and Marie Angelique, Marie Françoise, and Marie Joseph followed her. The four processed from the chapel and, as happened so often, left the abbess motionless and entranced.

The front door of the monastery was made of brawny planks of oak bound with hammered iron. It was locked and barred, and however many times Quent beat his fist against it there was no response. "Here," Nicole said. "We must try here. It is called the turn."

He did not answer her—they had barely spoken for days—but he looked at what appeared to be a small barrel set into the wall next to the door. A heavy brass bell hung beside the barrel's rounded bulge. Nicole took hold of the leather pull and shook it vigorously. A few moments later, though they could see no one, they heard a voice. *"Laudate Jesum Christum."* Praised be Jesus Christ.

"Per omnia saecula saeculorum," Nicole said. World without end.

"Qu' est-ce que vous voudrais, madame?" Angelique's heart was thudding against her chest. The accent of this visitor was not that of the locals. And she was young. Mère Rose had been saying for months that a postulant would come to join them. Perhaps today—

"I wish to be one of you," Nicole said. "To become a Poor Clare."

Angelique clasped her hands in excitement, then pressed them to her mouth to stifle a gasp. Praised be Jesus Christ indeed! *"Un moment, ma petite. Ne quittez pas."* The words tumbled out of Marie Angelique in an urgent rush. "One moment only. Do not go. *Un moment!"*

The little nun hurried from the turn and ran toward the chapel. It was early dawn and the high windows of the small choir let in a few beams of pink-tinged light. One seemed to be resting directly on the abbess, kneeling exactly as she had been when Matins and then the first Office of the day, Lauds, had finished. Angelique was not surprised. When *ma mère* was taken in this manner she could not control the length of what she called the wound of love. But for this . . . she would wish to be told this at once.

Angelique paused just long enough for a deep bow before the tabernacle, then turned and walked quickly to Mère Rose's stall. Her bare feet made no sound on the uneven stones. "*Ma Mère,*" she whispered. "I humbly beg you to forgive this interruption, *ma Mère,* but—"

"So she has come at last," Marie Rose said, opening her eyes. "Thanks be to God."

Quent lingered in the shadows at the rear of the chapel.

"*Magnificat anima mea Dominum.*" My soul doth magnify the Lord. The chant rose from behind the closely placed and heavily curtained iron bars that backed the altar. "He who is mighty has done great things for me, and holy is His name."

The disembodied voice behind the turn had given Nicole a worn old prayer book. All her responses were written there, the nun said. Nicole held the prayer book now, but as far as Quent could tell she wasn't looking at it.

"*Quia respexit humilitatem ancillae suae,*" the voices behind the bars chanted. He has looked on the lowliness of his handmaiden.

"*Ecce enim ex hoc beatam me dicent omens generationes,*" Nicole replied. She spoke the words clearly, without hesitation. All generations will call me blessed.

Sweet God Almighty, what kind of religion was this that locked women up behind iron bars and called it virtue? He couldn't bear the thought of leaving her in this place. It was dim. Nicole was meant for sunlight and laughter. For Shadowbrook. Not to be locked up forever a virgin. Was their world filled only with women? Perhaps not. A tall gaunt man dressed in a brown robe was kneeling in the tiny chapel. He seemed unaware of Quent's presence, but he hadn't taken his eyes off Nicole.

She was wearing the gray Quaker dress that Esther Snowberry had given her and she'd entirely hidden her hair under the plain white mobcap. She was nonetheless so beautiful she took his breath away. Maybe more beautiful than he'd ever seen her, glowing with happiness. She knelt in front of the small altar, gazing intently at a golden box.

Quent clenched his fists to stop himself from striding forward and carrying her away from this superstition and Catholic deviltry. There was no point. She was doing what she wanted to do. Damn you, Nicole. The devil take you. I'll not beg you to change your mind.

Still, he couldn't leave while he could yet look at her, kneeling with her head bowed in prayer so he could see the tender place at the back of her neck. A bird or birds, a hawk, a bear, a river of blood. Two almost identical dreams told to him by two entirely different men. What did it all mean? In spite of his distaste for popery, Quent found himself gazing at the altar and praying for an answer.

Père Antoine was conscious of the man behind him, but he did not need to look again to know the man was Uko Nyakwai, the legendary Red Bear. So Quentin Hale had come here, to Québec, to the place of the French enemy. In itself perhaps not so extraordinary. The trappers and scouts, all the *coureurs de bois*, moved freely over the land; like the red men, they had little use for legal borders. But that it should be Quentin Hale who brought the Franciscans the treasure they had all been waiting for was extraordinary. Père Antoine signed himself with the cross. The ways of God were truly remarkable . . . Lantak had sent word that the raid had been successful. He was claiming the two hundred livres he was owed.

The chanting of the Magnificat was finished. The voice of Mère Marie Rose came from behind the grille. "What do you wish, my child?"

"To follow Christ and live the life of the gospel," Nicole replied.

"Are you prepared to give your heart to Lady Poverty and follow Francis and Clare, to be hidden with God in the cloister?"

Oh yes, she burned to do exactly that. Accept me, *mon Dieu*. She did not look at the formal words of response. Her reply came from deep within her. "I am truly prepared, *ma Mère*. With all my heart and soul."

Mère Marie Rose smiled. Enthusiasm was natural in the young. And this one had spirit, she could tell simply from the sound of her voice. The black woolen curtains on their side of the grille made it impossible to see into the public chapel, and the turn permitted no glimpse of a visitor, but Angelique had been beside herself with delight when she announced the girl's arrival. "Her voice, *ma Mère*, it is lovely. I am sure she is a beautiful bride of Christ."

"We are concerned with a beautiful soul, *ma Soeur*, only that." It was her sacred duty as abbess to curb the remains of worldly attitudes in her daughters, but from the first day she had herself stepped inside the cloister, wearing the exquisite frock her darling maman had ordered made specially for the occasion (*"Each stitch sewn with one of my tears, ma chère petite, my tears . . ."*), Marie Rose had known how eagerly the nuns devoured the sight of a new postulant. A young woman coming to join them was, for the few moments before she was absorbed into the community, a glimpse of the world they had left behind. The latest fashions, the way women outside were dressing their hair . . . Oh yes, a tinge of it, the tiniest remnant, continued even in the heart of the holy abbess of the Monastery of Poor Clares of Québec. She would deny herself the evening collation in penance.

The abbess rose from her knees and bowed low before the tabernacle. As soon as she straightened she flicked forward the part of her veil that covered her face, which was to be used in any circumstance where a nun in solemn vows might be seen by one who was not a member of her community. The daughters of Marie Rose covered their faces as well. Then, hidden from the world they had left behind, the five nuns processed to the tiny door in the corner of the grille.

The keys at Marie Rose's waist were one of the marks of her authority, and her hand trembled slightly when she detached them from the cord that secured her gray habit and chose the one that unlocked the door. It swung wide on silent, well-oiled hinges. *Grâce à Dieu!* The girl was truly lovely. A fitting sacrifice of praise. Marie Rose's glance roamed beyond the new entrant, sweeping quickly over the poor little chapel. Père Antoine was there. Another man as well. She spent only seconds examining the world beyond her cloister, but with more interest than necessary, Mère Rose decided. She would discipline herself with greater than usual fervor this night. And skip the evening collation all week. Meanwhile, the postulant was waiting. "We welcome you, my child. Enter into the joy the world cannot understand."

Nicole drew a deep breath. She knew the black-veiled nuns must be intently curious about her, but mostly she was conscious of the eyes watching her from behind. Oh, yes. She had almost drowned in those extraordinary blue eyes. For-give me, my good God, if loving him is a sin, I will do penance for it all the days of my life, but I will never forget.

The nun stretched out both her hands. *"Entre, ma petite. Je tu invite."*

Nicole knew if she waited only a few seconds more, if she turned even her head, Quent would come for her. He would close the distance between them in two or three of his long strides and claim her and they would be together for whatever life God granted them.

"Qu' est-ce que tu désir, ma petite?" This time the question—what do you wish?—carried a hint of doubt.

Half a moment more, the space of one drawn breath. Quent behind her, and in front of her, a call that few heard and to which even fewer responded. Nicole's heart surged with unexpected joy. She had been chosen. "I wish to give myself to *le bon Dieu* as a Poor Clare." Her voice was firm and clear. She put her hands in the hands of the abbess and stepped into the cloister.

Quent glimpsed robust women with black veils over their faces. The creatures drew Nicole into their midst and the door closed. He heard a few muffled titters. It sounded like—good Christ, it was hard to believe—like a group of young girls giggling.

His fists were clenched and his jaws clamped together to keep him from howl-ing with outrage. Those iron bars are the only substantial thing in the place, he told himself. The rest is little more than a few stones piled atop each other. I could knock the whole thing down with my bare hands. But it might as well be a fortress. I'm never going to get her out of here.

Quent's huge body sagged with the weight of what he knew to be true. He didn't notice that now that Nicole was out of sight, the priest had turned and was staring at him.

Père Antoine could not get over his wonder. Uko Nyakwai had brought them a blessing from Almighty God. Holy Virgin, You have sent me a sign. I am unworthy but I am truly your humble and loving son and son of the blessed Francis, and you have sent me a sign that I've done the right thing. Sending Lantak to attack Shadowbrook. It will save many souls and lead to the glory of the Order.

And see how this Protestant heretic who is also many parts heathen gazes at the tabernacle as if he were truly praying. Perhaps he too can be saved. *Oui,* but that is in your gentle hands, Mother of God.

He could hear the voice of the Holy Virgin warning him: *Be cautious, my son, be jealous of my honor and the honor of the Church and your Order.* Antoine signed himself with the cross once more and slipped out of the chapel, leaving the Red Bear staring at the place he had last seen the young woman.

There was only one lookout lying on his belly at the crest of a hillock thick with pine trees. Quent crept up behind him and slit the brave's throat with one stroke of the dirk. The only sound was the gurgling of escaping blood.

That's for Lilac and Sugar Willie you murdering bastard. I hope the devil's waiting for you in hell. He wiped the dagger on the Huron's own breechclout and slipped it into the holster at the small of his back, then took the Indian's musket. Still making no sound, he moved closer to the camp.

The sun was directly overhead and the heat was brutal. The renegades hadn't made a fire. Two were sprawled underneath a tree, passing a jug of rum back and forth. One stood a few feet away, bending over Solomon the Barrel Maker.

He'd been stripped to his breeches. Even at a distance of ten strides, Quent could see that Solomon's bare back and shoulders were covered with the old scars of John's whipping, and fresh wounds that looked like burns. His boots were gone and his feet were bloody, the flesh torn and lacerated. He lay on his belly, his big body twisted into a deep, unnatural arch. They had tied a leather thong around his neck and his ankles and pulled it tight enough to raise both his head and his feet. The Indian standing over Solomon was pouring water over the lashing. As it dried, the leather would shrink and the ties grow tighter, contorting him into an ever more torturous curve, slowly but constantly tearing muscles and snapping bones. Quent had seen it before. It took most men three or four days and repeated soakings before they died. Judging from his position Solomon had been tied up for only a few hours. With luck, no permanent damage was yet done.

Quent held the long gun in firing position; the musket was also loaded and lying beside him. He could finish off two of the three renegades in as long as it would take to draw three breaths. The one remaining would be too busy looking for the source of the gunfire and a way to save his own skin to bother with the captive. His confusion would probably last the twenty or so seconds it would take Quent to reload, then he too would be dead. That left Lantak unaccounted for. He was by far the most dangerous. Not smart to move until he knew where Lantak was.

His gaze ranged over the campsite, always coming back to the thick stand of trees on the far side.

What had driven Lantak and his demented band to travel hundreds of leagues, much of it through the country of their enemies, to burn and murder and pillage the land of people they had never met and with whom they could have no conceivable quarrel? He'd seen Lantak once or twice, but they'd never tangled. The Huron could have no possible personal grudge against Uko Nyakwai. And as far as he knew, John had nothing to do with Québec, much less Hurons; it was the same for Ephraim and Lorene. Their world and that of Lantak were as far apart as America and the Japans.

None of it made any sense, but he had to find a way to make sense of it. Otherwise how could he be sure that the Patent and everyone on it would be safe from future attacks? Damn! He needed more time to think. He needed to talk to Corm.

Solomon groaned. He'd obviously been trying not to, but the leather ties were shrinking, and tightening as the sun dried them. The barrel maker's head and ankles had drawn closer together, increasing his agony. Quent could see his face clearly now. Solomon's left eye had indeed been gouged out, just as Thoyanoguin said. The empty socket was caked with dried blood; the old man's cheeks were sunken and his mouth drawn tight in a grimace of pain. He groaned again. The braves drinking in the shade beneath the trees laughed.

The one who had wet down the leather joined his companions. The jug passed to him and he upended it, taking a long drink of rum. Quent thought he saw some motion in the trees on the far side of the stream. Damn them all to hell. Lantak, where are you? Come out and fight like a man, curse your rotten hide.

He felt a prickling on the back of his neck and rolled swiftly onto his back, keeping the long gun in firing position and drawing a bead on the observer even before the motion was complete. A coal-black squirrel stood on its hind legs staring at him, swishing its bushy little tail and holding an acorn in its paws. Man and squirrel surveyed each other for a second or two, then the squirrel turned and ran away. Quent rolled back into his original position overlooking the camp in time to see one of the Indians get to his feet and stumble toward Solomon.

"Where are you going?" The words were slurred and uneven, as if the jug of rum had been circulating for some time.

"I have to piss." The renegade walking across the field pulled aside his breechclout as he spoke. "If we water this one some more, he will sing louder."

"Lantak said he wanted to be here at the end. He'll cut out your heart if you send the darkface to his ancestors too quickly."

"Lantak's not here. Besides, I do not need his permission to piss." The Huron stood above Solomon, holding his cock in his hand. A stream of urine played over Solomon's back and the thongs that tied him. The other two laughed heartily, even the one who had warned against killing the captive too quickly. The brave who was relieving himself changed position and directed his flow at the barrel maker's face. "You thirsty maybe? Here, drink this."

The others laughed louder. Quent's finger tightened on the trigger and he sighted down the five-foot barrel of the gun. The Huron didn't have time to release his grip on his cock. It was still in his hand when his head cracked like an overripe watermelon, spewing blood and brains.

"*Ayi!*" The brave who screamed reached for his tomahawk just as the ball of the dead lookout's musket parted his chest into two halves.

Quent dropped the musket and sprang to his feet, loading the long gun as he ran down the hill. A single stride to yank the cork from the powder horn with his teeth, two more to pour the black powder down the barrel, three to ram a wad and prime the pan. The third Huron had managed to load his musket but he was moving it in a wide and unsteady arc, still seeming not to know the source of the danger. Then he spotted Quent pelting down the embankment.

The long gun was now fully loaded and ready to fire. Quent raised it to his shoulder, still running, presenting a moving target and taking only the blink of an eye to get the renegade in his sights. The barrel of the musket swung in Quent's direction; Quent drew back the hammer of the long gun. The two weapons roared in the selfsame instant. This time Quent didn't brace himself against the long gun's mighty recoil, but allowed it to knock him to the ground. He continued rolling down the hill. The musket ball cut through the air over his head and landed some distance behind the place he'd been standing. The body of the renegade Huron crumpled headless to the earth.

Solomon's face was still wet with urine as he turned it to Quent, his remaining eye fixed steadily on the younger man. "I knowed all I had to do was hold on long enough and you be coming to get me."

"Absolutely, old man. I figured you knew that." The dirk sliced through the leather thongs, releasing the barrel maker from the unnatural arch. "Take it slow." Quent reached behind him and slipped the dirk into its sheath. He needed both hands free so he could support Solomon's shoulders with one arm and grab his legs with the other. "Real easy now." Gently, with infinite patience, he allowed Solomon's tortured body to unfold.

The barrel maker groaned. Quent waited until what he knew was a rush of excruciating pain had subsided, then asked, "Solomon, do you know where Lantak's gone?"

"I did not go far," a voice from across the clearing replied. Lantak stepped out of the trees. "I have come to meet you, Uko Nyakwai. Stand up and let me see the guest at my camp."

The renegade was some twenty strides away, on the other side of the field where the bodies of his two dead comrades lay. He held a long gun aimed at Quent. Quent knew it was loaded and ready to fire.

"So the brown robe told the truth." Lantak spoke the words without turning around, but he seemed to be addressing someone behind him. "I thought you were dreaming. I did not believe that a whiteface would come after a darkface in this manner. I was mistaken." He didn't move, not taking his eyes off the Red Bear for a moment. "I told you to stand up, Uko Nyakwai. Do it now. The gun, you will leave there on the ground beside you. If you reach for it I will kill you."

Quent still had hold of Solomon's arms and legs. He let them go. "Stay still," he murmured, his lips barely moving. "When I shout, roll away from my voice." Slowly, taking what felt like an infinite amount of time, Quent got to his feet. No gun, but his tomahawk hung at his waist. God-rotting hell! Why had he been so bloody quick to sheath the dirk? He couldn't risk reaching for it. Or the still more lethal tomahawk. And there was another unknown: Who was behind Lantak, and with what weapons?

"Walk toward me, Uko Nyakwai. Yes, like that. I wish to see your face when I kill you."

"Killing quickly is not your custom, is it Lantak? The storytellers say Lantak is like a spider who brings a fly into his web and offers many caresses before death. But perhaps that is only your way with old men and children and squaws? Maybe you do not have the courage to test a brave whose strength is like your own."

Lantak chuckled. "Do you think you can make me angry, Red Bear? That perhaps I will lose my temper and that will cloud my judgment? They say you are truly a Potawatomi brave. Perhaps that is so, but you are also a fool. You treat Lantak as if he were a child. No Real Person would do that. Yours will be the next corpse left for the vultures to find, not Lantak's. Every moment you remain alive you are a danger. If you have a death song, Uko Nyakwai, sing it now."

The barrel of the long gun had not wavered while Lantak spoke. Quent knew he was perfectly sighted. Lantak would not miss. Quent focused his mind on his interior spirit, calling up the strength to meet death. He saw everything with remarkable clarity. Even the small gesture Lantak made as his finger tightened on the trigger.

Quent's death song rose in him. He was a whiteness that first plunged into the bowels of the earth. Then the whiteness rose, reaching for light like a flower stretching to the warmth of the sun. He, his spirit, was the whiteness. He would cover the earth and protect all that he loved. He would sing his white song forever, and all that Shkotensi the Great Spirit had put inside him, all that made him who he was and not someone else, would live for eternity. He was a whiteness with the softness of new-fallen snow, and the cunning of the *wabnum*, the white wolf who hunts on ice. Lantak fired his long gun. Quent let his death song and his spirit go free, toward the bright light waiting for him, beckoning him.

The bullet crashed into the trees to Quent's left. Lantak stumbled and fell. Behind him Père Antoine shuddered, staring at the hand that had shoved the renegade as if it did not belong to him. He, Antoine de Rubin Montaigne of the Friars Minor, had saved the life of Uko Nyakwai, heretic and enemy of the True Church. The priest groaned softly.

Lantak released his gun and allowed his body to roll, coming to his feet with his tomahawk in his hand. He hurtled toward the priest with a roar of rage, the tomahawk swinging above his head in an arc of death.

"Lantak!" Quent was still suspended between two worlds, hovering, looking down on himself and on Lantak and the priest on the other side of the clearing. "Lantak! I am your enemy! Uko Nyakwai is over here! Why waste your time with a man in a squaw's frock?" Quent's own tomahawk was in his hand. In what seemed to him the slowest, most deliberate motion, he pulled his arm back. "I am over here, you madman!"

For a single heartbeat Lantak hesitated, torn between his rage at the priest and the knowledge that every moment Uko Nyakwai lived was a danger to him. Then he swung round and charged across the open ground toward the Red Bear.

Quent released his tomahawk. It whistled through the air in a deadly series of turns, gathering momentum as it spiraled toward the renegade. But though he'd adjusted the throw for the fact that Lantak was running toward him, he was spent from the release of his death song and this time his aim was not perfect. The knife-sharp edge of the stone blade buried itself in the renegade's left shoulder instead of his forehead, slicing through skin and muscle and lodging deeply in the bone.

The pain opened a pit into which Lantak could plunge to escape torment. But he knew it offered no refuge, only death. Lantak fought the lure of oblivion. He dropped his own tomahawk and reached up and pulled that of Uko Nyakwai from his flesh, sending it spinning into the dirt. He could not suppress a scream of agony, but it didn't stop him from pulling his knife and hurtling toward his foe.

Quent had his dirk in his hand. His rage erupted in a scream of hatred and he ran to meet his enemy.

Quent could not feel his feet in contact with the earth. To fight well, to feint and dodge and maneuver until he was close enough to cut out the heart of his foe, he must be able to read the enemy's movements with his moccasins. The ground would tell him which direction Lantak took before he took it, but it was as if Quent floated above its surface, separated from the source of strength and knowledge. He had freed his spirit to seek the next world, and though it had been called back, it had not entirely returned to this one.

Lantak sensed the Red Bear's weakness. For a moment it seemed to him that he could still emerge from this contest victorious. The renegade thrust forward with his right arm, ignoring the searing pain in his left.

Quent saw the blow coming and moved, but not in time to prevent the Huron's knife from slicing through the flesh of his side. He grunted once, then blessed the sting of the wound. It helped him to focus, to summon his soul back to his body, and when Lantak swiveled to the left Quent followed, ready to plunge the dirk deep into the other man's chest.

At the last moment Lantak pulled back. The handspan's length of the dirk's blade buried itself not in his heart, but in the same arm already on fire from the tomahawk's assault. He screamed again, and without another moment's hesitation turned and ran. Here on this day, he was no longer a match for the mighty Red Bear. But if he lived there would be other days. And revenge, when it came, would be sweeter for the delay. He ignored the pain and stooped to scoop up his long gun before he disappeared into the surrounding forest.

Quent could not follow him: his tomahawk lay on the ground where Lantak had flung it and his dirk was still buried in the renegade's flesh. By the time he got his gun . . . He glanced back at Solomon. The barrel maker was sitting on the ground cradling Quent's long rifle. "I got it, Master Quent."

"Very good, Solomon. Excellent. You hang on to it." He shook his head, trying to come back, reminding himself that he and Solomon were still not alone.

The priest hadn't moved since Quent first caught sight of him; he was white-faced and trembling with shock, hunched over, shaking like a leaf in the wind. Quent took a step toward him. "I appear to owe you my life, sir." The pit in the center of Quent's belly was closing, but his words still seemed to his own ears to travel an immeasurable distance. "I'd like to know your name."

"I am called Père Antoine, and— I could not let him kill you in cold blood in front of me. I could not."

"I'm glad to hear it, Père Antoine. But for you I'd be dead." Quent's voice strengthened. "The water in that stream over there is fresh and cold. Do you a bit of good just now." He touched the other man's arm, noting how rough the brown cloth was, and gently turned him in the direction of the brook.

"I could not see a man murdered in front of my eyes," Père Antoine said. "I could not." But Almighty God, how will you judge me for this? He is a danger to Holy Church. I feel it in the depth of my soul. But to see him killed in my very presence, with no opportunity to repent his sins so he must go straight to hell-fire . . . I could not. Savior, forgive me if I did the wrong thing.

Père Antoine stumbled toward the stream, leaning on his enemy. They reached the bank, and the priest bent over and splashed his face with the icy water. "Thank you, my son. I will offer prayers for your soul."

"I'm the one in your debt, Père Antoine. May I ask how you happened to be here," Quent watched the priest's face. "I saw you back there in the nuns' church, didn't I? The place I brought Mademoiselle Crane." He turned his head to look at the dead Indians in the clearing. "These renegades don't seem likely converts to Christianity. Nor Lantak either."

The cold water helped. Père Antoine felt more himself. He stood up, and his eyes were level with those of the redheaded giant. The priest was accustomed to being able to whither most men with the power of his glance. Not this one. Are you heathen or heretic, Red Bear? And do you know how close to death you just came? Do you care? "God's ways are not ours, my son. Who are we to say who is to benefit from the loving kindness of Jesus Christ, or the infinite goodness of His True Church? Now, I must be getting back to the town and my duties."

Quent moved aside, clearing the way to the path that led through the woods and back to the fortress city of Québec. "I will not forget this day, priest. Nor the fact that I'm in your debt." He spoke to the man's departing back. The priest merely raised a hand to acknowledge that he heard.

Solomon was still sitting on the ground, waiting. Quent went to him. "You goin' after Lantak?" the barrel maker asked.

"No." Quent took the long gun from Solomon's hands and slung it over his shoulder. "He's had too much of a head start. Besides, he knows these woods better than I do." But Corm knew them as well as Lantak did. Even with the old barrel maker slowing him down Quent wasn't more than a week's trek from Singing Snow. There were people there who could heal Solomon's wounds and if Corm was gone, Bishkek might know where. The temptation was strong, but it was hard to say how much time Solomon had left. Could be he wouldn't survive a week's trek. Could be he'd die before he ever saw the only place on earth that mattered to him. "I'd dearly love to get my dirk back," Quent admitted, "but if I don't get you home to Sally Robin sooner rather than later, she'll sing a hex on me."

Solomon chuckled. "She mighty will, boy. I trust she mighty will." It was the first time in years he'd called Quent boy rather than master. It felt good to both of them.

LEAF FALLING MOON, THE TWENTY-THIRD SUN
THE VILLAGE OF SINGING SNOW

It was nearly the end of September; the cold was settling in and the sun was never higher than the treetops of the far horizon. These days Cormac figured it to be about three o'clock when darkness arrived. A *Cmokmanuk* idea. If he'd never gone to Shadowbrook he wouldn't give a dog's fart for precisely what hour a thing happened or didn't happen. Or maybe he would. Maybe the white on the outside of him would have overwhelmed the red inside whether or not he ever left Singing Snow. *Ahaw,* yes, but if he'd made more room in his head for the *Anishinabeg* and less for the *Cmokmanuk,* maybe he would understand the meaning of the hawk and the little birds and the white bear and the white wolf. He shivered and drew the blanket closer around his shoulders, leaning toward the fire.

"Until he was eight," Bishkek said, "my bridge person son knew only the way things are here in this place of the Fifth Fire. Then he learned the *Cmokmanuk* ways and the cold moons chewed his bones and froze the water in his eyes, and the darkness was like a curse to him and he left us when the sun left."

Cormac couldn't look at his manhood father, much less answer him. How did the old man always know what he was thinking?

Bishkek shifted his position slightly to accept the pipe which had passed to him from the left. He drew long and deep, exhaling smoke in a slow stream before finishing his thought. "It is time for my bridge person son to go."

"I do not know more than I did when I came," Cormac murmured, his words meant only for Bishkek. "I have no answers, Father."

"*Ahaw,* you have. You know that the answer is not here."

"Where, then?"

Bishkek shrugged and passed the pipe to Cormac. Cormac drew deeply and held the smoke in his mouth, enjoying the heat and the taste of the tobacco. A boy of no more than six, the son of one of Bishkek's daughters, sidled up to him and leaned confidently into Cormac's body, sure of his welcome. "Do it, Uncle. Do the trick. Do it!" Cormac put his arm around the boy's waist and drew him close, at the same time exhaling in such a manner that the smoke made large and distinctive rings just visible in the glow of the fire. The boy's pudgy little hands grabbed at the fleeting images, destroying the thing he wanted simply by the act of reaching for it.

"You still have Memetosia's gift?" Bishkek asked.

"*Ahaw.*" The pipe had passed on and the little boy moved to another man in the circle. "I still have it." The medicine bag was buried deep in the earth beneath the place in Bishkek's wickiup where Cormac spread his sleeping blankets.

Bishkek started to say something, but Kekomoson the chief leaned forward.

There were four braves sitting on the ground between the chief and Bishkek and Cormac; Kekomoson had to raise his voice to be sure he was heard. *"Giyabwe."* I had a dream. "Last night I dreamed of *wabnum,* the totem of this brave who is different than all the others." Kekomoson lifted his chin in Cormac's direction. "The *wabnum* in my dream was the biggest, whitest wolf I ever saw. It was racing away from here, going toward the sun."

"Was there a hawk in your dream?" Cormac asked eagerly. "And a white bear?"

Kekomoson shook his head. "None of those things. Only the sun and the white wolf."

Bishkek nodded with satisfaction. "I have been telling my bridge person son that it is time for him to go. Before the end of the Leaf Falling Moon. Back to where he—"

"In my dream," Kekomoson interrupted, "it was as I told you. The *wabnum* was racing in the sun-coming direction."

"East," Cormac said. "Not south. Not toward Shadowbrook."

Kekomoson shrugged. A bridge person was a good thing for the People to have. And this one remained part of the village, a true son of the Fifth Fire. But a bridge person could be of little value if he stayed on one side of the bridge. "In my dream the *wabnum* went in the direction of sun-coming," he insisted.

"It is settled, then," Bishkek said. "Before the finish of Leaf Falling Moon you will go in the sun-coming direction."

"That way leads only to the ocean," Cormac muttered glumly. "Maybe I should drown myself."

"Be sure and take Memetosia's gift with you," Bishkek said as if he had not heard. "I do not want to be responsible for this thing that has no reason to be here."

Thursday, October 21, 1754
The Collège des Jésuites, Québec

The panels that lined the walls of the Provincial Superior's study had been brought from France. The wood was oak from the Ardennes forest, the carving the work of the talented *ébénistes* of Reims, the cathedral city of the province of Champagne. Louis Roget, Monsieur le Provincial, was from Reims. His family claimed descent from the holy bishop St. Remi, who in the fifth century baptized Clovis, first king of the Franks. There were Rémois counts as well in the lineage of Monsieur le Provincial, and no small amount of customary Champagne intrigue. As for Philippe Faucon, he'd been brought up in the court at Versailles where his uncle was Master of the Mews, and both his uncle and his father trained the king's hunting falcons. He'd long since learned that men, and sometimes women, had claws as sharp as any hawk. He wasn't surprised to discover that there were secrets hidden in the oaken woodwork.

Once before today, while he was rubbing the finest beeswax into the wood—on his knees, as a penance for returning late from one of his sorties into the countryside to sketch—the panel depicting the second of the Seven Sorrows of the Blessed Virgin had suddenly moved aside. Where the Flight into Egypt had been, there was now a framed view of the place in Québec Lower Town occupied by Père Antoine, the Franciscan priest, and two doors away the hovel that served as the monastery of his cloistered Poor Clares. In itself the incident involved no sin, but Philippe had spent much time examining the mechanism and marveling over its intricacies. That was what he had confessed to Monsieur Xavier Walton the fellow priest who regularly shrove him of his sins.

Walton was an Englishman who, following a long tradition, had left his schismatic country and joined the Society of Jesus in France. Xavier burned to return to his homeland and be martyred, and mourned that while it remained against the law to practice the Catholic faith anywhere in Great Britain and Jesuits were certainly not welcome in London, the days of public martyrdom at the Tyburn gallows were past. To make up for being born too late to be hung, drawn, and quartered, Xavier was rigorous in his observance of every penitential detail of the Jesuit way of life. But stickler for the Jesuit Constitutions though he was, he hadn't seen grave error in the tale of the moving panel and Philippe's interest in the mechanism. "It is only a sin to question the wisdom of our superiors, Philippe."

"But I do not. I was simply interested in how clever the thing was."

"Very well."

Philippe detected a hint of a chuckle in Xavier's voice. *Eh bien.* Earnestness was part of his nature. Other people often found it amusing.

"Put the whole thing out of your mind, Philippe. *Ego te absolve . . .*" And by the awesome power granted him at ordination to forgive in the name of Jesus Christ the Son of God, Xavier Walton had made the sign of the cross over his brother priest and absolved him of any sin there might have been in the business. Philippe had truly put the incident out of his mind. More or less. As much as he could. He was careful not to disturb again the Holy Family's Flight into Egypt when it fell to him once more to polish the wood paneling in the private apartments of Monsieur le Provincial.

Today was the third time since the great spring feast of Pentecost that the duty had been assigned to Philippe. "You will do the entire job on your knees, Philippe. And a few *Paternosters* might help the state of your soul. Obedience is the first virtue of a member of the Society."

But he had obeyed. He had burned the sketches. Six months' work, seven series of pen and ink drawings following the cycle of growth of various indigenous Canadian herbs, from the first wakening of early spring to the rich harvest of autumn, all ashes as his superior had commanded. His fault had been to utter a mild protest. "I'm told the king expects to see them, Monsieur le Provincial."

"Then the king must bend the knee to the will of Almighty God." As interpreted by the Provincial Superior of the Jesuits of New France, the voice of God to all his sons and, the Jesuit superior was convinced, to Madame de Pompadour and Louis XV. "You are too proud, Philippe, of these little pictures you make. A vigorous session with the beeswax is sure to be salutary."

Please, Blessed Mother of God, Philippe prayed, make me more humble. And please, if it be the will of your Divine Son, grant that Monsieur le Provincial does not forbid my drawing altogether. He rubbed harder on the wings that covered the face of an angel kneeling in adoration before the Divine Throne. *"Pater noster, qui es in caelis . . ."* The angel unfolded his wings.

Sacré Dieu! Philippe had to remind himself that the thing wasn't a miracle, only the talent of the Champenois woodworkers. Behind the angel's wings was a large, velvet-lined box. Lying in plain view was a letter written in an assured, clear hand. *Pompadour has decided. Dieskau and his troops arrive in early spring, as soon as the St. Lawrence thaws. He is to bring seventy-eight companies of regular soldiers, equivalent to eight British regiments, which is six more than they're sending with Braddock. Until then the diplomats continue to make mealy-mouthed talk of peace and—*

Philippe dropped the polishing rag and made a hurried sign of the cross, then shoved hard against the angel's wings, putting all his weight behind the move. The wings folded back into place. *" . . . sanctificetur nomen tuum. Adveniat regnum tuum. Fiat voluntas tua . . ."* The words of the Our Father tumbled out of him in an urgent flood. Thy will be done, but don't let it be Thy will that I must confess to seeing that document, *mon Dieu.*

It was not a sin, Lord. I did not seek to open the panel, I merely followed instructions to rub with vigor. I committed no sin, Lord. I have nothing of which to accuse myself. *"Je vous salue, Marie, pleine de grâce . . ."* Aves rather than *Paternosters.* The gentle Mother of God would know what was in his heart.

By the time Louis Roget returned, Philippe was on the other side of the room. *"Eh bien, Philippe, tout est bien?"*

"Oui, Monsieur le Provincial, tout est bien."

The Jesuit Provincial leaned close to the angel covering his face in adoration and studied the delicate carving. The single strand of his own black hair was gone.

He had lain it along one of the grooves in the folded wings, wedged in well enough so the act of simply polishing the wood would be unlikely to dislodge it. That would only happen if the hidden spring were triggered and the wings unfolded. So, Philippe my so conscientious *artiste,* now you know almost as much as I do about the plans being made in Versailles. And will you, I wonder, go running to your confessor? *Alors,* you must. Your scruples will permit nothing else. And what will the Englishman tell you? More important, what will he do with the information?

The Provincial rested his chin on the tent made of the fingers of both his hands. Xavier Walton will use whatever he is told for the good of his own country—but the good of England as he sees it. Which means he must side with Catholic France if there is to be another war, not with heretic Britain. *Eh bien,* that much is simple. The rest? For the moment I am not entirely sure how I will use the fact that Philippe Faucon has clandestine knowledge of the plans of the French navy. And that I know this, but he does not know that I know it. And all this was achieved while ensuring the spiritual well-being of those entrusted to me by Almighty God. Truly excellent.

There was a chess game set up in one corner of the room. The pieces were made of ivory and basalt and carved to represent the Christians and Moors of fifteenth-century Spain. Louis Roget always played both black and white, choosing each move as if he were totally invested in winning for whichever army he represented at the moment. This game had been in process for over a week. The Moors had only two pawns, a bishop, the rooks, and the king and queen left, and their king was in danger of being placed in check. Roget castled. The reversal removed the Moorish king from immediate danger, but sacrificed his queen. White's response was swift and decisive. Knight to knight seven. The Moorish queen was captured. Roget swept her from the board, then took the Christian white knight with the rook of the black Moorish king. The balance of the game was entirely changed. More thought was required.

The lightest touch opened the panel that let him gaze down on the Franciscan living quarters in the lower town. Poor Père Antoine. He was alone in Québec, with no brother priest of his own order to shrive him of his sins. The diocesan priests were few, and most of them were stationed in remote districts outside the city. And their penances were not, perhaps, muscular enough for an ascetic like the Delegate of the Minister General of the Friars Minor. In the normal way of things Antoine made his confession to a Jesuit. Particularly when a grievous fault weighed on his conscience. As it had only a few days before.

"Pray bless me, for I have sinned." There was a small curtained grille between penitent and confessor, but he had recognized the Franciscan's voice as soon as the first words were uttered. Normally that box was used by Xavier Walton, but the Englishman was ill that day and the Provincial had taken his place. Given how agitated the penitent sounded, he might have come even if he'd known it would be Louis Roget listening to him bare his soul. "I have lived for over a month with the knowledge that I have . . . that I may have betrayed Holy Church."

"Indeed? How did that occur?"

The Franciscan did not reply quickly. No doubt he recognized the voice of the Jesuit superior. Still, the seal of the confessional was perhaps the most solemn burden a priest carried. The Jesuit would be unlikely to commit the mortal sin of betraying that seal. "I saved the life of a man who is a heretic, and worse, an enemy of truth and the Gospel."

"All life is precious in the eyes of Almighty God. Even the lives of heretics. It is not for you to judge. How can saving even such a life as that be counted as a sin?"

"Because this man opposes the mission of the Church." Roget permitted himself a glance at his penitent. The Franciscan's head was bowed, and his shoulders sagged with the weight of his sin. He would not make less than an honest confession "The man I saved will do everything in his power to oppose us. He is a Protestant heretic, and if he has his way the Church will not be permitted to preach the Gospel to the Indians of the Ohio Country."

"I see. And how were you responsible for aiding this man's evil mission?"

"A heathen savage was prepared to shoot him. It seemed to me that I could not be witness to a cold-blooded murder, that I could not watch the heretic die with the sins of his heresy still on his soul and no opportunity to repent and save himself eternity in hellfire. I shoved the killer, just enough to spoil his aim."

The Jesuit took his time before speaking. He was administering a sacrament, acting *in loco Jesu Christe.* But for Your greater glory, Lord. I cannot betray the seal, but I can seek the knowledge necessary to advance Your most holy cause.

It was October and winter was upon them. Roget could see his own breath in the church air, but he could see as well the sweat beading on Père Antoine's forehead. "Who were these men? What were you doing in their company?"

"The man I saved is known as Uko Nyakwai, the Red Bear."

"Quentin Hale? The American *coureur de bois?*"

"Yes."

"And the would-be murderer?"

"Lantak, the renegade."

A pause, then, with not even a hint of sarcasm, "I am sure you were present for the purpose of trying to convert both the heathen and the heretic to the True Faith."

"As God is my judge, that is my ultimate aim in all things."

"If that is the case you have nothing to regret. Only perhaps that you do not sufficiently trust in the guidance of the Holy Spirit. In penance for that say fifty

Paters and as many *Aves*. And in the name of our most holy Lord Jesus Christ, I grant you absolution. *Ego te absolve in nomine Patris, et Filii, et Spiritus Sancti...*"

In his study, the memory of the confession emboldened Roget. He stretched out his hand. Black bishop takes white pawn. White queen takes black bishop. *Alors, échec et mat* in two moves. There could be no escape. The Christians had won. He tipped over the Moorish king. Then he went to his desk and rang the bell that summoned one of the lay brothers.

"You called for me, Monsieur le Provincial?"

"Yes. Please tell Monsieur Walton I wish to see him."

A few minutes later the Englishman stood before his superior. "You sent for me?"

"I did. You are a surgeon, Xavier, is that not correct?"

"It is, Monsieur le Provincial. I studied with the English Company in London before I went to France and joined the Society."

"I see. And did you ever actually practice surgery? Before becoming a priest, I mean."

"For a short time, Monsieur le Provincial. A year, perhaps a little less."

"A year. And are you any good, Xavier?"

"As a surgeon?"

"Of course."

Walton had little idea what they were talking about. Everything the Provincial was asking was already known to him. "I am not the finest surgeon in the world, Monsieur le Provincial. But neither am I the worst. Perhaps we should say 'competent.'"

A typical English answer. "You never wanted to come to Québec, did you?"

Xavier was startled by the sudden change of subject, but he recovered quickly. "I wanted to do whatever my superiors commanded me to do. They sent me here."

"But it wasn't what you really wanted, was it? You wanted to be sent back to England to say Mass in secret in the dark of night, and hide in priest holes, and eventually be captured by the heretic king's soldiers and sent to martyrdom at Tyburn Hill. Is that not so, Monsieur Walton?"

"There have been few martyrs made in England in recent years, Monsieur le Provincial. The English believe their Protestant heresy so well entrenched that they have far less fear of the True Faith. They mostly ignore Catholic priests these days, unless the prohibitions against the Faith are openly flouted."

"Hmm... Yes, that's what I hear as well. Still, it's martyrdom you're after, isn't it, Monsieur Xavier Walton?"

"If God were to judge me worthy, I— There are many opportunities for martyrdom here. Before we convert them, the heathen savages have methods every bit as efficient as those of the soldiers of the English king. Monsieur le Provincial knows that better than I do."

"Indeed, Xavier. I know most things better than you do. And as far as you are concerned, I speak with the voice of Almighty God. Is that not so?"

"It is absolutely so. If I have done anything to make you believe I thought otherwise—"

"No, no. I know you are a loyal Jesuit, Xavier. It's why I'm sending you to the American colony of Virginia."

The Englishman could only sputter in disbelief: "Virginia! But . . . I did not know . . . It never occurred to me . . . I never heard . . ."

"Get to the point, Monsieur."

". . . that we had a house in Virginia, Monsieur le Provincial. That comes as a complete surp—"

"We have no house in Virginia. It is an English colony, and as you and I have just been discussing, the Catholic faith is forbidden wherever England rules. No, no, my son. I am not sending you to Virginia as a priest. I am sending you as a healer. A surgeon. It is my belief, Xavier, that you will do a great amount of good in Virginia."

FRIDAY, OCTOBER 23, 1754
PORT MOUTON, L'ACADIE

The French called this land l'Acadie. It was Nova Scotia to the English, and Chignecto in the tongue of the Mi'kmaq, whose land it had been before the Europeans arrived. By whatever name, it was the easternmost point he could reach. Cormac had come to the edge of the world.

The ocean, dark and forbidding, pounded the shallow beach, kicking up white spray that reached ever higher on the incoming tide. The tang of salt was in his mouth and the cold nipped at his nose and fingertips. Behind him was a carefully tended field, its boundaries marked by a high, rounded ridge of grass, interrupted at regular intervals by wooden structures that appeared to be sheds of some sort. Cormac had never seen any fields quite like them.

A pair of brown and white cows stood a little distance away, intent on the last of the late autumn grass, paying him no mind. Beyond them, just visible in the gray of the dwindling afternoon, was the steep pitched roof of a *Cmokmanuk* house. No smoke, but he didn't have the feeling the place was deserted. The ghosts of thousands of warriors roamed this ground. *Anishinabeg* since a time too long to remember, then the Europeans. Nowhere was the land hunger between the French and the English more apparent and more vicious than here on the outer rim of this, their New World.

The wind was rising. Bishkek had given him a cloak made of elk hide, cured with great skill so the sleek black fur remained supple and glistening. Corm shivered and drew the cloak closer. He fancied there was the stink of powder and burning pitch on the wind. The smell of war.

A chain of forts surrounded him. In his mind's eye he could see them all. The Citadel of Louisbourg to the north was the biggest. It had been built by the French forty years before, captured by New England colonials in 1745, then returned to the French by treaty in 1748. Louisbourg guarded the entrance to the St. Lawrence River and thus to all Canada. To somehow compensate for so great a loss, the English began building Fort Lawrence just east of the Missaquash River, in plain sight of Beauséjour and Gaspareau, the two French forts that guarded the Chignecto Isthmus that joined l'Acadie to the mainland. Forty leagues up the coast from where he stood was the Halifax Citadel, a walled city populated by thousands of Protestant, English-speaking settlers. Halifax was heavily garrisoned.

Ayi! A river of blood might well flow from any direction in this place.

But what did it have to do with him? Or with Memetosia and his Suckáuhock. This was a *Cmokmanuk* struggle. Yes, he reminded himself, and you are half *Cmokman. Ahaw.* And you are also *wabnum,* the white wolf. And inside of you is a red man who knows that the path laid out in a dream must be followed. Otherwise even death will bring no release.

Cormac knew he had to find shelter. He couldn't travel much farther tonight. This hunt seemed to be over: he'd seen no hawk, no white bear. He'd dreamed nothing of any significance. The whole trek was a waste. Except that the foreboding of the original dream would not leave him. It sat in his belly as it had from the first moment he dreamed it. Every morning he woke to the same sense of urgency and the same dread still twisted his bowels. *Merde!* A curse on all dreams.

Kekomoson had said a *wabnum* running toward the place where the sun rises. "This *wabnum* can go no further," Cormac said aloud. "No further! Do you hear me?" He shouted the words at the relentless sea. Memetosia's medicine bag felt heavy around his neck. He struggled with the urge to rip it off and hurl it into the waves.

"*Est-ce que vous voulez que la mer vous répond, monsieur?*"

Cormac turned and his eyes met those of a woman almost as tall as he was. Hers were gray with black flecks, like polished stones found on a beach. She peered at him intently, clutching her blue knitted shawl with both hands to keep it from blowing away. She seemed to bend with the wind, like a willow, Corm thought, its trunk slender and supple enough to sway with any storm that came. "*J'ai pensé que j'etais tout seul, madame.*" I thought I was alone. "*Je m'excuse.* I didn't imagine I would disturb your cows. Much less their mistress."

She smiled. Her teeth were white and even, and the corners of her wide mouth turned up to show two dimples. "*Mademoiselle,*" she corrected. "And you did not disturb me or my cows. But it is late and getting cold. Soon it will be dark. Not pleasant, even, I think, for the fierce Cormac Shea. You must come home with me, monsieur. As you yourself just said—rather loudly I recall—you can go no further."

"You know who I am?"

"Of course. Who does not know of Cormac Shea?"

The scar made him easy to identify. "I'd be grateful for a night's shelter, mademoiselle. Perhaps I can offer some work in payment."

"I am Marni Benoit, and for a start you can help me bring these cows home."

The barn was attached to the house. It was full of the sweet smell of hay and warmed by the breath of the animals. A corner was occupied by a small flock of dark brown hens, and from a separate nearby shed he heard the snuffling of a pig. "You are well provided for, mademoiselle."

"Here in l'Acadie we provide for ourselves. And I told you, my name is Marni." She sat down on a little three-legged stool and began milking the smaller of the pair of cows while she spoke, leaning her head against its side as she rhythmically tugged on the teats, holding a bucket in place with her knees. "I prefer that to 'mademoiselle.' "

"Very well, Marni then." The position she'd assumed lifted her skirts, and he saw her ankles were slim and shapely above her heavy clogs. He wondered about the color of her hair. A white mobcap covered almost all of it, though the bit he could see above her forehead seemed quite fair. "Will you trust me to do the same service for Mumu?" he asked. As they walked back from the field she'd told him the smaller cow was Tutu, the larger Mumu.

"*Oui, si vous voulez.*"

There was a second milking stool hanging on a peg on the wall. As if it weren't in regular use, Corm thought as he reached it down. So far he'd seen no indication that anyone else lived on this remote farm with Marni Benoit.

"Mumu is not accustomed to strange hands, Monsieur Shea. You must be gentle, and at the same time on your guard."

"I will try to be both. But if you are Marni I must be Cormac. Corm, if you like."

She had finished with Tutu and straightened, quickly moving the bucket out of reach of the cow's swishing tale. "I like Corm. Yes, I shall call you that. And you are a very good milker. For a *coureur de bois* and a métis at that."

He was done, and he stood and handed her the full bucket of warm milk. "I didn't realize they knew so much about me in l'Acadie."

"They don't. I do. Come." Marni led the way into the house.

It was full dark now, and inside the only light came from the dull glow of the banked fire. "The logs are there," she said, nodding toward a supply of wood that had been moved into the house. "If you will stir up the fire, I'll get a lantern going. And then I'll fix some supper."

He turned to get a log from the stack she'd indicated and saw her remove her shawl and hang it quickly on a peg. When she lifted her arms he could see the swell of her breasts, despite the concealing blue dress and pinafore made of homespun flax. The gesture had shifted her mobcap and he could see her hair was a yellow so pale it was almost white.

"What did you mean when you said the others didn't know about me, but you did?"

"Only that around here very few care what happens beyond l'Acadie. They have heard stories, of course. Tales of the fearless métis who would turn us all out of our homes and let the Indians have everything."

"The Indians were here first. The Whites are destroying their way of life."

"So in return you would destroy ours." She shrugged. "It sounds to me like mostly everything men do. An excuse to fight."

The fire was blazing now and he felt truly warm for the first time in days. Watching her move about the kitchen was a delight. She wakened something in him that had been dormant for some time. This Marni Benoit was leading him back into his whiteness. For the moment, she was his Shadowbrook. "But the others around here, your family and friends, they do not know about my ideas?"

"No, not in any detail. As for my family, they are dead. And I have no friends."

"You live here alone?"

"Yes." She swung the crane that held a large black kettle into position above the leaping flames and ladled into it a portion of the milk they had just taken from the cows. "These days I prefer being alone."

"How come you know so much more than other Acadians?"

"Because unlike most of them I have not remained always in l'Acadie. I committed a great sin for an Acadian woman, Cormac Shea. I went to Québec. With a man."

The supper was ready. A thick wedge of hard cheese and a loaf of bread, and to drink, frothy spruce beer cut with the milk she'd warmed over the fire. The first *Cmokmanuk* food he'd had in months. The bread, made in the French fashion, with a hard crust and a soft chewy interior, particularly delighted him. "Québec was the first city I ever saw. I went there with my mother once. I was very little, maybe three or four. I don't remember much about it, except bread like this. It was very good, but yours is better."

"Thank you. Jean, my fiancé, was a baker. He taught me how to make it."

"You are to be married, then?"

"Was. I was to be married. Jean is dead."

"I'm sorry. How did it happen?"

She shrugged and leaned forward to refill his tankard with more ale and more warm milk. "He was run over. It was a foggy morning. He was delivering a sack of *batards* to the fine house of a fine Québécois. The carriage came quickly, the alley was too narrow to permit escape . . ." She shrugged again. "It is a common story."

"Not when it is your story."

They finished eating. Marni stood up and began clearing the table. "You can sleep over there." She indicated a corner beside the fire where there was a rolled-up mat and a neat pile of blankets.

"I don't want to discomfort you. The barn is fine if—"

"You will not discomfort me. My bed is above."

"You will have to let me do something to repay you," he insisted.

"There is always wood to be cut," she said, walking to the ladder that led to her bed beneath the peak of the roof. "I'll be glad of whatever you can get done of that."

He could get plenty done if he stayed for a time. He thought about it while he lay beside the banked fire and outside the wind howled and the sea could be heard crashing on the beach. No white wolf and no hawk and no white bear. But he had been sent east and traveled as far as he could in that direction. Now he might as well wait until the next step of the journey was revealed to him.

Chapter Fourteen

QUENT STOOD BESIDE the rushing stream. The five mighty oaks—Squirrel Oaks—were behind him. They separated him from the burial ground, but he could still hear the sounds of Jeremiah and Little George shoveling dirt onto Ephraim's coffin.

Everyone else had left. The Anglican minister and many of the other mourners had come all the way from Albany—John and Genevieve Lydius and their entire brood among them. Every slave was present, and all the tenants, even those from distant Do Good. The Kahniankehaka, too. Chief Thoyanoguin had arrived wearing his jacket trimmed in gold braid and his tricorne. A dozen braves had come with him. Such a large delegation paid Ephraim high honor. Like everyone else, the Indians stayed until the service ended. Only Corm wasn't there.

It was often Corm's way to move south before the great snows. Quent had hoped he'd show up as the autumn passed into winter, but so far it hadn't happened. Meanwhile, until three days earlier, Ephraim had seemed the same as he'd been since the summer, no better but also no worse. Then, three mornings past, Runsabout had gone to bring him his morning ale and found him dead in his bed. Too late to send word to Cormac, even if he was still at Singing Snow.

After they had gathered around Ephraim's grave and listened to the minister speak of resurrection and eternal life, John invited the mourners to stop by the Frolic Ground before departing. There would be johnnycakes to fortify them for the journey home, and a cup of punch lifted in Ephraim's honor. John didn't look at his younger brother when he spoke, and Quent knew the invitation didn't include him. That didn't matter, but his mother did. All during the funeral, each time he glanced up she was staring at him, defeat and despair all over her face. It was the first time he'd ever seen her look like that. When the minister had said everything he had to say and handed Lorene a clod of earth, she'd thrown it into Ephraim's grave and looked like maybe she wanted to die, too. Quent took a step toward her, but Lorene had turned aside. She'd never before closed him out like that. He'd known then he wouldn't be joining the others at the Frolic Ground.

The sound of shoveling stopped. "That'll rest him." Jeremiah's voice came softly from the other side of the oaks, traveling easily on the cold, dry air. Little George murmured an assent.

Quent heard the sound of their footsteps leaving the burial ground, which also contained the remains of his grandparents and a couple of aunts and uncles and cousins he barely remembered or had never known, and the small, long-worn-down mounds of the six dead children Lorene had borne but been unable to suckle to life beyond a paltry few months. Pohantis was there as well, buried a distance away from the others because Ephraim had insisted on that, and Shoshanaya, and Quent's son. The child was unborn, but he'd always been sure it was a son. Shoshanaya had said so and he believed her. All bones in the ground now. Soon Ephraim would be the same. The worms were probably already busy with his father.

He was dressed in a coat and breeches and a white shirt, his home clothes, but there was no longer any place for him to call home. Shadowbrook was John's now.

Quent stripped off the fine clothing and threw himself naked into the rushing stream. The frigid water came from high up in the hills, from the underground river that flowed through Swallows Children. Deliberately he swam upstream, fighting the intense cold and the swift current, taking perverse comfort in the struggle. The air was bitter and each sharp breath tasted of snow. At last, spent, he flipped over and lay on his back in the turbulent water and let it carry him back to the place he'd started, his heart racing less wildly now, his spirit calmed. He clambered ashore and pulled on his breeches and his silver-buckled shoes; everything else he left lying where it was. Then he headed for the big house.

Less than an hour later, in her dead husband's room, where she had been searching one last time for the bequest Ephraim had made but must have later destroyed, Lorene looked out the window and saw her youngest son leave the Patent. He had on buckskins and his long gun was slung over his shoulder. She watched him striding down the path toward Hudson's River until she could see him no more, then she sank to her knees, and for the first time that day, she wept.

Quent did not once look back. It was over. Shadowbrook was no longer his home. What next? He had buried his birth father, Potawatomi custom said he must now go at once to show respect to his manhood father. He should spend a year, twelve full New Moon Tellings, in Singing Snow. Take a wife there. Sire a child. Become a manhood father to a boy. Thus did life go on in the face of death. So had the Great Spirit Shkotensi made the world.

A great distaste rose in him, a protest that tasted of bitterness and rage. He was sick of old men dictating to young men how things had to be. Quent turned south, not north and headed for the Ohio Country.

FRIDAY, NOVEMBER 13, 1754
MONASTERY OF THE POOR CLARES, QUÉBEC

The refectory table was a single wide plank on a pair of trestles. The chairs of the nuns were low, backless stools. There were six of them, one for each member of the community. Nicole's was empty. She knelt on the other side of the table, on the stone floor, both arms outstretched before her, clasping the empty wooden bowl that should have contained her midday meal. "I accuse myself of falling asleep during silent prayer," she had admitted at the Chapter of Faults that convened that morning.

"That is a grave sin against the Holy Rule of our Mothers Clare and Colette," Mère Marie Rose replied. "You will beg for your dinner every day this week."

So she was here. Silently imploring her sisters—they were her sisters, Nicole reminded herself, they had become so exactly sixty-one days ago when she'd crossed from the world to the cloister—to share some of their food with her. Dear Lord, her arms were on fire, held out in front of her like this for so long a time. But she must not lower the bowl until it was filled. To do so was a sign that she wished to fast. That would be a holy thing if I could do it, *mon Dieu*, but forgive me, I cannot. Already the waist of the black dress she'd been given the first day had been tucked three times.

And I fell asleep when I was meant to be concentrating on You because our cell (a Poor Clare never referred to anything but her sins as her own since the nuns held all in common) is so cold at night that I shiver instead of sleep. If only I could have a blanket, *mon Dieu*, even just a little thin one, I would not be so—Oh! She had been concentrating so hard on this litany of complaints she'd almost lowered the bowl. That would signify that she meant to fast. Oh no, *mon Dieu*, please. I must eat. Forgive me my sins and strengthen my arms. For the sake of Your Holy Mother. Nicole gripped the bowl as tightly as she could and stiffened her arms yet again.

None of the other nuns paid any attention to the struggle of the young woman they called a postulant while they tested her fitness to become a novice member of the community. Until she took the habit, she was with them but not entirely of them, and each of the nuns tried to maintain a slight distance to protect her heart. It was desolation to lose a companion, a sister who gave up the struggle and left before making her vows. As for today, the punishment *la petite* was undergoing was something every one of them had endured numerous times. They knew it was kinder not to look. Besides, the Holy Rule forbade eye contact during meals.

Poor Clares ate no meat, and fish only on major holidays. This was an ordinary day; the martyrology read before the meal commemorated saints Vitis and Agri-cola, fed to the lions of ancient Rome. Today the black-veiled heads remained bent over servings of beans and oats cooked into a gruel, and for the monastic third portion—what they were served in place of meat—boiled turnips. The nuns ate quickly, but the refectory was so cold each woman could see her breath. The food congealed in their bowls before they could get it all down. When only a single spoonful remained each nun scraped it up and leaned forward and tipped it into Nicole's bowl. *"Que le bon Dieu vous récompense pour votre charité,"* Nicole responded each time. May God reward you for your kindness.

Mère Marie Rose waited until every nun had put down her spoon, then she stood up. The others immediately did the same, including Nicole. Thank you, *mon Dieu,* thank you that I am no longer kneeling on these stones. And that I can lower my arms. She held onto the bowl with her left hand and used her right to make the sign of the cross.

"In nomine Patris, et Filii, et Spiritus Sancti . . ." The abbess intoned the long Latin grace. When it was ended she picked up the spoon she had herself used and gave it to Nicole. Nicole's own spoon was at her regular place, clean and untouched. She must eat her cold dinner with the other woman's utensil, a fur-ther humiliation. "You may eat, child. And when you are finished you will clean the refectory floor. Soeur Angelique has left a brush and a bucket for you."

The nuns left the refectory in procession. When they were gone, Nicole downed every morsel that was in the bowl, tasting nothing, only grateful that the empty place inside her was a little less empty. Begging for her dinner meant that she did not get a slice of the rough brown bread, nor a glass of the thin, acrid wine that accompanied the meal for those who were not guilty of grave sins against the Holy Rule.

There was a bucket of sand in one corner of the room. Nicole carried the bowl and the spoon there and rubbed them clean, then replaced them on the refectory table, the bowl at her own place, the spoon at that of the abbess. She undid the cuffs of her black dress and rolled them above her elbows. When she took the habit she would roll back wide gray sleeves and fasten them to her shoulders with a single pin the way she'd seen the nuns do. And when would that be? She had no idea. The date of the Clothing, as it was called, was at the discretion of the abbess. When it comes, *mon Dieu,* I will wear a white veil and truly be your bride.

We will be married, Quent had said that day in Do Good, with the Quakers in the next room and the pain of betraying her sacred promise still burning in her heart. *Wait until I return and you will be my wife.* When he spoke those words, how clearly she had seen herself standing beside him in the Frolic Ground with flowers in her hair and her heart singing, then living as his wife in the beautiful house that was his birthright, and that she knew Madame Hale intended him to have, bearing his children . . . O Blessed Mother of God, surely you do not hold it as a sin that I wanted to say yes. Yes, yes, a thousand times yes. It can be no sin merely to have imagined marrying the man I love, Blessed Mother. Loved, she corrected herself. You cannot love him now. You have given yourself to God.

There was a thin film of ice covering the water in the leather bucket. Nicole resisted the urge to break it with the scrub brush and plunged both her chapped and reddened hands in first. Then she soaked the brush in the frigid water and knelt down and began to scrub the stones. *"Je vous salue, Marie, pleine de grâce . . ."* She whispered the prayer beneath her breath, it would help the task go more quickly. Never mind that her knuckles were bleeding. *"Vous êtes bénie entre toutes les femmes, et Jésus, le fruit—"*

"—de vos entrailles, est béni. Sainte Marie, Mère de Dieu . . ."

Nicole had not realized that another pair of hands was also scrubbing the floor until she heard a second voice join in the prayer to the Holy Virgin. It was little Soeur Angelique, whose job this usually was. Next to Nicole, Angelique was youngest. She had been last in the line of nuns to welcome her new sister that day in the chapel, but Nicole was sure it had been Angelique on the other side of the turn when she first arrived. Now it was Angelique who in her charity had given up her hour of recreation—the time when the nuns sat together around a small fire in the common room and talked and laughed without restriction—and come to help the sinful young postulant scrub the refectory floor. *". . . Priez pour nous pauvres pécheurs, maintenant et à l'heure de notre mort. Amen."*

Not just for us poor sinners, Holy Mother of God, Nicole added silently. I beg you to pray for Quent. Ask your Blessed Son that Quent may be safe and happy. Happy. She thought the word a second time as she continued to intone *Aves* with Marie Angelique. Then a third. Happy. So, was she asking the Holy Virgin to send Quent another love, another woman to stand beside him at the Frolic Ground with flowers in her hair? Yes, probably. The thought made tears prickle behind her eyelids, but her beloved needed someone and it could not be her, no matter how much her heart ached for him. *". . . Maintenant et à l'heure de notre mort. Amen."*

FRIDAY, NOVEMBER 13, 1754
THE SLAVE MARKET AT THE FOOT OF WALL STREET,
NEW YORK CITY

By God, and this New York was a city worth putting a pox on. Na like God-cursed Albany or Edinburgh. More like Glasgow, Hamish Stewart decided. A place where canny folk pursued business in every lane. God blight all cities, but this one was at least worth the spit o' the curse.

All the same, cities made him tired. And he wouldna be refreshed until he was laird o' Shadowbrook. A pox on the blighted, devil-sent rain that had made that day further off then he'd hoped. They said in Albany that Shadowbrook was ruined. But for his purposes, not ruined enough.

"Prime," the black auctioneer called out. "All prime, gentleman. Particularly this fine young Ashanti buck here." He pointed to one young man in the middle of the line, shackled to his neighbors with a short length of chain and, like them, restrained with leg and wrist irons. The auctioneer's black assistant prodded the lad with the tip of his bullwhip. The youth stumbled a few steps forward. "Prime flesh if I've ever seen it," the auctioneer repeated. "Look at those muscles. Plenty of labor in those arms. And look here." This time it was the auctioneer himself who stepped from behind the podium and used a long stick to raise the youth's loincloth, exposing his genitals "Plenty of labor here as well, if you've a mind to make use of it." The crowd of bidders erupted in laughter. The lad stared straight ahead.

Filthy business this, Hamish thought. Filthy. Maybe when the Patent's mine I'll— Na, I will not. Slaves and Shadowbrook. They go together. Why else is John Hale standing in the front waiting for something he fancies to go on the block?

One by one they went. The New York City slave market was the largest in the north, supplied by private slavers sailing their own ships through the Middle Passage, and famous throughout the colonies for giving buyers better value than they could get elsewhere.

"Prime, gentlemen, all prime!" The auctioneer danced along the line of shackled bodies, indicating each in turn with a tap of his long stick. "Look here, gentlemen! Look ye here! Ashanti! Ibo! Ibo! Fanti! What am I bid?" Back at his podium now, though not done with his huckstering; never mind that he too was owned by the owners of the slave market. "Here on Wall Street you see what you're buying before you part with your money. All prime, gentlemen! Prime! Come and bid!"

Hamish shivered. God's truth, and it was a soul-destroying thing to buy and sell human flesh, but the brass it made, that was a mighty thing. Any man could tell as much by the splendor o' these fine houses and grand ladies and gents o' New York City.

John Hale bid on an Ibo girl and got her for a hundred guineas. The lass was eight or nine, Hamish guessed. The auctioneer used his stick to push up the linen shift that was supplied by the owners o' the market for modesty's sake. Not a hair between her legs; wee breasts though, hard little ebony nuts just starting to form, the nipples not yet mature enough to stiffen with the cold. John nodded with approval, the shift dropped back into place, and she was his. Minutes later he was high bidder for two young lads, God blight his rotten soul, stepping up to make payment of four hundred guineas for his three purchases.

The man whose job it was to take the money, the casher, sat at a plank spread across two trestles at the far end of the auction block. Hamish edged a bit closer. Hale handed over a deerskin pouch and the casher took his time about untying it, then poured the contents onto the splintered wood.

There was a set of scales at his elbow, but it would only be used if there was doubt about the value of the odd assemblage of coins that passed for legal tender in these colonies. Money from every realm under heaven was in use since the Sassenach fools wouldna permit the Americans a mint and deliberately stinted the circulation o' their own guineas and sovereigns. That way anything the Americans wanted to buy had to come from Mother England, not some other country.

The casher separated Hale's coins with practiced fingers, using both hands, until there were short towers of French ducats and Dutch *daalders* and Portuguese *cruzados,* even a few Spanish pieces of eight. "To the value of four hundred guineas exactly," he said at last. "Done, Mr. Hale."

"Done," John Hale agreed. He reached into his pocket and withdrew a few more shillings. "Keep the three here for me a day or two. I'll collect them when I'm ready to return to Albany. And whatever's left over is for yourself and the auctioneer."

Regular buck o' the stuffed purse, he was. Ruined? By Christ Jesus, how could Shadowbrook be ruined if the new laird, God curse his blighted soul, could be payin' out four hundred guineas o' cash money for black slaves not three months after better than half his wheat crop had gone up in smoke?

John was vaguely aware of Stewart—as chance would have it, he'd seen the Scot earlier that morning, as he was leaving the Wall Street mansion belonging to his Devrey relations—but it was the three merchants standing to the side in the opposite direction that got most of his attention. James Alexander and Oliver De Lancey and the God-rotting Jew Hayman Levy. They had been there since the sale began, but had not placed a single bid this day. They had come to watch.

Power of the purse you may have, you bastards, but don't forget what you just saw. John Hale, master of the Hale Patent, stepped up to the auction block and paid top price for three new blacks. In cash money, mind. None of your paper rubbish. So don't be telling me that Shadowbrook isn't the collateral it once was, and that you won't be putting up the money as will buy the cane land that will change everything.

John turned his back on the casher's table. His hands were sweating—he shoved them into his pockets so no one might see them tremble—and his heart was hammering in his chest. He'd just paid close to every farthing the Patent had earned from what could be salvaged of the summer crop. It was worth it. Cane land was worth whatever gamble it took.

The Merchant's Coffee House did grand business after the sale ended. The long tables were crowded with bowls and mugs and tankards of drink, and the stools and narrow benches were crowded with the hindquarters of gentleman of every size and description. The smells of tobacco and ale and freshly roasted coffee beans mingled with the musk of traders invigorated by the morning's buying and selling. There was a steady hum of conversation as the patrons took each other's measure by the cut of a wig, the swagger of a blue velvet coat, or the sheen of green satin breeches. Finery and the display of it was the order of the day. This was New York City, by God. Not your prissy-mouthed Boston or your righteous, do-good Philadelphia. Since the Dutch founded the place a hundred and thirty years before—and surrendered it to the English forty years after that—this had always been a city with one purpose, the creation of wealth. The aroma that over-came all others in the midday bustle of the Merchant's Coffee House on Wall Street was the rich and seductive stink of money.

Black men and boys in long leather aprons hurried among the tables, serving pewter bowls of the dark, steaming coffee for which the Merchant's was famous, and offering other bowls piled high with Caribbean sugar. Each patron used long wooden tongs to take as many of the sticky, golden nuggets as he liked, sweeten-ing the black brew to his taste and to the stretch of his purse. COFFEE THREE PENCE A BOWL, SUGAR TUPPENCE PER MORSEL, a sign on the wall pro-claimed. A glass of punch or a tankard of ordinary ale could be had for a penny.

Hamish raised his hand and finally managed to attract the attention of one of the waiters. "Bring me an ale, laddie, and be quick." The black didn't seem impressed with the one-eyed stranger in the homespun jerkin. Hamish waited and nursed his thirst, and used his single eye and his two good ears, but not to the advantage he'd have wished.

John Hale was three tables to his left, deep in conversation with his maternal uncle, Bede Devrey. A short, stubby man with a head too big for his body, there was in Bede's face some of the look of his sister Lorene, but none of her grace. And what did that matter, Hamish thought, when he was the one inherited the fleet o' Devrey ships, and every one of 'em worth a fortune in the Triangle Trade 'twixt the colonies and Africa and England? Might well be it was Bede Devrey supplied the money his nephew spent this day to buy three slaves. But why? To impress the other merchants as watched every transaction. Make 'em lend more to John Hale, keep him afloat till next harvest. So Bede Devrey's sister would na finish her days wi'out a pisspot to call her own.

He dared na sit any closer, and it was impossible to hear what the uncle and nephew were saying at this distance. Everything he saw just deepened the mys-tery. Shadowbrook was not ruined enough. God's truth that was.

Time to leave this place. But not by blighted hell until he'd quenched his thirst.

Then he'd stay out o' sight until his night's business was finished; after that he'd take the first packet to Albany as would give him a bit o' deck space to stand on. Hamish's glance restlessly roved the room, his one good eye doing the work of two. The minutes passed and there was still no sign of the nigra meant to be bringing him his ale, while the coffee house grew ever more crowded, a steady stream of customers wedging themselves in where it seemed no more could fit.

The babble of conversation was a high-pitched and constant clatter. Mostly bawdy innuendo concerning the town's infamous whoremistress, a veiled creature they called Squaw DaSilva. The rest was all to do wi' business.

The Merchant's was the coffee house favored by those involved wi' the shipping trade and auctions. It was to the Exchange on Broad Street men went to talk o' the buying or selling o' land. More his sort o' transaction, that. A man could rely on land. It dinna disappear into the depths of the ocean, or reappear in bits and pieces along distant beaches a man never heard o' before.

The patrons of the Merchant's Coffee House did not share that sentiment. In the space of a few breaths Hamish heard at least four different men commit themselves to share the risk of a new vessel being built for the Islands trade, and two who were anxious to purchase an interest in the profit of a slave ship called the *Lauralee Haven.* "Leaks like a sieve, the *Lauralee* does," a third man called out. "You're fixing to lose your stones, Jack. But then, judging from the cut of your breeches, you've not very big ones to lose." And underneath the talk of fucking and finances, another theme, one that interested Hamish Stewart still more.

"The king said nothing when he opened parliament. Not a bloody word."

"You're wrong. He as good as made a declaration of war. He'd protect trade, he said, and the source of the nation's wealth. That's us, for the love of the Almighty. We're the source of England's wealth, and George knows it as well as his father did. He's sworn to protect us."

"Like he's been protecting us all along," a third man joined in. "Doesn't amount to a fart in the wind. Nothing's ever settled. Far as I can tell, the bloody French are true to their devious papist ways and get away with it. Keep taking a little more and a little more, and sometimes being made to give a small piece of it back, but at the end of the day they've got their hooks farther into us than they were before. Where's the protection in that?"

Hamish's ale arrived. He flipped a wooden penny at the young black who brought it, and drank half the mug in a single draught. "Another, laddie!" he shouted at the boy's departing back. "And best I'd na be in my grave a wee time afore it gets here."

". . . two regiments of five hundred each," a man was saying, his voice low and urgent, "under the command of the best possible man for the job, Major General Edward Braddock. They leave from Cork in a few weeks, and once they arrive each regiment is—" He broke off when the Scot called out his order, turning to face the stranger.

Hamish recognized the scrutiny and raised his half-empty mug. "Your health, sir."

"And yours." The other man was drinking coffee and he made a polite motion with the bowl. "I don't believe I've seen you here before."

"Aye, that's the truth. I've na been here before."

"And what brings you here now?"

Hamish swung his left leg over the bench on which he was sitting so he was in a better position to move quickly if he had to. "I do na mean to offend, you understand, but why would that be any concern o' yours?"

"We colonials are always interested in visitors from the mother country."

"Aye? Well, that's a fine sentiment, I'm sure. But if by mother country yer speaking of England, you mistake me."

"I didn't mean to say I thought you were English."

"Ach, I'm glad o' that. Since God's truth, I'm not."

"You're a Scot, of course. A Highlander, I'll warrant."

"A man o' discernment, sir. A Stewart o' Appin, to be exact." Hamish stood up and extended his hand. "Hamish Stewart's my name."

The man who'd been talking about troop movements stood as well, but he ignored the proffered hand. He was a head shorter than Hamish, and probably two stone lighter, but he was the younger. If it came to a fight, speed and stamina would be on his side. Hamish felt a great weariness rising inside him. He dinna want to fight. He wanted a peaceful life as laird o' the only place on earth he'd ever coveted.

John Hale appeared. "Here, what's happening? I know this man." Hale's black jacket and breeches—Albany style even if he hadn't been in mourning—were a startling contrast to the bright-colored plumage of the New York City popinjays.

"He was eavesdropping on a private conversation. And I believe he's a Jacobite."

Bede Devrey had followed his nephew. Apparently he knew the man who'd been speaking of London's plans. "For God's sake, Peter, it's nearly ten years since the rebellion. No one cares about Jacobites any longer."

The Merchant's had gone quiet, every eye watching the two men who seemed prepared to entertain them with a brawl. "Take it outside," someone called out. "No point in making trouble in here."

"No point in making any trouble at all," Bede insisted. "My nephew here is John Hale of the Hale Patent up Albany way. If he vouches for this stranger, that should be good enough for all of us. Even you, Peter."

"He's a Jacobite," the man called Peter repeated. "He said so himself. A Stewart of Appin. They fought against the king at Culloden."

"And were well and truly beaten," John said. "What's the point of—"

"Enough, by God!" Hamish's bowels were churning. The thought that any man, much less a creature like John Hale, should think Hamish Stewart needed defending was too much of an insult to be borne. He forced himself to speak in a normal tone of voice. "I thank ye for your good efforts, John Hale. But if this fellow," Hamish jerked his head in the direction of the one called Peter, "wants a fight, then he shall have one, wherever and whenever he chooses. As for me, I only came in to quench my thirst. And I've done that, so if it's to no one's disinclination, I'll be leaving."

He had to go. He could na pummel this Peter into butcher's meat, nor aim a kick or two at John Hale's blighted balls, much as he'd like the pleasure.

Peter stood between Hamish and the door. For a moment it wasn't clear he would give way and let the Scot leave, then he took a step back and cleared the path. It took all Hamish's self-discipline to walk past the other man. He felt the eyes of every man present watching him retreat.

Outside, Wall Street was all but deserted, and the cold air calmed him some.

"Stewart! Wait a moment!"

God's truth, and that was John Hale's voice. Blighted sodding hell and this was a bad day's work. A pox on this place. May Almighty God rain lizards and frogs down on New York City.

"What did he want?"

Hamish stretched his legs toward the few coals smoldering in the battered grate of the slop shop fire. The tavern was little more than a shack, but it was on Mott Street at the northernmost edge of the populated part of the city, beyond the wooden palisade the New Yorkers had erected in '45, at the start o' what they called the war o' the first King George. It was na a pleasant journey for all it wasn't far. The wind was howling a near gale. In here by this miserable wee fire it sounded as if it might rip out the tar paper windows and lift the thatched roof. " 'Tis a poor excuse for heat the landlord's given us for a *dreich* night like this one. Could you na ha' found a place wi' a bit more cheer?"

"Without doubt. Somewhere near the governor's mansion, in the court part of the town. Where Bede Devrey and John Hale are as like to see us as to piss. Don't make yourself sound a fool, man. I am never comfortable doing business with fools," John Lydius said.

God's truth, neither was Hamish Stewart. It was just the whole poxed day that had put him out of sorts and made him likely to complain about anything, whatever the excuse. Hamish twisted on the upturned crate that served as his seat. The proprietor stood a little distance away, busying himself with drawing an ale for a bald-headed dwarf who waited near the door, huddled in a threadbare cloak, stamping his feet and blowing on his hands for a bit o' warmth. The poor mis-shapen sod's chin barely reached the level o' the bar, and his bandy legs looked as if they might be going to break if the stomping dinna stop. "Landlord, if you'd bring a few more coals for this fire, your guests would na all be perishing wi' cold. Give this fine establishment a bad name, frozen corpses will."

The man finished filling the tankard and pushed it down the bar toward the dwarf, then disappeared out the back and returned cradling two large logs in his arms. It unnerved him that a pair of one-eyed strangers had shown up at the same moment on a night not fit for man or beast. Bound to be the devil's doing, that was. He had all he could do not to throw the wood on the fire and run for the woods. But a man had to take his opportunities where he found them. "I'll put one of these on the fire, if ye likes. Take yer pick. Cost yez a penny extra."

John Lydius reached into his pocket and came out with a couple of wooden coins. "Here's tuppence. Put 'em both on."

The logs were moldy with damp and seamed with pitch. They just smoldered and sparked, but the sight of them on the grate made it feel warmer. "Why did Hale chase you?" Lydius asked.

"Said he wanted to be sure I dinna need anything, seeing as how I was an Albany neighbor."

"And you believed him?"

"Of course I dinna believe him. What do you take me for?"

Lydius leaned back against the wall, folding his arms across his chest. He studied the Scot with the eye not covered by the black patch. Stewart's missing eye was a rough ugly scar on one side of his face and he made no attempt to hide it. Lydius calculated the chances of Hamish Stewart getting Shadowbrook to be forty out of a hundred. Not the best odds, but not the worst either. And now that Ephraim was dead and that horse's arse John Hale was master of the Patent, it might be the odds had improved. "That leaves me with the same question I asked originally. What do you think Hale wanted?"

Hamish had been asking himself that for most of the day. "God's truth. I do na know. Only to get a better look at me, I think. Take my measure. Because see-ing me down here in this poxed city struck him as na the ordinary way o' things."

Lydius nodded. "Whereas in Albany he pays you no mind. You're the Scot who rents the room above the gristmill from the Widow Krieger. Nothing worthy of note."

"Aye, that's the way it seems to me."

"Then tell me, in God's name, why you had to come down here?" Lydius slammed his empty mug on the rickety table between them. "Why expose—"

"Hold you tongue if you want to keep the use o' it." Hamish had not moved, but the menace in his voice was unmistakable.

Lydius sighed. Too late now to moan about this ill-advised visit. And John Hale, who up to now had shown not the slightest interest in Hamish Stewart, was alerted to the fact that the Highlander was skulking about on the periphery of his affairs. But was the Scot aware that John Hale was attempting to mortgage the Patent to buy cane land in the Islands, in that hellhole St. Kitts, God help them all.

And if you don't know Hale's plans, how do I use whatever advantage it might give me? How do I play you and John Hale off one against the other and come out owning the Patent myself?

Sweet Christ, it's a wild idea. Makes me feel I've drunk three bottles of sack. The same singing in my head and roaring in my belly. Genevieve would say, *Your reach exceeds your grasp, John Lydius, and that will be the ruin of you.* But the Hale Patent . . . sweet Christ Almighty. Ah, perhaps it's too much to hope for. Even with Quentin out of the picture. Didn't even come to the Frolic Ground to drink his father's health after the funeral.

Might be this was the time to bow out of the business, say a pox on both your houses and leave Hamish Stewart and John Hale to their fate. Could be the odds had shifted more in John's favor. But to own the Hale Patent . . . Do you hear the way my heart thumps at the thought, you Jacobite idol worshiper? No, not likely. You're too blinded by your own land lust to have a clue about mine. But if I make you an enemy . . . What forces do you command, you papist whoreson? Very well, say Genevieve has the right of it this time and I'm in waters too deep for swimming, say it's not possible to get the land, what about continuing to have you as an ally and business partner? At the very least it means a safe and steady way to ship guns to New France. Albany to Québec hidden in shipments of grain, and from there to the Ottawa and Mascoutin and Ojibwe and Potawatomi of the *pays en haut.* Christ Jesus, even a minor victory in this business, a small win, provides the opportunity of a lifetime.

Lydius watched Hamish swig the last of the rum and waited to speak until the Scot put down the mug. "You say Hale bought three slaves?"

"Aye, an Ibo lass canna be more than nine, with a hairless cunt and breasts like little black walnuts—"

"Not difficult to figure what he wants her for."

"—and two seasoned Ashanti lads. Paid four hundred guineas for the lot. In coins, mind." Hamish leaned over and spat into the fire. "Fit to vomit, it made me."

"Yes, seeing as he'd been all but burned out before this year's harvest. Odd, don't you think, that he could pay so much. Considering."

Aye, God's truth, it's odd. And would you na like to know if I had any knowledge o' that, any share in the bringing o' those Indians all Albany now knows were Huron from Québec. But you'll rot in hell before I'd trust you that far, John

Lydius. You're no better than the womb that bore you, a heretic bound for hellfire, but God's truth, you're useful just now. "The rain saved them the worst o' the blaze. And who's to say what Hale had put by from better times?"

"Who indeed?"

Wall Street was deserted at this hour of the night. John Hale stood a few strides from the front door of the fine house that belonged to his uncle Bede, just beyond the broad iron gates with the pineapple finials, unable to make up his mind. One of the servants had doubtless been instructed to wait up for him. He could ask for a glass of hot punch, or some rum with honey. Might be that would calm the churning of his belly and the thumping of his heart. Or if he chose he could find a tavern or an inn where the fires were not yet banked, the candles burned bright, and men passed the punch bowl and sang. He'd not yet heard the watchman calling the hour; it wasn't yet ten o'clock, for the love of Christ. No need to declare the night done unless he wanted to. Deciding what he wanted, that was the difficult thing.

No, by Christ, it wasn't. He wanted to kill James Alexander and Oliver De Lancey. And the Jew, of course. Sweet God in heaven, nothing would make him feel better than ripping Hayman Levy's guts out with his bare hands. Though the meeting not long ended had taken place in Alexander's office, on the ground floor of his elegant house in Hanover Square, it was Levy who'd done most of the talking. "Times have changed, John. Your father is gone, and those savages . . . We must be cautious, you understand."

He did indeed understand. And so did they. It was all nonsense, a stall. If his father were not gone John wouldn't have been in a position to offer the Patent as collateral and secure the loan. That's what all four of them had been waiting for these past two years, since he'd first come to them with the scheme. "Nothing is different than it was," he'd told them, his throat dry with insisting, sickened by the whine he could hear in his own voice. "The St. Kitts land is still available, and with it I can make us all rich beyond dreams."

"Of course, John. Of course. But we're men of business." Levy indicated by a nod of his head that he was speaking for all of them, while the others wagged their greasy chins in agreement. "Men of business, but honorable. We made you a promise and we'll keep it. As long as you see our need for something a bit more substantial."

As if the Hale Patent were not the most substantial thing on this earth. It was worth ten times the five thousand guineas he needed to secure his claim in the Islands, his share of the cane. Probably more. "Bright Fish Water was part of the original grant. It was given to my grandfather by Queen Anne. It has always belonged to the Patent."

"A good thing, too. How else could you make it over?"

Sweet Christ, the way Levy smirked when he said that. It had taken all John's control not to smash the little weasel's face. But it was Oliver De Lancey who put the matter beyond discussion. "My brother tells me there is much interest in the buying and selling of land in St. Kitts these days. I don't think you've much time to sit here and argue terms with us, Mr. Hale."

Sodding Oliver De Lancey's sodding brother was James De Lancey, Governor of the Province of New York. So what Oliver was saying was that if John Hale didn't choose to take the terms being offered by himself and Alexander and Levy, Hale's scheme was finished; not another merchant in New York City would dare to finance his plans. So he'd gritted his teeth and signed their God-rotting agreement, made over the top tenth of the Patent outright. Bright Fish Water and everything above the northern edge of Do Good were no longer part of Shadowbrook. The rest, every scrap of Hale land and Hale holdings, was pledged as collateral against the five thousand guineas needed to secure the plantation in St. Kitts. "Done, gentlemen." He'd managed not to let his hand tremble when he signed his name. And he'd waited for the cash.

God help him, it did not materialize in hard coin as he expected. "Excellent," Levy had said. "We will open the negotiation in the Islands, Mr. Hale. When everything is in place we will inform you." And he'd handed over a piece of paper, a copy of the note all four had signed, spelling out the terms of their arrangement.

God rot his perfidious soul. It had been all John could do to keep from snatching back the papers and ripping them to shreds. There had been a time, moments only, a few heartbeats, when that might have been possible. Then James Alexander, who was a lawyer as well as a man of business, had whisked them away. God curse all lawyers, particularly the canny Scots. *Never do business with a Scot,* his father had told him. *Get the better of you every time.*

And what about this other Scot, then? This Jacobite idol worshiper? Why did John have the feeling that Hamish Stewart had far more interest in the affairs of the Hale Patent than he should have. How long now since Stewart had shown up in Albany? A year or so. It was twenty-five years, since he had come to the Patent seeking to buy land and bring over a parcel of his Scottish Highland clansmen to settle on it. Ephraim had enjoyed playing with the notion, but in the end he refused to sell even a single blade of grass for the price the Scot could pay. Was his father spinning round in his grave now? Did he know John had just made over Bright Fish Water, and the Great Carrying Place, and the birch woods where the fattest pheasant were always to be found in the autumn, and the northernmost hills where the last of the fiddleheads and sparrowgrass appeared in the spring?

His mother would die of grief if she knew. And Quent? Quent would probably kill him.

"Ten o'clock on a dark and frosty evening." The watchman's voice rang out from a few streets away and his bell grew louder. Any minute now John would be asked to account for himself.

Sweet Christ, he must find some relief. Something to make the knots in his belly go away and calm the dread in his soul. A whore, perhaps. Plenty of whores to be had in New York City. But truth to tell, he could ill afford the two shillings a good one—young and pretty, with a face not marked by the pox and privates not stinking with the French Disease—was bound to cost.

The watchman's bell again. Closer. John thought a moment longer, then turned away from the Devrey gates and walked east on Wall Street, toward the slave market at the river's edge.

There was a black man asleep in a shed near the long row of holding cages that ringed the area adjacent to the wharves known as Burnett's Key. Most of the cages were empty now, the slaves they'd housed all bought and paid for and taken away by their new owners. John nudged the sleeping man with his toe. "You there, wake up. I've business with you."

Robby, the auctioneer's assistant, opened his eyes, and sprang to his feet. "What business might that be, master? Sales all be ended for the time. Don't be no new sale until the *Susannah* docks, master. Going to be at least a week 'fore she's here."

"I bought those three slaves this morning." John jerked his head in the direction of the cages. "You're boarding them for me until I'm ready to return to Albany."

Robby blinked the sleep from his eyes and nodded furiously. "Oh yes, master. I remember. I surely do. They be waitin' on you, jus' like you arranged."

"Fine. I want you to bring the girl here to me. For a time."

"The Ibo, master? Where you want me to bring her?"

"Yes, the Ibo. To the shed." Built of raw planks, the structure was bare of any comfort except a cot with a corncob mattress and a primitive fire pit with a chimney hole above it, but it would do. The way he was feeling now, anything would do.

"Yes, master. Robby gonna do that right away."

"Fine. But first throw a bit more fuel on that fire. Then bring me the girl and wait outside until I call you."

Robby walked over to the fire and picked up a shovelful of the Newcastle coal that traveled as ballast in the holds of the merchantmen that plied the seas between New York and England, and tipped it onto the smoldering embers in the pit. There was a low chinking sound, then a puff of dirty black smoke, followed by the hiss of the coals giving up the last of their moisture. "You wait right here, master. I be bringing her, like you say."

❦

Her name was Taba and she spoke no English. "Not a word, eh?" John asked. "That's the truth?" Taba stared at him, no sign of understanding even in the depths of her eyes. "Very well. I wasn't planning on talking much to you, anyway. Take that thing off." He mimed the motions of pulling her shift over her head. "Off."

She didn't move.

The guard's bullwhip was coiled in the corner. John picked it up. Good heft and excellent length. He fancied himself a skilled hand with a bullwhip. There wasn't a lot of headroom in the shed, but the leather lash uncoiled and released with a satisfying snap. He hadn't meant to touch her with it, only to indicate that he meant business, but his control wasn't perfect and the lash grazed her left forearm. The whip was tipped in lead and it laid open a cut that welled blood. The girl didn't make a sound. "Off," John said. "Or I'll cut the damn thing off you with this."

Taba pulled the shift over her head and dropped it on the dirt floor.

John nudged her with the handle of the bullwhip, turning her so she was full front to the glow of the fire. "Let's see what I bought, shall we? Spread your legs." He forced the whip between her thighs, prying them apart so she had to do what he wanted or fall on her face. "It appears I got you before the cutters did." He'd had a few African-born blacks over the years; their cunts were usually mutilated in ways he found disgusting. "Excellent," he said. "Full value for money. At least so far."

He could feel himself swelling, and some of the knot in his belly relaxing. He put down the whip, removed his jacket and loosed the buttons of his breeches, then took a step closer to the girl. She stared straight ahead, her eyes dead and face expressionless. John smiled. We'll see how long that lasts, little girl. He put both hands on her shoulders, forcing her to her knees. "We'll teach you a few simple tricks first, shall we? Something easy." He made broad signs to indicate the meaning of his words. "And I warn you, bite me even once and you'll wish you hadn't."

Robby sat on the cold ground staring at the East River lapping at the wharves, and at the masts of vessels anchored a bit offshore, listening to the sounds from the shed. A fair amount of time went by during which he heard only the grunts and groans of the white master, and something he couldn't quite place until he recognized it as the sound of retching. He grinned when he thought about what it likely was the little Ibo was choking on, but it was a long time after that before he heard Taba's first moan of pain. Then a few little screams, followed by one long one. Not so bad, he told himself. Wimmins always screams the first time. Only thing is, why she be goin' on screamin' that way? Going to wake the tars as is drowned in this here river since the beginning of time, she is, the way she's screaming. Ain't no fuck, first or fifteenth, is worth screams like that. Never mind. Ain't Robby's job to worry about a little Ibo is maybe getting more than she should the first time. Robby's job is to keep the slaves in line while they's in the pens and on the block. Long as Robby do that, the bullwhip stay in his hand not on his back. But those is some screams. Some screams.

There was no resistance when he finally threw her down on the corncob mattress and shoved himself inside her, and not a drop of blood in evidence a few moments later when he pulled out. "Little bitch," he muttered. "You weren't a virgin after all."

He'd make her scream, by God. And bleed, too. He picked up the coal shovel and rammed the handle into her vagina. Three times, four, all his strength behind each thrust. When he staggered back, gasping for breath and breathing hard, sweat pouring off him, he saw a narrow rivulet of blood making its way down her thin little thigh. "What do you think of that, then? Better then a cock, is it? Want some more?" She was silent, her face wearing that look of total apartness, as if she were not present. "I'll make you scream, you bitch slave."

A pair of iron tongs hung on the wall beside the fire. John grabbed them, and snatched up a red-hot coal. For the first time Taba's eyes betrayed her feelings. Not just fear but terror. She gasped and tried to roll off the cot, but he hurled himself on top of her pinning her in place with his knee. Then he pressed the live coal to her budding left breast and held it in place until the stench of roasting flesh filled his nostrils and Taba's screams filled the night.

Chapter Fifteen

THE ICY COLD rain pelted down mixed with snow, and to Philippe Faucon it tasted of salt. New France. God grant he might see the real France again some-day before he died. In Versailles in April the gardens were greening and spring flowers bloomed. The air of April was like a caress in Versailles, and the rain was sweet and full of summer promise.

He huddled deeper into the heavy black cloak. It had been given him by Mon-sieur le Provincial especially for this journey, but it had been made for a shorter man; the folds ended well above his knees and the lower half of his soutane was sodden. Philippe turned and glanced upward, shading his eyes with his hand to protect them from the slanted sheets of rain. The Upper Town was shrouded in cloud. He could not make out the steeples of the Collège des Jésuites, or the cathedral or seminary. Even the château of the bishop—much below the fortresses atop the hill—was obscured. The whole of Québec appeared to have disappeared and left nothing but these impoverished shacks clinging to the bank of the half-frozen St. Lawrence.

The river lapped noisily at the place the priest stood, a small wharf at the northern end of the harbor, upriver from the places where larger boats moored. The ice floes of winter were beginning to break up, enough so there was a passage over to Pointe-Lévis on the opposite bank, but the water was turbulent and angry and rough with whitecaps. The falling rain stabbed the surface like a hail of arrows. An hour he'd been standing here in the wet and cold and still no sign of the small craft Monsieur le Provincial had told him to expect. Blessed Mother of God, he was chilled to the bone.

The deerskin envelope with his sketchbooks crayons, and pens was clutched close to his heart beneath the cloak. A black leather satchel containing his clothes and his breviary, and a chalice and paten so that he might offer Holy Mass, was on the ground at his feet. A last look at the empty river, then Philippe hoisted the satchel and turned toward the town; there must be somewhere to wait out of the rain. The boatman knew he was collecting a Jesuit. He would come looking rather than incur the wrath of the powerful black robes.

A single cobbled street lined with fishermen's cottages fronted on the river, but no fishwife opened her door to beckon the priest inside. The *habitants* of the Lower Town were caught between the temperamental St. Lawrence from which they must wrest a living and the demands of the priests up on the hill who claimed dominion over their souls. They might not love the diocesan priests, but they thought of the black robes as arrogant oppressors.

Philippe turned into a narrow alley at the end of the road. He looked for an innkeeper's sign, hoping for a *petite bière*. He had not developed a real taste for the local brew, a powerful concoction of spruce, molasses, ginger, and Jamaica pepper, but it would warm him on a day like this. One door was marked with a rough cross that appeared to have been hacked into the raw wood with an axe. *Mère de Dieu!* Of course, the monastery of the Poor Clares. Philippe pushed and the door opened.

The public chapel was long and narrow, lit only by two small windows close to the ceiling, and largely empty except for a few battered prie-dieu scattered randomly about. It was only slightly warmer than the street outside, but at least he was out of the rain. Philippe blessed himself in thanksgiving and genuflected in the direction of the tabernacle. There was a strong smell of incense and burning candles. He heard the murmur of voices "Mystical Rose, *ora pro nobis.* Mother of Divine Providence, *ora pro nobis,* Mother of Mercy, *ora pro nobis.*" Philippe dropped to his knees on a prie-dieu and murmured the responses along with the unseen nuns. "Mother of all graces, *ora pro nobis,* Mother of Divine Hope, *ora pro nobis.* Mother of the Seraphic Order, *ora pro nobis.*"

There were faint rustling sounds from behind the grille and the nuns began to chant. It sounded like the chirping of birds rather than a melodious monastic choir. "*Quinque prudentes virgines aptate lampades vestras . . .*" The five wise virgins took their lamps and went to meet the Bridegroom.

Up on the hill it was said that the Poor Clares had a postulant, so they were six wise virgins these days. Or maybe not so wise. The damp was seeping into his bones. It was hard to imagine living walled into this hovel, forever separated from a big roaring fire, or a roast of beef turning on a spit, or even a glass of decent Burgundy. "*Veni sponsa Christi . . .*" Come, bride of Christ, accept the crown that has been prepared for you.

❦

Today Nicole took the habit. She had imagined that as a bride she would wear flowers in her hair. *Quent will wait in the Frolic Ground and I will come down the stairs of the big house, wearing a gown of lawn and lace sashed with ribbons, and there will be flowers in my hair.* There were few flowers in bloom in Québec in April. Soeur Marie Françoise, the keeper of the tiny garden behind the monastery walls. She had scoured the small square of earth and managed to find only three snowdrops and a few greening twigs. These she had woven together with some twine for Nicole's hair.

"What do you ask?" Père Antoine asked.

"*Mon Père,* I beg you for the love of God to admit me to the Second Seraphic Order, that I may do penance, amend my life, and serve God faithfully unto death."

Nicole wore the simple gray Poor Clare robe with the wide sleeves and the knotted white cord at the waist. As a postulant she had been given black felt slippers, now she was barefoot. That first day with Quent, when he threw her into the stream to stop her hysterics, she'd told him she wanted to be barefoot. Instead, later, when they were at Shadowbrook, he had given her moccasins of soft white leather, and put them on her feet with his own hands. His fingers had traveled up the calves of her legs and touched her knees and then . . . *Madame Hale will open the door of the house and I will step onto the great front verandah, then walk past the chestnut tree with the wooden bench circling the trunk. Quent will be waiting for me in the Frolic Ground. He will smile and put out his hand. I will take it.*"

Soeur Marie Joseph stepped from her choir stall and bowed deeply toward the altar and the tabernacle that contained the Sacred Host, then took her position at the cantor's lectern. "*O quam pulchra est . . .*" she sang in her clear and lovely voice. How beautiful it is to choose to be forever virgin, a sacrifice of praise.

Thank God she did not have to chant with her sisters. Nicole's throat was closed and her mouth was dry. Because I am so happy, she told herself. I am filled with joy because today I give myself entirely to *le bon Dieu.* From now on she was no longer a postulant whose vocation was being tested, but a novice, a nun in training. *In the Frolic Ground everyone will cheer when the wedding ceremony ends. Then my great red bear of a husband—called Uko Nyakwai by the Indians and my dearest darling by me—will kiss his bride. How insistent are the lips of my beloved, how sure when he takes what is rightly his.*

Mère Marie Rose left her choir stall. Nicole bent her head. The abbess removed the crown of flowers and little Soeur Marie Angelique brought the scissors. They were long and very sharp, with oversize handles that had once been painted bright blue but were now chipped and faded. Mère Marie Rose took them in her right hand, with her left lifted a hank of Nicole's black hair, and cut it as close to the scalp as possible. Angelique held open a small drawstring bag to receive

Nicole's curls. Two days before, when it was certain Nicole would remain in the monastery, the gray Quaker dress she'd worn when she entered had been cut up to be used for cleaning rags. A small piece had been kept aside and given to Nicole to stitch a *suaire à cheveux,* as the nuns called it, a shroud for her hair. Later, at the festive recreation period that would celebrate her new status, Nicole would throw the *suaire à cheveux* and its contents onto the fire.

The abbess snipped from forehead to nape of the neck and crosswise from ear to ear. Her scissors missed nothing. Nicole thought she must look like a lamb after shearing. Or perhaps the funny little hairless dog Grandmère always carried around in a bag. Soeur Celeste came forward and offered the abbess two folded squares of white linen. Mère Rose took the one on top and gathered the fabric in her hands and fitted it to the new nun. The wimple covered Nicole's head and neck and most of her forehead, allowing only her face to show. The abbess laced it tightly in the back. *"Quia concupivit Rex speciem tuam,"* Soeur Joseph sang. Thy beauty now is all for the King's delight.

Marie Rose's hand trembled slightly when she added the white veil and pinned it in place over the wimple. I am a foolish old woman, she thought, not worthy to be an abbess of the Poor Clares. But you have chosen me, *mon Dieu,* and you have chosen this child as well. And you have given to me the task of making her a saint so that many souls may be saved. I swear to you I will not fail.

"Veni sponsa Christi," the nuns chanted. Come bride of Christ, accept the crown that has been prepared for you. The abbess put both her hands on the shoulders of the new novice. "From this day forward, you will be known as Soeur Marie Stephane," the abbess said. Nicole had been named for the Church's first martyr, the man who soon after the Crucifixion had been stoned to death for proclaiming Jesus Christ the Messiah, the Promised One, the Son of God. St. Stephane had a very high place in heaven, the Church taught, because he had suffered so intensely for the glory of the Faith.

Mère Rose helped the new nun to her feet and led her to the door to the public chapel. She unlocked it and opened it wide. *"Vous pouvez aller si vous voulez,"* the abbess said. *"Vous êtes libre."* You can go if you wish. You are free.

Nicole turned to face the congregation. In the ordinary way of things she would have had family and friends come to see her make this most solemn commitment. If she were in France, perhaps, and if Maman had lived and poor Papa— There was a man in the back of the public chapel. A black robe. She had never seen him before, but Nicole addressed her words to him simply because he was there. "I, Nicole Marie Francine Winifred Anne Crane, make this decision freely, with no coercion and for no reason other than the love of Almighty God." It was so long since she had spoken all the names that had been given to her at baptism and Confirmation she had almost forgotten them. No matter. She did not have to remember them any longer. "From this day forward I am Soeur Marie Stephane."

Philippe could tell the girl was beautiful even though much of her face was covered by the wimple and the veil. And she looked . . . what? Not radiant exactly. Determined. *Alors,* it would take a strong will indeed to voluntarily lock yourself up in this barren place.

Nicole turned back to Mère Marie Rose, who had lowered her black veil over her face. The new nun knelt and the abbess put out both hands. Nicole lay hers on them. "I swear by Almighty God that henceforth you will be my mother and I will be your child. I will obey you in all things, unhesitatingly and with all my heart and soul. I swear this *au nom du Père, et du Fils, et du Sant-Esprit,*" she added. A solemn promise made in the name of the Father, and of the Son, and of the Holy Spirit.

The abbess made a large sign of the cross in the air over Nicole's head. "Come inside, my daughter," she said softly. "Your beauty now is all for the King's delight."

An hour later the rain had stopped. There was a thin sliver of blue in the gray sky, even a few sunbeams, when Philippe made his way aboard the small boat that had at last arrived. The man who owned it sailed regularly between Québec and Pointe-Lévis. "Sorry to keep you waiting, monsieur. But we have had much to contend with today."

Philippe had never had good sea legs. The crossing to Canada from France had been hell, nine weeks of extraordinary penance. This journey would take less than an hour, but already he felt the nausea beginning in his belly and a bitter taste rising in his mouth. "The weather, you mean?"

"Not the storm alone. Word is that the English are sending a fleet to intercept our shipping. We must be careful not to sail anywhere near where they may be."

"But surely Britain and France are not at war." The letter behind the angel with the folded wings had promised some six thousand troops in the late spring when the river was entirely navigable. If there were English ships in these waters, they were here for the purpose of intercepting those troops. But no one was supposed to know about the soldiers being sent to Québec.

The sailor was busy casting off the lines that tethered the boat to the dock. "We are not at war with the English yet, but the way they're all talking we may as well be."

"Then this is to be a dangerous journey?"

"To Pointe-Lévis? No, I wouldn't think so. Supposed to be a Mi'kmaq waiting to guide you the rest of the way to Fort Beauséjour. As to the danger . . ." The old seaman shrugged. "In this life who can say anything for sure, eh? But perhaps your black robe will protect you. Almighty God looks after Jesuits, no?" The sailor crossed himself ostentatiously. "Better find somewhere to lash those things you brought with you. Looks like the rain's coming back. Maybe even a real blow."

The little boat was rocking back and forth. Philippe maintained a white-knuckled grip on the rail that topped the bulwark. To make his way across the deck seemed impossible. *Lord, I know Monsieur le Provincial speaks with Your voice. Since he is sending me to Pointe-Lévis and then to l'Acadie, it is truly Your will that I go.*

The Acadians live under nominal English rule, the Provincial had told him, *but they are true to the Faith, and in their way, true to King Louis. You will reinforce those directions of their hearts, my son. You will strengthen them in resistance to heresy and heretical allegiance.*

Phillipe gribbed the rail. *I wish always to follow the instructions of my superior, Lord, but I do not know how I am to do such wonders as he commands. Eh bien, I am content to wait and find out. Only grant that I do not disgrace myself on the journey.* He'd no sooner made the prayer when he had to lean over the side and vomit.

MONDAY, MAY 10, 1755
FORT CUMBERLAND, ON THE BORDER BETWEEN
MARYLAND AND THE OHIO COUNTRY

"We meet again, Colonel Washington."

"So we do, Mr. Hale."

"Quent."

"Ah yes, you prefer that. Excuse me, I'd forgotten."

Both men were more interested in their surroundings than in each other. What they were looking at was a miracle of sorts. A huge clearing surrounded a vast fortified enclosure fenced by God knew how many felled oaks and murdered chestnuts. There were ramparts, barracks, magazines, walls pierced with loopholes just large enough for a single musket, and ten embrasures fitted with small cannon. Wills Creek, one of the first English trading posts of the Ohio Country, had become Fort Cumberland, marshaling place for the force being assembled under the command of Major General Edward Braddock of His Majesty's Coldstream Guards.

"A bit different than when you last saw it, I warrant." There was pride in Washington's voice.

"A bit," Quent agreed. "And not what I expected. I heard that both Braddock's regiments arrived shy at least two hundred men."

That didn't seem likely, judging from the bustle around them. A river of redcoats flowed through a heaving mass of provincial militia wearing the uniforms of Pennsylvania, Virginia, and Maryland and the different forms of transport that would carry them into battle. A group of young men dressed in the workaday outfits they wore on the farms and in the towns was assembled on the parade ground. They were the latest colonial recruits to become members of the Forty-fourth and Forty-eighth Foot, the pair of regiments Braddock had brought to the New World. A redcoat whose face dripped sweat beneath his bearskin was drilling them in marching order.

"Both regiments were light back in March when they landed," Washington agreed. "But they were permitted to subscribe American colonists to bring them up to strength."

"It appears they did well." It wasn't what Quent would have expected. There had been plenty of talk about the colonists doing their duty as Britons before the troops actually arrived, but American boys were never anxious to subject them-selves to the rigid discipline of the British army in which absolute adherence to orders was demanded, and severe whippings and sometimes death followed any infraction of the rules. That sort of unthinking obedience didn't seem to be in the native character. "Useful that these lads were feeling so patriotic," Quent said.

The tall Virginian didn't answer right away. He appeared intent on the exer-cises on the parade ground. Still lusting for glory, aren't you, Quent thought, despite that disaster on Great Meadows.

"Soon as he arrived the General met with Mr. Franklin of Philadelphia," Wash-ington said finally. "Mr. Franklin took things in hand and there's been no end of volunteers since."

Quent grinned. "So that story's true, is it?" Word was that Franklin had printed a shower of broadsides saying that if men and materiel were offered, the pay would be handsome. If they were not, London had authorized hordes of redcoats to descend on Pennsylvania—and probably the other colonies—and take what they wanted. Dozens of meetings were organized where Franklin's warnings were proclaimed and the alarm raised. It had been easy to rally the necessary volun-teers and supplies after that.

"Mr. Franklin was effective," Washington conceded, "though I admit he may have stretched the truth some. What matters is that both the Forty-fourth and the Forty-eighth are at full strength now. And the colonies have contributed their share of militiamen and supplies." He took a notebook from the pocket of his blue jacket and flipped it open. "As of this morning we have twenty-two hundred men, a hundred and fifty wagons, and I believe some half a thousand packhorses. The French are vastly outnumbered. They may well be preparing to leave the Ohio Country as we speak."

"Somehow, Colonel, I don't expect it will be that easy."

Washington smiled. "No, probably not."

"Definitely not. The French have a great many Indians fighting on their side. Unless Braddock can get enough braves to make a real difference, he's still outnumbered." Quent nodded toward a group of about fifty Iroquois standing a short distance away. Nowhere near enough, but a good start.

"And that's why you're here?"

"Can't think of any other reason a general would send for me." It had occurred to Quent that Washington might have recommended him, but the more he thought about it the less likely it seemed. It was common knowledge that the young colonel had brought six hundred Virginian fighting men with him but had himself offered to serve with Braddock as a volunteer. Meaning that, unlike his men, he got no pay. Still, he was well placed, one of two aides-de-camp. The young man was ambitious, he craved status as well as military glory. The last thing he'd want was for Braddock to hear the story of how, after they'd surrendered and been promised quarter, Jumonville and his wounded men had been slaughtered by the Iroquois while Washington stood and watched. The summons from Braddock had to have come because the general had heard of his reputation among the Indians.

Both Quent and Washington made themselves appear intent on watching the recruits train. Finally Washington cleared his throat. "Tanaghrisson, the one they called the Half King. I'm told he died a few months past."

"In their camp at Aughwick. That's his successor over there." Quent gestured toward one of the Iroquois. "The tall one with the striped face and all the tattoos. His name's Scarouady, he's an Oneida. They were part of the original Confederacy, back when it was just five tribes. Oneida are always among the fifty Lords that rule the League."

"Scarouady," Washington repeated. "I do find the names of these people hard to keep in mind."

"Some can be safely forgotten," Quent said. "Tanaghrisson, for example."

Washington hoped his flush would be attributed to the spring sun. "I agree. Let the dead rest in peace. By the way, when I heard you were coming I mentioned to the General that no one knows more about the Indians. I suggested he listen carefully to whatever you had to say."

"Generous of you. As I recall, I left you without a proper goodbye."

Washington smiled. "No need to talk about that either. New business to attend to, eh?"

Quent nodded, his eyes on the officer in the bearskin who was shouting commands at his charges, attempting to teach them to form themselves into the famous parallel lines that allowed British soldiers to fire a never-ending volley of musket balls into the ranks of an advancing enemy. The lads were trying, but the lines were undulating rather than straight. Moreover, the recruits were armed with sticks, not muskets. They were to pretend to discharge their weapons, then drop to their knees and reload pretty much in unison, while the line behind them pretended to fire over their heads, preparing to kneel and reload at the precise moment the front rank stood to fire. Both lines had too many men too swift to kneel and too late to stand. "They don't seem to have the hang of it, do they?" Quent asked.

"Not yet. But they will."

"Perhaps. And when they do? Will the French come out and meet them on the battlefield, do you think?"

"I see no reason to think them cowards," Washington said stiffly.

Because they're not, Quent thought. But neither are they fools. "Right. Where's this general London's sent to make the future safe for we poor colonials?"

"His tent's just over there. I'll bring you in and introduce you, shall I?"

"The one with those damned yellow stripes on his face, tell him." General Braddock didn't look at Quent when he spoke, just kept shuffling the papers on his desk.

"His name is Scarouady." Sweet Christ, how could a man come to wage war in this place, put his life and the lives of thousands of others in the way of a musket ball, and know so little about the Indians? "He's a Lord of the Iroquois League. A Half King. He's an important man. You need him, General Braddock."

The Englishman looked up and studied Quent through narrowed eyes, his lips pressed together in a thin line. "Need?" A few grains of powder from his wig had fallen to his shoulders. The general flicked them away. "I do not actually need any savage, Mr. Hale. A fact for which I thank the Almighty. It is unthinkable that His Majesty's entirely legitimate claims should be dependent upon heathen with painted faces and feathers in their hair."

Only the thought of those boys trying to pretend their sticks were muskets kept him from turning and walking out. "Whatever they look like to you, General, the Indians are formidable in a battle. And there are a great many of them fighting with the French."

"That's no recommendation to me, Mr. Hale. I have seen the French fight. And I assure you neither they nor your Indians will prevail over a well-disciplined line of British soldiers."

"And I assure you that this is America. Things are different here."

"So I believe," Braddock said softly. "But I repeat: You are to tell this Scarouady he must send his squaws and their papooses away. I cannot have them traveling with my forces. The warriors—braves—may stay. They might be a useful reserve. Always a bit of mopping up to do at the end of a battle. Now—"

"A bit of mopping up."

"Yes. As I said. Mr. Hale, I'm told you are a fearsome shot with that long gun, and a man of unimpeachable honor and decent family, as well as a practitioner of the peculiar skills required in this wilderness. And that you know as much about the red men as anyone in these colonies. And God knows, you are big enough and red enough yourself to terrorize most men, certainly the French. But all that said, I am in charge here and my orders are to be instantly obeyed. If you wish to stay, you must accept that fact. Now, sir, do you intend to be with us or against us?"

"If I were not with you, General Braddock, I would have left long since." But why was he with them? There were nearly a thousand braves aligned with the French at Fort Duquesne, Abenaki, Huron, Ojibwe, even Potawatomi and a number of Ottawa who had come with Pontiac. By every instinct Quent found himself on the wrong side of this damned fight. But he was English and American, not French and Canadian, and the best part of twenty-two hundred men were likely to die if he couldn't convince Braddock to see reason. "Your men have women with them. The wives of many of the officers, and the others, the laundresses and sutlers and such, all follow—"

"You need not mince words with me, Mr. Hale. There are the officers' wives, and as for the rest, we both understand what we're talking about. Whatever functions the women perform in the way of selling provisions to the men or doing their wash, they are essentially whores. But they are white and the men require them."

Besides, Quent knew, Braddock kept them under a close control no squaw would accept. The women, except for the officer's wives, were required to be present at the morning parade every day, and each time the rules were read aloud to them: *Any woman caught stealing or wasting supplies, death. Any woman caught giving or selling liquor to the Indians, 250 lashes. Any woman caught outside the boundaries of the camp, 50 lashes.*

"Troops can't be expected to be without females for months on end," Braddock said. "I employ a doctor to look after them, be sure they're not diseased. They do not parade around in broad daylight with their naked bosoms on display, or strap their infants to their backs, or relieve themselves in full view of officers as well as ordinary ranks. The squaws and their young are a disruption; I want them gone by nightfall. And while you're about it, tell the savages they are to quiet their nightly revels. All that whooping and hollering is keeping me awake."

"They are doing the war dance, General. If they stop, your difficulties begin. It means they've decided not to fight."

"Damn it, man, have I not made myself clear? I would rather have them than not have them, but neither my campaign nor its success is to be made dependent on savages. Now, take that Scarouady fellow my message about the squaws, and tell him and the other chiefs I will see them shortly."

"So, Uko Nyakwai, I would feel better about this war belt if it had come from you and not from this man Croghan."

"I am honored by the respect paid me by Shingas, the mighty sachem of the Lenape. But I remind Shingas that Croghan acts for William Johnson, and Johnson has been made the *Cmokmanuk* leader of all things to do with the *Anishinabeg.*"

Quent and the Delaware chief squatted in the shade of a chestnut tree a short distance from the walls of the fort. Shingas turned his head and spat on the ground. "I do not know this William Johnson. Do you speak for him?"

"I speak for his character." Originally from Ireland, Johnson was an Indian trader who had lived many years in the Mohawk Valley, not far from Shadowbrook. Quent had never heard anything to make him think ill of the man. "He has chosen a wife from among the Kahniankehaka. And they have made him a full chief."

Shingas spat on the ground. "I am little impressed by who is or is not adopted by the snakes."

"Then you will be pleased that there are to be a few less of them in this battle." Both men could see Scarouady and his fifty braves leaving the fort. Their families followed, looking neither right nor left, as stoic and dignified as the men. Outraged by the attitude of Braddock, the Iroquois had decided they would all leave.

Shingas nodded. "Perhaps, but were I this English war sachem, I might not feel the same. Tell me the truth, Uko Nyakwai, this Braddock, is he a fool?"

"I do not think so. But he does not know this land, or those of us who live here. Still, I am told he is brave and wise in battle."

"And I am told that he sends no word of his intentions to the French. Neither does the king in England tell the king in France that he means to make war on him in this place."

The *Anishinabeg* despised the notion of making war without first declaring it. Quent had to find an explanation. "I believe that is true. But the French occupy land that the English claim. According to the *Cmokmanuk* custom, they are within their rights to make them leave."

Shingas sat back on his heels. "Land the English claim . . . That is the meat I cannot chew. How can any man own something he cannot make or destroy? Land belongs to every foot that passes over it, *neya?*"

"It is their way. Not even Shingas the great sachem will change them."

"But does their way leave room for the *Anishinabeg* to go on living here? Tell me what you think, Uko Nyakwai, for I admit it is a question I cannot answer."

"The Lenape and the Shawnee and the Mingo all want the French to leave this valley, do they not?"

"You know that is so."

Quent did know it. That's why Croghan's war belts had been at least tentatively accepted, and why six chiefs—five now that Scarouady had left—had come to parley with Braddock. "The English will prevail if the braves of Shingas and the other war chiefs fight with them."

"And if we do not?"

"There will be more and more French. And more and more of their Huron and Abenaki allies."

Shingas picked up a twig and began drawing figures in the dust. "It is not just the Abenaki and the Huron who fight with the French. There are Ottawa at their camp. And Potawatomi. Is Uko Nyakwai no longer a son of the Potawatomi fire?"

"I will always be that, as Shingas knows. And I will always wear the amulet given to me by my dead wife's father, the great Ottawa chief Recumsah. But I am English, not French. And this is my homeland. Sometimes it is not entirely clear which side a man must choose."

"That is true, Uko Nyakwai. I too have relatives who build their fires near Fort Duquesne. In fact, I have visited there." Shingas tapped the British-style linen haversack that hung over his right hip. He had kept one hand on it since the conversation began. Something important was in that bag.

"Then you understand my dilemma," Quent said.

"I do. Now let us go and see if this war chief of the English understands mine."

Braddock peered at the plan of Fort Duquesne spread on his desk. "Ask him where he got this." He looked up at Shingas, pointedly ignoring the four other chiefs standing near the door of the tent.

"I have," Quent said. "And told you his answer. The drawing was made by one of the Virginians who was left behind as a hostage when Colonel Washington and his men surrendered Fort Necessity."

"But how did this savage get it?"

"Chief Shingas has relatives who are camped near the fort. While he was visiting them he was given an opportunity to smuggle this document past French lines and he took it. If he'd been caught with those plans he'd have been hung as a spy, General. He took a great risk to bring you this gift."

"Not so much risk, if his relatives are French allies. What if this is a ruse?"

"It's not. Shingas wants the French out of this valley."

Braddock opened his mouth to say something, but Shingas spoke first. "Tell him I and the others want to know what is to happen in this place if the British succeed in driving away the French and their Indians."

Quent had long suspected that Shingas spoke some English. Nevertheless, he continued to translate. "The chiefs have only one question, General. If they help you rout the French, what is to happen here in the Ohio Country?"

"Exactly what is to be expected, damn it. This is English ground. English people will come here and live. No savage will inherit our land."

There was not a flicker of understanding in the eyes of Shingas or the other chiefs, but they knew. Not just that Braddock was an imperious bastard, but that he despised them. Quent could feel their knowing. He repeated the words exactly as Braddock had uttered them.

"If we are not to have the liberty to live on the land, Uko Nyakwai, why does this man who calls himself a war chief think we should fight for it?" There was no anger in Shingas's tone, but Quent could feel the rage simmering beneath the calm of all five chiefs. Braddock had to feel it as well. Quent translated the question.

Braddock took a last look at the plan of Fort Duquesne, then folded the drawing and put it in the drawer of his desk. He stood up. "Tell these savages I do not need their help. I will drive the French from this valley because it is my duty to do so. Of that there is no doubt."

Quent turned to repeat the words. The five chiefs were already leaving the marquee.

TUESDAY, MAY 11, 1755
PORT MOUTON, L'ACADIE

Cormac sighted along the length of the arrow and released the tension in the tautly drawn bow. The partridge dropped near enough so he could hear the muffled thud it made as it hit the earth. Moments later he had gutted and bled the bird and tied it to the game cord that already held a duck and a brace of quail. Should be enough, even for Marni. She kept telling him the nicest thing about having him on the farm was all the fresh meat she could eat. Little enough time to hunt when she was running everything herself, she said, the implication being she could bag as much game as he could if she didn't have other things to do. He grinned and began walking back toward the farm.

Marni was waiting for him in the yard behind the house, rubbing a pinafore on a washboard. Thin whiffs of steam rose from the wash water. Nearby a black kettle was suspended above a fire made on the open ground. Her eyes lit up at the sight of the string of game. "You did well."

"Keep you from being hungry for a time," he said. It was cold enough so Corm could see his breath when he spoke. He reached over and stroked her hair. Lately, when they were alone like this, she had taken to ignoring her mobcap, letting her long straight hair fall free. It was the color of fresh wheat and reached halfway down her back. When they made love and she was on top the way she liked to be, her hair hung around them like a curtain, shutting away the outside world.

Marni ducked away from his touch and reached for the birds. She spent a few seconds examining his kill, then cooed with pleasure. "You didn't shoot them. You did it the Indian way."

Cormac slid the bow from his shoulder and released the quiver of arrows. "You prefer that, don't you? When I do things the Indian way."

"Some things I do," she agreed. Once, she'd made him show her how the Indians did it with squaws. He had her get down on all fours and he stood behind her and thrust himself into her. She'd hated it and they never did it again. "With bird killing, anyway," she said. "With a bow and arrow there are no pellets of lead to break your teeth when you least expect it."

"Shouldn't be any, no matter how the bird's killed. Not if it's cleaned proper."

She smiled again, her pink tongue darting forward to taunt him. "Clean them yourself if you do not like the way I do it."

"I like everything you do. Well enough, anyways." Again he reached out to stroke her hair and again she ducked away. "You're beautiful," he said. "That's why I want to touch you."

"But right now I'm busy."

"Leave off what you're doing."

"Why?"

"Because I want you to do something else."

"Later. When I finish the washing."

Corm shrugged and began to remove his hunting shirt. "Then you might as well scrub this, too."

He'd been on the farm less than a week when she surprised him in the wash yard, though both of them knew the encounter was pure calculation. It was the first time she'd seen him shirtless and she had found his lack of chest hair startling. "So it's true that you're half Indian," she'd said.

"It's true. Anyway, I thought you knew everything about me."

"I had heard . . . But the way you look . . . I thought maybe it was a lie."

"It's no lie. So what do you think? Would my scalp be worth the full ten guineas in Halifax? That's the bounty Governor Lawrence has offered for an Indian scalp, isn't it?"

"There's a better price than that on your head," she'd told him. "The Abbé LeLoutre at Fort Beauséjour, I hear he offers a hundred livres for the scalp of any English settler, and two hundred livres for yours. Twice that much if you are brought to him still breathing. So he can scalp you while you're alive, he says, and kill you after. But I do not go to Halifax. I have as little to do with the English as I can manage."

"But you're living on the English side of the line," he'd said.

Marni had shrugged. "My family's farm was here before the line was drawn. No one consulted us about where it would be."

For the Acadians, little had changed in the fifty years since most of l'Acadie had been ceded to the English. Seven months Corm had been here, and though as far as he could tell Marni never went near a church, most of her neighbors still practiced the Catholic faith, spoke French, not English, and swore only a limited allegiance to the English king. They said they would remain neutral if anyone took up arms against His Majesty, but they did not commit themselves to fighting on his behalf. Most important, they went on farming and being prosperous against all the odds. Those small sheds he'd seen when he came here were not for drying fish or storing apples as he thought. They were part of a remarkable system of earthen dykes that kept the seawater out and drained the rain from the wetlands, so eventually the salt marshes were washed clean and became sweet and were reclaimed for crops. The Acadians grew enough to amply feed themselves and had plenty left over to sell. And most of them secretly supplied the French forts before they traded with the English.

As for Marni and him, they were both outcasts. It was a fact that bound them to each other almost as strongly as the fire that had crackled between them the first time he accidentally touched her hand. She reached to take the shirt he'd suggested she wash. Corm tossed it aside and grabbed her and reeled her into his arms. Marni resisted for only a moment, then pressed herself to him.

Corm put his hand on her breast. "Inside," she said against his lips, pushing her tongue into his mouth between the words. "Inside. I want to be naked."

Later he slept. After about an hour Marni woke him with a mug of warm milk and spruce beer. "Here, open your eyes. You are acting like someone possessed. Shouting and arguing with ghosts. There can be no rest in such sleep."

He came awake instantly. "What did I say?"

"I have no idea. You were talking Indian."

Corm took the mug and drank half of it in one long swallow. "It's good, thanks. Are you going to cook me one of—"

The shout from outside cut off his words. "Peace be to this house and all who dwell therein." A stranger, and not far away.

Marni jumped up from her place beside his sleeping mat. Corm as well, and he reached for his long gun. "No," she whispered, talking while she bent over at the waist and twisted her long hair into a single coil, then stood and hid it beneath a mobcap. "It's a priest. I'll go."

"How do you know—"

"It's what they always say. You stay here. Hide in case I have to bring him inside."

She had gone out the door and pulled it firmly shut behind her before he had a chance to protest.

"Good day to you, Monsieur le Curé."

"And to you, mademoiselle. I came because I have not seen you at Holy Mass in the three weeks since I've been here."

A black robe. She had heard that one had come to replace old Curé Vincent at the church of St. Gabrielle in the village. "Perhaps if you had been here a little more time, Monsieur le Curé, you would know that I never go to church."

"You will lose your immortal soul, mademoiselle."

"Perhaps I have done that already."

So, Philippe Faucon thought, everything they said was true. She wasn't just a sinner, but a defiant one. He had little experience in the day-to-day care of souls, little idea of what to say in the face of such confirmed wrongheadedness. "Eternity is a very long time to spend in the fires of hell, mademoiselle."

Marni shrugged. "Perhaps it is only spent in the ground, Monsieur le Curé. Perhaps when we die we have only the grave to look forward to. I think we must take our pleasures in this life while we can."

"They tell me you live here alone."

"I do. My mother died many years ago, my father not long after. And I have no brothers or sisters."

"And you are not married?"

Marni smiled. "I am sure there are any number of people around here who will be happy to tell you the story of my betrothal, Monsieur le Curé. In fact, you must have heard it by now."

"Yes. It is a sad tale, but—"

"But dead is dead. As I have said. Now, Monsieur le Curé, is there something more I can do for you?"

Philippe nodded toward the house. "Perhaps if we go inside—"

"No."

So she did have someone staying with her. But was it really Cormac Shea?

"Mademoiselle has asked you to leave, monsieur. I suggest it would be wise to do so."

Marni turned as soon as she heard his voice. "There is no need. I am able to—"

"Go inside," Corm said. "I will deal with monsieur le curé."

"He's not an ordinary priest," she said.

"I believe mademoiselle means that I am a Jesuit." *Mon Dieu,* it was true. It was the métis Cormac Shea.

"A priest nonetheless," Cormac said.

"Most assuredly so. And I am concerned for the soul of Mademoiselle Benoit, here. And for yours, Monsieur Shea."

"You know me?"

"Everyone knows the most famous *coureur de bois* in Canada."

"Not quite everyone, Monsieur . . . ? Do you have a name?"

"Of course. Philippe Faucon."

Ayi! Corm's heart beat against his ribs. Faucon. In English, Falcon. A falcon was a hawk. And all in black like this one was, with his soutane and his cloak flapping about in the wind like wings. "Go inside." He turned to Marni, surprised at how his voice didn't give away the excitement inside him, or the fear. "Go inside," he said again. "Prepare something for the priest to drink. He has come a long way to warn us of the fires of hell."

"But—"

"Don't argue, just do it."

Marni's stone-gray eyes sent him a message of disapproval and resentment, but Corm's had become opaque.

To speak to her that way in front of the Jesuit . . . He had no right to order her about on her own farm. But he had. When she spread her legs for him she had given him the authority every man has over a woman once he lies over her. Cormac might as well announce to the black robe that she was a whore. She could feel her cheeks coloring bright red.

"Go," Corm said again. "Please," he added more gently, seeing how she looked. "We will come inside in a moment." And after she'd left, to the priest, "Faucon. Is that really your name?"

"Yes, of course. In France my family have been falconers for many generations." He did not add that his uncle was master of the king's mews. Pride was a sin. Even for a Jesuit.

"I think," Cormac said very slowly, "I have been expecting you, Monsieur Faucon."

"And how is that?"

How much should he tell this Jesuit? They were known to be perpetual schemers, deeply involved in all the politics of war and peace. In the normal way of things he would avoid them like the plague. But what was normal about a man dressed all in black and bearing the name Falcon arriving at Port Mouton, at the edge of the world, after Kekomoson had dreamed that Cormac must go east, and after Cormac had dreamed that he was to follow a hawk along a river of blood to where a white bear stood beside a covey of little birds? "Will you think me mad if I tell you that I believe we have business together?"

Philippe looked at the métis. He was handsome in spite of his scar. And his eyes . . . *incroyable.* He seemed to be seeing things that were not evident to others. The Jesuit made a hurried sign of the cross. "What business is that, monsieur?"

"I am not sure. And please call me Cormac."

"If you are not sure, then—"

"Wait. I said I wasn't sure, but I can tell you as much as I know."

"No man can do more," Philippe said softly. He had come to see if what they said was true, and if it was, to look with his own eyes on a man who was a legend. But now he was more than curious. He was enthralled.

"Some months ago," Corm said, "in the beginning of summer, I dreamed of a hawk following a river of blood. It came to a place where there were many little birds. A great white bear approached the birds and the hawk attacked the bear."

Philippe began to sweat beneath his cloak and his soutane. Despite the spring chill, rivulets of perspiration ran down his back. He was a priest, a Jesuit, but he had never sought out the mystical or attempted to probe the unknown. He had long ago resolved to do his duty, avoid sin, and hope for heaven after death. A quiet life, his sketchbooks, he had never asked for more . . . He wanted to turn and run. He could not. Cormac Shea held him in place with the strength of his glance.

Mon Dieu, I am not a man meant for a fight. You did not make me so. Not even strong enough to pit my will against a falcon's and prevail. *Come Philippe, she is hooded, and your gauntlet will protect you. She is only an eyas, a very young peregrine, and I have just begun to train her. The hens are best, you know, much better killers than the cocks. This one will be special. I've named her Lady of Steel. Here, take the jess . . . Remove the hood. Now, release the jess, launch her. The peregrine flew off, circling above Philippe's head, then, sensing his weakness, dived and began pecking at his neck and his shoulders while he crouched in terror, weeping, using the hand covered with the gauntlest to protect his face. His father softly whistled the peregrine back to fist and the boy was sent away in disgrace. Ever after the mere smell of the Mews sickened him.* "So," the priest asked softly, "in your dream, did the hawk overcome the bear?"

"I don't know. A white wolf ran out of the trees and charged the bear. Then I woke up."

"And this dream is significant?"

Cormac peered hard at the priest. The battle the man was fighting was evident. *Why are you so terrified, Jesuit? What have I said that has frightened you?* "Have you been long in Canada, Monsieur le Curé?"

"Five years. I go—I went frequently to visit the longhouses."

"Maybe you did not go frequently enough. The Indians, even the Huron, have much to teach the white men. Such as the fact that some dreams are very significant. Particularly if a man carries the name of a fighting hawk."

Philippe gestured toward the door of the cabin, desperate to end this talk of falcons. "I must speak more with Mademoiselle Benoit. She is—"

"You are the hawk of the dream. The black hawk that follows the river of blood."

"No. You're mistaken. I am not meant for such things. I do not—"

"Whether or not you are meant for it, you are the hawk. Now I must find out where the river of blood leads. And who is the bear."

Philippe clutched at his cloak, holding it together from the inside, and tried to stop shivering. "I cannot say, monsieur. You are mistaken in your assumptions. I am not a hawk and I cannot . . ." The words stuck in his throat. Six thousand troops and a flotilla of English ships deployed to intercept them. Surely enough firepower to turn the St. Lawrence into a river of blood.

Monsieur le Provincial had said Philippe must go to l'Acadie to strengthen the faith of the *habitants.* Had he come so far merely to chase after young women who had put their souls in peril by lifting their skirts? To become, though he was entirely unsuited to the task, the curé of L'Eglise du St. Michel, a backwoods parish in a forsaken part? What do you want of me, *mon Dieu?* Only make Your will known and I will do it.

"A river of blood," Philippe said softly.

"A flood," Corm said. "Blood that covered everything in its path."

The Jesuit felt the terror fall away. He let go of the cloak and withdrew one hand from the folds and made the sign of the cross. "Everything is for a purpose, monsieur."

That's what Xavier Walton had said before he left Québec for Virginia. *Remember, Philippe, Monsieur le Provincial does everything for a purpose. Nothing is an accident.* Ever since, Philippe had wondered if he'd been meant to find the letter speaking of the troops. Surely it could not be a surprise that the secret springs and hinges in the paneling would be released by vigorous polishing of the sort he'd been set to do. And would a man like Louis Roget forget that unlike the brothers, who usually did the cleaning, Philippe Faucon could read and write? No, not likely. "What is your place in all this, Monsieur Shea?"

"My name is Cormac. And I don't know my place. But I am the white wolf. It's my totem."

Old Geechkah the Huron had explained to the priest about totems. Philippe understood them to be not unlike the saints' names good Catholic parents gave to their children, and the amulets that sometimes went with the totems were like the medals or other symbols of devotion that Catholics often carried on their person. "And in your dream the white wolf attacked the bear?"

"The wolf was preparing to do so, yes. I think to protect the birds from the river of blood. But I can't be sure."

Nothing is an accident. "It is possible I have something to tell you, Cormac Shea." The Jesuit's mouth was so dry he could barely form the words, but once inside the cabin the story poured out; the promised troops from France, the presence of the English fleet, the way things were in Québec. At least the way he believed them to be. "I cannot be sure of such a thing, perhaps it is a great calumny . . . But Lantak, the renegade—"

"I know who Lantak is. What does he have to do with any of this?" Cormac was thinking of old Memetosia implying that Lantak was a métis, and of Memetosia's gift.

"The Franciscan," Philippe continued, "Père Antoine, he's called. I cannot be sure . . ."

"Yes, so you said. Tell me what it is you're not sure of."

"I think Père Antoine may be in league with Lantak. And that together they are up to no good." The cabin was not overly warm, but the Jesuit was soaked with sweat. "I saw Lantak and his renegade once, with their hair cut into scalp locks and their faces painted for war. I was told they went south to attack—I do not know who or where—because the Franciscan paid them."

"Lantak kills for pleasure. If he gets money as well he considers himself twice lucky. You think this Franciscan priest is some kind of spy?"

"I do not know." Philippe leaned forward, bent beneath the weight of his earnestness. "It makes no sense. I don't know what to think."

"No sense at all," Cormac agreed. "Let us leave it for the moment. Tell me again about the French troops."

An hour later Philippe Faucon had left the farm, and Cormac was preparing to do the same. "Where will you go?" Marni demanded. "Are you going to look for that renegade Huron?"

"Not immediately."

"What are you doing there at the fireplace?"

"I'm taking something I put here." He pried a stone loose and reclaimed the medicine bag of Suckáuhock. "As for Lantak . . . the master is more important than the dog. The Jesuit said Lantak was controlled by the Franciscan. Père Antoine. I go first to Québec."

"Bien! C'est parfait! Take me with you. I won't be any trouble. I know my way about the city. I can find a place to stay. There's a baker who will give me work and—"

"I can't take you with me. You'll slow me down too much. Besides, what about Mumu and Tutu? What about the pig and the chickens and—"

"You have been here all this time and you understand nothing."

Her normally pale skin was flushed dark red, and her voice shook. The obvious passion in her made the sap rise in him. It was all Corm could do not to grab her and have her right now on the floor in front of the fire. One last time before he left.

"I hate this place. It is my prison." Her breath came hard, making her chest rise and fall beneath the homespun frock and pinafore. "I should never have come back here. I do not care if the dykes break apart and this farm is washed out to sea."

He was rock hard but it was not simply lust. A great deal had already passed between them, but standing here with her, knowing he had no choice but to leave her, Cormac understood that he didn't just want to possess her to put out the fire between his legs, he wanted her to be his for always. He slipped the medicine bag around his neck and hid the pouch beneath his shirt. Then he went to Marni and put his hands on her shoulders. "I have to go. But I will come back. I give you my word."

His touch burned her skin. Through the fabric of her clothes, through all the layers that hid who she truly was, she could feel Cormac Shea's fingers on her skin.

Marni had exposed herself to him in ways she had done with no one else, not even sweet Jean the baker who was to have been her husband and who smelled always of flour and yeast. She reached up and traced his scar with a single finger. He did not pull away. "*Je t'aime*," she said. "*Je t'aime, Cormac Shea*."

"*Je t'aime*, Marni Benoit." He had not said those words before. Not to her, not to any woman. "*Je t'aime*, but now I must go."

"Very well. That I understand. Only I do not understand why you will not take me with you."

"Because I must travel very fast, and to do that I must travel alone."

"But why? If the black robe is correct and there are truly six thousand French troops on their way to Québec, and God knows how many English ships waiting to hunt them down, what can you do about it? Why should a war between the French and the English be a reason to separate us?"

"Because I am *wabnum*, the white wolf. It is my totem."

"And the white wolf approached the bear that was near the little birds." She had sat in this room with the Jesuit and Cormac and listened to her métis lover speak of his dream as if it were a thing as real as the table or the stools or the jug of spruce beer. As real and as important as she was. "You are sure?"

"I am very sure."

"*Alors*." She pulled away from him. "And I can't keep you here or go with you?"

"Not this time. But I will return, Marni Benoit. I will come back for you. You can rely on that."

Chapter Sixteen

TWENTY-TWO HUNDRED men, a hundred and fifty wagons, and five hundred packhorses carrying siege guns—monstrously heavy eight-inch howitzers and twelve-pound cannon—pushed their way through thickly wooded wilderness, over swampy morasses, and across rock-strewn mountains, cutting their own road as they went.

It was insanity.

"You have to tell him," Quent said. "He trusts you. You know it can't be done, not and come out the other end with men who are ready to fight."

"I've tried," Washington said. "He won't listen. The plan was made while he was still in London. And General Braddock takes his own counsel as best."

Washington stared straight ahead, his face grim. So you've learned something since the last time, Quent thought. Put that together with that insane courage of yours, you could be a formidable soldier one day. "Braddock's going to fail. If there was some way to make him understand that, maybe—"

"He's like someone who thinks they've spoken to the Almighty. Nothing can change his mind or convince him there's another way." Washington hesitated. "The General," he said at last, "has conceived a four-pronged attack. And this is only one part of it."

They were walking together behind a group of provincials whose job was to roll out of the way the trees the axe wielders felled. They did the work in a constant hail of cursing, sweating and groaning with the effort and the heat.

Quent drew Washington deep enough into the forest to muffle the sounds of Braddock's army spending its lifeblood hacking a road through the woods. "Exactly what are you trying to tell me?"

"When Braddock was back in Alexandria, he met with the governors: Dinwiddie of Virginia and Shirley of Massachusetts, and De Lancey of New York. But of course they have their various legislatures to contend with and—"

"Yes, very well. I don't want a lesson in politics. A four-pronged attack, you said. If this is one, what are the others?"

"Shirley of Massachusetts is to take two regiments and seize Fort Niagara. William Johnson is to lead his Mohawks and some colonials to Lake Champlain where they're to take Fort St. Frédéric at Crown Point."

Quent's heart slammed in his chest. By water Fort St. Frédéric was a three-day journey from Shadowbrook, a straight run from Lake Champlain into Bright Fish Water. "He is mad. There are settlements near both those objectives. Farms and homes and towns. It's—" He broke off. "Sweet Jesus Christ. Duquesne, Frédéric, and Niagara. That's three. And the fourth?"

There was a hint of bitterness in Washington's voice. "The fourth assault's to be made on the two French forts that guard the Chignecto Isthmus up in Nova Scotia. Beauséjour and Gaspareau. And there's something else. Apparently the French are sending reinforcements to Québec and London has dispatched a fleet to intercept them."

"They are all mad," Quent said again. "Look at what's happening right here. The column is so strung out it—"

"Gentleman, I take it you are both well? Not stopping here because of any illness, are you? If I can be of assistance . . ."

The English doctor appeared, the one Braddock kept in tow to look after the whores and hopefully keep his men from being laid low by the various diseases that accompanied fucking. "We're fine, Dr. Walton," Washington replied. "Thank you for your concern, but it's not warranted."

"Damned hot though, isn't it?" Xavier Walton mopped his face with a red bandanna that had been given him some months back by the first woman he'd treated. He'd painted her privates with a tincture of mercury and bled her from the thigh—all the while saying *Paters* in his head, reminding himself as well as the Lord that he was vowed to chastity, and trying to avert his eyes while still doing his duty. The bandanna was the brightest thing he'd ever owned. These days he wore a black jacket and black breeches. Had he been revealed as a Catholic priest, a Jesuit, no doubt Braddock would hang him as the spy he was. The thought was seductive.

I pray You will grant me martyrdom, Lord. But I will not take it unless you send it. Meanwhile I will do everything I can to be obedient to the command of my superior. "Hotter than any place in England, that's for sure," Xavier murmured.

"Hotter than hell," Quent said. "And it will get hotter. That's the one thing you can rely on, Doctor. Here in the Ohio Country it always gets hotter."

A four-pronged attack. Three of them to take place in heavily settled locations. Damn you to everlasting hell, Braddock. You're not just an arrogant bastard, you're stark raving mad.

A week later Braddock's army had gone no more than forty leagues. A brave, fully outfitted and painted for war, could run almost that far through the forest two days. "We are to be divided," Washington told Quent. He did not add that it had been his idea. "A third of the force is to stay behind with the heavy baggage. The rest will be what the General calls a flying column, and push on ahead."

"The women should stay behind as well."

"Some will," Washington agreed. "The officer's wives and a few of the older ones who might not keep up. The youngest and strongest laundresses are to be part of the advance column."

"No," Quent said. "They are in greater peril."

"The French troops won't attack women."

"I'm not thinking about the French."

"The Indians?" Washington asked.

Quent nodded. "Any that look as if they won't survive a forced march back to the braves' home villages will be killed, the others captured."

Washington looked at him curiously. "I thought you approved of the Indian way of life?"

"I do. But I'm not a captured white woman who never chose it."

The colonel nodded. "Very well, I'll tell the General what you've said. But I don't know that he'll agree. He doesn't think an army can function without its laundresses."

Nor, in Braddock's opinion, could it move through the forest in a way that took any notice of the nature of the terrain. The flying column was ordered to maintain army discipline. The officers were on horseback, the troops, scarlet-coated regulars and blue-uniformed Virginians alike, went on foot, marching in columns of four. Behind them came the light cavalry and the horse-drawn artillery. Thirty women and their assorted baggage brought up the rear. Neat. Precise. As if they moved through the settled farmlands of Europe, not the American wilderness.

"He is insane, this war sachem." Scarouady and seven of his Iroquois braves had decided to rejoin the campaign. They went ahead with Quent and Croghan and a few other scouts. "They are asking to be slaughtered. You know this is true, Uko Nyakwai."

Quent did know it, but he had yet to convince General Braddock.

In Canada, nearly four hundred leagues to the north, Beauséjour sat on the top of a hill facing the Missaquash marsh. It was a heavily garrisoned five-sided fort, with earthen ramparts ten feet high and emplacements for two dozen cannon, even a mortar. It should have been impregnable.

Except that on Sunday, the thirteenth of June, after the English forces had been more or less besieging the fort for almost two weeks, the cook realized he had waited too long to prepare the chickens that had been smuggled in five days before from a *habitant*'s farm. The poultry smelled, but there was no other meat for the commandant's mess. The cook prepared a strong sauce of vinegar and pounded almonds and a king's ransom in crushed black pepper, and masked the taste of the bad chicken so well that he received a number of compliments on the quality of the dish. Even the commander, Duchambon de Vergor, went out of his way to say how much he had enjoyed the meal.

At dawn on Monday, when an English shell fell on the latrine reserved for the use of the officers, six of them were straddling the holes and were immediately killed. Vergor, his own gut writhing with cramps caused by the bad chicken, considered his position. He had been put in command by the man in charge of procurement for all Canada, Intendant Bigot. Vergor knew a great deal about siphoning off supplies so they could be sold to enrich himself and his patron, but very little about war. Without his officers Vergor was helpless. He ordered a white flag to be raised and surrendered Beauséjour, and for all intents and purposes the whole of French-controlled l'Acadie. One of General Braddock's prongs had been driven home.

WEDNESDAY, JUNE 23, 1755
QUÉBEC UPPER TOWN

The little nun lifted her skirts as she climbed the steep hill. Cormac could see that she wore sandals and no hose. It was warm enough now, even in Québec, the river was free of ice and the air smelled of summer. He had been watching the nun since she left her monastery in the Lower Town, but he had yet to catch sight of her from the front. He stayed well back, shadowing the woman not because he was interested in her, but because he was following the Franciscan priest, Père Antoine, who was apparently following the nun.

If the Franciscan was a spy, as the Jesuit had suggested, he wasn't very good at it. The nun apparently hadn't spotted him, but anyone else would do so easily. Most *Cmokmanuk* were clumsy at such tasks. Not Quent, but he wasn't like most *Cmokmanuk*. The rest— The nun stopped halfway up the hill.

Nicole paused at the heavy iron gates in front of the château of His Excellency, the Bishop of New France. There was a rope hanging from a bell suspended from one of the gateposts. She could barely see it through the folds of the white veil pulled forward to cover her face. It was not necessary inside the cloister, only now when she had been sent into the street. "You must not be seen unveiled," Mère Marie Rose had said. "Never. Do you understand, Soeur Stephane?"

"*Oui, ma Mère.* I understand."

"I would not do this if it were not that the bishop himself requested it. His Excellency makes a special novena to Our Lady of Victory, for the Ohio Country, and he has decided that the altar breads he consecrates with his own hands, at his private Mass, are to be made only by the Poor Clares." The abbess could not keep the pride from her voice. "It is a great honor, Soeur Stephane. And only you can go. I have spoken with Père Antoine. It is not a violation of the Holy Rule since you have not yet made your vows."

Normally there was an extern sister, usually illiterate and unable to read the Latin prayers, who was a member of the order but not cloistered, who could be sent on errands outside the monastery walls. The extern who had come with Mère Marie Rose died soon after they arrived. So now there was only Nicole.

"If Père Antoine gives his permission, it can be no sin," she had told the abbess.

"None at all," Mère Marie Rose agreed. "The altar breads are to be delivered three times a week. Monday, Wednesday, and Friday. Promptly at the hour of noon."

"But, *ma Mère,*" the words had tumbled out of her. Nicole had not thought about how they would sound, until it was too late to get them back. "I will miss three dinners." Already the gray habit that had fitted her perfectly two months earlier needed to be carefully folded at the waist before she could tie it with the Franciscan cord. Otherwise it constantly worked its way free and dragged on the floor, a sin against the Holy Rule.

"You think too much about food, my daughter," the abbess scolded. "You will beg for your dinner today in penance."

"*Oui, ma Mère.*"

"And you should know that we will save your dinners for you on the days when you must go to the château, child. Do you not think that we have always your best interests at heart?"

Forgive me, *mon Dieu,* Nicole prayed as she waited for someone to come to the gate. I have sworn to trust Mère Marie Rose as my own mother. But oh, Ste. Vierge, can you please see that my dearest mother after you and my own darling maman saves me a bit of bread and a little glass of wine as well? She had never thought herself a glutton, but she was always hungry in this place. At least now that it was June it was warmer and she did not so much mind not having a blanket at night.

A footman in the white and gold livery of the bishop's household came to the gate. *"Oui?"*

"I have the altar breads from the Poor Clares. For His Excellency to offer Holy Mass."

"Ah, oui, bien sûr. Merci, ma Soeur."

It was the first time anyone had ever addressed her so. The nuns called the abbess *ma Mére,* and each other by the names they had been given in religion. Nicole felt a little prickle of pride. After everything, in spite of all the difficulties, I have kept my word, *mon Dieu.* I have become a Poor Clare and I will do penance for the rest of my life. She passed the small box through the bars of the gates and the footman took it. Time to go home, back to the monastery, and eat her cold dinner. She turned away from the gate, giving the skirt of the habit a little unconscious flick to keep it from tripping her up.

Cormac's mouth fell open in surprise. He knew that gesture. No wonder he had thought the small figure somehow familiar. It was Nicole Crane hidden beneath that all-covering white veil and that rough brown gown. *Ayi!* Maybe Quent was in Québec as well. She couldn't have come alone.

Nicole walked quickly, head down, inviting greetings from no one; passersby moved out of her way, offering her the deference of space. If Corm approached her he would be obvious, however careful he was. Still more daunting was the presence of the priest. Corm was in a doorway thirty strides from the gates of the bishop's château, completely hidden from view; Père Antoine was behind a tree directly across from the gates. Had she been less disciplined about keeping her head down and concentrating only on the hands folded at her waist, Nicole must surely have seen him.

She made her way down the hill, unaware of the two men following her. Then, in the Lower Town, the priest went one way and Nicole another. Corm hesitated only a moment before following not Père Antoine, but Nicole. For a few seconds he thought he'd been exceptionally fortunate. There was no one in the narrow, cobbled alley she turned into. He considered calling her name, but it was too dangerous. The business that had brought him to Québec was private. Corm strode forward, intending to catch up with her. He was still ten strides away when she abruptly opened a door and slipped inside.

Cormac swiftly covered the distance between where he was and where Nicole had disappeared. He found himself outside a door made of heavy oak planks studded with brass nails, with a black latched handle. He tried to open it, but the door was locked. Corm took a step back. The alley was full of shadows caused by the overhanging eaves of the ramshackle buildings either side. There was an odd half-barrel contraption set into the wall beside the latched door. He had no idea what it was for. On the other side was a second door, less forbidding than the first, not as heavy, with a rough cross carved into the wood. That door was not locked. Corm went inside what proved to be an empty and silent church and looked at what there was to see—the two small windows of plain glass, a few kneeling chairs, a bare altar, and behind it a grille and the heavy curtains. He would have to wait and watch and hope Nicole came out again.

Corm left the church and made his way toward the waterfront, keeping always to the shadows, every sense alert. He heard footsteps behind him and picked up his pace. He reached for the tomahawk at his waist but before he could free it Corm found himself enveloped in a crowd. People were pouring down toward the waterfront from the hills of the Upper Town.

"Les soldats sont arrivés! Vive la France! Vive la France Nouvelle!"

The troops had arrived. The British attempt at a blockade had failed.

"Fog," Corm heard someone say as the news spread from the decks of the ships to the waiting crowd. "Did the English in, the fog did. Only managed to capture one of our ships."

"And that only by lying."

The story circulated of how the officer aboard the French frigate *Alcide* had called out to the approaching English ship *Dunkirk,* "Are we at peace or at war?"

"And this pig English captain, he shouts: *'La paix, la paix!'* That's how he got close enough to attack the *Alcide.* They are all liars, *les Anglais.*"

"But he told the truth; he had no right to attack. We are at peace."

"Do you think so?" The speaker was a fisherman. "This does not look like peace to me."

Thanks to the loss of the *Alcide,* the arriving force was made up of slightly fewer than six thousand men, led by a general Jean-Armand, baron de Dieskau, who had already served with distinction in Europe. He was to be in charge of all things military in New France. With him was a new governor-general to rule in all civilian matters, Pierre de Rigaud, marquis de Vaudreuil. Vaudreuil had been born in Canada; he could be counted on to understand how things were here in the north.

So, Monsieur le Roi, Cormac thought, official peace there may be, but you are definitely showing your saber. Are you then the white bear? It was hard to think of Louis XV as any such thing. They said he was ruled by his mistress, the exquisite Madame de Pompadour, and that she arranged for other women to satisfy his prodigious sexual appetites while she involved herself in the affairs of state. They said that Pompadour was the true ruler of France. *Ayi!* How could he know that the white bear was not a female? Had not Bishkek first thought the bear might be Pohantis?

The Québécois were still arriving at the dock. Cormac could make out a cluster of Jesuits come down from their hilltop fortress, and not far away, though sep-

arate from the black robes, Père Antoine the Franciscan. Of Nicole or any other
nuns dressed as she had been, there was no sign.

In most Poor Clare houses there was a room called a parlor, divided by a curtained grille so the nuns could receive guests while not exposing themselves to the
outside world. The convent of the Poor Clares of Québec was too small and too
poor to have a parlor. But since the ending of the Council of Trent in 1563 a confessional had been obligatory for administering the sacrament of penance to
women. The one that served the Poor Clares was built into the grille behind the
altar, a small and narrow double-sided box with two doors. The one on the nun's
side could be opened only from the cloister. The one in the public chapel was so
cleverly crafted that the door could not be distinguished from the wall unless one
knew it was there.

Once inside the box, penitent and confessor were separated by a partition that
had a tiny square grille at eye level. The confessional was the only place in her
convent where the abbess could appropriately speak with Père Antoine. "It went
well?" she asked.

"Perfectly," the priest assured her. The wooden grille between them lacked a
curtain, but Père Antoine was careful to look only straight ahead and the abbess
had lowered her black veil so it covered her face. "The townspeople were careful
not to disturb her," he said. "And Soeur Stephane comported herself exactly as she
should."

Mère Marie Rose sighed with satisfaction. "She is almost too perfect. Sometimes I think that it is too great a gift, to be given such a perfect vessel of sacrifice.
I am not worthy."

"Nor am I," the priest agreed. "But it is not for ourselves, remember. It is for
Holy Church, and the Order, and for the salvation of Indian souls."

"*Oui, mon Père.* That is why I was so worried when this demand came from
His Excellency. To send her outside three times a week . . . Who knows what cor-
rupting influence might—"

"There will be none," Antoine said firmly. "It is the work of God, this order
from the bishop. Soeur Stephane will have repeated chances to face the tempta-
tions of the outside world and refuse to give in to them."

"Much strength will be required to do that." In those moments when she had
occasion to open the cloister door—however legitimately—did not Mère Rose
herself sometimes give in to an unfitting curiosity about life beyond her cloister
walls? The good God alone knew how much He asked of those who left everything for his love. "We must pray very hard to support her in this trial."

"Indeed. But perhaps we should do more than pray. I have been thinking . . ."

It was hot and airless in the cramped wooden box. And her hips were beginning to ache with kneeling in the restricted space. *"Oui, mon Père?"*

"Perhaps it is time to introduce the little sister to the discipline."

Mère Marie Rose did not immediately reply. It was not customary to require such a rigorous penance of a novice. In the Rule of the Poor Clare Colettines a nun was not to take the discipline until she had made her first vows. In matters of interpreting the Holy Rule for her daughters, the abbess had ultimate authority. None but the Pope himself could overrule her in some things, or question her in others. It was a great honor, but also a source of constant tension. Abbesses were the only women in the Church who did not submit to men always in all things.

A slight cough from the other side of the box broke the silence. "Only if you think it wise," Antoine said. "I defer to you in all things to do with your daughters, of course."

It was not only the Father Delegate who must be considered in this matter. The bishop could easily have been given enough altar breads to see him through the weeks of his novena. It was at His Excellency's insistence that a fresh supply was to be delivered three times a week. He was testing her, reminding Mère Marie Rose that every bishop was a king in his own diocese, whether or not he had permitted the establishment of a house of religious who answered only to the successor of Peter in Rome. "I will think about it," Mère Rose said. "And I will pray."

"I as well," Antoine promised. "But this matter of the trips to the château of the bishop, they are not, I think, anything for us to be concerned about."

Corm watched the alley all day on Tuesday but Nicole did not appear. On Wednesday, shortly before noon, the monastery door opened and she stepped into the street. How could he not have recognized her instantly? Now that he had, Corm was struck by how much Nicole was herself even in these strange clothes with her face veiled. He stayed well behind until she had cleared the alley and the road beyond it and started up the hill along the broad road known as the Côte de la Montagne. Then gradually he began closing the distance between them.

"Mademoiselle Crane . . ."

At first she did not register that the quiet voice was calling to her. She no longer thought of herself with that name.

"Nicole . . . It's me, Cormac Shea." Her shoulders stiffened and she paused and half swung in his direction. "No, don't turn around. Keep walking. Up ahead five strides there's a stand of fir trees. Go in there. Look as if you mean to relieve yourself."

This was the part of the journey that was most isolated, a stretch of road with no houses, not even cobbles, only hard-packed dirt beneath her feet. There was no one in front of her to see her disappear into the copse that was now just ahead. But behind her? No. Cormac Shea would not have spoken if there was any chance they were observed. She had trekked through the wilderness with him long enough to know that.

The fir trees were at hand. Nicole pulled her skirts tight to her and stepped off the dirt road onto the fallen needles that covered the earth beneath the trees. The copse smelled of urine and she saw a couple of suspicious little mounds.

"*Bonjour, mademoiselle.* I am glad to see that you got what you wanted."

He looked as she remembered him. Straight dark hair slicked back and tied behind his head, his face bronzed by the sun except for the white scar. "It is you," she murmured.

"Did you expect an imposter?"

She gave a slight shake of her head. "No, not really. I knew your voice."

"*Oui, après tout . . .*"

"*Après tout,*" she agreed. "But no thanks to you. You broke your word and left me behind." Oh! why had she said that? Now she had the sin of resentment to confess. Until this moment she had committed no sin and need tell no one of meeting Monsieur Shea. "Why are you here? Is it a secret? You must tell me?"

"Why would my presence be a secret?"

The arrival of the troops and of the new governor and Dieskau the great general had penetrated even the cloister of the Poor Clares. The nuns had spoken of these things the evening before during recreation. "There is talk of war. We are beginning a perpetual novena to Our Lady of Victory. If you—"

"You pray for French success?"

"Of course. So the Holy Faith may be proclaimed. The Indians must have the Gospel preached to them, Monsieur Shea—" Nicole broke off. Last night in her cell she had not been able to stop herself from thinking of the many things Quent had told her about the Indians. Père Antoine and Mère Marie Rose and all the authorities of the Church said that if the Indians died without baptism they could never enter heaven. For herself, she could not truly believe that. The Mohawk chief who had convinced Quent to take her to Québec—surely he was a good man who deserved heaven. It could not be his fault that he did not know that Jesus Christ was God. Would *le bon Dieu* penalize good people for their ignorance?

"Look, Mademoiselle Crane, I—"

"You must call me Soeur Stephane now. That is my name in religion."

"Soeur Stephane, then. I didn't come to argue with you about the afterlife. It's this one that concerns me. Quent brought you to Québec, didn't he?"

She nodded. "*Oui.*" She could not speak his name aloud. If she did it would burn in her mouth all day. The way it burned always in her heart. She had added that to the reasons for her life of penance, that her beloved, though a heretic Protestant, might be allowed to enter heaven.

"Where is he now? I must find him, it's urgent." Corm could feel Memetosia's deerskin medicine bag around his neck, beneath his hunting shirt.

"I do not think he is still in Québec," she said. "It's June. Monsieur Hale brought me here last September."

Cormac was startled. Somehow he had made himself believe that everything was coming together, that the answers he sought were almost available to him. Finding Nicole here meant he would find Quent close at hand. As for the arrival of the French troops at the same time, it was all a sign. Just as Kekomoson's dream and the appearance of Philippe Faucon had been a sign.

Nicole glanced anxiously up at the sliver of sky between the branches of the evergreens. The sun was almost directly overhead. "It is almost noon. They expect me at the bishop's château." She reached into the pocket of her habit and withdrew a small box. "Altar breads. For His Excellency. I must go."

Noon. Marni would be coming in from the fields about now. She would come back to the house and take a cold drink because the work had made her thirsty. And if he were there they would strip off their clothes and ring out a cloth in rainwater and bathe each other beside the fire. Then they would lie down on his sleeping mat and she would give herself to him and—

Nicole knew just from looking at him that he was very far away. What did that mean? What did any of this mean? She didn't know. "Monsieur Shea, please, I must go."

"How do you know Quent isn't still in Québec? Is his father still alive?"

"I do not know about the elder Monsieur Hale. He was alive when I left. But—" She broke off. Monsieur Shea knew nothing about the renegades attacking Shadowbrook. "I must go now. Truly. But on Friday I will be making this journey again, at the same time. I will meet you here and try to tell you more."

"You promise? You must promise me, Mademoi— Soeur Stephane." All the answers were waiting for him. He had only to pull the threads together and the pattern would be revealed. Then he could go back to Marni.

"I promise," Nicole said.

He left the copse first, whistling softly a few seconds later to tell her it was safe for her to come out into the road. Nicole continued on her way up the hill, with her head down and her hands clasped demurely at her waist, and the white veil swinging softly around her shoulders.

Chapter Seventeen

THE QUIET WAS deadly. The flying column had crossed the Monongahela and come upon relatively open country. They were, Quent realized, in an Indian hunting ground. Probably Lenape, possibly Shawnee. In either case it was a part of the forest where the underbrush was burnt off regularly to provide better accessibility to fodder and so attract more game. Braddock had been riding at the column's head, but Quent couldn't see him now. He turned, looking for the General, and spotted him trotting his horse rearward along the line of march, issuing orders as he went. The precise formation of the two regiments tightened in his wake. Officers called out orders and the drums beat faster. In response the soldiers picked up their pace.

Fort Duquesne was six leagues away. In country like this, for the flying column, three hours ahead. Possibly four. After so long and such a hellish march, the men were heartened by the nearness of their objective. Quent could feel their spirits rising. They were sure that after a siege they would take the fort, because Braddock said so. And to a somewhat lesser extent, so did Washington. Quent was a hell of a lot less sure. He raised his glance and searched the sky. Still no birds, not even a lone crow circling overhead looking for carrion. He studied the trees on either side, trying to see deep into the forest. Nothing. He heard no small animals scurrying, only the rhythmic thump of the drums, beating in unison, measuring the march. Both regiments carried their colors, the banners hanging limp in the hot, still afternoon. But there were watching eyes. Quent could feel them.

He was starting to move deeper into the forest so he could scout the right flank when Scarouady came up beside him. The Iroquois had been to the rear, checking on the column's end. "The women are just now crossing the river," he told Quent. Meaning the column's tail was a league or so behind its head. Satisfactory.

Except for the unnatural silence. Scarouady felt it as well. Quent could hear it in his voice. "These *Cmokmanuk* warriors," he demanded irritably, "can they not walk without the war drums?"

"Not and keep together."

"And our great war chief says they must stay together." The Iroquois Half King spat on the ground to show his disdain for Braddock's ideas.

Quent started to say something, then stopped. Another of the Iroquois—a Cayuga who moments before had snaked off to scout the left flank—was coming toward them, crouching and moving as rapidly as he could. Quent felt the prickles begin at the back of his neck. *"Hanio! Aiesahswatenien!"* Look! We're under attack.

Both the Half King and Quent dropped to the ground at the same moment. The other Iroquois braves did the same. Quent raised his head to look for Braddock. He was still on horseback and trotting along the margin of the march, but now he was going forward, heading for his customary place at the front. Washington was beside him. Jesus, God Almighty. "Colonel Washington! General!" Quent shouted. "We're surroun—"

The first arrow was aimed straight for Braddock. He was saved only because at that moment he turned to look for the source of the shouting voice. His horse wasn't so lucky. A musket ball took the animal out from under the general. Washington leaned down and offered his hand to Braddock, who took it and hauled himself into the saddle behind the Virginian. The two men pounded for the column's head.

There was a storm of arrows now and musket fire. There were war whoops, bloodthirsty screams that caused fear even in Uko Nyakwai, the Red Bear. God knows how the men felt who had never heard them before, and who had spent the last few weeks brooding on stories of Indian brutality and torture. Quent knew the only way to fight the fear of battle was to issue your own scream of challenge. *"Ahi! Neyezonya!"* He bellowed the Potawatomi war cry as he loaded the long gun.

Braddock and his officers were shouting commands that were mostly lost in the tumult. "Keep together! Keep them together. Bugler, sound the colors!"

The officer nearest Quent, an East Anglian he'd had an ale with most evenings since the march began, was urging his men into the parallel lines that in theory would allow them to deliver crushing volleys of musketry into the enemy ranks. "We can't shoot 'em if we can't see 'em, sir," a young American recruit protested. "We need to—" The boy's words were cut off by a musket ball to his chest. In seconds the officer's head had been blown apart and not one of his men still stood.

Quent crawled through the grass, pulling himself forward with his elbows, stopping every once in a while to fire at something he'd seen move among the trees, then pausing to reload. Braddock had found another horse. He was everywhere, continually trying to keep his men in close formation. "Stand your ground, boys. They can't defeat us as long as you stand your ground. Bugler, sound the colors!"

A boy with a bugle ran forward to stand beneath the banner of the Forty-fourth Foot and blew the notes that summoned the scattered forces to rally around the regiment's flag. Quent watched those who tried to obey being picked off by arrows and musket balls coming from the cover of the trees. Moments later one of them got the young bugler.

Quent shimmied his way along the ground until he was near enough for Braddock to hear him. "General! The men have to break ranks and take cover in the long grass and behind the trees!"

"Nonsense! Get out of my way, damn you, Hale! Keep together, men. You know what to do, now is the time to do it!"

Sweet Jesus! Quent felt the tall grass around him moving, alive with men using it for cover. It was the Virginians. He could identify them by their blue coats, and by the fact that they knew enough to get themselves into the woods and under cover. Washington didn't go with them. He remained at Braddock's side, in the direct line of fire. Quent saw the young colonel's horse shot out from under him. Washington snatched the reins of one that was riderless and sprang into the saddle. "Stand your ground, men!" Echoing Braddock's order and his confidence. "They can't beat us if we stand our ground!" The soldiers were desperately trying to follow orders. The result was to force them into an ever smaller square, an ever more defined target.

The men wearing bearskins were the enemy's prey of choice. The French may have felt constrained by the European custom of not deliberately killing officers, but their Indian allies had learned to pick them off one by one. The redcoats were helpless without them. They were trained to follow commands instantly and without question; without those commands no one had any idea what to do except try to obey Braddock and stand their ground.

In the woods on either side it was tomahawks and fixed bayonets and hand-to-hand combat between the Indians and the Virginians. Scalps were stripped from the living and the dead by both white men and red. An Indian came at Quent from the rear and he swung round, cursing the fact that he no longer had his dirk, and used his tomahawk to split the man's skull. Jesus God Almighty. The brave was Potawatomi. Quent felt nausea rise, then disappear as he took on a Shawnee seeking the most prized trophy of the day, Uko Nyakwai's red scalp. Quent dispatched the Shawnee and spotted a few Lenape behind him. Shingas and the other Ohio Country chiefs hadn't simply refused Braddock's war belt, they had been so disgusted with the treatment they received from him they'd decided to fight with the French.

The marching drums were silent now, but the sounds of the battle were deafening. Shouted commands, war whoops, and above all, the never-ending screams. Quent's long gun was useless in these close quarters. He fought his way to a tall tree near the cleared area, then climbed as high as he could. He had to squint to see through the smoke hanging over the battleground, but he could tell that the confusion was worse than before. Braddock was in the midst of it, riding what had to be his fourth or fifth horse and shouting out orders that his men now ignored, their terror too great. Many had thrown down their weapons and were running. Most were brought down by an arrow or a musket ball, others were dragged away by the braves. Quent knew they'd be tied up deep in the forest and reclaimed later. Captives were the most important thing any warrior could bring back to his village. The prisoners would be given the chance to prove themselves under torture, then a few would be adopted to make up for those killed here today. The rest would be killed and eaten.

The tail of the flying column had finally caught up with its head, but rather than reinforcing their comrades the new troops added to the general melee. The new officers too were quickly spotted and killed. The women were almost all captured. Four or five times Quent shot a brave in the act of dragging a woman into the forest, only to have another seize her while he was still reloading.

The ground was becoming a carpet of bodies, and parts of bodies. Quent could see a headless and legless trunk right below him, the red coat still intact, its buff-colored facings indicating a member of the Forty-eighth Foot. The pair of arms weren't from the same victim—the turned-back cuffs were yellow, indicating the Forty-fourth.

Quent got off another shot and took down a brave who had been hurtling toward one of the officers. The barrel of the long gun was smoking hot, but he reloaded in the space of twenty heartbeats. This time when he lifted the gun to his shoulder and tried to sight, he saw the doctor, Walton, moving on his knees among the bodies on the field. Sweet Christ, the man was mad. You couldn't minister to the wounded in conditions like these. Quent watched him for a moment, then swung the gun around to where a whooping brave—Abenaki from the look of him—was aiming his musket at Braddock. Quent fired, but he was a second too late. He saw the general go down. The Abenaki took a step toward his fallen victim, then the top half of his body separated from the lower, neatly sliced apart by Quent's blast.

"*Absolve peccatis, Domine.*" Absolve thy servant from all sin, Lord. Xavier Walton had been carrying holy oils about his person for just this eventuality. He kept them hidden in the pocket of his jacket and every few seconds moistened the forefinger of his right hand, then traced a cross on the forehead of a dying or dead man as he hovered over him, whispering Latin petitions for the salvation of his soul. Protestant heretics all of them, but his task was to give them the opportunity to renounce their sin. Who knew what thoughts of repentance might cross a man's mind in the final moment of life? *"Absolve peccatis, Domine."* He could do no less than to pray for these sinners, and hope that eventually they would be admitted to heaven. Any minute the martyrdom he had so longed for would come. Walton was convinced of it. Surely he would not escape. *This day you shall be with Me in Paradise.* You promised, Lord. *"Absolve peccatis, Domine."* The Jesuit crawled to the next red-coated body. His finger hovered above the man's forehead. It was the general. The front of his uniform was covered in blood, but Braddock was breathing.

"No doctoring now . . . have to get up. . . . a horse . . ."

Walton got his arms under Braddock's torso and dragged him across the ground, through the spilled entrails, bumping over bodies whole and dismembered, until finally he reached the scant shelter of a large oak whose branches almost reached the ground.

The Jesuit's breath came in hot, hard gasps; Braddock's were shallow and sounded as if he were expelling bubbles. Walton lay his hand over the general's chest and felt the rapidly beating heart but not the steady thump of fresh blood being pumped out of a damaged artery. The yellow facings of Braddock's red coat were stained neither by blood nor dirt. Walton's fingers were slick with Braddock's blood as he worked the buttons open, then pushed the coat aside. Holy Mother of God . . . Braddock had taken a musket ball directly to the chest. The breastbone had prevented total penetration and the musket ball was now acting as a plug, stopping the flow of blood. "You are a man favored by God, General Braddock," Walton whispered. "You should give thanks."

Braddock's eyes showed that he'd heard, but when he tried to speak no words came. The Jesuit pressed a finger over the wounded man's lips. "Save your strength. You are fighting for your life, and perhaps your salvation. Listen to me, and just nod. Do you renounce Satan and all his works?" Braddock's eyes showed panic. "I am trying to save your soul," Walton whispered urgently. "You are mortally wounded, man. Do you renounce all heresies and offer your full allegiance to Jesus Christ and His Holy Catholic and Apostolic Church?"

Braddock understood. Walton, the English doctor, was a Catholic and therefore a spy. He had no weapons; his only hope was to kill the man with his bare hands. Braddock lifted an arm, stretching toward Walton's throat. The gesture caused a fire to light in his chest, the pain such that a small scream was torn from him. Then he passed out.

Walton had seen the packet of papers wrapped in oilskin as soon as he parted the general's coat. He had made the man's salvation his first concern, but it was too late—or maybe too early—to save him from hellfire. His second duty was to aid the French forces in whatever way he could and help bring Holy Church and the authentic Gospel of Jesus Christ to this New World, and perhaps to speed the day when the heretical and schismatic king of England would be forced from the throne, and Xavier Walton's beloved country returned to the rule of those who avowed the True Faith. He reached for the documents and slipped them inside his own jacket.

"Dr. Walton!" Washington had found a fresh horse and dashed for the place where the general lay. He looked at the fallen man. "Is he dead?"

"Not yet, but dying."

"We must move him." Washington summoned two men and charged them with carrying Edward Braddock from the field. There was an instant when Braddock opened his eyes and frantically tried to signal that Walton was a traitor who must be immediately arrested or killed. "Don't agitate yourself, sir," Washington murmured. "Save your strength. We'll get you clear of all this." Braddock tried to reply, but produced only burbles through his bloodstained lips.

The job of command, Washington realized, had fallen to him. The place had become a killing field. "Buglers! Sound the retreat!"

Retreat wasn't difficult. The Indians had no interest in pursuing Washington and his soldiers. Instead the braves flooded the field and began looting and scalping corpses and wounded alike. Any heart they found still beating they cut out and ate. Their cries of triumph could be heard everywhere.

Deep in the forest Quent heard them as he systematically cut the bonds of one captive after another, the women first, then the men. He knew that he had only as long as the war cries persisted to finish the task. "Go," he whispered to each freed captive. "South's that way." Some would be recaptured, some killed, but it was the best he could do in this day of hellish misery and stupidity and death.

He'd told the others to go south because that was the quickest way to get out of the range of the French enemy and their *Anishinabeg* allies. For himself Quent had other concerns. As soon as he'd cut the bonds of the last captive, he headed north.

MONDAY, AUGUST 16, 1755
THE COLLÈGE DES JÉSUITES, QUÉBEC

"Excellent, Xavier! Truly excellent! I had no idea that sending you into the enemy camp would have such remarkable results." Louis Roget did not look up when he spoke. His glance was fixed on the French translation of the papers Walton had taken from General Braddock the month before. The quality of the information was staggering. *Merci, mon Dieu. I will be worthy.*

Roget stopped running his finger down the page and jabbed repeatedly at one sentence. "This bit here about the four-pronged advance, how does it compare with the original?" The Jesuit superior spoke a bit of English, but the written language was particularly difficult and he did not trust himself to correctly interpret every nuance. He had looked at the papers when Xavier first arrived, and listened to the priest's explanation, then demanded the material be translated into French. The task had taken his spy priest an entire day and most of the night as well. Xavier's eyes were rheumy with fatigue. "You did as I suggested?"

"I did exactly as you suggested, Monsieur le Provincial. I strengthened the words used to describe the proposed attack on Fort St. Frédéric."

The baron de Dieskau was in Montréal preparing to lead a combined force of four thousand French regulars and their Indian allies to Fort Niagara. Roget knew this because collecting such bits of information was his life's work, not because Vaudreuil and Dieskau had consulted him. They were under the impression that they could organize things in New France without taking into account the opinion of the Provincial of the Society of Jesus. "Come, Xavier, I hear something in your tone. You do not believe it was wise? I insist that you speak freely."

"I entirely agree that these new men must be fully alerted to the threat, Monsieur le Provincial." Xavier had made a great point of saying that the attack on Fort St. Frédéric was to be led by General William Johnson, and that he had thousands of Mohawk savages under his command. He reached for the bright red bandanna and swabbed at his forehead.

"An interesting choice of pocket cloth, my son."

Xavier glanced at the thing in his hand. "I apologize, Monsieur le Provincial. I did not realize. A woman . . . in the English camp . . . she . . ."

"Stop sputtering, Xavier. I understand." Walton still wore the coat and breeches of his Virginia adventure. "You will change back to your soutane now that you are at home. And the red pocket cloth will be retired. Now, about this . . . interpretation. You were saying—"

How could he explain what the Indians had done at the Monongahela? Xavier couldn't close his eyes without seeing them cutting the hearts out of men yet alive, and stuffing the still-beating organs into their mouths. Every night he heard the cries of the painted warriors and saw their arms and their chests running red with the blood of their victims. Almost a month now and he could rid himself of neither the horror nor the perplexity. *This day you shall be with Me in Paradise.* But the day had passed him by.

"What is it, Xavier? Something is bothering you, I can tell. Speak up, man. That's a direct command."

He was vowed to obey his superiors in all things that were not sin. "I cannot understand why God did not grant me martyrdom, Monsieur le Provincial. It was so close. If you could have seen what I saw . . . Men and women alike, slaughtered, hacked apart while they were alive, their hearts consumed raw—"

"Yes, I know. And you weep that your own heart still beats in your chest, not in the belly of some brave."

"Only because I have been given this desire for martyrdom. It has been with me since I was a boy. Such a thing must come from God."

"God demands that you do your duty like a good Jesuit, Xavier. The savages may indeed have carried things to extremes. They frequently do. But have you forgotten that they were fighting on the side of the king? Of New France?"

"*Non, Monsieur le Provincial, bien sûr! Vous avez raison, mais—*"

"*Mais rien!* How could you be a martyr for the Holy Faith if you died on the wrong side of the field of battle?"

The blood drained from Walton's face, leaving him as white as his shirtfront. "I never thought—"

"No, of course. But in such matters you need not think. I am the voice of God for you. Not myself," Louis Roget added quickly, "my office."

"I do not for an instant doubt that, Monsieur le Provincial."

"Then obey. I order you to stop mourning the martyrdom that passed you by. Give thanks that you have been allowed to serve the Church and His Majesty and our Holy Order so well." Roget tapped the translations. "These are magnificent, truly magnificent, Xavier."

The news of the great French victory that had preserved Fort Duquesne set church bells ringing in all Québec, From the mighty bells of the cathedral and those of the Collège des Jésuites to the bells of the Convent of the Ursulines at the Hôtel-Dieu and the single bell of the tiny Monastery of the Poor Clares.

Every bell had a name, and those who knew them could identify each one by its distinctive sound. The one belonging to the Poor Clares was called Maria. Its voice was sweet and true and clear. Nicole had learned only lately to ring the Maria bell. Soeur Joseph had been teaching her. *Slowly, ma petite Soeur, with the rhythm of your heart. It is like singing, no? When you ring the bell you make the music of the angels. Ringing the bell is an act of prayer.*

She could not follow the rhythm of her heart this day. It was thudding painfully in her chest. And she could not stop her tears. She had been crying when Mère Marie Rose found her, peeling potatoes for dinner, and sent her up to the bell tower. "Soeur Joseph cannot go. We need her in the choir for the *Te Deum*. I know you weep for joy, dear child, but you must dry your eyes and go and ring the bell."

How could she ever explain to the abbess, to any of her sisters? Not one of them had ever seen a battlefield. They did not know what she knew, what she had seen. So much blood, *mon Dieu,* so much pain. And the terrible screams of those who died in agony. She clasped the bell rope firmly with both hands and pulled slowly and surely, taking the movement as far as it would go, bending her knees to accommodate it as Soeur Marie Joseph had taught her, then rising, allowing the tension to ebb. *You do not let the bell go,* ma petite. *You guide the release as you guided the capture, slowly, with your body and with your heart."*

Her heart knew no release. It was with her beloved. I do not know if he was there, *mon Dieu,* in that terrible place of death. But I beg You to keep him safe. My life for his, my good God. I have given up my life with him and come here to offer You my small penances. Keep him safe. The top of the release came and the Maria bell of the Poor Clares of Québec added its voice to the general peals of joy.

In the choir the nuns heard their bell and Soeur Joseph intoned the opening notes of the Church's great hymn of joy: *Te Deum laudamus . . .*

The triumphal ringing of the bells had ended by the time the Provincial Superior of the black robes sat across from Vaudreuil, the newly installed governor-general of New France. "I am honored that you come to me, Monsieur le Provincial." Vaudreuil had lived eighty years, most spent in Canada, but many in France. He knew how things were arranged, and how they were meant to be arranged. The governor-general had already paid his obligatory call on the Jesuit residence. The hounds of hell could not have dragged him back a second time. Once was a courtesy, twice was submission.

Roget knew as well as his opponent when to sacrifice a minor piece in order to gain one that was still more vital. "It was important only that you have these papers as soon as possible. Protocol is of no matter in times like these."

"I agree, of course." Vaudreuil didn't want to appear too eager, much less too impressed, but he couldn't keep his glance from dropping to the French translations at least once every third word. "You are sure these things are accurate? A clever forgery could—"

"That is why I brought them myself, Monsieur le Gouverneur-Général. So that I could assure you that they were taken from the person of General Braddock by the man I sent for exactly that purpose."

"Braddock is dead over a month now." The dispatches describing the great victory at the Monongahela had been sent to every corner of the Empire. Vaudreuil had received his copy that morning, hence the great celebration throughout the city. "It is said the English buried him somewhere along the road."

"So I have heard." Roget piously signed himself with the cross. "May God have mercy on his soul. But before he died a member of the Society attended him and—"

"Braddock was a Catholic?"

"*Mais non, Monsieur le Gouverneur-Général.* As far as I know God did not grant the general the grace of conversion. Nonetheless, a member of the Society was with him when he was wounded. And this man took these papers from General Braddock with his own consecrated hands."

Jésus! Everyone said these black robes were formidable spies as well as meddlers, but to have one of their own inside the English camp!

"On the field of battle, Monsieur le Gouverneur-Général. While the English general lay bleeding from his wounds." Roget pronounced each word slowly, but without a hint of pride. "Of course I tell you all this only for your own information. So that you may be sure the documents are to be trusted."

"And the originals, Monsieur le Provincial? It was indeed kind of you to have the translations made for me, but—"

"The Jesuit who made them is an Englishman born and bred, Monsieur. And he has spoken French for the past twenty years. There can be no doubt of either his loyalty to our Holy Faith, and thus our king and our cause, or his understanding of both French and English. Is there a better translator in all Québec? Do you have someone here at your château who is more fluent in both languages?"

A pox on you, black robe. May your heart be cut out at the first possible opportunity. "*Bien sûr, Monsieur le Provincial. Bien sûr.* Still, the originals . . . I should send them to France. His Majesty will—"

"Of course. I entirely agree. As soon as this fracas is over and we know the high seas are safe, the originals must go to Versailles. Until then, I assure you, Monsieur le Gouverneur-Général, they are perfectly protected. I will take full responsibility."

"The responsibility for getting information to Versailles is mine, Monsieur le Provincial."

At once Roget bent his head in submission. "Exactly as you say, Monsieur le Gouverneur-Général. I will have the originals delivered to you immediately."

"Excellent. I am in your debt, Monsieur le Provincial. All New France is in your debt."

"I only do my duty, Monsieur le Gouverneur-Général,"

Vaudreuil rang impatiently for someone to show the Jesuit out. Quickly, before he gave in to his rage and cut out the man's tongue.

A strong inland wind greeted Louis Roget as he set out across the Place d'Armes, the wide plaza in front of the château. It had been calm earlier, a still and sunny afternoon, but during the hour he'd been with that old Canadian ruffian whom providence had seen fit to make a marquis a chinook had developed. He'd learned about chinooks since he'd been in this devil-spawned Québec. They blew almost gale force, but brought no relief from summer's heat. This wind was hot and dry, filled with grit and dust picked up as it descended the mountains and skimmed the prairies. The Jesuit had to hang on to his biretta and struggle to keep his sweaty soutane from tripping him up as he toiled up the hills to the Collège. No matter. If he could he would dance his way home.

General Braddock's papers would remain where they were, hidden behind the magnificent wall created by the *Champenois ébénistes*. Vaudreuil would ask about them a few times, but the governor-general would not go so far as to send armed men to wrest them from the clutch of the black robes. And failing that, he would not get them. Meanwhile he would act on the information supplied by Louis Roget because he dared not do otherwise, and it would serve him well. Vaudreuil would come to know what those before him had also had to recognize: there could be no governing New France without the cooperation of the Society of Jesus. *Grâce à Dieu!* Louis Roget had met the enemy and he had won.

From his window in the Château Saint-Louis Vaudreuil watched until the priest was out of sight. The Jesuit was a picture of holy modesty. Bastard. May you be staked out and left to die of thirst. May vultures pick at your flesh. Do you think I don't know that you despise me for not being French as you are French? For being Canadian? May you die a Canadian death, Monsieur le Provincial.

The governor-general turned from the window and grabbed the bell on his desk. The black slave he had acquired while he was governor of that hellhole called Louisiana appeared before it stopped ringing. *"Oui, Monsieur le Gouverneur-Général."*

"Bring me a glass of Burgundy. And talk to the apothecary. Have him add something that will soothe my stomach. Also, tell them to send the cook back to whatever wolf-pit he comes from. I cannot discharge my responsibilities if my digestion is challenged at every meal." It was his wife's fault. If she had not gone to Montréal to buy things she said she could not get in Québec, he would not be at the mercy of a kitchen lacking supervision and scheming to ruin him.

The slave scurried off. Vaudreuil knew it wasn't his dinner turning his bowels to water, nonetheless he felt better for doing something. Getting rid of the cook was not, however, enough. He reached for paper and a quill. He could not trust a secretary with such information as this. In fact, he could trust no one in the government of Québec. Every second person seemed to be under the thumb of the black robes. Those who were not, conspired with Intendant Bigot to make themselves rich by robbing the public purse. *Eh bien.* He had promised himself when he accepted this appointment that he would not waste his strength fighting battles that could not be won.

There is nothing to be done about *la grande société* and its larceny; Bigot's tentacles stretch too far. As for the Provincial Superior and his Society of Jesus . . . Not yet. Louis Roget is a thousand times more clever than Bigot. Is he clever enough to have forged a document and passed it off as the English battle plans?

Yes. But why? Whatever else you may be, Monsieur le Provincial, I believe you are truly a Catholic. You vie for power with me, and with this mad Franciscan whom I confess I do not understand, but I do not think you would do anything to assist the heretic English. If this information is then accurate, it must truly come from Braddock himself.

Vaudreuil was almost overcome by the hopelessness of it all. Battles you can win, he reminded himself. You are an old man and you took this assignment, undoubtedly your last, for only one reason. It is up to you to see that Canada is not lost to the English by the stupidity and pigheadedness and lack of understanding in Versailles. For the moment the man who can best keep Canada safe is headed up the St. Lawrence with four thousand French regulars, Canadians, and Indians to reinforce Fort Niagara. Where, If the Jesuit is to be believed, we are not yet to be attacked.

Alors. I have more reasons to believe Louis Roget than to disbelieve him. So you must go south, *mon ami le maréchal de camp.* To Lake Champlain, or even farther, to Lake St. Sacrement. Vaudreuil paused for a moment, trying to remember the old Indian name for that lake, the one he'd learned as a boy. Ah yes, Bright Fish Water. A long way away perhaps, but that is where they must confront this General Johnson and his Mohawks.

Vaudreuil hesitated a moment longer, ordering his thoughts, then dipped his quill in the fine jade inkpot that his predecessor had somehow left behind and began: *My dear Dieskau, I have it on no less than the authority of the Provincial Superior of the black robes that. . . .*

TUESDAY, AUGUST 31, 1755
THE SIGN OF THE NAG'S HEAD, ALBANY

"Lake George," Annie said. "That's what they's gonna call it. No more Bright Fish Water."

"They canna do that," Hamish protested. "It's been Bright Fish Water right along. The Sassenachs canna come along and name it for their bloody heretic king just 'cause they've a mind to do so."

"Lower yer voice, you Scots fool. Show some respect. It's the king's standard is right up there behind ye, remember. All around, if it comes to that." Annie jerked her head in the direction of the fort and the hills surrounding the town, and squirmed on the taproom bench so they were sitting a bit closer.

He could smell the sourness of her, and the sex. She'd just come in from the yard where she did her business. "It's him as told you about the name?" Hamish said. "That wee nubbin fancies himself a soldier that just left?" Yorkers, they were called, these fresh-faced young men in their blue coats with the bright red facings. Lads that could na wait to be slaughtered in the glory o' war. Christ ha' pity on 'em all. But may the Blessed Virgin bring victory to the French and the Holy Faith.

"Indeed. I've no idea what kind of a soldier he may turn out to be, but it's a fine strong boy he is in other ways." Annie laughed raucously and banged a coin on the table signaling for the punch bowl. "C'mon, you Jacobite papist, drink up and I'll buy you a refill."

Hamish gave her a black look, but he downed the last of his rum and let her ladle him a glass of punch when the bowl came. "Thin stuff," he complained after the first sip. "Canna serve to keep the cold from a man's bones."

"It's summer, you daft bugger. It's cooling you want, not heating."

He was not interested in discussing the weather. "You're sure," he said, "Lake George?"

" 'Course I'm sure. Way I heard, it's Johnson himself what said it. From this day forward," Annie rolled the words in a fair imitation of a man making a solemn proclamation, "this shall be Lake George."

A few of the blue-coated Yorkers standing nearby heard her and turned. One even lifted his mug of ale in salute. Hamish had all he could do to keep from walking over and punching the man in the face. He leaned toward Annie and spoke in a gruff whisper. "I don't care who this William Johnson fancies himself to be, with his blue-coated laddies pretending they're soldiers and God knows how many Mohawk savages ready to do his bidding. It's Bright Fish Water. As it's always been."

The force William Johnson was gathering to take Fort St. Frédéric at Crown Point had been assembling in and around Albany for weeks. But all Johnson had done was to send an advance party north as far as the Great Carrying Place and build Fort Edward. Edward, after yet another bloody Sassenach, the heretic duke o' York, Hamish thought. And God help him, he was o' two minds as to whether it was in his best interests to bide and let things develop as they might—which was the advice o' John Lydius—or run to Québec and warn that blackhearted Père Antoine o' what was to be. For the sake o' Holy Church, o' course. Though it might help his alliance with the Franciscan as well.

The conflict was eating into his gut. The thought of anything changing at Shadowbrook before it was his made it worse. Acid bile rose in his gorge. "What does John Hale say about it, then? It's you as should know better 'n anyone what's in the mind o' that piss-poor excuse for a man. What's he say?"

"Ain't seen him in a fortnight. But I can tell ye this. Don't matter none what John Hale says. He made over Bright Fish Water and the bit they call the Great Carrying Place, and a good deal more besides."

"In Christ's name, what are you talking about, woman? Made over to who? When?"

"Nearly a year past, in New York City. Leastwise that's what I was told." Annie sat back and watched the effect of her words. Jesus, but these men were something. Thought they were God Almighty soon as they had a stiff cock. Didn't realize it only made 'em easier to lead around. "Made it over to a Jew," she said.

"I don't believe you." Hamish downed the last of the punch and called for rum.

"Believe as ye like. It's the truth nonetheless."

"It's not."

The barmaid brought Hamish a large mug of rum. He gave her two coppers and an aimless pat on the behind.

"S'truth," Annie repeated. Aw, why was she doing this now? She'd known as soon as she heard the story that it was important, something she could use to make things a little better for herself. She knew she should keep quiet until she saw a way to do that. Instead here she was spilling the tale to this Scot. For no good reason except she wanted him to know she was something more than a stupid whore meant for fucking and abusing.

Almost two years the Scot had been paying her to talk about John Hale, that vicious rat. The month before he'd worn her down and made her tell how she had to let Hale piss on her 'fore he fucked her. She'd been feeling sorry for herself and needing someone as would listen to her woes. So she'd told him the whole thing and bloody Hamish Stewart laughed. Oh, he'd said sorry fast enough, but she knew he wasn't. Not really. He only said it so she'd go on talking. All right then, she'd tell him how his precious Shadowbrook—and did he think she was such a fool she didn't know that was what he wanted, though she couldn't see as how he'd ever get it—wasn't quite the prize as it had been before. "One of them sutlers as is all over the place selling things to the Yorkers, he told me. Worked for the governor's brother down in New York City he did. Oliver someone."

"Oliver De Lancey."

"Yes, that's right. Anyway this sutler, he was a footman for this De Lancey fella . . ."

"What about John Hale?" Hamish took a golden guinea from his purse and pushed it across the table. "C'mon, Annie lass, I always take care o' you when you do right by me. What did he say about John Hale?"

Annie swallowed hard. She wanted to snatch up the shiny coin before the Scot changed his mind. But what she knew was worth more. Her gut told her it was. And she'd never have a better opportunity. "A guinea ain't enough," she muttered. "Not for this story, it ain't."

"How's this then." Hamish put another golden lady on top of the first. Two guineas. Annie's mouth was dry and her palms were sweating, but she clenched her fists in her lap and shook her head. Hamish hesitated, then made up his mind. All his past investments in Annie had proved themselves worthwhile. "Very well," he said softly. "Five golden ladies. But only if I decide the information's worth that much. C'mon, lass, five guineas. 'Tis a fortune."

A fortune for the likes of her, that's what he meant. Thing is, it was. If she got five golden ladies she wouldn't have to come back to the Nag's Head for two months. Maybe longer. "Five guineas," she agreed. "But you puts 'em all on the table right now, Hamish Stewart. No promises, mind. Cash money."

Hamish turned to the wall and opened his purse and counted out three more coins, then turned back and added them to the stack. Annie covered the money with her hand, but he slapped his big maw over hers so she couldn't actually take it. "Not so fast, lassie." He leaned forward and fixed her with his single eye. "The truth. Otherwise I'll na be responsible for what I might do."

"It's all true. Just like the sutler told me." She craned her neck in all directions before she continued. No one was paying them any mind—they were both regulars at old man Groesbeck's after all—nonetheless she whispered. "John Hale was at a meeting in Oliver De Lancey's house, with another man whose name I don't know, and a Jew. Somebody Levy I think it was."

She'd been right about how important this story was. Annie knew it when she saw Hamish's cheeks turn a blotchy purple, and saw him draw his eyebrows close over his nose. Ah God, and aren't ye feeling a bit poorly now, my fine Scots cock-of-the-walk. Think Annie's for fucking and forgetting, do ye? We'll see.

"Hayman Levy," Hamish said.

"Yes. That's the name the sutler said." She chose her words carefully, watching their effect, feeling the thrill of power. "John Hale made over a whole piece of Shadowbrook to Hayman Levy. Back when he was a footman the sutler was right outside the door of the room where it happened. He heard everything. Even looked through the keyhole and saw John Hale sign the paper."

The blood was pounding in his ears, but Hamish's voice was steady. He let go of Annie's hand and wrapped both his around the mug of rum to disguise their trembling. Annie cautiously begin to slide the money toward the table's edge. Wanted to grab 'em up, Hamish knew, but she dinna quite dare. Damn Annie Crotchett to hellfire for holding him up for five golden ladies, but what she was telling him was worth the price. "Made the land over in return for what? Why would John Hale do such a thing?"

God's truth, not to pay for three slaves. The man couldna be such a fool as he'd sell a piece o' his birthright for the pride o' going to an auction and letting the men o' New York City see him buy three slaves he dinna really need. But Holy Jesus Christ Our Savior, the three o' em was there that poxed day watching Hale pay cash money for slaves not four months after he'd been nearly burned out.

Levy and De Lancey and the lawyer James Alexander. If there was land to be made over, a lawyer would be needed. "What did Hale get for the land?" Hamish asked. He made a gesture as if to take back the stack of golden ladies. Annie whisked them away and made them disappear down the front of her dress.

"I'm not sure," she admitted.

"Christ Jesus." Hamish spoke the words with as much venom as he could muster, but inside he was singing. If she dinna know what had made John Hale agree to such a devil's own bargain, than more than likely she was lying. "You'll not get to keep five ladies for such rubbish as that, Annie Crotchett."

"It's true. Every word of it." Her chest was heaving so she thought her paps might come out of her dress. Maybe this would be enough. Maybe she didn't have to tell Hamish the rest of the tale. At least not yet. Maybe once these golden ladies were gone she could come back and get more for the part of the story she still hadn't told. But why had he stopped watching her? Hamish had half turned and was staring down the room with his single eye. "Hey! What you looking at now?"

"Close your gob, lass. And keep it closed for a bit."

Annie half stood so she could see what he saw. "Jesus Christ," she breathed, settling heavily back down on the bench. "So he's come home, has he? They said he'd gone back to the Ohio Country for good this time."

Hamish scowled. The presence of Quentin Hale might complicate things, but the matter at hand was more urgent. "Keeps turning up like a bad penny, that one. But we canna allow him to interrupt our business, Annie lass. You were about to tell me what John Hale got for making a piece o' Shadowbrook over to Hayman Levy and his friends."

"No, I was not. I already told you, I got no idea 'bout that."

"Then I'll have my golden ladies back. Give 'em over or I'll shake 'em free."

"I earned them ladies fair and square, Hamish Stewart. I didn't—"

"You dinna tell me a story as makes any sense. And that means it's a bloody lie and I'll have my money back. Are you giving it to me or do I have to take it?" Hamish gripped her arm and stood up, dragging her up with him.

"Sit down!" Annie didn't realize she'd yelled until she saw a couple of heads turn. "Sit yourself down, Hamish Stewart." This time she whispered the words. "I never said I was finished, did I? There's a bit more to tell." She dare not hold back the rest.

"Get it spoke and done with, Annie Crotchett, or I swear I'll send a few more teeth where the front two went."

Instinctively Annie pushed her tongue into the gap where her teeth should have been. Wasn't a man did that. Went to a barber and had 'em yanked out, she did, 'cause they was aching so bad, but she didn't fancy losing any more. She took a deep breath. "John Hale signed a paper as gave the men in New York claim to the whole of the Hale Patent."

Hamish couldn't speak. When the words finally came they were a squeak, forced out through an almost closed throat. "He dinna do such a thing. He would na do such a thing."

"He did. He signed it. The sutler saw him. And they was all talking about cane land, down in the Islands somewhere. Cane land in return for the Patent, it sounded like. But the sutler wasn't sure 'bout that."

Hamish didn't say anything. He's going to explode, she thought, like a kettle when the lid's on too tight and the fire's too fierce. But when the Scot spoke, his voice was so low she had to strain to hear what he was saying. "Go," he whispered. "Get out of here."

"Who are you to tell me what I'm to do, Hamish Stewart?" Her arm still hurt from where he'd grabbed it. She rubbed the sore place, knowing she'd have a bruise there later. "I'll come and go as I please and don't you forg—"

"Get out o' my sight, you wretched she-witch. Now."

"You ain't got no cause to talk to me like that," she said. But she was standing up to go even as she spoke. "No cause, Hamish Stewart. I ain't—"

Hamish half rose. Annie turned and ran.

He sat down again. His legs felt na strong enough to hold him. Cane land in return for Shadowbrook. It made perfect sense, if you were John Hale and seeking only to show a profit on the Patent. A venal, cowardly, miserable excuse for a man, was John Hale. And if he went to Shadowbrook and killed him as he deserved to be killed, skinned him alive maybe, as if he were a rabbit on a croft, what would that gain? A hangman's noose, most likely. And there was Quentin Hale, no farther away than the front door o' this miserable tavern where a man couldna get a dram o' proper whiskey however much he needed it. Passing the time o' the evening when his stinking brother had signed away their birthright. Did Hale know? He couldna. Not and sit there like that, as if nothing were wrong.

Hamish reached the front of the tavern in six strides. Quentin Hale sat with his back to the wall. Old man Groesbeck was hunched across from him, straddling a small stool and leaning forward as if to hear better. The Scot put his hand on the landlord's shoulder. "Go tend your other guests. I've business with this one."

Quent looked up. The afternoon light was fading fast, and the Nag's Head was always stingy with candles. He could see a short hulk of a man standing behind Peter Groesbeck. "Take your hands off him or I'll do it for you," Quent said.

"Aye, laddie. I've no doubt you would," Hamish said softly. He removed his hand from Groesbeck's shoulder. "But there's better uses for your righteous rage. I can warrant that."

Groesbeck stood up. "I be leaving you two gentlemans to settle your own affairs."

"You do that." Hamish made no move to take the stool the Dutchman vacated. "Step outside wi' me, laddie. What I have to say is na for any ears but your own."

Quent squinted into the dimness. "I know you, don't I?"

"You did. But you were a wee bairn at the time. I doubt you remember."

"I do. Hamish something."

"Aye, Hamish Stewart. And you're Quentin Hale. Now come outside. You'll not thank me for telling my story in here."

It was dusk. A cartman drove a wagon up the cobbled road. A small group of Yorkers in their blue and red coats walked briskly toward the nearest gate in the stockade. The breeze carried a river chill and the first scent of autumn. "You gave me a dirk," Quent said. "I cherished it."

"Aye. I remember that I did. Still have it, do you?"

"Not anymore. But last time I held it, it saved my life." Someday, as soon as this insanity loosed by Braddock was done, he'd go after Lantak and get the dirk back. "I'm in your debt."

"Nay, laddie, you're not. Not for the gift o' a wee dirk. But you might be."

"And that's what you want to talk to me about?"

"Something you should know." Despite the chill Hamish was sweating. He wiped his face with the sleeve of his shirt. Fierce heat in summer and cold enough to freeze a man's balls in the winter. God's truth, he must be mad to want to remain. Except that Shadowbrook was here. "Your brother," he began.

"What about him?"

"He's forfeited your birthright."

"If I've a birthright it's this." Quent tapped the long gun hanging over his shoulder. "Nothing else."

"The law may say it's the elder who inherits, but it's Almighty God puts a man in one place and not another. That's how a birthright comes to be."

"You're talking of Shadowbrook."

"Aye. Just a wee bairn you were, but you sat up in front of your father most days when we rode out to see the place. From Do Good in the north to the sawmill at the southern end. You knew every blade o' grass grew on the land, and every bird in every tree."

This land be your pa's land, but it don't rightly belong to no human being. This land belong to God Almighty. It got a lot to teach you. No way you can have learned it all. Not yet. Solomon the Barrel Maker was a wise man. Quent hoped that John was letting him end his days in peace, with Sally Robin. "My father's dead. Shadowbrook belongs to my brother John."

"No," Hamish said. "It does na, laddie. Take my word on that."

"You're not speaking sense."

"I wish to Almighty God I were not. John Hale's given a lien on Shadowbrook to three New York businessmen. He means to trade the Patent for cane land in the Islands."

"You're lying. He wouldn't—"

"Ha' you na heard about this new name for Bright Fish Water? And is there na a new fort on the Great Carrying Place?"

"The fort's been built where John Lydius's trading post has always stood. Lydius leases the land from the Patent. Look, I admit Johnson makes free, but it's in my brother's best interests to allow him to do so. Temporarily. The French are a threat to—"

"The only best interests John Hale recognizes are his purse. He signed away Bright Fish Water and the Great Carrying Place and God knows what else, and promised to exchange the rest for cane land. He made a pact with Hayman Levy and Oliver De Lancey. Probably James Alexander as well. Though Alexander might only ha' been there to do the lawyering. I would na lie, laddie. Not about the Patent. If you think about your brother, you'll ken."

Quent claimed a horse from Hooghkerk's Livery on Market Street and rode hard all through the night. Not yet dawn when arrived; the house was an inky black shadow on a still dark horizon. "John!" He screamed his brother's name even as he pelted toward the stables. "John!"

The yells and the pounding of the horse's hooves woke Jeremiah and he stumbled into the stable yard. "Master Quent. What you be— Jesus God Almighty, Master Quent. You fair to killed this horse. I ain't never seen you ride any animal near to death like—"

"Look after him." Quent slid from the saddle and gave the black man the reins, then ran toward the house. "John! I've come to talk to you!"

Jeremiah led the horse toward the stable, making clucking noises, deliberately turning his back on whatever might be going to happen at the big house. Wouldn't be a good thing. He was sure of that.

There was a balcony outside John's room, just as there was outside the one that had been Quent's. His brother appeared, half naked; he must have pulled on breeches when he heard his name called.

"Come down here or I'm coming up there! You've questions to answer."

"Why the hell should I—"

"Down here or up there. Your choice. You've till the count of three to make it. Otherwise I'll take off your left foot." Quent unslung his gun and aimed and cocked it. "One, two—"

"Stop your foolishness. I'm coming down."

The Ibo child called Taba huddled beside the bed, her black eyes enormous in the half dark. She could see the man standing below the balcony. Not clearly, but clear enough. She could see the gun. Kill him, she thought. Please kill him. She held her breath, but the shot never came.

A thin band of pink ran along the horizon. Quent could make out John's features in the false dawn, his cheeks shadowed with black stubble and his eyes red-rimmed from too much rum the night before. "Did you do it?"

"Do what? What the hell are you—"

"Did you make over Shadowbrook in return for cane land in the Islands?"

Think, John told himself. He's armed and you're not. Besides, you'll never best him in a one-on-one fight, no matter what the weapons. What does he know? "Make over . . ." He spoke slowly, pausing between each word, giving himself time to make a plan. "Exchange Shadowbrook for cane land? Is that what you mean?"

"That's what I mean."

"No, of course not. I never did such a thing. Why would I?" You stupid oaf. What would I gain in such a transaction? You've no idea what a mortgage lien is, I'll warrant. But I need to know who told you your half-truth.

"At the Nag's Head, they're saying you exchanged the Patent for cane land."

"They say a lot of things in the Nag's Head. Most of it's lies."

"This too?"

"I already told you as much. Though why it's any business of yours isn't at all clear to me."

Quent's chest wasn't quite as tight and his breath came a little easier. He looked up and saw faces in most of the windows, all open wide to the approaching dawn. Corn Broom Hannah and Runsabout and Six-Finger Sam up in the dormers beneath the rafters. Kitchen Hannah at the kitchen door. And his mother. She'd come out onto what they'd always called the long balcony, outside the big room she hadn't shared with his father in all Quent's memory.

Lorene saw him looking up at her. "Quent," she said, "put down the gun. Please. Do it for me."

He hadn't realized he was still aiming it point-blank at John's chest. He dropped the barrel. "What about Johnson?" he asked.

"William Johnson? What about him?" John was breathing a little easier. His voice sounded more sure in his own ears. "He's nothing to do with Shadowbrook."

"They say he's changed the name of Bright Fish Water to Lake George. They say it's not part of the Patent any longer. That you signed it over to some men in New York."

John didn't answer right away. That's what alerted Quent to the lie. "That's ridiculous," his brother said finally. "I already told you—"

Quent dropped the gun and lunged forward. He got both hands around John's neck. "You bastard! You lying, cheating, foul bastard! How could you do such a thing? Why?"

John clasped Quent's wrists, trying desperately to wrench his brother's hands away from his throat. His breath burned in his chest and his vision blurred. He staggered, went down on his back. The iron grip didn't ease. Quent knelt over him. "Bastard! What else besides Bright Fish Water? What else?" A tiny part of his brain not blinded by rage realized that his brother could not answer because he was choking to death. And that Quent wanted to know—needed to know—the exact shape of the betrayal. He loosed his grip on John's throat and drew back his fist, but he didn't realize he'd actually hit him until he saw the blood welling from John's mouth. "What else?" The demand roared out of him. "What else?"

"Carrying Place . . ." The words were slurred and slow. John's tongue was rapidly becoming too big for his mouth.

"What else?" Quent's skin prickled and his heart thumped. The grieving was already beginning in him, a great gash that matched the wound John had made in the Patent. "What else?"

"Above Do Good," John muttered. "North land above Do Good."

Quent wanted to wail his anger and his pain, but he could not. It was stoppered inside him, his sorrow was tamped down by rage. "Who?" He spoke quite calmly. "Who'd you give the land to?"

"New York men. Businessmen. Had to. After the fire . . . Debts. Had to give something away to keep the rest." He couldn't get the words out fast enough or as clear as he wanted, as he knew he had to if he was to live. Quent's fury had gone from hot to cold and John knew it was the more dangerous for that. "Fire," he said again, struggling to be understood. "Fire near'y ruined uf. Had to ge' money to keep goin' . . . nex' year ha'vest."

Quent knew in his gut it wasn't the truth. He wanted to beat John to a pulp, spill his brains on the ground, and break every one of his bones. But it could be true.

"Quent." His mother's voice. Coming to him from the long balcony above his head. Just his name. "Quent."

He staggered to his feet and headed for the stable. Jeremiah would give him another horse. He would go north and do what he'd set out to do. Later he'd go to New York City, find whoever it was who had the northern part of the Patent now. Do whatever was necessary to get it back. "Jeremiah!" he shouted. "Jeremiah." The black man appeared holding a saddled mare. The gray he'd ridden out of the paddock that day of the fire, as it happened.

"You go away, Master Quent," the old man said, "for your mama's sake. Brother kill brother on this land, it be poisoned. Mark o' Cain that be. You go, Master Quent. For your mama's sake."

Quent swung himself into the saddle and rode away without looking back.

Upstairs, in John's bedroom, when she saw him stagger up from the ground still alive, Taba wept.

Chapter Eighteen

"FRENCH REGULARS?" Johnson asked.

The Mohawk scout shook his head. "A few. Mostly Canadians and *Anishinabeg.*"

Johnson made a soft sound under his breath. "This Dieskau does not sound like the usual sort of European general."

"But the Abenaki with him are the usual sort of *Anishinabeg,*" Thoyanoguin said.

The old man had cut his hair into a scalp lock. It looked out of joint above his timeworn face. The disparity gave Johnson a bad feeling about this campaign. The man the English called King Hendrick was over seventy by most reckoning, but nothing Johnson or his wife, who was also Kahniankehaka and a member of the old man's clan, had said could change the chief's mind. He was war sachem of the Kahniankehaka, the Keepers of the Eastern Door; if there was to be a battle on that doorstep Thoyanoguin would lead his braves into the fight. If it proved the last one, so be it.

The chief had put aside the tricorne and blue officer's coat he usually wore and was in full Iroquois battle dress: leggings, breechclout, and a double line of six blue dots across his forehead. His chest was bare except for the carrying strap of his musket. It was a young man's attire on an old man's soft and flabby body. Rolls of fat curled over the top of the tomahawk at his waist. "A blanket, old Father." Johnson held one out. "It grows cold." He did it out of respect, of course. But also he did not wish to see this travesty. It made ice in the marrow of his bones.

Thoyanoguin wrapped the blanket around his shoulders, grateful for the warmth. "The winds come early this year. You will not take Fort Frédéric for many moons."

"No, I don't think we will," Johnson agreed. "Next spring, perhaps."

"And the attack on Niagara? It too is delayed?"

"So I hear." The plans made in London were coming up against the realities of colonial life. Not just the thick forests and the lack of roads, but also the rivalries of the different governors and their legislatures stood in the way. "De Lancey refused to release the cannons from the Albany fort. And John Lydius was supposed to recruit men for the Niagara campaign, but not too many have appeared." More than likely Lydius had pocketed the bonus money meant for the recruits.

Thoyanoguin nodded. Even among the members of the Iroquois Confederation, sometimes you could not rely on cooperation. He had dreamed a river of blood covering the villages of the Kahniankehaka. Endless blood, covering the earth. And a hawk, and a tiny *raon*, and a great bear that Thoyanoguin had thought was Uko Nyakwai. Perhaps not. His scouts had reported sightings of the Red Bear heading north in the direction of Singing Snow. The Potawatomi were allied with Onontio. So maybe in the end Uko Nyakwai was more Potawatomi than *Cmokmanuk*. And maybe not the bear in his dream.

Johnson was squatting, making marks in the dust. It was a way he had of ordering his thoughts. Thoyanoguin had seen it before. He hunched down beside the other man. His old bones creaked and protested, but they still served. He leaned forward, studying Johnson's marks. There were two circles on the ground. Both had a few crosshatches within their perimeter.

"Say five hundred men in each group," Johnson said quietly, his words meant only for the chief. "Two detachments. They can cut off the French. A pincer movement."

Thoyanoguin ran his hand over his scalp lock. After so many years, the Great Spirit had given him one last opportunity. But pointless death was a waste. He stood and motioned to the scout who had brought the news of the French approach. "How many?" he asked.

The scout had already relayed his estimate, but he did so again. "A thousand. And half a thousand more. Nearly half the total are Abenaki and Caughnawaga Kahniankehaka. Only a few French soldiers. The rest men of Canada."

So there were fifteen hundred enemy approaching. And most were braves and *Cmokmanuk* from this world, not the Old World. Men who knew how to fight. It would not be like that thing they said happened two moons before on the Monongahela. These troops would not stand still and wait to be killed. Thoyanoguin looked again at the markings on the ground.

"Two groups of five hundred each," Johnson repeated. "A pincer movement."

Thoyanoguin shook his head. "If they are to die," he said quietly, "they are too many. If they are to fight, they are too few."

William Johnson considered for a moment. Then he stood up and ran his boot across the markings and scuffed them out.

The next morning, sitting astride a fine chestnut gelding, Thoyanoguin led out the combined war party of nearly a thousand Yorkers and two hundred braves—mostly Kahniankehaka, but also Mohegan and a few Mahican. Thoyanoguin despised the Mahican and had little use for the Mohegan, nonetheless he had claimed the honor of leading them all. However much Johnson disapproved he could not deny him. Now the old chief sniffed the air, trying to smell enemy blood. The scouts said two hundred French regulars waited up ahead on the wide road cut by Johnson's men during this long summer of preparation. But did this Dieskau mean to do what Braddock had done? Would they all simply wait to be killed?

Deep woods lined either side of the road. If it were he, Thoyanoguin knew, he would have placed—

"Oh nihotaroten?" What tribe? A voice from the woods, speaking in Kahniankehaka Iroquois. The Caughnawaga were deployed as he suspected. They were all around, but they did not wish to kill their own kind.

"We are of the Confederacy," Thoyanoguin called out. "Members of the Great League of Peace, leaders of all the *Anishinabeg.* Most of us are of the Keepers of—"

A shot rang out. *Ayi!* It had come from behind him, not from the woods. One of his own hotheaded braves, too stupid to wait. A Mahican, probably. And now it was too late. Many shots. The braves behind him were like partridge in the short grass, available targets, more and more of them fell to the ground with every volley of musket fire and arrows.

Thoyanoguin felt the hot white pain of a musket ball pierce his shoulder. He slid from the horse and stumbled toward the woods. At first two of the younger braves helped him, then he couldn't keep up and they scattered. Thoyanoguin ran through the woods until he saw a settlement up ahead. Women. His eyes were blinded by sweat and he had lost enough blood so that thoughts chattered in his head like rattling bones. The women who followed the Yorkers, he thought. The ones who did the washing by day and offered themselves at night when—

The first tomahawk had embedded itself in his flesh before Thoyanoguin realized he had lost his way and arrived at a camp of the enemy's women and boys too young to fight. The river of blood had reached here and would be swelled with his own. He was still alive when the boys took his scalp lock, but dead before they cut out his heart.

LEAF FALLING MOON, THE SIXTEENTH SUN
THE VILLAGE OF SINGING SNOW

"So now your birth father has passed to the next hunting ground, my white son?" Bishkek did not look directly at Quent when he asked the question.

"Yes, he is passed." Bishkek had always been able to read the thoughts of both his manhood sons. Quent wasn't surprised the old man knew it had been many months since Ephraim's death, and that they both knew Quent's visit was long overdue. "He passed in the Arriving Dark moon."

"Arriving Dark," Bishkek said softly. He and Quent squatted a short distance from the morning bustle of the village. Bishkek used the twig he held to scratch a number of lines on the ground, each one representing a New Moon ceremony. "No Sun, Deep Cold, Promised Light, Great Wind, Cracking Ice, No Fat, Much Fat, Thunder, Great Heat, Leaf Falling . . ." Bishkek paused and looked up. "Ten New Moon Tellings since your birth father passed. My whiteface son waited a long time to come and show respect to his manhood father."

"I know I should have come before," Quent said. "I could not."

"And you do not plan to stay until the Telling of the Last Fruit Moon, either." Bishkek's face was grim and he looked away from Quent.

Last Fruit corresponded to October. The Last Fruit New Moon Telling would take place in a little more than two weeks. If he remained in Singing Snow all that time, his mission would have failed. "No, Father. I do not."

"And have you a wife, my whiteface son? A birth son of your own?"

Quent shook his head.

"And you do not plan to find one here in the village, and put a bridge person child in her belly, or make yourself a manhood father to the son of another squaw, so that boy will come to know more of the *Cmokmanuk* ways even as he learns more of what it means to be an *Anishinabeg* man." Bishkek's voice displayed neither approval nor disapproval, but he did not smile. The words detailed Quent's solemn obligations to the village. So far all were unmet.

"All that you say is true, Father."

"And that is why you have taken so long to come to Singing Snow. So tell me," Bishkek said, "if you do not mean to honor our ways that you swore would be your ways, why have you come? Why have I held you in my heart since you were a little boy, and why has this village placed so much hope in the two bridge persons who were one with us. *Haya, haya, jayek,*" he said softly. So, so, all of us together. "Is it not so, my whiteface son?"

"It is so, Father. *Haya, haya, jayek.* I am always one with the people of Singing Snow. In my heart, always. In my spirit I am what you named me, Kwashko, he who jumps over fire." The memory of the Potawatomi brave he'd killed in the woods near the Monongahela was a sour taste in Quent's mouth.

"But now you are Kwashki," Bishkek said. "He who jumps back."

Quent shook his head. "No, never. I am one with you and with everyone in this place of the Fifth Fire. I am Potawatomi."

Bishkek looked at this man he had watched over since boyhood. Uko Nyakwai, the Red Bear. A terrible name, but it suited him. And a bridge person must be free to move forward and back. "Tell me why you have come," he said softly. "If I can do whatever it is you have come here wanting me to do, I will."

"Only tell me where I can find my brother."

Bishkek used his twig to draw a few more lines in the earth. Quent knew the marking symbolized something, but not what. "*Wabnum*," Bishkek said, nodding toward the scratches. "Cormac is the white wolf. My other bridge person son is on a sacred journey. He is following the dream he was sent. It is not for us to interrupt such a quest."

"I am part of the quest, Father. I have things to tell my brother. About the hawk and the white bear and the white wolf."

Bishkek looked up, mildly surprised that Quent knew so many of the details of Cormac's dream. "If you are part of the quest, how come you were not with him when he first came?"

"The dream was sent to Cormac when my birth father stood on the ground between this life and the next, Father. I could not leave him. But the Great Spirit sent Cormac the dream while we were both under the same roof."

"At Shadowbrook," Bishkek said. The word sounded strange coming from his mouth.

"At Shadowbrook," Quent agreed. "And I have important things to tell my brother about the little birds and the river of blood."

For a time Bishkek was silent. Eventually he nodded. "Kekomoson had a dream that sent Cormac all the way to the edge of the earth. Then my other manhood son came partway back. Now I am told by a brave who saw him there that he is in Québec."

SEPTEMBER 18, 1755

MONASTERY OF THE POOR CLARES, QUÉBEC LOWER TOWN

Mère Marie Rose had decided. She would introduce the sacrifice of praise to the discipline, as Père Antoine suggested, but in accordance with the Holy Rule of St. Clare, giving up nothing of her authority, or her responsibility to her youngest daughter.

The nuns were gathered together in the Chapter Room, where the important landmarks of each nun's life were acknowledged. Here they met weekly to accuse themselves of faults against the Rule—no Poor Clare ever accused another—and listen to the abbess's admonitions and corrections. Here each nun learned that she had been accepted as a novice and would be invested with the habit. When she was to be admitted to vows she was told in the Chapter Room. When she had kept those vows for twenty-five years her sisters gathered with her and the abbess in the Chapter Room and she was given a silver crown. If she lived long enough to reach the fifty-year mark, she wore a crown of gold. Soeur Marie Stephane had reached one milestone when she was clothed. Now she was approaching another.

Nicole knelt in the middle of the room, bent low, her forehead pressed to the stone floor, her hands clasped above her head. The posture was typical of the Poor Clares and was one to which she had grown accustomed this past year. "For the greater honor and glory of God," the abbess said, "the ever Blessed and Immaculate Virgin Mary, St. Joseph, our Holy Father St. Francis, our Holy Mother St. Clare, and all the saints, and for the salvation and greater sanctification of your soul, your holy profession will take place on the twenty-ninth day of September, the Feast of St. Michael the Archangel."

Nicole lifted her forehead from the floor, sat back on her heels, and stood. Little Soeur Angelique approached. "I wish you joy, dear sister," she murmured as she kissed Nicole ritually on both cheeks, then hugged her hard, "and the grace to persevere in the life." Soeur Joseph next, then Soeur Françoise, and after her the vicaress, Soeur Celeste. Each murmured the same message. "I wish you joy, dear sister, and the grace to persevere in the life." Joy was what she was supposed to feel. *Her own free will.* Over and over again she had said that, been told that. She was making these decisions of her own free will. Eleven days. Then I will make my vows and it will be final. Goodbye, my beloved Red Bear. Goodbye.

Marie Rose approached her youngest daughter and wrapped her arms around her. "I wish you joy, dear child. And the grace to persevere. For as long as it's necessary," the abbess added.

"When will it not be necessary, *ma Mère?*" She blurted out the question, startled by the abbess's words.

"When you are dead, dear child. That is the blessed release that comes to us all." There was a light in Mère Rose's eyes that only shone when she spoke of death.

TUESDAY, SEPTEMBER 28, 1755
THE WOODS OF POINTE-LÉVIS, ACROSS FROM QUÉBEC

The throaty, three-note cry of the northern loon echoed overhead. Corm and Quent looked up, then at each other. Both men laughed. "Damn bird could cause a problem," Quent said. Since they were boys they'd used the loon's call to pick each other out in a crowd, whether of trees or people. It worked fine down south where northern loons were a rarity.

"If you're going to be here much longer, it could be a problem," Corm agreed.

"Perhaps a chickadee," Quent said. "Not too many of them this far north. You any good at chickadees?"

"Good as you are, that's for sure. But there's lots of birds sound a bit like chickadees. And—"

"And what? C'mon, Corm. Spit out what's behind your teeth."

"You should not stay here long enough for us having a special signal to matter." The day was frosty, the early Canadian autumn announcing its arrival. They'd made a fire in the woods where they were leagues from any *habitants.* Corm held his hands over the glowing embers. "Best thing would be for you to leave these parts before the snows come."

"A little snow isn't going to bother me."

"No, but it will make you easier to track."

"I take it you mean Lantak."

They had been here talking for two days, since the cry of the northern loon identified Quent's arrival in Québec Lower Town. He'd found himself a secluded corner near the wharves and whistled the call every fifteen minutes or so. Corm discovered him after the fourth time, and one of the first things Corm told him was that Lantak was completely recovered from the shoulder wound of the year before. There was a tale that it had taken a long time to heal, because the wound rotted and was starting to turn black before Lantak found an old woman skilled enough with herbs to make him able to fight again. But since then he had attracted a new group of followers. There were always braves unwilling to follow the discipline of the Longhouse. Renegades were never in short supply. Lantak swore he would take Uko Nyakwai's scalp with his own dirk, then use it to cut out his heart and eat it while it was still beating.

"You think I'm getting old and infirm, maybe? You'd wager on Lantak over me?"

"If he hears you're in Québec, he and his braves will come after you. Nine or ten of them, last I heard."

"Sounds like a fair fight," Quent said.

Cormac grinned. Since they were boys, whenever the odds looked impossible, they said *Sounds like a fair fight.* This time the grin faded quickly. "It's not just Lantak."

"What then?"

"Seems to me that if your plan's any good, it needs to be put in place quickly. The longer you stay here, the more it's delayed."

"You're not sure about its being a good plan, are you?"

Corm grimaced. "The plan's good. Better than anything I've thought of, it's just . . ."

"*Haya, haya, jayek.* All of us together," Quent said softly. "Tell me your thoughts."

"I'm thinking that it's not like you to credit a dream. That part of you has always stayed *Cmokman*. Dreams don't have meaning for you."

"Sometimes they do." It was forbidden to discuss your death song, what it was or how it came to be, so he said only, "Old Thoyanoguin's dream was almost the same as yours." He'd told Cormac everything that happened at Do Good, how after the attack on Shadowbrook he hadn't intended to bring Nicole to Québec until he found Solomon and got him home, but then the Kahniankehaka chief had appeared and said Nicole was the hummingbird in his dream and the bear had to carry her as she asked or there would be terrible consequences.

"Thoyanoguin dreamed a river of blood," Corm said, repeating what Quent had told him.

"Yes. Exactly as you did."

"There is no way to know if his dream and mine are—"

"A river of blood," Quent repeated.

Corm shrugged. It was hard to argue about a dream. That was what made it such a mysterious and powerful thing. "This fight between the English and the French, you believe that is what it will become?"

"I believe it can become that, yes."

"But the English and the French fight all the time. This is nothing new."

"No. Listen with both ears, Corm. Before now it's been mostly Americans and Canadians doing the fighting. This time both sides are sending armies of regulars. That is a very different thing. What happened in the Ohio Country . . . Blood enough for any damn river."

Cormac shook his head. "The *Anishinabeg* won the fight on the Monongahela. I see that as a good thing."

"You're wrong. This time it was a very bad thing. The English cannot accept a defeat like that. They'll seek revenge. Last time they sent two understrength regiments. Next it will be four. Sweet Christ, maybe six or eight. And the French will have to match them. We *Cmokmanuk* are going to wage total war here, Corm, European-style war. Between us we will crush the *Anishinabeg*."

Corm was silent. "Care to tell me what's really bothering you about my plan?" Quent asked.

"Nothing about the plan. You speak with De Lancey down in New York, make a suggestion he's bound to be clever enough to understand, and I find Pontiac and talk to him . . . Nothing's wrong with either of those things." Corm hesitated. Dusk was settling, the dark thickening. A flight of starlings swooped down to treetop level, chattered, then rose and flew away. "But I'm to ask Pontiac to, convince all the *Anishinabeg* to fight on the side of the English—"

"Fight with the English or remain neutral," Quent corrected.

"Either way, it's damned difficult. Almost impossible. Pontiac's a war sachem.

You honestly think the Suckáuhock will convince him to fall in with this scheme?"

"It must," Quent said. "Besides, Pontiac's Ottawa. You're Potawatomi. In the beginning, one people." He was quoting the opening lines of a New Moon Telling. "Pontiac will have to respect your words and honor your dream."

"Respect is not the same as doing what you are asked to do. Listening is not the same as hearing."

Quent shrugged. It was true. "Say you're right and I'm wrong. Say the Suckáuhock doesn't move Pontiac to see things as we do. What is it for, then? Why did Memetosia give it to you?"

"I don't know. Some dream he had, maybe."

"That's what I think, too. So it's all part of the same plan. Memetosia's dream. Your dream. Thoyanoguin's dream." Quent waited, but Corm didn't comment. "Everything fits."

"If your plan is part of the dream, yes, you're right."

There was still doubt in Corm's voice, but there was nothing more Quent could say. Corm's dream, Corm's choice.

"You didn't find anything at the Lydius place?" Corm had been circling back and forth in the story for hours, weaving in and out of the long line of circumstances that had brought them to this place. "No explanation for the Huron who attacked me?"

"None. I told you, Genevieve and John were the same as always. And the same when they came to my father's funeral."

Corm winced. "I feel really bad about not being there for that. Miss Lorene—"

"She understands. Corm, what do you want to do? Are you with me on this or not?"

"I'm always with you. And getting Bright Fish Water and the Great Carrying Place back for the Patent, I know how important that is, but—"

"But you're not sure it fits into your dream."

"I'm not sure about any of it."

"I am," Quent said. "The hawk is the Jesuit priest you met in l'Acadie. I'm the bear. And you're the white wolf. I'm sure of all of it."

"I thought the bear was protecting the little birds, maybe it was the enemy."

"You only saw the bear, you didn't see him do anything."

That was true. "How come it wasn't a red bear in my dream?"

"How in tarnation should I know that?"

Corm poked at the fire and the embers flared. They'd come over to Pointe-Lévis the day before. Stole a boat because they didn't dare hire one for fear the boatman would talk about his two highly identifiable passengers, and rowed a quarter league across the water, to the woods of the southern shore, where they could talk as long as need be with little fear of discovery or distraction. Now the time for talk had come and gone. Corm stood up. "We do it."

"We do it." Quent stood, and they touched hands solemnly, palm to palm, to signify the pact was made.

"We can go south in the morning," Corm said.

"Day after," Quent said. "Tomorrow is Wednesday. You said she comes out of that place Monday, Wednesday, and Friday. I have to see her, Corm. Just once before I go."

"I said she was coming out three times a week. I didn't see her at all last week. Monday you came and I didn't look for her."

"But she could come out again tomorrow. What's one more day going to matter?"

"Thing like this, every day matters."

"Winter's coming, " Quent said. "The campaign season is finished for this year."

Pontiac had been in the Ohio Country at the time of the battle on the Monongahela. It was where Cormac was most likely to find him now. But it was true about winter not being the fighting season.

Corm crouched beside the fire. It had died down some while they were talking, and the chill was deepening as night approached. "Listen, there is another thing . . . something's happening in l'Acadie."

Quent began kicking at stray embers, encouraging the half-burned bits of wood to flare again. "What troubles you?"

"One of the Acadians helped me. Gave me a place to stay. This edict will be hard."

The only one of Braddock's four prongs that had succeeded was the taking of Beauséjour and l'Acadie back in June. For the last few weeks there had been stories that the English had posted notices saying the land and houses and livestock of the Acadians were forfeit to the king, and that the *habitants* were to be transported out of the province with their money and such household goods as they could carry. Like everyone else, Quent had heard the stories. "I can't think they're going to be able to enforce the order," he said. "The English have been threatening to deport the Acadians for years. You can put up a lot of notices demanding that people leave, but actually getting them off their land, that's not going to be too easy."

"Doesn't mean they won't try. Marni is all alone."

Quent stopped kicking at the fire. "Marni. So it's a woman you're worried about."

"Any reason it shouldn't be?"

"None at all." For Quent the most awkward part of their two days of talk had been telling Cormac how he felt about Nicole, but Corm had merely nodded as if he'd known all along. "No reason," Quent said. "I just didn't realize."

"What worries me . . . Her farm is way out at the edge of the peninsula, between Halifax and Port Mouton." Corm paused. "You ever been there?"

"No, not anywhere in l'Acadie."

"Then you won't know what I'm talking about."

"I know what you're talking about. What you're worrying about, as well. Has anyone actually seen any of these ships? Or does anyone have any notion of where they're to be taken?"

Corm shook his head. "I don't think so."

"It's likely all talk. And if it isn't, it won't be easy this time of year. Not with the freeze coming." He saw the look on Cormac's face, knew he wasn't convinced. "Look, there's no reason you shouldn't go back to l'Acadie and see she's all right."

"You reckon?"

"Yes. I told you, we have until the spring. A few days more or less this side of the divide, that's not going to count for much."

"You're right." Corm's sense of relief was enormous. He knew it showed in his voice and he didn't care. "I'll go to l'Acadie before I look for Pontiac." As soon as he said it he knew that he'd agreed as well to go back to Québec the next day and try and help Quent see Nicole.

The fire was nicely contained now, the embers glowing bright red. Quent put on another log. Sparks flared, then died away, and the dry bark crackled as it caught. Nice to be here like this with Corm, Quent thought, have a few hours when it wasn't necessary to worry about anything except the ordinary dangers of the woods. After tomorrow everything would change. What if she said yes, she'd come with him. If she agreed, he would not leave without her. If it slowed everything down, then so be it. Spring, summer, those were the times to make war. Both were over.

Quent blacked his hair with the ash of the fire, and Corm found him a farmer's traditional cloak. He didn't steal it exactly, he explained; he'd left a few sous in payment. "Nyakwai maybe now," he said. "But not so Uko."

Nothing to be done about Quent's size. He'd always be a bear, but he rubbed soot on his face to disguise the stubble of red beard. The cloak, though made for a shorter man, covered him from his neck to just above the knees. The disguise worked well. They rowed from Pointe-Lévis to the mainland, put the stolen boat back where they'd found it, and slipped into the shadows with no hint anyone had taken special note of their arrival.

"This is the place," Corm said when they got to the copse that flanked the deserted section of the Côte de la Montagne below the bishop's château. "I met Nicole here maybe six times. She always comes this way."

They waited, watching the dirt road, until well past noon, but that Wednesday she did not appear.

"I have to see her," Quent said. "I can't go until I do. There's time." He sounded certain, but there was a cold place in his bowels even as he spoke. I'm right about the war not starting again until next spring, he thought, but what about John? What if he makes his trade before I have a chance to stop it? Doesn't matter. I can't go without seeing her. She's no more than a hundred fathoms away, in that little hovel I could knock over with my bare hands.

Quent's thoughts were written on his face, and Corm read them easily. "She's shut herself away because she wants to," he said. "If she didn't want to stay, she wouldn't." He hadn't mentioned how thin she was, or how she covered herself in the white veil and wouldn't show her face. Or that he'd twice offered to get her away. *No one makes me remain, Monsieur Shea. It is my choice to be a Poor Clare. It is what God wills for me.* Corm paced to the edge of the trees, peering back toward the Lower Town, then paced back. "No sign of her. I warrant she's not coming today."

"I have to see her."

Corm shrugged. "We can try again on Monday if you want."

"Not we, me. You go to l'Acadie. Now you've shown me where the meeting place is, and what Nicole's route is, I can find her on my own."

"Your French is miserable. It will give you away."

"I'll manage," Quent insisted.

Corm believed him because he wanted to.

They started back toward the Lower Town and the harbor where, given Quent's disguise and the fact that the Québécois were accustomed to Corm's presence, they could chance hiring a boat to take them back to Pointe-Lévis. They were almost there when they heard the tolling bell. Corm recognized it at once. It wasn't coming from one of the churches of the Upper Town but from the Monastery of the Poor Clares.

According to the Holy Rule, it was the abbess who decided when a novice was allowed to make her sacred vows. The novitiate was a test. The abbess decided when it was over and whether the novice had passed, but in the end only the novice herself could determine if she wished to make the most solemn commitment a woman could undertake.

The symbols of vowed nunship or the freedom of the outside world lay on a table set in the center aisle of the choir. "Either of these things is available to you. This"—Mère Marie Rose indicated a square of folded black cloth and the knotted rope of the discipline beside it—"or this." She pointed to the key to the cloister door. "The choice is yours, child."

Nicole and Mère Marie Rose stood beside the table. Nicole had been ten days in retreat—speaking to no one, exempt from all her usual duties, spending every moment in prayer—while she contemplated her decision. Now her voice was firm and unhesitating. "With faith in Almighty God, and with prayers that the Holy Virgin and our Holy Mother St. Clare and our Holy Father St. Francis and all the saints will sustain my resolve, I choose to make my vows as a Poor Clare."

The abbess put out her hands. Nicole knelt in front of her and put her hands in those of Mère Marie Rose. "Soeur Marie Stephane," the abbess asked, "will you promise to live in obedience to our Holy Rule and to me as to Our Lord Himself?"

"I vow and promise God and you, *ma Mère,* that I will."

"And will you follow in the footsteps of Francis and Clare and cherish Lady Poverty, and own nothing and covet nothing and use only what we in this community hold in common, and only in obedience to the Holy Rule and to me?"

"I vow and promise God and you, *ma Mère,* that I will."

"And will you promise to keep yourself forever virgin for the love of Almighty God, to be a bride only of our Lord and Savior, Jesus Christ?"

Nicole thought of Shoshanaya's glen, and of Quent's lips on hers and his tongue in her mouth and his hand on her thigh. She held the thought for a moment, not flinching from it. Her hands were still in those of the abbess and the eyes of Mère Marie Rose looked into hers. Nicole did not look away.

Such incredible eyes the child had. They revealed her soul, but not her secrets. Mère Marie Rose was sure that Soeur Marie Stephane had secrets. What does it cost you, *ma petite,* to make this vow? What does it cost all of us? Do you think there is a woman here who does not sometimes ache for the man who might have lain over her and caused her belly to swell with child and her breasts to fill with milk? Do you imagine that any of us do not know what we have given up? Or what we have gained. "You must choose, child."

"I vow and promise God and you, *ma Mère,* that I will remain forever virgin." Nicole's voice was low, her throat tight with emotion.

"And will you hide yourself with Mary and our Holy Mother St. Clare in the cloister, here to remain until you die, and will these walls be to you as the arms of Christ the Heavenly Bridegroom, keeping you secret only to Him?"

"I vow and promise God and you, *ma Mère,* that I will remain hidden in the cloister."

Marie Rose felt the tension drain out of her. It was done. The sacrifice of praise had offered herself and been accepted. Now, as abbess, she could offer a return gift of infinitely greater worth. "And I . . ." Marie Rose's voice shook. Not me, child. Almighty God. I am only His voice this day. "I, if you keep this, promise you life everlasting." For five hundred years an abbess of the Poor Clares had been permitted to make that incredible assurance to her daughters. Eternal life. Perfect happiness forever and ever. A remarkable assurance for one human being to make to another, and the greatest of the many privileges won for her nuns by St. Clare.

The abbess let go of the girl's hands and drew a large sign of the cross in the air above her head, "In the name of Francis and Clare and our Holy Order, *au nom du Père et du Fils et du Saint-Esprit,* I, Marie Rose, Abbess of the Poor Clare Colettines of Québec, accept your vows of obedience, poverty, perfect chastity, and perpetual enclosure."

There was a document on the table, and a quill beside it. Marie Rose signed her name. Nicole rose from her knees and took the quill from the abbess and added her own: Nicole Marie Francine Winifred Anne Crane, in religion known as Soeur Marie Stephane. *Goodbye, my beloved Red Bear. Goodbye.*

"*Te Deum laudamus,*" the nuns sang, "*te Dominum confitemur . . .*" To thee, Our God, be praise!

Mère Marie Rose removed Nicole's white veil and lay it aside. She took the black veil of a vowed nun and placed it over the white wimple and pinned it in place.

"*Sanctus, sanctus, sanctus, Dominus Deus Sabaoth . . .*" Holy, holy, holy, Lord God of Hosts.

The discipline would not actually be handed over to Soeur Stephane until that evening. She would receive it a few minutes before midnight when the nuns would all kneel in single file here in the choir, wearing their thin gray night habits, and beat themselves in penance for the sins of the world and in petition for the needs of Holy Church.

"*Tu Rex gloriae, Christe . . .,*" Nicole's sisters sang. You, Christ, are the King of glory.

Nicole looked a moment at the length of thick cord with the seven knots. Marie Rose placed the crown of white flowers on her head. Now only one part of the ceremony remained. Soeur Stephane must announce to the world that she had indeed made these vows and assumed these obligations. Nicole picked up the document she had signed. The abbess led her to the cloister door and unlocked it.

Free and complete assent, given, and seen to be given. That's why today she faced the congregation with her veil thrown back so that everyone could see her, and know it was truly she. But we are in Québec, not France. I do not know a soul here, *mon Dieu,* except You, and my sisters, and the bishop's footman, and perhaps Monsieur Shea, if he is still— Oh. Oh my God. It cannot be.

Quent stood in the rear of the church. A *habitant's* black cloak hung from his broad shoulders and he had blacked his hair and his face, but Nicole never doubted it was him, only whether he was really there, or whether the devil had sent a vision to break her spirit and her resolve. Monsieur Shea was there as well, standing a little distance away. But no one could look at her as Quent did, and there was no other gaze in which she wanted so to drown.

Framed as it was by the black veil, the whiteness of her face was ethereal. Quent saw how her eyes had become dark embers in her pale face. She suffered in this place, but nothing could change her beauty, or alter her mind. He had heard every word she spoke behind the grille and the curtains, just as he had when he brought her here a year ago, when he saw her walk through that door rather than turn back to him. Quent knew he was powerless against whatever she found here, whatever she believed.

A great peace came over Nicole. What was happening was not of the devil, but of God. You sent him here today, *mon Dieu,* to test me one last time. She lifted the document she had signed and displayed it to the church. "I Nicole Marie Francine Winifred Anne Crane," she said and her voice did not tremble or falter, "in religion known as Soeur Marie Stephane, have made these vows of my own free will." Nicole turned in all directions, showing the document to any who cared to see. Finally she turned back to the cloister and stepped inside.

Goodbye, my beloved Red Bear. Tonight when I take the discipline for the first time it will be for you.

Chapter Nineteen

MARNI WORE TWO cloaks, her own and an old one that had belonged to her mother. The double layer of closely woven wool provided some protection against the sharp north wind coming in off the Atlantic. Despite that, she was both cold and hot at the same time. Her shoulders burned with the effort of swinging the *pioche* the whole day and the entire week before that. The rest of her was chilled to the marrow. One last section only, then it was done. She raised the heavy pickaxe over her head and brought it down. Again, and then again. Until she thought she would die if she had to do it one more time—and despite that struck twice more. The last short length of earthworks crumbled under her attack. *Finis.* She had salted the earth.

A century and a half earlier her seven-times-great grandfather had started the building of these dykes. Every member of the family since had nurtured and cherished and expanded them. The earthen ramparts that held back the sea were *les anges gardiens,* the things that made life in l'Acadie possible. Now, thanks to Marni, those built on this farm by the *habitants* Benoit no longer existed.

The tides on this coast were not so remarkably high as those of the great bay on the other side; nonetheless, with the dykes gone, the sea would sweep in at least four or five times a year, probably more. With nothing to hold it back the ocean would cover the fields her ancestors had tilled. In not too much time the earth would again be a salt marsh where crops would not grow. *Alors, vous avez votre forfaiture, Majesté.* She had given the English king that which he demanded. Her land. May it be as bitter to him as it had always been to her.

They said some of the men had been shot for breaking down the dykes before the redcoats came to march the *habitants* to the various disembarking places. In a few cases, after the wives tried to complete the task, they were shot as well. Never mind. It was unlikely the deed would be quickly discovered on a farm as remote as hers. Besides, what did she have to live for? And why would she anyway wish to remain in l'Acadie? Cormac had said he would return, but he had not. Six months since he'd left her, four months since Beauséjour had fallen. Corm would have heard the fate of l'Acadie. He would know about the edict of deportation. If he were coming, he'd have come long since.

Marni left the *pioche* where it was and headed back to the house.

She entered through the barn. Cold now because Mumu and Tutu could no longer warm the air with their breath. The cows were dead. She had shot them both herself, with the musket that had belonged to her father and to his father before him. The pig as well. She'd strangled each of the hens. The rooster had gotten away, but she doubted he'd live long. Not in the kind of place l'Acadie had become.

Dark was falling, rolling in over the horizon. Thick clouds had prevented any sunset this day, but now the night sky showed a red glow. There were many fires in the place of desolation that was l'Acadie. Some had been started by the redcoats as they hounded the *habitants* from place to place, forcing them out of hiding and herding them to where they were to wait for the boats. Other fires were set by the Acadians themselves.

There was an iron rake leaning against the wall of the barn. Marni picked it up and went inside. No need to remove either of her cloaks. She wouldn't be here long. She took the rake in one hand, the fireplace poker in the other. When she'd stirred up the fire, she dropped the poker and raked the glowing embers out of the hearth and spread them across the wide wooden planks of the floor.

She worked her way to the door, then dropped the rake and claimed the large drawstring bag she'd packed earlier. It held those few possessions she was allowed to take with her, and her money. She had forty livres saved from the days in Québec. For safety's sake it was not in the drawstring bag but in a pouch under her clothes and strapped around her waist. *Alors, c'est tout finis.*

The last thing she did was to pick up the crock of lard left from the previous autumn, when she'd slaughtered the pig before this one. Corm had been with her then. He'd helped her make sausages and cure hams and salt pork, and render enough pure white fat for an entire year of cooking. She had cooked little since he left. Plenty of lard remained. Marni raised the crock over her head and flung it to the floor. It shattered and shards of crockery thickly coated in fat went everywhere. A few landed directly on a burning bit of wood and sizzled nicely. Others, she knew, would soon send rivulets of melted lard toward the embers. Marni waited until she saw a few tongues of flame, then picked up her bag and started for Halifax.

After about twenty minutes she stopped walking and looked back toward her farm; there was a satisfactory red glow. The house, the barn, the dead animals—it would all burn. She'd heard that some women had actually murdered their own children rather than take them into the heretical English colonies to which they were being sent. Marni put her hand over her belly. Empty. She had prayed it would not be. After Corm left, she who did not believe had begged the Holy Virgin that she might be with child. That way, when he returned as he promised, there would be something to keep him besides love of her. But she was not with child. And Corm had not returned. So much for prayers.

Many of the *habitants* were said to be hiding in the woods, vowing never to leave their homeland. She couldn't wait to go. There was nothing here for her now. She had given her heart and her body to two men. Both had promised to love and cherish her, and both had proven to be liars. Jean was dead and Cormac was chasing a dream. So be it. She would reach Halifax by morning. She had seen two large ships sail by her farm the day before. That's what had made her choose this day to leave. Tomorrow, she hoped, she would be done with l'Acadie and promises.

The autumn cold bit his bones and the wind tasted of ashes. Corm stood where Marni's cows had been sheltered and looked across the charred stumps of wood that had once been the wall between the barn and the house. He was surrounded by a burnt shell. Only the stone fireplace remained intact. He could remember every one of the many times she had given herself to him in front of that fire.

He shouted, "Marni!" into the silence. An owl flew above his head, screeching its disapproval of the disturbance.

Damn bird had a point. It was dangerous to make so much noise. L'Acadie was crawling with redcoats. Corm had no difficulty avoiding them if he was simply concerned with getting from here to there, but now that he was convinced Marni wasn't at her farm, he'd have to go among them to find her, into the villages and towns where the *habitants* were being marshaled for deportation. Quent had said a mass exile wasn't easy to accomplish. Turned out it was bloody easy, as long as you were willing to do whatever was necessary.

It would have been hard for Corm to imagine that British soldiers would treat civilians like this, but he'd seen the desolation with his own eyes as he crossed the land between the Chignecto Isthmus and the Benoit farm. What houses still stood had been ransacked, in some cases destroyed. Burnt out like Marni's place, or simply left open and empty, exposed to the elements. The barns were another matter. The redcoats had waited to carry out their orders until much of the wheat crop of the summer had been brought in and stored, then they put the barns under guard and marched the people they'd turned into slave laborers off to await banishment.

Corm turned and headed north across the familiar fields, his way lit by bright moonlight. After a time he realized something didn't look right. At first he wasn't sure what, then he knew. The dykes were gone. The precise, rounded, earthen fences no longer stood guard between the fields and the sea. He cut to his right to look more closely; the dykes had been beaten flat, spread over the ground. The wooden parts of the structure were splintered.

A pickaxe lay a few strides away; it had to have been Marni who left it there. The last thing the English would want would be to destroy these farms. He knew them too well, knew how important land was to them, to all *Cmokmanuk*. Their intention would be to invite English settlers into l'Acadie. Land that would support crops, nothing would be more important than that. *Ayi!* If Quent's plan were going to work it would have to be put into effect soon. Otherwise it would be too late.

What was it she'd said to him the day he left? *I hate this place. It is my prison. I do not care if the dykes break apart and this farm is washed out to sea.*

He could feel the ghosts of all the Benoit clan looking down and cursing this betrayal. Maybe she felt them too. Maybe that's what had held Marni here on the land so long. "Marni!" he shouted again, even as he turned and walked backward, keeping his eyes on the charred remains of the house where they had been together and for a time no one else had mattered. "Marni!"

Not caring about the danger, Corm screamed her name until he was hoarse. Nothing and no one answered. Then, when he could no longer see even the jagged, burnt outlines of the pitched roof and low-slung barn, he turned again. Now looking forward, not back, he broke into a trot.

The village wasn't much, half a dozen houses, a small trading post and general store, and the church, the hamlet's main reason for existing. The sign read L'EGLISE DU STE. GABRIELLE; it had been nailed to the wall of the church, but someone had torn it down and left it lying in the grass. Corm walked past it and mounted the few steps to the door. It was not locked and he went inside.

The sanctuary was empty. Nothing had been touched. The pews, the stained glass windows doubtless imported from France, the altar built against the back wall, everything was as it had always been. But there were no altar linens, the sanctuary lamp had been extinguished, and the doors to the tabernacle were open, exposing to the empty interior. Corm had hoped that this was one of the marshaling places. He'd expected to find huddled crowds of *habitants* here, and to search for Marni among them. Instead there was nothing.

"*Bon nuit, Monsieur Shea.*"

He turned at the sound of his name. "*C'est vous!*"

"*Bien sûr. Je suis le curé.* Who else should it be?"

"I don't know, I thought . . ." The moonlight filtering through the stained glass windows provided enough illumination so he could see the Jesuit. Faucon was unshaven and his soutane was filthy, stained with dirt and mud. He was standing at the rear of the church clutching something. Corm couldn't make out what it was. "I expected to find many of your flock here. I thought perhaps Mademoiselle Benoit—"

"You know she does not come to church."

"Yes, but I presumed the *habitants* were being brought here."

"No," Faucon shook his head. "Not here. Everyone from this part of l'Acadie is being taken to the Halifax Citadel."

"And you? Where are you going?"

"I am told that I am free to return to Québec, and that there is never to be a Mass said here again. If that is so, I may as well do as they say."

"But I would think . . . Your parishioners, they must need you. Now more than ever."

Philippe shook his head. "No one needs me, Monsieur Shea. I told you, I am not permitted to say Mass or administer the sacraments. And priests are not allowed to accompany their parishioners into exile. Besides, I am not even Acadian. So I am of no use. Except, perhaps . . ." He stepped to a bench and put down the thing he carried—a deerskin envelope, Corm realized now that he'd gotten a better look—and opened it. "I have made a record, monsieur. To show them in Québec."

He had worked entirely in secret. Philippe knew the redcoats would confiscate his crayons and his sketchpad if they saw him, so he had waited until he was back in his rectory and alone and sketched from memory. The métis was the first person besides himself who had looked at these drawings. In the cold white light of the moon they were more terrible than they would seem in sunlight. The anguish on the faces of the *habitants* . . . Philippe had not realized he'd captured it so well. But yes, it was exactly how he remembered it being in Halifax.

In his pictures the women were all to one side, some with children clinging to their skirts, the men to the other. Redcoats stood between them with bayonets fixed to their muskets. "They said they would not separate families," Philippe said softly, "but they lied. Yesterday, when the ships left, many families were no longer together. See," he pointed a trembling finger at one sketch of a women kneeling beside a soldier who had a small boy by the arm. "That is Madame Trumante, and the child is her son Rafael. They were my parishioners here. She is a widow and the boy is four years old. She begged to be allowed to keep him with her, but they were put on different ships. No one knows if they were going to the same place."

"Yesterday, you say? The ships left yesterday?"

"Two of them. We are told there are more coming."

"Then everyone is not yet gone." Corm stopped looking at the drawings and grabbed the priest's arm. "That's right, isn't it? Some of the Acadians are still here."

"Oh, a good many of them, Monsieur Shea. Some are still at the citadel. Others hide in their root cellars and barns and even in the forests. The redcoats keep looking, but they cannot find everyone."

"Marni, Mademoiselle Benoit, do you know if she is hid—"

"Mademoiselle Benoit? Oh no, monsieur. She left yesterday. I thought you knew."

"You're sure? How can you be sure? Maybe she got away." He'd told her to wait for him, that he'd come back for her. Marni must have known he'd keep his word. "Marni wouldn't be easy to force onto any damned ship."

"It was not a question of forcing her, Monsieur Shea. Look." Philippe found the sketch of Marni he'd done right after he was made to leave Halifax. As soon as he'd come back here, hers was the first face he'd drawn. In his picture Marni was alone, wrapped in her cloak and standing on the ramparts of the citadel, with her back to the others, the miserable *habitants* begging not to be deported. Marni was looking out to sea and smiling. "Mademoiselle Benoit was, I think, happy to go. She did not like l' Acadie, Monsieur Shea. I believe you knew that."

Corm spent another week searching the entire peninsula, but the Jesuit had told the truth. He wouldn't find her because she hadn't waited to be found. Marni was gone. Corm headed south for the Ohio Country.

FRIDAY, OCTOBER 15, 1755
NEW YORK CITY

The acting governor of New York—the only governor, since the Englishman appointed to the task two years before had never troubled himself to come to the province—poured another glass of malmsey for his guest. "I am not entirely surprised by your report. I had heard much the same."

Quent had just completed a detailed description of the string of stupidities that had led to the massacre at the Monongahela. It was thirsty work and he was glad of the wine. He raised the glass in the direction of his host, then sipped. The malmsey was sweet and strong and very smooth. "Not the Canaries, I think," he said, "From Madeira?"

James De Lancey nodded. "You're a remarkable man, sir. You sit in my study in buckskins and moccasins, and I have it on good authority that you can paint yourself up to look like a savage and howl with the best of 'em. Indeed, that you regularly do so. But you can tell the difference between malmsey from one part of the Spanish Empire and another. Exactly what sort of man are you, Quentin Hale?"

"Many sorts," Quent said. "I believe it's called being an American."

De Lancey smiled. "Entirely true. It is something London has difficulty with, that we are true Englishmen, but Americans all the same."

"Apparently London has difficulty understanding many things in the current situation. How to defeat the French, for one."

"So it seems." De Lancey turned his head. Rain sheeted down beyond the window of the governor's mansion on the Broad Way. Be snow soon enough. "It's over for this year, at least. All Braddock's grand plans. Poor sod."

"I was never sure if the plans were his or made by his masters in London. In any case, whoever came up with those notions had no idea what our forests are like. Or the way the Indians who fight against us will—" Quent broke off. De Lancey knew what to expect, even if London didn't. The governor needed no further details. But Quent didn't feel he'd given Edward Braddock his due. "The general may have been ignorant of warfare in America, but he had as much courage as any colonial. Or any brave, come to that. I counted at least four horses shot out from under him that day. He never hesitated about getting up on another."

"And that young Virginian colonel," De Lancey asked. "What's his name?"

"George Washington. He's brave enough as well. Too brave, if the truth be told, still young and impetuous. But he's got a gift for leadership. Be a fine soldier some day."

"And will he," De Lancey asked, "make these same sorts of mistakes? The ones you accuse us all of—"

"I understood the plan was General Braddock's."

"Yes. It was. But he called all the governors together. Told us what he intended, asked our opinions." De Lancey shrugged. "Eventually we agreed."

"The general was accustomed to getting his way."

"But we"— De Lancey broke off long enough to fill their glasses a third time— "we were quite willing to give it to him. It's what we seem to do best, Mr. Hale. What London tells us to do."

"Then London must be informed that there's a better way."

"Exactly what are you proposing, Mr. Hale?"

"Quent, please." It was the second time he'd said that. He didn't think it likely James De Lancey would take him up on the offer. Not the sort of man to be on a first-name basis, even when he was invited. "I'm proposing that we get together enough of our American woodsmen to become rangers, fighting scouts if you will. Link them up with our redcoats and let the rangers use their specialized local knowledge to direct the attack on the French." God, it didn't sound very impressive. Not here in this elegant room. Not the way it had back on the Ile d'Orléans when he told Corm.

"That would require a great many woodsmen, Mr. Hale. I don't think—"

"I'm not saying the woodsmen could do it alone. But London's going to send more troops, aren't they? In the spring?" Quent leaned forward, trying to read the answer in De Lancey's face. If he were wrong about parliament's plans, nothing else mattered. His convincing Corm to try and enlist Pontiac in the cause, coming here, the whole thing was a wasted exercise. He hadn't yet gotten to the main thrust of his proposal, but there was no point in pursuing it if he were wrong about what they were intending in London. "After what happened on the Monongahela, surely they—"

"I'm not privy to London's plans, Mr. Hale. I doubt any of the governors are."

You're lying, you white-wigged fop, sitting there in your blue damask coat and your white satin breeches, with a ruby ring on one hand and an emerald on the other. You could be in any drawing room in London; would rather be, I warrant. You know damned well what your masters have in mind. "But you have an idea, Governor, some inkling . . ." Despite his certainty, sweat was starting to make rivulets down Quent's back. If London didn't value the colonies here as he assumed they must, if he'd been wrong about that . . . "Not privy to the details, perhaps. But you're bound to have an idea."

"I have a number of ideas," the governor admitted. "And you, I think, have a few as well. More than just these . . . what did you call them?"

"Rangers. American woodsmen who'll travel with the troops, and teach the soldiers how to fight Indian style."

"We have our Indians just as the French have theirs, do we not? The Iroquois and such like? Aren't they—"

"General Braddock saw little value in Indian allies and as a result he had few. A man with a different attitude could get more. Some Iroquois, no doubt, the Delaware and Shawnee. But that's not the same as what I'm proposing. The Indians—any Indians—have a different perspective from our own. They have no concept of taking territory or holding it. It's about captives for them."

"And scalps," De Lancey said, his distaste showing on his face.

"Yes," Quent admitted. Whites took scalps as well, for bounty if not for honor, but he didn't bother to say so. "Look, we do things differently. That doesn't make us wrong and them right, or vice versa. But in a fight like this, against the French and purely for territory, it means the help we can get from the Indians is limited. Thing is, the way our side is fighting isn't very useful either. Form up in two straight lines, shoot over each other's heads, keep up a volley so intense no enemy can resist it. Never run. Never break ranks. Not until the officer gives the command. That style of warfare won't work here, however many troops London sends."

"That style of warfare has served Britain well for more than a century, Mr. Hale. Why should they learn new tricks now?"

"Because this is America."

And that, De Lancey knew, was true. He was silent for a few moments. "Rangers," he repeated finally. "American colonials, most of them unable to read or write, common men with common notions, made superior to British officers." In practical authority if not in rank. And never in rank, the governor was sure of that. One of the great grievances of colonial troops asked to serve with British regulars was that the most junior red-coated officer automatically outranked the most senior colonial. De Lancey took a sip of his wine, keeping his sights on his visitor, staring at him over the rim of the glass.

"Call them special forces on special assignment. London must at least consider the plan. Look what the traditional methods have gotten them. Not a single success. Just dead—"

De Lancey raised a forestalling hand and set the wineglass on the table, then took a lace-edged pocket cloth from the sleeve of his ruffled shirt. "Let us give ourselves what credit we're due." Dabbing at his lips between the words. "We've pretty much driven the French out of l'Acadie."

"Not much of a return for so much loss."

The governor shrugged. "Something. And done without your rangers, if I may say so. More malmsey, Mr. Hale?"

"No, thank you. Look, they took Beauséjour by a freak, a once-in-a-lifetime accident." De Lancey looked as if he hadn't heard the story so Quent told him about the officers all having loose bowels and being in the latrine when the cannonball landed. "Something about a bad chicken. How many bad chickens do you think we can get the French officers to eat, Governor?"

De Lancey was smiling. "It's an amusing tale, sir, whether or not it's true. But say it is; say Beauséjour is not proof that the traditional means of warfare will succeed here. How do you propose convincing our colonial woodsmen to fight with the redcoats? That doesn't sound to me as if it would be a popular notion."

"It might not be, unless you could promise them that when they had defeated the French they would be free of any Indian attacks, that they and their families and their farms would not be harried by any red men ever again."

De Lancey put down his glass and sat forward, peering into his visitor's face. "In Christ's name, sir, how could you promise that?"

Quent felt his excitement start to build. He had De Lancey's full attention at last. "Because, sir, I can deliver an agreement with the Indians to share this land in peace. Once we throw the French out, they have Canada, and we have these English colonies."

There it was, in the open, the thing that Cormac Shea had been agitating for since boyhood, that a few other visionaries had suggested from time to time, that Quent had always known to be the only way his two worlds could coexist if somehow it could be made to happen. It was the first time he'd said it to someone he didn't already know to be convinced, and the earth, he noted, had not opened up and swallowed either of them.

De Lancey sat back and sipped his wine and studied his visitor. Quent watched him and waited. One of the logs on the fire bled a trickle of pitch. Leaping tongues of flame shot toward the chimney.

"If anyone else had brought me such a notion . . ." De Lancey's voice was low, the bluster and the false bonhomie both gone, "a notion that depends on getting a dozen different Indian tribes to agree to a single course of action . . . anyone else I'd have put out of my house as a madman. But Uko Nyakwai . . . Yes, perhaps."

"It's a workable plan," Quent said. "Maybe the only workable plan."

"Your friend, the métis with the Irish name, he's in this with you, I expect."

"Cormac Shea. You're well-informed, Governor. Not many people realize we're friends. Quite a few assume we're enemies."

"I would have said more than friends. I would have said almost brothers."

"As I said, sir, you're well-informed."

De Lancey shrugged. "The Hale Patent may seem to be its own kingdom, Mr. Hale, but it is in the Province of New York. It is my duty to know what goes on in New York."

How much gossip had he heard, Quent wondered. Tales of the two squaws, Pohantis and Shoshanaya. And he'd know Lorene Hale was a Devrey, with powerful relations here in New York City. Likely he knew about John as well and what sort of a master of the Hale Patent John was turning out to be.

De Lancey chose that moment to say, "I am remiss, sir. I have neglected to offer my condolences on the recent death of your father."

"A year now," Quent said. "But I thank you for your kindness. Governor, the business at hand . . . If I can deliver such a promise from the red men—alliance at best, neutrality at the least—until the French are defeated. Then what?"

"All the red men. That's what you said."

"Enough as will make the scheme work," Quent promised. The *Anishinabeg* who were longtime French allies, the Huron and the Abenaki and the Potawatomi among them, would be the easiest to convince. If they believed that once Onontio was defeated all Canada would be theirs as it had been before the Europeans arrived, they were sure to fall into line. As for the Ohio Country, he could convince Shingas and Scarouady. Hell, they were longing to be convinced. Most of the other chiefs—Mingo, Delaware, Shawnee—would come round after they did.

"It's a daring scheme, Mr. Hale."

"These times call for daring, Governor. Without it we shall drown in a river of blood."

"A river of blood. Yes, perhaps. Very well, say I accept your idea in principle, exactly what is it you wish me to do?"

"First, convince London to accept the rangers. Get a promise they'll abide by what they're told about how to fight here."

"That's the easy part, Mr. Hale. A few battles won will convince them. I take it that my second task is to secure a promise that after victory, we will not permit English settlement to extend into the lands now occupied by the French. That's what you have in mind, isn't it?"

Quent nodded.

"Remarkable," De Lancey murmured. "And considerably more difficult to do."

The acting governor's mind was racing, trying to blend this extraordinary proposal with what he already knew—and to see how both sets of intelligence could be made to work to his advantage.

De Lancey's most trusted source had told him that a new commander for the military here in America had already been appointed, that he had been instructed to operate under Braddock's original plan of attack, and that he was to be sent over with two understrength regiments and the authority to raise four thousand-man battalions here in the colonies. In other words, to do what was asked of him, this new man— John Campbell, earl of Loudoun, a Scot—would require thousands of American volunteers. Young men accustomed to the freedom of the vast American wilderness where they called no man master, and to farms where, however humble the holding, the farmer was a freeman not a tenant; boys raised on the give-and-take of town meetings and raucous colonial assemblies—such lads as these were expected to voluntarily submit themselves in the thousands to service in the British regulars where discipline was paramount and the lash ruled. It was a notion more insane than anything De Lancey had heard from Quentin Hale. John Campbell, earl of Loudoun would need to be a worker of miracles to put it into action.

Moreover, neither Britain nor France had yet declared war. Instead the French had made a great show of withdrawing their ambassador from London, claiming to have been attacked without provocation on the Monongahela; never mind that they had won. That diplomatic ruse would give them ample time to build up their navy and send over enough men and arms to protect Canada, as well as threaten every American colony from New Hampshire to North Carolina. Meanwhile William Pitt, the one man in England who might have brought some sense to this madness, was despised by the king and made an outcast by his enemies.

The silence continued for some time, broken only by the sounds of the crackling fire and the rain hitting the windows. Quent did not think it in his best interests to be the first to speak. Take as long as you need, Governor. You've only two rather simple ideas to get straight. We assign woodsmen to teach the bloody redcoats how to fight in America, and in return for not fighting with the French, we offer the Indians all of Canada once the battle's won. An end to war for both sides. You're not likely to hear a more audacious plan. And I doubt you've heard a better one. What remains to be seen is the size of the balls in those white satin breeches.

"Mr. Hale, I apologize if I seem to be changing the subject, but do you know the name William Pitt?"

Quent shook his head. "No. Should I?"

"No, perhaps not." You and Pitt . . . a pair of visionaries, who knows what you might have accomplished together? It's an intriguing thought. But Pitt's not really in charge in parliament, and you, sir, are a landless second son with only one advantage—the ability to make the Indians listen to you—and that is prized little by our masters in London. Still, your ideas are best not dismissed out of hand.

De Lancey got up and went to the window. They had been talking for nearly two hours, and it was almost eleven. The rain had let up some and the governor could see a bit of the fort and the harbor beyond it, and more of the grand houses across from his in this most fashionable part of the city. Many of the windows still had lighted candelabra glowing behind the curtains. They did not retire early here on the Broad Way in what they called the court part of town. "Remarkable," he murmured again. "Uko Nyakwai will deliver the red men and the woodsmen if . . ." De Lancey spun round and faced his visitor. "What else, Mr. Hale?"

"Why should there be anything else?"

"Because it has suddenly dawned on me that a piece of the puzzle is missing. What do you get in return for all this effort?"

"Oh, that." Quent sat back, stretching his long legs in their buckskin trousers toward the glow of the governor's fire.

"Yes, that," De Lancey said.

"Nothing that will cost you a farthing, Governor. I wish only to return to the *status quo ante,* for things to be as they were."

De Lancey had gotten over his amazement at a buckskin-clad woodsman who spoke like an educated man and knew one kind of malmsey from another. That he could also quote Latin was not a surprise. "What things?"

"The Hale Patent," Quent said. "My brother has made over to yours—"

"Which of my brothers?" De Lancey interrupted. "Oliver?"

"Oliver De Lancey, yes."

"I should have imagined as much. Very well, please continue, Mr. Hale. Made over what?"

"Certain lands that belong to us, and have always—"

"Lake George. That's what you're talking about, isn't it?"

"Bright Fish Water." Quent insisted on giving the lake its proper name. "I understand its strategic value, and that of the Great Carrying Place and the surrounding lands." Poor old Thoyanoguin being killed up by Bright Fish Water was a bad thing, but useful. The Kahniankehaka would not easily forgive the way it had happened, not in battle but at the hands of women and boys. They'd want revenge. Easy to get them to agree to fight with the English if they were handled correctly. Never mind. He'd deal with the Kahniankehaka later. Now was the time for convincing James De Lancey. "Use Bright Fish Water and the Great Carrying Place for the duration of this conflict, Governor. I understand the necessity—"

"I've heard we took an important captive up at Lake George."

Quent at once recognized the test. How much did he really know? How good was his information? "Baron Dieskau, yes, that's what I hear as well."

"It's true, then?" De Lancey prodded.

"It's true."

"A remarkable victory, wouldn't you say? Shows that we aren't getting everything wrong, despite what you say."

What it shows, Quent thought, is that despite his Kahniankehaka adoption and his Kahniankehaka wife, William Johnson is still more *Cmokman* than *Anishinabeg*. Thoyanoguin's braves were incensed about the way he died. They stood outside the fort where Johnson was holding Dieskau and jeered and cursed and promised revenge. The only sensible thing to do was to hand the baron over, but Johnson wouldn't do it. "General Johnson is doing what you'd expect a gentleman to do," Quent said. "Keeping his prisoner safe. But there may be a price to pay for that, Governor."

"What kind of a price?"

"I can't say exactly. But the Kahniankehaka, the Mohawk, they have a pretty strong sense of honor of their own. It's been violated."

De Lancey already knew one price being paid for the capture of Dieskau. Just yesterday he'd heard that the man the French were sending to replace the baron was an even more formidable soldier. "Louis Joseph, marquis de Montcalm," he said. "Ever heard of him."

Quent shook his head. "No, I have not. Governor—"

De Lancey knew he'd pushed as far as he could. Time to stop trying to get more information, or anything else for that matter, any kind of real commitment. Not without having the price spelled out and plain between them. "As you were saying, Mr. Hale?"

"Simply that I ask for your solemn word that when this is done and the French are defeated, you will make the Patent whole according to the original Royal Grant."

De Lancey was still standing at the window. He nodded, but the gesture was not agreement, simply a mark of understanding. Both men saw it as such. "What else?" he asked.

From the moment he was shown into De Lancey's study, Quent had known this would be the most difficult of the difficult things he had come to say. Time to play the final card. "John Hale and Oliver De Lancey have entered into an agreement to exchange the Patent for cane land in the Islands."

"I see. Cane land in return for the Hale Patent. It's an intriguing idea." And one that would give Oliver entirely too much power in the province. I wonder, Quentin Hale, for all your devotion to the place, do you have any notion what a piece of land like the Hale Patent could be if the French threat to the north were removed? "Mr. Hale, perhaps I've misunderstood and you can enlighten me . . . Surely only the owner of the property could enter into such an agreement. Is John not the elder son, the legal owner of Shadowbrook since your father's death?"

"He is."

"Well, then?"

"A man can do what is legal and still not do what is right, Governor."

"Indeed, Mr. Hale. Very well, I take your point. But I don't see how I—"

"I believe your brother and two of his friends are to share in the arrangement in return for putting it in place. I expect their reward is to be part ownership of the sugar plantation."

I'm sure that's what Oliver wants them to believe. But compared to sole ownership of the Hale Patent . . . Don't be a fool. No, De Lancey corrected himself, do be a fool. That suits my purposes. "Yes, that sounds entirely plausible." The governor left his place beside the window and returned to his seat. "And you do not wish this . . . arrangement, as you called it, to come to fruition?"

"I do not."

"No trading of land here for land in the Islands?"

"None. The Hale Patent must remain inviolate."

Just the day before, James De Lancey had put his brother Oliver's name forward to be the American correspondent of the London firm with the supply contracts for the entire British army in New York. The appointment was worth a fortune, thousands of pounds a year. And it was in the governor's gift. That would give him excellent leverage with Oliver. "I see your drift, Mr. Hale." De Lancey reached for the decanter of malmsey. "Now, I believe more wine is definitely called for. We must drink a toast to our—" He'd been going to say "bargain," but he broke off. Never wise to give too much too soon. He filled both glasses and raised his own. The firelight and the candlelight danced on his blue damask sleeve and the ruffled lace cuff of his shirt, caused his ruby ring to sparkle. "Our plans, Mr. Hale," De Lancey toasted. "And our good intentions. And, above all, the king."

Quent raised his arm. The buckskins had never looked more incongruous. "The king," he said. "And our plans."

WEDNESDAY, NOVEMBER 3, 1755
THE OHIO COUNTRY

A pile of arrows lay on the ground between Cormac the Potawatomi métis and Pontiac the Ottawa war chief. Corm wore a breechclout—first time since he'd left Singing Snow more than a year before—and beaded bracelets on his arms and ankles, and because there was a thin coating of frozen snow on the ground, the elk-fur robe that had been Bishkek's parting gift. He squatted and picked up one of the arrows and snapped it easily in half. Then he looked at Pontiac.

The Ottawa ran his hand over his head. Most of his scalp was shaved clean, except for a central tuft of hair braided with many beads and decorated with three feathers. "The last time we met my hair was long like yours." Cormac's hair hung to his shoulders and a single eagle feather was fastened in the back. "Now," Pontiac continued, "I wear the scalp lock of war. In the summer the Potawatomi fought beside the Ottawa and the Abenaki in the great battle not far from here. Where was Cormac Shea then?"

"I have been honored to listen to the stories of the bravery of Pontiac and his warriors. All Canada knows what you accomplished at the battle of the Monongahela."

"But you were not here then," Pontiac persisted. "Now you come and break my arrows. Why? Do you challenge me to fight?"

Cormac shook his head. "*Co.* I challenge you *not* to fight." He snapped another arrow into two halves, then gathered the rest and bundled them tightly together with a thin strip of leather. Finally he stood up. "Here, I return your arrows to you. Now, I challenge you to break them."

Pontiac took the arrows, but he made no attempt to break them in two. "I cannot," he acknowledged. "As long as they stay together, these arrows cannot be broken, *neya?*" Cormac nodded his assent. "As I recall," Pontiac continued, "when we were last together it was I who spoke of the strength that comes from union."

"*Ahaw,* it was indeed Pontiac who spoke wisdom on that occasion. That's why I'm here now. I have important things to say to Pontiac the great war sachem. I wish to demonstrate that I understand the lessons he taught when we met before." Corm touched the medicine bag that hung around his neck. It was the first time he had worn Memetosia's gift openly.

The white medicine bag with red symbols was the first thing Pontiac had noticed when Cormac walked into his camp. Now at last he could speak of it without appearing to have no manners, or worse, to doubt the strength of his own medicine in comparison to that displayed by the métis. "Those are the signs of the Crane People, are they not?"

"They are. This medicine bag was given to me by the ancient and great Miami chief, Memetosia. A gift for all the *Anishinabeg*." Half a dozen Ottawa braves stood near the two men. One spat on the ground the moment Cormac said the name Memetosia. The others made muttering sounds of disapproval.

"Potawatomi and Ojibwe and Ottawa, we are brothers," Pontiac said. "Once we were a single people."

"Ahaw," Cormac agreed. *"Haya, haya, jayek."* So, so, all of us together. The Ottawa would still know those words, however long the tribes had been separated.

Pontiac nodded. He did know them. "But the Twightwee, the Crane People, are nothing to do with us. Their fat is in my belly." Pontiac put his hand over his stomach and summoned a loud belch.

Pontiac had been with the war party three years before that had invaded Picka-willany, slaughtered every Miami there, and finally put Memetosia's grandson Memeskia into a pot and cooked and eaten him. Corm knew that. And he'd known it would be mentioned. He had a reply ready. "In the past the *Anishinabeg* had many reasons to be enemies of each other, to fight each other. Now, if they continue in that way, they will all die."

Pontiac threw down the bundled arrows. "This is a waste of time. Cormac Shea comes to my war camp to tell me things I already know."

"But I bring things others do not know." Once more Cormac touched the medicine bag. "There is snow on the ground and the *Cmokmanuk* stay in their forts and do not fight. It is a time for a wise war sachem like Pontiac to think and listen and make plans."

Pontiac was silent for a time. Then he nodded and turned and summoned one of the squaws standing nearby. "Prepare a place where I and my little brother Cormac the Potawatomi of Singing Snow may speak further of important things. Later we will eat."

Pontiac spread a blanket on the ground between them. It was the color of blood, with a bright blue border, and he arranged it with his own hands, not calling on a squaw or one of the younger braves to do it for him. Something in the Ottawa chief recognized that Cormac's Crane People medicine bag contained a unique treasure. Instinctively Pontiac paid it honor.

Corm waited until everything was ready, then he squatted and removed the medicine bag from around his neck and placed it in the middle of the blood-red blanket.

"Wait," Pontiac said. "First we will smoke."

More honor. Cormac did not allow his impatience to show. Pontiac lit the pipe, drew deeply, then passed it to Cormac. Corm sucked in the tobacco smoke, then opened his mouth and let it drift into the air of the waning afternoon.

"The calumet means peace," the Ottawa said. "It may be some time before we smoke again."

"This is a *Cmokmanuk* war. Why should the *Anishinabeg* spill their blood to serve the white man's ends?"

"You too are a white man, Cormac the métis."

"I am a bridge person. Inside me is a Potawatomi brave."

Pontiac nodded. "Since the *Cmokmanuk* came, there are many like you."

"Not so many." Cormac passed the pipe back to Pontiac and waited until the other man had smoked before continuing. "Now, in the peace of the calumet, I ask that the great chief of the Elder Brothers listen to me with both his ears." Pontiac's glance went to the medicine bag, but Cormac was not yet ready to show him what was inside. "The others, most of them, they fight to gain honor and captives and take back to their village many scalps and much treasure. But I do not think those are Pontiac's reasons."

"Fighting is our way." The Ottawa's tone was mild. "We are warriors."

It was Cormac's turn to smoke, but he did not immediately take the pipe. "*Co*, not this time. This is a *Cmokmanuk* war."

"You speak truth, little métis brother. But they are everywhere, they live among us like the mosquitoes, always biting, sucking our blood." Pontiac turned the bowl of the calumet into his hand and tapped the live ash into his palm, then rubbed it into the earth beside him. The time for smoking had passed; it was time to talk of whatever had brought Cormac Shea to his camp and whatever was in the Miami medicine bag. "A wise war sachem chooses his enemies at least as well as he chooses his friends. The English are like great dog turds that make a stink in every direction. The French are not flowers, but they stink less."

"Because they do not take so much land?"

"They take whatever they can get, but they do not prize it as much or hold it as long. The French are like trees with shallow roots: they can be moved. The English are like oaks: once planted, their roots reach to the middle of the earth."

The sun was dropping and both men felt the chill of the approaching evening. They could see the fires of the campsite, but not feel their heat. The cooking smells reached them, and the sounds of children playing a game that involved a repetitive chant and then many shouts. "It grows late, little brother. Say what you have come here to say."

Cormac summoned all his strength. "The last time we met you spoke of the need for the *Anishinabeg* to honor the old ways." Pontiac nodded. Cormac reached for the medicine bag and loosened the drawstring. "I have here a gift from the past. From the original ways of the *Anishinabeg*." He tipped the Suck-áuhock into his palm, then one by one he placed each of the dark purple Súki beads on the blanket.

They looked small and inconsequential on the square of scarlet, but Pontiac instantly recognized their great age and remarkable workmanship. "*Ayi . . .*" His sigh of pleasure came from somewhere deep in his belly. "They are beautiful. Memetosia the Miami chief gave these to you?"

"*Ahaw.*"

"Why?"

"I have asked myself that many times. I do not know the answer for certain, but I think it can only be that he was obeying a message sent to him in a dream."

Pontiac nodded. There could be no other reason for a chief full of age and wisdom, even a chief of the Miami, to give such a marvel to a member of another tribe that had nothing to do with his. And a métis at that. "*Ahaw.* That must be so."

Pontiac leaned forward and reached for one of the beads. Cormac grabbed his wrist. The Ottawa stiffened at the insult and started to pull away. "Wait," Cormac said. "I beg my Elder Brother to forgive my impertinence and to listen with both ears. I too have been sent a dream. In fact, two dreams. One I had while I was awake. The other came while I was sleeping." He let go of Pontiac's wrist and waited. It could be that he'd be in a fight for his life. Not that he'd have a chance in this camp of braves sworn to follow Pontiac, but he'd take a few of them with him before he went. Corm's hand didn't move, but it was directly in line with the tomahawk at his waist.

It seemed for a moment that neither man breathed. Then Pontiac spoke. "Tell me the sleeping dream."

There would be no fight, not here and not now.

I feel a great blackness between us, Ottawa, yet we have no quarrel. And I have a mission so I must put these thoughts out of my head. The future will come whatever I think or feel. My only course is to follow the dream. "There was a hawk," he began, "and a river of blood." He told of the little birds and the white bear and the white wolf.

Pontiac listened without speaking. When Cormac was finished he asked, "And the waking dream? What was that?"

"It came to me after I had fasted and meditated for many days. If the French could be driven from the north country, the place they call Canada, all the *Anishinabeg* could have that as their homeland. The English could stay here in the south, and we would both live according to our own laws and customs. And both would survive because of the separation."

Pontiac turned his head and looked at the woodlands surrounding them. Dusk had drained the fiery autumn color from the leaves, but the beauty of the place was still apparent. "You would give the dog turds all this?"

"I would give them what is necessary to allow the *Anishinabeg* to survive."

The Ottawa nodded. "In that, I agree with you. There is no doubt we are fighting for our survival. Only those who see no farther than the tips of their fingers mistake this war for anything else."

It was time for the hard choices to be made. Cormac picked up one of the Súki beads and placed it in the open palm of the hand he stretched toward the Ottawa. There was just enough light left to see the carving. "*Papankamwa,* the fox. I wish Pontiac to accept this. If he does, it will be his forever."

The Ottawa did not take it. "In return for what? In the old days Suckáuhock was used as we use wampum. Is my little brother asking me to accept a war belt?"

"It is a no-war belt. I am asking that Pontiac lead his braves and his people to where they can wait for the end of the war between the French and the English. And that he take this as well." Cormac picked up the bead that was carved with the spider symbol and placed it too in the palm of his outstretched hand. "Bring it to Alhanase, the Huron war chief who also fights with Onontio. Tell him what I have told you, and ask that the Huron, like the Ottawa, retire from this war and leave the *Cmokmanuk* to kill each other without our help."

"So that in the end we can all go to the frozen land of ice and snow and the *Cmokmanuk* get our homeland." Pontiac spread his arms wide to indicate the woods of the Ohio Country where his ancestors had been since the Great Spirit put them on this earth. "In the end the dog turds get what is ours."

"In the end we survive." Cormac could feel in his belly that Pontiac did not believe in the meaning of the dreams. He was in turmoil, but despite what he felt and the length of time he had held out the hand offering the Suckáuhock, Cormac's arm did not tremble. He held it steady, as if he were passing it over Potawatomi the Sacred Fire, proving the strength of his manhood. "The fox and the spider are for the Ottawa and the Huron. I myself will take the racoon to the Abenaki."

"And you think they will make you welcome and agree to do what you ask?"

"I think they will rejoice at the thought of land they no longer need to share with intruders who bring them disease and trouble and wars not of their making."

"But there will still be *Cmokmanuk* here. The English are to remain, according to your dream."

"Not in Canada. It is a vast place. There is room for all of the *Anishinabeg* to hunt in Canada."

"It is a frozen place," Pontiac insisted. "Mostly snow."

"Not all the year and not all of it. And the hunting is magnificent."

Pontiac made a sound in his throat that represented a grudging sort of agreement. "The sickness, and the white man's goods that the Real People now believe they cannot do without . . . knives made of metal not flint, clothing of cloth not skins, firewater, none of that will have gone away."

"Those *Anishinabeg* who wish to continue to trade with the *Cmokmanuk* will do so. We must make a new way for the future, Elder Brother. We cannot change the past."

"And the other beads?" Pontiac was looking at the four beads on the blanket.

"They are for the Lenape and the Kahniankehaka."

"Shingas and Scarouady," Pontiac said, knowing immediately the chiefs Cormac had in mind. "Who will speak to them? Not you, I think. Uko Nyakwai?"

"He knows them better than you or I."

Pontiac turned his head and spat on the grass. "He is not even half *Anishinabeg*."

"He is a full Potawatomi brave by adoption. That has always been our way. Does Pontiac deny the right of a tribe to adopt whom they will?"

Pontiac didn't look at Cormac, but he shook his head. He couldn't deny truth.

"You know that Uko Nyakwai wears the amulet given him by the great chief Recumsah, your uncle. Whatever your quarrel with my brother the Red Bear, it is not—"

"My quarrel is that he is *Cmokman*. And English."

Neither fact could be denied. Better to let go the matter of Pontiac's animosity toward Quent. His arm was on fire, still stretched in front of him; he wasn't sure how much longer he could hold the position, but if he put down the beads he had conceded the advantage. "The *Anishinabeg* can survive in Canada. If we remain as we are, the French and the English will crush us between them." They were Quent's words, but Cormac knew none better.

Pontiac continued to ignore the offer of the Súki beads. "For your plan to succeed the English must win this war. Even if both sides fight without our braves, how can you be sure of that?"

"The English have more men and more guns and more food and—"

"And they fight for more," Pontiac said quietly. "They fight for the right to land, and for the English, land hunger can never be satisfied."

"They will agree that we have Canada," Cormac insisted. "If it means they must fear no further attack from any of the *Anishinabeg*, they will agree. Does Pontiac agree?" The Suckáuhock was still on offer in his outstretched palm.

"Is it enough," Pontiac asked softly, "to say I will try to see how this thing can be made to work?"

Cormac did not hesitate. "It is enough."

Pontiac reached over and took the two beads. Cormac's palm was empty, but he did not immediately drop his arm. "My Elder Brother is sure?"

Pontiac watched the hand that remained stretched out toward him. He spoke slowly, knowing the test was not over until he said the final word, wondering how much longer the métis could hold out, half wanting him to fail, half impressed with his strength. "Your Elder Brother is sure that he will examine this thing in all its parts, and try to make it real. The north for us. The south for them." Pontiac hesitated as long as he dared. If he forced the trial beyond its natural limits it no longer counted for anything. "I will try," he said at last.

Cormac dropped his arm. It throbbed and quivered from wrist to shoulder, but that didn't matter now. He was as light-headed as if he had already achieved the final victory. *Cmokmanuk* in the south, *Anishinabeg* in the north. Blessings on the Great Spirit and his white wolf totem and Miss Lorene's Sunday morning Jesus God. He had maintained his Potawatomi honor, and possibly enlisted a powerful ally.

Neither man said anything while Cormac returned the other beads—the turkey and the elk and the possum and the racoon—to the Miami medicine bag and replaced it around his neck. The bag felt different, lighter. When Cormac got to his feet he nearly stumbled. Pontiac paid him the courtesy of pretending not to notice.

The rich odors of the cooking fires made Cormac's mouth water and he looked forward to the meal. Stewed beaver, from the smell and the last of the season's fresh corn. He was being treated as an honored guest and the Ottawa were known as fine cooks. It was said they flavored their food with dried sumac, but when squaws of other tribes tried the same tricks they did not produce the same taste. The Ottawa cooks had secret— *Ayi!*

Corm saw himself lying on the ground at Singing Snow with the Midewiwin priestess leaning over him. *Because the leaves of a tree turn red in the time of the Great Heat Moon does not always mean the tree is a sumac.* That's what she'd said and neither he nor Bishkek had known what she meant. Now he did. A thing might look like one thing but have an entirely different taste, because in reality it *was* something else. The brave who attacked him in the sweat lodge had looked like a Huron and smelled like a Huron, but that didn't mean he was a Huron. Perhaps he had disguised himself as a snake because that was what he wanted Cormac to think. *"Ayi!* It could be so."

He didn't realize he'd spoken out loud until Pontiac turned to him. "What could be so?"

"Nothing. I was just thinking that in dreams, sometimes things are not exactly what they seem to be."

"That is true. But put these thoughts aside now, Little Brother. It is time to eat and to talk, and later to smoke and sing and dance. The winter is coming. Then it will be the time to prepare for war. Or"—Pontiac touched the pouch at his waist where he had put the Suckáuhock—"to prepare for no-war."

WINTER, 1755–1756
LAC DU ST. SACREMENT

A time to plan and listen, and think about war and prepare for war.

The French troops billeted at the northern end of Bright Fish Water, the lake they called Lac du St. Sacrement and the British now called Lake George, began work on a fort meant to be as impregnable as Fort St. Frédéric on Lac du Champlain. At first it was to be called Carrion, for Philippe de Carrion who had once maintained a trading post on this land. It was Vaudreuil back in Québec who rejected that idea. "Despite what passes for commerce these days, I will not name a fort after a smuggler." Eventually they settled on Fort Carillon, for the pealing sound made by the outlet of the waters of the lake. It was a compromise made necessary because Vaudreuil also rejected the suggestion that they use Ticonderoga, the Iroquois name for the high rocky promontory between Lac du Champlain and Lac du St. Sacrement. This new *maréchal de camp*, the marquis de Montcalm, had the usual French disdain for all things Canadian and Indian. No point in alienating him so soon after his arrival.

Bright Fish Water was frozen solid by early January. Eight leagues to the south, in the thin clear air of winter, surrounded by a mostly leafless forest temporarily empty of enemies, the Yorkers heard the sounds of French axes whistling through the air and felled trees crashing to the ground. They too took up their hatchets and saws.

The Yorkers began by constructing a fleet of the flat, raftlike boats known as bateaux. Fast and simple to build, they were strong enough and big enough to carry at least twenty soldiers, as well as the heavy artillery that must sooner or later determine the outcome of this as yet undeclared war. Meanwhile, General Johnson sent out scouts who returned with the information that the French were also building bateaux, and constructing a mighty fort. The Americans set about constructing a fort of their own.

It had four bastions and was set on a steep rise. One side faced a cliff that fell sharply to the lake below. To protect the other three exposures they dug a dry moat around log walls thirty feet thick and fifteen feet high. Johnson said the fort was to be named for the two royal princes. Most of the Yorkers, whose sweat and backbreaking labor had made this thing, were born and bred Americans and had less regard for the royals than an Anglo-Irish transplant like the general. Still, Johnson was in command and he prevailed. The new fort was named William Henry.

Book 3

The New World and the Old

1757

Chapter Twenty

THE HALLS OF the Collège des Jésuites were paneled with the finest woods. The floors were of red and white and black marble. The brothers kept everything spotlessly clean and gleaming, nowhere with more care than in the broad and colonnaded south corridor that passed by the private apartments of Monsieur le Provincial, where Philippe Faucon now walked silently reading his breviary. Old Brother Luke was twenty strides ahead, shuffling forward with large cloths tied to his feet, telling his beads as he polished the floor. His sibilant whisper could be heard clearly in the otherwise silent hall. *"Je vous salue, Marie, pleine de grâce."* Men became Jesuit brothers rather than priests because they were unschooled and could therefore not fulfill the priestly obligation to daily read the Divine Office. They prayed the rosary in French, while each priest of the Society read the Latin Hours by himself, fitting in the duty among his other chores.

It was Sunday. Philippe had no chores. He would have liked to be off sketching in the countryside, but he and Luke had been left to look after things while the rest of the community was away at a reception in the château of the governor-general. Ten strides from the door of the apartments of Monsieur le Provincial Philippe began the third psalm of Vespers for this feast of St. Mary Magdalene: *Quis ascendet in montem Domini? Innocens manibus et mundus corde.* Who can ascend the mountain of God? He with a clean heart and innocent hands.

The words chilled him. Philippe did not believe his heart clean or his hands innocent.

"Sainte Marie, Mère de Dieu," the old man ahead of him murmured. It was not appropriate to do menial work on a Sunday, but Brother Luke had long since decided that polishing the floor while he walked was not actually labor and had dispensed himself. *"Priez pour nous . . ."* His purposeful shuffle carried him for-

ward, past the door of the Provincial's study and around the corner into the corridor leading to the Retraite de Ste. Anne, the community's private chapel.

Philippe slowed his pace still further. He knew that when Luke reached the
door to the chapel he would pause, remove the cloths tied over his shoes, and go
inside. The old man spent hours in devout prayer. He was quite possibly a saint.

A few moments passed. The sounds of the whispered rosary grew fainter, then
died away. Philippe heard the squeak of the one hinge that defied all their efforts
to silence it; even a novena to Saint Anne herself had produced no results. The
squeaking hinge meant Luke had opened the door of the Retraite. When it
squeaked a second time Philippe knew the door had been closed.

Alors. In practical terms he was alone in the house. He did not remember the
last time such a thing had happened. It was a sign from God.

He closed the breviary and lay it on a nearby table, then hurried forward and
without hesitation grasped the handle of the door to the Provincial's study. It
turned easily. He had told himself that if the door was locked that too would be
a sign from God. He would make no effort to force his way inside, simply accept
that what he was thinking was grave sin and prepare himself to do penance to
expiate it. But Louis Roget had not locked the entrance to his private apartments.
The door swung wide at Philippe's first touch. The wondrous carvings of the
ébénistes of Reims were spread before him.

Straight ahead was the panel that depicted the Flight into Egypt, which if he
touched it in the proper place would swing wide and give him a view of the Lower
Town and the wretched monastery of the Poor Clares, and the hovel where Père
Antoine Rubin de Montaigne lived. On his right was the panel with the angel
whose wings covered his face as he knelt in adoration before the Divine Throne.
Philippe, too, put his hands over his face.

Lord, I wish to do Your will. His heart thumped wildly, his hands were icy cold.
But it could not be the will of God that the night terrors would not leave him, that
his grieving and sense of failure, were like a scrofulous growth in his belly which
no amount of prayer or sacrifice could relieve. *It is not your fault, Philippe.* That's
what Xavier Walton told him each time he confessed the same sin of betrayal. *You
did not desert the habitants of l'Acadie. They were sent away by the heretic English
soldiers, may God have mercy on their souls. The English forbade you to accompany
your parishioners. What were you to do?*

What he had done was the only thing he'd known for certain was right and the
thing God expected of him. He had borne witness, using the small talent that had
been given him to document the sufferings of those entrusted to his care. And the
moment he arrived here, back in the Collége, he had turned his drawings over to
Monsieur le Provincial.

It had rained the afternoon of his return. Philippe remembered being soaked to the skin as he walked up the Côte de la Montagne. No one knew he was coming so no calèche had been sent for him, and by his lights his vow of poverty—however loosely it was interpreted among Jesuits—prohibited him from hiring a cart and cartman. He remembered dripping puddles of water when he stood right here in this very room, facing his superior and clutching the deerskin envelope that contained his drawings.

"Welcome home, Philippe. You would perhaps prefer to dry yourself and change before we speak."

"No, Monsieur le Provincial, with permission. I wish at once to give you these things."

"Your drawings." Roget could not quite suppress a sigh. "Yes, of course."

Philippe opened the envelope and spread his sketches on the gleaming surface of a mahogany table. "This is what I saw, Monsieur le Provincial. Exactly as I saw it."

For some moments the only sound was of rain thudding on the lead roof. Louis Roget had looked a long time at the drawings. Finally he made the sign of the cross and Philippe saw his lips move and knew that Monsieur le Provincial was praying for the *habitants,* asking God that the sufferings of the Acadians might be rewarded with the joys of heaven. When he finished he gathered up the drawings, handling them, Philippe thought, with a certain tenderness. He had never before seen Louis Roget be tender. "You have done well, my son. I shall take charge of these now."

Almost two years, and Philippe had heard nothing more. His record, the only thing he could give those parishioners who had been put in his care, had been stifled. At least that's what he thought had happened. Twice he'd tried to ask Monsieur le Provincial what had been done with his drawings. Both times the question was answered with an icy stare and the reminder that it was not his place to concern himself with the decisions of his superiors. But, *mon Dieu*, this thing gives me no peace. I have to know.

Philippe crossed to the panel of the angel kneeling in adoration and pressed on the wings. The wall parted and a drawer slid forward. It was lined with velvet and deeper than he remembered, crammed full of papers. This time nothing had been left open for him to see.

The rasp of the Retraite's squeaking hinge was unmistakable. Impossible! Brother Luke never left the chapel after so short a time. There was a second squeak as the door closed again. *"Je vous salue, Marie . . ."* Luke had left the Retraite and was retracing his steps, coming back toward Philippe.

He had not closed the door to the Provincial's study. He raced toward it, resisted the urge to slam it shut, closed it carefully and soundlessly, and pressed his throbbing forehead against the coolness of the wood.

Luke's footsteps grew louder. *"Priez pour nous pauvres pécheurs—"* The words stopped.

The old man was standing right outside Monsieur le Provincial's study. He had stopped reciting the rosary. But Luke never stopped; decade after decade rolled out of him, a constant stream of petition. Philippe leaned all his weight against the door. Perhaps if Luke tried it and it did not give, he would assume the study was locked. The handle, however, did not turn. Philippe put his hand on his chest and counted his own heartbeats. They seemed to him loud enough for Luke to hear. He had reached nine when the river began again to flow. *". . . maintenent et à l'heure de notre mort. Sainte Marie, Mère de Dieu . . ."* Brother Luke continued on down the corridor.

Philippe had promised himself he would not look at anything else in the drawer. He wanted only to know if his drawings were there, if Monsieur le Provincial had, as he suspected, hidden away the record of the sufferings of the Acadians. He could be wrong. Louis Roget was a thousand times more clever than Philippe Faucon. Perhaps he had sent the drawings to Versailles, or even to the pope in Rome. Perhaps Louis Roget, like Philippe, was waiting for the English to be publically accused of the terrible things they had done.

The sketches made in hiding in the little Eglise du St. Gabriel in those dark days of terror and turmoil were tied together with a black ribbon. They had been placed in the rear of the secret drawer. Philippe knew without doubt that they had been there since, in keeping with his vow of obedience, he had presented them to his superior.

He carried the drawings to the mahogany table and untied the ribbon, turning the sketches over one by one, flipping through them quickly, tears streaming down his cheeks as he saw again the anguish he had been trying to forget. There were Madame Trumante and Rafael, her four-year-old son, sent away on separate ships, unlikely to find each other ever again. There were the women cowering on one side of the hall and the men on the other, the redcoats between them with fixed bayonets. Not just exile, but separation, whole families destroyed, for no other reason than that their tormentors wished them ill. *Alors,* even Mademoiselle Marni Benoit, standing on the ramparts and looking out to sea smiling, the one *habitant* who seemed glad to leave her homeland. The record he had made was intact, but no one had seen it except himself, his superior, and of course Cormac Shea, that night when the métis had arrived looking for Marni.

There was a drawing in the pile that had not been made by him. It had been caught in the black ribbon and lifted out of the drawer when he removed his sketches. A map of some sort, with dotted lines to indicate the depths and the positions of shoals and reefs and little numbers scattered all about. So perhaps a navigation chart. Both. A map and a chart. The artist had not wished to be bound by convention. And though the thing was old and yellowed, it was meticulously drawn with ink and a quill.

Philippe held the sketch to the light, squinting so he could read the signature. *Mon Dieu!* Ignace Loualt? *Que magnifique!* He was holding a drawing made by one of the most famous names in the Society. Loualt had been among the Jesuits who accompanied Champlain when Québec was established in 1608. This drawing must therefore be 150 years old.

At first Philippe could not orient himself to the artist's point of view, but after a few seconds he realized he was looking at the St. Lawrence River and the earliest beginnings of Québec Lower Town. *Alors,* the big tree, the oak with the large wound in its trunk left from a bolt of lightning . . . it is still there. Loualt drew this from the shore just below the falls. *Bien sur.* It is the river passage between Ile d'Orléans and Ile Madame, the place they call La Traverse. *No merchant ship larger than a hundred tons can maneuver through La Traverse, and even then only with the aid of one of the experienced local pilots. Everyone knows that's why we are impregnable here in Québec.* He had heard the statement more times than he could count. *No British warship can sail upriver and threaten us, they cannot pass La Traverse.* It was an article of faith in Québec. He had no doubt it was true. But why would Monsieur le Provincial have such a map as this hidden away?

The Society was immensely proud of its history in New France. The breviaries of the first Jesuits to come here were on display in the public rooms of the Collège. Their battered birettas, two with holes said to be made by the arrows of hostile Indians, were in a glass case beside the entrance. There was even a reliquary containing a fragment of bone said to have come from a Jesuit who had been tortured and killed by the Huron. But this map, this document straight from the pen of Loualt himself, why should it be hidden away?

Because whoever saw it was in possession of a secret. No other explanation was possible.

Philippe was no longer conscious of where he was, or the moral danger of his position. He was drawn into the heart of the drawing by his pure love of lines on paper. He turned it this way and that, examining it from every angle. Loualt the artist, his brother Jesuit, seemed to speak to him. See, I am bearing witness with my gift for art. As you have borne witness, to the trees and flowers and grasses of this place, and to the Indians, and to the sufferings of the *habitants* of l'Acadie. In my own way, in my own time, I did the same. Because, my brother, a thing is not always as it seems, or as people say it is. But the truthful eye of the artist, that does not fail.

Mère de Dieu . . . Loualt had made a chart of the channel through La Traverse.

Philippe's hands shook. *Only with the knowledge of local pilots,* everyone said. *They have secrets that are passed from father to son. There is no other hope of find-*

ing a way through. It was not true. Ignace Loualt had provided all the knowledge necessary. The cross-hatching identified the various shoals and—he was no expert in these things—perhaps even a reef. The numbers were fathom markings, indications of depth. But were they accurate? They had to be. Loualt must have made the soundings himself or he would not have committed the results to a permanent record.

We Jesuits are always thorough and precise. Do all for the greater glory of God. We are taught that from the first day we enter the Society. No shoddy efforts, no half measures. So, since it must be accurate, with this thing one could navigate La Traverse— *Mon Dieu . . .*

Philippe made the sign of the cross. He closed his eyes and prayed that when he opened them he would not see what he thought he'd seen. But when he looked a second time the numbers on the chart had not changed. *Mon Dieu,* I am not a seaman. But I have heard it said over and over since I came to Québec seven years ago: *La Traverse is not only too fierce and too narrow for English warships, it is nowhere deep enough. The smallest frigate cannot get through.* But here I see with my own eyes that according to the soundings of Ignace Loualt, priest of the Society of Jesus and companion to Champlain, the channel is plenty deep, only crooked and difficult to locate.

He had to sit down. The closest chair was the one usually occupied by Monsieur le Provincial. Philippe sat in it, holding the map in both trembling hands. Québec Harbor was not inviolate. It could be entered by English warships. The redcoats would separate husbands and wives, mothers and children, and banish them to some terrible place where they could not receive the sacraments and save their souls.

He looked across the room to the record he had made of the sufferings of the Acadians, still spread out on Monsieur le Provincial's beautiful mahogany table. Tears rolled down his cheeks and his shoulders shook, but he was careful not to allow his sobs to be heard.

"You left this in the corridor, Monsieur Philippe. I thought you might need it."

Philippe took the breviary from Brother Luke's wrinkled hands. *"Merci, mon Frère."* The old man nodded and went to his place in the refectory. Philippe set the breviary on the table beside the boiled egg and rich, dark beef bouillon of the Sunday evening collation. He lifted the cup of broth and drank, carefully avoiding any glance at the head table where Monsieur le Provincial sat.

The Provincial was equally careful not to look directly at Faucon, though he did not miss what had passed between the priest and the brother. Did you by chance leave your breviary in my study, Philippe? *Non,* I do not think so. If you had Luke would not have found it. It is not Brother Luke who disturbed the hair in the angel's wings. And only you and he were in the house. *Au fond,* you left your breviary somewhere else. Near my study, perhaps. And the saintly old brother who thinks ill of no one has simply assumed that you forgot it.

The brother in charge of serving the evening meal approached with second helpings. Roget had a mind to refuse for the sake of self-discipline, and because the crisis in the matter of food grew worse every day. The fisheries were managed for the good of France, not Canada. Most of the catch was salted and sent to the mother country. The growing season in this place was short, and the *habitants* came of stock selected for fishing and trapping skills. They were not, God help them, natural farmers. Worse, Bigot offered them so little for what wheat they did grow that they preferred to hoard, and to sell on the black market. As a result the bread in the town bakeries was of terrible quality—the flour was augmented with ground peas—and rationed to a few thin slices per person per day. For meat, the *habitants* were reduced to slaughtering their horses.

Such deprivation was not apparent in the refectory of the Jesuits. They baked loaves of the finest white bread from excellent flour presented to them by Intendant Bigot, who also frequently supplied them with sides of beef. All, of course, for the sake of his soul. What would be gained by refusing such gifts? Bigot would not turn around and give the food to the poor.

The brother stood in front of his superior, head bowed, holding the tureen of bouillon, waiting to be told if Monsieur le Provincial wished a second helping. The rich aroma of the broth was irresistible. Roget nodded and two ladlefuls of the soup were added to his cup.

The Provincial did not always eat here in the refectory with his sons. Frequently his status required that he dine with those in Québec who, like himself, were in positions of great authority. Though they were not, of course, anything like himself. What did he have in common with the likes of a stunted little charlatan like Bigot, or that old Canadian who fancied himself an aristocrat, the marquis de Vaudreuil? The Provincial sighed. It was his duty to associate with such people for the greater glory of God, just as it was his duty to do all in his power to promote the welfare and spread of Christ's Holy Catholic Church, not simply here in this brutal Canadian wilderness, but in all of New France, most particularly the more hospitable lands to the south. He had known almost from the moment he arrived on this side of the ocean that the future lay in the Ohio Country and the territory known as Louisiana. They would be not just the heart, but the spine of New France. From there the Holy Church and the Society could spread west. Whatever happened, such treasures must not be given up to the English. Certainly not to save this harsh land. But now, with a Canadian as governorgeneral . . . Patience, he reminded himself. The time will come.

Eh bien, he had been patient with his wounded falcon for a very long time. And did I trap you today, *mon pauvre Philippe,* you who wished to hide here in the Society because you could not face the rigors of the mews and then discovered that a Jesuit does not have even a falconer's gauntlet with which to protect himself? Only the grace of God and his own wits.

Did I leave my apartments unlocked simply to tempt you into the sin you have now committed? I think I simply forgot. I am guilty of an oversight, nothing more. And if you had merely satisfied yourself that your drawings were still in my possession and gone away, I could perhaps leave you to the punishment of your own overscrupulous conscience. But as it is . . . And you took not just the damning pictures which will excite Vaudreuil and the rest of the Canadians to defend with still greater fervor their kingdom of snow, you took Loualt's chart as well. So I must act. After evening prayers, I think. Leaving you a little more time to agonize over your sins will make it easier in the end.

The bell chimed, signaling the end of collation. Monsieur le Provincial rose and led his sons in a brief grace after meals. When it was finished they left the refectory in silence, but not in procession. Jesuits were not monks. They did not move through their house in liturgical conformity. Each man went where he wished for the few minutes until the bell would again summon him to the church for evening prayers.

Philippe returned to his small room and reclaimed his deerskin envelope. It was a warm summer's night; he would have no need of a cloak. The bell rang. Philippe walked not to the church where his community gathered, but to a side door that gave out on the street that ran beside the west facade of the grand Collège des Jésuites.

Philippe pushed open the door of the little public chapel of the Poor Clares. Père Antoine knelt in the back. The Jesuit breathed a sigh of relief and made the sign of the cross in thanksgiving.

He had nearly panicked when he found no one at the Franciscan's cottage. He had made no other plan, no decision except that he must somehow enlist the aid of the only man in Québec he was sure was not in league with Louis Roget. But how wise was the good God. Here in this place sanctified by the prayers of these remarkable nuns, it would be better, easier. He had been brought to confront Père Antoine in a situation perfectly suited to the occasion. It was yet another sign that he was doing the right thing.

The nuns were chanting Compline, the final Hour of the day. Be on your guard, their singsong voices told him, for the devil like a roaring lion goes about seeking whom he may devour. Philippe knew it was true. But surely the devil could not follow him here to this holy place. The Fallen One could not survive among these women who had given up everything for the love of Almighty God. The Jesuit dropped to his knees beside the other priest.

Antoine turned and looked to see who had joined him for night prayers. *Alors!* Something remarkable is happening. Jesuits do not go about in the Lower Town in the evenings. They dined with the rich and powerful in the grand houses above. And this one looks as pale as if he has stood at the gates of hell. I think, my brother priest, that Louis Roget does not know you are here at this moment. And that if he did know, he would not be happy. *Eh bien.* We will pray together now. When you wish to talk you will let me know. Perhaps you will even tell me what it is you carry in that envelope you hold so close to your heart.

The chant continued for another while. *"Nunc dimittis . . ."* Now, Lord, you can dismiss your servant. Both priests kept their gaze on the altar and appeared to be entirely focused on the prayers. At last the service ended with a hymn to the Virgin. *"Salve Regina,"* the nuns sang, *"Mater misericordiae . . ."* Hail Holy Queen, Mother of mercy, our life, our sweetness and our hope.

Philippe heard the soft sounds of the women's bare feet on the stone floors as they left the choir, singing as they went to their cells. *"O clemens, O pia, O dulcis Virgo Maria."* Only because their monastery was so small could he hear the final loving notes of the nuns' entreaty to the gentle and merciful Mother of God.

Antoine turned his head. Both men still knelt, leaning only on their faith. "Do you wish to confess, Brother?"

Philippe shook his head. "It is past time for confession, Père Antoine. At least of the sort you mean."

"You know my name, *mon Frère,* but I do not know yours."

"I am Philippe Faucon."

"Ah yes, the Jesuit who makes the beautiful drawings. I have heard of you." Antoine nodded toward the envelope. "Have you brought me some of your drawings?"

"I have brought you the truth about *les Anglais.* And the means to save Québec."

Antoine's belly knotted and his heart raced. Mother of God, grant that I make no mistake. "Those are grave matters, brother. Maybe it is better if we go to my—"

"I wish to remain right here, in the presence of the Holy Sacrament." The eyes of the Jesuit and the Franciscan were locked. Neither looked away. "Antoine Rubin de Montaigne," Philippe said, "as you are a priest of God and He is your judge, are you a spy for the English?"

It was the most extraordinary question anyone had ever asked him. Antoine took a deep breath before he answered. "As God is my judge, I am not. What would give you such an idea?"

"You conspire with the evil renegade Lantak. You send him to make war on your enemies."

"On the enemies of Holy Church. Only for the sake of the Gospel." Antoine's chest roiled and his palms were sweaty. *The Jesuit knows something truly momentous, and he does not trust Louis Roget with the knowledge. You have brought him here to me, mon Dieu. Let me make no mistakes.* "*Mon Frère,* I swear to you on my immortal soul that I am a loyal son of the Church and of France."

"So help you God?"

"So help me God."

Philippe was very calm. He was the avenging sword of St. Michael the Archangel, the voice of both prosecutor and judge. Now he came to a verdict. The Franciscan might not speak the entire truth, but he did not lie. He was not a spy, and the best interests of the Holy Faith were uppermost in his mind and heart. Philippe began to tremble. He had risked so much. Now, at the end, he must risk everything.

"Please," Antoine pleaded, "*Frère Philippe,* you are ill, I think. Let us go to my cottage. I cannot offer you much, but I have some *petite bière.* It might—"

"We will finish our business here, Père Antoine. Then it is best that we leave separately. And with great care." Philippe opened the envelope and withdrew the contents, his drawings and Loualt's. Antoine took them eagerly and started to thumb through the pile. "No," Philippe commanded. "Do not look now. Put these under your scapular. Take them back to your house and study them there. No one must know you have them."

Antoine looked quickly at the door to the street. It was shut, and the only windows were high up on the walls. "We are entirely alone, *mon cher Frère.* Calm yourself."

"Later I will be calm. First tell me, do you know what is said about La Traverse, the impassable channel—"

"—only the local pilots can navigate. Of course."

"*Bon.* That is as I expected. I counsel you to look very carefully at the old map, Père Antoine." The Franciscan began again to leaf through the papers. "*Non!* I told you, not here. Not yet. What I have given you is truth, whole and entire. It is a dangerous thing; guard it well. I swear that when you see what you have, you will understand." Holding his now empty envelope Philippe stood up. "Remember, wait a little before you leave. Then be sure you are not followed, go straight home, and lock your door before you examine the drawings I have given you. After that, my brother priest, for the love of God and his Church, do what is right and necessary."

Was this Jesuit mad? No, probably not. For nearly two years Antoine had frequently felt himself followed and watched. He watched Faucon walk unsteadily toward the door, a black wraith who seemed lost inside his soutane. At the last moment the other priest paused and turned to him. "Pray give me your blessing, *mon Père.*"

The Franciscan made a sweeping sign of the cross in the air that separated the two men. "Go with God, Philippe." The door of the chapel closed behind the Jesuit.

Followed, by someone or something that wished him ill. How long had he suspected but told himself he was being foolish. *Mon Dieu,* You protect me despite my own folly. And now . . . Panic threatened. Antoine clutched the precious drawings and looked about the poor and all but empty chapel for a place to hide.

Louis Roget waited for the length of three *Paters* and three *Aves.* No one had left the monastery chapel after Philippe, but he could not trust such scant evidence.

Nearly nine o'clock, but still bright as day. In Canada even the sun did not behave in a normal fashion. In summer it lingered too long and in winter it almost did not come at all. *Eh bien,* some things were as they were. He could not wait for the shadows of night to protect him. Besides, there was nothing suspicious in a poor fisherman of the Lower Town visiting the chapel of the holy Clares to pray before retiring.

The Provincial congratulated himself on the wise decision to spend the few moments after he realized that Philippe had not appeared for evening prayers changing into the clothes of a *habitant.* He pulled the broad-brimmed black hat farther over his eyes, then, walking with the constant stoop of a man who had done physical labor his entire life, he crossed the alley to the door of the chapel and pushed it open.

Inside was dimmer than the street. Roget removed his hat and genuflected toward the altar while he waited for his eyes to adjust to the gloom. When they did he saw no one, just the scattered prie-dieux, the altar prepared for the morning's Mass, and the flickering sanctuary candle. Behind everything was the forbidding iron grille with its heavy curtains, hiding the nuns from the outside world.

Was there no confessional in this place? Surely even Poor Clares must confess. He looked, but he saw nothing that appeared to serve that purpose. And no one. Philippe had been alone when he came here, and *grâce à Dieu,* when the tortured falcon came out of this place, he still had the leather envelope that must have held his stolen drawings and the map of Loualt. I should have destroyed both long since, *mon Dieu,* but the work was so exquisitely done. Such talent. I had hoped that sometime in the future, when it was not so incendiary or important, their art would add to the glory of the Society, and thus to You. Forgive me my weakness.

In the confessional built so cleverly into the grille that no one unfamiliar with the ways of cloistered Poor Clares would recognize it for what it was, Père Antoine held his breath, and thanked the Virgin for the inspiration that had brought him here to wait as Philippe Faucon said he must before leaving the chapel. The confessional door was open just a crack. Thank God he had dared that much. No mistake, it was Louis Roget. Antoine pressed to his heart the drawings he still had not properly seen.

Monsieur le Provincial hurried back into the street and paused for a moment, deciding what to do next. At one end this alley of the Franciscans emerged onto the broad Côte de la Montagne that climbed the hills to the Upper Town; at the other it led to a narrow, twisting road that rose much more steeply to the cliffs high above the river. That was the direction Philippe had taken. The Provincial had seen the last flick of the hem of his falcon's soutane go around that corner. Now, still in the measured pace of a man exhausted by the burden of surviving in this place, Louis Roget made his decision and went after him.

Philippe walked along the steep cliffs west of the walls of the Upper Town. The headland was a flat plain divided into small farms where a few *habitants* grew vegetables. In Québec they said those same fields had first been planted by another companion of Champlain, Abraham Martin; that was why they were called the Plains of Abraham.

Had Abraham Martin known these footpaths as well as he did? What about Loualt? Yes, probably so. The ordinary people knew them as well. Philippe had sometimes seen women making their way among these narrow byways, using shortcuts because of their heavy loads. This way down to the inlet below, for example, this faint declivity in the cliff face. It wasn't truly a path, but here if one were careful and used the saplings for purchase, it was possible to climb down the sheer side of the promontory and reach the sheltered cove. It was the only possible descent for leagues in either direction.

Philippe looked down at the majestic river, racing away from Québec toward somewhere better. He started down. I can only put everything in your hands, *mon Dieu,* and ask your Blessed Mother to intervene to save my soul.

He knew the name of the cove, why could he not remember it? Ah, yes. *L'Anse au Foulon,* the Fuller's Cove, where the women dug the clay that they rubbed on newly woven cloth to give a supple finish. The narrow crescent of beach was covered in shale. He left no footprints as he walked across it and into the river. There was a moment's shock when the cold water lapped around his ankles, but Philippe went forward, into the broad and deep St. Lawrence, holding the deerskin envelope above his head. When the water reached his waist he began to sing, his voice loud and clear and full of hope. *"O clemens, O pia, O dulcis Virgo Maria."*

From his place high on the cliffs above l'Anse au Foulon, Louis Roget continued to tell his beads as he heard the last notes of the hymn to the Virgin, then saw the water close over the falcon's head. I could not save him, Lord. I was too far away when I realized what he intended to do. Surely you will forgive his grave sin of suicide. He was a wounded soul, too weak to survive. I will tell the others that I have sent him back to l'Acadie to see if he can be of any assistance to those few *habitants* who remain; that he wanted to go. Indeed he insisted on it. They will think him yet another Jesuit hero. And I thank You that he has taken those wretched drawings with him. Monsieur le Provincial made the sign of the cross over the water where he had last seen the Jesuit, then turned and made his way back to the Collège des Jésusites.

TUESDAY, JULY 24, 1757
MONASTERY OF THE POOR CLARES, QUÉBEC

"It is impossible."

"It is necessary."

Mère Marie Rose could not believe she was being asked to consent to this thing. "*Mon Père,* forgive me, but what you ask . . . Soeur Stephane is a nun in vows. She has sworn to God to remain always enclosed, and—"

"And when the Saracens threatened Assisi," Antoine interrupted, "what did our Holy Mother Clare do? She climbed to the parapets, holding the monstrance that contained the Holy Sacrament. She repelled the invaders and Assisi was saved. Is that not exactly what happened, Mother Abbess?"

"Yes, but—"

Antoine heard the slight doubt in her voice and pressed his advantage. "There are no buts. It must be as I say." The confessional was stifling. It took all his stamina to summon the breath to continue the argument he had made for the last ten minutes, and at least twice a day for the two days since the drawings had been given into his charge. "St. Clare showed her face to the world because the safety of her city and her Church required it. Is she not the example you and your daughters have sworn to follow?"

"But Soeur Stephane is so young, so untried as yet in our life. She has not been here three whole years. Why not Soeur Angelique, or Soeur Joseph?"

"Soeur Stephane is the most clever of your daughters." Antoine had been confessing the little nun since the moment she arrived in Québec; he was convinced of her intelligence and resourcefulness. The ability to think and act quickly might be required for his scheme to work. "Besides, only she speaks perfect English. So if by chance she were intercepted she could—"

"*Mon Dieu!* You told me there would be no danger." The abbess made a quick sign of the cross, and begged God that she might endure the pain of kneeling here as long as it took to protect her authority and the souls of her daughters.

"I said, *if* something should happen, *ma Mère*. But she need go only as far as Montréal." Père Antoine mopped the sweat from his face with the hem of his scapular. "Mère Marie Rose, listen to me very carefully. I have information that shows how the most terrible disaster can come upon this city. If we do not prevent it, New France is finished. The Church is finished here. Heretics will overrun this land and millions of souls will perish."

Sacré Coeur! That she should be asked to take on herself the responsibility for such a thing. Mère Marie Rose trembled. The voice of the priest continued to hammer at her conscience. "If I could go myself I would do so in an instant." Now his voice was less commanding, more pleading. "I am watched, Mère Marie Rose, suspected. I cannot go. Is a vow made by one young woman—a vow, I might add, that I am entirely and legally able to temporarily dispense—more important than that?"

"If we could wait until September, when Soeur Stephane will renew her vows as we all do every year. I could let her go before she has again made her promises. For a few days she would not be in vows at all."

"By September, *ma Mère*, the vultures might well be picking over our flesh."

Marie Rose told herself she was shaking with fatigue, not fear, and that the tears that ran down her cheeks were caused by exhaustion, not surrender. "I have been given the care of this girl's soul, *mon Père*. I cannot lightly ignore that responsibility."

Her voice gave her away. Antoine knew he had won. *Grâce à Dieu.* "Not lightly, *ma Mère*. After much prayer and consultation with your confessor, who is the Delegate of the Minister General in Rome. For the good of thousands and the glory of God."

Much prayer indeed. She had prayed without ceasing since Père Antoine made his proposal two days before. And this morning, during Lauds, the very same image had come to her, of Holy Mother Clare standing on the walls of Assisi, facing the world and repelling the Moslem invaders who had almost overrun all Europe, by holding up the monstrance that contained the Sacred Host. "Very well." She whispered the words, beating her chest in penance as she spoke them. For my fault, for my fault, for my most grievous fault. "Very well, it will be as you say."

"God is speaking through you, Mère Marie Rose. You do what is right."

Chapter Twenty-One

SHABA-SHABA-SHABA. The sound of little bare feet on the earth. Taba feet. *Shaba-shaba-shaba.* Keeping no count of the days and nights, or the difference between them. Only run. When you stop, climb into a tree and sleep. Portion out the hardtack and jerky you took from Kitchen Hannah's stores. Make it last.

Shaba-shaba-shaba. Don't make a sound. No little gasps for air, no sucking-in sounds to make the spit come, no matter how thirsty you are. Something feels dangerous about these woods now. Got to get away from whatever is in these woods wasn't here before. No sound. Just *shaba-shaba-shaba.* Bare feet flying over the earth. *Shaba-shaba-shaba.*

Soft black earth. Black night woods. No moon and no stars woods. A path, narrow as ever it can be, but soft and springy. Been here since before Jeremiah and Solomon the Barrel Maker and Six-Finger Sam were born. They were the oldest people she knew, but Taba was sure this path was older. *Shaba-shaba-shaba.*

Clemency the Washerwoman had taught Taba most of what she knew about Shadowbrook. Clemency said Taba had been three years a Hale slave, "So don't you be grieving for your home place no more, child. It be time you stop all that." But it didn't matter how long it had been. Taba remembered her village and the lake, and the fish she caught that last day. And the slavers. Only mostly she didn't think about them. Clemency was right about that. Stupid to keep thinking about what could never be changed. Like Ashanti slavers and Master John and the things they did to her.

"You got to be smart you gonna survive, little missy Taba. And smart means not thinking no more 'bout how things was. Just thinking 'bout how they be. And knowing what the white folks know, and some things they don't. That way you get to keep the inside-free alive. Right here where it counts." Clemency touched

Taba's heart when she said that, but she didn't feel a nice soft pap that could feed a baby some day. *Shaba-shaba-shaba*. No soft round mound with a pink circle around the dark baby-suck. She had one pap and one hard, rough lump. It took a long time until she told Clemency how that lump came to her. Then one day while the Washerwoman was putting Taba's hair into so many tiny little plaits Taba couldn't count them, she did. Clemency didn't talk when Taba told her the story, but she had plenty to say when she told the others that night sitting by Kitchen Hannah's fire. And when she finished, Runsabout said that when Master John got hard between his legs he was a crazy man. Did things no natural man who was right in his head should do or would do. White or black.

Shaba-shaba-shaba. Taba had heard them talk because she was behind Kitchen Hannah's big fireplace at the time. They didn't know Taba was there, not even Kitchen Hannah, who had said Taba could go to that sleeping place behind the fire whenever she wanted.

Shaba-shaba-shaba. She was smelling a lake smell. She knew there was a lake in these parts. Taba had never seen it, but she had heard the others talking about a lake that used to be Bright Fish Water but was called something else now. *Shaba-shaba-shaba.*

"Poor little thing," Corn Broom Hannah had said that night. "Too bad not having two paps don't put him off wanting her in his bed."

"Ain't nothin' gonna put Master John off nothin' if he don' want to be put off. Master John, he don't be a natural man. And he don' change for nothin'." Those were Runsabout's final words. But even if Master John never changed, Taba did.

Shaba-shaba-shaba. She came to a place where there was a big wall inside herself. A high stone wall, big as the walls of the Guinea fort where the slavers kept her until the white men and their ships came. *Shaba-shaba-shaba*. She had to be free outside, had to be on the other side of that wall. The inside-free that Clemency and the others talked about, that wasn't enough.

Black as tar here in the woods. Blacker than in the big house cupboard where she hid until everyone was asleep the night Master John had left for Albany. He wasn't home so she didn't have to go to his room that night. The women, all except Kitchen Hannah, they slept up in the place they called the long room under the roof, and when Master John wasn't home Taba could sleep up there too, comforted by the sound of the others' breathing. But that night she didn't go to the long room after all the candles were snuffed out and the fires banked. *Shaba-shaba-shaba*. That night she stayed in the cupboard until it was dark and everyone was sure to be asleep. She knew the others were so used to her not sleeping in the long room they wouldn't miss her, even though Master John wasn't home. If she was going to get over the wall, find the outside-free, this was the time to try. *Shaba-shaba-shaba*.

That night when she crept across the Frolic Ground and headed off to find her outside-free, the only thing she knew for sure was that she wasn't going the Albany way. *Shaba-shaba-shaba.* No idea where this way was taking her, except that it didn't go to Albany and it took her away from Shadowbrook. *Shaba-shaba-shaba.* Nine sunrises and sunsets. Maybe ten. Could even be twelve. She wasn't really counting. Besides, it had rained so much and there were so many clouds covering the sun and the moon you could hardly tell when the days came and when they went. One thing she was sure about, nobody was following her. She had the outside-free now. No Master John. That was as free as she needed to be.

She'd come to a village sometime. She could smell a lake and in her home place a lake meant fish so—"Oh!" A small, right-out-loud scream. Squeezed out of her when she stumbled over a rock and fell. Before she could get to her feet and keep running, she was grabbed and lifted and imprisoned in the crook of a strong arm. After she'd come so far. The grief welled up in Taba so big and so fast she thought she'd drown in it, drown in all those tears she dare not cry.

"You must be stark raving mad, lassie. Dinna you ken there's soldiers and savages in their hundreds prowling this forest?" The words were whispered right into her ear, but Taba couldn't understand them. Whoever her captor was, he didn't speak like anyone she knew in her home place or here.

The girl kept trying to squirm out of his grip, struggling with more strength than Hamish Stewart would have thought possible for such a wee thing. He held onto her nonetheless—head down, body tucked firmly under one arm, the way he'd heft a bale of oats—and pressed back into the hidden cave that gave him cover and a vantage point. The bairn made a hissing sound and tried to beat on his thigh with her fists. Hamish clamped his free hand over her mouth and held her tight with the other, then lifted her so he could press his lips to her ear again. "Quiet. Otherwise the pair o' us will finish up wi' no hair and boiled for broth."

The lass struggled a few seconds more, then calmed some. Black as a lump of coal, she was. That's why she'd got this far with no painted savage behind her swinging a tomahawk. And thank God for thick clouds covering the moon and the stars. *Might be my hair would na still be on my head if it had na been such* dreich *weather these past few days. Has to be this wee gel's a slave from Shadowbrook. Running away, from the look o' it. God's truth, she chose a bad direction to run in.*

Hamish had been many times in these woods. He knew the lay of the land so well he could see it in the dark. Fort William Henry was less than a league distant; he'd discovered this hiding place several months before, and taken refuge in it earlier that evening when he spotted an advance scout of Canadians and savages circling behind the fort. He'd toyed with the notion of speaking to one of the Canadians, explaining that he was a Catholic and a Jacobite, that he was on their side. But talk, he'd realized sometime since, would not get him off this hilltop. He'd simply have to wait and choose his moment to make a break for freedom.

With the wee gel in his charge he had to think again on what was to be done. The weather was changing. Hamish felt wind in his face, fierce and sudden, blowing in off the water and clearing the clouds as if a great broom were sweeping the sky.

Moments later a round summer moon had risen above the trees and lit the land and the lake and the entrance to Hamish's hiding place, which was formed by an outcropping of boulders at the edge of the flat field where the fort's garrison grew beans and maize and cabbages. God's truth, e'en if you were staring straight at the rock face, you wouldna ken the cave was there. Not unless you tried to wedge yourself between what seemed like a narrow fissure in the granite, the way he had one day because it was pelting hale and e'en a tiny bit o' shelter seemed better than none. The grotto was beyond the crack, six strides in length and three in width. Not much, but in some circumstances, enough.

Hamish moved deeper into the cave, glancing down at the girl still tucked under his arm. She wore a calico frock and her black hair was a mass of tiny plaits. "Listen, lassie," he whispered, "if I take my hand away will you promise na to shout or scream?" He barely breathed the words, spoke them slow and separate so she'd understand. "You're safe wi' me, lass. And not safe out there." He jerked his head to indicate the forest and the fort and the lake. "Do you ken?"

Taba nodded. She didn't understand his words, but his tone was kind. Maybe he was what Runsabout called a natural man. Yes, he was a natural man. She knew it in her bones.

Hamish put his finger over his lips. He felt some relief when she nodded. Still he hesitated a moment before releasing her from his tight grip and setting her on the ground. When he did, she stood where he'd placed her. Dinna move and dinna make a sound. Thank God, lassie, whatever else you may be, you're na a fool. Because heaven as my witness, if you were mad enough to run I'd let you go. Choose to die, lassie, and you can die alone.

Two seconds went by. Three. Hamish held his breath. Finally he exhaled and crouched down, motioning to her to squat beside him. There was bright moonlight now; he could see the fort to his right and beyond it, across a marsh, an entrenched camp on a hill called Titcomb's Mount. The Sassenachs had made the camp to protect the wide military road they'd built through the forest. The road connected Fort William Henry with Fort Edward, ten leagues to the south. The camp overlooked the lake, and if the French attacked, that's where— Sweet Mary in Heaven and all the Blessed Saints, protect us.

Hamish stared at the wash of moonlight on the water and hurriedly blessed himself, trying to hold back the vomit his churning stomach wanted to expel. God's truth, he'd rather a thousand times face another Culloden Moor than what he was looking at.

The wee lass sucked in her breath. Hamish put his arm around her again, more for comfort than capture this time. The wind that blew away the clouds had stirred ruffles of whitecaps on the lake, but they were no deterrent to the massed canoes floating toward the fort, each one filled with naked savages painted for war. Mother o' Heaven, there were Indians as far as he could see. He'd heard it said there were two thousand o' them gathered at Fort Carillon t'other end of the lake. Sure to Almighty God, every one was on Bright Fish Water this night.

The bateaux of the French garrison came into view behind the canoes, some moved by paddles, some by sail, many roped together for strength and stability. They rode low in the water, almost sinking beneath their cargo of heavy siege guns and hundreds of uniformed French regulars. Hamish tried to count the total number of craft and gave up when he passed two hundred and fifty. Since war was declared in May of '56, the French and their Indian allies had won nearly every battle. The Sassenachs werena likely to reverse the trend this time. They were facing an armada.

The fleet floated toward the fort, then halted and held steady just out of cannon range. It was a maneuver of breathtaking skill, as if a wave had rippled backward and been arrested before the crest. Hamish glanced at the fort. He detected no motion, but their lookouts would have seen what was coming and by now the entire garrison would be under battle alarm. Bloody heretics they were; still, it was hard not to feel some pity. He knew there to be twenty-five hundred men in Fort William Henry. Redcoats—the Thirty-fifth Foot, whose officers had brought their families, maybe a hundred women and children—as well as Yorkers, and militiamen from New England and New Jersey. Some forty rangers as well; woodsmen sent to scout, and to teach the redcoats a trick or two about fighting in the wilderness. God help them all, the force on the lake had to be at least three times that number.

The rangers must ken as well that no escape through the forest was possible, that the woods were full of Canadians and their Indian allies. The sutlers going back and forth between Albany and the fort peddling their wares, trading as much in talk as in combs and corn and musket balls, said the rangers had been sent by Quentin Hale. Hamish got the same information from Annie Crotchett. These days she sold her favors to as many redcoats as locals, given the numbers of 'em camped in the hills around the town, and just last week Annie had told him the Red Bear had been summoned to London, no less. To tell their bloody lordships how to make war like Indians, as if the Sassenachs needed any training in savagery. The blood rose in Hamish, reminding him of his hot hatred of all things English, but it cooled when he looked from the fort to the lake. He was seeing the makings of a slaughter. Sweet Savior in Heaven, he'd not have thought there could be so many painted barbarians in one place.

Four piercing notes from a horn rolled up the hills one side o' the water and down the other. The strangeness o' the thing made drops o' cold sweat form on his skin. A French horn in these American woods. He half expected the skirl o' the pipes next. The horn sounded a second time. In response the Indians in the canoes began beating their drums and whooping and screaming. Those in the forest behind the fort replied with shouts and drums of their own.

Hamish put his hand on the lass's shoulder. Her whole body heaved with every breath she drew, but she made no sound and it was plain she dinna mean to bolt. God alone knew how she'd got here through a forest bristling with white men and red, all intent on dealing death, but it was fitting that it was he who'd caught her, not some howling savage. The gel was bound to be Shadowbrook's property. And Shadowbrook, he reminded himself, magnificently, unbelievingly, was his. Pinned between two halves of a war he might be, but by Christ Almighty, he was at last the laird. And this wee lass, like everything else on the Hale Patent, belonged to him. Now all he had to do was stay alive to claim his prize.

THURSDAY, AUGUST 9, 1757
FORT WILLIAM HENRY

Days and nights filled with the scream of cannon fire and musket fire and Indian whoops and curses hurled in French and English. And death.

In all of the civilized world it was agreed that however badly the defenders were outnumbered, as long as a fort's walls and bastions were intact, honorable surrender was not possible. By the time the sun came up on the tenth day of the siege, the top of the bastions of Fort William Henry, the ones facing the French guns, had been entirely shot away.

At noon that day the front gate of the fort opened and a white flag was raised. A drummer beating a solemn tattoo marched ahead of a red-coated lieutenant colonel on horseback. A musket ball had shattered the Englishman's left foot. Despite that, he was the best man for the job. His French was flawless.

Montcalm's tent was a large marquee of three poles, with walls that reached above a tall man's shoulders and elegant campaign furniture. The general was joined by half a dozen of his most senior officers, five Indians in the full battle regalia—warbonnets and the like—that marked them as chiefs, and a handful of translators. In deference to the wound of the Englishman, everyone sat. There were not enough of the hastily unfolded leather-covered chairs to accommodate all. The Indians squatted at the fringes of the meeting.

The Englishman's name was Young. He and Montcalm did the talking. Quiet, courteous speech, no need for bluster, because both men knew the battle was over and the English had lost. Fort William Henry had fewer than seven hundred soldiers fit for duty. Three hundred had been killed since the engagement began, the rest had fallen to an epidemic of smallpox raging since mid-July. All the English cannon and most of their mortars had burst from overuse or been disabled by shot, while the whole of Montcalm's thirty-one cannon and fifteen mortars and howitzers were intact, now entrenched, and ready to open fire together. Up to now only some of the guns had been in action, and that portion of the French firepower had been almost more than the English could resist. Facing the entire battery meant surrender was the only option. That's what had decided the vote taken among the fort's officers earlier that morning.

The marquis de Montcalm had no interest in prisoners. The harvest had been poor in Canada this year and the year before, and the policies of Intendant Bigot and his *grande siéty* had made a bad situation horrendous. Montcalm had barely enough food to feed his own men and dole out a bit to the Indians. "You have fought bravely, monsieur. I offer you the honors of war and safe passage to Fort Edward." Young nodded in acknowledgment of Montcalm's compliment. "In return," the Frenchman continued, "for eighteen months parole."

Generous terms. The defenders of Fort William Henry would be allowed to leave with their colors flying and in possession of their small arms and their personal effects. For their part, the British and the colonials must give their solemn word not to fight against the French for a year and a half. "We will take the fort at once," Montcalm continued. "Your garrison will go over the ravine to the entrenched camp and spend the night there. At first light tomorrow a detachment of my soldiers will escort you to Fort Edward."

It was a journey of some three leagues. "We have many sick," Young explained. "They are not fit to cross from the fort to the camp. The journey to Fort Edward would be impossible."

"*Pas de probleme, Monsieur le Colonel,* they may stay where they are. We will look after your sick and wounded and send them to you as soon as they have recovered. Now, there is as well the matter of French and Canadian prisoners taken by you since the start of the war. They are to be returned to us."

"*D'accord, mon Général. Mais . . .*" Young shot a quick look at the Indians.

Montcalm followed his glance and nodded. He summoned three of the translators and spoke to them quickly, repeating the terms of the surrender. In turn, the translators, two Canadians and one Indian, explained them to each of the chiefs in his own language.

Alhanase the Huron spoke French and did not require a translation. Still he listened carefully in case he had misunderstood what he'd heard earlier. He had not. He rose. The other chiefs did the same.

"They understand?" Montcalm asked anxiously. "They agree?"

"They understand perfectly," one of the translators assured him.

"And agree," Montcalm said again.

This time it was Alhanase rather than one of the translators who replied. *"Il a parlé, Onontio."* Onontio has spoken. *"Il a arrangé les choses à la Cmokmanuk.* He has arranged things the *Cmokmanuk* way. *"Nous comprenons."* We understand.

Alhanase and the other chiefs knew their young braves would not be so accepting of this outrage. They had fought well, for nothing but meager rations and a few gifts given when they had first agreed to once more take up the tomahawk on behalf of Onontio. Now the enemy was beaten, yet Onontio's warrior sons were being denied the fruits of their victory. They would have no plunder, no scalps, the fat of their enemies would not fill their empty bellies, and worst of all, they would have no captives to bring home to replace the many who had died. A father—Onontio—did not behave in such a manner.

As arranged, every member of the English garrison able to walk or ride left the fort a few hours after the terms of the surrender were concluded. They filed out under the gaze of restless braves, who mocked and taunted them, making threatening gestures that the English pretended to ignore. A broad ravine separated the fort and the camp where they were to spend the night. The moment they crossed it a number of braves rushed into the fort. The rangers had made sure to bury whatever rum the garrison didn't take with them, but the Indians found it, and drank it, complaining mightily at how little plunder was to be had in the all-but-empty fort. Only one thing worth having had been left behind.

The braves made their way to the infirmary and slaughtered and scalped the wounded. There were some protests, but the Canadians who were supposed to be caring for the sick mostly stood back and watched.

Just before sundown more bands of braves entered the camp on Mount Titcomb, many more than the French regulars who stood guard duty. "Stave the kegs. Hurry," someone murmured. The word was passed and holes were bashed in the eleven barrels of rum the English had brought with them, the contents allowed to soak into the ground. The *Anishinabeg*—Potawatomi and Nipissing and Ottawa and Huron—did not need more drink. Their blood was heated with rage that having accomplished so much, they were to be repaid with so little. For a time they prowled the camp, demanding clothes and jewelry and making threatening gestures. They paid particular attention to the women, playing with their long hair as if reminding them of the possibility they could lose it. Eventually the French guards turned them out.

Alhanase the Huron stood apart and watched. The medicine bag that hung round his neck contained a rare thing, a single blue-black Súki bead carved with a spider, ancient and beautiful. A reminder of the old days, of a time when the *Anishinabeg* lived alone and made both war and peace in their own fashion. There were some Ottawa here, but only a few, and those not led by Pontiac. Perhaps the powerful Ottawa war chief was correct. Perhaps separation could bring the old days back. Perhaps if the English were allowed to win they would divide the earth of this place they called the New World between themselves and the Real People. Like the others, Alhanase had trusted the French, accepted their war belt, but Onontio was not a father if he asked his sons to fight and die and get nothing in return. Perhaps this was to be the last battle.

Even so, Alhanase knew, it was not yet over.

At dawn a detachment of three hundred French soldiers led the English down the road toward Fort Edward. The redcoats and the colonial militia marched behind them. The defeated men carried their muskets, but in accordance with the terms of the surrender no ammunition and no bayonets. The women and children were in the rear of the long line, at least a league behind the armed French who might protect them.

Hamish and Taba watched from their hidden grotto, their stomachs cramping with hunger. Their combined jerky and biscuits had run out three days earlier. Hamish's canteen had been dry still longer. The Scot had managed to collect a bit of rainwater during a night's downpour, and two cabbages and four ears of maize from the fort's garden on the one foray he'd risked. They'd survived on that, and on luck. Last night a painted Indian had found the entrance to their hiding place. A sudden darkening of the light was all the warning Hamish had. Hamish figured it to have been the brave's surprise at discovering the cave that gave him time to plunge his dirk into the Indian's throat before he could shout. He'd pulled the corpse the rest of the way into the grotto so it would not be found. Sharing the cave with a dead body gave him and Taba less room than they'd had before, but he knew it was better than what waited for them if they tried to get away. They would be butchered alive, like the Sassenachs Hamish was watching die on the road below.

Could be hunger had made him light-headed. Maybe that's why the sight of the Indians attacking the unarmed English seemed like a dream. Hamish watched it without any real feeling, as if it were a mummery at a summer fair in the Highlands when he was a lad.

The women and children were dealt with first. They were guarded only by a few Canadians who stood by and did nothing while young wives in their prime were captured and carried off into the forest, and older ones were tomahawked and scalped. Babes and the very young were hacked apart and thrown aside; only the older ones were taken alive. From where he watched the Scot could see their mouths open, but it seemed to him he could not hear the screams. Maybe because he did not want to hear them.

The provincial militia came next. Most were made to hand over their clothes and their muskets as if they were bargaining for their lives, or thought they were. A few managed to escape naked into the woods, the rest were tomahawked and scalped and left for dead. After a time the chaos spread far enough so the redcoats farther up the column understood what was happening in the rear and doubled back to do what they could, though with no shot for their muskets it was not much. At last the French soldiers at the column's head turned around and tried to restore order. By now the savages were screaming and whooping and dancing. There was no hope the French could simply command them to leave off, but no one gave the order to fix bayonets, much less to fire. They couldn't, Hamish knew; not unless they want to lose the allegiance of the savages. And that was their best advantage in this war where, taken all together, the English outnumbered them many times over.

Screams of triumph and terror echoed off the forested hills, and when silence came it was because there were no more Sassenachs or Americans to be killed.

Hamish and the girl stayed hidden another day, surviving on a few filched carrots and some ears of maize that Hamish got by chancing another crawl on his belly to the edge of the garden in the field and back again. The odor of roasting and boiling meat rose from every side and competed with the stench of the rapidly decaying Indian corpse that shared the grotto with them. It was the first time Hamish ever knew himself not to salivate at the smell of cooked flesh. Maybe because it was the slaughtered Sassenachs the Indians were cooking and eating. Once he saw a brave offer a French soldier a joint fresh from the fire and dripping with fat. The man recoiled and the savage and his friends laughed.

Hamish saw other vigorous discussions between the French and their Indian allies. He could tell they were bargaining, but not what for, or what the outcome might be. The next morning the Indians began to leave, sated with blood and laden with plunder, piling it into their canoes and at the last moment bringing their captives out of the woods, roped together with cords around their necks.

As soon as the canoes were out of sight the French and the Canadians set to work demolishing the fort and dragging as many dead bodies as they could find to the center of a huge pyre. They set it alight and left; the blaze burned most of the day and a good part of the following night. In that firelit dark Hamish took the girl by the hand and led her away from the grotto. They walked upright now because he was sure there was not a soul left alive in the vicinity, except for themselves and the wolves coming down from the hills to feast on what carrion remained.

There was game and fish aplenty in the woods. Hamish had his dirk. Hunger was no longer a problem, though it was a while before either of them could eat. The memory of what they'd seen had closed their bellies and their mouths. The girl told him her name, Taba, and he said he was Hamish—"I'm your master now, lass. And you've naught to fear if you do what you're told"—but little else. He did not think she knew he was taking her back the way she came until, after an eleven-day trek, she saw Shadowbrook sitting atop its gentle rise, its white walls turned to pink by a fiery sunset in the hills behind.

Taba screamed and tried to run but Hamish had expected that. He was on her before she could get away, hoisting her like a sack of oats as he had that first night, and carrying her forward despite her desperate attempts to break free. "Easy, Taba lass. I told you you'd naught to fear and I dinna lie. Just be easy while I attend to what's necessary."

"So, Hamish Stewart the Scot, returning my property. I'm delighted, man, though not more than I'm surprised. I just ordered the broadsides and—"

"She's not your property. And I dinna see any broadside."

"You couldn't have. I just ordered them printed and put up around Albany," John Hale said, ignoring the first statement. "There's a reward of ten guineas for the return of my runaway Ibo slave, Taba. You shall have—"

"Keep your money, John Hale. What you have on your wretched self is yours as well. I'll na take it from you. And you can pack your personal things and take them besides. You've an hour to get ready and be gone."

"In Christ's name, Stewart, what are you talking about?"

They were in the small square room off the front hall where Mistress Lorene spent most mornings planning the household's work. Her desk was against one wall. There was a serving table beside it with sides that lifted to make it larger. More times than she could count, Taba had polished both until she could see her face in the golden grain.

She was curled up under the desk now because it seemed the only thing to do. Mistress wasn't here, but mostly she was kind to Taba. Maybe her kindness was in this place. So Taba crawled under the desk and tried to think of kindness covering her up.

"I dinna wish to incommode your mother. She can take a few days to pack if she needs them."

"I think you're mad," John said quietly. "But it's no affair of mine. Get out, Stewart. You're welcome to the reward since I promised it, but with or without your ten guineas, get out of my house and off my land."

"I'm not mad, however much you might wish it, you God-rotting heretic bastard. The Hale Patent is mine." Hamish reached into the pocket inside his hunting shirt. He'd been carrying the deed since he'd been to New York City the month before. "Every scrap o' the original grant," he said, offering the papers to Hale. "Including Bright Fish Water and the Great Carrying Place." That's why he'd gone up there to see the condition of the fort and see if it made any sense to insist the Sassenachs withdraw immediately. No need to worry about that now. Burned to the ground the fort must be. Na a trace left by now.

"The three of 'em signed. Oliver De Lancey, Hayman Levy, and the lawyer Alexander. And it was witnessed by the governor o' New York Province, James De Lancey himself." Hamish said, holding out the bundle of papers. "Take a look, John. Do my heart good to see you read the thing."

John did not want to touch the papers. If he actually held them and read them, this nightmare might turn out to be real, not simply a feverish dream caused by too much rum. But the names. The three names. By God in heaven, how could this lout of a Jacobite with one eye know that De Lancey, Levy, and Alexander held a lien on the property? He put out his hand, doing his best to keep it from trembling, and the Scot slapped the sheaf of papers onto his open palm.

"Take your time, you blighted bastard. I'll enjoy seeing you ponder every word."

John staggered a few steps to the desk and sat down. Taba pushed herself back against the wall.

John untied the papers and opened the top one. It seemed to be the original lien that he'd signed nearly three years before. Patience, James Alexander had advised last spring. The run-up to war and the war itself, that's what the delay was about, that's why they had not yet succeeded in finding suitable land in the Islands. Things were bound to change eventually. Jesus bloody Christ, that was his signature on the bottom no mistaking it. "How did you get this?" The words came out high-pitched and shrill, like an old man's croak.

Hearing the shock in Hale's voice was a fine thing. Almost as fine as watching him go pale when he realized what he had in his hands. Telling him what had been done was even better. Hamish savored every word. "Wi' money, o' course. How else does a man get what he wants? Read the next one, why don't you? It's the making over o' the lien to me. Paid in full, it says. Right at the top."

John put down the first sheet and unfolded the second. "This is an outrage! It can have no standing before any judge in—"

"It's got every standing, you blighted bugger. Do you think I'd o' come here wi'out? Ha' you not yet figured what I've been doing in God-rotting Albany these past four years? Or how I've been planning and working for this since the day your father first showed me the place. It's mine, you twisted heretic. It's the Stewart Patent now."

Hamish reached for the papers, but this time John was the quicker. He grabbed them with one hand and crumpled them into a tight ball. Jumping to his feet he looked wildly around for a place to dispose of them. The fireplace was the obvious choice, but it was August. There was no fire.

Hamish's roar of laughter filled the room. "You're every bit the feeble-brained idiot Annie Crotchett says you are. What do you take me for, man? Do you think I'd hand o'er the only proof o' my ownership to you? Governor De Lancey had copies made o' the entire transaction. They're lodged wi' him, under his private seal. I said you'd an hour to get out. You've used the half o' it. If you want to take anything wi' you other than the clothes you're standing up in, you'd best see about packing."

John lunged. Hamish was expecting it. He moved quickly to one side, spinning around as he did so. They finished facing each other, the Scot with a dagger in his hand. John, with no weapon but his rage.

"Come on, you God-rotting heretic," Hamish taunted. "Come after me and I'll send you straight to hell where you belong. I canna wait to claim the privilege."

The last time John had seen a dagger of that sort it had been in his brother's hands, and, it was this very same Scots bastard who'd given it to him. "Quent!" The word burst forth like a curse. "My brother sent you here."

"Your brother's nothing to do wi' this. I'll deal wi' him as well. But later. Right now it's your turn." Hamish pushed forward; all his weight on his leading leg, and swung his arm in an underhanded thrust. The six-inch blade of the dirk sliced through the flesh of John's left underarm in an upward curve, severing the muscle and stopping at the bone of the shoulder.

John staggered backward, screaming in agony and collided with the brick of the fireplace wall. The heavy brass and iron poker hung on a hook. He swung it free with his right hand and lunged again, still screaming, swinging the poker above his head.

Hamish waited until the last possible second, then stepped to his left. John came after him again. He landed one blow that opened a cut above the Scot's empty eye socket. Hamish thrust forward, but this time the blade of the dirk sliced through only the cloth of John's shirt. Hamish twisted out of the way of the poker's next assault, skidded on a slick of blood, and went down.

John stood above him, one leg either side of the Scot's prone form, and raised the poker over his head.

Taba had crawled out from under the desk when the fight began. She didn't know when she'd reached for Mistress Lorene's silver scissors, but they were in her hand. Master John, he was going to kill Hamish. Hamish said he was her master now. But if he was dead, it was Master John again. And not a question in Taba's mind about which one was better.

She hurled herself at John's back, holding the scissors straight out in front of her. The poker began its descent toward Hamish's skull. The Scot snapped his legs wide apart, destroying both the force and the direction of the poker blow and bringing John Hale down in a sprawling heap; Hale's head hit the floor with such force the crack was audible. Hamish roared and sat up, ready to throw Hale's body off to the side. Taba had no opportunity to check her forward motion and no time to register the changed positions of the two men. The scissors plunged into Hamish's chest to the hilt of the fancy silver handles.

"Little George, take a wagon and go to the sawmill." Lorene's voice was like a cold wind cutting through the heat of hate in the room.

She had stood in the open door since her son's bloodcurdling scream had brought her running down from the linen room where she'd been folding blankets. The house slaves were all clustered behind her. She knew they were there without having to turn her head. They were straining to see over her shoulders into the chaos beyond. "Little George," she repeated, "you take a wagon and two fast horses. Go to the sawmill and get Sally Robin. Tell her Master John's been attacked and his arm's nearly cut off so she'll know what to bring. Clemency, take the child away. I don't think she's hurt."

For a few heartbeats nothing happened. The thought crossed Lorene's mind that perhaps no one would obey her.

Lorene was quite sure Taba had not just wounded Hamish Stewart, but killed him. The Scot's eye was open and staring at the ceiling and his chest wasn't moving. Taba had stabbed him to death with the silver scissors that had belonged to Lorene's grandmother Sally. They had been a gift from her mother on Lorene's wedding day. Like Sally Robin had been a gift from her father. Two special pieces of property to bring with her to Shadowbrook when she came as a bride. And now? Full circle perhaps. That had been the beginning of her life here and this might be the end, the moment when the slaves would decide to be slaves no longer. "Did you hear me, Little George?"

"I heared, mistress. I be back soon as ever I can be. With Sally Robin." His pounding steps ran down the hall toward the back door and the stable beyond.

Thank you, Lord. "Jeremiah, you and Sam had best see about getting the man who attacked Master John out of here. We'll bury him, but not up by Squirrel Oaks. Out behind the pigsty, I think. Hurry now." Her voice soft, cajoling rather than commanding. "Be harder to move him once he stiffens."

The men did not rush to obey her. Maybe Little George doing what he was bid was the last time she would be heeded in this house.

Lorene's heart pounded and her body trembled. She did not think her legs would hold her if she tried to move, but she knew she had to make the effort. One step, then two. She walked forward, toward her unconscious son and his dead assailant, still issuing orders in that soft, sure voice that betrayed none of her tur-moil. "Corn Broom Hannah and Runsabout, you'll help me with the master. We won't try to move him until Sally Robin comes, just make him comfortable. Kitchen Hannah, we'll need hot water to deal with his wound. Clemency, what are you waiting for? I told you, get that child out of here."

Taba hadn't moved. Lorene had no doubt of what the girl's intentions had been. She even knew why. That was perhaps the only part of what had happened here this evening she was sure she understood. "Clemency, do as I say. The child's all but lost her wits."

A third step. A fourth. Lorene did not turn around to see if the slaves were doing what they were told. She had reached her son and she knelt beside him and lifted his head onto her lap. Such a sweet baby, he'd been. Who would believe, knowing the man he'd grown to be, that she had so rejoiced in his survival? Her dear boy. At least that's what he'd been then. With one hand she pressed the edges of John's wound tightly together, and with the other used the skirt of her pink and white calico frock to begin sopping up the blood.

Clemency came in and bent down and gathered Taba into her arms and Lorene allowed herself a small, soundless sigh of relief. It would be fine now. As long as she had the Washerwoman on her side the others would surely follow. Clemency, Lorene knew, was the keeper of their souls.

Jeremiah and Six-Finger Sam came into the room and began dealing with the body. Lorene watched them, saying nothing, her thoughts a jumble of questions without answers. Hamish Stewart, almost a quarter century after he'd spent three weeks with them dead in her house, dead in her house at the hands of a Patent slave. Dear Lord, why? What had brought him here in the first place? What possible quarrel could he have with John? "Runsabout, those papers by the fireplace. Get them for me."

The girl did as she was told. Lorene looked up and smiled when she took the papers from Runsabout's hands, pleased by the slave's unquestioning obedience. Her heart was beating less furiously now. John was flushed and feverish, but he too was breathing easier and the bleeding had stopped. He would live and Sally Robin would know what to do for his arm. No more questions. Everything would be fine.

Chapter Twenty-Two

"SO, *MA SOEUR*, you have waited a long time for me, I am told."

"Not so long, *mon Général*. Four days only."

Nicole sat with her hands folded in her lap. Her veil was thrown back as it was worn inside the monastery. Mother Abbess had said she was not to cover her face. "You are, for these few days—a week perhaps, however long it is until you return to us—dispensed from your vows, Soeur Stephane. You will wear your habit because it will protect you, but you are, *en effet*, no longer . . ." She stopped, as if she could not bear to speak. The abbess had already explained that while she was away from the monastery Nicole's vow of enclosure would exist only in her heart. "Père Antoine says you must . . ." Finally Mère Marie Rose found the strength to ask the question that most tormented her. "*Ma petite*, after you do this thing that is, I am absolutely certain, the will of God, you will return to us?"

"*Bien sûr, ma Mère!*" Nicole had been astounded. "I have sworn. I would never break my word to Almighty God, or to you. Never. *Jamais, jamais, jamais.*"

"*Jamais*," the abbess repeated. Then, for the first time, she touched Nicole's cheek.

The little nun looked lost in her own thoughts. Montcalm cleared his throat to gain her attention. "The Grey Nuns have been treating you well?"

"*Oui, mon Général.* They have been entirely too kind." The sisters of Notre Dame had a home for foundlings and the destitute in the Hôpital Général of Montréal. It was a short walk from this grand house where for the past four days, since the marquis de Montcalm's return to the city, she had sat and waited for him to find time to see her. It had been arranged—by Père Antoine, she presumed, since he had arranged everything else—that the Grey Nuns would give her hospitality as long as she was in Montréal. The room they gave her was one reserved for visits from their benefactors, who, they assured her, were the finest families in

New France. It was no doubt so. The guest room of the Grey Nuns had a feather-bed, and numerous quilts piled high on a shelf within arm's reach. It was summer, she did not need the quilts, but she had slept under one each night. Just to remember how it felt. *Mon Dieu,* I am a wretched sinner. When I am back in my cloister I will beg for permission to take the discipline every night.

"I regret that you have been kept waiting, nonetheless. Now, Soeur Stephane, what have you brought me that was so urgent it could not be put in the hands of anyone else?" His aide had tried a number of times to take whatever it was she wanted to give the marquis, but the little nun was adamant.

The aide had reported her exact words. "I have sworn to Almighty God, monsieur. From my hand to that of Monsieur le Général."

Now that it was no longer necessary Nicole was embarrassed by her obstinacy. "I apologize, Monsieur le Général, but—"

Montcalm waved aside her words. "I understand, *ma Soeur.* You are a soldier under orders, no? And your *Général* is indeed the most high command to which we must all answer."

He had some charm, this man of war. But then, they always did. Papa had been charming as well. Before the barbarities of the battle and after it. It was only during battle that he, that all these soldiers, gave in to their animal nature. And how the crowds cheered them for it. The marquis de Montcalm had returned to Montréal in triumph. The entire populace stood in the street to welcome him with shouts of approval. Women threw flowers at his feet. As for the bloodshed and the desolation . . . War was always the same.

Nicole reached into the deep pocket of her brown habit and withdrew a narrow tube of black oilcloth no longer than the span of her two hands, and as thick as three of her fingers. It had been pinned inside so there was no danger of it being lost. Nicole had no idea what it was, only that she was charged to literally guard it with her life. *For the sake of a million souls, Soeur Stephane. For the glory of Almighty God and Holy Church and our Seraphic Order.* Of what value the life of one young woman compared to such a vast responsibility? None.

"I present you this on behalf of Père Antoine Rubin de Montaigne, the Delegate to New France of the Minister General of the Order of Friars Minor. Père Antoine begs to inform His Excellency that what is contained herein is of the utmost importance to the defense of New France." Every word exactly as she had been instructed. Nicole breathed a silent prayer of thanksgiving. The important part of this trial was over. She would deal with the many wounds to her conscience once she was back in her monastery.

"So, the defense of the whole empire? Nothing less? That is surely a heavy charge for such a young nun." Montcalm started to untie the ribbons that secured both ends of the tube of oilcloth.

"Not as heavy as yours, Monsieur le Général. I will pray every day for your success. And that this war might soon end." Nicole stood up. "If you will excuse me, it is time I returned to—"

"Sit down, *ma soeur*. I insist. I must show you at least some hospitality in return for your patience. And for your bringing me something so important it bears on the defense of all New France." The marquis rang the bell on his desk.

A footman appeared, so quickly she knew he had been waiting right outside the door. Nicole had no choice but to sit down.

"Bring some wine," Montcalm instructed. "And some of the biscuits we had yesterday. And some of those sugared almonds. *Vitement, s'il vous plaît.* We have kept the little nun waiting with no refreshments. She will wonder if we are all peasants here in Mont—"

"Monsieur le Général, please, I assure you, nothing is necessary. I must return to the Grey Nuns. They are expecting me."

"Of course. I will send you in my private carriage. And you will bring the good sisters some gifts as well. Two extra bottles of wine," Montcalm told the footman. "The Lafite of 1749. And biscuits and almonds for the Grey Nuns as well as for us. *Vite, vite!* What are you waiting for?"

The presence of the little nun calmed him. It was absurd. She was probably the age of his youngest daughter. But there was something about her. Something . . . Montcalm searched for the word. Gracious, he decided. She has a natural grace. And *mon Dieu*, I have seen little enough of grace these past days.

The house Montcalm had chosen as his headquarters overlooked the Champ-de-Mars. Today no soldiers drilled there. The parade ground was full of Indians, the Potawatomi and Nipissing and Ottawa and Huron who had been with him at Fort William Henry. And whatever captives remained. Some of the savages had ignored the bargain he'd offered before they left the killing ground they had made of his battlefield of honor.

The general rose from his chair and walked to the window, peering down at the activity below. Nicole watched him. He was not as tall as Papa had been, and his belly was round and stuck out too far. Not as impressive in his uniform as Papa had been in his. What would the marquis think if he knew she was the daughter of an English officer?

"Do you know what it is they are doing out there, *ma Soeur?*"

"I am told that on your instructions the government of New France is paying ransom to the Indians for the English captives. So that they may be returned to their homes."

"*Oui.* You are told correctly, *ma Soeur.*"

"It is a wonderful act of Christian charity, *mon Général*. You will be given a great reward in heaven."

"It is a pitiful gesture," Montcalm whispered. "An attempt to salve my conscience for what I must do in this barbaric place where my allies are savages without whom I cannot do my duty to my king."

Nicole did not think she must comment. He was looking out the window and he did not seem to speak to her. His French, she noted, had the lilt of Provence about it. Grandmère had once had a cook from that part of France. She too spoke in that singsong way, ending each word with what Nicole thought of as a little upturned breath. But the dishes that came from her kitchen . . . A *confit de canard* to which had been added cloves and garlic, and a thin bread topped with onions and tiny salted fish. Nicole sighed. More *culpas* to confess when she was again in Québec. Memories of such food were not appropriate for a Poor Clare.

Montcalm turned away from the bustle on the Champs-de-Mars. Nothing to be gained by watching. Or reproaching himself still further. Attend to the little nun. "So where is that footman with our *goûter*? Ah, he arrives just as I mention him. Excellent. Leave everything. I will serve the good sister myself."

The servant set the tray on a gilt side table and left the room. The general busied himself with pouring wine into two small goblets of exquisite crystal. "It is from my private cellar, *ma Soeur*. I cannot say from my very own vineyards. At Candiac—that is my home in Provence—I have magnificent olives and almonds, but not great grapes. Our soil and our climate are not the friends of wine that one finds in Bordeaux. Try this, *ma Soeur*. You will enjoy it, I'm sure."

She could not refuse the wine the marquis de Montcalm had himself poured for her. One sip only. A little one. Then she would find a way to dispose of what was left. A small penance, because— *Mon Dieu.* How long since she had tasted such a wine. "It is truly delicious, Monsieur le Général. Truly."

"Yes, it is. These almonds, as well. We grow them at Candiac, then we send them to Montargis to be sugar-coated. Do you know them?"

"When I was a girl, my Grandmère . . ." No, she must not speak of such things. She had made her choices. "The abbess of my monastery, Mère Marie Rose, she is from a place not far from Montargis. She entered the Poor Clares there. Before she came to Québec to make our foundation. Do you know our monastery, Monsieur le Général? We are very small and poor, but—"

"I am told you are very holy women, you Poor Clares." Montcalm's mood suddenly changed. He almost whispered the next words. "I require your prayers, Soeur Stephane."

"We pray for our brave soldiers every day, Monsieur le Général. You can rely on that."

"And for me personally. Will you be my personal emissary to *le bon Dieu, ma Soeur*?"

"*Absolument, mon Général.*"

"*Bon.*" Montcalm returned to his desk. He shot another quick glance toward the parade ground where the conclusion to the filthy business that had ended the battle of Fort William Henry was taking place. At least as much of a conclusion as he could arrange. He could not restore to life dead women and children, or unarmed soldiers massacred in cold blood after he had given his word they would depart unharmed. "The prayers of a Poor Clare. I shall sleep better for knowing I have them. Now, you have not finished your wine, *ma Soeur.* Come, we will drink a toast. *Vive le roi. Vive la France.*"

She could not refuse to drink a toast to the king and to France. Nicole drained her glass.

"Now, let me see what you have brought me." Montcalm sounded again like a commander-in-chief. He opened the tube of oilcloth and spread the paper it contained on his desk and leaned forward, studying it. After some moments he reached for a magnifying glass. "Then I will myself take you in a carriage back to the convent of the good Grey Sisters. And we will bring them two bottles of this excellent Bordeaux as well as some of—"

Nicole could see that what she had brought the general was a drawing, but from where she sat, not what kind. Nor could she imagine why any drawing would be the key to the salvation of a million souls. She did not wish to know. It was not her place or her responsibility. *Mon Dieu,* I wish only to return to my cloister. But did she? Sitting here with the taste of that exquisite wine still in her mouth, was she not so tempted never to return that the temptation, even if resisted, was itself a sin?

General Montcalm rang the bell on his desk. The footman arrived. Something had changed. Nicole knew it. She could tell that the footman did as well, simply by the way he stood as he waited for instructions. "Take the good nun downstairs and put her in a carriage. Send my compliments to the Grey Nuns, along with two bottles of the Lafite. *Adieu, ma Soeur. Merci.*"

He did not look at her when he said goodbye. And he had forgotten about the sugared Montargis almonds for the Grey Nuns, or that he was going to go with her to their convent. Nicole knew how thrilled the sisters would have been to have such a visit. Too bad. "*Adieu, mon Général. Je vous remercie.*"

She started to follow the footman out of the room. Montcalm's voice stopped her. "Soeur Stephane, a moment longer." Nicole turned to look at him. "*S'il vous plaît, ma Soeur . . .*" he added in a whisper.

She had to go closer to the desk to hear him. "*Oui, mon Général?*"

He was staring not at her but at the thing she had brought him. It was a map, a nautical chart of some sort. She could not help but recognize such things; she was a child of the military, after all. Nicole wanted to squeeze her eyes shut. I do not wish to know what it is that has so changed the mood of this powerful man, *mon*

Dieu, Or why it is so important that Père Antoine and Mother Abbess sent me out of the cloister and away from my vows. Do not ask me to know such things.

"You will not forget to pray for me, Soeur Stephane?"

"Never. You have my word."

Montcalm nodded and made a gesture of dismissal, and Nicole followed the footman out the door. In the carriage she busied herself telling her beads. She refused to think about the fact that for some reason best known to himself, Père Antoine had sent to General Montcalm as a matter of the greatest urgency a chart of the waters around Québec Lower Town.

FRIDAY, AUGUST 31, 1757
THE HALIFAX CITADEL IN NOVA SCOTIA

Much had changed in l'Acadie. Most of the Acadians were gone; English land was no longer crawling with French spies and sympathizers. But much was the same. The blasted infernal miserable weather was as dreadful as Lord Loudoun had been told while still in London. "The weather might play you havoc, John. But we're quite sure you'll prevail."

John Campbell, earl of Loudoun, the man sent to replace General Braddock and take charge of the war, was less sure. Fog for the entire month he'd been here, and before that his great invasion fleet, more than a hundred ships under sail and carrying six thousand troops, had sat in New York Harbor waiting for its naval escort. He'd left without the escort in the end, though the ships had caught up with them when they were halfway to Halifax, and they'd arrived without incident. Didn't make any difference. More bloody waiting, that's all; this time for the navy reconnaissance ships that were to tell him what exactly he faced farther north at Louisbourg.

Sweet Christ, not more than he could handle, he hoped. Louisbourg was the object of the exercise, the first stone that must fall if Canada was to be taken. A hundred nights running he'd studied the situation—more, if he counted the time in London doing the planning. Built on a tongue of land between Cape Breton and the open Atlantic, Louisbourg faced a sea that boiled like a cauldron where it met an iron coast, continually white with foam and shooting jets of spray that disappeared into a mist that never entirely went away. And if the natural conditions weren't miserable enough, there was the wall. More than five leagues of wall. Surrounding a town that housed four thousand people and was garrisoned with three battalions of French regulars, one of the poxed *Volontaires Etrangers*—the formidable Canadian troops—two companies of artillery, and a varying number of woodsmen.

"In all, some three thousand troops," Admiral Holburne said. "Besides officers, of course." Holburne and Loudoun sat across from each other at the dining table in the governor's mansion, which Loudoun had commandeered on his arrival.

"Of course." Loudoun's stomach growled. Sweet Christ, he hadn't waited this long only to be told what he already knew: the size of the garrison had not changed. Another, louder protest from his belly. Had to be the beef at lunch. Tough as hide. And the delay, of course. More than a month lost to foul weather would turn any man's stomach. But however long the news had taken to get here, it wasn't bad. No major reinforcements at Louisbourg meant his force outnumbered the enemy two to one. "And in the harbor?" he asked.

Admiral Holburne did not look at him. The better part of a second bottle of Rhenish wine was gone. At the moment the naval man's glass was empty. They were ashore in the governor's mansion. Loudon had commandeered it upon his arrival, and in these circumstances Loudoun outranked Holburne and was host; he leaned forward and poured a refill for the admiral. "Come on, man. Might as well tell me. What's waiting for us in the harbor?"

"Eighteen French ships of the line, fully armed. And five frigates."

Loudoun set down the wine and stared at his guest. He opened his mouth, then closed it again. He'd been told to expect three ships, maybe four, no frigates. Eighteen fully armed ships of the line. Jesus bloody Christ.

Holburne mopped his face with a linen pocket cloth. The man perspired in visible showers. Repulsive and fascinating at the same time. "We tried to prevent them getting through," he said. "We could not. Most arrived in the past fortnight. The weather . . ."

Loudoun got to his feet and walked to the window. Nearly the entire French fleet had come to bulwark Louisbourg while he'd sat waiting for the British navy to pull their thumbs from their own arses. There was bright sun now. And the sky as blue as a tart's best cloak, not a cloud to be seen. He'd been here well before the reinforcements and it availed him nothing. The weather had defeated— Perhaps not. Perhaps he was being an old woman. He spun around. "Holburne, as one military man to another, tell me what you think about the situation."

Before today Holburne had known Loudoun only by reputation. A Scot by birth, but a Campbell, a clan that frequently sided with the crown. And look what it got them. Those the other Highlanders didn't slaughter became earls and commanded his majesty's forces in America. "It's entirely your decision, milord. The fleet will support you in whatever plan you follow."

Loudoun returned to the table and leaned on it with both arms, forcing the other man to look straight at him. "Don't mouth porridge at me, Admiral. I asked what you think. For the love of God, man, there's no one here but the pair of us. Express yourself."

The Scot's face was as white as the ruffled stock below his chin. For his part Holburne knew he was the color of raw beef. Damned wine always made him hot as a whore's tit.

"I see you're not going to answer me, Admiral." Loudoun straightened and reached for the bottle. Only one glass remained and he poured it for himself. "I can't compel you. I just thought it might help to hear your—"

"There's no hope of succeeding, milord. Not at any attempt on Louisbourg at this late season of the year." The words were out of his mouth before he knew he was going to speak them. Cowardice, failing to do one's utmost against the enemy, was a capital offense. It meant a firing squad. Holburne poured sweat.

Loudoun didn't speak for long seconds; when he did, his voice was low and even. "Very well. Let me ask another question. What about Québec?"

"What about it, milord?"

"Could we take it? Bypass Louisbourg, where they expect the battle, and go straight to the heart of the matter. One devastating blow that will bring New France to its knees." He had been toying with the idea for the last couple of days. Probably the wine talking, and his frustration at the long delay. "What about it, man? Could we take Québec?"

The admiral mopped his face. He could feel beads of sweat dripping from his nose and his chin. "Not without taking Louisbourg first, milord. And even then . . ."

"Yes."

"My honest opinion, sir, as a man of the sea, is that we can never take Québec with warships. We can't get through La Traverse, the channel that lies off—"

"I know where the bloody passage lies, Admiral." There was a real edge to his voice now. Does the thought of any battle turn your britches brown Holburne? "But if we are never to take Québec, how are we to win this war?"

"By containing them up there, milord. By making the French withdraw to their fortress city and leave everything else to us. To do that we must take Louisbourg."

Sensible advice and what Loudoun's better judgment also told him. Québec was forever out of reach. Louisbourg was indispensable to victory. But nothing could change the fact that the entire campaign season had been lost to him. He pulled a square of linen from his sleeve. "Here man, use this. Your own is sodden. And thank you for your honest advice. I value it."

"Milord, I don't mean that I won't—"

"Do your duty. I know that. What's at issue here is my duty, Admiral, not yours. Thanks to your intelligence I learn that I must attempt to bring ashore on one of the most dangerous coasts on this continent nearly His Majesty's entire regular army in America. And I must do it facing a naval force superior to that you can provide me, under constant threat of the worst weather Almighty God has sent to plague Christendom, at a time of year when it can be counted upon to deteriorate from whatever parlous state we find it in when we arrive. It becomes rather clear put that way, doesn't it, Admiral?"

Holburne nodded.

Loudoun drank the last of the Rhenish and went to the door. Two heavily armed marines waited in the hall. "You there, find Captain James and tell him I want him. Immediately."

When the door was again closed, Holburne asked: "May I know your decision, milord?"

"You may. I shall tell James to prepare the fleet to sail."

"For Louisbourg?"

"No, of course not for Louisbourg. You are entirely correct, sir; it is far too late to undertake a campaign against Louisbourg. We shall return to the godforsaken province of New York in the stubborn and ungrateful and barbaric American colonies. God alone knows what we'll find when we get there, but it can't be any worse that what we're leaving behind."

LEAF FALLING MOON, THE NINTH SUN
THE VILLAGE OF SINGING SNOW

"We have waited long to see you, my bridge person son."

"I have been far away, Father. It took time to return to the home of my heart."

Bishkek made a sound of disgust. "Many times I am told you were seen in Québec. It is not such a great distance between that city and this fire."

Cormac had expected the reproach. He could not tell his manhood father that he had been as far south as Carolina looking for a white woman. "I found the hawk, Father. The one in my dream. At least I think it was that one."

"It is not likely that you will have been sent to look for two hawks. So?"

Corm shook his head. "He told me many things, but I still do not know who the white bear is. Kwashko says it is him, but—"

"My other whiteface son is a red bear, is he not? Has his hair turned white since I saw him?"

"No, Father. He is still Uko Nyakwai. That is why . . . But even if he is correct, I do not know if the threat to the little birds is finished."

"Red Bear," Bishkek muttered. "Disgusting name." They squatted near a cooking pot suspended over a fire tended by one of Bishkek's many daughters. "*Wisnawen,*" the old man demanded, "*yawukne?*" The squaw shook her head. The food was not yet ready. Bishkek stood. "Come, we must go to see someone."

"Who?"

"The squaw priest."

"The one who nearly stabbed me?"

"Nearly is not important. The flint did not go into your heart, did it?"

"No but—"

There was no wind, but an unseasonably biting cold. Bishkek pulled the blanket he wore closer around his shoulders. "Come. Otherwise by the time we return the food will be cold."

They began walking. Bishkek looked up at the sky. It was gray and heavy. *"Pkon,"* he muttered. *"Nagic."* Snow soon. "My bridge person son must not be here when the snow comes."

"Leaf Falling is too early for snow."

"Perhaps the clouds do not know which moon it is. Perhaps they do not care. Tomorrow or the next day it will snow. You must leave before the first flakes come."

"You always say that. But I am not a squaw or a child. It does not matter if it snows. If I want to leave, I can still—"

"Be quiet. Do you think you are the only one who has dreams?"

They had walked as far as the dome-shaped wickiup the village had erected for Shabnokis the Midè squaw priest. Having her near Singing Snow was a good thing; not having her actually living among them was even better. Everyone knew that the priests of the Midewiwin often caused trouble.

There was no sign of Shabnokis, but they could hear her chanting. *"Wa hi, hi, hi. Haya, haya."*

"She is praying," Corm said. "Better we go away and come back tomorrow." He wasn't sure why the thought of another session with Shabnokis was so unpleasant, only that it was.

"I already told you, you must leave tomorrow."

"Yes, before the snow." Corm's tone made it obvious how unlikely he thought that to be. "But the priest is busy. She won't like it if we—"

"She chants because she knows we're here. So we'll be impressed with how holy she is. Praying all the time even when no one is around." Bishkek cupped his hands around his mouth. *"Ho! Jebye. Kteshyamin."* We have come.

The chant stopped and the blanket that covered the door of the wickiup was pushed aside. Shabnokis looked older than Corm remembered her. Her hair was entirely white and she wore it in two plaits that hung over her shoulders. "Why do you make so much noise? I knew you were coming and I know you are here. I was praying for that one, the scar-face." She jerked her head in Corm's direction, but spoke of him as if he were not present. "He needs prayers."

Bishkek's look darkened. "Then make many prayers. As many as he needs." *Ayi!* Just like the Midewiwin. Always reminding you how important they were.

And impossible to know when they spoke the truth and when they were only boasting. Still, better to be sure. "Many prayers," he repeated. "I will send an elk-skin tomorrow. It will snow soon. You will need it."

Shabnokis cocked her head at the gray sky. "Leaf Falling is too early for snow."

So, she did not know as much as he did. Nonetheless. "I did not come here to talk about the weather. Tell my son what you told me."

Shabnokis shrugged. "I have told you and the others many things. Besides, I am old and I forget much."

"Two elkskins," Bishkek promised.

"Father, I don't—"

"Be quiet. I brought you here to listen, not to talk."

Shabnokis came toward them. "Good skins," she said. "Not shabby with half the fur gone."

"The best," Bishkek assured her.

The squaw priest squatted on the ground and motioned the two men to join her. Corm tried to keep his distance, but Bishkek pushed him closer. The woman wore a buckskin shirt much like that of a *coureur de bois*. The laces that closed the neck were not done up and he could see the wrinkled skin of the flat place above her drooping breasts. No whole-skin otter bag. Maybe she left it in the wickiup because she knew this wasn't a ceremonial visit. Meaning Bishkek must have arranged everything ahead of time. Which was a little odd since Corm had arrived in Singing Snow without warning and not more than an hour earlier.

"A priest of my lodge, a Miami, died in Thunder Moon. Before the Telling," Shabnokis said. Corm realized he had lately been too long and too steadily among the *Cmokmanuk*. He automatically translated that to two months ago, early July. "I was among those who attended his ending."

The squaw priest closed her eyes and began humming softly to herself. "*Wa, hi, hi, hi.* It was a bad ending," she whispered. "He died slowly, with his belly on fire. Before the spirit left him he kept repeating the same thing. *Papankamwa, esipana, ayaapia, anseepikwa, eeyeelia, pileewa.*"

"Those are Miami words," Bishkek supplied.

"I know." Corm looked from his manhood father to the squaw priest. She had just repeated the Miami names for racoon, elk buck, spider, fox, possum, and turkey, the symbols carved on the Suckáuhock. It was not possible that Bishkek could have told her those things. For one thing he would never betray Cormac. Never. For another, he didn't have the information. Bishkek had always refused to look at the Súki beads. Corm's heart began hammering in his chest. "This priest who died, was he named Takito?" Genevieve Lydius's priest, who'd put Cormac to sleep for three days and nearly got him killed.

"No, I told you before. The one called Takito is not from my lodge. I would never be at his ending. This one was—" Shabnokis broke off. "He is not yet dead six moons. I cannot speak his name. It is anyway not important. *Eehsipana, ayaapia*—"

"You already told me the six animal names. What else did he say?"

Bishkek made a sound of disapproval. *"Cmokman,"* he muttered softly under his breath, hoping Cormac would be reminded that he was acting white, not showing proper respect. Then, louder so the squaw priest would be sure to hear, "Two elkskins, remember. The very best."

Shabnokis shrugged. She would allow the scar-face's impertinence to pass, at least this time. "The fire in the dying priest's belly," she said, "it came from two things. One was the evil spirit who was slowly taking away his life. It was so big a spirit that his belly stuck out this much." She used her hands to indicate a great swelling. "The other was from the shame of making a bargain with a *Cmokman* dog turd priest and not keeping his word."

Ayi! Finally some information he could use, though Corm was pretty sure he could guess the rest of the story. "What bargain?"

The squaw priest grunted to show her disapproval of yet another interruption, then continued. "A long time ago the priest of my lodge went to Québec. He met with a dog turd priest and told him that the Miami chief Memetosia was in Albany at a powwow with the other tribe, the English *Cmokmanuk.*"

That meant the Midè and Christian priests had met in 1754, the same year Memetosia gave him the Suckáuhock. Corm's chest roiled and his heart thudded against his ribs. "You said they made an agreement. What—"

Shabnokis turned to Bishkek. "Did you never teach this one any manners?"

"Comamden ezhawepsiyan." He can't help being as he is. "Three elkskins." Then, so she wouldn't think he made too easy a bargain: "Small ones."

"Big," she corrected.

"If big, only two."

For a moment it seemed she would continue to haggle, then Shabnokis waved her hand to dismiss the discussion. "Two big," she agreed. "When he was in Québec the Midè priest promised the dog turd he would get him something rare, something that would make many *Anishinabeg* do his will. He said so when he was dying. We all heard it. Next he told how he had tried to keep his word, but he couldn't do it. The brave he sent to get the thing he had promised never returned. Even though the priest of my lodge had told the brave that a terrible curse would be on him and his family if he did not."

"He couldn't return," Corm said quietly. "I took his scalp and left his body in the river to feed the fish."

Shabnokis nodded. "So the spirits told me. That is why I repeated this thing to your manhood father."

"Two more questions," Corm said. Bishkek sighed, but Shabnokis did not demand any more elkskins. "This Midè priest," Corm asked, "the one who died, what did the *Cmokman* priest give him in return? Why would he agree to betray the *Anishinabeg* in this way?"

"For money. To buy firewater." She turned her head and spat on the ground. "He could not live without firewater. And that is what made an evil spirit come into his belly and grow it out to here." This time her hands made the swelling even bigger.

"*Ahaw.*" Corm had no difficulty believing that a man could need alcohol more than he needed life or honor. He had seen such things before, and not just among Indians. "Do you know the name of the priest?"

"I told you, he is not dead six moons. I cannot—"

"Not him. The *Cmokman.*" It had to be the one they called Père Antoine. Philippe Faucon had told him that the Franciscan was some kind of spy for the English.

Shabnokis shook her head. "I never heard his name. I know only that he was a black robe and—"

"No, a brown robe! It must be a brown robe!"

"Do you think I have so many elkskins that you can be as rude as you wish?" Bishkek exploded.

"Stop berating him," Shabnokis said. "It is as you said. He cannot help being as he is. There is too much white in him to change."

Corm leaned forward, making sure she could see into his eyes. "My heart"— he put his hand over his chest—"my heart is *Anishinabeg.* All that I do is for the good of the Real People."

"*Ahaw,*" the squaw priest agreed softly. "I know. That is what the spirits say. But the dog turd who made the bargain with the priest from my lodge was a black robe. The highest of the black robes. I cannot change the truth to make it what you want to hear."

Corm started to get up. He needed to be alone, to think through this information. "Thank you. I will—"

"Wait. There is something else."

"What else?"

"Only two elkskins," Bishkek warned. "Big ones, but only two."

"Two," Shabnokis confirmed. "Anyway, this is for your bridge person son. The spirits have told me to tell him this: The one you are looking for, the squaw. She eats *kokotni.*"

Cormac stared at her. *Kokotni* was alligator.

"Why do you look so black and eat so little?" Bishkek demanded. "Is my daughter's food no good in your belly?" More than half Corm's portion of dried corn stewed with venison was uneaten.

"Lashi's food is fine, Father. My thoughts fill me up and leave no room for eating."

"A black robe, not a brown," Bishkek said softly. "This is important?"

"It means that for two years I have been watching the wrong priest."

The old man shrugged. "So now you can watch the right one. The spirits tell us things in their time, not ours. They do not make mistakes. Besides, it is good to know about the one you thought was a Huron, no? That too was something you did not know before."

"Yes. It is very good to know that. I had already figured out that when she said not all trees with red leaves were sumacs, she meant the brave might only be pretending to be a Huron, but now . . . It is better to have the whole story, not just a part."

"*Ahaw.* The Suckáuhock that Memetosia gave you, you still have it?" Bishkek nodded toward the medicine bag around Corm's neck. "I see you still have the medicine bag with the Crane People's symbols."

"Yes, but only one bead is left. *Pileewa,* the turkey."

"And the others?"

"I have given them away. To the chiefs of different tribes."

"And are those gifts the reason it is said that in the *pays d'en haut* the *Anishinabeg* will accept no more war belts from Onontio?"

"Perhaps." Lashi had come to collect his uneaten food and she looked at him reproachfully. Corm murmured an apology.

Bishkek waited until the squaw was gone before continuing. "And is your gift the reason they have the dying-without-skin illness in the *pays d'en haut*? Our own people and the Nipissing and Ottawa and Huron, they are all sick with this thing. Did the Súki beads bring them a curse?"

"*Co!* The beads are from our past. They are a treasure, not a curse." Corm realized that Bishkek had been puzzling over this question for some time. "The dying-without-skin disease, Father, is a white man's disease. They call it smallpox. No one knows where it comes from, but—"

"Sickness comes from the spirits. How can you be sure it was not your gift that—"

"Father, smallpox can be passed to another person if he touches something that belonged to one who was already sick. I have heard it said that in the Fort called William Henry there were many soldiers sick with smallpox. And the *Anishinabeg* who fought there took scalps. So maybe—"

"The scalps they won, honorably, in battle, that is what gives them the dying-without-skin disease?"

"I think so. *Ahaw.*"

Bishkek was silent for a long time. If your enemy could kill you even after he was dead and you took his scalp, what kind of a world would this be? This was the purpose of a bridge person, to explain one side to the other. Sometimes, though, he would rather not have the explanation. Some questions, he decided, are not just too big to answer, they are too big to ask. "Come, we will smoke. But not with the others yet." The men of the village had gathered around a large fire and were passing a pipe. "Here first. By ourselves."

Cormac watched the old man prepare a pipe and light it from the embers of Lashi's cooking fire. Bishkek took the first deep puff, then passed the pipe to him. Corm drew the fragrant smoke into his mouth, held it, then exhaled in the rings that in the past had so amused the young boys of the village. "Tell me something," Bishkek said, smiling when he saw the smoke shapes in the firelight. "What Shabnokis said about *kokotni,* what did she mean?"

Ayi! He should have known the old man wouldn't let that pass without comment. "I knew a woman. I have been looking for her. I think the squaw priest was trying to tell me where she is."

"This *kokotni,* it is a beast I have heard about, but I have never seen it."

"It is a fierce thing that lives in the rivers far south of here. I've never seen it either," Corm admitted. "Only heard stories."

"And this woman, is she a squaw or a white woman?"

"White." He would not lie to the old man, though he knew how much Bishkek hoped his manhood sons would choose squaws as wives and bring them to live in Singing Snow.

"She must be very brave if she eats this fierce beast."

"Or very hungry." Corm smoked, then looked over at the others who sat, and smoked and spoke of better things. He could hear the laughter. "The youngest son of my sister Lashi, I wish to send him on a journey."

Bishkek turned and looked for the boy called Pondise, Winter, because he had been born in the moon of No Sun. "How long a journey? He has only just passed to manhood."

"It is a far way," Corm admitted. "He will be gone for two moons, perhaps. But if he is clever, it won't be dangerous. I cannot do it myself because I must return to Québec and see if I can learn more about the black robe."

"Pondise is very clever. And he often hunts alone, going a far distance, and always returns with a kill. But you must speak with his manhood father if you wish to send him away. I do not have authority over him any longer."

In the end it was decided; Pondise would go on the journey the bridge person wished him to take. Corm could see how excited the young man was at the

prospect, even though he tried hard to look grown-up and impassive. "If you succeed in this thing it will be good for all the *Anishinabeg*," Corm promised.
Pondise did not say anything, but he stood very tall.

The next day Corm took Pondise to the edge of the village and spent a long
time telling him what he must do and how he was to do it. He drew maps indicating the location of New York City and how Pondise would get there. And they
discussed how he would protect himself in that great city of the *Cmokmanuk*.
Finally Corm wrote a note on a strip of bark and put it in a medicine bag he hung
around the boy's neck. "Only to Kwashko," he cautioned. "You must give the message to no one else."

There were no clouds that day, but when the sun was as high as it got in this
Leaf Falling Moon, Bishkek came to where Cormac and Pondise spoke, looking
agitated. "Have you not finished yet? My bridge person son must leave. You told
me you had to get to Québec, to find out about the black robe. Why are you still
here?"

"I thought tomorrow—" Corm began.

"*Co!* Not tomorrow, now. Go. I am your manhood father, do you openly dis-
obey me?"

Corm had no idea why the old man was so agitated, but he knew that somehow his presence was the cause. "I will leave as soon as I have eaten, Father."

Bishkek looked up at the sun and nodded agreement.

The clouds rolled in while they ate the midday meal. Then came the squalling
winds. The first snow fell just as Corm stood up to go. Bishkek saw two flakes
catch in the eyelashes of his bridge person son as they said goodbye. He watched
Corm walk away, and only when he could see him no longer did a tear escape and
make its way down his seamed old cheek.

His dream had been very explicit: If here in this village the snow falls on the
child of Pohantis, you will never again see him alive.

Chapter Twenty-Three

THE FRIGATES OF Loudoun's failed expedition to Louisbourg flanked either side of the entrance to the outer harbor. The vessels rode at anchor, every sale furled, nonetheless they took a considerable amount of wind. The two-masted schooner *Catherine Rose* had to trim canvas and tack repeatedly to navigate the channel. Devil it matters, the schooner's captain thought. The tide's behind me, the sun bright gold overhead, and the ocean's like a turquoise bauble in the belly of a honey-skinned whore. " 'Tis a fine day to come home, I warrant, Mr. Hale," he called out.

His only paying passenger leaned on the forrard rail, eyes fastened on the oncoming shore. "A fine day indeed, Captain," Quent called back. "Mighty fine. And my thanks for an equally fine voyage."

A remarkable voyage. They had not once seen a French flag. God bless the Royal Navy; they had virtually blockaded the entire Atlantic. And what the navy might miss, those legal pirates, the American privateers, did not. Thanks to them, the *Catherine Rose* had sailed home without incident, and both the captain and his passenger brought back the cargo they'd gone after.

The schooner was laden with the finest goods London had to offer, and three men and five women who had given themselves into ten years' bondage to pay their passage. The captain would sell them as indentured servants in New York for at least six times what it cost to bring them across the ocean. By long tradition the profit of that venture was his own. As for the hard goods, the silks and satins and fine furniture and kegs of port and malmsey, they would be offered at the Exchange. Four fifths of whatever return they made would be divided among the half dozen or so men who had formed the consortium that built his ship. Out of what remained he had to pay the crew and bear the cost of any necessary refit.

Not to worry, he told himself again. He'd do well enough this time. What with the indentures and the extra thirty guineas the man they called the Red Bear had paid for passage, well enough indeed.

Quent's cargo was of a different sort, but he was equally satisfied. "A fine day," he called out again though no one was paying him any attention.

The crew were busy in the rigging, reefing still more sail, slowing the ship's passage through the narrows and into the inner harbor. Quent heard the call, "Helmsman! Two degrees starboard!" and felt the almost immediate response as the *Catherine Rose* picked up a northeasterly tack and headed for the southern tip of Manhattan. Half an hour later he stood on West Dock with the city spread out in front of him—it didn't look anywhere near as big or as important after nearly four months in London—waiting for his land legs to return, and trying to remember what direction he must take to get to the governor's mansion.

There was a crush on the dock, people coming and going. Still, compared to London, not much of a crowd. A man jostled his elbow and Quent moved aside. The man followed, tugging this time at the tails of Quent's fine green velvet coat. He'd bought it before he sailed for London and worn it ever since. Indeed, he'd become so accustomed to the close fit of satin breeches he almost didn't remember the feel of buckskin trousers.

"Mr. Hale? 'Scuse me, sir. This be for you."

Quent took the folded slip of paper. *Please allow Pipps to escort you to my home. It is a matter of some urgency.* The note was signed *B. D.* Quent's brow furrowed.

"Bede Devrey," the messenger offered helpfully. "Your uncle, sir." He was a small ferret of a white man, probably an indenture, and barely reaching to Quent's elbow. Two of his teeth were so elongated they looked like fangs.

"I take it you're Pipps?"

"I am, sir." The man looked around furtively. "It's best if we move on, sir. There's others might know you were on the *Catherine Rose*."

"Indeed. Does that matter?"

"I think it does, sir. Your uncle gave me to understand it did, sir."

"Very well, let's move on, then."

Pipps made a gesture toward Quent's bag, but Quent hefted the canvas satchel before the other man could touch it. They headed toward an alley on the right. Quent sensed Pipps' relief as they disappeared into its shadows.

"Thank you for coming, Nephew."

"Your note said a matter of some urgency. My mother—"

"My sister is well. She came to see me a fortnight past, and spent three days with us. It is John who has been ill."

Quent shrugged. No point in pretending concern for John's health. Everyone knew the bad blood between them.

"Your brother has lost the use of his left arm. He was ill of the wound for many weeks, but I'm told you have a clever herbalist at Shadowbrook who—"

"Sally Robin. As clever an herbalist as can be found."

"That, it appears, is true. And fortunate for John. He will live, though as I said, with only one arm that's any use to him."

"Thank you for informing me." But that's not why you plucked me off the dock like some special treasure, much less why my mother made one of her rare visits to her girlhood home. "May I ask how you knew I was on the *Catherine Rose*, Uncle? I didn't think her to be a Devrey ship."

Bede chuckled. "She's not, more's the pity. But once you were on the water you were in my world, Nephew. It's my business to know what's afloat and where it's headed." They spoke in his office, on the ground floor of the grand Wall Street house built by his father, the slaver Will Devrey. The walls were hung with drawings of Devrey ships and the charts that tracked their passage. The fleet had grown to twenty-three vessels, and since his father's death, Bede Devrey, the eldest son, owned the lot.

"Yes, of course. But in that case . . . The governor is expecting me, sir. At least he is expecting that I will report straight to him the moment I return. If you knew I was to arrive, he must—"

"It will be a cold day in hell, Nephew, when I don't know more than James De Lancey about what an Atlantic tide will wash up on these shores. Now, let me get you a glass of something. Nancy will wait dinner until our business is done." Apparently he still wasn't prepared to say what that business might be. "Your voyage was untroubled?"

"Entirely so. The Atlantic is ours."

"The shipping is safe enough these days. But here on land . . . Brandy, do you? Not too early in the day?"

"Never too early for your fine brandy, Uncle. Thank you."

"Welcome indeed. Health, lad. And the family." Both men lifted the bulbous glasses into which Bede had poured a generous portion of the pale gold spirit. The heady scent was as pleasurable as the first taste. Quent had been offered nothing as good in all his time in London.

"Last of the French cognac in my cellar," Bede commented after the first smooth sip. "And sad to say, there's no hope of replenishing it until this damnable war's done. That arrogant Scot, Loudoun . . . Can't see why London leaves him here. The bugger sailed off to take Louisbourg in June, already too late if you ask me, and came back three months later empty-handed, with his tail between his legs."

Quent kept his face impassive. Loudoun was to be recalled—the letter informing James De Lancey of that fact was in his bag—but Quent said nothing. Not
until he knew if this summons had to do with his uncle wanting information
rather than having any to share. "The news about Louisbourg reached London
just before I left. A shame."

"Worse. A disgrace. Meanwhile . . . I take it you heard as well about the massacre at Fort William Henry?"

"I did."

"Well? What do you think of—"

"Papa," the door burst open. A young man stood there, tall and slim, with hair
as red as Quent's, proof that both were descended from the woman known as Red
Bess, their great-aunt. "Papa, Mama wants to know how long you'll be. So she
knows about the dinner."

"I see. And she sent you, not one of your sisters, to inquire?"

"Actually, she sent Celeste, but—"

"I thought that more likely."

"But I told her I'd go."

"Indeed." Bede turned to his guest. "You're the attraction, you realize. My children
are bursting to get a look at the legendary Uko Nyakwai. You remember Samuel?"

"Of course." Quent stood and offered his hand. The boy shook it fiercely. This
one was a twin, Quent reminded himself, though he looked nothing like his
brother. And there were two little girls. At least they had been little when he last
saw them. Must be young ladies now. "How are you, Sam?"

"Well, thank you. Cousin Quentin, at dinner, will you tell us about the Indians? They say you know all the terrible things they do. And that you went to London to tell the government how we can make them pay for the massacre up at
Fort William Henry. You'll tell us all about it, won't you?"

"I left for London before that fort fell, Sam. And because the Indians are different from us doesn't make them wrong and us right."

The boy's eyes darkened. "But up at Lake George, they—"

"It's Bright Fish Water." Quent couldn't help himself. The thought that young
men in New York City were learning to call a part of the Patent by a false name,
along with all the other untruths they were raised on—that the tribes were heathen savages, never to be trusted, filthy—it grated on him. "That lake's on Hale
land. It's always been called by the old Mahican name, Bright Fish Water."

"All the same, what I mean is that—"

"Go away, Samuel." Something had obviously changed Bede's mood from
indulgent father to head of the house. "Tell your mother I will inform her about
dinner as soon as I can."

"But Papa, I only want to know if—"

"Go!"

The boy left, shutting the door behind him. Bede apologized for the interruption. "I'm not bothered," Quent said. "Growing up in a big city like this, he must be curious about the rest of the province. Particularly knowing that the Patent is in the family. Maybe he—"

"It's not."

"I'm sorry, Uncle Bede. I've lost the drift. What's not?"

"Shadowbrook, it's no longer in the family. That's what your mother came to talk to me about, and why I had to see you before the bloody governor did. Your brother has pissed everything away. The De Lanceys' have gotten control of the Hale Patent."

"Are you a card-playing man, nephew?"

Quent shook his head. He'd eaten little of the excellent dinner Aunt Nancy's cook produced, and heard nothing of the children's chatter, though he was fairly sure he'd managed to answer their countless questions—as he answered this one, without much distraction from his own bitter thoughts. "No, Uncle, I am not a card-playing man."

"Pity. Bluffing is a skill you'll be needing, Quentin. You've a few cards to play, but you must not show them too soon."

That had been one of Bishkek's manhood lessons: . . . Your enemy must never see in your eyes the direction from which you plan to attack. "I don't play at cards, but I can bluff well enough, Uncle."

Bede studied him for a few seconds, then nodded. "Yes. I expect you can."

It was nearly five o'clock, most folks were indoors digesting their dinners and the streets were as empty as the streets of New York City ever were. Quent could hear the ring of his boots on the cobbles of the Broad Way. He was conscious of Pipps behind him. "He'll follow on," Bede had explained. "When you need me, go to James De Lancey's window and signal. Pipps will come and let me know." The servant did a fair job of following; not as good as even a very young brave, but fair. According to Bede, it was a skill the little man had learned in London where picking pockets had been his trade. "Very useful, is Pipps. There's three years left on his indenture, but I've been paying him a wage this past twelvemonth. Keeping him happy so he'll want to stay. And leave my purse in my pocket meanwhile."

The early dark of oncoming winter was settling when Quent reached the governor's mansion at the foot of the broad, tree-lined avenue. He walked up to the imposing front door and lifted the large brass knocker.

James De Lancey considered the papers spread on his desk. The majority bore official seals, a few—the most important—were headed with William Pitt's personal crest and signed by his own hand. He considered as well the man who had brought him this welcome news, clad in a velvet coat and satin breeches. The outside matched the inside for once. "Excellent, Mr. Hale. You have brought me excellent news."

Quent nodded. "Your servant, Governor."

De Lancey stood up. "Well then, if there's nothing else . . ."

"Sit down."

"I beg your pardon."

"I said sit down, Governor. Our business is not yet finished."

"London's taught you impudence, Mr. Hale. I suggest you not take that tone in my—"

"If remaining as governor is what you wish, then I suggest you stop talking, take your seat, and pay attention."

De Lancey's face reddened. "How dare you—"

"Don't talk, Governor. Just listen. I want the leases, both sets. The ones signed by my brother and yours as well as Levy and Alexander, and the ones making the Patent over to Hamish Stewart."

The governor had regained his composure. "I rather thought that was what this was about. I regret I cannot comply, Mr. Hale. Those are legal documents left with me for safekeeping. They belong to others, not to you."

"We had an agreement, you and I. Made in this very room—" Steady, Quent warned himself, steady. He heard Bishkek's voice in his head: *In battle the fire-heat of anger is suitable for braves. For the chief there must be the snow-cold of wisdom.*

"We had a discussion," De Lancey said. "No promises were asked or given, and no oaths taken. Besides, I did not make any of these arrangements. I was simply a witness."

"The Hale Patent belongs to me."

"I remind you that you are not the eldest son."

"I am my father's son, sir, and a Hale. For now that's quite enough." Quent nodded toward a tall clock standing across from the governor's elegant writing table. Painted cherubs cavorted in a painted garden at the clock's base. Two more carved in brass rode the bob of the pendulum as it swung rhythmically from side to side. "You have thirty seconds, sir, to give me what I require. I shall start the count."

"Thirty seconds?" the governor repeated incredulously.

The pendulum had completed three swings. "Twenty-seven now."

"Or else what, Mr. Hale?"

"Or else a letter I wrote before coming here will be delivered to His Excellency the Secretary of State, William Pitt. It's on a Devrey ship that leaves with the evening tide—about half an hour from now—and will be in London in less than a month."

"I might have known Bede Devrey was party to this outrage. And exactly what does your letter say, Mr. Hale?" It was said softly, with no hint of panic. De Lancey was neither a fool nor a coward.

"It says that I have proof you conspired with John Lydius to deliver faulty muskets to the Yorkers who joined His Majesty's soldiers for Braddock's campaign in the Ohio Country, as well as those provided for conscripts sent to defend Fort William Henry. That you were thus in some measure responsible for both massacres, and that the corruption of your stewardship in this province cries to heaven for vengeance. Something to that effect, at any rate. There are seven seconds remaining, Governor."

"It's not true, therefore you can have no such proof."

"It is true. But even were it not, are you aware of the mood in London after so many defeats, Governor? Have you any notion of how desperately the government needs a goat that can be made to bear its sins?"

"Why should William Pitt believe a landless second son who has chosen to live as a woodsman and—"

"The Secretary and I spent many hours together, Governor. I have his complete confidence *precisely* because I am not a man of politics or property. Lacking ambition in your world, and that of Pitt, that gives me all the bona fides I require. And your writ runs from London, or it runs not at all. Now, sir. Your time is up."

Quent rose and went to the window and pushed aside the damask draperies.

"What the devil are you doing?"

"Signaling to my uncle's man. So he can go down to the docks and let the Devrey captain know the letter's to be delivered."

"I don't believe you."

Quent threw open the casement. "Pipps! Are you there? Come closer so His Excellency the Governor can get a look at you."

"Right here I be, Mr. Hale, sir."

"Excellent. Now, I wish you to—"

"Wait!" De Lancey's command came out in a harsh whisper.

Quent turned to face him. The governor stood behind his desk, leaning over and supporting himself with the knuckles of both hands. "Wait," he repeated. "What you're doing makes no sense at all."

"It makes perfect sense." Quent glanced toward the clock with its unrelenting pendulum. "You'd best go now, Pipps. Tide's getting ready to turn."

"I said wait, damn you! There's a good fifteen minutes before the tide turns."

And you, sir, are mine. I've won, damn your lying hide. I've won! Excitement roiled Quent's belly and made him want to roar with triumph. *You have accepted my measure of the situation and it's urgency, adopted it as your own. Meaning I have you as securely as if your still warm scalp was in my hand.* He had never before experienced the thrill of a serious battle fought without a gun or a tomahawk or a knife, using not even his fists, only words and ideas, fashioning them into clever feints and parries that his enemy could not avoid. It was intoxicating. "Pipps, you'd best leave. Be sure and tell—"

"You won't have the Patent, whatever I do." De Lancey shot the words at him from across the room. "The holding will simply revert back to your brother John."

"I'll tell you one more time, De Lancey, I, too, am my father's son. And my brother, whatever else he may be, is a Hale." *John must die. For the Patent to survive, not only must I prevail here, now, in this room, John must die.* "I am asking you one last time for those deeds, sir."

Pipps stood by the open window, listening to everything, grinning, his long, fanglike teeth on display. "Won't take me more'n a few minutes to run down to the docks, Mr. Hale, sir. Be a bit o' time left. Not much, mind, but a bit."

De Lancey moved out from behind his desk. A picture of his country seat on Bouwery Lane a few miles north in the rural Manhattan fastness hung above a mahogany console set against the opposite wall. The governor swung the painting aside and revealed a locked cupboard which he opened. Inside was a box, also locked. The governor carried it to his desk.

"Still time," Pipps said at the window. "But it's getting short. I'll be going in less'n a minute or so."

"Shut up, you evil-looking blackguard," De Lancey snapped. Then, to Quent: "I am not accustomed to being spied on by common riffraff peeking through my windows."

"Back off, Pipps. But wait nearby."

"Yes, sir. As you say, sir."

De Lancey had the box unlocked and open. He removed two packets of documents and held them out. Quent took them, untying each bundle in turn and examining the papers quickly but thoroughly. The entire history of the double transaction was in his hands. If these papers were destroyed, it would be as if neither sorry bargain had been struck. "Tell me something, Governor, why did you agree to sell to Hamish Stewart? He can't have paid you half what the place is worth." Quent glanced again at the signatures on the bill of sale. A quartet of scoundrels as rotten as any he'd ever heard of. "Not an eighth of its worth," he said, noting the price. "Why?"

"Why should I tell you anything?" De Lancey was very pale. Quent could smell the fury in him, and the self-disgust because he'd been forced to surrender.

"Indulge me, Governor," he said softly. "Why the sale for too little to a man you could easily have crushed and discarded?"

De Lancey shrugged. There was no harm in telling now, and it was worth it to inflict a bit of pain on this arrogant red devil. "Stewart's the one arranged to have Shadowbrook burned out by the Canadian savages. He thought no one knew, but of course I . . ." The governor made another of those dismissive gestures meant to indicate his all-seeing authority. "Granted, the rain saved the Patent from as much ruin as was intended, but—"

Not just the rain, Quent thought, but the fact that Nicole and I were in Shoshanaya's glade. She couldn't have run off to a nunnery if I'd taken her in that cursed glen. Quent forced his thoughts away from Nicole. They were a distraction. Worse, they softened him.

"—the attack was the first wedge." De Lancey enjoyed the look of anguish in Quentin Hale's eyes. "Opened the wound, so to speak. Everything fell into place after that. Hamish Stewart was a useful tool. No reason not to let him think the Patent his. For a time, at least."

"A device to get John out of the picture," Quent said. "And leave you to manage things as you chose when you were ready." The governor nodded. "Stewart's untimely death must have caused you some disappointment," Quent added.

"I am not surprised that you know he's dead, Mr. Hale. Your mother came to visit her brother very recently, and your uncle can hardly have failed to inform you of all the Patent's vital business."

"I would never expect to surprise a man so well-informed, sir. At least not in such particulars." Quent spoke as he carried the second set of deeds, the one awarding the Patent to the Scot, to the governor's lively fire and tossed them into its heart. "I'm told Stewart's buried on our land. Out behind the pigsty."

"A detail I shall carry forever in my heart."

Quent watched the last traces of the deed that had made the Patent over to Hamish Stewart char, curl, blacken, and finally disappear. He looked over at the other papers that had occupied this visit, the ones from London that still lay on the governor's desk. "You understand what Pitt's plans mean, do you not?"

"Oh yes. Massive, irresistible force. That's what you advised, isn't it?"

"Indeed. But the idea had already been in the Secretary's mind. My suggestions were warmly received."

"Then we shall get very rich here in New York. Very quickly. Properly fought wars do that for men of business, Mr. Hale. You are aware of that fact?"

"Entirely aware, Governor. Which is why I wish to make you a proposition."

De Lancey was immediately wary. "What sort of proposition?"

"Twelve percent of the Patent's profits for the next four years. You and Oliver to share equally."

"I think," the governor said slowly, "you must be mad." He indicated the set of deeds Quent still held. "You have what you came for, Mr. Hale. Why should you—"

Because your reaction tells me what I most need to know, bloody James De Lancey. There are no other copies of these damnable papers, no further way you and your poxed brother can claim the Patent. "Because, sir"—nothing in Quent's tone gave away his triumph—"I would far rather have you as an ally than an enemy. As you've said, trade will be brisk over the next few years. There are many ways the Acting Governor of New York can assist a provincial farmer who wishes to profit from that trade."

De Lancey was silent for some time. Quent counted eight swings of the cherubs riding the pendulum. "Fourteen percent," the governor said finally.

"Done."

"I will draw up an agreement." De Lancey flipped the tails of his coat as he sat down and reached for a quill.

"No need," Quent said. "My uncle and I have done so already. Only the exact figure needs to be filled in." He turned to the still-open window. "Pipps, you still there?"

"Right here, sir."

"Please go at once to my uncle and ask that he might attend us here at His Excellency's residence. And Pipps—"

"Yes, sir?"

"Tell him the figure is fourteen."

De Lancey leaned back in his chair, the quill still in his hand. "You are a remarkable man, Mr. Hale. May I ask what was to be your final offer?"

"Sixteen percent," Quent admitted with a grin. "Now, sir, I suggest you send for your brother Oliver. I'd like his signature on our agreement as well."

"Oliver's up in the country. At his house in Bloomingdale. It will take the better part of two hours to—"

"Oliver's drinking at the Sign of the Black Horse over on William Street, sir. Not ten minutes from here."

"How do you know that?"

"I was trained by the Potawatomi. All braves are taught to scout out the battlefield before they attack."

De Lancey swallowed the bile that filled his mouth. Fourteen percent. Less than what he'd hoped for, and by Hale's own admission, less than he could have had. But it was a good deal better than nothing. He rang for a footman and sent him to summon Oliver. "All as you arranged it, Mr. Hale," the governor said softly. "But may I ask, having taken care of my brother, what you plan to do about your own?"

"Nothing. There is no need. For the time being John will run the Patent as he always has." *John must die. For the Patent to be safe, John must die.*

De Lancey raised his eyebrows. "He's nearly run it into the ground so far. What use to me and Oliver is fourteen percent of nothing?"

"Not even John will fail to make profit in the present circumstances, Governor."

De Lancey looked again at the papers from London. Both men heard the clatter of the front door knocker, then Bede Devrey's hearty tones saying that His Excellency had sent for him. "We shall soon find out, I expect," De Lancey said as he rose to greet his new guest.

Quent nodded. He had won—the joy of that made his pulse race and heated his blood—but a battle only, not the war. *John must die.*

FRIDAY, OCTOBER 27, 1759
ALBANY

The tobacco smoke was as thick as ever; the noise, if anything, louder. It had been two years since Quent had been in the Sign of the Nag's head, but little had changed. The chalkboard on the tavern wall still offered the day's selection of food—the oysters were a shilling a dozen, outrageous—and the air was heavy with the yeasty scent of ale and the honey of rum.

As for old man Groesbeck, he looked younger. Must be the amount of brass he was taking in now that Albany was full of redcoats and militia. He stood not far from the front door, tapping a new keg. The bung gave at the third whack, and the foamy brew erupted into the pail below. Good beer, the smell and the color attested to it. Those patrons near enough to observe sent up a cheer. Groesbeck plugged the hole with a pewter spigot. Landlord's duty done, he made way for one of the barmaids.

He'd spotted the Red Bear as soon as he came in. Now he made his way through the throng. "Good evening to you, Quent. It's been a long time."

"Too long, Peter. I'm parched."

The landlord turned and shouted, and one of the mugs of new beer was passed forward. Quent offered a penny, but Groesbeck waved it aside. "No, no, not after so much time we are not seeing you. Besides," he added with a grin that showed his missing teeth, "tuppence I'm charging these days."

"Yes, and I see the oysters have doubled in price as well. Business must be very good."

Groesbeck's grin widened. "Many customers, *ja*. The Yorkers and the redcoats, they all come. Sometimes the officers, even."

Give it a few months, old man, and you'll have so much custom you'll surely think you've died and gone to landlord's heaven. "What about the old customers, then? Do they continue to drink here?"

"Why not? We still give them the best food, and drinks to full measure. No water in the punch, neither."

"Ah, that must be the attraction for the canny Scot, then. Have you seen him lately?"

Groesbeck cocked his head and looked up at Quent. "The one who used to live by the Widow Krieger? With one seeing only?" He clapped a hand over his left eye.

"That's the one."

"Why you want to know about him?"

"We had some business together last time I was here. Interrupted a conversation you and I were having, as I recall."

"*Ja, ja.* I remember. He's dead, that one. Happened up at your place. Some kind of quarrel with your brother."

He'd found out what he wanted to know, how the death of Hamish Stewart was interpreted locally, and he need not pretend to mourn for a man he barely knew. "My brother's not hard to argue with."

Groesbeck's look darkened. "Not so bad when it's another man, a fair fight. With a woman, even a —"

"What woman?"

The landlord jerked his head to the back of the taproom. "Annie the whore. She was a friend of the one-eye. She's here tonight. First time in three weeks."

Quent nodded his thanks for the information and the beer and began making his way toward the rear. A path was instantly cleared for him. A few people nodded or murmured a greeting or slapped his arm in welcome, mostly locals who had known him since he was a boy. The rest kept a respectful distance.

Annie Crotchett sat in her usual place in the rear of the taproom, near the door to the yard. Her right eye was swollen shut; her left was blacked, but usable. She saw Quentin Hale making his way toward her and waved away the two Yorkers who had been keeping her company. "Go on about yer business, lads. Annie's got a special caller. Another Hale, as I live and breathe. The famous one."

Quent nodded to the Yorkers as they left, and straddled one of the stools they'd left vacant. "Good evening to you, Mistress Crotchett."

"It's Annie I'm called. Even by the likes of you, Quentin Hale."

Her face and neck were marked with bruises just beginning to fade to a sickly yellow. "Very well. What happened to you, Annie?"

"What do you think? Your bloody brother came at me with a fireplace poker. Nearly killed me he did. Good as killed me." Gingerly she shifted her backside around on the bench and hiked up the skirt of her frock; both feet in their striped, knitted stockings were at odd angles to her legs. "Broke both me ankles, your poxed brother did. Won't walk never again, the quack says. Ain't no use hoping, 'cause it ain't gonna help. Wouldn't be here tonight except old Harry over there carried me. How am I supposed to earn my living if I can't stand up or walk out to the yard? Much less hold myself up long enough to let a man—" She broke off, trembling with misery, putting her hand over the little pile of coins, mostly coppers and wooden pennies, that had been accumulating in front of her as each of her former customers stopped by to wish her well and make a small contribution in memory of good times past.

Sweet Christ. "You know it was John Hale who did this?"

"Of course I bloody know it was John Hale. Been a regular customer since I can't remember when, your poxed brother. Wish to God I'd never seen him, but a fat lot of good that does me now."

"Why, Annie? Why did he turn on you now?"

Two fat tears escaped from her swollen eyes and rolled down her cheeks. "Said I told. Said it was my fault Hamish knew—"

"Hamish Stewart?"

She nodded, but didn't look at him when she whined, "I told John I didn't know nothing to tell Hamish, but he didn't believe me. How could I know when or why 'bout business happens down to New York City? Ain't never been nowhere but Albany. Never."

Quent knew she was lying. John must have known as well. Still, to beat a woman until she was crippled . . . . "You know Stewart's dead, don't you?"

More tears. " 'Course I knows that. Your poxed brother killed him. Hamish was a good man. He never—"

The man who gave a little boy a dirk and showed him how to use it was good enough once. But Stewart had finished up a covetous bastard who sold his soul to land hunger. Quent dug into his pocket and came up with a handful of coins, a golden guinea among them. He spent little when he earned and managed to put nearly everything aside, but his last paying job had been a brief stint as a scout in the Ohio Country a year past. The money he put on the table in front of Annie was pretty much all he had left. Nonetheless he said, "There will be more. You have my word you won't starve."

If that was true, Annie thought, if she could give up fucking for money and eat anyway, Christ Jesus it was worth it. Worth everything.

Outside the Albany palisade, in the woods that bordered the north road, the three-note call of the loon echoed softly twice, then a third time. Cormac appeared from the shadows of a stand of spruce.

"*Nekané,*" Quent said. Little brother.

"*Sizé.*" Elder brother. Corm pressed his palm to Quent's. "*Ahaw nikan.*" My spirit greets you.

"*Bozho nikan.*" And mine, you.

"Took you long enough to get here," Corm said. "I've been in these woods every night for almost a week."

"Your note said ten o'clock, before the Telling of Arriving Dark. It's still Last Fruit far as I know."

The message written on the strip of bark had been pressed into Quent's hand as he came out of the governor's mansion the night he got back the deeds to Shadowbrook. The Indian who gave it to him had what looked like blue Mohawk tattoos on both cheeks, but he'd whispered "*Nikan, Kwashko*" as he brushed past. A Potawatomi greeting using Quent's sacred Potawatomi name. "That was Lashi's boy wasn't it? Bishkek's grandson."

"Yes, Pondise. The Mohawk thing was his idea. He said he thought it would be better to look like a snake among their allies."

"New York City people can't tell one Indian from another. And they're terrified of them all. Bede was with me when Pondise appeared." Quent chuckled at the memory. "The old boy nearly fainted. I tried to find Pondise again later. Couldn't do it."

It was Corm's turn to laugh. "That's because you're becoming white through and through. Look at you. How long since you've had on buckskins?"

"Too damn long," Quent admitted. "Nearly five months, I reckon. Not very sensible to go around London looking like a woodsman." As if he needed to apologize to Corm. "You have to fit in."

Not here in Albany. Quent knew he could have changed before he left the city, or on the boat coming up here. The only reason he hadn't was because he didn't want to.

"Tell me about Pitt," Corm said.

"We've got everything we wanted. Everything, Corm. The French don't know it yet, but they're finished. The *Anishinabeg* will have Canada." The thrill of it rose up in him the way it had back in London when he realized that Pitt had been convinced. "The Indian way and the *Cmokmanuk* way; they're going to survive side by side. We'll learn from each other." Quent was suddenly conscious of being in the open, on a well-traveled road. He looked around. "Let's go somewhere we can talk."

Corm led the way deeper into the woods to a spot he'd already scouted. The night was unseasonably mild, but the place he'd chosen was in the lee of a boulder taller than either of them, protected from any wind that might rise. The ground was cushioned by a deep layer of blue-green spruce needles. Corm sat, leaning against the face of the huge stone, watching Quent, knowing he had to let him take his own time and tell the story in his own way.

Quent opened the canvas bag that had accompanied him on the journey from

America to England and back again. His long gun came out first. Then his buckskins. "Let me change, then we'll talk."

There's a war inside him, Corm thought. Always has been, in some ways. But now he's being sucked into the world of men who wear city clothes, men of power. White men.

"I feel like I'm back in my own skin," Quent said when the breeches and the velvet coat were packed away.

"They're both your skins," Corm said. "Almost as much as they're both mine."

"Maybe," Quent agreed, but he didn't want to talk about such things; there was too much else to tell. "I'll start with Pitt. I was in London nearly two months before I got to see him. I—Christ Almighty, Corm, what a place London is. You can't credit the numbers of people, or how they look, or the goods in the shops, or the traffic in the streets. There are so many carriages you can't count the number on even one stretch of road, any stretch of road. And the women . . . They're something, Corm. Remarkable."

"You thinking of going back there? Settling there, maybe?"

"In London?"

"Yes."

"Of course not. I want to tell you what it was like, because I went and you didn't, but . . . I'm an American, Corm. The time I spent in London only made that more clear. The English and us, there's a difference. Besides, this is my home. I could never go so far from Shadowbrook."

"You were going to tell me about Pitt," Corm reminded him.

"Yes. As I said it was more than eight weeks before he saw me, and just as well, as it turned out. It gave me a chance to find out how things stood. Seems Pitt's been in and out of favor for years. He takes the part of the next king, the Prince of Wales, more often than that of the prince's father. George II has no choice in that, by the way. Eldest son's the next king. Always."

"I know." Miss Lorene's history lessons, no telling when they suddenly came in handy.

"Thing is, there's bad blood between George and his son. And Pitt, he's close to Wales, which makes the king detest him more. All the same, he's finally given Pitt complete charge of the conduct of the war. Had to. The people demanded it."

"Doesn't sound like it's much use being king."

"Sometimes, no, it isn't. George's people come from Hanover over in Germany, and France is at war with Hanover as well as us. The king always wants the main British military effort to go toward helping his relatives in Europe rather than us colonials here in America."

"I take it Pitt doesn't agree."

"Absolutely not. He's got this idea that what matters is building an empire,

America and India. Thinks if England loses either to France, Great Britain's as good as finished. A toothless lion, he said. 'But that need not happen, Mr. Hale. I can save this country and I must, because no one else will.' That's what he told me, Corm."

"Is it true?"

"I've no idea about India, but here . . . Yes, I think it is true." Quent grubbed about until he came up with a handful of small stones. "Look, this is how it's to be." He positioned three of the stones in a triangle on the earth between them. "Say this is Fort Duquesne down in the Ohio Country." He pointed to the right bottom stone. "It guards the way to the rest of the French territory south and west."

"Louisiana, you mean." That was the only place Corm had ever heard of where people ate *kokotni*. If Marni were eating alligators, she had to be in Louisiana.

"Yes," Quent agreed. "Louisiana. And all the land to the west the French claim. The key to their holding it is Fort Duquesne. If we take that, they're finished."

"Braddock already tried to take Fort Duquesne. We know how that came out."

"Yes, but Braddock was sent over with fewer redcoats than he needed and told to make up his strength with colonials. That's never going to work. I told Pitt as much, but frankly he already knew. Massive force, that's his plan. There'll be so many of them to take Duquesne the French won't stand a chance. Besides"—Quent looked at Corm, watching his reaction—"I hear it's a lot more difficult for Onontio to get his war belts accepted by the *Anishinabeg*. You know anything about that?"

"Later," Corm said. "Finish about Pitt first."

"Fair enough. First thing to go will be Duquesne. We'll take it with the biggest guns you ever saw, and overwhelming numbers of redcoats."

"There'll be some local help as well. Your old friend Washington, he's raised a new regiment, the First Virginia. A force to be reckoned with, they tell me. Better than that ragtag bunch of farmers he had with him back in that cursed glen."

Quent nodded. "We're all a little wiser than we were four years ago. Pitt's gotten the parliament in London to agree to help pay colonial soldiers a living wage. Washington can recruit real officers, men with some experience, for the First Virginia." He pointed to one of the two stones that remained. "Second objective is Carillon."

"The fort up on the French end of Bright Fish Water?"

Quent nodded.

"How did you get him to make that a major objective?"

"Ticonderoga is critical for the corridor between Canada and the Ohio Country. Take Carillon and you cut New France in half."

And the fact that it was better not to have French forces five days' march from the Patent was simply a bonus. Well earned, Corm thought. Quent deserves something for all he's done for the English. "Same plan?"

"Same plan." Quent chuckled. "I just came from the Nag's Head. There's so much custom old man Groesbeck's like a pig with his snout in the swill. When he sees what's coming he may die of joy." Quent swept the second stone away with the edge of his palm. "Thousands of redcoats, and we turn the French out of Ticonderoga. We'll be in complete control of everything between Lake Champlain and Bright Fish Water."

"The Huron," Corm said quietly, "they call that stretch between the lakes the Great Warpath. Because it led them to their enemies."

"Call it what you will, once we take Carillon, it's ours."

Corm pointed to the single stone that remained. "And what's this?"

"Two things, actually," Quent said. "Louisbourg and Québec. Force," he said quietly. "Irresistible force. The whole bloody English navy if that's what it takes." He scooped up the remaining stone and flung it into the trees. "Québec falls and Canada is ours."

Corm stiffened. He felt a sudden chill despite the mild night. "Ours? Do you mean that Canada will be British?"

"Only in a manner of speaking," Quent said. "I didn't mean to imply the English *Cmokmanuk* would replace the French. I told him, Corm. Everything you've always said, everything we agreed on. The *Anishinabeg* get Canada and the *Cmokmanuk* stay down here on the land the English hold now. In return, peace between us and the Indians, no more frontier harassment, no raids. We draw a line and everybody stays on their own side."

"I know you understand," Corm said softly. "What I'm waiting to hear is that your friend Pitt also understands."

"Pitt's a friend to himself only, I suspect. But about Canada . . . We talked four evenings running, about the war, everything." In the Palace of Westminster Quent had been led to Pitt's private apartments through the most splendid corridors he'd ever seen, lit with an uncountable number of candles, alive with Turkey carpets glowing in colors he'd never imagined. "That last night, we talked of nothing but the *Anishinabeg*. He wanted to know all about them, to understand their ways. What happened up at Fort William Henry, it concentrated his mind—"

"—on the fact that Indians are bloodthirsty savages," Corm broke in, suddenly fierce. "That's what the whites are saying. Not just in New York and the rest of the colonies. The French are equally as ignorant. Montcalm wrings his hands and pretends not to understand how the 'savages' could have gone back on his word. His word, mind you, not theirs."

"I admit, it was pretty hard for them to understand in London as well. But as for Pitt . . . He's not a closed-minded man, Corm. I think he understood in the end. I really do."

"And he agrees? We'll have Canada?"

It was maybe the first time Quent had heard Corm align himself entirely to his Indian heritage. "He agrees that whites and Indians have to find a way to live together if there's ever to be peace and prosperity in America."

"Did he give you his word Quent?"

"He promised me he'd try, Corm. He swore he'd bend every effort to make it happen. It was the best I could get, so I took it."

It was the same thing Pontiac had said when he accepted the Súki bead with the spider carving, that he'd try. *Cmokman* or *Anishinabeg,* sometimes to try was the only promise possible. "There's something else." Corm found another stone and held it out in his open palm. "This attack on Québec. Presuming the English warships get close enough to do any damage, it's the Lower Town they'll smash first. You given that any thought?"

Quent nodded. "I have. That convent is not a hundred paces from the harbor."

"Closer, maybe."

"*Ahaw.*" It was the first time either of them had slipped into Potawatomi. "*Wijewe,*" Quent said. "I got Pitt's word on that as well. When the time comes to take Québec, I'll be there."

MONDAY, NOVEMBER 5, 1757
SHADOWBROOK

John must die. Not now, though. The night he confronted his brother about the exchange of Shadowbrook for cane land, Jeremiah had said: *Ain't no good going to come from spilling your brother's blood. Mark o' Cain that be. Don't you do it. For your Mama's sake.* The mark of Cain didn't bother Quent; John had to die to preserve the Patent. *John must die.* But about his mother, Jeremiah was right.

Lorene sat at her bedroom window the way she did so often these days; Taba sat on the floor not far from her, mending a piece of fine lace with the careful little stitches her mistress had taught her. Lorene looked out and there was Quent, walking up the path.

Lorene flew down the stairs and out the door, rushing to meet him before he got to the house—only partly because she hadn't seen her youngest boy for such a long time.

"Where's John?" he asked. If he came on his brother suddenly, without being prepared, he wasn't sure what he would do. John must die, but he didn't want it to be today, like this, with his mother watching.

"He's not here. Quentin, I've so much to tell you. There's so much you don't know." Her blue eyes were dark with anxiety, and her chest rose and fell with quick, sharp breaths.

"Calm yourself, Madam. I know more than you think. I saw Uncle Bede before I went to see the governor."

"That vicious, evil man. That snake. I wish—"

"Calm yourself," Quent said again. "I've dealt with James De Lancey."

"Dealt with him how? He has the deed to the Patent, Quent. The De Lanceys played John for a fool. Oliver sold the deed and lien to Hamish Stewart, but Hamish is dead, and the Lord alone knows how long it will be before the De Lanceys' claim—"

"No. They won't claim anything." Quent drew her to the wooden seat that circled the big chestnut tree in front of the house. The unseasonable autumn warmth had changed to the damp cold more normal for the first days of November. Quent opened his bag and pulled out the green velvet coat and put it around his mother's shoulders.

She drew it close. "Is this yours, Quent? I don't believe I've ever seen it."

"It's mine. Bespoke in New York City. So I could look like a diplomat in London."

"Indeed." She was examining the stitches on the lapel. "It's fine work. I expect our New York tailors did you proud, even in London."

"Proud enough." He'd felt like a country cousin despite the clothes. Not one person he met was as big as he was, for a start. And not just the accents different, some of the words as well. We're growing farther and farther apart, American Englishmen and English Englishmen. God knows how it will turn out. "Madam, listen, there's much to say and not much time. Is John likely to interrupt us?"

"Not for some hours. He's gone to the sawmill to talk to Ely about timber we need for repairing the stable, and to have Sally Robin look at his wound. Uncle Bede told you—"

"Everything. Don't fret. How is Ely?"

"Well. He's to be married again. The Widow Krieger from Albany."

"Good, that's a fine thing." Quent remembered Ely's daughter and her husband and the tiny baby, and the way the sawyer had looked as he stood over their bodies. "The sawmill must be lonely after so much loss. And the Frankels, how are they?"

"Very well. But John thinks perhaps we won't have enough work to keep the gristmill and the sugarhouse busy next year. He says we may not be able to plant as much or trade as much and—"

"John couldn't be more wrong. About that like so much else. Madam, you're shivering. Come, let's go inside."

It was well past the dinner hour but Kitchen Hannah plied him with johnnycakes and biscuits, and ham and parsnips and potatoes baked into a pie. "Still warm enough," she told him. "Don't you be leaving any, saying it be too chilled to be good."

"It's delicious, Hannah. Thank you." When she had gone, he pulled his chair closer to Lorene's. "Madam, I want to be gone before John gets back. Else . . ."

"I know. But he's your bro—"

"We haven't time to talk about John. Just listen. You must see to it that every field is planted in the spring. Grow plenty of wheat, never mind what John says, and take in as much sugar as you can beg or buy. Tell Moses Frankel he's to make rum with the lot. As many jugs as they can manage. And don't send any more to Do Good than you must."

"We're doing less and less trade at Do Good. The Indians seem to be withdrawing from us. At least that's what Esther Snowberry says and she never lies."

"Give Esther my warm regards. And don't worry about the Kahniankehaka, they've got their own concerns at the moment." Some months back, before he went to London, Quent himself had given a Súki bead to Scarouady. He had accepted *ayaapia*, the elk buck, on behalf of the entire Iroquois Confederation. Just to be sure, Quent had also given *eesipana*, the racoon, to the Kahniankehaka. "Just do as I say, Madam." Quent dropped his voice, speaking in a low and urgent tone. "Next summer, everywhere in the province but particularly here, will be teeming with redcoats. More than you've ever seen, more than you can imagine. They'll need to be fed and supplied with drink and housed. You must have a quiet word with Ely and leave John out of it if you can. Tell Ely he's to cut and plank as much timber as possible over the winter. There will be barracks needed. The wood to build them can be sold from Shadowbrook."

"Quent, I do not doubt that you know things about London's plans, but if we can indeed turn all this profit, what good will it do? The De Lanceys—"

"James and Oliver De Lancey will share in our profits, Madam. But not to any undue extent."

"No, you don't understand. John made everything over as part of some mad scheme to get cane land. With Hamish Stewart dead it must be the De Lanceys who own the Patent. John says no, that with Hamish dead it's reverted to him, but—"

"John is right." The words were bitter in his mouth. Everything he'd done had given the Patent back to his brother. *John must die.*

He handed her the original of the document she'd found crumpled up in the cold fireplace the night Hamish Stewart died. Lorene looked at each page, her eyes skimming the tiny print, then fastening on the signatures. Oliver De Lancey, James Alexander, Hayman Levy, and John Hale. "But are you sure, Quentin, that it is now the only copy? And what of the deed that gave Hamish Stew—"

"Stewart's deed no longer exists. I burned it myself. And yes, I'm sure this is the only copy of the papers John signed."

She turned away as if hearing him say it pained her. "Your brother didn't mean to give up the Patent, only to add land in the Islands to what we already have."

"It doesn't matter now. Things are as they were."

"Yes, some things are. I am very pleased, Quentin. But . . . do I want to know how you accomplished this?"

"It was nothing dishonorable, Madam."

"Do you think I care for honor where snakes and liars and cheats like the De Lanceys are concerned? I do not." She fairly spat out the words. "I would see them all in hell and dance over their graves. But they are not fools. Your brother, perhaps, but not the De Lanceys, and not you. What did you have to trade to get control of the Patent, Quentin Hale? That is my question."

"James De Lancey cares more for power than money, Madam. And Oliver pretty much does his brother's bidding. I made certain alliances in London, and London is the source of the governor's writ here. So, fourteen percent of our profit for the next four years, Madam. It will not be difficult with so much coming in. And better to have the De Lanceys as allies than as enemies."

She nodded. "Your father would have said the same thing. But what am I to tell John?"

"As little as possible. John must not know the Patent is entirely free and clear again. It will make him impossible to control."

"How can I keep such a thing secret?"

"You have been keeping secrets all your life, Madam," he said softly. "This one is probably easier than some."

Lorene was silent for a time. She put her hand over his. "He will know nothing. Not until you say he may."

"Until this war's over and I can come home and . . . deal with things." *John must die.* "You can manage this, Madam." He smiled. "You've always been able to manage the Hale men."

Lorene nodded but did not return his smile. The price for arranging things as she knew they must be often turned out higher than she wished to pay.

"One last thing," Quent said. "The Scot. The De Lanceys were using him, of course, and he was so besotted with his desire to possess the Patent he let himself be used. But I need to know if he said anything other than that he was the new master of Shadowbrook. Stewart was a Jacobite with alliances to the papists in Québec. I don't want any surprises. Could that have been why John killed him?"

"John has said nothing to me of such a thing. I don't believe Canada was ever mentioned. And your brother didn't kill Hamish Stewart. Taba, a little Ibo slave, did. She was bought after you left, so you don't know her." Lorene told the story.

"This Taba," he asked when she finished, "is she still here? Perhaps it would be best if she were sold on."

Lorene shook her head. "No. That's not necessary. She is a fine seamstress. I am training her up myself; she'll be useful for many years. John won't— I gave him to understand that she had saved his life," Lorene said mildly, only her eyes speaking the darker truths. "He will not punish her for running away. And he's stopped . . ." She let the words trail away.

Something else he could safely leave to his mother. He stood up. "I must go."

"When will you come back?" Lorene asked when they stood by the front door.

"As soon as I can. After this war's over for sure." *John must die.* "I nearly forgot, Madam. There's a woman in the town, Annie Crotchett. She's no better than she should be, but thanks to John she's lost what livelihood she had. She's usually at Peter Groesbeck's tavern. I promised a guinea every month or two. Can you find it? You always did have a bit put by the rest of us knew nothing about."

Lorene smiled and lay her palm alongside his cheek. "Any woman not an utter fool does the same. I'll find a bit for Annie Crotchett and see she gets it."

The easy part was done. What remained was a great deal more difficult.

Book 9

Québec

1758–1759

Chapter Twenty-Four

NEARLY SUMMER AND it was still shivering cold in this perverse hell the devil had fashioned off the coast of Canada. Quent was in one of the most forward boats, stomach churning, blood roaring in his ears, praying this would not be another false start. There had been three aborted attempts, the men loaded into two hundred landing craft, then called back because they could make no headway.

Each longboat was manned by twenty oarsmen and carried sixty-three soldiers, plus a drummer lad amidships to beat the stroke. They were twigs tossed about on the thundering waves, their flat bottoms and lack of serious heft continually punished by the boiling surf. Icy fog and whip-sharp salt spray added to the misery of men drenched to the skin, peering into the mist hoping for a sign of the beach with the smell of their own fear and their own vomit filling their noses.

Behind the flotilla of landing craft was a vast array of fighting sail: twenty-three ships of the line, eighteen frigates, and a fleet of transports. They had been crowding the horizon for eight days, waiting for the fog to lift. And when it didn't, trying anyway to put ashore the eleven thousand British regulars and American provincials, militia, and rangers intended to take Louisbourg.

Quent put up his hand to shield his eyes from the spray. His glance raked the approaching shore. Earlier he'd gone in a smaller boat with Jeffrey Amherst, the general in charge of the troops, and brigadier James Wolfe, the colonel Amherst most relied on, to scout the coast. The army men had hoped for great things from his woodsman's instincts, but he'd seen nothing that suggested a landing place even halfway hospitable. Tired of waiting, Admiral Boscawan used his command prerogative—*I remind you, General Amherst, that I'm God Almighty while we're on the water*—chose a cove that looked likely, and sent the boats out for a fourth time.

Quent peered at the thin ribbon of coast. It yielded nothing. He thought he heard someone shout his name and turned his head, but it was only the wind's cry. Wolfe was in the prow of the boat on the right, seated just behind a sailor who was crouched over the craft's single swivel gun. He clung to the gunwales with both hands and his customary look of determined agony.

Another wave was building. Quent saw it rippling toward them and braced himself. The sailor manning the oar to his right muttered "holy God, holy God, holy God" over and over again, the words marking the rhythm of his strokes, keeping time with the drummer's tempo. The longboat was sucked into the wave's belly, lifted to a dizzying height, then slapped down with a spine-shuddering thud. The oar on Quent's right clattered loose in its lock because the praying sailor had been washed overboard. Quent thought he spotted the man's bobbing head a few arm's lengths away, beyond the reach of even a fully extended oar. Quent slid into the vacant position and took up the stroke. The drummer boy had lost his sticks, but he'd resumed the beat with the flat of his hand. The rowers quickly got the cadence back. The pull was not as hard as Quent expected. The tide was with them, only the weather their enemy. At least until they made landfall.

Despite the fog, the French had seen the great spread of canvas filling six leagues of the horizon. Louisbourg's defenders were dug in at every possible landing point on Ile Royal. They waited until the boats were close to shore, then rained down a deadly storm of grape and musket fire. The landing crafts' single swivel guns were no match for such a fusillade and the soldiers' muskets were mostly too wet to be of any use. The sea turned red with blood, and the screams of the drowning and dying shuddered in the air.

Quent looked to his left. There was a bit of coast, only a narrow strand strewn with rocks, but out of the range of the cannon. "Colonel Wolfe, over there!" he screamed into the wind.

Miraculously, Wolfe heard him and squinted in the direction Quent was pointing. "Quite right, Mr. Hale!" he shouted. "Excellent!" His voice was lost in the pounding surf and the roaring wind and the screech of gunfire, but it didn't matter. He raised his hand. The boats sheered off to the left and the landing proceeded.

By morning there was calm and bright sun, and the boom of the French guns was replaced by birdsong. Quent led Wolfe and some of the other officers along the line where he and five hundred rangers had engaged the enemy during the night, driving them back behind the walls of the citadel because they knew if they didn't go they'd be cut off. The defenders had left their cannon behind. And about a hundred bodies. Every one had been scalped.

"Do you take scalps, Mr. Hale?" Wolfe asked. "I know it is the custom in this country, but do you do it?"

"The rangers fight like Americans, Colonel, in a manner suitable for our terrain, and conditions, and way of life. That's the value in having them."

"I understand that. But you, personally? I'm told you're a gentleman. Do you scalp your enemies?"

Quent stared at him, unflinching. "Every chance I get, Colonel Wolfe. One way or another."

Wolfe had hair as red as Quent's own. No chin, however, and eyes that looked as if they might pop out of his head. And he was ill almost all the time. But according to Pitt, the man had the courage of a tiger.

In India the tigers are something remarkable, Mr. Hale. The most clever and ferocious beasts you can imagine. So tell me, what do you think would occur if a tiger fought a bear?

I'm not sure, sir. But if they both fight on the same side, does it matter?

Wolfe was still looking at the mutilated bodies. "I am surprised there are so few Indians among them. I see just two. Have you any explanation for that, Mr. Hale?"

"As far as I could tell last night, there were only some Mi'kmaq and Abenaki. Not many. Not like before."

"It's true, then? The Indians have deserted the French?"

"A good many fewer have been willing to accept Onontio's war belts, that's true." He hadn't tried to explain the Suckáuhock to William Pitt—*I can deliver what I promise, sir. How need not be your concern*—and he wouldn't try with James Wolfe.

Wolfe was looking at him, waiting for more. Quent stared back and said nothing. Finally the Englishman turned to look again at the scalped bodies. After a moment he signaled to a young ensign. "Organize a detail to bury them."

A New Englander stepped forward, wearing the green jacket affected by many of the ranging auxiliaries. Some, a Colonel Rogers the most famous of them, had adopted military titles to go with the self-styled uniforms. Quent preferred his buckskins and his ordinary name. But none of the rangers stood for much in the way of ceremony or deference. "Beg pardon, sir, but that's not necessary."

Wolfe turned his iciest stare on the speaker. "Perhaps you Americans leave bodies to rot. We English do not."

"That's not what I meant, sir. We'll burn the corpses."

"Burn . . . It's barbarism, I will—"

"No, Colonel, it's not. The stink of all that burning meat will get back to the fort. Put the fear of the Almighty in 'em. You might say we're returning the compliment they paid us at Fort William Henry."

Quent's belly knotted. Even the woodsmen, closest to the Indians and their ways, didn't understand. Separation was the only hope. Thank God for Corm's notion of how it could be achieved, and his persistence. And the Suckáuhock.

It took ten days before all the supplies were unloaded. The operation splintered more than a hundred small boats on the rocks of the iron coast, but in the end they got everything ashore, including the heavy guns and cannon. When Amherst finished preparing his camp, the better part of a morning was required to walk from one end to the other.

On the eighteenth of June everything was in place and the siege of Louisbourg began. Before the first shots were fired General Amherst sent a basket of pineapples to the wife of the fort's commander, along with a note apologizing for the noise of his guns.

MONDAY, AUGUST 5, 1758
QUÉBEC LOWER TOWN

The Maria bell of the Monastery of the Poor Clares tolled in mourning. Nicole pulled and released the rope with careful concentration, all the while saying the Miserere, uniting her spirit with those of Dear Abbess and her sisters praying in the choir.

Louisbourg had fallen. Almost as terrible, the brave French soldiers who defended the great fort had been refused the honors of war by the English. They were to be sent to England as prisoners of war, and the eight thousand women and children and civilian men who had lived behind the walls of the citadel were being deported to France. "But *ma Mère*, who has ever heard of such a thing?" Soeur Angelique's eyes were wide with horror when she heard the news at the afternoon's recreation. "Why send away the people who did not fight? That is not done."

"It is done by the English." Mère Marie Rose was embroidering. Even during the day's hour of relative freedom no Poor Clare sat with idle hands. "Just as they banished the Acadians. At least these poor people of Louisbourg are sent home to France, not delivered to the American colonies where they must live among heretics and be little better than slaves."

"The Acadians are English subjects." Nicole had ventured the explanation tentatively. Did they think her any less loyal to the French cause, the Catholic cause, because of her English father? "I do not defend what was done. Never. But the English could not send the Acadians to France because they were not supposed to be French any longer."

"*Les Anglais* are beasts." Soeur Françoise, who seldom raised her voice above a whisper, practically shouted the words. "*Cochons!* Pigs! Every one of them."

Not my Red Bear, Nicole thought. But these stories of the American rangers who fight with the redcoats and the militia, who whoop like Indians when they kill and take scalps like Indians . . . Is my Red Bear among them? That night beside the fire in the Shawnee camp, when he danced and went off with a squaw into the woods, he was entirely Indian. But with me, in Shoshanaya's glade . . . She bent forward, plying her darning needle with ferocity and letting her veil fall forward to hide her burning cheeks. Forgive me, *mon Dieu,* forgive my wicked distractions. "Is any explanation made for sending the civilians to France, *ma Mère?* Do we perhaps know if this is some tactic of the war?"

Clever, Mère Marie Rose thought, just as Père Antoine said. Almost too clever to be a nun. What do I see in your eyes, *ma petite Soeur?* Something, I think, that is not in the eyes of the rest of us. "We are told nothing. Perhaps they wish to empty all Canada of the French."

Then she sent Nicole to toll the Maria bell in memory of the passing of the souls of the brave French soldiers who died defending Louisbourg, and for the misery of the survivors.

Pull on the rope slowly and with total attention. Remember, ringing the bell is an act of prayer. Bend your knees as you take it down. Release it with equal care. And because you toll not victory but defeat, wait for two strophes of the psalm before you ring it again.

Miserere me, Deus. Have mercy on me, O God. *Quoniam conculcavit me homo.* For man has trodden me underfoot.

To empty Canada of all the French had been Cormac Shea's plan. She'd heard him and Quent arguing about it once. And later Monsieur Shea had explained it to her, when Quent wasn't around to contradict him. "It's the only way there will ever be peace in the New World. Canada for the Indians; the rest of it, the part the English have now, the whites can keep."

"It seems harsh, Monsieur Shea. On the Canadians. Is there no—"

"Not as harsh as the alternative. The only other way the whites can live here without being constantly at war with the red men is to kill every Indian they can find."

Conculcaverunt me inimici mei tota die. My enemies have trodden on me all day long. *Quoniam multi bellantes adversum me.* For they are many that make war against me.

Before summer's end the bells of Canada tolled again in mourning, this time for the fall of Fort Frontenac on Lake Ontario. The chain of forts that stretched from Canada to the Ohio Country was broken. "Protestant heretics can now overrun the Ohio Country," Marie Rose said, her eyes filled with tears. "How will the poor Indians ever hear the true Gospel of Christ and His Catholic Church?"

If they live at all, Nicole thought. If, as Monsieur Shea said, the white men do not find it necessary to kill every Indian they find.

WEDNESDAY, OCTOBER 23, 1758
A MEADOW NEAR THE VILLAGE OF EASTON
IN PENNSYLVANIA COLONY

It was a gray, overcast day following three weeks of unrelenting rain, but at least this afternoon was dry. Cold, though. Corm had wrapped a blanket over his buckskins and stood by himself at the fringe of a large clearing in the eastern Allegheny foothills. He was an outsider here, a Canadian and a Potawatomi. Neither group had any standing in this powwow. Not like Quent. In this place he was Uko Nyakwai, the legendary Ohio Country woodsman, much more than he was Kwashko, the adopted Potawatomi brave, or Quentin Hale, gentleman. Corm watched Quent go from group to group, speak a few words, and move on.

Use the Suckáuhock to convince the *Anishinabeg* to fight with the English or stay neutral. Corm's efforts with the Ottawa and the Huron and the Abenaki had been mostly of the stay-neutral variety. Quent was urging alliance.

Five hundred *Anishinabeg* from thirteen nations had gathered beneath trees whose wet leaves shimmered with the red and gold of autumn. The Indians, many chiefs in full and solemn ceremonial dress, competed with them for splendor. The Delaware sachems Teedyuscung and Pisquetomen, who was the brother of Shingas, sat together. Corm counted sixty of Teedyuscung's braves lined up behind him. Pisquetomen had only half a dozen councillors, but all the authority, Corm figured. Months before, Quent had given the Súki bead carved with *pileewa*, the turkey, to Shingas; it was almost a certainty that for this meeting he'd have passed it to his brother. Pisquetomen was a civil chief, Shingas a war sachem. Now was the time for Pisquetomen. Maybe Shingas later.

The Iroquois had judged the meeting important enough to send chiefs of the individual tribes, rather than a single delegate to represent the Great Council of the Six Nations. Quent had already greeted Nichas of the Kahniankehaka, and the Seneca chief, Tagashata. Now he walked among the observer-delegates from the many small nations the Iroquois controlled. Corm identified Nanticoke, Tutelo, Chugnut, Minisink, Mahican . . . *Ayi!* Could even the snakes hold so many to whatever was agreed? Yes. Probably. They had been doing it for a very long time.

And now they had the power of *Eehsipana,* the racoon, and *Ayaapia,* the elk buck, to add to their authority.

He saw Quent press palms with a Nanticoke, then begin working his way toward the edge of the assembly. A tall white in the blue coat of the Virginia provincials stopped him and Corm recognized George Washington. Washington and Quent moved a bit to the side, speaking earnestly. After a time they parted and Quent hurried toward Corm. When he got close his face split in a huge grin. "I think—"

"—it's going to be good," Corm finished for him.

"How do you know that?"

"Because you've let your *Cmokman* spirit rise from your belly and mark your face."

Quent chuckled, then grew serious. "Listen, you don't think . . . It's not just for the *Cmokmanuk,* or for Shadowbrook. You know that, don't you?"

"I know that. What did your friend Washington have to say?"

"He's getting married. A Martha someone. A widow with two children, not to mention a fine piece of land that just happens to abut his."

"When's the wedding to be?"

"In January. He's resigning his commission and going to stand for a seat in the Virginia House of Burgesses."

Corm started to say something, then stopped. "Teedyuscung's turn," he said, motioning to the chief who had walked to the center of the circle. "Could be we're about to get to some real business."

They had been on this meadow for five days. One harangue had followed another, but most had been of an almost ritual nature, the orators showing their prowess, vying with each other to catalog a list of grievances with which everyone was already familiar. *It is clear you white men have made this war. Why do you not fight in your Old World or on the sea? Why do you come and fight here in this World that is New to you, but Old to us?* In true *Anishinabeg* fashion all the tribes had put their best talkers first. The English had sat through speech after speech trying not to let their impatience show. Now it was time for those who wielded real power to make their ideas known.

Teedyuscung carried a string of wampum in his left hand. Slowly, with deliberate motions so everyone could count the number of turns, he wound it six times around his right wrist. Four turns had been the highest they'd seen so far. The Delaware chief was signaling that he had something to say of major importance.

"Uncles"—he was looking at the Iroquois chiefs who had conquered his Delaware so long before—"you may remember that you have placed my people at Wyomink and Shamokin." Teedyuscung gestured to his right and left, indicating the two nearby valleys.

"Then sold the land out from under them," Corm muttered.

"Good old snakes," Quent said. "Always to be counted on. Listen, Washington told me—"

Corm put up a hand. One of the Iroquois, an Oneida, had risen while Teedyuscung was still standing. He too had made six loops of wampum. He spoke quickly, with many gestures. Corm wasn't sure he'd understood. "Did he say what I think he said? That the Great Council will let the Delaware continue to live in those valleys?"

Quent's Oneida was better, more practiced because of all the time he'd spent in these parts. "Yes, that's exactly what he said."

"But just letting them stay won't be enough. That's typical Iroquois arrogance. If the Delaware think the snakes can sell them out again whenever they want, it won't—"

Quent put a hand on his arm. "Calm down. It's not going to be like that this time. Wait." A white man stood up and walked to the center of the circle. "He represents the Penns," Quent whispered. "The family." The man began looping a string of wampum around his wrist. He got to six turns—matching Teedyuscung and the Oneida—then ostentatiously added a seventh.

"*Ayi!* He'd better have something to back that up."

"He does. Both ears, Corm. It's important."

The white man nodded in the directions of the two speakers before him, Teedyuscung and the Oneida chief. "I have heard what has been said by my Indian brothers. I wish it to be known that I speak to them with the voice of the Penn brethren to whom the English king gave this land."

There were impatient murmurings from all the Indians who had understood, joined by others as soon as the words had been translated for them.

"That's not going to make them any happier," Corm began. "You know—"

"Will you please shut your mouth and listen? He's giving all the land west of the mountains to the Iroquois. Officially. On behalf of the Penn Family."

"How do you—" Corm broke off. It didn't matter how Quent knew; it was clearly what had happened. A number of the Iroquois stood up. They were obviously delighted, smiling and nodding.

"What about the Delaware?" Corm demanded. "Look at them. They seem ready to walk out."

"Ssh . . . Here comes the best part. That's Denny, the governor of Pennsylvania."

Governor Denny started to speak, then realized he'd forgotten his wampum string. He looked around. An aide rushed forward with a rope of the tubular white beads, whispered something in the governor's ear, then went back to his place. Denny began making loops of wampum around his wrist, his gestures clumsy and unpracticed, but clear enough to be counted. Seven turns. He was saying his words were as important as those of the man who had just given the Iroquois a gift worth a king's ransom. He faced the Delaware. They looked at him intently, waiting.

"I wish to tell our friends the Delaware that the chiefs and the people of Pennsylvania mean to kindle up again the old council fire in the city we call Philadelphia."

Neither Teedyuscung nor Pisquetomen said anything, but the braves and councillors behind them began murmuring among themselves.

"We invite our friends the Delaware to send representatives to that Philadelphia fire," Denny added.

There was a collective intake of breath as everyone, *Anishinabeg* and *Cmokmanuk*, realized he was offering to negotiate directly with the Delaware in future; their claim to this land in the Delaware Valley was being officially recognized by the whites. It was a dramatic change: for many years Pennsylvania had refused to negotiate with anyone other than the Great Council, meaning they saw the Delaware as subject to the Iroquois.

Pisquetomen sat cross-legged on the ground, in the front rank—but he turned his head so he could look at the snakes he despised, however many times he might call them his uncles. The Iroquois were staring straight ahead, making no objection to Denny's words. Clearly they had known about the offer and given their consent, but that didn't mean they could be trusted. Pisquetomen fingered his medicine bag and felt the outline of the blue-black Súki bead carved with *pileewa*, the turkey.

Nichas the Kahniankehaka sachem was also seated in the front rank, and he also wore a medicine bag. He touched it, his gaze meeting that of Pisquetomen the Delaware. Uko Nyakwai said the Kahniankehaka had accepted *eehsipana*, the raccoon. The Red Bear was always truthful. Nichas inclined his head. The gesture was barely perceptible. Probably no one else had seen it, but Pisquetomen had no doubt of its meaning. The Great Council was promising to honor the agreements made here, swearing to do so by the power of the ancient beads that carried the spirits of all their ancestors.

The brother of Shingas the mighty war sachem waited a moment more. If Teedyuscung objected to his speaking for all the Delaware he would say so now. There was no objection. Pisquetomen got to his feet and faced Governor Denny. "The Delaware accept your invitation. We will be glad to share the warmth of the old fire with our brothers in Philadelphia."

It was done. One way or another every Indian in the Ohio Country had promised to withdraw their allegiance from the French and, if asked, accept war belts from the English. Corm's heart pounded in his chest. He turned to look at Quent. "Good plan," he said softly.

"Good dream," Quent answered.

Three days of celebration drinking and feasting and whooping and dancing ended the Easton Conference. Corm and Quent were invited to the Kahnianke-haka fire. They went as white men, wearing buckskins not breechclouts. On the last night they sat together, a slight distance separating them from their Kahni-ankehaka hosts. The sparks of the many fires rose like the fireflies of summer, and the smell of roasting meat put both men in mind of feasts long past. "How long since you've been in Singing Snow?" Quent asked.

"Twelve moons. Leaf Falling last year."

"That's bad."

"*Ahaw,* it is. You?"

"Worse. Not since before we met in Québec. Has to be three years. You heard anything about Bishkek?"

"Nothing. But he must be well. Someone would come looking for one of us otherwise. Pondise probably. He found you before, in New York City no less."

"*Ahaw,*" Quent agreed. "Pondise is pretty good at looking. Speaking of which . . . You ever find that Acadian woman? Marni?"

"Marni Benoit. No, I haven't found her."

"Still looking?"

"*Ahaw.*" Corm got to his feet. "I'm still looking."

Three weeks later the French who occupied Great Forks, the place where the Allegheny and the Monongahela rivers joined to form the Ohio, faced an oncom-ing force of the English and their Indian allies that outnumbered them five to one. The French garrison set Fort Duquesne alight and fled. The prize General Braddock and fifteen hundred men had died trying to capture was taken without a shot. Within hours the English began building Fort Pitt on the rubble of Fort Duquesne.

Word of this latest disaster reached Québec on a bleak December day in the first week of Advent, when all the prayers of the Divine Office begged God for a savior to come and ransom mankind from the captivity of sin. Mère Marie Rose told her nuns the news at the recreation that followed their Monday dinner of stewed cabbage and, for each of them, a sixth part of a well-boiled duck egg left in the turn by a kind *habitant.*

"Dear Sisters," the abbess announced as soon as the bell for recreation began, "the duck egg was the gift of a benefactor. It was for third portion." She went on to the concerns of the outside world. "I must tell you the sad news that Fort Duquesne has fallen to the English."

"But what is to happen?" Soeur Joseph demanded. "How—"

"We will do more penance. And pray harder for our soldiers, and for the poor heathen souls who will now be exposed to the Protestant heresy."

"And what of us here in Québec, *ma Mère*?" Soeur Angelique's eyes were enormous—she was glowing with happiness. "Will the English come and kill us all, and make us martyrs who go straight to heaven?"

"I think you must wait a bit longer for martyrdom, *ma chère petite.* Québec is inviolable. No English warship can pass through La Traverse."

Nicole's heart beat fiercely, but she did not look up from her darning. A chart of the waters around Québec. So important that the defense of all New France depended on it and delivered by her into the hands of Monsieur le marquis de Montcalm.

"Besides"—Soeur Celeste this time, practical as always—"whatever is to happen, martyrdom or anything else, you must wait until next summer, Angelique. It is almost winter. There will be no more war for the time being."

Chapter Twenty-Five

THE CANOE GLIDED across the barely moving water of the bayou, carried on the sluggish current. Mostly Corm sat with his paddle across his knees, dipping it into the water only when he needed to adjust direction. A *Cmokmanuk* cabin on the right bank, he'd been told, hidden in the trees. He must look with both eyes if he was not to miss it.

It was easy to miss anything here. The moss hung in whispering ropes that obscured and distorted the landscape. The only sound was the low hum of insects, and the occasional call of some bird he didn't know. It was like being in a different world, like the chanting at a New Moon Telling. *Haya, haya, jayek,* so, so, all of us together. The bayou too made your heart beat to a different rhythm, but not because you were one with others. Bayou Isolé was as lonely as its name. Marni's place in Louisiana, if he ever found it, seemed to be at least as remote as her farm in l'Acadie.

A couple of times he almost drifted into sleep, then pulled himself back with a surge of fear that he could be lulled into such a dangerous lapse in a strange place. Probably didn't matter. He'd spent a couple of days with some local Choctaw and they were friendly enough; alligators were the only thing to worry about, and so far he hadn't seen any. *The one you are looking for, the squaw. She eats* kokotni.

There was a slight bend up ahead. He put his paddle in the water to make sure the canoe handled the turn properly. That's when he saw her.

Marni was by herself, crouching in the shallows by the bank. Her pale skin was more gold than he remembered, tanned by the sun of this place, and she'd woven her wheaten into a single braid that hung down over one shoulder. She had a basket under her arm, and it looked like she was washing whatever was in it in the water of the bayou. She looked up, startled when the prow of the canoe breached her vision.

"*Pierre? C'es toi? Je n'ai pas pensé que*— Oh." It was a sound between a gasp and a sigh, as if the air had been forced out of her chest by a great weight. "Oh."

"Hello, Marni." Corm used the paddle to move the canoe toward the shore.

"Oh." Then she simply stared.

There was a rope coiled in the bottom of the canoe. He picked it up and gestured toward one of the tall trees on the shore. "*Aide-moi.*"

She didn't say anything, but after a time, when he thought he could hear his heart beating, or maybe hers, she nodded and stood up. She'd hiked the skirt of her dress up almost to her waist and her long legs were bare. He could see the droplets of water pearling on her thighs. They were almost the same color gold as her face. Did she go naked in this place? Like a squaw.

Marni left her basket on the shore and approached the canoe and stretched out her hand to take the rope. Their fingers touched when he gave her one end. She made that same breathy sound then quickly turned away and waded ashore. Corm fed her the slack and she looped the line around an overhanging branch and made it fast. He climbed out of the canoe and went ashore. "Aren't you going to say anything to me? Not even, 'Hello, Cormac'?"

"I . . ." She stopped, ran her tongue over her lips. "I didn't . . ."

"You didn't expect ever to see me again."

"Not just that. I didn't think you were real. Not until I touched your hand."

He looked around at the landscape that was so different from the one where they'd been together. "It's hard to know what's real in this place."

"How did you find me?"

"An old woman in my Potawatomi village—"

"Singing Snow?"

"Yes, Singing Snow." He had forgotten how much he'd told her during those long winter nights when the whole world contained only the two of them. "Shabnokis. She told me the woman I was looking for ate *kokotni,* alligator. Had to be here."

"I never ate an alligator."

"She didn't mean 'ate' exactly. It was just a way of telling me where you were."

"Why?"

"I don't know." Marni's question startled him. He wasn't sure exactly what she was asking. "I went to see her about something else, then she—"

"I meant why were you looking for me. Why now? It's almost four years."

"I never stopped looking."

Marni shook her head. "Don't lie. I waited. You didn't come."

"Yes, I did. The embers of your house were still warm when I got there. I found the curé, Monsieur Faucon the black robe. He had made a drawing of you standing on the ramparts at Halifax waiting for the British ship. He said he'd seen you just a couple of days before, but that you'd already left. In his picture, you were smiling."

"I hated l'Acadie. You knew that."

"Hated it so much you couldn't wait another few weeks? I told you I would return. Why didn't you trust me?"

"It had been six months since the banishing started. I knew you'd have heard about it. I figured if you were going to come, you'd have come by then."

"You figured wrong."

She turned away without answering, yanking down her dress so the skirt covered her legs. She picked up her basket. "Come to the house," she said. "I'll make you something to eat, then you must go."

"Just like that? After I've come all this—"

Marni strode off, not listening to him. "Are you coming?" she called back. Corm followed her.

The house wasn't far, but he'd never have seen it. It was tucked cleverly into the trees, and the clearing that served as a garden was in the rear. It wouldn't be visible from the bayou unless you knew it was there.

Marni stopped before she opened the door. "How did you find me here?"

"I asked some Choctaw." He reached out and touched her plait with one finger. "When I described the color of your hair, they knew exactly who I meant. Besides, they said there aren't many white women around here."

"A few whores," Marni said. "Over by Bayou Septembre. They service the fishermen."

She started to push open the door. Corm stopped her. "Is Pierre, a fisherman?"

"*Non*," she said. "*Pas un pêcheur.* Pierre traps. Snakes mostly. Just now he has gone to Nouvelle Orléans to sell his skins. Of course, the war . . ."

She broke off, catching her lower lip in her teeth. He had seen that gesture a hundred times in his dreams. "Marni, I—"

"It was the war you expected, wasn't it? The reason you could not stay with me but had to—"

A voice from inside the house stopped her words. "*Maman! C'es toi?*"

There were two little girls. Twins, Marni said. "Yvette and Cécile." Neither looked anything like her, nor did they look as young as they must be if—"Do not look so startled," she murmured. "They are five. Their mother died when they were born. They were eighteen months old when I came."

The one called Yvette took the basket from Marni's hands and squealed with delight. "So many, Maman! We will have a feast."

"Yes, a feast. This is Monsieur Shea. He is a friend from l'Acadie. He will eat with us. Go, get things ready. *Vite!*"

The children prepared the table. Marni made a kind of corn gruel cooked with some of the saladings from the garden out back, and boiled the creatures she had been gathering from the bayou when he first saw her. "*Les écrevisses.*" She held up one that had turned bright red now that it was cooked and showed him how to strip away the shell. "It is the tails you eat. They are very good."

Corm agreed that they were, but he could force down only a few, and a little of the gruel. His stomach was cold and knotted. The laughter of the little girls, the way they clung to her and the way she looked at them . . . He was not afraid of Pierre, the trapper of snakes. Not of any man. But Yvette and Cécile terrified him.

Marni looked at his half-eaten plate before she cleared it. "They will sleep soon. Then we will talk."

At dusk, when the twins were settled in their bed, Marni led him back to the bayou. They sat with their backs against one of the trees, some ways distant from the water. "It is not safe at night," she said. "That is when the alligators hunt."

"What kind of a place is this? How did you get here?" He was asking a great deal more. They both knew that.

"The bayou, all Louisiana, is a forgotten place," she told him. "The people who come here, they are forgotten people. France has, I think, less interest in them than they had in the people of l'Acadie, and that is certainly very little. The women are whores, mostly. The men are usually former prisoners who were sent here because no one knew what else to do with them. There are not enough whites to be a threat, so there is little trouble with the Indians."

"This Pierre, he was a prisoner?"

Marni shook her head. "No, a settler. One of the few. His wife was pregnant with the girls when they made the crossing. It was very hard. Then, to bear two . . ."

"They are not your responsibility." He knew how stupid the words were as soon as he spoke them, but he could not call them back.

"You know that is not true. A Choctaw squaw was their wet nurse for the first year. They were still babies when Pierre brought me here. I am the only mother they know."

"How did you meet him?"

"The ship brought me first to Providence from Halifax. I was sent to live with a woman who thought I was her slave. Fortunately I had taken money sewn into the hems of my cloaks when I left the farm. I used none of it to buy food or blankets on the ship. The others did, but not me."

He did not ask how she had managed instead. Better not to know.

"I left Providence after two weeks. Eventually I got to Charleston."

"I looked for you there. Two years ago I was in Carolina looking for you. I had heard some of the Acadians were there."

"Two years ago I had already left. I met Pierre in Charleston. He had hoped to sell his skins for better money, but the war had dried up trade even there. He brought me here."

"And in return you agreed to raise his children."

"It was not like that."

"This Pierre, do you—" Corm broke off. He did not want to know if she loved the snake trapper. "When you are together," he said instead, his voice a fierce whisper, "is it like it was with you and me?"

"No, it is not." Spoken softly, the words bearing no weight of inference. "It is different." She lay beneath Pierre without moving, simply permitting him the freedom of her body. He asked for nothing more and she gave nothing more. So it had been with Jean, the first one, and the others, the men on the journey without whom she would not have survived. Only Cormac had been different. That is why when she saw him floating toward her on the bayou she had thought she was seeing a ghost. Because of all the fevered dreams, and the times after Pierre rolled off her when she shoved the bedclothes in her mouth to keep from wailing aloud her grief. "Pierre is my husband," she said. "We were married by a priest in Nouvelle Orléans before we came here."

"I thought you didn't go to church." It was the only thing he could find to say. Her words were like knives cutting his flesh, but there was too much *Anishinabeg* in him for him to allow the pain to show.

"Cormac Shea, listen to me." She turned toward him, putting her hand on his arm, the first time she'd voluntarily touched him since he appeared. "I had two choices, wife or whore. I chose wife. Pierre is a good man. The children love me and I love them."

"We could have had chi—"

"No, we could not. After you left, I prayed I was with child. I never pray, but I did then. I wanted something of you to be growing in my belly more than I have ever wanted anything in my life. It did not happen. Not then. Not before then. And it has not happened since. I am barren. Yvette and Cécile, they are a gift to me, from the Virgin perhaps. They are the only children I will ever have."

There was just enough light left for him to see the tears streaming down her face. He touched them. She put her hand over his scar. They stayed like that a long few moments. Finally she said, "Take me. Then go."

FRIDAY, JUNE 20, 1759
QUÉBEC LOWER TOWN

As soon as the river was free of ice, Père Antoine adopted the custom of walking every day along the top of the cliffs. His destination was always the same, the place below the town where, to take the south channel and approach the harbor of Québec, a ship must pass between Ile d'Orléans and Ile Madame, the place of La Traverse. Why were there no new batteries on little Ile Madame? He was not a military man, but surely anyone could see that it was the perfect place for cannon to guard the channel. Why not at least some naval ships to patrol the river at this spot? Because they think it is impassible for warships, that without a local pilot no ship can navigate La Traverse, and that even with one, anything larger than a hundred tons is disallowed. But Montcalm knows better since I sent him the chart. Why is nothing happening?

Today is Friday. I am to hear the nuns' confessions. I will have an answer.

The Delegate of the Franciscan Minister General ran back toward the Lower Town, brown robe flapping about his ankles.

"Bless me, *mon Père,* for my sins are many." Nicole made the sign of the cross. "Twice this week I—"

"Why did you lie to me? Do you not know that by doing so you imperil your immortal soul?"

Père Antoine did not look at her, but his fury was evident even without the punishment of his burning gaze. Nicole made another hurried sign of the cross. Holy Spirit help me to find the right words. "Never, *mon Père.* About anything. I have never come into the confessional and lied to—"

"Ha! You think to trip me up by clever expressions and twisted arguments. I did not say you lied in confession. You lied when you told me you saw le marquis de Montcalm. You never met him. What did you do with the thing I gave you to give to him? Did you perhaps throw it in the river at Montréal and think no one would ever—"

"*Mon Père,* on my soul, on the souls of my dead parents, I gave the little tube directly into the hands of Monsieur le marquis. I saw him open it and study the—" She broke off. That was the one thing she had never admitted, how much she knew of what she had brought to Montréal.

"You are convicted out of your own mouth, Soeur Stephane. A busy man like monsieur le marquis, he would not keep you with him while he opened the thing I sent. He would go at once to a private room. You would be sent from his presence." Père Antoine wanted to weep. It had been a huge mistake not to go himself to Montréal. He had allowed his fear of being seen and outfoxed by Louis Roget to cause him to make an enormous mistake. That he had made such an error in such circumstances was unthinkable. Worse, unforgivable. "For your penance, Soeur Stephane, you will take the discipline every night for a month alone in your cell. You will recite ten times the Miserere, and during the entire duration you will not cease to lash yourself and beg God and His Holy Mother and all the Saints to intercede for New France and make up what your cowardice—"

"I will do everything you say, *mon Père*, for I am certainly a sinner and deserve this penance. But I swear to you that in this matter I do not lie. I gave the thing you sent to monsieur le marquis. I saw him open it and study it. He had insisted that I stay and he had opened a bottle of wine. A Lafite Forty-nine. It was the most delicious wine I have ever tasted. Monsieur le marquis also told me about his estate in Provence. It is called Candiac and there he grows olives and almonds, but no grapes. He told me how they send the almonds to Montargis to be covered in sugar and how—"

"*Mon Dieu!* It is not possible."

"But it is possible, *mon Père*. It is true. I swear to you, I—"

Behind the grille of the confessional Nicole saw the priest put his hand to his forehead. "I know," he whispered. "How would you know such things if the marquis had not himself told them to you? And here in the confessional . . . I think you would not lie here, *ma Soeur*. It is the explanation I prefer, but it is not, I think, possible."

"I would not take an oath and break it, *mon Père*." Nicole shifted her weight slightly. Even for her, thin as she was, the confessional was so narrow that just entering it was a penance. Every one of her sisters was plump and round. So was Dear Abbess. How did they manage to be so on such a stingy diet? "Prefer to what, *mon Père?*"

"To the notion that knowing what he knows," the priest whispered, "Montcalm does nothing. It means he does not want to do anything."

Still worse was the news Antoine heard when he had finished confessing the Poor Clares and went out into the street. Tall ships flying the Cross of St. George had been spotted downriver of the Ile d'Orléans. The fleet stretched as far down the St. Lawrence as anyone could see.

"*Tant pis, mon Père*," one of the fisherman told him, almost chuckling, but not, Antoine thought, with humor. "*Cela ne fait rien.* They will stay until it gets cold and the ice threatens and they must turn around and go home. They cannot pass La Traverse." The man turned his head and hacked a globule of yellow phlegm into the gutter. His cheeks were sunken and his eyes red-rimmed. Three consecutive harvests had failed in Canada, and still Bigot fattened the quail for his table on pure wheat. In the town the *habitants* were rationed to four thin slices a day of bread that was three-quarters pea flour. "*Le bon Dieu* protects us, *non?* Isn't that what you priests always say? And if we die? What of it? Heaven is waiting, *non?*"

WEDNESDAY, JUNE 25, 1759
DOWNRIVER OF ILE D'ORLÉANS

He was General Wolfe now, the hero of Louisbourg. A major general only in America and a brigadier general elsewhere, to avoid giving offense to all those officers so much older than he. But most important, he was the man Pitt had selected to lead the attack on Québec, even after the new general insisted on the unheard-of privilege of choosing his own staff for the expedition. Cock-of-the-walk, Quent thought, watching Wolfe standing at the forward end of HMS *Richmond*'s fo'c'sle, glass to his eye. He can't help it. The haughtiness is bred into him.

Sometimes the slight figure turned right, toward the shore of the mighty citadel itself—Quent had no glass, but as far as he could tell the sheer cliffs were unbroken and unscalable. More often Wolfe looked straight ahead, studying the turbulent waters of La Traverse, blocking the only way to bring the fleet within shelling distance of the town. Wolfe snapped the glass closed and turned to Admiral Saunders, in command of this mission as long as it was afloat. "So, sir? What plan?"

The cluster of officers standing near the two men didn't actually press forward, but you could feel their intensity. They're listening with both ears, Quent thought. Hell, so am I. In Christ's name, what does he mean to do? If we bring that pilot we captured up here in chains, and expect he'll—

"I don't trust the Canadian pilot," Saunders said. "And I expect you don't either, General."

"The pilot has every reason to guide us well, Admiral. If we founder, he goes down with the rest of us."

"Is there then no chance," Saunders asked softly, "that he's a patriot?"

"He's a Canadian," Wolfe said, as if that settled the matter.

And you, Quent thought, are an arrogant fool. Never mind that I'm here at your personal request. If it weren't that Nicole were here, I wouldn't be either. He dropped his glance, hoping his disgust wasn't evident in his face. One of the men standing beside him cleared his throat. Quietly at first, then with more force. The admiral turned his head. "Yes, Cooke? You've something to add?"

"I spoke with the Canadian pilot, sir, when the rangers first brought him to us. And last night, I took one of the small boats and—"

"And who, pray, was master of the *Three Sisters* when you were off in a small boat?"

Cooke nodded toward his ship, lying a ways upriver. "The same master who cares for her now, sir. As ably as any man I know."

Wolfe wasn't interested in the rivalries of the seamen. "With respect, Admiral, might we hear what this officer has to say?"

Saunders nodded.

"I can take us through, sir," Cooke said. "At least I'm fairly certain I can. I'd like to try if you'll permit it."

"What about the depth?" asked another of the masters who had been summoned to this council of war. This one had command of HMS *Goodwill*, a third-rater with only eighty guns, but still a draft greater than any merchantman. "I have it on reliable authority that no ship drawing more than—"

"The draft is adequate for the *Goodwill,* sir. I promise you."

Saunders looked at him, trying to decide if he dared trust him. In God's name, how could Cooke know so much more than the rest of them? He couldn't be more than thirty. Sailed on merchantmen until a few years back, and only had four years in the service. Too damned young for command, whatever those fools at the Admiralty thought. "Even if the draft is sufficient, Captain Cooke, do you not think that the French are expecting us? We will be fair game for—"

"I see no evidence that they're expecting us, sir." Out of the corner of his eye Cooke caught sight of Wolfe's nod. He was flooded with courage. "Let me try with one ship for a start, Admiral. If she gets through, we can bring the others. I can do it, I'm quite sure."

Holy God Almighty, Quent thought. He really does think so. "A suggestion, Admiral. If I'm permitted . . ."

"Ah yes, Mr. Hale. The native voice. Go ahead, man, tell us your suggestion."

Quent thought of Nicole, of how close she was and how much danger she might be in, and swallowed his bile. He jerked his head toward the Cross of St. George flying from the masthead. "Take down the English flag, sir, and fly the French. It should allow you to get close enough to answer any enemy fire with your own."

"Devious, you Americans," Saunders murmured. "Is it Indian-style to approve of sailing under false colors?"

Hell take you, you insufferable bastard. As if the same trick hasn't been employed a hundred times by your precious Royal Navy. "Indians don't have flags, Admiral. That's why they use war paint and tattoos to identify themselves."

"Are you suggesting my sailors should—"

"It's an excellent idea," Wolfe interrupted. "A French flag. Just until we get through La Traverse. I believe we can dispense with tattoos and war paint."

Saunders looked at his other officers. Everyone nodded assent.

❧

The admiral decreed that HMS *Goodwill* should make the first attempt. Wolfe insisted on being aboard; Saunders went as well. At the last minute Quent was invited to join them; a whim of Wolfe's, no doubt. The man seemed always to want him around, rather like a charm insuring good fortune, but at the same time appeared to despise him.

They took up their positions on the quarterdeck. "You have the helm, Captain Cooke," Saunders said. "For the duration of the passage," he added, feeling the barbed glance of the *Goodwill*'s actual master.

"Aye, sir."

To Quent's eye Cooke didn't seem unnerved by either the scrutiny or the difficulty of the task. Saunders hadn't said what would happen if he failed, but it didn't need saying. If Cooke survived a shipwreck, he'd be hung from the nearest yardarm as the man who had caused it. On the other hand, not likely any of them would survive a shipwreck in waters this turbulent. Summer it might be, but even from the triple-decked height of the *Goodwill*'s topside Quent could feel the chill rising off the river.

Cooke armed himself with a quill and a sheet of paper fixed to a board, and pressed into service one of the young powder monkeys—a boy of eight who during battle ran flannel-covered cartridges of powder from the stores to the guns. The lad's job this day was to follow Cooke about with a pot of ink. "Helmsman, steady as she goes," the young captain called out. The journey had begun.

Two sounding boats traveled with them, lying off each side and hoisting different color flags to indicate the channel, but mostly it was Cooke's instinct that guided their passage. In the heart of La Traverse the current reversed itself and flowed upstream, or so it seemed. The river was a seething, heaving mass of entrapment, a place of unending turbulence. Despite that, Cooke would spy one particular ripple and call out a change of direction. "Helmsman, half a degree to port!" To Quent, even to the other mariners, the ripple had looked no different from any of the others. "A ledge," Cooke would murmur, making note of it on the chart he was drawing. "Rock, not mud or gravel. Extreme danger."

"In Christ's name," Quent asked, "how do you know?"

"I smell it, Mr. Hale."

Quent sniffed. "I don't smell a damned thing."

Cooke chuckled. "When we land the troops, Mr. Hale, you will know where the infernal Indians are and what they have in mind. I won't smell anything then. And— Helmsman! Larboard a degree! That's where the channel is, not straight ahead, by Christ!" More marks quickly drawn on the evolving chart.

The passage was a zigzag and not wide, but deep enough. When the *Goodwill* drew level with the lower point of the Ile d'Orléans, they struck the French colors and hoisted the red and white St. George's Cross. It didn't seem to make any difference. No one opposed them and not a shot was fired to prevent their progress. Sixty English ships went through La Traverse in two days. Forty-nine were warships, the rest were transports carrying in addition to their crews eighty-five hundred soldiers and the provisions and ordnance they required to place under siege the Citadel of Québec, the fortress city of New France.

Chapter Twenty-Six

"*EH BIEN, MES* amis, *les Anglais sont arrivés.*" Vaudreuil's announcement was entirely unnecessary. Four men were gathered in the Château Saint-Louis: the governor-general and three guests: Pontbriand, the bishop, Intendant Bigot, and Louis Roget. They knew the English had arrived. All Québec knew. They had tried using fire ships to burn them out, and *le bon Dieu* had sent a fierce squall that wrecked two of their frigates. Neither served to drive them away. Wolfe's army was encamped on Ile d'Orléans, facing the town from less than half a league across the river.

"Fewer than nine thousand, I'm told." His Excellency the Bishop of New France was well looked after by Bigot, nonetheless he was rail-thin and his eyes were surrounded by perpetual dark circles. The bishops before him had spent more time in Paris than in Québec. Pontbriand had tried to do his duty by remaining here, but ever since he had permitted Père Antoine to bring his Poor Clares, things had gone from bad to worse, or so it seemed. Cloistered nuns devoted entirely to penance . . . surely such women should bring blessings raining down from heaven, not English warships that mysteriously found their way through La Traverse. *Alors,* such things were in the hands of *le bon Dieu.* "You have twice as many men, do you not, *mon Général?*"

Montcalm shook his head. "Not quite, Excellency. If your figures are accurate—"

"I have them on superb authority, *mon Général.*" The bishop stifled his sigh. His priests were a constant worry. Many of them were Canadian firebrands who too often put country above Church. He had instructed them to remain neutral whatever happened. He might as well have commanded the tides to flow in reverse. "I am informed by a patriot on Ile d'Orléans," His Excellency murmured.

Montcalm shrugged. "If the patriot can count, and if there are not still more fighting men aboard the ships, then yes, we perhaps outnumber the English. Still . . ." He had sixteen thousand men, but fewer than half were French regulars, troops he could rely on. Most of the rest were Canadians. Montcalm had seen boys of fifteen in his camp alongside men of eighty, all burning to defend Canada. God help them if a battle actually came.

"How many Indians?" Vaudreuil asked.

"A thousand perhaps." Montcalm was busy studying his fingernails.

"So few! I thought—"

"The savages are not to be relied on, Monsieur le Général. Their beliefs as well as their customs will always be a mystery to us. I have heard talk of magic—some precious stones that tell them they are not to fight with Onontio."

Louis Roget stiffened, then made himself relax, but not before the bishop noticed. His Excellency had not taken his attention from the Jesuit since the meeting began. "You know something of this matter, Monsieur le Provincial?"

"No, Excellency. How could I?"

"I have no idea, *mon cher Roget.* But you Jesuits, you know everything, *non?*"

The Provincial allowed himself a small smile. "Not quite everything, Excellency." *Papankamwa,* the fox. *Eehsipana,* the raccoon. *Ayaapia,* the elk buck. *Anseepikwa,* the spider. *Eeyeelia,* the possum. *Pileewa,* the turkey. Five years now, but Roget could still hear the Midewiwin priest in the forest not far from here, chanting those words over and over, the names of six magic stones. The black robes, he promised, could have them for a price.

The Jesuit had, of course, never believed in the magic. But it wasn't necessary that he believe, only that the Indians did. That fact alone would have given him enormous power over them, if, of course, he had the stones. The amount he offered must have seemed a king's ransom to the Midè priest, but the savage had never appeared to claim his prize. Perhaps someone else offered him more, or perhaps the stones never truly existed. Roget turned away from the bishop's intense scrutiny. "It seems to me the Indians can always be convinced to fight, *mon Général.* Fighting is in their nature. You might try a bit more persuasion."

"With respect, Monsieur le Provincial, in a siege such as General Wolfe clearly intends, the savages are useless."

"Never useless," Vaudreuil said, but not Louis Roget thought, with much insistence. The Jesuit looked from Montcalm to the governor-general, his eyes probing for any new information. There was none. Each had an instinctive position. Versailles had made him a marquis, but Vaudreuil was a Canadian and he would always choose to fight like a Canadian. He had wanted to move the entire populace out of the city, send them to Trois Rivières or Montréal, and leave the defense of Québec to men who would hide behind trees and harass the enemy when they least expected it. And take scalps. Roget suppressed a shudder of distaste. It did not matter what Vaudreuil wanted. Word had come from Versailles in May. The governor-general was to defer to Montcalm in all matters that pertained to the war. *Au fond,* things were as they were. As for Montcalm . . . Not the best family, certainly, but French, and a traditional soldier. "Exactly what sort of siege do you speak of, *mon Général?*"

"The sort with which we military men are familiar. The *siège en forme,* Monsieur le Provincial," Montcalm proceeded, as if speaking to a young cadet. "One surrounds on three sides, with the aid of certain entrenchments brings one's guns ever nearer, and—"

"It is not possible to surround Québec on three sides."

"Exactly. You make my point, Monsieur le Provincial. It needs only that we wait. When the winter approaches, the soldiers and sailors of His Britannic Majesty will leave."

The bishop cleared his throat "We were told with equal authority that the English could not pass La Traverse."

"Not by me, Excellency." Montcalm faced all three, the Jesuit and Vaudreuil as well as the bishop. He did not flinch. "I have left such matters to local wisdom. What would I know of the waters surrounding Québec?"

Père Antoine waited across from the Château Saint-Louis keeping to the shadows of one of the grand houses surrounding the Place d'Armes. He was shivering. Not so cold a day, but this trembling would not leave him. He felt hot at the same time, as if he were burning up with fever. His fingers moved automatically, counting off the beads of the rosary as he told his *Aves.* He had been here a long time, four recitations of the seven decades of the Franciscan Crown. Never mind. He'd seen them all go into the château, the bishop, and Louis Roget, and monsieur le marguis de Montcalm. They would have to come out sometime. *"Je vous salue, Marie . . ."* On the other side of the square, the central door of the château opened and a pair of liveried servants took their places on either side.

The first man to appear was the bishop. His departure was marked by a flurry of ring kissing and signs of the cross sketched hurriedly in the air. Antoine had positioned himself so that his view of the château would not be obscured when a carriage approached. The one that did so now was pulled by four horses and covered with much gilt; it displayed the seal of New France as well as the arms of the Episcopal See. The bishop lifted the skirts of his red robes, then waited while the servants positioned themselves on either side. A footstool was put in place. His Excellency placed one velvet-clad foot on it, then, with the aid of the footmen, disappeared into the coach's interior.

Louis Roget used the fuss surrounding the departure of the bishop to slip out the door and hurry away on foot. Père Antoine watched him for only a moment. For once the Jesuit was not the focus of his interest.

The door of the Château Saint-Louis remained closed for the duration of five more *Aves*. He was midway through a sixth—"*Sainte Marie, Mère de Dieu, priez*"—when the marquis appeared. The footmen snapped to attention. Another carriage rolled forward. Antoine darted across the square.

"Good day to you, *mon Général*."

"Who are you?"

"I am called Père Antoine."

"Ah yes, the Franciscan. I thought—" Montcalm stopped speaking. *I present you this on behalf of Père Antoine Rubin de Montaigne, the Delegate to New France of the Minister General of the Order of Friars Minor. Père Antoine begs to inform His Excellency that what is contained herein is of the utmost importance to the defense of New France.* "Not just any Franciscan, are you? You are the Delegate of the Minister General. Is that not correct, *mon Père?*"

"*Oui, mon Général.* I am unworthy, but I have that honor."

The door to the carriage was open. The footmen were waiting. "Come," Montcalm said. "Ride with me to Beauport. We will talk on the way."

"I expected this visit before now, *mon Père.*"

"I did not wish to intrude myself into such a business, *mon Général*. I am a simple son of St. Francis. I do not—"

"You are Antoine Pierre Rubin de Montaigne, sir."

"No longer, sir. Now only Père Antoine, a humble priest."

Montcalm shrugged. "*Eh bien.* What then does this humble priest wish of me? I am very busy, *mon Père*. As you are perhaps aware, there is a war. And the English are at our doorstep."

The carriage of the marquis was a much simpler affair than that of the bishop. It was entirely black, the only relief being the Montcalm coat of arms emblazoned in gold on the door. There were black curtains on the windows, but they were pushed back. Antoine could see the fortifications that were everywhere. Eleven thousand men had dug fifty leagues of trenches and erected countless campsites and redoubts. They had worked night and day for five weeks—Montcalm had not issued the order to fortify the Beauport shore until the end of May—and despite endless rain which left behind a plague of flies, the men built a line of defense from the place where the St. Charles River entered the St. Lawrence, near the château of Intendant Bigot in Québec, to the massive and impassible Montmorency Falls above the village of Beauport. Everywhere Antoine looked there were gun batteries trained on the river. There were rows upon rows of tents, even a few wigwams. "So much, *mon Général.* Such a huge effort. Now, after they have come. And to protect La Traverse, nothing. Not even one battery on little Ile Madame."

"You forget, *mon Père,*" Montcalm said softly. "La Traverse was believed to be impassable."

"But you knew better, *mon Général.*"

"No, I did not. How could I contradict those who were born here in Québec?"

"Do you deny that the little sister brought you the chart made by the Jesuit Loualt? That it showed—"

Montcalm raised his hand. "I deny nothing, *mon Père.* Here in this carriage there is no need to deny anything. In a more public place . . . That, of course, would be different."

The two men looked at each other. Neither glance wavered. "To my face," Antoine said at last. "You are a man of incredible arrogance, Monsieur le Marquis de Montcalm. Have you no fear for your immortal soul?"

"I am, *mon Père,* a man who knows the difference between spiritual realities and those of a military nature. You speak of a battery at Ile Madame. It would have been useless. Even a pair of batteries facing each other across the entry to the channel would have been useless. Forty warships would have been required to defend La Traverse. I do not have forty warships, my dear Pére Antoine, because in Versailles the lovely Pompadour does not concern herself with Canada. And the king—I apologize for offending your religious sensibilities—concerns himself with nothing except his cock. That is the reality."

"And the souls of the heathen? Do you have no concern for the millions who thanks to you may never hear the gospel preached to them and never attain salvation? Do you realize that if—"

"I leave such things to you, *mon Père.* And to *le bon Dieu.* Surely God is sufficiently concerned with souls not to need my poor assistance."

"You speak heresy, sir. I warn you again, you put your own soul in peril."

They had arrived at the small manor house Montcalm had made his headquarters. The carriage slowed, then stopped, and a footman appeared at the door and started to open it. The marquis waved the servant away. "I will give you one sop for your conscience, Père Antoine, though why it should prick you, I do not know. You did what you thought best, and I did likewise. We will both be judged at the appropriate time, *non?*"

The priest started to speak. Montcalm raised his hand. "Hear me out. I promised you a piece of information. It will do you no good with anyone in Québec. You are already believed to be a fanatic, as you know. Vaudreuil doesn't trust you, and neither, I think, does the bishop. Roget hates you, and Bigot is barely aware of your existence. Still, for your own peace of mind, and because I am grateful for the effort you made—even if I chose not to act on it in the manner you hoped— the defenses of Québec are without a break. There is no place for Wolfe to attack us. He can shell, and he will. But unless we give him a battle, he cannot have one. I do not intend to give him a battle, *mon Père*. When the winter comes the Admiral Saunders and the General Wolfe will go away, because if they do not they will be frozen in place in the river and we will pick them off at our leisure. With, I am sure, the assistance of those local Indians in whom our esteemed governor-general has such faith. Meanwhile the supplies of the English will be long gone, and those we do not kill will starve to death."

"But all of this could have been avoided if—"

Montcalm held up his hand. "I am not finished. I am told, *mon Pére*, that your concern is for the Ohio Country. Millions of heathens, you said, just waiting to be saved. I am not sure they can ever be civilized, much less made into Christians, but on the matter of the importance of the land south of us, we are in agreement. The Ohio Country and Louisiana are the future of New France on this continent. If we were to lose this realm of ice it would be unfortunate, perhaps, but not the defeat of the empire."

The marquis reached for the door of the carriage. It seemed almost too much effort. He was weary. He had made exactly this argument in documents sent to Versailles during the winter. He had begged His Majesty for permission to withdraw from Canada and defend the Ohio forts and Louisiana, and he had been refused. The folly of that decision was already apparent, at least to him.

Amherst prepares to take Fort Carillon. If it falls—*eh bien,* when it falls—the English will also take Fort Niagara and then Fort St. Frédéric. The entire corridor will be theirs, and I can do nothing because the chinless general has pinned me and my army here in Québec, and I must defend this place whether or not it is worth defending. If I could have avoided this by using the map you undoubtedly stole, my fanatic Franciscan, I would have done so. It was not possible, but I can see in those half-mad eyes of yours that you will probably never believe me. So I must pull your fangs with a trifle more firmness.

"Don't bother to get out of the carriage, *mon Père*. We have finished our business. I will have you driven back to the town. Please give my compliments to the delightful Soeur Stephane. Ah yes, one thing more. If you are thinking that she can corroborate your fantastic story about a map . . . I will deny her as readily as I deny you. And since I have learned that her father was an English officer, I do not think she will command more trust than you will. *Au revoir, mon Père*. I commend myself to your prayers."

And I, if you keep this, promise you life everlasting. In all Christendom a Poor Clare Abbess was the only woman who could speak those words to her nuns, but her legacy included another extraordinary privilege. A Poor Clare abbess could bless her community with the Sacred Host, just as a priest did.

Because, five hundred years before, Holy Mother Clare had taken it on herself to carry the Blessed Sacrament to the ramparts of Assisi and repel the Saracen invaders, Mère Marie Rose was permitted to open the door of the tabernacle from the nun's side of the grille and remove the elaborate monstrance that held the large white wafer. She did so now, and turned to face her nuns. They bowed their heads. The abbess raised the monstrance above her own, then brought it down to chest height. *"Au nom du Père, et du Fils, et du—"* Marie Rose stopped speaking.

Soeur Celeste waited for the space of two heartbeats, then raised her head. The eyes of Dear Abbess were closed. She was motionless, holding the monstrance at her left side. *She feels again the wound of love,* Celeste realized. *But like this, with the Holy Sacrament in her hands . . .* Celeste was the vicaress of the community, the second in command. It was up to her to decide what to do. Normally, when it was during the Office or some other prayer, it was simple. She led the sisters out of the choir and allowed *le bon Dieu* to care for the nun He so favored. But now, with the Sacred Host in her hands . . . what if, overcome as she was, the grip of Mère Marie Rose gave way?

The mighty St. Lawrence was a red torrent, a river of blood. Hundreds tumbled in the rushing waters, all screaming in agony and weeping with despair. And hovering above, holding the river back so it could not engulf Québec and sweep thousands of more souls into a plunge to everlasting hellfire, there were five nuns. "There should be six, Lord. Why only five?" Soeur Stephane was missing. She was off to one side, by herself. Very still, and her veil was crowned with a wreath of flowers. "Truth is where it is, Marie Rose, whom I have made abbess. I have given you charge over the souls of these nuns, but only to act in My name. To honor the truth I show you, not the truth you expect."

The moments went by. Mère Marie Rose did not move. Soeur Celeste was not an abbess; for her to touch the monstrance when it contained the Sacred Host was a grave sin. How much worse, though, was the thought that, entranced as she was, Mother Abbess might drop the Glory that she held. Celeste rose from her stall and approached the altar. *"Ma Mère,* please. You must come back to us. For at least as long as it takes to return the monstrance to the tabernacle. Mère Marie Rose, please . . ."

"Blood," the abbess whispered. "A river full of blood and torment. Soeur Stephane . . ."

Startled, Celeste turned to look at the youngest nun. Soeur Stephane knelt in her stall, head bowed, apparently unaware that she had anything to do with the vision of the abbess. "She is here, *ma Mère,* do you wish me to—"

"I wish that you would return to your stall, Soeur Celeste. What are you thinking of?" The abbess's eyes were wide open now, and she was staring at her second in command with astonishment. "You give a bad example, *ma Soeur.* It is against the Holy Rule."

Celeste bowed her head and in acknowledgment of the reprimand touched her heart. "I humbly confess my fault, *ma Mère.*" She turned and went back to her stall.

Marie Rose waited until Celeste had resumed her place. *"Et du Saint-Esprit,"* she intoned, concluding the benediction. Then she turned, replaced the monstrance in the tabernacle, and genuflected. Give me strength, Lord, she prayed. Don't let the sisters see me tremble as I walk back to my stall. A torrent of blood. And Soeur Stephane, so young to die . . . Save us, Lord, we perish.

Wolfe's guns could not shell the town from the Ile d'Orléans, but he believed Québec would be in range from the heights of Pointe-Lévis on the opposite shore. Monckton, his senior brigadier and a Yorkshireman accustomed to plain speech, said that couldn't be so. "If the guns could do them damage from this elbow," he bent over the map the two were studying and indicated Pointe-Lévis with a blunt finger, "surely they'd have fortified it."

"Why is it, General Monckton, that if I say black, you say white?"

"Begging your pardon, General Wolfe, I do not. I merely wish to point out that—"

"That we should accept French wisdom. Which, I remind you, also said we could not navigate La Traverse, or bring anything through that was bigger than a hundred tons."

Like a rat he was, an ugly little white rat with pink eyes. God rot Cooke for ever showing them the way through that God-rotting channel, and Wolfe for being the first to support the notion. No telling him anything now. "There's not a single battery on the whole of the south shore, General Wolfe. Not a gun. That has to mean that the French engineers believe—"

"I do not, sir, mean to conduct this campaign according to the beliefs of the French engineers. We will take Pointe-Lévis and bring up our guns."

"A man, *ma Mère,* at the turn." Angelique was at her most wide-eyed. "He demands to see whoever is 'in charge in this place.' I directed him to the chapel, but he refused to go."

"Yes, I expect that is so. He did not ask for me by name?" The governor-general had sent two emissaries in the past four days, and the marquis de Montcalm one. All three had been extremely respectful, however insistent.

"No, *ma Mère*, he asks only for a person with authority."

Marie Rose was at her writing table, preparing a testament that was to be sent back to the founding monastery in Montargis once she and all her nuns were dead. Soeur Stephane might be the first, but surely they all faced the same fate. "Tell him he must come back tomorrow. I am too busy to come to the turn just now."

Angelique did not leave. "I humbly beg, *ma Mère* . . ."

"*Oui?* What is it, child?"

"The man, *ma Mère*, his accent . . . I do not think he is like the others. I think perhaps he has been sent by . . ." Angelique's voice dropped to a whisper. "General Wolfe, *ma Mère*. Possibly. I mean, I cannot—"

"Did you smell no brimstone, Soeur Angelique? Feel no heat of the devil's fire?"

"On no, *ma Mère*. I do not mean—"

Marie Rose put down her quill. "Very well, *ma Soeur*, I will go to the turn."

"I will come with you, *ma Mère*. I will bring holy water and—"

"I will confront the devil alone, Soeur Angelique. You may go back to your chores."

The little Angelique was quite correct. The man spoke French badly, and with an English accent. So, a man sent by the General Wolfe? Not likely, but entirely possible. "Please, monsieur, I wish to be certain that I understand. If you would kindly repeat—"

Quent marshaled all his patience. "I am telling you, madame, that you and your nuns are in grave danger."

"On whose authority do you say this, monsieur?"

"On the authority of common sense, madame."

Marie Rose leaned her forehead against the wood of the turn. Only for a moment, and only because she was alone. It was imperative that none of her nuns know how weary she was. "Apparently common sense has become a much more common virtue since I have entered the cloister. You are the fourth person to tell me of our danger, monsieur."

"Then why are you still here?"

"May I ask, monsieur, what business that is of yours?" A question only to gain time. While she considered. Could it be him? Yes, it was possible.

"I am concerned for you and the other nuns, madame."

A stranger with an English accent who does not know how to address a nun. The very large redheaded man who brought Soeur Stephane that first day. "Are you perhaps most concerned for one of my nuns, monsieur? One in particular." Holy Spirit, grant me wisdom and discernment. And let him not hear the pounding of my heart. "If that is so, I can assure you that we are all of one opinion."

Jesus God Almighty. Was there no reasoning with the woman? "Madame, the English soldiers have taken Pointe-Lévis. They are now directly across from you. They are not of your religion, madame, and they will not respect your way of life. You must all leave this place. The Lower Town in particular is not safe."

The redcoats had made up a ditty. They sang it all the time, made up verses to suit whatever bellicose mood took them:

And when we have done with the mortars and guns,
If you please, Madame Abbess, a word with your nuns.
Each soldier shall enter the convent in buff,
And then never fear, we will give them Hot Stuff!

Even Wolfe had laughed at this latest version.

"Madame, do you hear me? I truly think—"

"I think, monsieur, that you have put yourself in some peril to bring us this warning, and I am sure that God will reward you for your kindness. Now it is best if you go away."

"And will you do the same, madame?" He stamped down his frustration with her obstinacy, not letting himself shout the words.

"No, monsieur, we will not. We have taken a vow to remain enclosed in this place. If we are to die here, then so be it." Angelique and Françoise were both making a novena to petition for martyrdom. Joseph had started another. Her request was for quick martyrdom, without being tortured first. It was Stephane who said she was quite sure English soldiers would not torture nuns. All, Marie Rose thought, a matter of definition. "Good night to you, monsieur. I shall hold you in my prayers."

"They have all but emptied the Lower Town of *habitants*," Quent told Wolfe. "Your ammunition will be wasted, General."

"Never that. Makes the men feel good to fire their guns. Besides, it'll put the fear of God in the enemy. Still . . . You're sure about the locals?"

Quent nodded. "Very sure."

"You've been over there, haven't you?"

"Yes."

"Bloody damn. I might have known. How did you manage it? The way you look, I should think you'd be easy to spot."

"There are ways, General."

No one would have thought much about an Indian standing in the alley, leaning into the turn conferring with the invisible nuns. The man with Huron face-markings and blacked hair, wearing a smock and breeches, would be assumed to be one of the Christian Indians from the Jesuit missions come to aid in the defense of Québec.

"Yes, of course," Wolfe agreed. "Many ways I suppose for a man of your talents." It was Hale who had convinced him to have the redcoats' jackets made a bit freer and shorter, so they weren't as restrictive. And putting the light infantry in those caps with the black cloth under the chin, that was an excellent idea. Kept the men a bit warmer when they were belly down on the ground. " Mr. Hale, I have been thinking. Why can't our troops wear their knapsacks higher and fastened across their backs the way the Indians do? That would be an excellent accommodation, don't you think?"

"Excellent, General Wolfe. Leaves both hands free."

"Yes, my thought exactly. I shall issue the command. Mr. Hale, will you go again?"

"Sir?"

"To Québec, Hale. Will you go again on my behalf? See if you can tell us by what manner we can get up those damnable cliffs."

Quent fixed him with his most intense stare. "If I find a way, I'll tell you. But this idea of shelling the Lower Town, General, it's really not—"

Wolfe had already turned away.

SATURDAY, JULY 12, 1759
POINTE-LÉVIS

Not yet dawn. Wolfe stood on the battlements, wrapped and muffled against the rain and the chill and the nagging ache in his lower belly, doing up the buttons of his breeches. Sweet Jesus, what wouldn't he give for a proper piss, one without the burning. A lot. But not everything, by damn. Not Québec. I'll have this prize if I have to stay here until November. And if there's nothing left but rubble by the time I take it, well, that's their choice.

He raised his hand. The grenadiers in their tall mitered caps ran forward and lit the charges, then dashed out of the line of fire. The bombardment of Québec began with a hail of cannonballs that fell into the river. The officers in charge of the shelling called out the adjustments to be made and the reloading began.

The goal was simply to have their ammunition reach the shore. Everyone assumed that even if the French engineers were wrong and General Wolfe was right and cannon could do damage from this distance, only the Lower Town would be in peril. When the gunners finally found their range, the first direct hit was at the very top of the escarpments, on the Collège des Jésuites. The men sent up a huge cheer, then broke into song.

Quent heard the boom of the cannon and the tumult of success from a distance. Since dawn he had been prowling the forest between the camp and the village of Beaumont, stopping every once in a while to whistle the call of the northern loon. There was no response. Even if one came he couldn't be sure it would be Corm who'd appear. The woods were full of Indians, and Canadians who'd disguised themselves as Indians. The redcoats had taken to posting double pickets after a number of single sentries at the perimeter of their camps were found killed and scalped.

In God's name, what did they expect? Gentlemanly conduct, Wolfe said. Quent whistled again, and heard only silence. Wolfe said it was the scalping he couldn't stomach. Death was to be expected in war, but mutilating the corpse . . . that wasn't how gentlemen fought. Hell no, gentlemen did their damage from a distance. The chinless bastard bloody well knows he can't take Québec by shelling it; he admits he's only doing it to keep the men occupied. What about—Quent heard the faint scuffling sounds of moccasins touching the earth.

There was an enormous maple tree to his left, with a trunk too big for him to get his arms around. Quent ducked behind it and waited, tomahawk in hand. He had his long gun, but it was almost useless in these circumstances. The sound of a shot would bring hundreds of the enemy converging from every direction. A few more moments went by. Maybe he'd been wrong. No, he could hear it more clearly now. The steady drumming of running feet. Moments later a half dozen Abenaki went by in single file. They were heading away from the English camp, not toward it, so he felt no need to engage them. How come Lantak and his renegades hadn't shown up and given him a chance to settle that old score? No sign of him so far, and probably not going to be. Outlaws like Lantak skulked about on the fringes of things. They weren't likely to relish a clash of this magnitude.

Quent waited until the Abenaki were out of sight, then whistled the loon's cry once more. There was still no answer.

THUNDER MOON, THE THIRD SUN
THE VILLAGE OF SINGING SNOW

Bishkek was staring at him, at least so it seemed to Corm. His manhood father was in a square box made of woven twigs. A log for his chin to rest on had been fixed across the open top. Bishkek was dead.

Every member of the village sat on blankets spread on the ground—squaws and small children in one place and men and boys in another, Bishkek's burial box between them—and ate the feast of stewed corn and berries and bear fat. No one spoke. The only sounds were made by Shabnokis and her drum and her chanted prayers. "He is not here in this body," she had told Corm when he arrived that morning. "His spirit has left this worn-out thing behind. But"—she had gestured to the air above their heads—"he is still here with us. He will not go to the next world for a time."

"How long?" Corm asked.

He meant how long had it been since the old man died. The Midewiwin squaw priest thought he was asking about the afterlife. "Until his bones are dry and in the pit with the others, his spirit will be in the village. Ten moons, maybe twelve. You must stay until then."

"I can't. I mean no disrespect to my manhood father, but I am—"

"Listen to me, bridge person. This old man stole your death." Shabnokis read the disbelief in his eyes. "I am telling you exactly what he told me. The last time you were here, when we spoke of *kokotni,* when was that?"

"Leaf Falling. Not the one just past. The one before that."

"Yes, that was the time when the snow fell while the trees still had leaves."

"I remember."

"Before then your manhood father dreamed that if the snow fell on you while you were in this village, it would be the last time he would see you alive. That Leaf Falling, the snow fell on you."

Corm remembered how anxious Bishkek had been for him to go. "A few flakes only. I was already leaving."

Shabnokis made a sound of disgust. "Do you think a dream is only half true? Bishkek knew you were cursed. He fasted and made many prayers to take the curse from you to himself. Now"—she turned to look again at the corpse in its burial box—"you are alive and he is dead, because he offered Shkotensi his life for yours. You will stay until the second funeral."

Corm shook his head and tried to explain, but Shabnokis had ignored him and began again to beat her drum and chant her prayers. She continued all day while the family prepared Bishkek's body for burial, and while the village feasted.

A squaw came to the men's blanket with a huge second portion of the corn and bear fat stew, scooping it from her tin cooking pot onto the flat wooden board that sat on the ground in the middle of the circle of braves and elders and young boys. The pot was a *Cmokmanuk* thing, traded for skins. The old art of making pots of clay was almost forgotten. Corm thought of Pontiac the Ottawa and his concern for the changes among the *Anishinabeg,* and touched the Crane People medicine bag that hung around his neck.

The honor of giving Bishkek his second helping fell to Corm as the eldest male relative. If Quent were at the feast the privilege would be his. The others waited while Corm scooped up a portion of the steaming food in his two hands, carried it to the burial box, and put it on the ground in front of his manhood father. Once Bishkek had been fed the other men eagerly dipped their fingers into the stew. They did not speak, but ate with enthusiasm, wiping their greasy hands on their chests after each mouthful. Corm managed only a few more bites. *I wish I had seen you before your spirit left your body, old Father. I wish I had come even one day sooner.*

When he arrived in Singing Snow Bishkek had not been dead for long. The old man's corpse was still propped in a corner of the wickiup, leaning against the wall with the knees drawn up almost to the chin so he would stiffen in the proper position for burial. Bishkek's daughters had dressed him in soft moccasins with no beadwork, because that was the Potawatomi way, and leggings made of fine elkskin cured without hair, and a breechclout of the same material. Corm had touched his manhood father's hand and found there was still some warmth.

"I looked for you everywhere among the *Cmokmanuk*," Pondise said. "To tell you Bishkek was sick and that you should come home quickly. I left after the Cracking Ice Telling and did not return until the Telling of Much Fat."

The boy had devoted two months to the search, much of April and May. "I was in a place very far from here," Corm said. "It is no shame that you did not find me." He'd spent much of that time with the Choctaw, trying nearly every day to see Marni alone, and mostly failing. When he did catch her without the snake trapper or the little girls, she refused to talk to him and sent him away. Finally he'd gone.

"I did not find Kwashko either," Pondise added.

"He is in Québec with the redcoats."

Corm heard the surprised murmuring of those who were crowded into the wickiup watching him pay his last respects to Bishkek. "First we will bury my manhood father," he told them. "Then I will explain."

By afternoon the corpse was rigid. Now Pondise and Corm painted Bishkek's bare chest and his face in the red and black colors of a Potawatomi brave going to war. Corm thanked the Great Spirit that he'd at least arrived in time to perform this service for his manhood father. He thanked Miss Lorene's Jesus God, too. Just in case.

When the war paint was finished, it was the turn of Bishkek's granddaughters to do him homage and they wound many strings of wampum around his neck and his arms, so in the next world it would be known how highly he was valued.

Then Kekomoson had come into the wickiup, carrying a headdress made of black beaver fur with two long quills of gray eagle feathers and another, smaller cluster of red feathers from the breast of a rare bird. Because he was the chief Kekomoson put the headdress on Bishkek. He watched while Corm placed the old man's bow in the burial box with him, and Pondise brought a quiver of arrows and put it beside the bow.

When everything was ready four braves carried the burial box from the wick-iup to the death feast and put it where it now stood, between the eating places of the men and the women, and Shabnokis told Bishkek that they were gathered to eat with him for the last time.

When everyone had eaten as much as they wanted, the squaws took what was left away and the men smoked the calumet. Then Corm and Pondise spent the night sleeping on the ground beside Bishkek's corpse. Because it was Thunder Moon and warm, the daughters and granddaughters slept there as well. In the morning the same four braves who had carried the burial box to the feasting place lifted it again and brought it to an open area that had been prepared for first burial. Everyone followed in procession, with Corm and Pondise leading. The squaws came behind, carrying many parcels wrapped in skins and some that were large enough to require a hide for covering.

The hole prepared for Bishkek was deep enough so that the base of the casket could be set in it and it would stand firm for as long as necessary. "See," Lashi said, "he can look back at the village and see us." Lashi was Pondise's mother and Bishkek's youngest daughter; she had been his favorite. She put a woolen shawl in the casket with her father. It was bright red—*Cmokmanuk* work, like the metal pots—and Bishkek had brought it back for her the one time he visited Québec. "So he won't be cold," Lashi said. Corm added his tomahawk and Pondise a metal skinning knife. Corm wished it were made of flint, but he said nothing; Pondise had given what he considered his most valuable thing.

One by one the rest of the old man's kin put in his burial box something he would find useful on the journey to the next world, then a conical lid woven in the same manner as the box itself was fit snugly over the top and tied down with leather thongs.

Ixtu the Teller came forward and began the story of Bishkek's ancestors and how he came to be here in this place when it was his turn to die, and of his grandson and his two manhood sons. He did not say that one of the manhood sons was not here to honor his manhood father. If he added that to the Telling it must always be part of the story, but perhaps not a true part. The bridge person had promised there was an explanation.

They were all waiting for Corm to speak; he could feel their eyes watching him. He knew too that they were thinking that Bishkek's male line was threatened. Nei-

ther Quent nor Corm had ever planted a seed in the belly of any squaw in Singing
Snow, and Pondise was still too young to marry.

Maybe it wasn't Marni who was barren. Maybe his seed had no strength and
could not make any woman's belly swell. But the hot juices of his manhood had
never failed him. Besides, he hadn't been Marni's first or her last. Damned whore.
Damned barren whore. But knowing she would never be his was like a festering
wound stinking inside him. The way Bishkek's flesh would stink as it fell off his
dead bones. That's why the burial box was not woven too tightly. The air had to
get in and help rot the flesh and dry the skeleton. When the maggots had eaten
away everything that could putrefy, the whitened bones of his manhood father
would be taken out of the burial box and put into the great pit with the bones of
everyone else from Singing Snow. And at that second and final funeral they would
chant the same words they chanted at every New Moon Telling: *Haya, haya, jayek.*
So, so, all of us together.

When Ixtu was finished with his Bishkek Telling the bundles that the women
had carried to the burial site were opened and all of Bishkek's possessions were
given away. Corm got the old man's calumet, and Pondise the sealskin tobacco
pouch and all the tobacco that was in it. The other men in the village divided
Bishkek's blankets and the furs that kept his wickiup warm in the winter. Those
that had needed a full hide to cover them were his birch sleeping frame and the
cooking pots that his wife had left behind in his wickiup. Old-style clay pots, they
hadn't been used for all the years since her death. After their mother was gone
Bishkek's daughters cooked for him in the pots their mothers-in-law gave them.
Because neither Corm nor Kwashko nor Pondise had taken a wife in the village,
there was no one to inherit the cooking pots of Bishkek's wife. "I will keep them
in my wickiup until the squaw to have them is chosen," Kekomoson said. Corm
was furious with Quent for not being there to share the disapproval. Even though
that was as stupid as saying he hated Marni Benoit and Pierre the snake trapper
was welcome to her.

"Now it is time I explain why Kwashko my whiteface brother is not here,
though he honored his manhood father and honors everyone in Singing Snow.
It is the story I came here to tell," Corm added. "If Ixtu and Shabnokis agree that
it is proper, I would like us to sit on the ground here so that Bishkek too can hear
my words."

The Teller and the Midewiwin priest consulted, then said it was permitted.
Everyone sat on the ground and Corm began the story of his dream and the gift
of Memetosia the Miami chief, and of the great war that the English and the
French *Cmokmanuk* were fighting. "And when it is over and the English have
won, all the *Cmokmanuk* will leave this place and it will be for the *Anishinabeg*,"
he finished. "That was the meaning of my dream, and whatever dream it was

that caused Memetosia the Miami to give me the Suckáuhock that comes from long ago."

Corm took the medicine bag with the crane symbols from around his neck and gave it to Kekomoson. "Inside is the Súki bead marked with *eeyeelia*, the possum. It is the last of the stones and I have kept it for my people and my village, because the *Anishinabeg* half of my bridge is here and will always be here."

Chapter Twenty-Seven

TWO BUILDINGS IN the Lower Town had miraculously withstood the day and night bombardment of the city and become symbols of hope for the *habitants,* the little church of Notre-Dame-des-Victoires and the Monastery of the Poor Clares. Now, after nearly two months of punishment, they too were gone. A huge fire fanned by a northeast chinook had spread from the Lower Town to the Upper. The bucket brigades were endless and useless. For days afterward the air was choked with smoke and a thick black cloud covered the sky in every direction.

Quent stood in the gathering dusk of the evening, looking at the rubble that was all that was left of the monastery. He could still feel heat rising from the stones. Probably the only time the God-rotting place had ever really been warm. *"Les religieuses,"* he demanded of a *habitant* poking through the remains. *"Où sont les religieuses?"* The man looked at him oddly—Quent wasn't sure if it was his stiff and unconvincing French or his appearance—and shrugged, muttering something about not being God and therefore not required to worry about nuns.

He was going to grab the man and beat some information out of him if necessary, when he heard the three-note whistle. Jesus bloody Christ, Cormac Shea. It took you long enough. Quent whistled a reply, and waited. The scavenger began backing away, stooping to retrieve a large sack before squeezing between two big boulders into what had been the alley beyond the front door. *"Allez, larron!"* Quent called after him. He wanted to add that he would do something terrible to the man if he caught him here again, but he didn't have sufficient French.

Routing the looter had kept him from hearing Corm's answering whistle. Presuming there was one, and that it was really him, not a bird confusing the issue. Quent whistled again.

"If you were my enemy you'd be dead by now," a voice whispered from just over his left shoulder. "You must be losing your touch."

"My mind, more like. Where in hell's name have you been?"

"In Louisiana for a time. And since the beginning of Thunder Moon, in Singing Snow. Bishkek is dead."

Quent felt the grief rising in him. And the shame. "God-rotting hell . . . Were you there for the funeral?"

"The first funeral, yes. I promised I'd try and return for the second." The promise hadn't satisfied Shabnokis or anyone else, but it was the best he could do.

"I should have been—" Quent broke off. He should have done many things, and not being at Bishkek's funeral was only one of them. Right now, not even the most important. "I came on this God-rotting expedition so I could protect Nicole. Look what a fine job I've made of it."

There was a loud boom before Corm could answer. After an hour or so's rest the bombardment had started up again. The shells lobbed from Pointe-Lévis exploded overhead like fireworks, their flashes illuminating the devastation. Corm looked around, spotting a half-buried section of the iron grille he remembered from behind the altar. "She's not dead, is she?"

"No, I'm sure not. I've found no evidence of any bodies. I think the nuns left soon after the shelling started." He told how he'd urged them to go before the bombardment began, and how they'd refused to budge. "The abbess said they had taken a vow to remain in this place, but I don't think she had any idea how bad it was going to be."

"You didn't see the priest, Père Antoine the brown robe?"

"No. I've been looking for him." The constant barrage of English shells had become background noise. They ignored it much as the Québécois had ignored it for seven weeks.

"His house is . . . was in this same alley, three doors nearer the harbor. I suppose it's a total ruin as well."

"Everything's a ruin."

Corm reminded himself that it had to be that way if the *Anishinabeg* were to have Canada. All the *Cmokmanuk* things must be destroyed so they would leave and not come back. Still, the destruction he saw sickened him, the white half of him anyway. Easier to talk about something else. "You get your dirk back yet?"

"Not yet. There's been no sign of Lantak."

"Other Indians, though? Fighting with the French?"

Quent heard the bitterness. "Not many. Fewer than there might have been. It wasn't likely the Suckáuhock would be perfect, Corm. Nothing ever is."

"If the English had said what was to happen, if they'd made a proclamation about Canada being for the *Anishinabeg* after they won the war, it would be perfect then."

"That's not their way, saying things flat out like that."

"Why not?"

"I'm not sure, but in London they call it diplomacy. It's how they do things."

Corm walked to where the old alley used to be and watched the shells being lobbed from the opposite shore. "Are the English going to storm the Lower Town?"

"That's the one thing they're certain not to do. The French could just pick them off from the heights. Wolfe wants a battle, but on his terms. He's got to get his army up the cliffs before they engage."

"That won't be easy." The steep cliffs either side of the city were of monumental height. The only other approach was the Côte de la Montagne. If Wolfe's army tried to fight its way up that road they'd be slaughtered by troops on the walls above. A turkey shoot, with the outcome assured.

"Impossible," Quent agreed. "At least that's how it looks so far."

"I take it you're staying over the way with the redcoats." Corm jerked his head to indicate the English camp on Pointe-Lévis.

"Yes." Another round of cannon fire punctuated his answer.

"Go back there. Let me look for Nicole. When I find out something, I'll come and tell you."

"Corm, I—"

"Go. Even got up like a Christian Huron you're too easy to spot. The *habitants* will tear you apart if they get the chance."

"I wouldn't blame them," Quent said softly.

In the middle of August, after Wolfe had been shelling Québec for over a month without luring Montcalm into the battle he craved, he had declared his so-called restraint at an end and loosed the rangers on the surrounding countryside. Their orders were to burn every house and barn, but not harm women and children or destroy churches. Only Indians and Canadians dressed as Indians were to be scalped. Having issued the order his conscience was apparently clear. The rangers went off singing about giving the locals hot stuff, and Quent had to live with the knowledge that it was thanks to him they existed. He'd gone on as many of the raids as he could because his presence went some way toward protecting the *habitants* from the worst excesses, but he couldn't be everywhere, and even his towering authority sometimes wasn't enough.

"Go on over to Pointe-Lévis," Corm said again. "I'll find out where she is, then come and tell you."

❧

Quent waited until Corm had started for the Upper Town, then went to do some investigating on his own. The house belonging to the Franciscan priest was three doors down the alley. It appeared to be remarkably intact. The front wall looked much as it had when the houses either side of it still stood. The closed door was rough and thick, made of ill-planed oak. There was no bell, and if there had been a knob, it was no longer there. Quent thought of knocking but was struck by the absurdity of the gesture. He put up his hand and felt the marks made by the axe that had originally fashioned this door from a single massive trunk. When he pressed lightly it easily fell backward, as if someone had recently propped it in place. He had the sensation that he was being watched.

He had a tomahawk, and a skinning knife. His long gun would have attracted too much attention, and besides, no Christian Huron from one of the missions would have such a weapon. He took the knife from his belt.

It was full dark now, and the waning moon had not yet risen, but there was enough starlight for him to see that behind its deceptive facade, Père Antoine's house no longer existed. Like its neighbors it was a pile of stone and splintered, charred wood. Quent's glance roved over the debris; he couldn't shake the feeling that it was somehow wrong. This place looked as if someone had deliberately wreaked further destruction after the English bombs and shells had done their work. In the far corner there was a gleam of light low down near the stone chimney breast that was still intact above what had been the fireplace.

Quent picked his way toward it, unable to shake the feeling that he should be careful not to cause any loud or unexpected noise. Jesus bloody Christ! For all his care he'd nearly walked straight into a beam. It lay at a precipitous angle from a remaining corner of the roof to what would have been the hearth. It was as thick around as he was, and black with the smoke of more than the most recent fire. Had to have been one of the original ceiling joists. He glanced up. The dark was deeper where a large wedge of masonry hung between a section of the house's north wall and the top of the beam he'd almost dislodged.

Despite the gloom, he could still make out the shimmer that had attracted him to this part of the ruined room. He knelt down, stretched his hand toward the source of the glow, and touched something hard and cold. A large golden goblet of some sort, set with what were probably precious stones about the rim. Beneath it there was a flat golden plate, also bejewelled. No ordinary looter would have left such booty behind.

"Not things a brown robe should have, *neya?*"

The voice came from deep in the shadows. "Lantak."

"Yes, Uko Nyakwai, Lantak. Get up. And keep your hands above your head. I have been waiting a long time to see you again. It would be sad if we had no time to visit before I kill you."

As before, the renegade Huron had a long gun when Quent had none. The barrel end was an arm's length from Quent's face, near enough so he could see Lantak's finger on the trigger. He rejected any thought of summoning his death song. An enemy this close was within range of attack. "I've been looking for you, Lantak. Over on the western shore where the scalps are. I didn't think to find you prowling the ruins of old battles like scavenger vermin."

"I take the scalps I wish to take, Uko Nyakwai. Lantak is not to be used to fight a *Cmokmanuk* war."

"But like a squaw you come to where the battle is long ended to pick up what the braves have left behind."

"I do not mind your insults, bear dung. I will remember them when I am cutting out your tongue. Leave the gold where it is. Go over there." Lantak jerked the long gun in the direction of the corner formed by the angled beam.

Now. It was the best opportunity he would have. The beam was hip height where he must pass it. It would give way if he shoved, and the remains of the roof would come crashing down. Quent took a step, preparing himself to fall in the direction of the blackened beam. Then he saw the priest. Pére Antoine sat on a stool in the corner formed by the angle of the ruined walls. He was bound and gagged and both his eyes had been gouged out; the empty sockets still bled. The flow nearly covered the wound where his nose had been cut away.

"You see we have a brother at this feast," Lantak said behind him. "I am glad he still lives to welcome a second guest."

If he brought down the chunk of masonry overhead the priest was a dead man. Quent barely managed to check his planned fall in time, praying that he hadn't lost the advantage by allowing Lantak to read the motion of his body. Apparently not. The long gun prodded his back. "Go!"

Quent stumbled ahead, deliberately exaggerating his faltering movement to gain more time, speaking even as he repositioned himself. "You are truly a squaw, Lantak. You torture like a squaw, delighting in screams rather than death."

"We will see soon who is the squaw, bear dung, and who screams. The brown robe at last pays for saving your life. My totem has brought you here to watch him die before you die yourself. "

Quent waited a heartbeat more, long enough so that Lantak once again prodded him with the barrel of the long gun. At that instant, while his forward thrust took Lantak's balance for the space of half a breath, Quent dropped to one knee and threw himself at the Huron's legs. The long gun went off, whether involuntarily or by design was impossible to tell. The bullet whistled over Quent's head and the gun's recoil threw the renegade backward toward the hearth.

Quent hurled himself after Lantak, landing on top of him. The Indian stretched both hands for his face, clawing at his eyes and his hair. Quent shouted a Potawatomi war cry as he ignored the grasping fingers and wrapped both hands around Lantak's neck. He'd managed to get only one knee on Lantak's chest, not enough to bring his full weight to bear on his enemy. When the Huron grabbed his wrists his grip was like iron. Lantak arched upward with more strength than Quent would have believed him to have, and used the entire wiry length of his body to break Quent's hold. When he rolled free he screamed a war cry of his own and staggered to his feet. Quent lunged for him again, but Lantak evaded him. Now both men had knives in their hands. Each of their next thrusts drew blood. They grappled and once more broke apart as each fought for a hold that would allow him to slit his opponent's throat. Then, somehow, the Huron was behind Quent, wrapping him in a death hug strong enough to squeeze the life from his body. Quent reached up and got both hands behind Lantak's neck, and with an effort so massive it seemed to stop his heart, swung the Indian over his head and hurled him forward.

Lantak's body hit the beam. There was a great rumbling sound, followed by the crack of breaking stone, and the corner of the roof that had been held aloft only with the beam's support fell in a crash that shook the dirt floor.

The blood pounding in Quent's head blinded him for many seconds, and his ears were ringing as if he'd stood next to a firing cannon. He shook his head to clear it and the ringing subsided; he could see again as well. It was not only the last of the roof that had fallen when the beam was dislodged, the stone chimney breast had come crashing down as well. If he'd been even a step to his right he'd have been buried by the falling rock.

The collapse had opened much more of the little house to the sky. The starlight shone on the place where Lantak had been when he was crushed by the beam and the toppling roof. The only part of him that showed was one arm. Sweet Christ, what about the priest?

Quent clambered over the debris, telling himself it was best if the Franciscan had been killed as well. No man would want to live in his condition, even a papist priest. Still he was sickened by the fact that the brown robe had saved his life, and he might have repaid him by causing his death.

Père Antoine was only half buried by the rubble. His legs were entirely covered, but his torso was clear of the debris. He was alive. Quent managed to get close enough to release the gag that remained in place, and use the piece of soft leather to wipe the blood from the priest's face. "Oh my God . . . I'm sorry . . . I never . . ."

"Not your fault," the priest murmured. "Mine. I came back to get my chalice and paten."

"I can dig them out of the rubble. Bring them wherever you—"

"Not important now. Want . . . pray." He murmured a string of Latin words Quent couldn't understand, then smiled. "*Oui, mon Jésus, oui . . .*" he whispered.

Then a few struggling gasps and a request Quent had to bend closer to hear. "My beads, bring them to the nuns."

Quent looked for the beads and found them attached to the priest's belt, miraculously intact. By the time he'd freed them, Père Antoine was dead.

He sat back on his heels for a moment, letting himself catch his breath, then crawled over to the corpse of the renegade Huron. When he pulled on Lantak's extended arm it came free, attached to nothing. Quent flung it aside and began hefting the chunks of masonry until at last he could drag the Indian free of the rubble. He examined the body thoroughly, but didn't discover what he wanted. Disappointment was a metallic taste in his mouth and a cramp in his belly. If he didn't find the dirk now, it was gone forever. Either Lantak had carried it on his person or he had traded it long since for liquor or a woman or whatever else he wanted. But he remembered Corm saying that Lantak had sworn to take Uko Nyakwai's scalp with the Red Bear's own weapon.

He kicked at more of the splintered wood and broken stone where the Indian had died, and unearthed the dirk on the third thrust, feeling its carved handle through the soft leather of his mocassin. Quent reached down and grabbed it, thrilled at the familiar feel of the weapon in his hand. Then, for Solomon the Barrel Maker and Sugar Willie and Lilac and Big Jacob, and for Père Antoine, he used it to take Lantak's scalp.

Louis Roget knelt in prayer in the ruins of the Retraite de Ste. Anne in the Collège des Jésuites in the Upper Town. Most of the roof was caved in and part of one wall, but unlike the main church the little chapel was still intact, including the stained glass windows depicting the life of the mother of the Virgin. So too was the exquisite statue of Anne that had been carved by the *ébénistes* of Reims and sent as a gift from the Jesuits of that city to their brother priests in Québec. The saint still stood high above the altar, looking down on the destruction.

The Provincial was alone. His priests and brothers were out in the town, offering what help they could to the battered and half-starved *habitants*. There was a bed of sorts in what remained of Roget's apartments, but he had resolved to spend the night guarding the Retraite. Tomorrow Bigot was to send skilled workmen to remove the stained glass and take the statue down from her place, and carefully pack the treasures for transport to Louisiana. An enormous pity if, having withstood so much, these gems were snatched by looters just before they could be salvaged.

Mon Dieu, I do not believe it is a sin that I refrain from asking for a French victory here in Québec. This kingdom of snow, *mon Dieu,* I have looked at it with all the intelligence granted me, and I am convinced it is worthless.

"*Bon soir, Jésuite.* Sorry to disturb you at your prayers."

There was a candle beside the tabernacle that contained the Most Holy Sacrament, and the glow of starlight entered through the smashed roof. Together they provided enough light for the Provincial to see the man who stood at the edge of the shadows. A woodsman in buckskins and a hunting shirt, but not just any *coureur de bois.* This one had a long scar that immobilized one side of his face. "This is a house of God, Monsieur Shea. To come here intending theft, or worse, violence . . . You imperil your immortal soul."

"My soul is my worry, Jésuite, not yours. But I have no interest in your treasure, and no intention of harming you unless you make it necessary. All I want is information. Since you know who I am, you won't hesitate to give it to me."

"That depends. What sort of information?"

"The Poor Clares. Where have they gone?"

Roget made the sign of the cross, slowly and deliberately, then rose from the half-broken prie-dieu he had dragged out of the rubble. "You have said it yourself, Monsieur Shea. I am a Jésuite, a black robe. The Poor Clares are Franciscans. What would I know of— *Mon Dieu!* Are you mad?"

Corm had turned to face the statue of Ste. Anne and he held his tomahawk over his head in throwing position. "I can cut her in two with ease from this distance, Jésuite. You Catholics place high value on your statues, don't you? And this one is supposed to be especially valuable."

"She is the work of the finest *ébénistes* of Reims. You are well-informed for a métis, Monsieur Shea."

"Not as well-informed as I want to be. I promise, your statue will be nothing but splinters by the time I'm finished with her. You have until the count of five. Where are the Poor Clares?"

"Will you tell me why you want to know?"

"No. Two, three—"

Roget shrugged. It was certainly not a secret worth protecting with the Reims Ste. Anne. "All the nuns of the city are in the Hôpital Général with the Augustinian nursing sisters, Monsieur Shea. At least, I know the Ursulines have been there since their convent was bombed out of existence. I presume the Poor Clares have gone to the same refuge. You may have noticed that there is little else standing in Québec."

Corm tucked the tomahawk into the belt at his waist. "I've noticed. I saw your trunks outside as well, Jésuite. Care to tell me where you're headed?"

"That too is not a secret. If it becomes necessary, I and my community go to Louisiana as soon as we can find a ship." He saw the métis stiffen. "That interests you, Monsieur Shea?"

Corm shook his head. "No. Why should it?"

Alors, something in the way he held his head, the eyes that did not look at him . . . The métis was lying. Perhaps this one was not the rough half-breed he appeared to be. Roget suppressed an unseemly smile. This was not a game he had expected to play, but possibly one worthy of engagement. He, of course, would be black. White had already opened. "Tell me why you are so concerned about the Poor Clares, Monsieur Shea. A few women who spend their lives doing penance, why should they interest you?"

"A friend of mine's with them. I just want to be sure she's not hurt."

"Allow me to venture a guess, monsieur. Your friend, she is the one they call Soeur Stephane, *non?* The young one whose father was an English officer." Black knight to Queen's pawn four.

"You are as well-informed as they say you are, Jésuite."

"Sometimes better." You have given me an opening, métis. If I can maneuver into a position that allows me to take a pawn or two, your ranks will be open to attack. *"Papankamwa,"* Roget said softly, *"eehsipana, ayaapia, anseepikwa, eey-eelia, pileewa."*

Cormac listened to the names of the symbols on the Súki beads with no change of expression. "I already know you offered to pay the renegade Midè priest for the Suckáuhock, Jésuite, I took the scalp of the man you sent to kill me."

Alors, échec to the black king, but only a temporary setback. "I sent no one to kill you, Monsieur Shea. I had no idea that was the plan of the man who offered me the stones. But at least now I know they are truly as important as he said. Most of the Indians have deserted Onontio because of the stones. Is that not correct?"

Corm shrugged. "Give me one good reason why Indians should fight and die in your white man's wars, Jésuite. Maybe they're just getting smarter."

"Indians fight and die for scalps and captives and loot, Monsieur Shea. Unless something more important has been offered them. It is that thing that interests me. Do you know what it might be?"

"If I did, do you think I would tell you?"

Roget's fingers found the beads of the rosary that hung at his side. You have sent me a remarkable opportunity, Mère de Dieu. Grant that I make no error. "You might, monsieur. If in return I could offer you something of equal, perhaps greater, value."

"I don't trust you, Jésuite." Corm's heart thundered in his chest. This was a white man's game, he knew that. The only thing he didn't know was if he were white enough to play it. "If there's to be a trade, both sides have to see what's being offered."

Endgame. To threaten white's king, black must expose his own. "Your General Wolfe," Roget began, "he must meet General Montcalm if—"

"Wolfe's not my general."

"Ah, but in this matter I believe he is. I have the feeling, Monsieur Shea, that like the Indians, you withhold your allegiance from Onontio in this *contretemps*. Is that not correct?"

"I'm half Indian, Jésuite. A métis, as you continue to remind me."

"Indeed. So if your people do not on this occasion fight with their French allies, it must be because they wish the English to win. And if the English are to win, General Wolfe must meet the General Montcalm on the field of battle. Is that not true, Monsieur Shea? The military men inform us Québec is a fortress, not a fort. It cannot be taken by the traditional *siège en forme*."

"Even if what you say is true, what does it have to do with our trade?"

Roget felt a surge of triumph. The métis had committed himself. "It has everything to do with it. Let us speak plainly, monsieur. If Wolfe does not get his battle, he must leave when winter approaches. On the other hand, to force Vaudreuil and Montcalm to fight, the English must threaten the Upper Town in such manner that our two reluctant warriors are convinced a battle is the only choice. To achieve that, the English troops must be not at Pointe-Lévis or Ile d'Orléans, or wreaking havoc among the *habitants* in the countryside, or even swarming in the Lower Town. They must be up here where we are, massed at the city's gates. Wolfe has already made a number of attempts to gain the heights, and been beaten back because he chose the wrong places to try his assault."

Je vous salue, Marie, pleine de grâce. The beads slipped rapidly through Roget's fingers. The prayer to the Virgin was a thing happening automatically somewhere in his being, like the beating of his heart, or the breath entering and leaving his body. "I can tell you the correct place. And you, Monsieur Shea, can tell General Wolfe."

"And in return, Jésuite? What do I give you?"

The métis spoke very softly, but he had taken a step forward. Close enough now so Roget could see the vein that throbbed above Cormac Shea's scar. It was the only clue, but on the strength of it black must commit everything, the queen and both rooks. "I already stated my request. I deal in knowledge. It is the only weapon I have with which to further the cause of God and His Holy Church. I wish, monsieur, to understand the power of the stones. What have the English promised the Indians in return for their staying out of this fight?"

"Canada."

. . .et Jésus, le fruit de vos entrailles . . . "Please, repeat that. I believe you said—"

"I said that when the English win this war, they will give Canada to the Indians. They'll keep the land to the south where their colonies are now. Whites and reds will be separated. So they can both live in peace and follow their own ways and customs."

Louis Roget loosed his hold on the rosary. His fingers were too slick with sweat to continue rolling the beads. He could barely speak for the force of the blood pounding in his ears. *Échec et mate.* His victory was more complete than he could have imagined. With Canada finally lost to them, even the cretins in Versailles would see the need to concentrate all their energies on Louisiana and win back what they had lost in the Ohio Country. Why not? They would have plenty of help from the Indians. There was no way the English would honor this bargain. English settlers would flood Canada as soon as the French were no longer in control. And once they were betrayed, *alors,* the savages would be more ready than ever before to adopt the French cause as their own. Not just the Ohio Country, *mon Dieu.* Possibly the English colonies as well. New York and Pennsylvania and Virginia . . . all of them, even perhaps the place they called New England, open to the Holy Faith.

"I'm waiting, Jésuite."

"Waiting, Monsieur Shea?" Roget's voice sounded thin in his own ears. The enormity of it, the sheer audacity. Only saints dared so much. But saints were rewarded with a golden crown.

"Yes, for your side of the trade."

"*Bien sûr* . . ." Roget brought himself back to the moment at hand. If the full glory of his vision was to be realized, there were things, however difficult and even distasteful, that he must do. "Monsieur Shea, you know the place, the heights, called the Plains of Abraham? West of the city, near what before this bombardment were the gardens of the Convent School of the Ursulines." He waited until he saw the other man nod. "Very good. If you follow the cliff road past those gardens and past the plains you will come to a place above a cove called l'Anse au Foulon. That is where there is a path I'm told the laundresses sometimes—"

Corm shook his head. "I am not interested in what you are told, Jésuite. Words aren't enough. Show me."

Roget hesitated. The statue of Ste. Anne, the stained glass . . . *Eh bien,* surely having given him so much, the Mother of God would protect these treasures. And if not, so be it. The ways of God were not the ways of man. He understood now why he had been forced to watch the sad and sinful event of the wounded falcon's suicide. "Come with me, Monsieur Shea. I will show you the place I mean."

Corm watched Roget swing his long cape around his shoulders. Then, just before they left: "Jésuite, one more thing. If you are trying to trick me, I will take your scalp while you are still alive, then cut out your heart and eat it." Maybe not *Cmokman* enough for diplomacy, but *Anishinabeg* enough for that.

"I do not doubt it, Monsieur Shea. Now, let us go."

Saturday, September 13, 1759
The St. Lawrence, above Québec

It was the darkest reaches of the night. Dawn was a few hours away, and the last sliver of an old moon had already disappeared. The river was swollen by the torrential rains of the past three days, the ebbing tide running heavier than usual. The longboats moved with it, and with the rowers' instincts. The oarlocks were padded, and on Wolfe's orders the drummer boys who usually beat the stroke were silent.

The shoreline was unguarded but there were sentries on the cliffs. One of them thought he heard something and squinted to see better in the darkness. Nothing at first. Then . . . yes, a black-on-black shadow, and the sound of water lapping against oars. *"Qui vive?"*

The men in the boats heard the call and froze. If they were discovered, French gunners the entire length of the cliffs would pick them off from overhead. There was no way the longboats could outrun them or hide.

The sentry waited for a reply. None came. The God-cursed damp of the endless rain had all but closed his throat. He cleared it and tried again, louder this time. *"Qui vive?"*

Wolfe was in the lead boat. He nodded to the young captain with the Seventy-eighth Highlanders, who spoke perfect French. *"La France et vive le roi!"* he shouted. Wolfe was pleased with his forethought. He'd identified enough French speakers among his troops to scatter them throughout the longboats. But if a password was demanded . . . Quentin Hale was in Wolfe's boat, and the American had his long gun to his shoulder trying to sight the French soldier so far overhead.

The sentry on the heights did not trouble himself about passwords, he only thought about how empty his belly was and how long it had been so. He felt a surge of relief. *Merci, mon Dieu.* For days now they had been promised a convoy of supplies from Montréal. He sprinted along the clifftop to the next post. *"Ce sont nos gens avec les provisions. Laissez-les passer."* His voice reached the British on the water as the faintest of echoes. It was enough. They rowed on.

Moments later Wolfe's longboat and three others had landed at l'Anse au Foulon. Four others missed the landing and were carried farther down, but there was no time to worry about them now. "Mr. Hale"—a whisper so faint Quent had to strain to hear it though he was standing right beside the general—"where is your friend's route?"

Some of the men had already started to clear a ravine that had been filled with scree and tree trunks. Corm had been very clear. That wasn't the footpath. "The ravine's a feint, meant to shift attention from the real thing. Seven long strides farther on. Easy to miss, and as steep as the way up Big Two, but it'll take you to the top."

Quent hadn't come with Corm to see the place for fear they'd be spotted and the alarm raised about interest in the Foulon cove. The only difficult part was convincing Wolfe that Corm was absolutely to be trusted; in the end he convinced himself. Quent figured it was the Englishman's desperation that made him accept Corm's assurance of a way up the cliffs. Time was running short, winter was coming, and Admiral Saunders would insist the fleet leave. Besides, whether or not he took Québec wasn't as important to the chinless general as that he got the quick and glorious death he craved. Sick as he was as often as he was, maybe it was understandable.

Quent paced off the distance and studied the portion of the cliff he faced. It was exactly as Corm had described, a narrow declivity that you could think of as a footpath if you used your imagination. Climbed almost straight up. That's what had made Corm think of the way they used to take up Big Two when they were boys. Impossibly steep, but if you were surefooted, you could do it. Except at Shadowbrook there were no enemy soldiers lying in wait when you got to the top.

The first team had already been chosen, sixteen of the most nimble redcoats led by a Colonel Howe from the Fifty-eighth Light Infantry. Howe was almost as big as Quent himself, and equally as agile. He and his men appeared at Quent's side. A faint drizzle had started but there was no point in waiting. If the heavy rain returned, they hadn't a chance. Howe nodded. His lead men fixed their bayonets and the climb began.

There were no enemy soldiers at the top of the Foulon path, only a small detachment housed in a few tents. They had posted no lookout, or if they had, he had deserted his post. The fight was over quickly. When it was done Quent saw one of the redcoats use the tip of his bloody bayonet to take a scalp. Apparently he'd developed a taste for it. Howe came over, cleaning his musket, not even breathing hard. "Well done, Mr. Hale."

"Well done yourself, Colonel Howe. But one of the French soldiers got away, I saw him running toward the town." Quent touched his long gun. "He was out of sight before I could get off a shot. Do you want me to go after him?"

"I think not, Mr. Hale. The whole point of the thing is to get them out here, isn't it? Now, time to invite the others."

The colonel walked to the edge of the cliff. He struck a flint and flashed a signal to the general and the men on the beach.

By the time Wolfe and two hundred more soldiers stood on the heights it was four o'clock and a false dawn lightened the sky. The only resistance was a battery of French guns shooting ineffectually from some distance away. Wolfe sent Howe and his men to silence it. In the cove below, the longboats kept landing, and wave after wave of soldiers were sent clambering up the path.

There were more showers, but so far not the downpour they all feared. Meanwhile Wolfe had reconnoitered and chosen a place to await the enemy. He gave the signal. The men formed up with more confusion than usual, finding their places according to the familiar companions either side. Finally, as silently as it was possible for such a large body to move, Wolfe's army marched on Québec.

By the time the sun rose, seven British battalions were drawn up in battle order across the open ground facing the Rue St. Louis, two leagues from the town's western wall. Five more battalions were on the river or in the cove, taking their turn to scurry two by two up the path to the heights. A twenty-man guard protected the open ground at the top of the climb, but farther on toward the town sharpshooters harried them from the surrounding woods. They were mostly Indians, Quent figured, and possibly a few Canadians, but as yet there was no sign of Montcalm's army. Maybe the soldier Quent had seen run from the encampment atop the Foulon cove, hadn't made it to the town. Never mind. The British would announce their presence soon enough. A pair of stalwart sailors had managed to manhandle a couple of brass six-pounders up to the heights. Quent saw the cannon in place and knew he couldn't wait any longer. "The hospital, General."

"Ah, yes. As we discussed. Take ten men and go, Mr. Hale. Please give my compliments to the Mother Superior. You may tell her the nuns and their patients can count on my protection."

The August night when the Poor Clares had at last consented to leave their monastery, Père Antoine had murmured a decree of exclaustration over each nun as she passed beyond what had been the cloister walls. "By the power vested in me by the Minister General in Rome, I dispense you from your vow of enclosure, for as long as it proves necessary." Consequently, while in the Hôpital Général, Nicole did not cover her face with her veil, nor did any of her sisters. They all took part in the work of caring for the ill and the wounded and the dispossessed and desperate who, since the bombardment began, had crowded into the spacious hospital founded to care for a better class of sick than were served by the Hôtel-Dieu. By the grace of God, the Hôpital Général was beyond the range of the British guns.

Big as the place was, it wasn't big enough. How could it be? The first refugees to arrive were the nuns' families. They were lodged in the sheds on the extensive grounds. When more *habitants* came, the barns were emptied and turned into dormitories for mothers with young children. When the Ursulines could no longer remain in their ruined monastery, they too sought shelter with the Augustines Hospitalières. They were given the rooms of the resident nuns, who themselves now slept together in shifts in a small vestibule near the front door. Soon there were six hundred *étrangers* within the hospital walls. It was only because the Augustinian Superior, Mère St. Claude, was extremely well connected—her father had been governor of Trois Rivières and her brother carried the title King's Lieutenant of Québec—that Bigot had given them sufficient food for so many. When Poor Clares arrived and were housed in the tiny icehouse near the largest well, they were six hundred and six. With such a huge burden it was imperative that everyone help. Mère Marie Rose said she and her nuns would take on the task of filling the large tin jugs with water from the well and carrying them to the hospital kitchen. This morning, immediately after the chanting of Lauds, it was Nicole's turn.

She filled two of the large metal canisters—each held the equivalent of ten ordinary bottles of wine—and hefted one in either hand. The icehouse was separated from the main hospital building by a copse of trees divided by a cobbled path that led directly to the kitchen door. Nicole walked as quickly as she could, struggling with her heavy burden and thinking of the small pleasure that waited at the end of the journey. At this hour the Hospitalières would be stirring a few handfuls of barley into the vegetable cooking water of the previous day to make a broth that would serve as breakfast for the sickest patients. She would be glad of the few moments she could spend near the warmth of the stove. Summer was definitely past. Already she could see her breath in the air.

She saw a flash of movement out of the corner of one eye in the scarlet-leaved maples to her left. Nicole turned her head. Nothing. She must have imagined it. She was perhaps getting dizzy. It was foolish to think she was strong enough to carry two jugs of water on one trip. Better to have brought one and then gone back for the other.

Quent saw her look in his direction and caught his breath. Should he approach her here? Sweet Christ, he wanted to. He couldn't believe his luck. This was a perfect chance to see her alone. The others were waiting for him to scout the area before they took up their positions, but maybe there was just enough time for a word or two. Père Antoine's beads were in his pocket; he'd use the fact that he had something to give her to extract a promise she'd talk with him later. He needed to speak with her almost as much as he needed to breathe.

The dirk was in his hand. Quent slipped it into the familiar place at the small of his back, pleased with how right it felt. A lot of things would go back to how they'd been, when this damnable war was over. No, they'd be better than before. He stepped out of the cover of the stand of trees.

The sound of a musket exploded in the early morning stillness. Nicole fell.

Quent hurled himself forward, then dropped to his knees across her body, shielding it with his own. The sniper who had shot from the trees on the other side of the icehouse had to have been aiming at him. Now the bastard was reloading to finish the job. Quent's long gun was already loaded, and up on his shoulder. But he could see nothing to shoot.

The redcoats came running, summoned by the sound of the musket. Quent heard their booted feet tramping through the stand of maples behind him. As soon as they appeared on the path he shouted, "Sniper. Over in those woods across the way. Cover me while I get her out of here."

Three redcoats stood shoulder to shoulder, making themselves into a human wall between the far trees and Quent and the fallen nun. The others ran off to either side to give pursuit from behind the cover of the trees. A few months ago they wouldn't have known to do that. Behind the protective backs of the stationary soldiers Quent gathered Nicole into his arms. She was breathing. Thank Christ Jesus, she was alive. But her face was ghostly white and he could see the tiny blue veins that marked the lids of her closed eyes. The rough gray gown she wore was sodden. One of the tin jugs had shattered, the other had overturned and spilled when she dropped it. He felt something dripping over his arm as he lifted her, and saw blood splashing on the cobbles. He sprinted toward the hospital.

Three nuns had gathered in the doorway, all staring wide-eyed at him and the red-coated soldiers in his wake. Another older sister approached behind them. "Back to your work, *mes Soeurs*. At once. *Pas vous, Soeur St. Louis.* Go and tell the abbess of the Poor Clares that one of her nuns has need of her. *S'il vous plaît, monsieur,* you will follow me."

Quent hesitated, watching the one called Soeur St. Louis hurry toward the kitchen door. "Out there, madame." He jerked his head toward the copse and the cobbled path. "I can't be sure the soldiers have yet made it secure."

"That's as may be," the nun said. "A Poor Clare should not die without the comfort of her abbess."

The marquis de Montcalm surveyed the enemy from horseback, his green and gold uniform shimmering in the soft rain of early morning. When the news of an English landing had first reached him he hadn't entirely believed it. He was exhausted; he'd been up all night supervising the defenses of the Beauport shore where the English attack was expected. He had taken the time to finish his tea and change his clothes before going to consult with Vaudreuil. *Eh bien,* who could blame him? The man who brought him the word from the cliffs above l'Anse au Foulon was almost incoherent, hysterical. Clearly he believed in his own news. But an English landing on the heights west of the town . . . He and the governor-general agreed it was, if not impossible, most unlikely. Unfortunately, according to the evidence of his own eyes, it had happened.

The plateau was less than a league wide, and the redcoats lay on their bellies across its breadth. They did not move and they made no acknowledgment of the

French troops scurrying into position across from them. *Ils ne devraient pas y être.* They should not be there. But they were.

The Indian and Canadian sharpshooters continued to harass the enemy from the edges of the battlefield, firing from every hill or ravine or clump of trees, but there was simply not enough cover for them to do any real damage. Meanwhile, the French line moved as quickly as it could into position behind their general. Colonial troops and militia to the right and left, the white-coated French regulars in the center. Montcalm decided he would command the regulars himself. They would hold, whatever happened.

A sixth part of a league from the enemy, Wolfe could hear the crunch of his own boots as he walked the line. The only other sounds were the occasional explosions from the snipers' guns and the thudding of his heart. God be praised, it was exactly as he'd dreamed it. No matter that a musket ball had already shattered his wrist. An aide had stopped the bleeding with a tight bandage; he didn't feel the throbbing pain. Everything had been done as he ordered. Four and a half thousand troops had wheeled themselves into battle formation on the open plain. He'd arranged them in two shoulder-to-shoulder ranks, one behind the other. The distance between the parallel lines was exactly one long stride. Three lines would have been better, but he didn't have enough men to do that and cover the full width of the field. Never mind, he'd lived thirty-two years only to prepare for this day. Each soldier had loaded his musket with a double ball and every bayonet was fixed, and they'd had time to do all that before the French even knew they were there. Now they were lying down so the sharpshooters couldn't pick them off as easily, watching the enemy, and waiting. No one moved. Whatever happened, superbly trained as they were, they would not move until he gave the command. And he would wait to do that until the French charged.

"The silence, sir," a young infantryman murmured.

Wolfe crouched down to hear better. "Yes, what about it?"

"It's eerie, sir."

"You're right, lad, it is. And they know we're here now, so there's no need for us to be so damnably quiet." Wolfe stood up and summoned a runner and gave an order. Moments later the drums and the fifes began. And soon after, at the particular request of one of the Scots, he permitted the skirl of the pipes. A mournful sound to him, but nothing fired up the Highland regiments more effectively.

"She has taken a musket ball in her upper thigh, *ma Mère.*" The surgeon was a young man from Trois Rivières. He had been visiting an aunt and uncle in Québec when the bombardment began, and remained to offer what help he could. "It would have gone much deeper except that of the musket ball passed through the water can and some of the velocity was lost."

"The thigh," Mère Marie Rose repeated. "Must she then lose her leg?"

Nicole gasped. "No, please!"

Marie Rose bent toward her. "We did not believe you were conscious, *ma petite.*"

Nicole didn't answer. She was staring over the shoulder of the abbess. Quent stood in the shadows near the door, but she could still see him. He could not be in the Hôpital Général of Québec, so she had died and this was heaven. But surely in heaven she would not have so much pain. Purgatory, perhaps. How good of *le bon Dieu* to permit her the sight of her love in purgatory. "Hello, my darling Red Bear," she murmured. "It gives me great joy to see you. Promise you will not let them remove my leg. I wish to go to heaven with both of them." Then she closed her eyes.

Mère Marie Rose put her hand on the forehead of the girl she had tried to make a sacrifice of praise for the glory of the Holy Faith and the winning of the Ohio Country. Soeur Stephane's skin was burning hot.

"The body struggles to fight the poison of the gunshot, Mother Abbess," the surgeon murmured. "We must remove that poison before it defeats her. I will have to make the cut very high, near the hip."

"You cannot simply remove the musket ball?"

"I would not dare. Her thighbone is shattered. Even after the ball is out, the poison will be left to do its damage. The whole leg will turn black and the poison will invade her entire body and she will die."

"Very well. Do what you must."

"No." Quent stepped toward the table where the surgeon was opening his case. There were three saws of different sizes fixed to the inside lid. "I'm sorry, but you heard her. It's not what she wants."

"Monsieur, remember your promise." Mère St. Claude the nun in charge of the hospital. It was she who'd said he could stay. "You gave me your word that you would not interfere, monsieur. You must understand that this young nun has given herself entirely to God in the person of her abbess. Mère Marie Rose will decide what is to be done."

Quent took another step, putting himself between the surgeon's saws and Nicole, and addressed Mère Marie Rose. "There are ways to prevent the poisoning of the blood the surgeon speaks of. I can bring Nicole to the best herbalist alive, tomorrow or the next day, at the latest. You don't know me and there's no reason you should be—"

"I do indeed know you, monsieur." The abbess Rose had to tilt her head to look into his eyes. He was the tallest man she had ever seen. Stephane had called him her Red Bear. There could not be two. "I believe we have spoken before. At the turn, *non?*" Quent nodded. "You came to warn us we must leave our monastery. And as we both see, you were correct."

"I did not wish to seem arrogant, madame. Not then and not now, but—"

She raised her hand. "We need not continue to argue, monsieur. It is the time of Soeur Stephane that we are wasting." She turned to the surgeon. "You will remove the musket ball, nothing more. It will be as Soeur Stephane requested. If she is to go to heaven, she will arrive with both her legs."

"Not a shot," Wolfe ordered. "Not until we can count the buttons on their jackets." The line remained immobile. The pair of cannon that had been brought to the battlefield were fired repeatedly and did some damage. The Canadian sharpshooters and their Indian allies were also still active. In terms of the battle that would come, neither meant anything. Wolfe knew that. So did Montcalm.

The French general rode up and down his lines, making adjustments, then changing things back. "*Mon Général,* how much longer?" one of his officers asked. Indeed, it was the only question. Action must come, however much he had tried to avoid it. The regulars were stoic, and would remain so. But the Canadians, the savages . . . he did not trust them to wait much longer. Reinforcements must be on the way—Vaudreuil had held back fifteen hundred troops—but how long would it take them to arrive? Two hours, possibly three? He murmured an evasive reply and moved on.

There was a burst of fire from one of the English cannon, followed by another from the second. Four men fell together in a heap. Another was cut in two and his body fell in opposite directions. The corpses were dragged out of the way and the gaps in the lines filled, but Montcalm heard the undercurrent of unease. No that was not entirely correct, he felt it. He wheeled his horse around and faced the center of the line of Québec's defenders. "*Alors, mes enfants, la gloire et arrivée.*" So much dread in his belly, still he did what he knew he must. He was a man of the military. It was his job. God help him, it was his destiny.

Montcalm tugged lightly on the bridle of his horse and the animal turned once more to face front. He raised his sword, held it upright for as long as it took him to commend his soul and the souls of his men to the Holy Virgin, then pointed across the plain to the English. Instantly the regimental bearers unfurled their flags and the drummers beat the charge.

The soldiers gave a tremendous cheer, releasing the terrible tension of the long wait, and took four rapid steps forward, more or less in unison. Montcalm looked right and left and breathed a sigh of relief. So far at least, the line held. And *mon Dieu,* the sun. At this moment it arrives. It is a sign.

Wolfe, too, felt the sun's warmth as it broke through the clouds. The plains were bathed in light. He could clearly see the French advance. "Lieutenant, bring the men to their feet!" A long wave of scarlet and tartan rippled into position along the open field.

The French were close enough to see every detail of the enemy formation. The snipers from the hills had joined the charge as best they could. Montcalm still led, but he was conscious of the wavering line behind him. The regulars knew to go forward at parade ground pace; the militia followed their Canadian instincts and ran toward the enemy. In seconds the front lines were too far ahead and the left flank too far back, and some of the men had stumbled and fallen on the rough ground, increasing the havoc.

Eh bien, nothing can now be changed. I have the army I have in the conditions that exist. Dictated by Wolfe, who has outgeneraled me. But I will not give the command to fire until we— A shot rang out from behind. A Canadian, it has to be. May God rot his soul in hell.

As he feared, the gunshot was taken as a signal. A great volley followed, but they were still too far away to do any real damage. Montcalm saw a few English go down, but others took their places and those either side stood rigid. Sainte Vierge, what must we do to break their ranks? We must charge. It is the only hope. Montcalm turned his head to shout encouragement and saw that following their usual custom, having discharged their guns, the wretched Canadians had thrown themselves on the ground and were rolling to the side to give themselves time to reload. The men coming behind them now had another obstacle to trip over. He wheeled his horse around and plunged into the melee, shouting the orders that would bring his troops back into formation.

Wolfe watched and counted off a full minute in slow, deliberate seconds. Then he gave the command that brought his lines three steps forward and slightly turned so they would present a smaller target. Another count, to twenty this time, but it felt like an eternity. Still the discipline of the redcoats was perfect. "Highlanders!" Wolfe shouted. "One knee!" The order was obeyed and passed down the line; the front rank knelt while the one behind it remained erect. "Prepare to fire!" Every musket was shouldered. The French still came toward them, shooting wildly now, but not a single English gun answered. Until, at last, when they could indeed count the brass buttons on the coats of the enemy, Wolfe shouted the command: "Fire!"

In the middle the muskets were discharged simultaneously, their double balls cutting through the French lines in great bursts of skin and bone and sinew and showers of blood. On the right and left flank, where the command must be relayed because of distance, the English soldiers fired platoon by platoon. The result was a volley that seemed to go on and on, the death and chaos it caused neverending.

Vaudreuil was at the north end of the plains, well out of the field of battle, in a calèche, still not convinced he should commit to this battle the fifteen hundred men he commanded. He saw the English line take another step forward. The screams of the dead and dying were too loud for him to hear the command to fire a second volley, but obviously it had come. Once more the redcoats in the front dropped to one knee and discharged their muskets while those behind fired over their heads. Involuntarily the old man clasped his hands over his ears. He could not help it. The roar was like a gigantic cannon from hell. It was a madness, all of this. If the Canadians and the Indians had been allowed . . . *Alors!* Some small comfort. Wolfe was down, his officers clustered around him and dragging him out of the line of fire.

Montcalm's right flank broke, the Canadians running to take cover in the woods where they knew they would at least live to fight on, while screaming their Scots war cries and swinging their claymores, the Highlanders took off after them. A group of Canadian militia made a stand in the military bakery that stood just outside the city's gates. Their bravery bought the fleeing French army enough time to reach the walls and take shelter in Québec, though every one of the Canadians paid with his life. And finally, the end. Half an hour after monsieur le marquis had pointed his sword at the enemy, the gates of the fortress city were again closed and locked. What was left of the army meant to defend New France was behind the walls. Montcalm was with them, still on his horse, but he had taken a musket ball to the gut on the field, and during the retreat English grapeshot had ripped open one of his legs. *Alors.* I think my life leaves with all this blood, *mon Dieu.* I shall be sorry never to see Candiac again. Or to taste the sugared almonds of Montargis.

Wolfe had sustained two hits, one in the belly and one in the chest. He lay on the battlefield, his cape spread beneath him, covered in blood and breathing with difficulty. A soldier kneeling beside him could think of nothing to do except report the rout. "They run, General. My God, how they run!"

"Who is running? Not our—"

"It's the French, sir. Everywhere. They're all running away with our lads hot after them."

"God be praised. I die in peace."

Quent was made to wait in the garden while the surgery proceeded. He heard echoes of gunfire and the shouts of the crowds who stood on the ramparts watching the battle, but it was as if everything happened in a dream. Nicole was enduring the agony of the surgeon's knife because she had taken a bullet meant for him. The sister in charge of the apothecary had brought wine, but nothing else to dull the pain. "Our laudanum, *ma Mère,* it is gone. I have looked everywhere for more, but—"

"Do not disturb yourself," the one they called Mère Marie Rose had said. "Soeur Stephane will offer her suffering to God."

Heaven help him, he'd never understand the way they thought.

He looked up. The Poor Clare abbess was coming toward him. She had a black knitted shawl wrapped around her shoulders, but her feet were bare. He'd noticed when he saw Nicole struggling toward the kitchen with the water cans her feet were bare also. In Canada, at the onset of winter. Perhaps madness was a contagion.

"She lives, monsieur," Marie Rose told him. *"Le bon Dieu* has seen fit to leave her with us for a time."

"Can I see her?"

"Not yet. She is sleeping. Soeur Celeste will remain with her, and the nursing sisters of the hospital will care for her. We are doing everything that can be done, monsieur." The abbess turned her head in the direction of the battlefield. "You may go back to your war."

"I believe it is over, madame." He'd heard no gunfire in some time.

"So quickly," Marie Rose whispered, then, looking at him: "I take it the French have lost?"

"I think so. There's a crowd watching from the tops of the walls. I've heard no cheers in some time."

She bit her lip. The gesture made her seem almost human. "I pray," she said, "the river does not run red with blood. I saw it that way, but perhaps I was mistaken."

Quent stared at her. "You and Corm and old Thoyanoguin."

"I am sorry, monsieur, I do not understand . . ."

"Neither do I." He reached into his pocket and pulled out Père Antoine's beads.

Marie Rose's eyes opened wide in astonishment. "You are a Catholic, monsieur?"

"No. They belonged to the priest called Père Antoine. He asked me to give them to you."

"Where is he? We have heard nothing for days and—"

"He's dead."

The abbess made the sign of the cross, but she did not seem surprised. Quent handed her the beads and she held them in one chapped and reddened hand. "We will pray for his soul. And yours, monsieur."

❧

They did not allow him to see her until Tuesday, three days after the surgeon had done his work. When at last he was shown into her room, Nicole was propped up on many pillows, deathly pale, her face etched with lines of pain, but she was smiling. "Dear Abbess tells me you saved my life, Monsieur Hale. I would have bled to death if you hadn't been there."

A young Poor Clare he hadn't seen before was present, her head bent over some sewing. Probably didn't understand a word of English. Damn, he didn't care if she did. "That bullet was meant for me. As for saving your life, I didn't do it so you could go back to calling me Monsieur Hale. I thought we'd put all that behind us long ago." She blushed. It was wonderful to see the color in her cheeks.

"This is Soeur Angelique," Nicole said, switching to French. "My sisters have taken turns staying with me night and day."

"But I must leave you now." Angelique looked doubtfully at the enormous man who seemed to occupy all the space in the tiny room. "Dear Abbess said I must come and tell her as soon as you were awake and Monsieur Hale had come. If you like, I can ask one of the Augustinian sisters to—"

"Everyone is much too busy to be worried about me, Angelique. Besides, there is nothing to fear from Monsieur Hale. We are old friends."

Quent waited until the other woman had gone, then took a step closer to the bed. Nicole was wearing a gray robe and a black veil. "Do you wear these same clothes waking and sleeping?"

"They look the same, but we have different sets for night and day."

Her right hand lay outside the coverlet. If he simply stretched out his fingers, he could touch it. "Nicole, I must tell you how I feel. I—"

"No, please. Do not say anything from your heart. Not now when I am so weak." She felt the tears coming but she did not have the strength to brush them away. "Tell me what has happened. Angelique says there was a battle and we lost."

"Yes. But—"

"What of monsieur le marquis de Montcalm?"

"He is dead. So's Wolfe, the English general."

"And Québec?"

"The terms of surrender were signed this morning. Nicole, we must—"

Marie Rose came into the room. Soeur Celeste was with her. "I am glad to see you well enough to speak, *ma petite,* and I believe Monsieur Hale was about to say you must speak of the future. He is correct." She went at once to the bedside and sketched the sign of the cross on Nicole's forehead. "That you have survived so far is a miracle, my child, but if you are to live, we must send you away."

"But *ma Mère,* I am a nun. I have taken vows. Where can I—"

"Your vows are due to be renewed in a matter of days. I shall not accept them." *Soeur Stephane apart from them, by herself with flowers in her hair. She had thought it meant the girl was to die. Perhaps it meant something else. It was only necessary that she do what* le bon Dieu *willed. In that way it was she, Marie Rose, Abbess, who was the sacrifice of praise.*

Nicole stared at the woman into whose keeping she had placed her immortal soul. *"Ma Mère,* do you tell me that I am rejected? By you and by God? Do I not, after all, have a vocation to be a Poor Clare?"

"I believe you had such a vocation, child. And that now it is over. Our Lord has himself told me this."

"But why does He not tell me?"

The abbess smiled. "I think he does, *ma petite.* For the moment you are still my daughter, so you must tell me the truth. Are you happy to be with us?"

"Yes, of course—" She broke off, then tried again. "I have felt that I was doing God's will."

"And you shall be rewarded for that. But you have never been happy, child. The rest of us, we are joyful to be Poor Clares. There is no place we would rather be. But you . . ." The abbess glanced at the man she too now thought of as the Red Bear. He'd had the good sense to move a few steps away into the shadows and leave this business to her. "You, Soeur Marie Stephane who must now again be Mademoiselle Crane, you have always had a divided heart."

Nicole could no longer hold back her tears. "I have tried to do what is right, *ma Mère.*"

"I know. And God knows. And now what is right is that you must leave. Monsieur Hale tells me he can bring you to safety, and that you will be well cared for in this place called Shadowbrook."

"Sally Robin," Quent said quickly, "you remember how skilled she is with cures."

"I remember." Dear God in heaven, did she not remember everything? Had she not remembered for every minute of every day of the past four years? Nicole did not permit herself to look at Quent, only at the abbess. "But if I stayed with you and my sisters, *ma Mère,* surely I would also be cared for."

"If I kept you here I would be failing in my obligation, to you and to the other sisters. I do not know how much Monsieur Hale has told you, but the governor-general has left with the last of the troops. We are told he goes to the fort at Jacques Cartier to regroup. This morning Québec surrendered to the English. There are now thousands of redcoats within our walls and they prepare to spend the winter. We have little shelter and less food. Things will be very difficult here. If I can arrange that there is one less invalid to look after, it is my duty to do so."

"How is she?" Corm was waiting for him outside the grounds of the hospital. "I heard Nicole was shot."

"Yes." Quent was too drained to explain how it had happened. "A surgeon took a musket ball from her leg. She's alive, but the doctor is afraid the wound will turn poisonous and kill her. I'm to take her to Shadowbrook."

"To Sally Robin," Corm said. And when Quent nodded: "Does she want to go?"

"Frankly, I don't know. She—" The sounds of a fife and drums interrupted his words. The last of the French forces were leaving the city. They had been granted the honors of war—the first time that courtesy had been extended since the massacre at Fort William Henry—and they marched to the ships waiting in the harbor to take them to France with their arms shouldered and their flags flying.

Quent and Corm watched without speaking until the last of the procession had disappeared down the Côte de la Montagne. "The militia aren't with them," Corm said.

"They took off for the garrison at Jacques Cartier before the terms of the capitulation were arranged."

"And the redcoats just let them go."

"Be reasonable, Corm. They had no way of knowing if the city would surrender of if they must mount a siege."

"What about the women and children? Are they to remain?"

"I haven't heard anything else."

"Not me either. But they have to be sent away, as the women and children of Louisbourg were sent away. It can't work any other way."

"I know. Listen, I was thinking of talking to General Amherst, he's up at Bright Fish Water. After I get Nicole to the Patent I can see him. He's in command of the entire expedition, Corm, and he—"

"I heard the surrender terms promised the *habitants* they could keep their religion and retain their property."

"I didn't actually see them. Far as I know, you haven't either."

"Not with my own eyes. But everyone's talking about it. And about how if they can just get through this winter, things won't be so bad."

"Corm, listen—"

Corm shook his head. "I've been listening. And what I hear is that it's not going to work. Not the way we were promised. The *Cmokmanuk* have lied to the *Anishinabeg* one more time."

"I don't know that and neither do you. I know how it looks right now, but remember Louisbourg. And Easton." Corm looked anguished. Quent put a hand on his arm. "In London, when I spoke with Pitt . . . He understood, I know he did. It's just the English nature to do things in a roundabout way."

❧

The entire fleet had to leave before the river froze. Admiral Saunders was not averse to allowing some ships to go immediately. The *Three Sisters* under James Cooke would be one of the first; she was to sail at the end of the month. It presented no difficulty to take Quentin Hale and the young woman for whom he'd requested passage.

They came aboard at midday on the Monday the *Three Sisters* was to sail. The crew were occupied with preparations for getting under way. Quent carried Nicole in exactly the manner in which she'd been given into his arms by the nuns, shrouded head to toe in blankets, only her face showing. The ship's company paid them little attention and he did not himself get a proper look at her until they were in the small cabin to which she'd been assigned.

"One of the laundresses who was with the troops will be traveling back with us. She'll look after you. And of course I'll never be far." She did not smile. She was in pain, he knew, and frequently feverish, but he'd give a lot to see her smile. "Listen," he added, "taking you to Shadowbrook to recover needn't have anything to do with you and me. What I'm saying . . . If you no longer feel—"

She turned away from him. "Please, I want to rest now."

"Yes, of course. Only let me make you more comfortable." He moved aside the blankets that covered her head. "Your veil's gone." The words were startled out of him.

"Today is the Feast of St. Michel the Archangel. I was to have renewed my vows. I did not. Mère Marie Rose tells me I am no longer a nun, so I may no longer wear the veil."

Her black hair was raggedly cut and as short as a man's. It made her eyes appear to be enormous purple-black coals in her white face. "But you still feel like one, don't you?"

"I am not sure what I feel. Except very tired."

There was a single small porthole on the wall beside her narrow bunk. He glanced out and saw the coast of Québec passing out of sight. They were under way.

Book 5

The Covenant

1759–1760

Chapter Twenty-Eight

QUENT STOOD ON the deck of the *Three Sisters* as she approached Burnett's Key on a raw, damp day in early autumn. The news of Wolfe's great victory had arrived before them. New York's streets were hung with red and white bunting, and everywhere the king's standard snapped in the stiff breeze. Nicole saw none of it. She was confined to her cabin, burning with the fever that had attacked her two days out of Québec.

Quent leapt ashore before Cooke's ship had been made fast, and came back an hour later with his uncle Dr. Caleb Devrey. The brother of Bede and Lorene, he had diagnosed Ephraim's dropsy five years before. "Why wasn't the leg removed?" he demanded after he'd examined her. "Don't they know in Québec that gunshot wounds poison the blood?"

"The surgeon wanted to do just that. She wouldn't have it."

Caleb Devrey was a tall scarecrow of a man dressed entirely in black. He had removed his cloak while he attended to the patient, now he swung it back over his shoulders. "Then she has written her own death warrant. Will you bring her ashore? I expect Bede will make a place for her if you wish. She'll be more comfortable until the end comes."

"No." Quent's hands were gripped into fists, and his rigid stance reflected his unwillingness to concede defeat. "I promised to take her to Shadowbrook."

In the afternoon he prowled the waterfront taprooms and alehouses and was eventually able to secure passage on a schooner headed up the Hudson on the dawn tide. When he carried Nicole aboard the new vessel—shrouded in blankets, and twitching violently in his arms, murmuring incoherent bits of Latin prayers—the crew looked surly and displeased. Tars were notoriously superstitious and shipboard deaths were always thought to be portents of doom.

Rain and cold followed them upriver, but also a favorable wind. They were in Albany in three days. Though at times Quent despaired, Nicole lived. One more change was required, to a small nondescript boat with a single gaff-rigged mast. It was owned by a tar named Henry Morris who knew him and Shadowbrook, and frequently made supply runs to the Patent's wharf. The boat had one tiny airless cabin belowdecks where a narrow bench spread with rough, none-too-clean blankets served as the only bed. Quent lay Nicole on it and sat on the floor beside her, leaning against the bulkhead, praying for death to hold off for another few hours.

He was alone with her now. The laundress who had come with them from Québec had taken one look at Albany, still bursting with redcoats and provincial militia, and decided to remain. Quent watched over Nicole for the four hours of the journey, wiping her hot face with wet cloths and making sure her restless and tormented movements didn't hurl her out of the makeshift bed. Once, Morris poked his head through the hatch to see how his passengers were faring and Quent took the opportunity to ask, "What news of my brother?"

"None I know of. John Hale's pretty much same as always, except more of it. Drinks at old man Groesbeck's when he's in the town. These days that's usually three weeks out o' any four."

John must die. "And Shadowbrook?"

"Patent's doing fine. Miss Lorene's seen to that. No need to worry 'bout Shadowbrook."

You spill your brother's blood on this land it be poisoned, Master Quent. Mark o' Cain, that be.

They arrived at sunrise. A glorious golden light flooded the red-gold autumn landscape. Morris tossed a line over the bollard and made his boat fast to the Patent's wharf with practiced ease, then poked his head through the hatch to the cabin below. "We're here and it's a fine day above. You want me to go up to the house and get some help?"

"Please," Quent said, rubbing his reddened eyes and feeling his tiredness full on for the first time since they'd left Québec. "Ask them to send for Sally Robin first thing. Say it's a matter of urgency."

Nicole had been sleeping more naturally for the past hour, but when he once more gathered her into his arms she felt featherlight, almost insubstantial. For a moment he feared she wasn't breathing, then he felt her heart beating against his own. "Stay alive," he murmured fiercely. "I haven't brought you all this way to be cheated by death now."

When Quent carried her up to the deck Sally Robin was waiting.

"I can't believe my luck, you being here at the big house."

"I been here some weeks now. Mistress be poorly."

"How bad?"

"Not too bad, Quentin," Lorene said, coming slowly onto the wharf from the big house path. She walked with a cane and leaned on the arm of Six-Finger Sam. "Sally Robin's been magicing me well with her potions, and now that you're here I'm sure to be better still. Am I correct in thinking that's Mademoiselle Crane bundled up in all those blankets?"

"Yes, it is. She took a shot meant for me in Québec. The surgeon wanted to remove her leg, but she wouldn't let him do anything except take out the musket ball. Now she's burning with fever. Uncle Caleb saw her in New York and said gunshot poisons the blood and she must die. Even if he's right, I promised her Sally Robin and I meant to keep my word."

"Caleb doesn't know as much as he thinks he does. Besides, I always believed Mademoiselle to be of good, strong stock. The right sort for Shadowbrook. I'm glad you've brought her home, Quentin."

"Nothing's arranged," he said, taking her meaning. "I don't know if—"

Lorene held up her hand. "Time for all that later. Sam, you take—"

"Let me, mistress." Sally Robin took a step forward before Six-Finger Sam could and reached out her arms. "Don't look like she be very heavy, and I needs to hold her against my heart to tell what it is should be done. You give her to me, Master Quent. Sally Robin be looking after her now."

Quent relinquished his precious burden and Sally Robin hurried up to the house with Sam in her wake. Quent hung back, walking at his mother's pace and giving her his arm to lean on. "How long since you've needed a cane?" he asked.

Lorene shrugged. "A few months, maybe. I'm tired, Quent, nothing more. It's been a great deal of work."

"I hear you've done exceptionally well. I'm sorry I wasn't here to assist you."

"I quite enjoyed it, and yes, we've done well. You'll see."

"John?" he asked. It had to be faced. Now was better than later.

"He's not home. He seldom is, Quent. Your brother is . . . less than he was. I know no other way to put it."

But Shadowbrook was more. He could tell as soon as they approached the front door. Sally Robin had already disappeared, but Kitchen Hannah and Runs-about and Corn Broom Hannah were all waiting by the open front door, their smiles wide with pleasure. "Welcome home, Master Quent."

The morning sun poured into the spacious hallway. Ever speck of wood displayed a recent coat of paint or polish and the pewter chandelier shone. From where he stood he could see into the great hall. The furnishings had fine new coverings, and Turkey carpets gleamed against the wide chestnut floorboards. Each of the three fireplaces in his line of vision was heaped high with logs and blazing. Since no one knew he was coming, clearly this was the usual state of things at the big house these days. Quent turned to his mother. "Well done, madam. Very well done indeed."

Kitchen Hannah rushed off to get food and Corn Broom Hannah opened the door to the little room off the hall where Lorene had her writing desk. "I got everything ready for you in here, mistress."

Quent saw a bed against one wall. "Are you sleeping down here these days?"

"Sometimes, when I am late at my desk. Now enough about me. Tell me about Québec and the battle. It must have been splendid."

"I didn't see it. I was at the hosp—"

His words were interrupted by a knock at the door. It was Sally Robin, and she was smiling. "Come to tell you there ain't no black, Master Quent. The leg, it be hot as the rest of her, but it don't be turning black."

"That matters?"

"It be a good sign, Master Quent. You remember what you told me when you went off to get Solomon back from those Indians took him away?"

"I said you should have hope but not certainty."

"Yes indeed. And that's how it be now. You got reason to hope, but we can't be no ways certain."

"Fair enough, Sally Robin. And whatever happens, thank you."

He was home and so was Nicole.

Lorene waited for Sally Robin to go before she spoke. "That time after we were nearly burned out, when you went off to get the Barrel Maker rather than stay and help, I was bitter, Quentin. I felt you had given the Patent and all of us into John's less-capable hands for nothing but your pride. But you were right. Solomon's been a rock to me these past two years. I could not have achieved half as much without him."

She reached for her ledgers, eager to show him the shape of those accomplishments. "We were prepared when they came, Quent. Thanks to what you'd told me."

The wave of redcoats that engulfed Albany in 1758 and 1759 had slept in barracks built with lumber milled at Shadowbrook, the troops fed with grain grown at Shadowbrook, and it was the Patent's rum that went into a goodly portion of the grog required by the British Navy. "That does for the sailors," Lorene explained. "The Army's quartermasters are more interested in ale. Since we have never had much land in hops, I couldn't at first see how we could produce enough to make the trade worthwhile. Then I found the most extraordinary little man, Quentin. Stands no higher than my waist and not a hair on his head, but he has a fine brewery some ways south in Chappaqua. He grows more hops than he requires, and since our two enterprises are far enough apart to be no competition to each other, we came to an arrangement."

"Is the sugarhouse big enough for so much enterprise?"

"It wouldn't have been. That's why I had Solomon build a brew house out behind the stables. I made Taba the laundress and put Clemency full time to making ale. She's remarkably good at it, but Clemency's old and we must look to the future, so I've given Little George into her keeping. She's been teaching him brewing for over a year now. We produce enough to sell our ale directly to the redcoats, as well as supply the official requests. They call at Do Good with some regularity."

Quent chuckled at the thought of Esther Snowberry running a taproom, but Lorene said it wasn't like that. "It's but a small outlet to service travelers. They can't drink on the premises, only have their jugs filled, then take them away."

It seemed a Quakerly compromise. "If Little George is learning brewing, who's helping Jeremiah in the stables?"

"One of the Ashanti lads John bought same time as Taba. He has a most unpronounceable name, so we call him Tall Boy. He's almost your height, Quentin. Quite the tallest nigra I've ever seen."

"Good with the horses?"

"As good as he needs to be." She became quite busy with closing up the ledgers and putting them back on the shelf above her desk. "I don't go about the place much. There's plenty to keep me occupied right here. And John's not at home all that often." Then, rushing on before he could comment: "So we're stabling mostly draft animals now, for plowing and cart work. Tall Boy's plenty good enough with that level of horseflesh. And I've put a few more fields to hops. The dwarf is cooperative, but in the long term we don't wish to be dependent on any supplies but our own."

Three o'clock, dinnertime, and Groesbeck's taproom at the Sign of the Nag's Head was filled to overflowing. The smell of squirrel stew hung heavy in the air, mingling with the smell of yeasty ale and fiery rum and the sweat of hardworking men. Henry Morris wedged his way into the crowd and called for the punch bowl, downing two cups one right after the other when it came, and paying for them with a couple of shiny coppers picked from the handful of coins he'd been paid for ferrying Quentin Hale and the young woman upriver to Shadowbrook. Waste of good Hale money, that was, might as well o' buried her where she was as pay for her passage. But rich folk had their own way o' goin' on. And these days the Hales were rich enough. Hell, everyone was richer than they'd been a few years back. Even himself, if the truth be told. Rich enough to buy a hot dinner here in the tavern, and not settle for a morsel from the pie-woman's wares out on the street.

He was hungry and there was no place to sit at the front. Morris worked his way through the throng until he found a vacant place at a long table hard by the rearmost fireplace, nearly out the door to the yard where the whores did their business. "A bowl of that good stew I smell," he yelled. "And an ale to wash it down." The serving woman signaled that she'd heard. Morris pulled out a few more coins in readiness, salivating at the thought of what good eating squirrels were just now. Chock-full of acorns, they were, and thick with the fat they'd stored to see them through the coming winter.

A log of applewood too green for proper burning crackled loudly when a pocket of sap caught, and rolled forward to the edge of the hearth. The man next to Morris stretched out a leg to kick it back but couldn't reach. The man slid out of his seat to do the job properly. Another slid instantly into his place. "Hey! I'm sitting there!"

"Not now, you're not."

The man by the fireplace knew John Hale's reputation for violence. Besides, he'd already finished his dinner. He reclaimed what was left of his mug of ale and went away muttering about them as felt they were better than the rest. John turned to Morris. "I'm told you made a run up to my place last night."

"Aye, I did that."

"I'm also told it was my brother hired you."

"There's some around here with mouths bigger than they should be." Morris leaned back to let the serving woman put down a wooden bowl filled with steaming stew and a pewter tankard of ale. She scooped up the coins he'd left on the table and backed away. The tar picked up his spoon and began eating.

"Some as know who butters their bread," John said. His left arm hung by his side and he used his right to lift it onto the table. "What I want to know, who'd he have with him?"

"Can't say. Didn't get a good look."

"But he wasn't alone?"

"Folks pay for passage, I don't ask questions. Just brings 'em where they want to go."

John took the knife from his belt and with his right hand began cleaning the fingernails of the useless left. "Plenty of competition on the river these days, isn't there?"

The tar waited until he'd finished chewing a particularly succulent morsel of squirrel. "Aye, but enough work for all."

"Did you know we're to build an extra landing place on the Patent this year?"

"Hadn't heard."

"You have now. And with all the transport available, I can be as choosy as I like deciding who lades from my property and who does not."

Morris turned his head and spat two small bones onto the floor. "Near as I can tell, it's the mistress says who ferries for Shadowbrook and who don't." Then, before John could answer: "Your brother had a young woman with him. Never heard her name. Not worth learning it neither. Burning with fever, she was. Near as I can tell, Quent brought her to Shadowbrook so's he could bury her there."

John stared at nothing for a few moments, then got up and pushed his way through the mob to the front door.

Ten o'clock. Quent climbed the stairs, feeling the heaviness in his legs and thinking that a night in his old bed under Shadowbrook's roof would make a world of difference. He started down the hall, then paused outside the room where they'd put Nicole. The door was ajar and he could see her small form in the bed. A black girl sat beside her, sponging her face. She must be the Ibo John had bought. She looked up and saw him, and left her patient and came to the open door. "You be wanting me, master?"

"Only to ask how she is."

"Sleeping. And the fever be not so fierce. Sally Robin put something in the water I be using to keep her cool."

"Where is Sally?"

"Down below, master, getting something for mistress. Some bedtime thing she be bringing her most nights."

"So you're in charge up here?"

"Only till Sally Robin comes back, master. But Sally Robin, she be learning me how to do things for sick folks and I be doin' everything she says."

"Good, that's fine. You're Taba, aren't you?"

"Yes, master."

Fourteen or fifteen, maybe. Not pretty, but there was intelligence behind her eyes. "I'm glad to meet you, Taba. My mother speaks highly of you. You take good care of mademoiselle and we'll be well pleased."

"Yes sir, master. I best be goin' back to her now."

The lure of his bed was irresistible. Quent walked toward it, heard a sound, and glanced over the banister to the floor below. Sally Robin was hurrying across the hall, carrying a steaming glass of liquid. He waited just until he saw her knock at Lorene's door, then stumbled into his room. The bed had been turned down and his dressing gown was spread beside it on the chair. Corn Broom Hannah, or Runsabout, doing for him as they always had. Reminding him he was supposed to be a gentleman, at least when he was at Shadowbrook. Hell with it, he was too tired to get undressed. Still in his buckskins he fell on the feather mattress and was instantly asleep.

Downstairs Lorene murmured, "Come," when she heard Sally's tap on the door.

"Hot drink for you, mistress."

"Thank you, Sally." Lorene was sitting up in her bed, covered with a lace and linen nightdress full enough to hide her unnatural thinness. She'd removed her mobcap, and her hair, more gray than brown these days, hung in a single plait. She took the glass and a first sip of hot milk and honey, and whatever other herbs Sally Robin put in the drink to make her sleep. "I don't know what I'd do without you and your potions. How is your new patient?"

"Some better. Taba be with her."

"Good. You've got to get her well, Sally Robin. For the sake of the Patent as well as for Master Quent. She'll be a fine mistress for you all."

"I like the mistress we got. So do everyone else."

Lorene smiled. "I look better to all of you now that you know I'm about to go, don't I?"

"Don't you talk that way, mistress. You got to think happy thoughts. That be doing as much for you as any brew."

Lorene glanced at the shelf above her desk. There was a blue glass bottle beside the neat stacks of ledgers. It was tightly closed, with a coating of wax covering the wooden stopper. "I'm happier because of your brews, Sally Robin. Knowing that if the pain gets too bad I don't have to endure it is a comfort."

The black woman followed her mistress's glance. "Not yet," she said firmly. "There be plenty Sally Robin can do 'fore you open that there bottle."

"Not yet," Lorene promised. But maybe sooner rather than later. Particularly if Nicole can be made well and I can see the Patent in Quent's hands, with a wife who will look after him as well as Shadowbrook. I'm coming, Ephraim. You shan't have to wait much longer.

Despite Sally Robin's potion, Lorene had not slept a night through for many weeks. The pain was bearable by day; at night it threatened to overwhelm her. She looked at the blue bottle with longing. But if she could hold on a few weeks more, just until she was certain that Nicole would live, or if she did not, that Quent would remain without her, then she might—

She heard the front door open. There was only one person who would let himself into the big house by the front door in the dark of night. She got up to meet him. "Good evening, John."

John looked up the stairs to the faint light that showed beneath the door to the corner bedroom. "The Frenchwoman?"

"Mademoiselle Crane, yes."

"Why did he bring her here?"

"She was wounded in Québec. Quent brought her home so Sally Robin could look after her."

"Not his home," John muttered. "Needs to ask me before he puts my slaves to his work."

She could smell the rum on him even though he remained standing near the door. Pity the horse hadn't thrown him before he arrived. A broken neck in the woods would have been a thousand times easier than what would happen now. John started for the stairs. "Where are you going?"

"Have to see my brother. Welcome home the prodigal son. Like it says in the Bible, madam. You know all about the Bible, so now you can kill the fatted calf. Or something like it. Make a great feast because my brother is home. Only right that I go upstairs and welcome him."

"He will kill you, John." Her eldest son had one foot on the steps. "You mean to kill Quent, I know that. But that is not how it will be. He will kill you." And for the rest of his life he will feel shame and bitterness over it.

John hesitated, his body sagging slightly. His back was to her and she could not see his face, but Lorene could smell the fear on him. Poor John, she wanted to weep for him. God knew how many times she had wept for him, many fruitless tears that had changed nothing. He was what he was. If it were her fault, God help her. She'd face justice soon enough. "Come sit with me for a bit. I am poorly, John. You and Quent have the rest of your lives to settle your differences."

He turned. "I am sorry you are unwell, madam."

"It will be over soon," Lorene said, gesturing to the open door of her room. "Meanwhile I've a good blaze going. And some fine brandy sent by your uncle Bede. You and I haven't had such a visit in a long time."

John looked once more up the stairs to the place where his brother slept. Fear and hatred mingled in him, making his gut roil and his mouth taste of ashes. "Uncle Bede's brandy sounds a fine thing," he muttered as he followed his mother into her room.

In the morning Quent woke to the sound of Sally Robin's voice. He ran down the stairs knowing what it was had summoned her song even before he saw her standing in the door of Lorene's room. Quent pushed past her. Lorene lay on her bed. She looked peaceful. John was sprawled in a chair beside the fire. His legs were on the edge of the hearth, his head lolling sideways. He might have been asleep, or in a drunken stupor, but Quent knew he was dead.

Sally Robin's song ended and she came into the room. There was a decanter of brandy on the table beside Lorene's bed, and an empty blue bottle. "What is that?" Quent demanded when she picked it up and put it in the deep pocket of her apron.

"Only a potion I made for the mistress. Something as would help rest her when the pain got too bad. She was dying, Master Quent. Sooner or later, that don't make much nevermind."

He looked at his brother. "John . . ."

"He be dying too. We all is, you know that."

"But here, like this. I—"

"Let it be, Master Quent. Your mama, if she was here, she tell you to let it be."

The double funeral took place at Squirrel Oaks the following day. They buried Lorene next to Ephraim. Pohantis was some distance away, but across from them both. John's grave was beside those of his six dead brothers and sisters. Quent had decided not to wait for a minister from Albany, so he read from the Bible himself, and Sally Robin sang.

"My go-to-heaven song, that be," she told him afterward. "It be peaceful where she is, never you mind about that."

"And John?"

"I don't know, Master Quent. And you don't neither. Your mama, she didn't want you to worry overly 'bout your brother John."

He'd always known that was true. He simply hadn't realized how much.

The slaves stood on one side of the burial ground, the tenants on the other. Ely Davidson was there with his new wife, and all the Frankels. Tim was still not married, but Ellie had a second husband. She was Ellie Frankel Bleecker Hodges now. Larky Hodges was a boot maker, a skill not before in good supply on the Patent, so Lorene had been well pleased by the union. Ellie's stomach stuck out so far Quent had to stand to the side of her to accept her condolences. "We're gonna miss her a lot, Quent. I swear I don't know what the Patent will do without her." Then, the question that was on everyone's mind: "You plannin' on staying?"

"I'm staying, Ellie." He spoke up loud enough so pretty much everyone could hear. The collective release of tension was almost a physical thing. "I'll have to go away one more time. For a month, maybe, in the spring." Whatever happened, he must be at Bishkek's second funeral. "But I'm master of the Patent now. Shadowbrook will be the same as always. For everyone."

Some things would be different, however. Quent walked over to the young Ashanti who worked in the stable. "You're the one they call Tall Boy?"

"That be me, master."

"What's your real name? What did they call you back in Africa?"

"White people no be saying my name, master. Tall Boy, that be fine."

"Try me," Quent said. The slave hesitated. "A direct question deserves an answer. What's your African name?"

"Ajibwamemelosu."

Quent smiled. "It's a lot to say, I'll grant you that. Will it be all right if we call you Ajib?"

In five years, since the net had dropped over him when the slavers raided his village, no one had asked Ajibwamemelosu's permission for anything. "Ajib be fine," he said. "I be mighty pleased you call me Ajib."

Two days after Lorene and John were in the ground Nicole's fever broke. She opened her eyes. *"Ma Mère, je voudrais—"* Then saw the black woman leaning over her and remembered. She was no longer a nun; God had rejected her. "You're Sally Robin, aren't you? The one who sings those incredibly lovely songs."

"I sing some, that be the truth, Little Mistress."

Nicole wanted to ask why Sally called her that, but she had more urgent needs. "Please, I'm so thirsty."

"I 'spected that. Got some nice stuff brewed up for you right here." Sally Robin held a mug of lukewarm tea to Nicole's lips, brewed of bark and flowerbuds and sweetened with honey.

"Thank you," Nicole murmured. "I think I want to sleep now. Could you sing me a song, Sally Robin?"

"Special rest-easy-and-get-well song," Sally promised. She was only partway through it when Quent came and stood in the doorway behind her.

He waited for the song to end before he spoke. "How is she?"

"Very tired, Master Quent. But Little Mistress, she be fighting a big fight with the poison in her, and she won. She sleepin' natural now. That be a good thing."

He came and stood by the bed. "Do you all call her Little Mistress?"

"Yes."

"Whose idea was that?"

"Can't rightly say. Now you go away and be patient, Master Quent. Soon as Little Mistress be able, I be calling you to come."

The next day he was summoned to her bedside. "Nicole, I'm so happy to see you like this." They'd put a mobcap over her shorn hair, and dressed her in a fresh white linen nightdress. She smelled of lilacs, not sickness. Quent reached for her hand. "Sally Robin says you're going to get well."

She did not pull away from him, but her hand lay motionless in his. "I am very grateful to you. And to Sally Robin. More grateful than I can ever say. I will pray for you both every day."

They were alone, and he leaned closer and grinned at her. "I'm glad of your sweet prayers, precious heart, but don't expect me to be satisfied with only them. I'll show you other ways to thank me, soon as you're well enough."

Nicole turned her head away and didn't answer.

It was pretty much the same every time he visited. Eventually she was well enough to be carried to a chair beside the window, and by the first week of the new year she was taking a few tentative steps, leaning on the furniture or on someone's arm—Sally Robin's or Taba's, or even his own, but always she was as distant as she'd been that first day. Quent brought her two canes he had made from elmwood. "I think they are the right size. I measured while you were sleeping."

The sticks were beautifully carved and rounded and smoothed by his own hands, as he'd done with the boards he'd brought to build the place above the waterfall in Shoshanaya's glen. "Thank you. I'm very grateful for everything."

"For the love of Almighty God, Nicole, it's not gratitude I want. I love you. I think you love me. Despite everything, I still believe that. In Shoshanaya's glen, you wanted—" The look she gave him was so stricken he broke off. "You did," he murmured. "I know you did."

"I was breaking my vow. All those people died because of it."

"But you kept your vow. The abbess said you had. I heard her. You kept your vow and now God has sent you back to me."

"I wish I could believe that," she whispered. "I cannot. Go away, please."

Weeks went by. He visited her at least once a day, but he never saw her smile. In April, when the snow was mostly gone but the ground was still frozen and there was not yet any sign of spring, he went into her room at midday but found her gone. Stricken with sudden terror, Quent tore through the house yelling Sally Robin's name.

"I be right here, Master Quent. What you be wanting of old Sally?"

"I can't find Nicole. Little Mistress, Sally. Where is she?"

"She be wanting to visit your mama's grave, master. Little George, he fix her a horse and she go off a little past breakfast time."

"A horse? I had no idea she was well enough to ride."

"Little Mistress be well enough to do mostly whatever she wants now. On the outside, master, that lady, she be nearly entirely well."

"Then why—"

"That lady she don't be feeling herself part of this world, Master Quent. Little Mistress, she be between this world and the next."

"Can you sing her back, Sally Robin?"

"I be trying, but my song don't be big enough. Little Mistress, she be so busy looking into the beyond-after, she ain't got no time for the now-here. You got to find some way make that little lady know she got her feet solid on the good earth, Master Quent. Sally Robin done all she can. Up to you now."

Quent saddled a horse of his own and galloped off toward Squirrel Oaks. He had an insane fear that she had secretly left the Patent, and that he'd never see her again, but he was still half a league away from the burial ground when he saw her standing on the cemetery hill, silhouetted against the afternoon sky. "Nicole!" He screamed her name into the wind. "Nicole!"

She turned and waited for him, unmoving. He rode up beside her, then slid out of the saddle.

"I wanted to pay my last respects to Madame Hale. I am very sorry I was not well enough to attend the funeral. I brought her the first forsythia of the season. You can make them flower early if you cut them and—"

Quent pulled her to him and stopped her words with his mouth. Nicole stood rigid in his arms. "You love me," he said finally. "I know it."

"I do, I have never denied that. I always will love you."

"Then why—"

"I am not free to love you or any man. I took a vow."

"And kept it. But—"

She reached up and put a finger over his lips. "I will make you a bargain, Mons—Quent. I know the Patent needs a mistress. I will be that, but I can never be your wife."

Jesus God Almighty, a devil's bargain. How could he agree to such an unnatural covenant? If he did not, she would leave. "Very well. But—" The idea was born full in him without his having examined any of it's parts. "Nicole, I saved your life, didn't I? Bringing you here so Sally Robin could look after you, isn't that why you're still alive and walking on both your legs?"

"Yes, and I will always pray for you."

"I want something more than your prayers. I want you to make me a promise. In June I will go to Singing Snow."

"The Potawatomi village where you and Monsieur Shea were—"

"That's right. I want you to come with me. Give me your word, Nicole. You owe me that. Give me your word that you'll come." *You got to find some way make that little lady know she got her feet solid on the good earth, Master Quent.*

"Very well," she said. "You have my word."

Chapter Twenty-Nine

Much Fat Moon, the Fifth Sun
The Village of Singing Snow

"*HAYA, HAYA, JAYEK.*" Every member of the village stood in a circle, arms linked. The whitened skeletons in the open pit were tumbled together. Bishkek's bones had been placed on the heap only minutes before, but Quent could no longer tell which ones belonged to his manhood father. "*Haya, haya, jayek.*" So, so, all of us together. The rhythm of the chant owned him. He was no longer aware of Corm, standing beside him, or of Nicole a short distance away.

When the burial of the bones was completed, he came back to earth enough to see how solemn she looked. The ceremony had clearly moved her. "It must be very strange to you," he said.

"Not as strange as I expected." She had become so accustomed to seeing him dressed as the master of the Patent she had forgotten how broad his naked chest was.

"I don't understand."

"It is pagan and heathen, at least that's what I'm supposed to believe. But it was . . ." She searched a moment for the word. "It was holy. I am sure it was of God."

"It makes me happy for you to see that."

Nicole smiled at him for the first time in all the months since Québec. "I am sure I look even stranger to everyone here than they do to me." She had on the same simple gray frock and white mobcap she wore at Shadowbrook. "Never mind, we shall become accustomed to each other. What happens next?"

"I need to speak with Corm. Lashi will look after you. Later there will be a feast."

❧

"They aren't going to do it. There are thousands of redcoats all over Canada—Québec, Trois Rivières, Montréal crawl with soldiers. But every French white still alive is right where he's always been."

Quent wanted to hold out some hope, but he'd never lied to Corm and he wasn't about to start now. "Pitt wrote to me. He reminded me that he'd only ever said he'd try. He faces huge opposition in the government. Despite all he's done, there are plenty who want to be rid of him."

Corm leaned over and spat on the ground. It was an entirely Indian way of saying what he thought. "Pontiac agreed to try as well. But he succeeded and Pitt failed."

"It's not over yet," Quent said. "Maybe things will still—"

"Jeffrey Amherst hates every red man he sees, and he has garrisons to sustain from Carolina to Québec. He does it by offering a bounty to any as poach game in *Anishinabeg* hunting grounds. As long as Amherst's in charge, it's over."

Quent wanted to disagree, but he could not. "It will be enormously difficult for them to leave Amherst in charge. The battalions were never up to strength. Now, with deaths and casualties and plain old desertions . . . He grows weaker, Corm. He has to."

Cormac looked at him. "Do you really think so?"

"I do. He's trying to recruit local lads, of course, but you know that seldom produces much."

"Not in the colonial character, soldiering?"

"Not in the English fashion. Not blind obedience to standing still and being shot at when there's a whole forest ready to offer shelter. And not doing things for fear of the lash and the noose." He put his hand on Corm's shoulder. "I know how discouraged you are. I can't blame you. But could be things are going to change now. Maybe just in ways we didn't expect."

"Change, yes. But not for the *Anishinabeg*. At least not the kind they were hoping for."

"You can't be—"

Corm held up his hand. His disappointment was too bitter for this day in this place. It would poison their last visit with the spirit of Bishkek. "Let's talk about something else. Nicole looks fine. Pretty as ever."

"She is that."

"But?"

"She wants no part of me. Still says she's bound to her vow to be a nun."

"Crazy," Corm said. Then Shabnokis came, beating her drum and announcing the beginning of the feast.

Nicole came shyly out of Lashi's wickiup. She was dressed in a squaw's buckskins, leggings and a short dress, and her hair was plaited, the braid hanging over one shoulder and finished with a cluster of bright-colored feathers.

"You look splendid," Quent told her.

"I wasn't sure you'd approve."

"Why not?"

"I'm not sure. Pretending to be something I'm not, perhaps."

"Is who we are a matter of what we wear?"

She was startled. "No, of course not. I just—"

"You're you, Nicole. Whether you're wearing the black veil of the Poor Clares, or a mobcap in the big house, or beaded buckskins." He fingered the neckline of the bodice. She couldn't be wearing corsets beneath this outfit. The time when she dressed herself in Pohantis's white skins, she'd known enough not to wear them then and when he lay over her for those few moments before she told him everything was different, he'd felt her flesh soft and yielding and unrestrained.

How familiar his fingers felt on the bare skin between the lacings of the dress. How right for this time and this place. As the veil had been right for the monastery.

I have tried to do what is right, ma Mère.

I know. And God knows. And now what is right is that you must leave.

He saw the shadow pass over her face. "What are you thinking?"

"That I do not understand very much." Then, before she could say more, Lashi came and pulled her away. It was time to eat and the women must be separated from the men.

After the meal there was the calumet, and then, she knew, there would be the dance. Would the women choose a man as they had in the Shawnee camp and go off with him? And if they did, what would she do? I cannot, however much I want to. It is a sin. Help me, *mon Dieu*.

The drums began, many this time, and not with the prayerful solemnity of the earlier ceremony. Corm came to where she sat beside Lashi and leaned down and said, "This part's joyful. We're celebrating Bishkek's passage into the next world."

"Monsieur Shea, please, tell me . . . That other time, when we were in the camp of the Shawnee and all the women chose a man to be with, is it . . ." She knew herself to be bright red. She could feel the flush, and see her embarrassment reflected in Cormac's wide grin. If only they were not so far north and it were not June, at least it would be dark.

"Not quite the same here. We Potawatomi have our own ways. But don't worry. I'm sure you're going to enjoy everything that comes next." He left her then and she saw him speak a few words to the one they'd told her was the chief, though she could not remember his name. Then the drums became more insistent and she could think of nothing except the way the beat seemed to keep pace with her heart, and how Quent looked as he danced with the others. All the women chanted. *"Ahaya, haya, haya . . ."*

Quent watched her moving with the other squaws; they had linked arms with her and she could not avoid it. Her lips were slightly parted and her eyes shone and he could see from the way her chest rose and fell that she felt the excitement of the others. He was heavy with wanting her, and sick with fear that when the dance ended nothing would be changed. *You got to find some way make that little lady know she got her feet solid on the good earth, Master Quent.* There was no place on earth more good or more solid than Singing Snow.

The circle moved and he had no choice but to move with it; for a time he had his back to Nicole and the other women. When he next saw her Kekomoson stood in front of her. He was offering her the old clay cooking pots that had belonged to the wife of Bishkek.

Nicole looked up at the chief, trying to look respectful. Doesn't he know I don't understand a word of his language? Surely Lashi must tell him. Or Quent or Monsieur Shea. She was enormously relieved when she saw both men coming toward her.

Corm moved faster than Quent. "It's a gift," he told Nicole. "You can't refuse if you want to be polite."

"Oh no, why would I refuse his gift? Tell him I'm honored. Please say these things are beautiful and I am proud to have them." Nicole reached out and took the stack of clay cooking pots. A loud cheer went up from everyone in the village. Then the drums were beating more furiously than before and the chief had dragged her to her feet and was walking her toward Quent.

There were more words she didn't understand, and Quent grinning at her, and finally saying, "Kekomoson wants to know if you wish to give the pots back."

"Oh, no, why should I? Please tell him I'm most grateful for his kindness."

He knew he had to tell her, but just then, the way she looked and how much he wanted her . . . I'll explain later, he promised himself. When we're alone. "You have to dance with me now," he said. "That's the way you say thank you for the gift of the pots."

"But I still limp. Besides, I don't know how."

"It's easy, I'll show you."

She held the pots in her arms and he put his hand on her shoulder to lead her to the fire. The drums continued to beat. Corm had picked up two rattles and he shook them in the same rhythm, and the squaws chanted as before. *"Ahaya, haya, haya."*

"Why is Monsieur Shea circling us like that?"

"It's the way it's done. Come on. Don't think so much. Just move."

She was halting at first, then a bit more sure of herself. He worried that her bad leg would let her down and he put his arm around her waist to support her. "Don't drop the pots, that's very important."

She turned to him and this time her smile was like sunlight and her body moved in unison with his. Quent led her around the fire three more times, then away from the campsite into the woodland beyond. The chant followed them. *"Ahaya, haya, haya."* Nicole still held the clay pots that had belonged to the wife of his manhood father.

"We're married," Quent said.

"What?!"

"The Potawatomi don't make much of weddings. But when a brave chooses a squaw, his mother gives her cooking pots. And if she accepts them, then she's saying yes, she accepts the brave. Those pots belonged to the wife of my manhood father, Bishkek. She's dead as well. So Kekomoson took the pots to keep them until either Corm or I chose a squaw."

"And you told him you chose me."

"Not exactly. Corm did."

"Quent, I . . ."

"Stop talking, damn you. I have listened to all your talk for months. Hell, I've listened for years. But the reality is that we're both alive and we're both here and we love each other."

They were sitting beside a stream and he turned to her and put both his arms around her and forced her to lay back with the weight of his body. Nicole knew she should pull away, that he would not force himself on her if she resisted, but for only the length of one kiss . . . That could not be such a terrible sin.

Quent loosed the laces of the squaw dress, and felt the soft flesh of her breast against his palm.

"No, my darling. I cannot. It's a sin."

"No, it isn't. I told you. We're married."

The catechism she had learned at maman's knee had spoken of marriage as a sacrament, one that the couple bestowed on each other. The priest was merely a witness. She turned her head to free her mouth from his. "Quentin Hale, will you love me forever? Will I be your wife under God?"

"Forever and ever," he promised. "Under any God, Potawatomi or Christian or—"

"Ssh. There is only one God, my darling. However we choose to worship. I will be your wife, Quentin Hale. Forever and ever."

"Forever, starting now," he whispered and covered her body with his.

Epilogue

The World of Tears

1763–1769

FOR THE FIRST time ever the *Anishinabeg* united under a single leader. Faced with the broken promises of the English and Jeffrey Amherst's refusal even to supply them with food or tobacco or guns or powder, Pontiac rallied his people in a great effort to bring back the French. He called together a powwow of Ottawa, Chippewa, Huron, and Potawatomi—more than four hundred chiefs and sachems—and they listened to the Ottawa sachem and remembered the words of the prophets who had told them that unless the Real People turned back to their old ways they were doomed, and soon they danced a war dance that was unlike any other. *Papankamwa, eesipana, ayaapia, anseepikwa, eeyeelia, pileewa . . . So, so, all of us together.*

Fires burned and whites died from Niagara in the north to Carolina in the south. Miami joined the rebellion, and Lenape, and Kickapoo and Seneca and Shawnee. *So, so, all of us together.* Fort Sandusky fell, and Fort Wayne, and Fort Venango and Fort LeBoeuf. After two months, when Fort Edward Augustus in Green Bay was taken, the English had lost every stronghold in the *pays d'en haut* and the Ohio Country except for Fort Detroit and Fort Pitt, and both were under siege. *So, so, all of us together.*

Amherst sent a troop of handpicked soldiers including rangers to Pontiac's camp near Fort Detroit, but the *Anishinabeg* were waiting for them and the creek where the two forces engaged ran red with blood. Bloody Creek, it was called after that. Cormac Shea, who had been beside Pontiac from the first moment of the great rebellion, was among those who died there, but no one took his scalp. Pontiac brought the body of the métis back to the camp and it was honored and buried, but the Ottawa knew that without his *wabnum* his war had lost its heart. He offered to treat with the English, but hatred of the red men was now strong in the hearts of Amherst and the others. Pontiac's offer was refused, and the other tribes no longer believed in his leadership and gradually they deserted. For the red men, life in the sun-coming part of the earth had all but ended. Most moved west, but the *Cmokmanuk* followed and the Real People began their sad journey over a long trail of tears.

In 1763 the Treaty of Paris was signed and only Louisiana was left to the French. The Jesuits were well established there by then, but one, Louis Roget, went for a walk one day and was found a week later, scalped and missing his heart. So Vaudreuil's curse had borne fruit: Roget had escaped Canada, but he had died a Canadian death.

Vaudreuil himself was imprisoned in the Bastille for a time, but later exonerated.

Bigot was found guilty of fraud and banished from France.

Mère Marie Rose and her four daughters from France, returned to the monastery in Montargis. History forgot them and the Poor Clares dated their origins in Canada to the founding of a monastery in Québec more than fifty year's later.

Pontiac was killed in 1769 by Peoria *Anishinabeg*.

In the big house at Shadowbrook there was laughter and birth and death and hope, and bonfires that burned in thanksgiving when word came in high summer of 1776 of the glorious Declaration of Independency pronounced in Philadelphia. In July of 1788, confident that the Bill of Rights for which they had so long argued would be added to the proposed document establishing a union of all the former colonies, the delegates to the Assembly in Poughkeepsie agreed that New York State would ratify the Constitution. The people who tilled the earth, on small farms as well as the huge patents of the north and plantations of the south, would join with the people of the merchant cities from Boston to Savannah. Together they would set out on a great and daring experiment made possible in part by the terrible war they had fought and won twenty-five years before.

The mists of dawn still hung over the Patent when Quentin Hale and Cormac Shea Hale, at twenty-two his eldest son, climbed to the top of Big Two, but by the time they had erected a pole and run up the flag with thirteen stars that Nicole had stitched with such care, the sun had risen on a new and glorious day.

Haya, haya, jayek. So, so, all of us together.

Acknowledgments

Like every author, I stand on the shoulders of those who have preceded me. I could not have written this book without the assistance of a great many others, and an abbreviated list appears below. Two, however, were truly stars to navigate by: *1759 The Battle for Canada* by Laurier L. Lapierre, McClelland & Stewart, Inc., which provided a wealth of insight and information about Québec of the time, including the story of a secret Jesuit map of *La Traverse* in the hands of and ignored by the great Montcalm; and *Crucible of War: The Seven Years' War and the Fate of Empire in British North America, 1754–1766* by Fred Anderson, Knopf, which introduced me to the tale of Washington in Jumonville's Glen and which brilliantly told the war's story from the other side of the border. Others were *The Middle Ground: Indians, Empires, and Republics in the Great Lakes Region, 1650–1815* by Richard White, Cambridge University Press; *Indians and English: Facing Off in Early America* by Karen Ordahl Kupperman, Cornell University Press; *Into the American Woods: Negotiators on the Pennsylvania Frontier* by James H. Merrell, W.W. Norton & Company (where I learned about bridge persons); *Montcalm and Wolfe: The French and Indian War* by Francis Parkman, DeCapo Press; *A People's Army: Massachusetts Soldiers and Society in the Seven Years' War* by Fred Anderson, University of North Carolina Press, *Empire of the Bay: The Company of Adventurers That Seized a Continent* by Peter C. Newman, Penguin USA; *A Few Acres of Snow: The Saga of the French and Indian Wars* by Robert Leckie, John Wiley & Sons; *The Indian Tribes of the Upper Mississippi Valley and Region of the Great Lakes: As Described by Nicolas Perrot, French Commandant in the Northwest*, University of Nebraska Press; *Redcoats Along the Hudson: The Struggle for North America 1754–63* by Noel St. John Williams, Brassey's, Inc.; *The Founders of America: How Indians Discovered the Land, Pioneered in It, and Created Great Civilizations* by Francis Jennings, W. W. Norton; *The Ordeal of the Longhouse: The Peoples of the Iroquois League in the Era of European Colonization: British Military Sites from Albany to Crown Point* by Daniel K. Richter, University of North Carolina Press; *The Great Warpath* by David R. Starbuck, University Press of New England; *Redcoats, Yankees and Allies: A History of Uniforms* by Brenton C. Kemmer, illustrated by Joe Lee, Heritage Books; *Sons of a Trackless Forest* by Mark A. Baker, Baker's Trace Publishing. (Mark Baker is the re-enactor and student of the period who taught Daniel Day-Lewis how to fire a long gun for the Twentieth Century Fox film, *Last of the Mohicans.*)

The Internet was an indispensable resource. I found there dictionaries of Native American languages, reproductions of maps and documents, the wisdom of the nation's many re-enactors of the colonial period (surely one of the great underutilized resources for those seeking authenticity in historical film and fiction), histories of numerous Native American tribes, and countless accounts of the time of the story without which the world within these pages could not have come into being. It would be impossible to list every website I visited, many over and over again, but anyone interested in retracing this path need only put subject headings and keywords into the major search engines and follow the links. Bravo.

Finally, in keeping with the biblical promise that the last shall be first, warmest thanks to my agents, Henry Morrison and Danny Baror, my superb editor, Sydny Miner—who once again has given me back a better book than I gave her—and a special note of thanks to Andrée Pagès for that rarest of treasures, sensitive and enlightening copyediting.

I am indebted to you all.

About the Author

Beverly Swerling is the author of the critically acclaimed *City of Dreams*. A writer, consultant, and an avid amateur historian, she lives in New York City with her husband.

Shadowbrook

1. *Shadowbrook* is a sweeping epic of the French and Indian War and the way it changed the lives of the American and Canadian colonists, as well as marking the beginning of the end of the traditional life of the Native Americans known as the Eastern Woodland tribes. How were you brought into the story? Were you surprised that the book began with the Poor Clare nuns and their corporal discipline? Did you find the practice shocking? Did you see this as in any way connected to the unfolding story of the brutality of war and the different cultures of the colonials and the Indians?

2. Look at the book's narrative style and the use of interior monologue as narration. What effect does this have on the reader? On the story? Why does a writer employ such a device? How does a love story figure into a book of historical fiction? What effect does Nicole and Quent's relationship have on the story? Were you surprised to learn about slavery in the north and the existence of the patents, in other words, the northern plantations? After the Huron renegades attacked, do you think Quent should have stayed and helped them save Shadowbrook? Was he right to choose instead to go after Solomon the Barrel Maker? Would you have done that?

3. Did you understand the feeling of the Indians about what they called "Bridge People?" Do you think the history of Native Americans in our country would have been different if a divide such as the one Quent and Cormac tried to establish had come into being? Would it have worked? Was it fair?

4. The book's main characters are Quent, Cormac, and Nicole, all of one generation. In what ways are they like the generation that preceded them, represented by the characters of Ephraim and Lorene? Are John Hale and Hamish Campbell more alike than they are different? What about Père Antoine, the Franciscan, and Louis Roget, the Jesuit?

5. *Shadowbrook* is rich in minor characters and their stories. Did you enjoy Swerling's wide canvas or find it confusing? How does the author assist the reader with character recognition? Could you "hear" the voices of the different characters, and did that make the story more alive for you?

6. Dreams move the story forward because they motivate the characters. What are the similarities between Cormac's dream and that of the Mohawk chief, Thoyanoguin? Do you think that Quent really believes in either? If not, why does he do what the dreamers ask of him?

7. Consider the different roles of women in the story. What kinds of lives are available to poor women with or without husbands? What about rich women? Do you see similarities between Lorene Hale's choices and those made by Annie Crotchett? What about Nicole's choices, or those of the abbess, Mère Marie Rose, or Marni's choices? What would you have done if you were any one of them? In the end, who do you think had the most power?

8. History says that it is because Britain won the French and Indian war that the American colonists began thinking about independence. Did this book help you understand that? If you were living in that time, would you have been attracted to the notion of independence?

9. What differences do you see in the way modern Canada developed vs. the United States? Do you think the history related in this story had any role in that?